IN A DISTANT GALAXY,
THE PEACEFUL PLANET LORIEN
WAS DECIMATED BY
THE BRUTAL MOGADORIANS.

The last survivors of Lorien—the Garde—were sent to Earth as children. Scattered across the continents, they developed their extraordinary powers known as Legacies and readied themselves to defend their adopted home world.

The Garde thwarted the Mogadorian invasion of Earth. In the process, they changed the very nature of the planet. Legacies began to manifest in human beings.

These new Garde frighten some people, while others look for ways to manipulate them to their benefit.

And although the Legacies are meant to protect Earth, not every Garde will use their powers for good.

I AM PITTACUS LORE.
RECORDER OF THE FATES,
CHRONICLER OF THE LEGACIES.

I TELL THE TALES OF THOSE
WHO WOULD SHAPE WORLDS.

BY PITTACUS LORE

THE ◇ LORIEN LEGACIES REBORN ◇

Novels

GENERATION ONE

THE LORIEN ⇌ LEGACIES

Novels

I AM NUMBER FOUR

THE POWER OF SIX

THE RISE OF NINE

THE FALL OF FIVE

THE REVENGE OF SEVEN

THE FATE OF TEN

UNITED AS ONE

The Lost Files Novellas

#1: SIX'S LEGACY

#2: NINE'S LEGACY

#3: THE FALLEN LEGACIES

#4: THE SEARCH FOR SAM

#5: THE LAST DAYS OF LORIEN

#6: THE FORGOTTEN ONES

#7: FIVE'S LEGACY

#8: RETURN TO PARADISE

#9: FIVE'S BETRAYAL

#10: THE FUGITIVE

#11: THE NAVIGATOR

#12: THE GUARD

#13: LEGACIES REBORN

#14: LAST DEFENSE

#15: HUNT FOR THE GARDE

The Lost Files Novella Collections

THE LEGACIES *(Contains novellas #1–#3)*

SECRET HISTORIES *(Contains novellas #4–#6)*

HIDDEN ENEMY *(Contains novellas #7–#9)*

REBEL ALLIES *(Contains novellas #10–#12)*

ZERO HOUR *(Contains novellas #13–#15)*

GENERATION ONE

BOOK ONE OF THE ◇ LORIEN LEGACIES REBORN ◇

PITTACUS LORE

HARPER

An Imprint of HarperCollins*Publishers*

Library of Congress Control Number: 2017932862
ISBN 978-0-06-249374-3 (trade bdg.)
ISBN 978-0-06-266689-5 (intl. ed.)
ISBN 978-0-06-268175-1 (special ed.)

17 18 19 20 21   PC/LSCC   10 9 8 7 6 5 4 3 2 1
❖
First Edition

CHAPTER ONE

KOPANO OKEKE
LAGOS, NIGERIA

THE WEEK BEFORE THE INVASION, KOPANO'S
father, Udo, sold their TV. Despite his mother's fervent
prayers for his father to find a new job, Udo was unemployed,
and they were three months behind on rent. Kopano didn't
mind. He knew a new TV would manifest soon. Football season was coming and his father wouldn't miss it.

When the alien warships appeared, Kopano's whole family
crowded into his uncle's apartment down the hall. Kopano's
first reaction was to grin at his two younger brothers.

"Don't be stupid," Kopano declared. "This is some bad
American movie."

"It's on every channel!" Obi shouted at him.

"Be quiet, all of you," Kopano's father snapped.

They watched footage of a middle-aged man, an alien

supposedly, giving a speech in front of the United Nations building in New York.

"See?" Kopano said. "I told you. That's an actor. What's his name?"

"Shh," his brothers complained in unison.

Soon, the scene descended into chaos. New York was under attack by pale humanoid creatures that bled black and turned to ash when they were killed. Then some teenagers wielding powers that looked like special effects showed up and began to fight the aliens. These teenagers were only a little older than Kopano and, despite the madness their arrival had created, Kopano found himself rooting them on. In the coming days, Kopano would learn the names of the two sides. The Loric versus the Mogadorians. John Smith and Setrákus Ra. There was no question who the good guys were.

"Amazing!" Kopano said.

Not everyone shared Kopano's enthusiasm. His mother knelt down and began to pray, feverishly muttering about Judgment Day until Kopano's father gently escorted her from the room.

His youngest brother, Dubem, was frightened and clung to Kopano's leg, so Kopano picked the boy up and held him. Kopano was short and stout like his father, but well muscled where his father was paunchy. He patted Dubem's back. "Nothing to worry about, Dubem. This is all far, far away."

They stayed glued to their uncle's TV day into night. Even

Kopano couldn't maintain his good cheer when the footage of New York's destruction was played. The broadcasters showed a map of the world, little red dots hovering over more than twenty different cities. Alien warships.

His father scoffed when he saw the map. "Cairo? Johannesburg? These places get aliens and not us?" He clapped his hands together. "Nigeria is the giant of Africa! Where is the respect?"

Kopano shook his head. "You don't make any sense, old man. What would you do if the Mogadorians showed up here? Hide under the bed, probably."

Udo raised his hand like he would slap his son, but Kopano didn't even flinch. They stared at each other until Udo snorted and turned back to the TV.

"I would kill many of them," Udo muttered.

Kopano knew his father to be a boastful man and an unrepentant schemer. It had been years since Kopano responded to Udo's big talk with anything but scornful laughter. However, Kopano didn't so much as chuckle when his father talked about killing Mogadorians. He felt it, too. Kopano itched to do something, to save the world like the guys he'd seen fighting at the UN. He wondered what happened to them. He hoped they were still out there, fighting, turning maggot-aliens to dust.

The Loric. How badass.

The second night of the invasion, Kopano stood outside on his uncle's veranda. Never had Lagos been this quiet.

Everyone was holding their breath, waiting for something terrible to happen.

Kopano went inside. His brothers and uncle were still blearily staring at the TV screen, watching horrific reports of a failed Chinese assault on a Mogadorian warship. His father slouched in an armchair, snoring. Exhausted, Kopano collapsed onto the futon.

He dreamed of the planet Lorien. Actually, it was more like a vision than a dream, the whole thing unfolding like a movie. He saw the origin of the war that had traveled to Earth, learned about the Mogadorian leader Setrákus Ra, and about the brave Garde who opposed him. The saga was like something out of Greek mythology.

And then, suddenly, he awoke. But Kopano wasn't on his uncle's futon in Lagos. He sat in a massive amphitheater alongside other young people from many different countries. Some of them were talking to each other, many were frightened, all were confused. They'd all experienced the same vision. Kopano overheard one boy say that a moment ago he was home eating dinner, he'd felt a strange sensation come over him and now here he was.

"What a bizarre dream this is," Kopano remarked aloud. Some of the nearby kids murmured agreement. A Japanese girl seated next to him turned to regard Kopano.

"But is this my dream, or your dream?" she asked.

Then new people appeared out of thin air, all of them seated at the ornate table in the room's center. Everyone in the audience recognized John Smith and the other Loric from TV and YouTube. Questions were shouted—What's going on? Why did you bring us here? Are you going to save our planet? Kopano stayed quiet. He was too in awe and he wanted to know what his new heroes had to say.

John Smith spoke to them. He was confident in a humble way. Kopano liked him immediately. He told them—the humans sitting in the gallery—that they all had Legacies.

"I know this seems crazy," John Smith said. "It also probably doesn't seem fair. A few days ago, you were leading normal lives. Now, without warning, there are aliens on your planet and you can move objects with your minds. Right? I mean . . . how many of you have discovered your telekinesis?"

A lot of hands went up, including the Japanese girl's. Kopano looked around, jealous and disappointed in himself. These other kids were learning telekinesis while he was sitting around watching TV.

A glowing Loric girl at the table with a strangely echoing voice displayed a map of Earth with locations marked. Loralite, a stone native to Lorien, now grew in these places. Those with Legacies—Human Garde, like Kopano was supposedly—could use these stones to teleport across the planet. They could join the fight.

"I obviously can't make you join us," John Smith said. "In a few minutes, you'll wake up from this meeting back wherever you were before. Where it's safe, hopefully. And maybe those of us who do fight, maybe the armies of the world, all of us . . . maybe that will be enough. Maybe we can fight off the Mogadorians and save Earth. But if we fail, even if you stay on the sidelines for this battle . . . they *will* come for you. So I'm asking you all, even though you don't know me, even though we've royally shaken up your lives—stand with us. Help us save the world."

Kopano cheered. He clenched and unclenched his fists. He was ready!

Suddenly, the evil Setrákus Ra was shouting threats, his black eyes scanning the room, his gaze boring into everyone. People started to disappear, blinking out of the dream. Kopano woke with a start, sweaty, his head aching.

Little Dubem was the only one still awake and he was staring at him. "Kopano," Dubem whispered. "You were glowing!"

The next day, with his family once again gathered around the television, Kopano made his announcement.

"The Loric visited me in my sleep. John Smith himself asked me to come join them in the defense of Earth. They showed me a map of the world with the locations of stones that I may use to teleport to them. One of them is located at Zuma Rock. I must go there immediately to meet my destiny."

Dubem nodded along solemnly while the rest of Kopano's family stared at him. Then his father and uncle broke into laughter, soon joined by his brother Obi.

"Listen to this one!" his father shouted. "Meet his destiny! Shut up now, we can't hear the news."

"But I saw him," Dubem said, his small voice shaky. "Kopano glowed!"

Their mother made the sign of the cross. "A devil has invaded our house."

Udo regarded his son through eyes narrowed to slits. Kopano stood tall, chest puffed out, hoping to cut a striking figure.

"Okay, Mr. Superhero," said Udo measuredly. "If you are an alien now, please show us your powers."

Kopano took a deep breath. He looked down at his hands. He didn't feel any different than he had yesterday, but that didn't necessarily mean the great powers of the Loric weren't lurking within him, right?

With a flourish worthy of a martial arts movie, Kopano thrust his hands towards his father. He hoped that his telekinesis would come rushing forth and knock his old man out of his chair. But while Udo flinched at the sudden move, nothing else happened.

Kopano's uncle laughed again and slapped Udo on the back. "Your face! You looked like you might crap in your britches!"

Udo scowled, then snorted in Kopano's direction. "You see? Noth—" His father's face suddenly contorted in anguish. Udo clutched at his chest, feet kicking out in front of him in spasms. His eyes went wide in panic. "My insides!" he screamed. "My insides are boiling!"

Kopano's mother screamed.

Kopano and his brothers all rushed to their father's side. Their uncle took a frightened step back. Kopano grabbed his father's arm.

"Father, I'm sorry! I don't know what—"

His father slapped him on the side of the head and grinned. Just like that, he was miraculously recovered and already turning back to the television. A practical joke.

"You stupid boy, I'm fine. Or perhaps my alien powers are just greater than yours, hmm?" He waved Kopano away. "Go on. See to your mother. You scared her bad."

Kopano slunk away. Had it really all been a dream? What would he have done with Legacies, anyway? A boy from Lagos rushing off to save the world? Even Nollywood didn't make movies with premises so far-fetched.

Little Dubem clasped his hand.

"I believe you, Kopano," his youngest brother whispered. "You will show them all."

At least, for a few days after his embarrassing announcement, Kopano's family was too glued to the news to mock him. But then the invasion ended, suddenly and brutally, with the nations of Earth coming together to simultaneously attack every Mogadorian warship. Meanwhile, the Garde, the ones who had invaded Kopano's dreams and promised him bigger things than Lagos, went to the Mogadorians' secret base in West Virginia and killed Setrákus Ra. Kopano imagined being there, fighting alongside the Garde, and melting Setrákus Ra with his fire-breath.

Fire-breath, Kopano had decided, would be his Legacy.

When the news broke that Earth was saved, they celebrated in the streets. His father hugged him close as they danced down the road, fireworks going off overhead. Kopano couldn't remember the last time Udo had hugged him like that. Not since he was a boy.

But the next day, it started.

Alien son, go down to the market before school and pick up the items I am thinking about right now! Use your telepathy!

Alien son, did you finish your homework?

Alien son, use your telekinesis to get me a beer, eh?

Kopano grinned through it all, but inside he seethed. His unemployed father had nothing better to do than sit home all day and think up ways to humiliate him.

Worse still, his bigmouthed brother, Obi, had spread the word around school. Soon, Kopano's classmates were teasing him, too. A stall in the marketplace had started selling rubber Mogadorian masks, hideous gray things with empty black eyes and tiny yellow teeth. A group of his older classmates chased Kopano through the halls wearing these masks and, when they caught him, they used rolls of duct tape to bind him to one of the football goals. They took turns kicking balls at him.

Until one day, when Kopano stopped a football in midair. When that happened, they all ran away screaming.

"Finally," Kopano whispered to himself as he began wriggling free. "Finally."

It had been three months since the invasion. Kopano, it

turned out, was a late bloomer.

That evening, he strode into his family's apartment to find his father napping on the couch. With his little brothers watching, Kopano used his telekinesis to levitate the couch high above the floor. Then he screamed, "Fire! Fire! Father, get up!"

His father sprung upright, swung his legs off the couch, and fell five feet to the floor. As he groaned and picked himself up, staring aghast at the couch still floating above him, Obi and Dubem cackled with laughter. Kopano simply grinned at his father, squaring his shoulders in the same noble way he had on that humiliating morning months ago.

"You see, old man? What did I tell you?"

Udo stumbled over to his son, a smile slowly spreading on his face. He grabbed Kopano's cheeks and pinched. "My beautiful alien son, you are the answer to all of our problems."

Many months later, when Kopano finally made it to America, the psychologist Linda Matheson would ask him what life was like back in Lagos, before he came to the Human Garde Academy.

Kopano would think about his answer for a long moment before answering.

"Well," he said, "I guess for a little while I was a criminal."

CHAPTER TWO

THE PATIENCE CREEK SURVIVORS
AN UNDISCLOSED LOCATION

FOR THOSE FIRST HUMAN GARDE WHO DID ANSWER John Smith's call to arms right after their visions, the invasion wasn't as glorious as Kopano had enviously imagined.

The story of Patience Creek wasn't reported on the news networks. The battle there didn't make it into any of the retrospectives made after the invasion. It was kept secret. Remembered by only the survivors.

Patience Creek was a secret government facility in Michigan where the Loric hid out after the invasion, plotting their counterattack on the Mogadorians. They were joined by a host of military personnel and a handful of Human Garde, those who had answered John Smith's telepathic plea or who had otherwise crossed his path.

Daniela Morales. Stone-vision.

Nigel Rally. Sonic manipulation.

Caleb Crane. Duplication.

Ran Takeda. Kinetic detonation.

There were others, but they didn't survive the assault when the Mogadorians discovered Patience Creek. Most of the military didn't make it out alive either. John Smith himself was nearly killed. It was bloody and brutal and not at all heroic. The ordeal showed John Smith that maybe the humans he'd recruited weren't ready for a full-scale war. They needed training that the Loric didn't have time to give them. Not then, at least. The humans needed protecting.

So, John Smith sent them away.

"Bloody Guantanamo Bay," Nigel groused.

Daniela rolled her eyes. "This isn't Cuba, man."

Nigel bent down and gathered a handful of bright white sand. He opened his fingers and let the grains blow across the crystalline blue ocean. The sun beat down on him—skinny bordering on bony, pale, a sunburn growing around his bleached mohawk, his cheeks pocked by persistent splotches of acne. He wore a black Misfits tank top in defiance of the heat. He gestured from the waves to the austere military base two hundred yards away—their accommodations for the last few days—and looked back at Daniela.

"Ominous military base on a tropical island," Nigel countered. "Where do you think we are?"

"It isn't that ominous," Caleb said. He brushed a hand across his buzz cut and skipped a stone into the ocean. Biscuit, Daniela's Chimæra, the shape-shifting Loric animal

12

who preferred the form of a golden retriever, bounded into the water after the rock. "There's a snack bar."

"Not ominous to you, mate," Nigel replied. "You grew up in one of these places, didn't ya? And besides, your uncle's running the show."

"Guantanamo's where they bring the bad guys and shit," Daniela told Nigel. "We aren't prisoners. This is just a stop-over." She looked at Caleb. "Right?"

Caleb's uncle was General Clarence Lawson. He'd been called out of retirement and put in charge of coordinating the armies of Earth with the Loric during the invasion. Since then, it had seemed to Caleb like his uncle was await-ing orders. Like he didn't know what would happen next.

Back at Patience Creek, Caleb had acted as his uncle's bodyguard. "In case any of these aliens get out of line, you're the ace up my sleeve," Lawson told his nephew. Caleb didn't think he could go toe to toe with John Smith or one of the Loric, but he didn't argue. It had been his uncle's idea for Caleb to pose as twins. He was having problems controlling his duplication Legacy—a second body would pop out of him without warning—so it was better for his clone to sim-ply hide in plain sight.

Since they arrived at the island, Caleb had dinner with his uncle every night in the man's windowless office. These meals were largely silent, especially after one of Caleb's duplicates manifested and hurled a plate of food into his uncle's face. Since Patience Creek, the dupes were becoming harder to control. Rowdier. With minds of their own.

Caleb didn't tell anyone this. He kept his mouth shut, like a good soldier.

To Daniela, he simply nodded. "You're probably right."

Nigel snorted. He didn't buy anything that Caleb said. He turned away, watching his own Chimæra, the raccoon-shaped Bandit, root around for seashells.

Daniela clapped her hands together. "I just want to get back to New York, man," she said. "Find my mom. Do something useful."

They all nodded in agreement, even the silent Ran Takeda, the Japanese girl sitting in the sand nearby with her turtle-shaped Chimæra, Gamora, lightly stroking the back of her hand across his craggy shell. This was their life—watching news feeds of the aftermath of the invasion, eating microwaved military base food and hanging around on the beach. Sometimes, they practiced their telekinesis, copying the rudimentary games Nine had hastily taught them during their brief training session with him. They looked ahead, hoping they could eventually be of some use. And they tried their best not to think about Patience Creek.

Eventually, Daniela and Caleb drifted away, leaving Nigel alone on the beach with Ran.

"So, what do you think, silent and violent?" he asked. "We princes and princesses or prisoners?"

Ran looked over at Nigel. "I don't think anyone knows what we are," she said after a long pause.

Nigel grinned. He still couldn't get over Ran speaking in her precise English. He thought she'd been mute when he first met her at the Niagara Falls Loralite stone and all the way through the ordeal at Patience Creek. Everyone assumed that she couldn't speak English.

She had saved his life back at Patience Creek, maybe more than once, and so he stuck close to her. He started to notice the keen way her eyes tracked conversations happening around her.

And then he caught her smiling during one of his colorful rants. He confronted her and she admitted that she could speak English. Why hadn't she said anything sooner? Because no one had bothered to ask. As far as Nigel knew, the others were still under the impression that she was either mute, couldn't understand them or both.

That was how their alliance started. In the days after her confession, with nothing to do but sit on the beach and wait for news, Nigel and Ran got to know each other better. He told her about his dreary past in London, and she told him about her shattered life in Tokyo. They found they had something in common.

Neither of them had lives to go back to.

Nigel crouched down next to Ran and scratched under Gamora's chin. "Of course they gave you the Chimæra named after a Godzilla monster, right? Bit stereotypical, innit? Thought the refugees of the advanced alien society would be better than that."

"I don't mind. I have always liked turtles." She looked at him evenly. "You do not need to complain about everything, Nigel."

Nigel sighed, glancing over his shoulder to where Daniela and Caleb had meandered down the beach. "You agree with me, though. That this situation we find ourselves in is bloody mental."

"Yes," Ran replied.

"So, you could speak up about it," Nigel pushed. "Get my back when soldier-boy tells me everything's peachy. I mean, you gotta start talking to the others eventually, yeah?"

Ran gazed out at the waves, thinking.

"I did not think I would survive the invasion," she said at last. "All I wanted to do was fight. There was no point to talking, to making friends." She paused. "After we came here, I kept it up so that General Lawson and those watching over us would speak freely around me. Our situation is a strange one, as you said. We need to know who we can trust, nakama."

The four of them spent weeks on that island in a weird limbo while the rest of the world shakily recovered from the invasion.

Then, finally, they watched from the beach as a squadron of black helicopters arrived at the base. The choppers carried military personnel and posh people in suits and bookish-looking types with crates of high-tech equipment.

"The unholy triumvirate," Nigel observed. "Soldiers, senators and scientists."

"Something's going to happen today," Caleb said.

"No shit," replied Daniela.

General Lawson spent his entire day in meetings with these new arrivals. The Garde twiddled their thumbs until almost sunset, when Lawson finally called them into one of the base's dull conference rooms. Arranged on the table were a bunch of glossy brochures, all of them depicting a beautiful blond teenager in the process of lifting a chunk of brick wall over her head, freeing a family that had been trapped underneath. The caption read: *OUR PLANET—OUR PROTECTORS—EARTH GARDE.*

"A delegation from the United Nations arrived today," General Lawson began without fanfare. "A decision has been made regarding—"

"Hold up," Daniela interrupted, tapping one of the brochures. "Why does this bougie girl look so familiar?"

"That's Melanie Jackson," Caleb answered.

Daniela stared at him blankly.

"The first daughter? You know, of our president?"

"Oh yeah," Daniela said. "She's strong, huh?"

Nigel squinted at his copy of the Earth Garde pamphlet. "Lotta makeup for a spontaneous act of heroism."

General Lawson pinched the bridge of his nose and pressed on. "Ms. Jackson is the first enrollee in the Earth Garde program, a UN-administered initiative to train and deploy you LANEs—excuse me, you Human Garde."

LANE was a term first coined by the US military, possibly by Lawson himself. Depending on who one asked, it meant either Legacy-Augmented Native Earthling or

17

Legacy-Afflicted Native Earthling.

Daniela smirked. "That what they're calling us now? Human Garde?"

Lawson sighed. "It's simple and less . . . offensive than LANE, apparently. There are PR gurus involved. Not my area of expertise."

"Oi," Nigel broke in. "Did you say deploy? As in, like, stormtroopers?"

Lawson began again. His patience for being interrupted had grown exponentially since he started working with Garde. "Participating countries, which include England and Japan—" He looked in Ran's direction. "Ah, damn. Forgot to get the interpreter in here for this."

"Not necessary," Ran said. "Please. Continue."

Everyone stared at her except for Nigel, who belted out a laugh. General Lawson puffed out his cheeks and shook his head, taking Ran's revelation in stride.

"As I was saying, the Earth Garde program has been agreed upon by most UN member nations. All Human Garde from participating nations will be required to register with Earth Garde and undergo training and observation at the Human Garde Academy, which is currently under construction in California." Lawson slid packets across the table, filled with forms and dense contracts. "The legal details are in here. If you want, we can have your parents flown in before you sign anything."

"Bollocks to that," Nigel said with a snort, thumbing through the pages.

Caleb exchanged a look with his uncle, then shook his head. "That's okay."

Ran and Daniela said nothing, both their families unaccounted for since the invasion.

"Once you've undergone training at the Academy and proven you won't be a danger to society, you'll be deployed to an Earth Garde unit. Not as stormtroopers," Lawson said, with a glance in Nigel's direction. "No one faces a combat situation until they're at least eighteen years old and hopefully by then the remaining Mogadorians are routed and the world's a goddamn utopia." The old military man smirked. "As outlined, your time with Earth Garde will be spent doing humanitarian work. Currently, Melanie Jackson is assisting with the cleanup efforts in New York. Daniela, I know you're from there and you've already demonstrated excellent control of your powers. I've arranged for you to skip the Academy and go straight to Earth Garde. Help rebuild your city."

Daniela's eyes widened. Although she didn't talk about it much, they all knew she was still holding out hope that her mom would be found somewhere in the rubble of Manhattan. The hospitals there were overwhelmed, many neighborhoods didn't yet have power restored and survivors were still being found. It was possible.

She looked at the other three Garde. Back at Patience Creek, she had promised John Smith she would protect them. But the invasion was over. She'd kept her word. Nigel grinned at her, and Ran nodded once.

Daniela reached across the table for a pen. "Where do I sign?"

Nigel leaned back in his chair and studied Lawson. "Right, then. Who's going to be in charge of this Academy thing? You?"

Lawson shook his head. "No. My job was the war, and the war is over. The UN has appointed someone better suited to training people of your unique abilities."

"Yeah? Who's that?"

✧ ✧ ✧

The Americans lobbied hard to host the Academy. With everything the United States had done to coordinate the counterattack against the Mogadorian warships, none of the other world leaders were in a position to push back. The Academy would technically be on international soil, the entire thing UN-funded, with Peacekeepers handling the security.

Fifty miles north of San Francisco, the secluded Point Reyes was chosen as the location for the Academy, the people of California and the National Park Service generously gifting the land to the United Nations. With a promise to be as eco-friendly as possible, building began immediately on the coastal cliffs of the former nature preserve.

"Damn, dude. Place is going to be huge," said the young man as he surveyed the construction, hundreds of workers already clearing earth and laying foundations, bulldozers and cranes rumbling across the landscape. "How many students we expecting?"

The older man standing next to him glanced up from his tablet. He pushed his glasses up his nose. "Last count they'd registered more than one hundred Human Garde. Finding new ones every day."

The young man whistled. His long black hair was tied back in a sloppy man-bun. It was windy here and he kept having to push rebellious strands of hair out of his eyes. He'd seen the blueprints and now, looking at the land, he tried to picture what the Academy would look like. Two dormitories each capable of housing five hundred students, a cul-de-sac of town houses erected for faculty housing, a school building equipped with state-of-the-art computers and laboratories, a recreation center, a training complex designed by the military, a sports fieldhouse, solar power and a tide-power generator. All that nestled between the fir trees of the valley and the rocky cliffs of Drake's Bay. Not so unusual, a private school in the middle of nowhere, albeit this one would be surrounded by miles of electrified razor-wire fence, its perimeter patrolled by round-the-clock security.

"What are you thinking, Professor?" Dr. Malcolm Goode asked, emphasizing the title that his young friend had negotiated for, despite never actually finishing high school.

The young man rubbed the spot where his prosthetic arm joined his shoulder. The thing still itched him like crazy.

"It's no penthouse," Nine said. "But I guess it'll do."

CHAPTER THREE

TAYLOR COOK
TURNER COUNTY, SOUTH DAKOTA

THE CLOSEST THING TO ACTION TAYLOR COOK SAW during the invasion was when a pickup truck filled with local boys rumbled by her family's farm and asked her father if he wanted to go to war.

"We're headed to Chicago, see if the army needs our help," announced the driver, Dale, the manager of the local grocery store. "Kill some of these goddamn aliens."

"Uh-huh," Taylor's dad, Brian, replied. "That right?"

Brian stood on their porch, his arms crossed skeptically. He and Taylor had run this farm together ever since Taylor's mom had run off. She knew what her dad's stance meant—it was the same as when one of the farmhands did something stupid. Her dad had an abiding patience for foolishness that Taylor didn't exactly share.

From a few steps behind her father, Taylor assessed the contents of the pickup truck. There were three men stuffed in the cab and another four perched in the bed, all of them carrying rifles and dressed in hunting fatigues. There was something almost comical about this bunch going off to fight aliens with bright orange reflectors glued to their shoulders. This whole day—warships, invaders, superpowers—it felt like a crazy dream to Taylor. She was scared, sure, have to be insane not to be. But that didn't stop her from smirking at her neighbors' makeshift posse.

One of the boys in the back of the truck caught Taylor's eye. "See something funny?" he asked. She recognized Silas, her father's main farmhand. He was in his early twenties, dark hair slicked back by a gloss of gel, a cigarette dangling from his lips. Taylor tossed her blond hair over her shoulder and crossed her arms, unintentionally copying her dad's posture.

"Have you seen the size of those spaceships?" she asked, meeting Silas's gaze. "What're your hunting rifles going to do against that? Jesus, they've got guys who can fly."

"The flying guy's on our side," Silas responded.

"Whatever," Taylor said. "I'm sure he's waiting for you to come save him, Silas."

"Better than sitting around doing nothing, anyway," he muttered.

"Running off to get killed, that's what you're doing," Taylor said. "You'll probably fall out of the back of that truck before you even hit the state line."

Some of the other boys in the back of the truck snickered. Silas seethed and fell silent.

"Folks on the news say we ought to stay in our homes," Brian stated coolly, sparing Taylor a glance over his shoulder. "Go home to your families for Pete's sake. It's a ten-hour drive to Chicago and who-knows-what. Safer to wait this out."

"It's the end of the world," Dale countered, his meaty arm hanging out the window. "We at least gotta go down swinging. Figured it wouldn't be neighborly if we didn't stop by and ask you to join us."

"Well," Brian replied with a sigh, "you asked. I'm staying right here, with my daughter. If you fellas insist on rushing off to do something dangerous, hell, you'll be in my prayers. I hope to see you again."

"Good knowing you, Brian," Dale said, throwing the truck into drive.

"I won't be in to work tomorrow, Mr. Cook," Silas yelled out as the truck started to pull away.

"Wouldn't expect you to be, son," Brian replied.

Taylor and her dad stood in silence, watching the truck careen up their dirt driveway and back the way it had come. When it was out of sight, their land was peaceful again. A butterfly floated by. The hogs squealed rambunctiously in the barn. To Taylor, it didn't look like the planet was in jeopardy.

"You don't think it's really the end of the world, do you?" she asked her dad.

"Don't know, sweetheart," Brian said calmly. Nothing shook her father, not even these so-called Mogadorians. "You want some ice cream? Might as well eat it, just in case the power goes out."

So, Taylor and her dad spent the invasion in front of their television, glued to news reports from the major cities. When the cable feeds occasionally cut out, they played tense games of Connect Four and Scrabble. Except for feeding the animals, they let their chores go and instead ate all the junk food in the house. Taylor tried to call and message some of her friends to see how they were doing, but the cellular networks were down. The farm started to feel like an island far removed from the battles taking place all over the world.

And then, just like that, it was over. The Mogadorian leader was killed, the warships went down and the Loric were hailed as heroes. The death toll was high, especially in the major cities, but those numbers seemed almost made-up to Taylor, like the entire invasion had taken place in a different universe. No one from Turner County died. When Silas slunk back to the farm a week after the invasion, she learned that he and the morons who took off to Chicago in their pickup truck had been turned back by the National Guard at a gas station on the Minnesota border. They spent the invasion getting drunk.

Within weeks, things were pretty much back to normal, at least in Taylor's part of the world. She saw the stories about human teenagers getting Legacies, about Mogadorians waging guerrilla warfare in Russia, about new laws that would apply to how extraterrestrials like the Loric would have to behave on Earth. None of this changed her daily grind. A war with her alarm clock, a few quick chores, school, dinner, homework, repeat.

At school, they called an assembly—all 158 students at the high school packed into the gymnasium—to talk about Earth Garde. It was a law now that anyone who developed Legacies needed to report them to their local authorities. Taylor had read about the Academy they were constructing for Human Garde in California. She didn't understand why the UN had to build that in America, or why the president and other politicians had pushed so hard to host. Anyone with Legacies was getting pulled out of their regular schools and sent there.

The guidance counselor asked if any of the students had experienced "visions" or "out-of-body experiences" because apparently those were things now. Taylor couldn't believe that the teachers were talking about this stuff so casually, like they'd just been plucked out of a comic book.

In the hall after, some boys joked about their "night visions" and Taylor groaned and rolled her eyes, secretly feeling relief that everyone at her school was normal.

"We're taking a road trip to Chicago this weekend to see the crashed warship," Taylor's friend Claire told her on the bus one day, a few months after the invasion.

"What?" Taylor replied. "Really?"

"I saw some girls on Insta, they got so close, that ugly-ass ship is like right behind them. So many likes," Claire continued. "Maybe if I get close enough, I'll score some Legacies."

Taylor rolled her eyes. "I don't think that's how it works."

"They're alien powers! No one knows how it works!" Claire laughed and nudged Taylor's ribs. "Come on. Like you don't want telekinesis or whatever."

"And get sent away to their weird alien Academy?" Taylor snorted. "No thanks."

"You'd probably get to meet John Smith," Claire replied. "He's so hot."

"Really? He always looks like he's about to cry in all those pictures."

"He's soulful! You're such a downer," Claire said without any malice. "So, do you want to come with us this weekend or what?"

Taylor didn't know how to explain to Claire that she liked their peaceful bubble of Turner County without sounding lame. So she lied about having too much work due and how her dad needed her help. She didn't need an up-close-and-personal view of an alien warship. Too real.

"It's like, everyone's already treating what happened like it's totally normal," Taylor said to her dad over dinner that night.

Her dad shrugged. "That's just people, hon. Given enough time, they can adjust to damn near anything. A few hundred years ago, if you'd shown folks an airplane or a cell phone, their heads would've exploded. I thought getting wireless internet out here on the farm would be the most awe-inspiring thing I saw in my lifetime. Pretty cool to be wrong."

"Wasn't so cool for all the people who died," Taylor said, pushing some corn around on her plate.

"No, that's true," her dad replied gently. "It can be a lot to wrap your head around. But we're safe here. You know that, right? Ain't nobody bothering little old Turner County."

Her dad was right. Taylor was comforted that Turner County remained pretty much unchanged in this brave new world. The articles she read about teenagers with Legacies speculated that everyone who was going to get the enhanced abilities had already gotten them—that it was a side effect of the war triggered by the Loric and that now it would stop.

They were wrong about that.

And eventually, her dad would be proved wrong about Turner County.

CHAPTER FOUR

THE CESSNA CAME IN LOW OVER THE TINY ABORIG-
inal village, sought the dusty runway and bounced through
a landing on the hard-packed ground. Nearby, a group of the
villagers huddled around a fire and prepared a freshly killed
sea turtle for dinner. They stuffed the spear-holes in the animal's shell with twigs and then buried it beneath coals so
that the meat inside the shell would cook. They paused in
their work to exchange glances as the plane's engine rumbled
to a stop. It was dusk and they weren't expecting visitors.

For this village, tiny was perhaps an understatement.
Only fifty aboriginals lived here, in the train-car-shaped
houses just a stone's throw from the Timor Sea. The walls
were made of corrugated steel, these all painted vividly with
images of stingrays and turtles and colorful dots and stripes.

Dogs that straddled the line between stray and domesticated weaved in and out of the mango and banana trees, barking at the plane.

Jedda, the village's matriarch, eyed the plane warily from the steps of her home, smoking a pipe. She was in possession of the village's lone satellite phone.

Even if she had called for help right then, it would not have arrived in time.

From inside the airplane, Einar watched the villagers shuffle about. He could tell they were uneasy. He was nervous, too. This was his first operation on behalf of the Foundation and he badly wanted it to go smoothly. Needed it to go smoothly. He wondered if this little village even knew that there had been an alien invasion, if they knew how much the world had changed in the last four months. He could see the glow of a TV set inside one of the houses. They weren't entirely cut off from society out here in the bush.

Still, he wondered if they even understood what they possessed.

Einar's gaze drifted away from the villagers and towards a tree where the fat leaves seemed to shift oddly on the wind. Not leaves. Those were bats. Dozens of them hanging upside down from the thinning branches.

He suppressed a shudder. It wouldn't be good to show weakness. Not considering his present company.

Sandwiched into the small plane with Einar were six very nasty-looking men. Mercenaries. All of them dressed in black body armor and carrying excessively large machine guns. Their leader was a Norwegian named Jarl, red-bearded with bulging neck muscles, a hooked scar that ran from his eye to the corner of his mouth. He and his men hadn't been much for conversation during the journey. The Blackstone Group weren't used to having a seventeen-year-old in charge of them. Einar wondered how much the Foundation was paying them.

Einar stood and delicately rolled up the sleeves of his shirt. He looked at Jarl. The men knew their orders; he didn't need to go over them again. Instead, he pointed at the ser-rated combat knife strapped to Jarl's belt.

"May I?" Einar asked.

Jarl handed him the knife handle first. Without hesitating, Einar gritted his teeth and dragged the blade across the inside of his forearm.

The villagers were taken by surprise when Einar stum-bled off the plane. A young, pale-skinned boy, dressed in sharply pressed chinos and a white dress shirt, carrying a stylish attaché case, his brown hair parted from the side. Some rich gubba whose plane lost his way? An intern from one of the mining companies that were always trying to buy up their land?

Bleeding from a cut on his arm. Deep and getting all over his shirt. The guy held up his arm.

"Hello? I'm sorry. Can someone help?"

Only half the aboriginals spoke English, but they all got the gist. They exchanged looks. One of the boys tending to the turtle—no more than fourteen, dark-skinned, with a mane of curly black hair—started immediately toward Einar. Jedda barked something at him in Yolngu Matha, a warning, but the boy waved her off.

He couldn't explain it, but he felt an overwhelming urge to help this injured white boy. He felt like the stranger was an old friend.

"I'm Einar," he said. "Do you speak English?"

"Yeah. I'm Bunji," the aboriginal replied. He took Einar's arm in his hands, his touch gentle despite the calluses on his palms. "What ya doing way out here?"

"Lost," Einar replied. "Lost and hurt, as you can see."

"Not for long," Bunji declared, unable to keep the pride and excitement out of his voice.

Some of the other villagers had edged closer. They always wanted to watch Bunji use his gift, which he'd first discovered when his older brother had accidentally cut his hand on a fishing line.

Bunji pressed his hand onto Einar's arm, not mindful of the blood. He squinted, and Einar felt a wave of warm energy wash into him. The sensation that followed was like a pleasant tickle.

When Bunji took his hand away, Einar's cut was gone. His arm was healed.

"Remarkable," Einar said, smiling at Bunji. "My friend, can you do this?"

Einar held up his attaché, then let it go. The case floated there, suspended in midair by telekinesis. Some of the villagers gasped. Bunji grinned and laughed.

"You! You're like me!" The aboriginal reached out with his own telekinesis and levitated a handful of nearby stones. He floated them around the two of them like tiny meteors orbiting a planet.

"Indeed," Einar said, and opened his floating attaché, produced a tranquilizer gun and shot Bunji in the neck. All the rocks he was levitating fell out of the air.

By the time the stones hit the ground, Jarl and his men were stepping off the plane, their guns clicking as the safeties were flicked off. They took care of the villagers while Einar carried Bunji to the plane.

The Foundation would be pleased.

CHAPTER FIVE

THE PATIENCE CREEK SURVIVORS
AN UNDISCLOSED LOCATION

AFTER DANIELA LEFT FOR NEW YORK, THE REMAIN-ing Human Garde spent three idle months at the island military base, basically in limbo while they waited for construction of the Academy to finish. Ran and Nigel played a lot of chess, using their telekinesis to move the pieces around the board. Caleb started to grow his hair out and kept to himself. Ran's room was right next to Caleb's and, at night, she could hear him talking to himself—arguing with one of his duplicates—but she never mentioned this to anyone.

Nothing much happened at the base. Apparently, the only job of the military personnel stationed there was to watch over the three of them. Around the world, other newly discovered Human Garde endured similar holding patterns, waiting for the Academy to officially open. The days blended together.

Until, two days before they were to depart for California, they came for the Chimærae.

"Colonel Ray Archibald has been assigned to lead security at this new Academy. He's a good man. Held down NORAD during the invasion. I briefed him on the three extraterrestrial creatures you and the others are in possession of. It's the colonel's opinion—and Earth Garde backs him up on this—that the animals pose a liability."

General Lawson stoically imparted all this to Caleb from behind his desk. Caleb sat opposite, perfectly at attention as usual. Regal, his hawk-shaped Chimæra, was perched on his forearm, his talons a gentle pressure. Idly, Caleb stroked his Chimæra's feathers.

Two scientists sent by the UN hovered at the edge of the room. One of them held a cage made of bulletproof glass, the airholes on the sides no bigger than pinpricks. The other wore latex gloves and brandished a syringe filled with some kind of sedative. They both watched Regal nervously, although the Chimæra paid them no attention whatsoever.

"Oh," was all Caleb managed to say to his uncle.

"Over the next six weeks, that Academy's going to be filling up with more than a hundred Human Garde, wild-ass teenagers all, from dozens of different countries. It's going to be a logistical nightmare keeping that place safe without adding shape-shifting monsters into the mix. You get me?"

Caleb nodded.

"Plus, we don't know what diseases these Chimærae could be carrying. They can transform into damn near anything. The Loric didn't think much of our environment when they set all this loose," Lawson continued.

Caleb looked into Regal's face. The bird cocked his head and flexed his beak. He didn't look sick to Caleb, but his uncle probably knew best.

"Okay," Caleb said, unable to keep some glumness out of his voice.

"It's just temporary," Lawson said. "Until the lab coats have a chance to check these beasts over, make sure they aren't a risk. You'll get Regal here back once he's been cleared."

"I understand," Caleb replied, swallowing. "I . . . have you told Ran and Nigel yet? They won't . . . I don't think they'll like this very much."

"I hoped that you'd help me convince them," Lawson said. "I know those two are . . . headstrong."

Caleb snorted. "They won't listen to me."

"Well, we aren't really having a discussion," Lawson said with a stiff shrug. "This is the way it's gonna be. They'll fall in line."

At a wave from Lawson, the two scientists approached Caleb and Regal. Caleb felt Regal's talons tighten on his arm, the Chimæra shifting uneasily. He held his free hand out towards the scientist with the injection.

"Better let me do it," he said. "He doesn't trust you guys."

The doctor seemed relieved to hand over the injection

to Caleb. Regal's dark eyes blinked, his head cocked, as he looked from Caleb to the needle.

"Sorry, buddy. I know this sucks," Caleb whispered to his Chimæra, hopeful that his uncle wouldn't overhear, or at least wouldn't judge him for being soft. "It's for the best, I guess."

Regal let out a squawk when the needle went in. Caleb thought it sounded more like sadness than it did pain, but he beat back this thought. Just like he beat back the duplicate that was trying to leap out of him, bundle up Regal and sprint as far away as possible.

Once Regal was peacefully asleep in his cage, they went in search of the other Garde and their Chimærae. Caleb had trouble keeping his shoulders from slumping on the way.

They found Nigel first, lounging in the hammock he'd hooked up in his room, listening to some screeching punk rock through a pair of oversized headphones. Bandit, surly-looking as his owner, rested on Nigel's belly with his furry legs up in the air.

"Mr. Rally, we need a moment—," Lawson began.

Nigel spotted the scientists—their gloves, the cage, the needle. He read the sullen look on the face of that goodie-two-shoes Caleb. He got the picture quickly.

"My arse! Run, Bandit! Escape the bloody fascists!"

Bandit listened. He dove off Nigel and transformed in the air, shrinking down to a mouse. He scurried toward the nearest air vent, the scientists too mesmerized by the transformation to react.

Not Caleb. He had orders. With a flick of his telekinesis, he shut the vent, cutting off Bandit's escape route. Then he plucked the fleeing Chimæra up, holding him telekinetically aloft, gently, his legs kicking. Bandit started to transform into a larger form—dark fur, claws and fangs. Before things could get any further out of hand, Lawson snatched the tranquilizer syringe from the frozen scientist and jabbed it into Bandit's morphing haunch.

"Young man, I appreciate your loyalty to this animal, but Earth Garde has determined—"

Lawson made it only that far through his lecture before Nigel punched him in the jaw.

Nigel was scrawny and hadn't thrown a lot of punches in his life, but what his punch lacked in power it made up for in passion. Not to mention the element of surprise. The blow caught Lawson off guard and sent the old man stumbling back. He ended up flopping right into Nigel's hammock, his legs kicked awkwardly up in the air.

Two duplicates sprung forth from Caleb and grabbed Nigel by the arms, pinning him up against the wall.

"You're just making things worse, Nigel!" Caleb yelled, the duplicates echoing his words.

"Shove it up your ass, ya sellout wanker," Nigel replied. Then he took a deep gulp of air and bellowed, his sonic manipulation Legacy making his next words loud enough to rattle the walls, not to mention make everyone in the room wince and stumble.

"RAN! THEY'RE STEALING THE CHIMÆRAE!"

Nigel's siren-like scream reached Ran all the way on the beach. She sat cross-legged, peaceful up until that point. Gamora basked in the sun next to her. At Nigel's scream, Gamora craned his stout neck to look up at Ran. She frowned thoughtfully, gently scratching Gamora under his chin.

"Better go into the water," she told him in Japanese. "Find me when it is safe, my friend."

Gamora seemed to understand. He trundled to the shoreline, glanced back once and then plunged gracefully into the ocean. Ran sighed.

Their departure for the Academy wasn't off to the best start.

CHAPTER SIX

KOPANO OKEKE
LAGOS, NIGERIA

WORD OF THE INCIDENT ON THE FOOTBALL PITCH traveled fast. Kopano was famous. Yesterday's tormenters were today's spokespeople, telling all their friends that Alien Boy Kopano was for real. Despite his mistreatment at their hands, Kopano didn't harbor any resentment towards those witnesses to his big day. In fact, he regarded them fondly, like a reluctant baby bird might view the cruel mother that launched him from the nest. Kopano didn't hold a grudge.

Everyone wanted to see what Kopano could do. "Prove it," they kept saying, the same challenge over and over. "Prove it."

By the end of the next school day, Kopano's face hurt from grinning. He'd spent much of the day doing tricks—levitating desks, juggling objects, even flying a couple of his screaming classmates through the lunchroom. His teachers were in awe, uncertain what the protocol was in matters of superpowered disruption. Kopano was one of their better students, usually quiet and courteous, so they let him have his day. After dismissal, the principal pulled him aside.

"What is happening to you is very good," the principal said. "You will be the pride of Nigeria. But please, Kopano, you must understand, this is a place of learning. You must try not to be so distracting to the other students."

"Not to worry," Kopano boasted. "Soon, I will be joining the Garde in America."

Kopano went home and told his family about what the principal said. His mother shook her head wearily. She'd spent the entire day at church. She told Kopano that she was praying for his safety, but Kopano was certain that meant she was trying to pray away his Legacies.

"Be careful, Kopano," his mother warned. "If you keep making a spectacle of yourself, they will come take you away. Or worse."

Kopano knew what his mother was talking about. Ever since the invasion, he'd been devouring every bit of news about the Loric and the changes they'd wrought. He had begged his father to drive him to Zuma Rock, where an outcropping of Loralite stone had grown, but Udo complained it would be a waste of time since the UN Security Council had set up a base there and weren't letting just anyone take tours. Also, Udo reasoned, the government might snatch him up if they got that close.

The prospect excited Kopano. The Americans had just finished building a school with the support of the UN that eventually all Human Garde from participating countries would be required to attend. It was only a matter of time before he would leave to begin his training with the other Garde.

That was what worried his mother.

"They will steal my child away to America and turn him into one of the aliens," she moaned.

"I want to go, Mom," Kopano said. "I'm not turning into an alien."

His parents ignored him, Udo dismissing his wife's concerns with a wave of his hand. He paced back and forth across their living room, a man possessed of a great idea.

"We have nothing to worry about," Udo said. "Kopano isn't going anywhere."

"You dumb man! You know how people in Lagos talk. Everyone already knows what he is . . ."

"Yes, they talk, that's true. But I know how to make it so that nobody important listens. The good people of Lagos will respect our family's privacy," Udo concluded. Kopano knew this meant his father would generously bribe as many people as necessary, although he wasn't sure where the old man would scrounge up the money. "And if this principal doesn't want our son in his school?" Udo stomped his foot. "Then we will give the man what he wants."

Kopano sighed, deciding not to argue. The Academy wasn't open yet, anyway. Let his parents have their way for now; eventually Earth Garde would come for him, no matter how many palms his father greased.

The next day, Udo made good on his promise. Instead of school, Kopano found himself sitting shotgun in his dad's old Hyundai, stuck in Lagos's bumper-to-bumper morning traffic. Already, the sun was hot overhead. The car's air conditioner needed fixing.

"Okay, I have come along," Kopano said with a sigh. "Now tell me what crazy scheme you have planned."

"It is not a scheme!" Udo yelled, pounding the horn as another driver cut him off. "You have a reputation now, Kopano. We would be stupid not to take advantage of that."

"What do I have to do?"

"Nothing! That is the beauty of reputations." Udo glanced in his son's direction. "Yes. That is good. Make that mean face just like that."

Kopano turned to look out the window. His gaze drifted to a roadside stall where a thin man with shifty eyes sold what he claimed were authentic alien artifacts. To Kopano, they looked like broken hunks of common electronics— toasters, TV parts, melted cellular phones—the kind of crap one would find in a dump. He shook his head again.

They drove across the bridge to Victoria Island, the slumped and crowded buildings of Kopano's neighborhood replaced by glittering skyscrapers, many of which were still under construction. A few of the wealthier kids Kopano went to school with lived on the island. Kopano also knew that this was where many of the foreign corporations set up—the banks and oil companies and real estate developers. A banner overhung the street reading *WELCOME TO AFRICA'S BIG APPLE.* Kopano rolled his eyes.

His father parked them in front of a fat hexagonal building. The windows were tinted gold, their glow reflecting onto the sidewalk and street. Udo told Kopano to wait, hopped out of the car and sauntered by the security guards at the door. He returned with a backpack slung over his shoulder, which he tossed into the backseat.

"What's in there?" Kopano asked, once they were driving again.

"None of our business," his father answered. "We are only deliverymen."

Kopano made to reach for the bag, but his father shouted and slapped his hand, accidentally swerving into the opposite lane. Kopano laughed. If he really wanted, he could wrestle the bag away from his father using telekinesis. But, he decided then, maybe it was better he didn't know. This work Udo had involved him in wasn't exactly battling Mogadorians for the fate of the world, but at least there was some excitement, a cloak-and-dagger feeling, like he was a spy. Kopano didn't want to ruin it by finding out they were ferrying bank contracts or something equally boring.

They drove halfway across the city, far away from Victoria Island, into an area where the roads were cluttered with potholes and the ramshackle buildings looked like they were jostling each other for room. Scrawny street vendors peered hungrily into their car. Kopano sat up a little straighter.

Udo parked them in front of a block where the buildings had collapsed in on each other, like a house of cards after a strong wind. The area was blocked off by police tape. A sign advertising the property developers who promised to revitalize the neighborhood was covered in graffiti.

Kopano spotted a group of men picking through the debris. Most of them looked like vagrants, sweaty from work, not much older than him. Supervising them was a chubby man in a hard hat who stood out all the more because of his wrinkled white suit.

Kopano turned to his father. "What now?"

Udo rolled down Kopano's window. "Give him the bag." He stopped Kopano from getting out of the car. "Use your powers!"

Kopano frowned. "Are you serious?"

"Just this one time," his father insisted. "Then they will know we're for real."

With shaky control—he was still mastering his telekinesis—Kopano lifted the bag from the backseat, floated it out the window and into the waiting hands of the man in the white suit. His whole crew had stopped to watch. Kopano got a kick out of how their mouths hung open in awe.

Days, and then weeks, went on like that. There were always more mysterious errands to run, an increasing volume of men in expensive suits and glittering sunglasses nodding their approval at Kopano's telekinetic deliveries. It got so that Kopano was going to school only a couple of days each week, and then only at the insistence of his mother.

He didn't show off anymore, so busy was he catching up on schoolwork. His teachers didn't make a fuss over his absences; they assumed it had to do with his training as a Human Garde, and Kopano suspected that Udo had played a role in that. He heard whispers about special treatment from his classmates, but no one had the guts to say anything to Kopano's face.

His father was, once again, an important man. All thanks to Kopano.

"Safest courier in Lagos!" he heard his father brag on the phone. "No one else will have their deliveries protected by a genuine superpowered Garde!"

They worked the banks, the oil companies, the developers. They delivered to hotels and hovels, to the slums and to resorts. Sometimes, they took duffel bags from policemen and delivered them to embassy employees. Kopano visited parts of Lagos he'd never seen before. He never looked in the bags, never asked what they were transporting. The family once again had a TV in their apartment. The rent was paid. Soon, his brothers would be transferred to better private schools. It was not America, it was not the Garde, but Kopano told himself he was doing good, at least for his family. He practiced a steely look on his deliveries but had a hard time keeping the grin off his face.

It was months before someone decided to test him.

Udo was navigating them to their drop-off, their sleek, newly purchased gray Lexus badly out of place in one of Lagos's more hardscrabble neighborhoods. Kopano had long ago gotten used to the slums. He didn't quite feel comfortable there but had begun to feel like their car was a bubble of protection.

Kopano noticed how suspiciously devoid of life this block was. He opened his mouth to say something. That was when a pickup truck accelerated out from the alley and slammed into the back of their car.

They were spun around. His father shouted. Kopano's ears rang.

When they came to a stop wedged against a street sign, Kopano saw them. Five men in bright red balaclavas. There were two in the truck and three on foot. They were all fit and Kopano thought they looked young but couldn't quite tell because of the masks.

"Bastards!" Udo shouted. "My car!"

The men descended on them. His father tried to drive away, but the Lexus sputtered. One of the men smashed through the driver-side window with a tire iron and began to punch Udo in the face. Another smashed through the back and grabbed the duffel bag they were transporting. Kopano watched all this in shocked disbelief.

Kopano's door was ripped open and two of the men dragged him into the street. One of them laughed; Kopano thought he sounded like a hyena. That was when he came to his senses.

He thrust his hands out and sent his two attackers flying with a burst of telekinesis. Their bodies looked like rag dolls as they hit a nearby wall.

The man punching his father stopped doing that and flung his tire iron at Kopano. The metal bar struck Kopano in the back of the head, caused him to stumble. He touched his scalp and found no blood. He was surprised by how little it hurt.

Kopano picked up the tire iron with his telekinesis and whipped it back at the man. He ducked out of the way and the tire iron crashed through the window of a vacant building across the street.

Another man jumped onto Kopano's back. Kopano ducked his shoulders low as if he were play-wrestling with his brothers, and threw the man off. He got back to his feet fast, but Kopano was ready, his fist cocked back.

Kopano was stout and had been in a few fights before, but he didn't expect the punch to knock the man fully off his feet. He didn't expect to hear the crunch of the man's jaw breaking. He looked down at his fist. It was as hard as a brick.

"Stop this!" Kopano shouted. "I will only keep hurting you if you force me to!"

One of the men he'd tossed into the wall rushed forward with a butterfly knife and stabbed Kopano in the stomach.

"Kopano!" yelled his father, spitting blood.

Kopano looked down. Where there should have been a wound, there was only a hole in his shirt. The knife's blade was folded up like it was made from paper.

His skin. It looked normal, but it was as durable as titanium.

Kopano backhanded the knife-fighter away from him, eyes wide with sudden fury. "You would have killed me! For what? For what?"

"Kopano!" his father shouted again, as Kopano loomed over his would-be murderer. "The bag! He's getting away with the bag!"

Kopano whipped around, spotted the man who'd taken the duffel bag sprinting down the street, laboring under the weight. The runner was already nearly a hundred yards away. Kopano squinted, tried to bring his telekinesis to bear. He'd never used his Legacy at this distance. He thrust out his hand, a telekinetic shove—and flattened the windshield of the car nearest the runner. The thief glanced over his shoulder, then hooked down an alley. Gone.

"I . . . I missed," Kopano said. The other thieves had used his distraction to scurry off, except for the two Kopano had knocked out.

"You let him get away!" his father barked. He came around the car, kicked one of their fallen assailants and tore off his mask. Neither of them recognized the guy. He was nobody. "Come on! We have to get out of here."

On the ride home, Kopano rubbed his knuckles and forearms. His skin didn't feel different. His sense of touch was unchanged. Yet, he knew, there was a new hardness lurking within him. He wondered if his new Legacy was a result of the jobs he'd been doing with his father.

"I do not think we should do this anymore," he said quietly.

"What!" his father bellowed. "Do you not understand what just happened, boy? We lost a delivery! The next job is the least of our worries. We will need to make amends and quickly."

Kopano didn't know what that meant. He shook his head and stared out the broken window, hot air rushing into the car. "This is not what I wanted," he said.

His father snorted, ignoring him. They rode home in silence.

That night, when he tried to sleep, Kopano could hear his father's pleading voice through the walls. Udo had been on the phone almost nonstop since they returned home, talking to whatever mysterious big man was in charge of the package they'd lost. He spoke in a meek voice that Kopano wouldn't have thought his father capable of. Kopano tossed and turned, Udo's wheedling apologies the worst kind of lullaby.

Kopano must have drifted off, because he did not hear the door to his room open, nor notice the shadow that padded across the floor. His eyes snapped open only when a cool hand pressed over his mouth.

"Kopano," a voice said. "It is time to go."

CHAPTER SEVEN

TAYLOR COOK
TURNER COUNTY, SOUTH DAKOTA

TAYLOR DISCOVERED THAT SHE WAS ONE OF THEM on the Wednesday morning when she reached for her buzzing alarm clock and accidentally sent the thing flying across her bedroom. The clock smashed against the wall, made a squawking sound like a dying goose and was silent. Taylor was 99 percent sure she hadn't laid a finger on it.

"Okay, get a grip," she told herself. "You were still half dreaming. It was an accident. You're freaking out over nothing."

Taylor held her hand out toward the broken alarm clock, gasping when it levitated and floated back to her.

"Dad!" she shouted.

Brian didn't hear her. He was already out of the house. Taylor threw open her bedroom window and gazed out over their small farm. The barn doors were open, her dad probably in there feeding the hogs.

A dented pickup truck made its way up their dirt driveway. That would be Silas. He got out of his truck, hair slicked back as usual, a pack of cigarettes rolled up in the sleeve of his flannel shirt, like a dingy version of some old movie star. Over the last few months, ever since she spoke up to him during the invasion, he'd started looking at Taylor in a new way, a creepy way. He always made a point of telling her how much she'd grown. He saw her watching and waved.

Taylor shut her window. Took a step back.

"This isn't happening," she told herself.

It'd been almost a year since the world got crazy. Things had been normal here, though, just like Taylor had hoped. She'd even gotten comfortable with the idea of aliens and superpowers in the world. But now . . .

"I . . . I can't be one of them."

But she was. Taylor realized she hadn't used her hands to shut her window just then. She'd used her mind. She went back to the glass, peering out, praying that Silas hadn't noticed anything. Taylor watched him saunter into the barn like nothing had happened and breathed a sigh of relief.

"Okay. Okay." She looked down at her hands. They were shaking. "Nothing has to change."

Taylor decided then and there that she would act like nothing happened. She got ready for school. Wiping steam off the bathroom mirror after her shower, Taylor studied her reflection. Blue eyes, wavy blond hair, a small nose and

PITTACUS LORE

rounded cheeks. She didn't look any different than yesterday. Granted, every day she looked more and more like her
mother, a fact that annoyed Taylor. But there was no physical manifestation of her telekinesis.

Telekinesis. A year ago that word was strictly in the
vocabulary of comic book readers and science fiction fans.
Now it was everywhere. The telltale sign of a Garde developing their powers. There were PSAs on TV about what to do if
you spotted someone using telekinesis. Taylor never thought
she'd be one of them.

She would hide. There were fewer than ten thousand people in all of Turner County. Those government people she
saw on TV would never come to South Dakota looking for
one of their so-called Human Garde. Her dad had said no one
would bother with their little town.

"Going to school!" she yelled into the barn as she half
jogged down the driveway to where the bus waited. Usually,
she'd never leave without giving her dad a hug and a kiss,
but Silas was there, lingering in the barn's doorway waiting to take the tractor out, and even though Taylor knew he
was just eyeballing her in his usual pervy way, she felt extra
exposed that morning and couldn't bring herself to get too
close.

Taylor zoned out in her history class, daydreaming about
the fiery images she'd seen of the invasion, imagining herself
there, clumsily floating around a broken alarm clock while
pale aliens shot at her with lasers. She got scolded, her classmates giggling after the teacher called her name five times.

53

At lunch, her friends told her that she seemed distracted and Taylor brushed them off, making an excuse about not sleeping well. When the kid in front of her grabbed the last peach iced tea from the drink cooler, Taylor nearly used her telekinesis to snatch the bottle out from under his fingers, then immediately felt ashamed. Whenever she needed to reach for something, she could feel the telekinesis urging her to use it. Ignoring the ability was like not scratching an itch. It frightened her how much the telekinesis already felt like a part of her, an instinct she had to fight against.

"It'll get easier," she promised herself in the bathroom mirror as she washed her hands. Then she floated a paper towel to herself from the dispenser, screamed in frustration and stomped her feet.

Sooner or later, she would screw up and someone would see her. Unless she learned how to bury this power deep inside her, make like it never existed. But already that felt like keeping an arm tied behind her back.

On the bus ride home from school, Taylor stared mutely out the window while Claire rambled on about some boy. She watched Turner County glide by and then imagined the bus carrying her onwards, all the way to California and that bizarre Academy for Human Garde. If they caught her, that's where she'd end up.

She had promised herself that she would never leave Turner County.

Inevitably, this led Taylor to remembering the last time she'd seen her mom. She was nine years old and they were at the bus station in Ashburn. Her mom wore jeans that Taylor thought were too tight, a tied-off plaid shirt and a red bandanna in her hair. All the rest of her clothes were stuffed into the backpack she carried on her shoulder.

"You're coming back, right? This isn't forever," Taylor had said to her mom.

"Oh, honey," Taylor's mom said, and touched her gently on the cheek. "You can come visit me whenever you want. Minneapolis is only a couple of hours away."

Young Taylor glanced over·her shoulder to where her father sat in their truck, watching them, a baseball cap pulled low to hide his eyes. She looked back to her mom.

"But how will I get there?" she asked. "I'm nine."

Her mom smiled. "You'll see one day, Tay. A person can't stay in Turner County forever. Even if it hurts now, you'll come to understand."

Minneapolis was just Taylor's mom's first stop in her flight from South Dakota. She kept going farther and farther east—after Minneapolis was Madison, then Chicago, and the last Taylor heard it was Philadelphia. Taylor never ended up visiting any of those places. Her mom promised that one day Taylor would understand, but she didn't want that day to come because it'd mean she was like her mother. She'd take over the farm from her daddy, just like he'd taken it over from his daddy.

Her dad made patty melts and French fries for dinner that night. She got the feeling that he had noticed her hasty departure that morning and thought maybe she was mad at him, so he cooked one of her favorite meals. Taylor hugged him while he was frying up the burgers.

"There's my girl," her dad said, sounding relieved.

Over dinner, Taylor studied her dad. He was a handsome man with his half day's growth of beard, brown hair graying at the temples, lean and tan from all the work around the farm. He'd never remarried after Taylor's mom, not even a girlfriend as far as Taylor knew, although the single ladies in the county still sent over cookies and pies on a regular basis. She got teary-eyed while picturing a scenario where she'd have to say good-bye and leave him here all by himself.

Brian caught Taylor looking at him and rubbed a hand across his cheek. "What is it? I got slop on me?"

She laughed. "No, you're all good, Daddy."

"If you say so." He kept looking at her. "What about you? You all good?"

She nodded. "Yeah. I'm fine. Just tired."

Then, Taylor reached for the salt and the little glass shaker slid across the table right into her waiting palm.

They looked at each other.

After a long silence, Brian said, "Well, I'll be damned." Finally, Taylor started to cry, big heaving panicked sobs, and her dad came around the table to hold her. "Come on, now. I always knew you were a special one and this just proves it."

"I don't—I don't want to be special!" Taylor replied through her tears. "I like our life here! I don't want anything else!"

Taylor's dad rubbed her back. "Come on, now," he said

quietly. "I saw them say on TV that the ones who get powers are the best among us. That they're destined to be important people."

"I saw that same show, Dad! The one lady said all that flowery bullcrap, and the other guy said it was all random. An alien lottery. And I didn't want to win!"

"Well," her dad said calmly, "I choose to believe the bit about destiny."

"Are you not listening? I don't want a great destiny. I like it here. With you I don't want to go to their dumb Academy."

"Then you won't have to." Her dad nodded once, like he'd just come to this decision. "You don't have to do anything you don't want to do."

"But it's a law now. You're supposed to . . ." She swallowed. "You're supposed to turn me in."

Brian shook his head. "Not in a million years."

"But someone else could see," Taylor said. "You don't know how hard it was today at school to control myself. All day, I wanted to use it. I'll slip up."

Brian considered this for a moment, studying Taylor, who was studying her hands like they'd suddenly become foreign.

"Just us and the hogs out here, most times," her dad said slowly. "Maybe if you practice doing your alien-thing around the house, it'll be easier when you're out in public."

"Ugh. Please don't call it my alien-thing."

"Sorry. Your Legacy."

Taylor frowned. All day, she'd been thinking about ways to suppress her telekinesis. Maybe her dad was onto something. Maybe instead of ignoring her power, she could exhaust it in the moments when it was safe to use, get it out of her system.

"It's worth a try," she admitted.

"Besides," her dad said, picking up the saltshaker and wiggling it through the air, "I think it's pretty cool to watch."

For a month, Brian's plan worked. Taylor used her telekinesis around the house—she floated her homework books out in front of her while she studied, poured herself glasses of water in the kitchen while standing in the living room and spooned sugar into her dad's morning coffee while flipping eggs. Her control began to get more precise, the tasks she could complete more complicated, the objects she could lift heavier. And while it felt like a part of her was asleep whenever she went to school or when Silas and the other farmhands were around, Taylor found it easier and easier to keep from slipping up in public.

But then came the day of the accident.

CHAPTER EIGHT

NIGEL BARNABY
THE HUMAN GARDE ACADEMY—POINT REYES, CALIFORNIA

SHE WAS PLAYING THE CLASSICAL MUSIC AGAIN. Nigel heard it as soon as he walked into Dr. Linda's office. Daintily plucked violin strings, whistling woodwinds . . . and was that a bloody oboe? Nigel couldn't tolerate that, so he reached out with his Legacy, grabbed hold of the sound waves rolling out of Dr. Linda's stereo and bent them until they were a jangling mess of out-of-tune squeals.

Dr. Linda narrowed her eyes at him and turned off her stereo. "Nigel, we've talked about this. If you don't like the music, you can ask me to change it."

"Where's the fun in that, love?" Nigel replied as he flopped down on Dr. Linda's comfortable couch, hugged a pillow to his chest and put his combat boots up on the armrest.

Dr. Linda's office was on the top floor of the administration building, the windows south-facing with a captivating view of the blue-glass bay. She kept the room open and bright, the walls covered in splotchy abstract paintings meant to evoke reactions from her patients. Her degrees, one each in psychiatry and developmental psychology, both from Stanford, hung over her neatly kept desk.

"We've also discussed respect for my space," Dr. Linda admonished, eyeing his boots. She was a short woman, barely five feet tall, with a cherubic face, graying brown hair cut in a bob and thick-framed lavender glasses that made her look like a naughty librarian. Nigel liked her, which was why he went out of his way to get on her nerves.

"What shall we talk about this week?" Nigel asked as he swung his feet to the floor. He slouched low, his long legs reaching across the space so he could almost play footsie with Dr. Linda. Not that he would. He idly flicked the barbell in his septum—his newest piercing, the thirteenth in his head alone. "Perhaps your love life for a change, eh, Doc? I'm bored talking about me, me, me, all the time."

Dr. Linda regarded him levelly. "You know I record these sessions, right, Nigel?"

"Sure. So you can keep it all straight for that bestseller you're gonna write, yeah?" Nigel used his Legacy, changing the pitch and timbre of his voice so that he sounded almost exactly like Dr. Linda. "I forced two hundred teenaged Garde to discuss their wet dreams. Here are my findings."

Dr. Linda was, as usual, unperturbed by his sonic manipulation. "I do not make you or any of the others discuss their quote-unquote wet dreams," she said dourly. "We could, though, if you'd like."

"Well, you certainly called my bluff," Nigel said, smirking as he worked a finger around the collar of his moth-eaten Suicide tank top.

"When I attempted to listen back to our session from last week, I couldn't hear anything on the recording," Dr. Linda pressed on as if he'd never interrupted. "Was that your doing, Nigel?"

Nigel tugged on his lip ring, not sure whether to fess up or lie. Eventually, he threw on his customary devil-may-care grin and nodded. "Sorry about that, Doc. Didn't realize my powers would flummox your recorder."

"What exactly did you do?"

"Neat bit of business, actually. I put us in a sound bubble." Nigel was unable to keep the pride out of his voice; this was a new application of his sonic manipulation Legacy. "Made it so nobody outside our little circle of trust could hear."

Dr. Linda tilted her head. "Are you worried people might be listening to our sessions? I assure you, these are kept completely confidential."

Nigel tucked his chin down and looked at the therapist skeptically. "If you say so, Doc. You live on campus, right? Over in the little faculty village?" He knew she did, so he kept going. "And you don't ever get the feeling you're being watched? Like every mirror's got a bloke with a clipboard hiding on the other side?"

"That's an interesting observation," Dr. Linda responded.

That was the token neutral statement she deployed whenever Nigel set off one of her therapy alarm bells. He kicked himself for giving her something to work with. "Do you think those feelings of paranoia might be rooted in your time at the boarding school?"

Nigel groaned. He'd been seeing Dr. Linda every week since he first arrived at the Human Garde Academy. You couldn't see a woman like Dr. Linda that often for almost a year and not let a few secrets slip.

So, much to his great regret, Nigel had told Dr. Linda about the Pepperpont Young Gentlemen's Preparatory Academy. "After that fuckin' helltrap, superhero training school is easy-peasy," he'd told her at the time. Nigel had recounted the details of his four years at Pepperpont grimly—the uniforms, the stiff professors, the chores, the very particular tie knots. "But you could get all that from Dickens, eh?" He went into the darker details. The rich boys with bad taste in music. The rich boys who wanted to get experimental with him, then pretended like it never happened, then beat the piss out of him every day for months. The endless teasing, name-calling, abuse. The time that they stripped him, shaved him and dropped him out of a second-story window.

"Like prison," he'd explained, "except instead of knowing how to fix up a shiv from a toothbrush, all these blokes knew the rules of cricket. Future barristers and brokers, the lot."

When the invasion happened and Nigel discovered he'd developed telekinesis, he released himself from the custody of Pepperpont. He found an open tattoo parlor to push clear the holes in his ears that had started to close, bought an updated wardrobe at a thrift store and pledged to live the rest of his days as the alien-fighting punk rocker that lived inside him, the same badass gorilla the nice people of Pepperpont had tried so hard to tame.

There was a warship over London. That's where his parents lived, although at the time they were in Zurich on a ski trip with his older sister and her stockbroker fiancé. If they tried to call him during the invasion—"Surely, they tried to locate you; you're their son," Dr. Linda had said—Nigel was long gone by the time they rang. He hadn't seen them since. There were visiting days at the Academy, but Nigel refused to add them to the list. He couldn't forgive them for Pepperpont.

"Perhaps you have lingering anxieties from your days there," Dr. Linda said in the present. Nigel had spaced out. "Even though you're safe here, perhaps you still feel the need to keep a part of yourself walled off."

"Yeah, you got it in one, Doc," Nigel replied. "Bloody breakthrough."

Dr. Linda raised an eyebrow. "How's it going with your roommate?"

A sudden change of topic. Nigel hated when she pulled that.

"Fine," he said. "The same. Whatever. Ask him yourself. Captain America's got his weekly head shrink scheduled right after me, doesn't he?"

"Have you reached out to him? Last week, you promised

you would visit the dining hall with him at least once a week."

Nigel folded his arms. Any chance of him becoming besties with Caleb went out the window that day on the island, when he helped turn their Chimæra over to the government. Nigel held a grudge, but Dr. Linda was persistent about trying to mend that relationship. "He apologized to you, didn't he?" Dr. Linda pressed when Nigel remained stubbornly silent.

Nigel grunted. "So?"

"So, I think forgiveness might be a good skill for you to work on, Nigel."

Nigel scowled. He thought about Caleb and their months spent rooming at the Academy together, surrounded by dozens of other Human Garde. Nigel was popular around campus—his classmates remembered him from the shared vision during the invasion, they knew he'd gone to fight the Mogs. The legend about how he and Ran had taken down a Mogadorian skimmer at Niagara Falls grew and grew—in every telling, they killed more Mogs, battled against greater odds. The other Garde who were there—Fleur and Bertrand, who had died at Patience Creek—were omitted from the story. Nigel didn't stop the tale from circulating. He liked having a reputation, even though it came at the expense of some real-life pain.

And maybe he'd let slip, when the other Human Garde were first getting to know each other, that Caleb was a government plant who would report their every action to the

Earth Garde administrators. So what? It was true, wasn't it? Caleb spent more and more time alone in his room rather than with his fellow Garde.

Well, alone wasn't exactly right. Caleb had the duplicates, after all.

"He doesn't have any friends. Still. After all this time," Nigel complained.

"Which is why you should reach out to him."

"What's that they say about a bloke, huh? A creep who can't make friends . . ."

"Do you think the boys at Pepperpont thought of you that way, Nigel?"

"Aw, that's a bloody low blow, Doc. Totally different scenario."

Dr. Linda regarded him evenly. "Is it?"

"I never did anything to those wankers as bad as what Caleb did to me," Nigel said defensively. As she stared at him, unspeaking, Nigel heard his tone of voice change. This wasn't his Legacy at work; this was the whiny boarding school aristocrat coming out. "This my therapy hour or Caleb's? I'm starting to wonder."

"What else would you like to talk about, Nigel?"

"How about me having to come see you every week?" he replied sharply. "Me and Ran, Caleb—we're the only ones on campus who see you all the time. People might start to think we're bloody abnormal."

"They will not."

"They definitely already think that about Caleb."

"You know very well why you're monitored more closely than the others. Precisely because you've been exposed to a life-and-death scenario."

"It wasn't even all that traumatic," Nigel muttered, thinking back to the brutal fight at Patience Creek. "I never think about it."

"No more nightmares?" Dr. Linda asked him.

Another little fact Nigel should have never let slip; he had a reccurring dream of being pursued down a smoky hallway by the mad Mogadorian woman who'd hunted them.

"No," he lied.

"Then I suppose you are cured," Dr. Linda replied. "See you next week."

In the posh waiting room outside Dr. Linda's office, Nigel found Caleb waiting for his appointment, seated next to one of his duplicates. The two were huddled close, apparently deep in a whispered conversation that cut off as soon as they noticed Nigel. It looked like Caleb had been scolding his clone.

"He wanted to eavesdrop," Caleb said sheepishly, gesturing to his duplicate.

"Uh-huh," Nigel replied, raising an eyebrow. "You're gonna want to cut that shit out, mate. It's not couples therapy. Wouldn't want the doc thinking you're a freak."

Caleb nodded in agreement. "Yeah, Linda says I shouldn't . . ." He trailed off, looking at his clone. "Never mind. He was just leaving."

The clone kept its gaze on Nigel, even as Caleb began

to absorb it. The process still made Nigel's skin crawl. The clone went transparent, like a ghost, and then slowly flowed back into Caleb. There was always a moment when they were back together but still overlapped slightly that would give Caleb a blurry four-eyed look, like a person coming apart. Nigel suppressed a shudder. He wasn't the only one on campus who Caleb unnerved, as evidenced by Dr. Linda pushing Nigel to be friends with the aloof duplicator.

When there was only one of him, Caleb stood up. He patted Nigel companionably on the shoulder—these Americans were always touching, high-fiving, back-patting—then brushed by him, into Dr. Linda's office. "See you back at home," Caleb said, as he closed the door.

Nigel wondered, not for the first time, if tonight would be the night that an army of Calebs held him down in bed and smothered him.

CHAPTER NINE

TAYLOR COOK
TURNER COUNTY, SOUTH DAKOTA

THE ACCIDENT HAPPENED ON A SATURDAY, THE DAY dry and sunny. "Got lucky with the rain," Taylor's dad reported. "Good baling weather."

The Cooks owned ten acres of hayfield, just enough to feed their own animals every year and maybe sell a few left-over bales to their neighbors. The weekend before, Brian and Silas had cut the field, raked the stalks into rows and left them out to dry. Today, Brian would attach the small baler to the tractor and ride over the rows, while Silas and a couple of other farmhands would trail behind, collecting the freshly made bales and lugging them to the barn. As usual, Taylor's job would be to direct traffic. Left to their own devices, Silas and the others would stack the bales nonsensically, like the year they'd piled the hay right where the tractor was always parked. Her dad hadn't realized until after the farmhands had left and he had to move every bale himself before he could get the tractor in the barn.

"You know," her father mused over breakfast, "we could do this whole thing just you and me. Probably only take us until noon. Nobody'd even break a sweat."

"Dad." Taylor rolled her eyes.

"My superpowered farmhand would be the envy of all our neighbors," he said with a laugh. Brian stroked his chin, suddenly deep in thought. "Probably save us a lot, actually. Could get to some of those projects I've been putting off. Well, you could, anyway, and I would supervise." He winked at Taylor. "This place might actually turn a profit."

"We do just fine," Taylor said. "Besides, if you cut Silas loose, how would he afford those butt-ugly tattoos?"

Brian chuckled. "Come on, now. Don't put that boy's 'artwork' on me. Making me think I oughta fire him for his own good."

"So, you had at least one smart idea this morning," Taylor replied with an easy smile.

Taylor had first noticed Silas's latest tattoo a few days earlier, when he made a show of sitting at their kitchen table, easing off the bandage and applying some salve to the raw, pink flesh of his forearm. The tattoo depicted a coiled serpent bursting forth from within a circle, its dripping fangs bared; as if in response to the snake's emergence, a scythe swung down for the reptile's throat. Taylor had eyed the tattoo skeptically. She imagined Silas walking around the fields, lopping the heads off of garter snakes for fun.

"You like it?" He'd caught her looking and immediately perked up.

"Not really," she said, and left the kitchen, but not before she caught the disappointed look on his face.

The farmhands showed up while Taylor was washing the dishes. There was Silas, of course, along with Brent and Teddy. Brent was around her father's age, plump, with a bushy brown beard. He was a distant cousin of hers, on her mom's side, although they weren't very close. He'd been helping out on the farm since before Taylor was born; Brent and her father had an easy camaraderie, even if her dad sometimes called Brent "shiftless" behind his back. Teddy, on the other hand, was a guy who'd gone to community college with Silas, muscular, quiet and sweet, a hard worker, basically Silas's complete opposite. Silas had gotten Teddy the gig on the Cook farm and Taylor always suspected it was because Silas knew he could pawn off some of his own work onto good-natured Teddy's broad shoulders.

That afternoon, Silas insisted on working without a shirt, even though the hay surely made his skin itchy. Taylor watched from the porch as he and the others hauled bales back to the barn. Once he worked up a good sweat, his ropey muscles caked with dirt and golden flecks of hay, Silas sauntered over to the porch for a drink of water. Taylor cringed.

"You hurt my feelings the other day," he said to her.

"How's that?" she replied with a sigh.

Silas held up the arm with the snake tattoo. "Making fun

of my tattoo. This one's important to me, y'know?"

"What is it? Some death metal band?"

"Naw, nothing like that—"

"Look, it's fine as far as tattoos go, all right?" Taylor said, hoping to end the conversation. "Just not my thing."

Silas leaned against the porch bannister. "You like a clean-cut type, that it? Like them boys you go to school with?"

Taylor's skin crawled, but she looked back at him steadily. In the past, she would have endured Silas's gross come-ons in silence. But now, even though she was keeping her power secret, the telekinesis made her feel safer. Bolder.

"Maybe you could get one of those Chinese characters next."

Silas perked up. "Oh yeah? You like those?"

"Yeah, maybe we could get an English-to-Chinese dictionary and see if they've got a symbol for 'creep.'"

Silas forced a laugh, then made a point of giving Taylor a once-over. "Come on, now. I ain't no creep. Nothing wrong with having an appreciation for the finer things in life."

Before Taylor could respond, they both heard shouts from the field.

"Help! Silas! Help!"

That was Teddy screaming. Taylor was off the porch in a flash, sprinting towards the field, Silas close on her heels.

The tractor had blown a tire and rolled over. Taylor's dad was either thrown or jumped clear. Either way, he lay a few yards away, not moving, facedown in the dirt. To make matters worse, Teddy had been too close to the baler when the tractor pitched and gotten his sleeve tangled in the machine. The baler could pull you in and strip your skin right off if you weren't careful, especially when it wasn't upright. Bloody welts were already forming on Teddy's arm where he struggled against the baler; Brent had his arms wrapped around Teddy's waist, doing all he could to keep him from getting shredded.

"Son of a bitch!" Silas yelled as he joined Brent in trying to free Teddy. "Turn that thing off!" he shouted at Taylor.

Without even thinking about it, Taylor used her telekinesis to throw the power lever on the baler. The machine wheezed to a stop. The three farmhands fell in a heap as Teddy's arm came free, Teddy crying tears of relief.

Luckily, in the chaos, the farmhands hadn't noticed Taylor use her Legacy. She rushed to her dad's side, fell to her knees beside him and rolled him over, her telekinesis helping with his weight. Taylor saw a gash on her dad's forehead from where he'd landed on a rock. There was a lot of blood—one side of her dad's face was caked in copper-tinged mud. Worse than just a few stitches. Taylor thought she could see a bit of bone peeking out through all the grime and gore.

A strange calm settled over her. She knew what to do.

Taylor pressed a hand to her dad's forehead, felt warm energy flow through her and into him and watched as his wound miraculously closed. Seconds later, his eyes fluttered open and she breathed a sigh of relief.

"Hell, what happened?" he asked blearily.

Taylor felt eyes upon her. She turned slowly, saw the three farmhands all standing there and staring at her. Their eyes were wide, their mouths agape. They'd seen what she did.

"You're . . . you're one of them!" Silas exclaimed.

"Hold on, I can explain," Taylor replied, her mind searching for a convincing lie.

Silas took off, running as fast as he could back towards the house. Taylor and the others watched, puzzled, as he sprinted to his truck and took off up the dirt road.

"That'll be trouble," her father said, sitting up. He touched the front of his shirt—nearly soaked through with blood—and shook his head in disbelief.

"Don't see what got into him. I didn't see nothing to be scared of," Brent said, her cousin turning to look meaningfully at Teddy. "You see anything, Ted?"

Teddy continued to stare at Taylor, his mouth open. Brent elbowed him.

"Yeah, uh, I mean, no," Teddy said. "Didn't see nothing."

"Double wages for today," her dad said to Teddy as he slowly climbed to his feet. "For the trouble."

Taylor stayed quiet through it all, her eyes on the dusty trail left by Silas's quick exit. She should've been amazed by what she'd done—healing a massive gash with just a touch!—except there was already a heavy seed of anxiety growing in her stomach. The way Silas had looked at her, not leering anymore but repulsed . . .

Well, the secret's out now, she thought, surprised to feel some small glimmer of relief. Whatever happens next, at least there's no more hiding.

Taylor snapped her attention to Teddy when he stepped forward and sheepishly held out his bloody arm. "Maybe I could also not see you doing your magic for me, Taylor?" He smiled shakily. "Please?"

For a week, Taylor and her dad waited for the other shoe to drop. Silas stopped showing up for work and wouldn't return phone calls. Taylor kept waiting for a battalion of soldiers to come and take her into custody, but after another week went by as if nothing had happened, she began to get hopeful.

"Maybe he didn't tell anyone," she told her dad over breakfast, although the words rang hollow.

Her dad's brow furrowed. He pushed his food around his plate, his appetite diminished since the accident.

"It ain't so much the telling that worries me," her dad said after a moment. "It's who he tells."

A few days later, Teddy showed up at the farm. He'd been picking up Silas's shifts since he disappeared, but it was Sunday, the day the Cooks didn't have help. Brian met him on the porch and Taylor eavesdropped at the door.

"I went out in Sioux Falls last night," Teddy explained. "Saw Silas. He was with a strange bunch of fellas, Mr. Cook. He saw me, came over, started asking about Taylor."

"Government types?" her dad asked.

"Nuh-uh," Teddy replied. "Y'know them Bible-thumping sort that go door-to-door sometimes, all intense and in your business? These guys looked like them but . . . meaner. Gave me the heebie-jeebies, so I got outta there quick. Then, this morning, I seen some of them same guys driving around town. Figured it wouldn't be right if I didn't come out here and warn you."

After Teddy left, Mr. Cook got his shotgun out of storage. He sat out on the porch with the weapon across his lap and waited.

"Who do you think they are?" Taylor asked.

Her dad grimaced. "Don't know." He paused and she could tell he was debating how much to tell her. He touched the spot on his forehead where there should have been a scar from his fall off the tractor. "When all this first happened with you, I did some research into . . . you know, how things are now. There's some people out there, crazy people, with nasty ideas about kids with your gifts."

Taylor's hands shook. "Maybe we should call somebody. The police, at least."

"They'll take you away." He looked over his shoulder. "You want that, Tay?"

She shook her head. She didn't want that. But she didn't want her father to get hurt either.

"This is our family's land," her dad concluded resolutely. "Ain't nobody pushing me around on our land."

They came at nightfall.

Taylor's dad hustled her inside when the first set of headlights came into view. She didn't go far—she was the one with the Legacies, after all—her dad had only his shotgun and a single box of ammo. Taylor peeked out from behind the screen door, watching the vehicles come.

They made a show of driving up, coming in abreast of each other like they were in formation, riding roughshod over the fields. There were a couple of RVs, some pickup trucks, a handful of motorcycles and a big van like cops would use to haul prisoners. Spray-painted on the sides and hoods of some of the vehicles was that same snake-and-scythe symbol that Silas had tattooed on his forearm.

Her father stood on the porch with his gun ready as the men got out of their cars and formed a perimeter. Taylor assumed they were mostly men, anyway—she couldn't see their faces. Many of them wore gasmasks. Some of them opted simply for bandannas covering their mouths and noses like outlaws. Taylor didn't know what to make of the metallic headgear some of them sported. Looked almost like tinfoil hats. Taylor scanned the crowd but couldn't pick out Silas from their number. There were about thirty of them.

"You people are trespassing!" her father yelled. He made an effort to keep his voice steady, but Taylor could tell he was scared.

The men were armed. Pistols and machine guns and assault rifles. Her dad's shotgun was loaded with buckshot.

A man came forward from the crowd. He wore a black bandanna, a coal-colored duster and no silly headgear. His curly hair was salt-and-pepper. He held his hands up as if to keep things calm.

"Mr. Cook, isn't it? Brian Cook? Can I call you Brian?"

Her dad pumped his shotgun in response.

"Now now, Brian, don't go doing anything rash. We didn't come all the way out here to hurt you. On the contrary! We came to protect you."

"Protect me from what?"

"Why, from that thing living in your house," the man answered.

Taylor thought about the clips she'd seen of the Garde fighting during the invasion. They used their telekinesis to rip the weapons right out of the hands of their enemies. She could do that if she focused.

Except there were an awful lot of guns out there.

She looked down at herself and gasped. There was a red dot on her chest. Someone sighting her through the screen. She ducked behind the door frame, heart pounding.

"They always told us in Sunday school that the devils lived down below, but we know now that's not the case, don't we, Brian?" the man was saying. "They came from the stars. Descended just like Lucifer did. Seeded the world with their sin. Now that corruption's growing, manifesting in ways that defy the laws of nature. Satan, he wants you to see those powers as miracles. He wants you to worship these supposed guardian angels. But I know my Bible, I remember the words of Corinthians—"

"Jesus," Taylor's dad said. "Don't you ever shut up?"

The preacher sighed. "We're here to Harvest the sin, Mr. Cook. Your daughter, she didn't choose to have that filth possess her, and my heart goes out. It's a shameful and ugly business. But we got to do what God commands and Harvest these false prophets before they get a chance to grow. You go ahead and stand aside now, so we can do God's will."

While the man spoke, Taylor's dad half turned and hissed in her direction. "Taylor, you run out the back now."

"No, Dad."

"I love you, now you run—!"

Taylor's dad aimed his shotgun at the preacher.

He fired. And, at the same time, a dozen other guns fired back. *Pop-pop-pop.* Their peaceful farm, now a war zone.

And then, a moment later, the night sky filled with fire.

CHAPTER TEN

KOPANO OKEKE
ZUMA ROCK, NIGERIA

"DOES FATHER KNOW ABOUT THIS?"

Kopano's mom stared at him. "What do you think?"

She drove a car borrowed from one of her church friends, Kopano buckled in beside her. He could not remember the last time that he saw his mother drive. She hunched over the wheel, the color drained from her knuckles. She kept checking the rearview mirror, worried they were being followed.

It was Akuziem, his mother, whose cool hand had pressed over Kopano's mouth and awoken him in the middle of the night.

She had already packed a bag for him.

She led him past the living room, tiptoeing in a way Kopano found overly dramatic. His father was passed out in the armchair, a half-empty bottle of ogogoro in one hand, his cell phone clutched in the other. Finally done making apologies for their lost delivery, Udo had drunken himself into a stupor. When Kopano stopped to stare at his father, Akuziem grabbed his arm and yanked him down the hall.

"Say good-bye to your brothers," his mother whispered.

Kopano looked at her with alarm. "Are we in trouble, Mama?"

"I am sorting it out," she whispered back, then waved him forward impatiently. "We must be quick."

Kopano crept into the narrow bedroom that his little brothers shared. Obi stretched out on his back and snored relentlessly, while little Dubem huddled close to the wall with a pillow pushed over his head. Kopano kissed Obi on the forehead, the boy not even stirring. He couldn't reach Dubem's face, nestled as it was in his pillows, so he settled for squeezing his youngest brother's little arm. Dubem rolled over immediately, tired eyes trying to focus.

"Kopano? What's wrong?"

"Nothing," Kopano replied too quickly, his smile forced. "Just saying good night."

Dubem eyed him skeptically. He soon noticed the canvas pack slung over Kopano's shoulder. "Is this it? Are you going to America?"

Kopano sensed his mother's shadow watching from the doorway. Only then did it dawn on Kopano that spiriting him away to the Human Garde Academy was exactly his mother's plan. He had waited months for this day, but he never expected it to come so abruptly. He had imagined a going-away party with all their neighbors invited along with his friends from school, and then a tearful parting with his family at the airport. When would he see his parents again? His brothers? Would they be all right without him? Kopano wiped the back of his hand across his eyes.

"Yes," he told Dubem. "Don't tell Father until morning. He'll be mad."

"I will keep your secret," Dubem said, then sat up to hug him. "Good luck to you, brother. Write me letters."

◇ ◇ ◇

The streets of Lagos were far less crowded after midnight, the bumper-to-bumper traffic and daredevil drivers of the daylight hours gone, although the cavernous potholes that needed careful navigation while the sun was up were even more dangerous now. Kopano found the deserted roads ominous. There were so few other cars that he wondered what sort of sinister people were hidden behind each set of passing headlights. In his mind, he concocted stories for them—criminals and vigilantes and fugitives like him. Was the boy who'd tried to gut him driving around out there, looking for vengeance?

"Father's gotten us in trouble, hasn't he?" Kopano said to break the silence.

"Not just Father, hmm?" his mother replied, then adjusted the rearview mirror. "Or did he force you to go along with his stupid scheme? You, with your powers . . ."

Kopano crossed his arms. "I thought . . . we needed the money. I didn't expect what happened to happen."

She tossed her head, dismissing Kopano's words. "Too late now, my son. You and your father angered some very bad people. Powerful people. And all your father can think to do is drink and cry on the phone and beg mercy. So, you and I will fix this. We know people more powerful than these so-called big men."

"Who? Who do we know?"

"The United Nations," his mother replied firmly. "Your friend John Smith."

Kopano stared at her like she'd gone mad. "They will take me to the Academy in America, Mama, not the rest of you."

"I know that. I also read the articles that say the families of your kind will be protected. So, you will go to America, and your new keepers will take the rest of us somewhere safe."

Kopano pretended not to notice the way his mother said "your kind," as if he was no longer Okeke, no longer Nigerian, no longer human.

It was more than a ten-hour drive north on the A22 to Zuma Rock, where the Loralite stone had grown and the United Nations had set up a headquarters. Kopano offered to take a turn behind the wheel, but his mother refused. She relaxed some once they left Lagos behind. They both did.

Kopano dozed off and awoke to the sound of hoofbeats. It was morning. A group of boys rode their horses on the side of the highway, racing their car, whooping and slapping riding crops against the flanks of their skinny mounts. Akuziem honked her horn in irritation and stepped on the gas until the jockeys fell behind them. They were in a rural part of the country that Kopano had never seen before. He had never even been out of Lagos. Once again, the reality of his situation dawned on him.

He was going to America.

They only stopped twice, both times for gas. His mother still wouldn't let him drive. She didn't take any food—Kopano bought a bag of potato chips and two large oranges from a stand when they passed through Auchi—but Akuziem only gulped deeply from the bottles of water she had the foresight to pack. His mother was hard-eyed, squinting into the sun. She'd remembered the water but forgotten her sunglasses. To Kopano, she looked like a woman on a mission. She drove fast.

"Are you so eager to get rid of me?" Kopano asked his mother, only half joking.

His mother's mouth tightened in a frown. "You are my son," she said, but Kopano could hear the doubt in her voice. Akuziem must have been aware of that, too, because she reached over to grab Kopano's hand and repeated herself with more conviction. "You are my son. I wish none of this had happened to you. But you are on a journey from God now. We must accept that."

By afternoon, they approached Abuja. The highway was crowded, although nothing like the traffic of Lagos, and Kopano felt comfortably anonymous. His stomach turned, however, when Zuma Rock came into view. For a long stretch, the road pointed right at the stone monolith,

Zuma Rock casting a shadow, its dull gray surface eating up the sun. Around Zuma Rock the land was green and hilly, not mountainous like one would expect, which made the 725-meter-high stone stick out all the more. To Kopano, Zuma Rock looked like God above had dropped a meteor in the middle of Africa and left it there. Zuma Rock made sense as a place where the aliens would choose to have their Loralite grow. It was as otherworldly a place as one could find on Earth.

As they drove closer, the newly built man-made feature of Zuma Rock caught Kopano's eye. A swath of the parkland around the giant rock had been recently converted into a military base camp. Scaffolding ran up and down the side of the rock face; even from this distance, he could see a small elevator going back and forth to the top of Zuma Rock. A helicopter circled overhead.

Akuziem's expression didn't change as they got closer. In fact, she looked even more determined than ever to see this through, her eyes locked on the checkpoints that loomed ahead.

There were detour signs. Large notifications in many languages that Zuma Rock was closed to the public. The traffic thinned around them, the other drivers following the curve around Zuma Rock and into the capital city of Abuja. Kopano's mom pressed onwards, ignoring the signs. Soon, they were the only car on the road.

They drove towards a group of Nigerian soldiers lounging in their Humvees, their vehicles arranged to create a loose roadblock. Kopano glanced at his mother. She slowed down but showed no sign of stopping.

"Did you tell them we were coming?" Kopano thought to ask.

"No," his mom replied.

Kopano stared at the soldiers, who were now paying attention to their little car. They were guarding a site of great power. Kopano was worried they would start shooting at any moment.

Kopano's mom rolled down her window and waved. The soldiers waved back, and she simply drove around them. Kopano nodded at one of them as they went by. The soldier lit a cigarette.

Kopano laughed in relief. "Just like Father says! If you act like you belong, you can get in anywhere."

"I packed your bag for you, Kopano," his mother replied stiffly. "I did not leave room for your father's wisdom."

The soldiers at the next checkpoint weren't so lackadaisical. They wore the light blue berets of UN Peacekeepers and manned a heavy iron gate that blocked the road to Zuma Rock. A very pale man with a bad sunburn and red eyebrows raised a gloved hand to stop them and approached their car.

"You have to turn around, lady," the soldier said with what Kopano thought was an Irish accent. "Place is closed to the public until further notice."

"My son is one of them," Akuziem countered stiffly. "He has the Legacies."

The soldier glanced at Kopano and then rolled his eyes.

Apparently, this happened a lot. "Sure he does. Look, there's no reward, you get me? You got a strapping young lad here, that's true, but the docs'll take one look at him and know you've wasted everyone's ti—"

Before the soldier could finish, Kopano used his telekinesis to float his beret into the air. The soldier took a step back, wide-eyed, and waved his hands above and below the beret, as if checking for strings.

"I could lift something bigger, if you want," Kopano offered with a smile.

"Not necessary," said the soldier, already getting on his walkie-talkie.

The soldiers ushered their car through the gate and allowed them to park in the shadow of Zuma Rock. A knot of men and women—some soldiers, but also some scientists in lab coats and a few people in business attire—speed-walked toward their car.

"I love you, Kopano, no matter what happens," his mother said.

"I love you too," Kopano replied.

Kopano would not speak to his mother again for some time. He was glad they had that moment, even if his mother's words were cut with the edge of doubt, as if she still wasn't entirely convinced Kopano was still Kopano.

What happened next was a whirlwind of activity. They were welcomed enthusiastically by the UN representatives and quickly separated. The people in the suits gravitated towards Kopano's mother. There were documents for her to sign on Kopano's behalf—visa applications, emancipation agreements, surveys of which vaccinations he'd received. The suits asked for her address in Lagos, the names of his father and brothers, and assured her that they'd all be brought somewhere safe.

"There will be a cure, yes?" Kopano heard his mother ask one of the men. "You do all this research with them so you can eventually find a cure."

Kopano's heart sank, but soon a barrage of questions from the scientists made him forget his mother's words.

How old are you? When did your powers first manifest? That long ago? All this time, right here, under our noses! Did you experience the vision of John Smith? Have you been practicing on your own? Why didn't you come sooner?

Kopano got the feeling that the science team stationed at Zuma Rock hadn't had much to do. They were thrilled to have him, nodding and smiling and writing down everything he said as if it were of the utmost importance. They showed him into their encampment, then brought him into a high-tech laboratory that was meticulously clean.

Any strange feelings or poor health? Depression? Anxiety? Have you used your Legacies in any hostile situations?

Kopano described yesterday's attack. The scientists didn't judge him for his year spent as a superpowered courier. One of them, the only Nigerian in the room besides Kopano, shook her head in sympathy. She understood.

A pair of doctors administered what seemed to be a very ordinary physical. The only speed bump occurred when they tried to take a sample of Kopano's blood. The needle pierced just the first layer of Kopano's skin when his Legacy kicked in. The syringe crunched and crumpled before it could reach his vein. Three times they tried with the same result.

"Is it possible for you to turn that off?" one of the doctors asked.

"I don't know," said Kopano. "It's brand-new."

"We've been told that when dealing with Legacies, it's helpful to visualize the desired result," one of the observing scientists suggested. "Perhaps imagine that you want to have your blood drawn."

"I do want to help," Kopano replied with a smile. "But who in this world has such a strong imagination that they can pretend to like needles?"

Everyone laughed. After a few more broken needles, the doctors gave up, settling instead for hair and skin samples, plus a few fingernail clippings. Apparently, his fingernails weren't made of the same stern stuff that lurked beneath his skin.

His physical complete, the initial ruckus of his arrival dying down, many of the scientists went off to quietly evaluate their data or video-chat with colleagues about the boy with impenetrable skin. Kopano was left alone with the Nigerian scientist.

"They're very excited," she said, gesturing after the other scientists. "You're the first Human Garde we've seen here."

Kopano puffed out his chest. "I am excited too."

Her name was Orisa, she was in her late twenties, with huge brown eyes and tightly arrayed braids. She was an employee of the World Health Organization who had volunteered to transfer to Zuma Rock when the "alien manifestation" occurred.

"Do you want to see it?" she asked.

They rode the elevator up the side of Zuma Rock, the little cage rattling in the wind. At the top, they were greeted by a pair of soldiers, both armed with automatic weapons and paperback novels.

"I guess guarding a rock on top of another rock doesn't take much attention," Kopano remarked.

Orisa smiled. "Honestly, until you came, this was the most boring assignment ever."

The outcropping of Loralite grew from the top of Zuma Rock like a tree of stone. Veins of the glittering cobalt-blue substance spread like roots beneath Kopano's feet. The Loralite growth was seven feet tall and reminded Kopano of a tidal wave in the way that it shot up sharply and then curved back over itself. He remembered what John Smith had said in the vision all those months ago—imagine another place with a stone, touch its glowing surface and the Loralite would teleport you across the globe.

Kopano couldn't help himself. He reached forward, hand outstretched.

Orisa pulled him back.

"Don't do that," she said. "You might teleport away on accident."

"I would come right back," Kopano promised with a crooked grin.

"Not all the Loralite growths are as secured as this one," she said. "Anyway, they say you Garde must be able to picture where you want to go."

"I can picture America. That's where I'm going, right?"

"Yes, but not by teleportation. You will be flown there." She caught Kopano's look of disappointment. "Old-fashioned, I know. But at least the plane is private."

"My father would be jealous," Kopano muttered with a smirk. He held out his hands towards the stone again, not to touch it, but like one would reach toward a campfire.

"Do you feel something?" Orisa asked, producing a notebook from her lab coat.

"Yes," Kopano replied, struggling at first to put the feeling into words. "It pulls me. I feel—I look at it, and I know it does not belong here. I should think of it as alien and strange." *Like the way my mother looks at me*, he thought but didn't add. "But instead, it feels natural. I know this stone like I know the sky."

There was a mountain of paperwork waiting for Kopano downstairs. They asked Kopano to read what he at first thought was a book but turned out to be a contract, the huge document stamped with the UN logo, written in a dense legalese and filled with subsection after subsection. He looked to Orisa for help.

"Basically, it says that you agree to enter the custody of the United Nations and that, after a period of training and once you turn eighteen, you will be conscripted to the Peacekeep-ers' Earth Garde division for a five-year term of service," the scientist summarized. "It also lays out the laws that Garde must abide by, that you agree to be held accountable for your actions and that you won't hold your home country or the United Nations responsible should anything happen to you."

Kopano nodded once, flipped to the last page of the mam-moth contract and signed where indicated.

"Can I see my mother now?" he asked. "I'd like to say good-bye."

Orisa's brow furrowed. "Oh, I thought you already . . . she left, Kopano. The soldiers brought her to a hotel in Abuja. After she told us of your troubles; the rest of your family is being gathered as we speak." She glanced at her watch. "Your plane will be coming soon, but I could have her brought back . . ."

Kopano shook his head. "No worries," he said, and forced a smile.

She had left him. He would begin this great journey alone.

CHAPTER ELEVEN

TAYLOR COOK
POINTS IN BETWEEN

BEFORE THE SHOOTING STARTED, WHEN THE COS-
tumed zealots with their snake-and-scythe tattoos were still
making their way to the farm, while her dad was alone on
the porch sitting watch with his shotgun in his lap, Taylor
Cook decided to call the hotline.

"You have reached Earth Garde North America, how
may I assist you?" a lady operator said, her voice kind but
detached.

Taylor sat on the floor with her back against her bed,
hands cupped around her cell phone, even though there was
no chance her father could overhear. They advertised the
hotline on TV and on billboards and all over the internet.
The commercials featured young people practicing telekinesis, or accidentally setting trees on fire with Legacies. Any

Human Garde or extraterrestrial activity was supposed to be reported.

"I can hear you breathing," said the operator. "Hello?"

Taylor worked some moisture into her mouth, then finally spoke.

"I'm one of them," she said. "A Garde."

"Okay, honey," the operator replied briskly. "What makes you think that?"

"What—what makes me think that?" Taylor blinked. "I can move things with my mind. My dad, he got a cut on his head, and I healed it."

"How old are you?"

"Fifteen."

"I'm showing your location as South Dakota. Is that correct?"

"Yes, but listen, we need—"

"What you're going to want to do is get your parents to drive you on down to Denver. That's the evaluation center nearest to you. They'll take a look at you there, assuming what you say is true. We used to send out investigators, but we got too many pranks. If you've got video evidence of Legacies, you can upload it to our secure site. Let me give you that address . . ."

Taylor's mouth hung open, stunned by the woman's casual tone, the mundanity of it all. She raised her voice, hands shaking.

"You don't understand! There are people . . ." She got control, overcompensated and started to whisper. "There are people coming to hurt us. To hurt me."

There was a pause. When she spoke again, the operator wasn't so dismissive. She must have recognized the tautness in Taylor's voice.

"If you're in danger, honey, you should call nine-one-one."

"I know, I know. But . . . but my dad's worried you'll come take me away if we tell. It all started with this jerk with a weird tattoo—"

"Stay on the line, please. I'm contacting emergency services in your area."

"Wait—"

The line went quiet except for a series of clicks. Seconds stretched on. Taylor felt her palms getting sweaty.

"Okay, this is strange," the operator said, suddenly back in Taylor's ear. Her flippant tone was replaced with a gravity that rattled Taylor. "We can't get a response from the sheriff station in your area."

"Oh God."

"Help is on the way," the operator said. "If you can get to a safe place, you should do so."

An hour later, the Harvesters encircled their house. Taylor's father stood alone on the porch, rifle in hand, listening to a preacher dressed like an outlaw give an impromptu sermon on Taylor's "sinful" condition.

Help still hadn't arrived.

Guns went up. Her father got off one shot. Dozens of Harvesters fired back, the sound like a drumroll. Taylor dropped to the floor, huddled against the wall next to their front door. She expected shattering glass. She expected the *chunk-chunk-chunk* of bullets eating away at the wooden walls of her house. She expected not to make it through the next few seconds.

Instead, there was a sudden silence.

And a glow. A warm, orange glow, like fire. It was as if the sun had risen.

Taylor peeked out from behind the door frame. In the strange, fiery glow, Taylor noticed what she at first took for a swarm of gnats hanging a few inches from her father's rifle. His buckshot, she realized, suspended in midair, the heavier silver rounds fired by the Harvesters likewise stuck glittering over their front yard. Taylor glanced down at her hands—for a moment, she wondered if the stress had caused her Legacies to trigger, like the day her father rolled the tractor. But no, she realized, she wasn't capable of such a spectacular feat of telekinetic control.

The glowing young man floating over her driveway was.

Taylor heard the pitter-patter of rain. It was the bullets, falling harmlessly to the ground.

"Drop your weapons or I'll drop them for you," the glowing figure said.

Taylor recognized him immediately. The entire world knew John Smith's face. His sandy-blond hair had grown out from the picture they always used on the news and a patchy beard covered his cheeks. Seeing him there, floating fifteen feet in the air, his hands glowing with fire that spread up to his forearms, it was like a comic book come to life. Even the Harvesters, who moments ago had seemed so threatening, gawked up at the leader of the Loric. It was said that he possessed every possible Legacy, his powers near godlike, and that he'd single-handedly destroyed at least one Mogadorian warship during the invasion.

What in the hell was he doing in South Dakota?

Well, the operator had said she'd send help.

Brian dropped his gun as commanded, the clatter of his rifle against the porch breaking the stunned silence.

The Harvesters weren't so ready to comply.

"The devil himself is among us, brothers and sisters!" the preacher shouted through his outlaw bandanna. "The source of the infection that corrupts our young!"

The Harvesters trained their guns on John Smith. He didn't flinch. A second later, instead of a volley of gunfire, screams of surprise filled the air. With his telekinesis, John Smith had ripped the weapons away from the mob, a number of trigger fingers broken in the process. The disarmed Harvesters watched as each of their guns folded and twisted until they were nothing but useless metal rings.

"You aren't allowed to hurt us!" someone shouted. This was true. The UN had passed a resolution that any Garde— Loric or Human—couldn't use their Legacies against other humans, except in cases of self-defense.

With a demonstrative flick of his wrist, John Smith sent the crumpled guns flying towards the Harvesters' vehicles.

Antennas snapped, tires exploded, windshields shattered.

"I'm not hurting you, just your stuff," John Smith told the shaken Harvesters.

Even with their faces hidden, Taylor sensed fear from the Harvesters. Many began to back away towards their damaged vehicles. They'd completely forgotten about her and her father.

John Smith floated gently to the ground.

"Lie down," he commanded the Harvesters. "The authorities will be here soon."

They ran.

A tremor rumbled out from where John Smith stood. It was aimed away from their house, but Taylor could still feel the reverberations. The trucks and RVs flipped over like turtles. All of the Harvesters were knocked to the ground. Some of them stayed down like John Smith commanded, but others scrambled to their feet and sprinted towards the road. She noticed the preacher hobbling off her property, a Harvester under each arm half carrying him.

Taylor stood next to her father, watching the action from the porch. She reached out and grasped his hand.

"Wow," Brian said.

"I—I called them," she said. "I turned myself in."

"You saved our lives," Brian said.

"He saved our lives," Taylor replied. "He . . ."

Taylor trailed off when she realized John Smith was looking at her. He wasn't pursuing the fleeing Harvesters. At first, she thought he didn't want to leave her and her dad alone with the ones who had surrendered. But there was something about that look—he was stopped cold, staring at Taylor, almost like he'd seen a ghost.

Flashing police lights appeared in the distance, racing towards their house. The Harvesters wouldn't get far. She hoped.

"Um, hey," Taylor said, waving a hand to break John Smith's daze.

He shook his head, blinked away whatever memory had overtaken him and focused up.

"Sorry," he said after a moment. "You . . . remind me of someone. Are you all right?"

Taylor and her dad nodded in unison, both of them dumbfounded.

John Smith glanced at the overturned cars. "Sorry about the mess," he said. "I'll help clean this stuff off your property."

Brian laughed in disbelief at that.

"You saved our lives," Taylor said.

John Smith shrugged. "Earth Garde didn't have a team close enough and I was in the neighborhood."

"You were in South Dakota?" Taylor exclaimed.

"Canada, actually."

"Pretty big neighborhood."

He smiled. "Guess so."

Taylor kept an eye on the defeated Harvesters as she stepped cautiously off the porch. John Smith seemed kind and, in a way Taylor couldn't quite explain, deeply melancholy.

She had read an article about his time spent hiding out in a small town in Ohio before the invasion and how he tried to live a normal life. Maybe he would understand . . .

"Hey," she said, keeping her voice low so the Harvesters wouldn't overhear. "Is it possible to say . . . ? I don't know . . . that this was all a big misunderstanding? Could we tell the authorities that I don't actually have Legacies?"

John Smith raised an eyebrow. "But you do."

"Yeah, but . . . I don't want to go to the Academy." Taylor glanced over her shoulder. "I don't want to leave my dad alone."

John Smith studied Taylor for a moment, his mouth tightening, and then he looked down at his feet. He shook his head.

"I'm sorry," he replied. "That's beyond my power."

Taylor never got to see if John Smith made good on his word to clean the Harvester vehicles off their property. An armada of cops and FBI showed up—apparently, their local sheriff's station had been taken over by a second crew of Harvesters, so help had to come down from Sioux Falls— and they were soon joined by an unmarked government helicopter. A pair of Earth Garde representatives rode in on the chopper, local law enforcement immediately deferring to them. They instructed Taylor to pack a bag, which she did slowly and reluctantly and with a lot of help from her father. Then they were hustled onto the helicopter.

Taylor left the farm behind. As the chopper rose up, she looked over the remnants of the battle. She caught sight of

John Smith signing autographs for a group of local cops. She thought he glanced up in her direction, but she couldn't be sure.

Taylor and her dad were taken to the processing center in Denver. The building was located at the base of Pikes Peak, that location chosen because an outcropping of Loralite had grown at the mountain's top. They were greeted by a bunch of fast-talking lawyers, military brass and hypercurious scientists. They drew Taylor's blood and asked her to use her telekinesis to push on a piston as hard as she could in order to gauge her strength. She felt a strange mix of relief and disappointment when she caught a glimpse of a researcher checking the box for "average" next to "telekinetic strength." After that, there were the forms, an endless pile of them—pledges and agreements and waivers.

"Should we have a lawyer present for this stuff?" her dad asked, staring blearily at the latest document thrust before him. The two of them hadn't been given a chance to sleep and Taylor wasn't sure whether this was an oversight or on purpose.

"Mr. Cook, I am your lawyer," replied the middle-aged man sitting across from them in the bunker-like conference room.

"Oh," her dad said. Taylor could tell he was overwhelmed by everything that had happened. He was a trusting man, smart, but slow and considerate with his words. He was completely out of his element here. And Taylor—well, to her, the entire experience was like a waking nightmare. She thought about all the things left undone: her work around the farm, her essay on *Othello*. She hadn't even gotten to say good-bye to her friends.

"What if I refuse to sign this crap?" she asked their supposed lawyer. "Do I get to go home?"

The lawyer took off his glasses and cleaned them, an excuse not to look Taylor in the eyes. "By law, if you don't sign the agreements in full, your condition will necessitate a period of quarantine."

"Quarantine?" exclaimed her father. "But didn't you hear? She heals people!"

"Yes, but that may not be all she can do," the lawyer replied archly. "There's still so much we don't know about Taylor's condition. The health of the general public has to be taken into consideration."

"How long would I have to be in quarantine?" Taylor pressed on stubbornly.

"Indefinitely," the lawyer replied. "You would be the first, so the process would require some . . . figuring out. At the Academy, on the other hand, you will have a world-class education and receive the proper training for your Legacies. You won't be allowed off campus until you've turned eighteen, but your father will be allowed to visit once a month."

Taylor thought about using her telekinesis to slowly tighten the lawyer's tie. She could probably fight her way out of there. But what would be waiting for her? Years as a fugitive? Her father's life ruined? More Harvesters?

"Your family's farm will also be protected," the lawyer continued, as if reading her mind. "So another incident like last night's can be avoided."

With tears in her eyes, Taylor signed the paperwork. She was now property of the United Nations. An enrollee at the Human Garde Academy.

She was still massaging the pen indentation out of her signing hand when they whisked her off to a secluded military airfield on the outskirts of Denver. There was a private jet waiting for her. Taylor pressed her face into her father's shirt. She'd been fighting back tears during the entire process and now could feel them spilling over. He hugged her, whispering into her ear.

"Come on, now. Don't let these people see you cry. You gotta be strong, Tay."

"I don't want to go," she said, her words muffled into his chest. "I don't want to leave you all by yourself."

"Aw, I'll be just fine," he replied, although she detected a tremor in his voice. "Imagine all the good you can do, running around with that John Smith fella and his crew. You're gonna make me so proud."

And then it was time. They led her across the tarmac, up a set of roll-away steps. Taylor gazed back at her father, waved and then she was sealed inside. Minutes later, buckled into a plush leather chair, Taylor was off the ground, on her way to California in a private jet. Less than twenty-four hours had passed since Teddy had come by their farm to warn them about the Harvesters. To Taylor, it felt like days. She was exhausted, but too anxious to sleep.

There was one other person in the passenger section with her. He was black, built like a linebacker, handsome, with wide eyes that made him seem perpetually curious. She didn't feel so bad staring at him because he was staring at her, a big, doofy grin on his face.

"Hello," the boy said at last. His English was slightly accented, almost British.

"Hi," Taylor replied uncertainly, nearly too tired for socializing.

"I'm Kopano," the boy continued. "What's your name?"

"Taylor."

He switched to the seat right next to her and enthusiastically shook her hand.

"They told me we were making a detour to South Dakota to pick up another passenger—what a relief! I've been alone on here for half a day. Very boring." He held up his hands like he was taking her picture. "My first American friend. Just like the pretty girl they put on cereal boxes. Very classic."

Taylor felt herself blush, not really sure why. She couldn't think of any cereal boxes with girls her age. "And you're from . . . ?" she asked, changing the subject. "England?"

"Nigeria," the boy said proudly. "So, you are Garde, too, eh? I have never met anyone like myself."

"Me neither." Taylor paused. "Actually, I take that back. I met John Smith last night, but I guess that's a little different."

"John Smith!" Kopano shouted. "My hero! How tall was

he? Taller than me? You must tell me everything, Taylor. Right away."

So she told him, starting from the day she first discovered her Legacies. With Kopano's huge smile and enthusiastic nods, it was easy for Taylor to tell her story. It came pouring out of her. Taylor was amazed she managed to get through it without crying.

"I saw John Smith the one time, during the telepathic vision. His speech was amaz—"

"I'm sorry," Taylor interrupted. "The what?"

"During the invasion, when we were all called to action," Kopano said. Seeing Taylor's blank look, he slapped his knee. "Oh! You became Garde after the war. So, more of us are still being made, eh? Very interesting. Very cool. Let me tell you what happened!"

Kopano told her about what he'd seen during the invasion, how eager he'd been to help fight, but how his Legacies were slow to develop. He told her how he'd been roped into working a shady job with his father until finally escaping for the Academy. Taylor thought she'd gotten her emotions in check, but when Kopano told her about the way his mother looked at him like he was something from another dimension, Taylor got choked up. She tried to hold it in, but a big guffawing sob escaped her and then she started crying again.

"What did I say? What did I say?" Kopano asked in a panic.

"Not you . . . ," Taylor said, wiping her face. "It's just all so much. We shouldn't have to go through this. I hate what's happened to us. I liked the life I had! I don't want to leave it all behind to go to this stupid Academy where I don't know anyone . . ."

"You will know me," Kopano declared. "We will be partners in carving out our great destiny as the stars have foretold it!"

"What stars?" She stared at him. "I don't want a great destiny."

Kopano smiled crookedly and Taylor realized he was kidding about the stars and destiny. Well, if not kidding, then not completely serious. Kopano locked eyes with her and made his face grave.

"A great destiny for me, then, and an ordinary and boring destiny for you. Together, I believe we can achieve this."

Taylor laughed in spite of herself. "You're nuts."

Kopano extended his hand. "Let us make this alliance official. Once we reach California, we will watch out for each other. You will make sure that I stay on the path to historic greatness, and I will make sure that your life is as unexciting as possible."

Taylor smirked. "So, what? If I find like a cat stuck in a tree or something, you want me to come find you right away?"

"Yes! Exactly! Damsels in distress, in particular." Kopano stroked his chin. "I would like them to become my specialty."

Taylor rolled her eyes.

"And in return," Kopano continued, "I will make sure you are assigned extra homework by our new teachers. I will remain constantly vigilant of the spectacular happening and make sure you are far, far away when it does."

"Okay, Kopano," Taylor said with another laugh. She shook his hand. "You've got a deal."

"Excellent!" he replied. "This, I believe, is the beginning of a great friendship!"

By the time they reached California, Taylor had fallen asleep with her head on the large boy's shoulder.

CHAPTER TWELVE

ISABELA SILVA
THE HUMAN GARDE ACADEMY—POINT REYES, CALIFORNIA

ONE OF THE BOYS ON THE SOCCER FIELD WHISTLED loudly when he spotted Isabela walking along the sideline. She paused and half turned, aimed a scornful glare in the whistle's general direction and shouted in Portuguese, "You will whistle much higher once I've cut off your balls!"

Simon walked beside Isabela, his short legs struggling to keep up with her long, purposeful strides. He was French, hairy for a fourteen-year-old, with a tousled mane of dark brown curls atop his overlarge head. Simon was in the process of learning Portuguese—it would be his fifth language after French, English, Spanish and Italian—which meant he'd been shadowing Isabela almost constantly these last few weeks. She tolerated Simon. Unlike most of the other males attending the Academy, he wasn't constantly trying to hit on her. Simon wasn't in her league and he knew that; Isabela admired his self-awareness.

"My obscenities aren't great yet," Simon said breathlessly. "What are 'colhões'?"

"Balls," Isabela replied in English.

"Ha," Simon said, then adjusted his belt. "And ouch."

"You should probably keep that stuff to a minimum when we meet the new recruits," Caleb said stiffly. He had been following a few steps behind Isabela and Simon. "We want to set a good example."

Isabela and Simon exchanged a look, then stifled laughter. Caleb noticed this, but said nothing. He was aware of his reputation—behind his back, the other students had nicknamed him "Hall Monitor."

"I heard one of these new kids is from Africa," Simon said excitedly. He rolled a crystal-blue pebble across his knuckles, the stone freshly charged with his Legacy. "I hope he doesn't speak English."

"Why must we all speak English, anyway?" Isabela complained. She tugged at the beaded bracelet that fit snugly around her wrist. One of the beads—the aquamarine one that emitted a slight glow when the sun hit it just right—was charged with Simon's Legacy. As long as she kept in contact with the bracelet—and the bead maintained its charge—she could speak and understand English. At least, Isabela consoled herself, the bracelet Simon had made for her wasn't a total fashion disaster.

"Because this is America," Caleb replied.

Isabela groaned in response.

The trio had drawn orientation duty for that day's two new arrivals. Simon was always one of the greeters—his Legacy made him particularly useful in that regard. Isabela and Caleb were chosen to give the tour because they both had empty rooms in their three-person suites.

"I don't understand why we even need roommates," Isabela huffed. "This campus is huge. There are entire floors in the dorms that we aren't even using! We could all have our own suites with two walk-in closets."

"I don't need that many closets," Simon replied with a shrug.

"No one needs that many closets, but wouldn't it be nice to have them?" Isabela asked. "Wouldn't it be nice to not share a bathroom?"

"Dr. Linda says it's good for us to socialize," Simon replied. "Chores are also healthy, apparently."

"Ugh, don't talk to me about that old cow," Isabela replied.

"I like Dr. Linda," Caleb said.

"You would," Isabela replied sharply.

Dr. Linda, the Academy's resident expert on mental health, was in charge of their room assignments. Isabela had asked her over and over again for reassignment, not because she disliked her roommate—Ran was about as quiet and respectful as one could hope for around here—but because Isabela valued her privacy more than most. The therapist always responded with the same psychobabble about support systems and bonding. Isabela didn't see how sharing a bathroom with two other girls would turn her into a better person, but whatever.

"This new girl better be as clean as Ran," Isabela said with an edge in her voice. "And quiet, too. We have a good arrangement, me and her. She keeps clean and meditates all the time, and I do whatever I want."

"Yeah. Sounds great," Caleb replied dryly.

A helicopter swooped overhead, circling around for a landing. Isabela sighed again. Now her hair was all out of place.

"We're late," Caleb said, walking faster.

"I'm sure Dr. Goode is already there," Simon replied. "He's got that thing about greeting all the new kids."

Dr. Malcolm Goode was one of their science instructors. When he wasn't teaching them chemistry and physics, Dr. Goode headed up the Academy's research staff. He studied their Legacies, helping the students better understand what they could do. He had a son of his own with Legacies, although he didn't attend the Academy. Isabela wondered how he'd gotten so lucky to avoid the monotony.

With Caleb now in the lead, the trio made their way down the path that led out to the helipad. The day was sunny and breezy, like it always seemed to be on these coastal cliffs. Sometimes, Isabela missed the sticky heat of Rio de Janeiro, parading around the Zona Sul in her bikini and sarong, looking for trouble. The wind here chilled her, made goose pimples on her light brown skin and forced her to wear more clothes than she would've liked. She shoved a curly tangle of dark hair out of her face.

The helipad was constructed in an open field to the east of the Academy. From here, Isabela could see the woodlands that created a buffer between the campus and the fence erected to protect them. When she was particularly bored, she liked to visit with the UN Peacekeepers who patrolled the perimeter. The soldiers were always sweet and stammer-prone—she was beautiful and possessed superpowers, a combination that drove ordinary men to speechlessness. The power to make even grown men nervous was intoxicating.

It was during one of those visits, casually flirting with a group of idle guards, that Isabela realized how easy it was for a person with her Legacy to escape from campus. She'd dipped down to San Francisco a half-dozen times since then, sometimes alone and sometimes in the company of Lofton, the handsome Canadian currently wrapped tightly around her little finger. His eighteenth birthday was quickly approaching and he'd recently been notified that the administration thought he was ready to graduate. They would have to make at least one more excursion to the city before he left the Academy to join Earth Garde.

Then, she'd need to find a replacement.

Ignoring Simon and Caleb, Isabela daydreamed about the little bar she and Lofton had found in Haight-Ashbury, the one that didn't bother checking IDs. She closed her eyes, let the sun heat her cheeks and imagined the boozy tang of margarita on her tongue.

The newbies waited for them next to the UN chopper, its propeller still making a slow rotation. Just as Simon predicted, Dr. Goode had arrived ahead of them.

"Kopano and Taylor," Dr. Goode introduced the new kids. "This is Simon, Isabela and Caleb. They'll show you around and get you settled in. You're in good hands."

Isabela quickly sized up the new recruits. The first was a sturdy African boy with a wide grin, the type that thought the Academy would be superhero camp. They got plenty of those. Next to him was a frightened-looking all-American girl. Isabela thought Taylor might almost be pretty if not for the huge bags under her eyes.

Caleb made sure to properly shake hands with the two new arrivals. Isabela didn't miss that he held Taylor's hand a little longer than necessary. The new girl smiled shyly. Caleb let go only when Isabela loudly cleared her throat. She gave Caleb a look of acidic amusement. These American boys. Always so obvious.

"So, you guys both speak English, huh?" Simon asked, sounding disappointed. He stuck the smooth pebble he'd been playing with back in his pocket.

"Simon's Legacy is quite unique," Dr. Goode explained to the blank-faced Kopano and Taylor. "He can charge objects with knowledge. Whoever touches an object thus charged can then access that information as if it were stored in their own neurons."

"Amazing!" Kopano stared down at Simon with reverence.

"It's especially useful considering Simon is a hyper-polyglot."

"Hyper-what?" Taylor asked.

"I learn languages easily," Simon explained. "Even before the Legacy."

"Isabela is using one of Simon's creations now," continued Dr. Goode. "She isn't a native English speaker, but the bracelet allows her to understand us as well as communicate seamlessly."

Isabela held out her arm so they could get a closer look at her bracelet.

"Pretty," Taylor said.

"Not so much when you need to wear it every day," Isabela said, adding dryly, "but it's worth it to understand all the interesting things you're saying."

"It lasts forever?" Kopano asked.

Simon shook his head. He was puffed up from all the attention. "I have to recharge them every week or so. Most people have me charge like a watch or a necklace."

"Sometimes he screws up and implants a memory along with the knowledge," Isabela said with a sly smile. "My last charge came loaded with a traumatic vision of young Simon wetting the bed."

Simon groaned and stared down at his shoes. "I'd had a lot of water when I was charging that one up," he complained. "Anyway, I'm getting better at filtering."

"May I try one?" Kopano asked.

Simon kicked around in the grass until he found a small gray rock. "Give me a second," he said, then closed his eyes and concentrated. Slowly, the stone changed colors, taking on an otherworldly glow that slowly faded to a barely perceptible twinkle. After a minute, Simon opened his eyes and offered Kopano the stone. "It's not my best work. Usually takes a lot longer . . ."

Kopano grabbed the stone and squeezed. "Now what?"

"Tu me comprends?" Simon asked.

"Oui!" shouted Kopano. "Je parle Francais!"

While the boys messed around, Dr. Goode excused himself. This was another of Dr. Linda's policies—after the UN orientation process that involved endless encounters with smelly bureaucrats and pushy scientists, the Academy's on-site headshrinker believed it important to get new arrivals among their peers as soon as possible. If Dr. Linda had her way, they'd spend the whole day playing icebreakers and doing trust-falls with these wide-eyed newbies. Isabela didn't know about Caleb and Simon, but she had better things to do.

She turned her attention to Taylor. The girl watched with tired amusement as Kopano and Simon had a rapid-fire dialogue in basic French. She didn't seem at all aware that Caleb was still staring at her. Isabela knew by the way his mouth worked in silence and the nervous movements of his hands that Caleb was getting ready to talk. Well, at least this might be amusing, she thought.

"Where are you from?" Caleb eventually managed to ask Taylor.

The question startled her. "South Dakota."

"Oh, cool. I'm from Nebraska." Caleb appeared puzzled about what to say next. "Our states touch."

"Yep," Taylor replied, an eyebrow raised. "They sure do."

"Cool," Caleb said. "So . . ."

The conversation was too painful, even for Isabela's dark sense of humor.

"Thrilling!" she said, gliding in to grab Taylor by the elbow. "Come now. Let's leave these drooling bobos to their silly games and get you settled in. You look completely exhausted."

Taylor glanced in Kopano's direction, like she was nervous to leave him behind. After a moment's hesitation, she allowed Isabela to whisk her towards campus. "Nice to meet you!" she called over her shoulder to Caleb.

"Yeah, you too," he said. He watched Isabela lean in close to Taylor and whisper in her ear, probably telling her something malicious about him.

"Our states touch. Real smooth talk, Casanova. That was embarrassing."

Caleb's shoulders tightened. He looked in Simon and Kopano's direction. They'd both fallen silent and were staring at him.

He turned in the opposite direction and found his own face mocking him. A duplicate. One had popped out without

Caleb even realizing.

"This is why we never had a girlfriend," the duplicate said, sneering at Caleb. "Because you're such a sad los—"

Caleb absorbed the duplicate. He took a deep breath and then turned to Kopano, pretending like nothing had happened.

"Should we get on with the tour?"

CHAPTER THIRTEEN

TARGET #3
MANILA, THE PHILIPPINES

TWO WEEKS EARLIER, AN EARTHQUAKE STRUCK THE
Philippines. A 6.2 on the Richter scale. The quake resulted
in rough waters off the coast, waves just short of tsunami
level. Five hundred died during the tremors and more
during the subsequent floods, the casualties worse in the
densely packed slums of Tondo and San Andres. Thousands
were injured, many more than that displaced.

The world sent aid. The Red Cross, Doctors Without Bor-
ders, UNICEF, International Relief Team and others were
on the scene, tending to the injured and helping the locals
rebuild.

Earth Garde was there, too. Two of the young Human
Garde along with thirty of their UN Peacekeeper handlers.

It was just the opportunity the Foundation had been waiting for.

Einar sat at an outdoor café amid Manila's bustling downtown. If not for the broken window behind him, one would never know there had been an earthquake there. The buildings in the wealthier parts of the city were reinforced, history teaching the inhabitants to prepare for the worst. Einar sipped his coffee and admired the patchwork architecture—colorful and glassy modern building competing with old Spanish and French architecture.

The air was humid and sticky, not Einar's preferred climate. He tugged at the neck of his powder-blue Habitat For Humanity T-shirt. Looking down at himself—the dumb shirt, his khaki cargo shorts, his brown flip-flops—Einar had to stifle a groan. He hated the outfit, but at least it kept him anonymous. Just another good-hearted young person here to volunteer.

He glanced over at the girl sitting at the table next to his. Another foreigner. Saudi Arabian. A zebra-print hijab framed her pretty face, her long-sleeved dress a matching black-and-silver. She daintily sipped from a cup of tea.

"This heat doesn't bother you," Einar said, pushing his own coffee away from him.

"I'm used to it," Rabiya replied lightly. She cringed as a man rushing down the sidewalk bumped into her table. "It's the crowds that get me."

"Won't be long now."

Einar much preferred working with Rabiya to the brutish Blackstone mercenaries. Their first mission on behalf of the Foundation had taken them to Shanghai. China didn't participate in the Earth Garde program, preferring instead to keep control of their own Garde. However, the invasion followed by the ongoing problems with Mogadorian insurgents on the Mongolian border had kept China from properly organizing and securing their Garde. Thanks to Rabiya's Legacy, they had easily accessed the Chinese research station and acquired their target—Jiao Lin, a healer. The mission was made even simpler when they discovered Jiao actually wanted to defect, the girl welcoming the lifestyle the Foundation could offer her.

It was always better when the targets saw reason, Einar thought, his mind drifting to Bunji and what had become of the Australian boy since Einar plucked him up from the outback.

He had a feeling today's target might prove uncooperative.

"Do you think this will be enough?" Rabiya asked him. "Enough . . . healing power?"

Einar glanced around. "Be careful what you say in public," Einar admonished gently. Her cousin was sick, dying slowly, and Einar knew this weighed heavily on Rabiya's mind. He smiled at her, using his Legacy to make sure Rabiya found his words and gestures properly reassuring. "This will be enough. I know it."

It had better be, Einar thought. Attacking Earth Garde

directly, even if their tracks were properly covered, would have consequences.

Einar's earpiece crackled to life. "Target incoming," said Jarl's gravelly voice. Einar gazed up at the nearby rooftops where he knew the mercenaries were positioned. He couldn't see them; they were too well hidden.

"Ready," Einar replied into the microphone hidden in his shirt collar. Rabiya, overhearing, set down her tea and pulled her bulky purse into her lap. She nodded to Einar.

From within one of his cargo pockets—he'd had to leave his attaché case at home for this mission, unfortunately—Einar produced a padded box. Inside was a small device, the size and shape of a large thumbtack. He pricked his thumb with the sharpened end, then bumped his fingernail across the barbed shaft that made the thing extra painful to remove. He knew what that felt like. He resisted the urge to touch his own temple and suppressed a shudder—Rabiya was watching him.

"You're going to chip him," she said.

Einar nodded. "Safest way."

Rabiya shook her head disapprovingly. "I don't like those things."

Einar said nothing. He traced his thumb across the device's flat head—the microchip and power source—and found himself thinking of Bunji again. They'd had to chip the aboriginal boy when they first brought him back to the Foundation. He was out of control. That was months ago, and there were . . . unfortunate side effects.

"Target at your location," Jarl said in his ear.

"I see them," Einar replied through his teeth.

The Earth Garde team was impossible to miss. A cavalcade of black SUVs drove up to the hotel across the street. A crowd was already amassing out there. It was the same thing as yesterday and the day before, for as long as Einar had been here, watching and waiting.

"They love the attention," he muttered.

Melanie Jackson hopped out of one of the trucks, smiling brightly for the camera-waving onlookers. There were smudges of dirt on her cheeks from work at the rebuilding sites, but her curly blond hair looked perfect. The quintessential poster girl for Earth Garde, never one to miss a photo op. She took selfies with the crowd, even lifting some of them up with her superstrength. The Foundation's research indicated that enhanced strength was one of the more common Legacies—common, but not desirable. Not like healing.

Melanie's partner, Vincent Iabruzzi, was slower exiting the truck and less enthusiastic about interacting with the crowd. The Italian looked exhausted, drained after a long day of healing the injured in the slums. The boy was barely eighteen, round-faced and a little pudgy, with a mane of kinky black hair and a shadow of beard. The Foundation's reports indicated that he'd been given the unfortunate nickname of "Vinnie Meatballs" by the so-called professor who ran the Academy. Einar supposed he could see the reason.

With his telekinesis, Einar floated the pronged microchip into the air. It was like a silver bug weaving through the air.

No one noticed it. Not until the little device bit into Vincent's temple.

He yelped and made to swat at his face, but that yelp quickly turned into a scream. His limbs jerked as the chip sent an electromagnetic shock into his brain, the signal specifically designed to disrupt the part of a Garde's brain that fired when they used their telekinesis. The chip induced seizures, loss of muscle control and sometimes temporary blindness.

"Vincent?" Melanie shouted, pushing away from her now-frightened fans. She reached out to her fellow Earth Garde but stopped short when three tranquilizer darts zipped into her neck and shoulders. That would be Jarl and his Blackstone snipers.

"Rooftops! Rooftops!" shouted one of the Peacekeepers. They drew firearms and tried to cover the dazed Garde, pushing them back to the safety of the cars.

A gas canister rocketed down from a rooftop, shattering a windshield. A second one soon followed, exploding in the middle of the street. The crowd was screaming now— panicked and choking from the tear gas, trampling each other, creating confusion for the Peacekeepers.

Everyone at the café was running for cover except Einar and Rabiya. She opened her purse, retrieved a gas mask and pulled it on. Then, she handed one to Einar and he did the same.

"Shall we?" Einar asked.

The two of them strode into the choking orange gas

towards where they'd seen Vincent drop. Any fleeing civilians who got in their way got roughly shoved aside by bursts of telekinesis. They found Vincent prone in the road, drooling, his body twitching. Two Peacekeepers stood over him protectively, tears streaming from eyes swollen by the gas. The two soldiers still managed to get their weapons raised in Einar's direction.

With his telekinesis, Einar twisted their arms around. The soldiers pointed their guns at each other's heads and fired before they even knew what was happening.

Einar knelt down and touched the back of Vincent's neck. The boy was sobbing. "Hush now," Einar said. "You're with friends."

Rabiya extended her hand, an eerie blue glow emanating from her palm, visible even through the thick blanket of gas.

Seconds later, they were gone.

CHAPTER FOURTEEN

ISABELA SILVA • TAYLOR COOK
THE HUMAN GARDE ACADEMY—POINT REYES, CALIFORNIA

ISABELA KEPT A TIGHT HOLD ON TAYLOR'S ARM, vaguely worried the fragile-looking girl would pass out. She didn't need that. On one hand, she wanted to be done with this tour so she could find Lofton and make plans for the night. On the other hand, Isabela rather enjoyed talking and was eager to get a read on her new roommate. Would she be cool? A tattletale? A nighttime crier? Isabela needed to know.

"So," Isabela started as they walked back towards campus. "What do you do?"

Taylor's tired mind worked slowly. "Do? I don't know what you mean . . ."

Isabela scoffed. "Get used to that question, my dear! Everyone will want to know. What is your Legacy?"

"Oh. I'm a healer, I guess. What about you?"

Before Isabela could answer, a golf cart zoomed across their path. The driver was a young UN Peacekeeper. The passenger was a middle-aged man with thinning hair gone gray at the temples. He wore a severely starched and medal-bedecked uniform and he looked, to Taylor, like a solid block of ice. He briefly glanced at the two girls as his cart sped by. Even though they were simply walking around, the man's look made both of them feel like they were about to get into trouble.

"Who was that?" Taylor asked.

"The warden," sniffed Isabela, snapping off a mocking salute. "Colonel Ray Archibald. UN Peacekeepers. Head of security. He makes sure no one gets in and none of us get out."

"He seems nice," Taylor said dryly, glancing after the colonel as they approached campus.

"Look, there," Isabela commanded, pointing at two large buildings on either side of the main walkway. "Boys' dorm and girls' dorm, okay? You'll be rooming with me and Ran. We're on the third floor. It's not bad. Good light. I hope you won't be dirty."

"I'm . . . no, I'm not," Taylor replied. "I won't be."

"Perfect."

Isabela pointed out the other important landmarks—the administration building where they took their classes and where the faculty held office hours, the student center where meals were served, the gym, the military-grade training center. She gestured towards the cul-de-sac-style clump of small cabins set a distance away from the dorms, explaining that the faculty lived there. Taylor's neck started to hurt from all the head-turning, Isabela's finger speeding around the grounds.

"How do classes work?" Taylor asked.

"They are boring," Isabela replied.

"Not really what I asked, but okay."

Isabela sighed. "They'll give you some tests. Sit you down with an academic adviser. Figure out if you are smart or dumb. Which is it, by the way?"

Taylor was taken aback. "Which . . . um? Smart? I guess."

"Hmpf. Arrogant," Isabela replied. Taylor couldn't tell if she was joking. The fast-talking Brazilian had already moved on, lowering her voice. "If you make it seem like you're uneducated, they will give you easier classes. I took algebra in Rio, now I'm taking it again. Very simple."

"Oh," Taylor said, nodding slowly. "I, um, I don't think I'll lie."

"Suit yourself," Isabela replied. "There is a lot of homework. They like keeping us busy. At first, I thought, why would I do this stupid shit, huh? What can they do? Suspend me? Call my parents? We are basically prisoners. What can they do to us?"

"What can they do?" she asked.

Isabela tossed her hair. She recalled her first few weeks at the Academy, when she had pushed the buttons of every authority in place, trying to find out how much she could get away with. Her experiments had paid off.

"First, they will take away privileges," Isabela said, ticking off her fingers. "Make the recreation center off-limits, exclude you from movie night, allow you to eat only the boring food in the dining hall. The chef here is very good, surprisingly, so that one hurt a little." Isabela watched Taylor, gauging her reaction.

"Okay . . . ," Taylor replied, slightly amused by how Isabela puffed up with pride at her tales of misbehavior.

"After all that, I still wouldn't do the work they asked of me," Isabela bragged. "I was ready to live like a monk. There's a decent beach here if you hike down the cliff. I figured I could spend my time down there until all the boring shit was over and they sent me off to be in Earth Garde. But then they started to punish my roommate and my classmates. Until Isabela does her work, they said, the student center will be off-limits to everyone."

"Oh, wow," Taylor said. "So you gave in?"

Isabela dramatically pressed the back of her hand to her forehead. "They found my weakness. I could not stand being unpopular."

Taylor's shoulders slumped when Isabela finished her story. She still held out hope that her new reality would dissolve like a bad dream and she'd find herself back on her farm in South Dakota. Isabela pinched her cheek as they approached the student center. Taylor flinched.

"Don't put on such a sad face," Isabela chided. "It makes you ugly."

Taylor blinked, startled. "Um, sorry."

"I shouldn't tell you these stories. I'm a bad influence. Anyway, life here is very boring, more boring than you'd expect considering the things we can do. Homework, at least, helps pass the time." She squinted at Taylor. "You don't want to be here, do you?"

Taylor met her gaze. "Is it that obvious?"

"Maybe you were thinking about getting yourself kicked out, hmm?" Isabela asked in a knowing singsong. "Don't bother. You're Earth Garde now."

Taylor noticed a tall woman emerging from the nearby administration building. She was probably in her thirties, although it was hard to tell with her wrinkle-free mahogany skin. The woman carried a tablet computer, her fingers dancing across the screen as she walked towards the faculty housing.

Isabela followed Taylor's gaze. "That's Lexa. She's in charge of cybersecurity or something. Later, you'll have to meet with her and give her access to all your social media accounts and emails."

"What? Why?"

Isabela rolled her eyes. "For our own good, they say," she replied, then lowered her voice. "I think she is secretly Professor Nine's sexy older girlfriend."

"Who's Professor Nine?"

"Ha! You will see."

Isabela led Taylor into the student center. The two-level atrium was clean and brightly lit. At one end of the room was an open kitchen, a few hot trays out for midday snacking. Long tables filled the room, with smaller booths on the balcony level. About thirty students were present, most of them a crowd of young men watching a soccer game on a wall-mounted flat-screen TV, although there were some students trying to study quietly on the second level.

"You said you came from South Dakota, yes?" Isabela prodded the quiet newbie, trying to wring some small talk out of her. "They made me learn all the states in geography. That's one of the boring middle ones, yes?"

Taylor's mouth tightened. "Some people think so."

"Lots of cows and stuff, right?" Isabela didn't wait for Taylor's defense of South Dakota, continuing on obliviously. "Did you have cliques in your little high school?"

"No," Taylor said with a tired roll of her eyes. "We Midwest barbarians haven't learned such complex social concepts yet."

Isabela picked out an orange from a fruit bowl, then raised an eyebrow at Taylor. She held up her arm, reminding Taylor of the bracelet charged with Simon's Legacy. "Sorry, the translator doesn't do well with sarcasm. Also, if I seem rude, please understand, it's just the language barrier."

"Oh. Oh no, you're fine," Taylor replied half truthfully. "I'm just exhausted."

Isabela smiled. There was nothing wrong with Simon's Legacy-powered translator. Isabela punctured the orange with her fingernail, peeled it and offered Taylor a slice. She gestured towards the group of boys watching soccer, noting with no small amount of satisfaction that a few of them had turned to subtly check her out.

"The boys here, they are probably the same as the boys where you're from. Dirty and stupid." Isabela waved at the group watching her and Taylor, then led her new roommate back towards the door. "They all gravitate together like smelly, immature meteors. But there are some differences. The Americans tend to hang out more with the Americans. We foreigners outnumber you here and it makes you all—" She slipped into a cartoonish southern accent. "Y'all, hmm? It makes y'all uncomfortable. Am I making you uncomfortable, pard'ner?"

"We don't all talk like that," Taylor replied with a raised eyebrow.

Isabela shrugged blithely. "Sounds like it to me. Anyway, the ones designated for combat—that means they have violent powers—they also tend to cling to each other, like the star athletes might, always trying to one-up each other. They are our jocks."

"Jocks I get," Taylor said.

"The ones who are close to graduating, they will pursue you the most, always flirting, because they think it's their last chance to get some before they go off to be Peacekeepers, you know? Pigs! Well, some aren't so bad." Isabela wrinkled her nose. "I am supposed to be showing you where the library is, but this is the stuff that really matters, yes?"

Taylor was surprised to find that she was smiling. Short of slapping the girl, there was no other way to respond to

Isabela's irrepressible bluntness. Also, it was good to talk about mundane things—like boys—instead of contemplating the stranger side of her new surroundings.

"You sound like you're making a nature documentary or something," Taylor said. "Like, the lady who went to live with gorillas."

"Sometimes it feels that way!" Isabela replied with a dazzling smile. "Observation is my hobby."

Isabela led Taylor out of the student center and took her down the walkway towards the training area.

"We girls, our cliques are much different. Many get tight with their roommates, whispering secrets long into the night." She flashed Taylor a sharp look to communicate that this would be out of the question. "There are the goody-goodies who do all their work. I thought maybe you were like this at first, but now I'm starting to think there's more to you. Maybe a secret rebel."

Taylor chuckled. "No. I'm definitely a goody-goody."

"That's okay. At least you aren't the brooding type. Like Ran. We get a lot of those, too. Boys and girls. Simon calls them little Bruce Waynes, but this is a reference I do not understand."

"That's Batman. His parents died and he became a super-hero."

"Yes, yes, I know. I choose not to understand these silly pop culture phrases. Everything is like . . ." She shifted into a stoner accent. "Whoa, man, this is just like that movie or that TV show or who cares."

Isabela popped another orange slice in her mouth, tossed the peel away on the lawn and began ticking off fingers again.

"Then there are the artsy types, the hippies who want to use their Legacies to fix the world, the ones like me who don't give a shit and—oh, the tweebs."

"What's that?"

"A person who's only developed their telekinesis," Isabela explained. "They stick with each other, commiserating about what losers they are, waiting for their big moment. They are like virgins, but worse." She flashed Taylor a devilish look, her tone growing conspiratorial. "We had another healer before you. Vincent from Italy. He's off with Earth Garde now. You will be very popular. The idiot boys, they're always hurting each other. And you're much prettier than Vincent."

They entered the training center. In a huge grassy area cordoned off by a safety net, a handful of Garde practiced using their telekinesis to launch bricks at straw dummies carrying plastic machine guns. Low-tech, yes, but why waste the resources on gear the young Garde were just going to destroy? Everyone knew that Professor Nine had designed much of their training material himself. All the equipment— from the mundane straw dummies to a reprogrammable obstacle course with a vicious AI—had been inspired by Nine's own training methods when he was their age.

To Taylor, it was like stepping into another world. Her eyes darted from a girl shooting a torrent of frost from her hands that was cold enough to ice over a small pool to a boy who punched through the solid ice and lifted a massive chunk over his head. She jumped when a scrawny bleached-blond punk let out a piercing screech that exploded a pane of glass. Isabela smirked when the new girl shied back, half hiding behind her.

"Chaos, no?"

"It's . . . it's very intense."

"Eventually, you'll get used to the madness."

Nearby, a crowd had gathered around two boys. They stood twenty feet apart, hands outstretched towards each other, both of them sweating profusely despite not moving at all. One of them was small, barely thirteen, with dark hair and almond eyes. The other appeared to be almost eighteen, tanned, with fried-looking dreadlocks and a lean surfer body. Taylor watched them with her eyebrows furrowed. Isabela noted her interest with a sly smile.

"Checking out my boyfriend?" she asked.

"What? No." Taylor replied quickly.

"It's okay. He'll be graduating soon. Mentally, I'm already moving on."

Taylor tilted her head and made a show of examining the smaller boy. "Really? He looks young to be graduating," she said innocently.

"Not Miki!" Isabela replied with offense before she realized Taylor was joking. "Aha. So you are funny."

"I was just wondering what they're doing," Taylor said.

Isabela made a face. "A stupid game the boys here

invented. They call it Thrust. Probably because they aren't getting any." She waved her hand in the direction of Miki, the diminutive Inuit, and her boyfriend, Lofton. "They are pushing on each other with their telekinesis." She sighed. "Lofton is good-looking, but not very smart. Everyone knows Miki is strong for his size. Telekinesis is not about muscle, it is about willpower."

As soon as Isabela finished her sentence, there was a sound like dry wood breaking and Lofton was thrown across the room, overwhelmed by Miki's telekinesis. Some of the onlookers used their own Legacies to catch Lofton and set him down gently, but he came up cradling his wrist.

"Case in point," Isabela said with a dismissive wave of her hand. "Dummy probably sprained his wrist again."

"Oh. Should I . . . ?" Taylor started forward, but Isabela grabbed her shoulder.

"No, no. Once they know you'll heal them, they'll be hounding you nonstop. Are you ready for that today?"

Taylor rubbed her face. "Um, not at all."

Isabela dismissed Lofton with a wave, then dragged Taylor out of the training center. "Let him go see the nurse and then later he can lie to me and tell me he won his silly game while I rub ice on his muscles."

"You know, you never told me . . . ," Taylor began.

"What is my Legacy?" Isabela finished her question, leading her towards the dorms.

"Yeah," Taylor replied with a quick laugh. "Guess superpowers aren't one of my go-to conversation topics."

"That will change soon." She stopped, turned to Taylor and covered the other girl's eyes with her hand. "Close your eyes."

"Okay . . ."

"Now open them."

Isabela was gone.

In her place was Taylor.

"Howdy, I'm from South Dakota," Isabela said, her voice now Taylor's. "I like cheeseburgers and fireworks."

Taylor screamed. Then, she clapped both her hands over her mouth, embarrassed by the other students now peering in their direction.

Isabela grinned with Taylor's face. She knew how convincing her shape-shifting could be. She'd gotten Taylor perfect, right down to her threadbare hooded sweatshirt and ugly old sneakers.

Taylor finally managed to collect herself. "Wow," she said at last. "Do I seriously look that tired?"

In the blink of an eye, Isabela was back to her tanned and beautiful self. She still grinned. Most people, when she stole their shapes, tried to tell her that she wasn't getting it quite right. Not Taylor. She was chill enough to make a joke about it. Isabela liked that. She decided, much to her own chagrin, that she kind of liked this new girl. That was something of a personal milestone. With the exception of Ran, who she warily tolerated, Isabela didn't like any of the other girls on campus. Despised them, in fact. This half-clever, self-deprecating American, though—well, she might make a worthy apprentice. A project.

Isabela put her arm gently around Taylor's shoulders and guided her to the dorms.

"Yes. Let's get you a nap," she said, then leaned in close to Taylor and whispered, "And when you're ready to escape this place, I will show you how."

CHAPTER FIFTEEN

RAN TAKEDA

THE HUMAN GARDE ACADEMY—POINT REYES, CALIFORNIA

MONDAY MORNING FOUND RAN TAKEDA IN DR. SUSAN Chen's weekly Adjusting to the New World course. Dr. Chen was in her midthirties, pretty, with her hair always arranged in a fastidious braid. She was Chinese by way of Canada and, like most of the Academy's faculty, academically impressive; she held dual PhDs in world literature and behavioral science. Ran enjoyed Dr. Chen's literature class but liked these weekly New World meetings even more. The discussions were always freewheeling and wide-ranging—last week, they'd spent the entire session debating what to do about the Mogadorians in the Arctic internment camps. Ran wasn't much of a participator, but she liked listening to the debates, and especially the way Dr. Chen made complicated real-world problems of life and death seem like they could be solved right there in the classroom with rational debate.

This week, Dr. Chen had written "Constructive vs. Destructive Legacy Use" on the board. In the seat next to Ran, Nigel yawned dramatically.

"Look around at your classmates," Dr. Chen began. "What do most of you have in common?"

Ran pushed her overgrown black bangs out of her eyes and did as she was told.

She looked first at Nigel. Her nakama. The literally loud-mouthed punk who Ran knew was secretly fragile. Nigel did the talking, Ran did the listening. Nigel caught her staring at him and made an ugly face. Ran subtly raised an eyebrow. In their secret language of facial expressions, Nigel would interpret that correctly as amusement.

In the next seat over from Nigel was Lisbette. From Bolivia. Capable of creating and projecting ice.

Caleb Crane. America. The duplicator.

Omar Azoulay. Morocco. Immune to fire and capable of breathing it like a dragon.

Lofton St. Croix. Canada. His skin projected razor-sharp quills at will.

Nicolas Lambert. Belgium. Enhanced strength.

Maiken Megalos. Greece. Enhanced speed.

And on and on, around the room Ran went, until she arrived back at herself.

Ran Takeda. Japan. Girl who blows things up.

"Combat," Ran said under her breath.

Nigel raised his hand, getting Dr. Chen's attention.

"Oi, I got it, Susan," he said, and Ran's mouth tightened in disapproval. She didn't like the disrespectful way he insisted on addressing their instructors, but Nigel was Nigel. "We're all a bunch of considerable badasses, aren't we? Take over the bloody world with this bunch, couldn't you?"

Some laughter from the rest of the class. Dr. Chen nodded in patient agreement with Nigel's bluster.

"Exactly, Mr. Barnaby," she said. "These seminars weren't put together at random. This group, in particular, intentionally includes those with advanced control of Legacies that Earth Garde deems combat-oriented. One day soon, when your training here is completed, you'll be placed into a division of Earth Garde Peacekeepers and potentially be deployed into dangerous situations. War zones, riots, Mogadorian insurgents. That is your future."

"Heck, if that's the case, shouldn't we have this class in the training center?" Lofton spoke up in his lazy surfer drawl.

Ran felt her ears go red. Thanks to her roommate Isabela and the Academy's inadequate soundproofing, the mere sound of Lofton's voice made her blush with discomfort.

"Yeah. After your lecture on all the horrible things we'll be facing, most of us could probably use the extra training time," Lisbette said. She cast an envious look in Ran's direction. "Some of us haven't beaten Professor Nine's obstacle course yet."

"Correction. Only one of us has done that solo," Nigel

said, looking in Ran's direction as well, his face filled with pride. She pretended not to notice either of them.

"But that is exactly why we're here," Dr. Chen said. "Just because you're expected to be soldiers doesn't mean that has to be the sum total of your lives. As I've said before, you must remember that you are not weapons. You are people. And like all people, but especially Peacekeepers, you must aspire to be above violence. Today, I want us to think about how your violent Legacies might be used in unconventional ways, towards altruistic or beneficial purposes. Have any of you considered that?"

The room went silent. Ran looked down at her hands, both of them splayed on top of her desk.

"Approach it simply," Dr. Chen pressed. "What is one way that you could use your Legacies where no one would get hurt?"

"I can lift heavy things," Nicolas said at last, uncertainty in his voice. "Like, help build houses and stuff, right?"

"Good," Dr. Chen replied. "That's a start."

"We can all do that, brother," Nigel replied. "That's what the telekinesis is for, innit?" At a look from Nicolas, Nigel held up his hands. "Don't get me wrong. Unlike me, you're strong enough to be the beams in a skyscraper. Muscles from Brussels the sequel over here. But what can you lift with your hands that the rest of us couldn't lift with our minds? Nah, mate. That Legacy o' yours is good for punching. Strictly punching—"

"Thank you, Nigel," interrupted Dr. Chen. "Do you have

any thoughts on your own Legacies?"

"Oh, I'm easy-peasy. I can help the deaf to hear. I can shout tornado warnings across small towns. I can auto-tune rap songs."

"Ice sculptures," Lisbette said suddenly.

Dr. Chen turned in her direction. "What was that?"

"Um, I've been making ice sculptures in my spare time," Lisbette elaborated. "For fun. I can do that."

"Auto-tune? Ice sculptures? Dr. Chen's not asking about useless tricks," Maiken scoffed. "There's a water shortage in some countries, Lisbette. God. Ice melts. You can create water."

"Oh yeah," Lisbette said. "That too."

Dr. Chen held up a hand. "Now, hold on. Let's not discount artistic applications. One could argue that art is an altruistic use of one's Legacies, with intangible benefits to society."

"Hell yeah," Nigel said. "I'd rather have the Sweet than some bloody water, that's for sure. Follow your inner artist, Lizzy."

Caleb raised his hand. "Organ donation."

Dr. Chen turned to him. "Could you elaborate on that, Caleb?"

"Well, I can duplicate myself," Caleb explained. "So, a surgeon could perform an operation on one of my duplicates, take the organs and give them to someone in need."

Lofton made a face. "Do those clones of yours even have organs, dude?"

Caleb blinked. "I mean, I obviously haven't dissected one, if that's what you're asking."

Nigel gave Ran a look—the same slack-jawed and cross-eyed expression he broke out whenever his roommate did something weird. She gently tipped her head in response, reminding Nigel that he was supposed to be making an effort with Caleb. Unlike Nigel, she never blamed Caleb for the episode months ago with the Chimæra. He was just following orders.

"Mate," Nigel started in a gentler tone than the one he'd used with Nicolas. "Don't your duplicates disappear when you get too far away from them?"

"Yeah," Caleb replied. "But my range is getting farther . . ."

Nigel rubbed the back of his neck. "Right. But, uh, assuming them clones even have hearts and livers and whatever, wouldn't those organs just disappear when you absorbed them back up? You'd leave some poor sot with a hole in his belly."

Caleb nodded slowly. "I hadn't considered that."

"This is gross," complained Maiken.

"We might have to spend a little more time workshopping that particular idea," Dr. Chen diplomatically told Caleb. "However, Caleb's on the right track. That's exactly the kind of outside-the-box, nontraditional thinking that I hope to inspire in you." Dr. Chen's pacing brought her over to Ran's desk. "What about you, Ran? Any thoughts?"

Ran tensed up.

"No," she said quietly.

Dr. Chen smiled. "Come on, Ran. There're no wrong answers here. There's got to be something you can add to the discussion."

Ran felt the eyes of her classmates upon her. She racked her brain for something to say. With a touch, she could render an object's molecules unstable. When she released an object thus charged, it would explode with all the concussive force of a grenade. What were the altruistic and beneficial applications of that?

That's when the flash occurred. All of a sudden, Ran's mind went hot and she was back in Tokyo. Buried under a pile of rubble, the roof of what used to be her family's small apartment on top of her, her little brother crying somewhere close. Trapped. Suffocating. She shoved against the debris with all her might. The telekinesis that Ran hadn't even discovered yet triggered and the chunks of roof went sailing off her. Some of them—the ones she'd been touching— exploded. She staggered to her feet, blood in her eyes, not sure what she'd just done.

Ran was the only Garde known to have manifested her telekinesis and primary Legacy at the same time. Such a trivial fact meant nothing to Ran now and meant even less back in Tokyo.

"Ran?"

She couldn't hear her brother crying anymore.

"Ran?" Dr. Chen asked again.

The vision passed. She was back in the classroom, everyone staring at her. Her desk vibrated beneath her fingers.

Ran glanced down, saw that she had begun to charge the polished wood desktop. With a deep breath, she pulled that energy back inside her, narrowly averting an explosion.

"No," she said again, firmly, and this time Dr. Chen accepted that answer. Her teacher moved on, but not without a lingering look of concern for Ran.

After the seminar, Ran strode purposefully across the lawn towards the girls' dorms. It had been a few weeks since she last experienced a flashback like the one that overcame her in class. Foolishly, she'd begun to hope that they were fading, the visions of Tokyo during the invasion relegated to an occasional nightmare. Not so. Ran wished she were harder. More in control.

Nigel caught up to her. He looped his hand through her arm, matching her pace.

"All right, then," he said casually. "Nice day for a speed walk across campus, innit?"

Ran didn't respond. Nigel was adept at interpreting her silences, though. She didn't mind his presence.

"How's the new roommate?" he asked, each of them having gotten new additions to their suites over the weekend. "Mine's a real sweetheart. Excitable sort. Told me they're gonna write about us in history books. I can get behind that. A welcome change of pace from ol' Caleb, who I might very well find pulling guts out of a clone when I get back to our room."

"Mine seems kind," Ran replied. "Overwhelmed. Very tired."

"Getting the tour from Isabela would wear out a marathon runner."

"Yes," Ran responded noncommittally. "She is a healer. A good Legacy."

The atmosphere around them changed. It was subtle—the noises from other passing students became muffled and fuzzy, while their own soft footfalls in the grass sounded louder thanks to a lack of background noise. Nigel was using his sonic manipulation Legacy. He put them in a bubble so that no one would be able to hear them.

"We gonna talk about what happened in class, love? Or are we just gonna dance around it?"

Ran pressed her lips together. She knew Nigel got a kick out of it when she played up her own robotic nature.

"I do not dance," she replied stiffly.

Nigel snorted, but kept giving her that concerned look. "You had one of your episodes, didn't you?"

"Yes."

"You not taking those meds Dr. Linda prescribed?"

"No."

"Why not?"

Ran stopped. She turned to look at him. "Are you taking yours?"

After learning about what happened to them during the invasion, Dr. Linda had prescribed both Ran and Nigel the same antianxiety medication. Ran remembered how Nigel had clicked their two identical pill bottles together like they were cheers-ing. Now, he flashed her a sly smile.

"Nah. You know they made me tired. I gotta stay functional."

"As do I," Ran said.

"So we're both full Cuckoo's Nest," Nigel observed with a shrug. Then, his face got serious again, an expression Ran wasn't used to seeing on his pockmarked cheeks. "Look, you know I tell you all my shit . . ."

"Yes," Ran said.

"But if I'm ever talking too much, if you need to get something off your chest, you know I'm your man, right?"

Ran smiled. A rare thing. She put both her hands on Nigel's bony shoulders, carefully avoiding the spiky studs sewn onto his denim vest.

"You are my man," she said. "Do not worry about me."

Nigel laughed brusquely and looked away. "All right. We had our moment, didn't we? Let's go back to silently repressing our feelings, yeah?"

Ran let her hands drop away and they resumed their walk across campus. Nigel's words were stuck in her head, a couple of random phrases that hinted at some bigger inspiration.

Gotta stay functional.

Repressing our feelings.

Ran stopped walking.

"I have to go back and see Dr. Chen," she said suddenly.

"Huh? About what?"

But Ran was already jogging back towards the administration building. "I will see you at dinner!" she called over her shoulder.

Ran found Dr. Chen still in the seminar room, tidying up for the next class. The jog back hadn't come close to winding her and Ran had a habit of entering rooms quietly. When she finally spoke, her soft voice made Dr. Chen jump.

"I have an answer."

"Oh, wow—Ran. You scared me."

"I am sorry about class before," Ran said, believing Dr. Chen was referring to the near explosion at her desk.

"It's okay," Dr. Chen replied kindly. "So, you gave my question a little more thought?"

"Yes," Ran said, a tinge of excitement in her voice. "The best way for me to benefit society using my Legacy—the only way, I believe—is for me to stop using it entirely."

"Well, Ran, that's not exactly the point of the exercise—"

"Please inform the other administrators," Ran concluded. Her message delivered, she was already halfway out the door. "I will no longer blow anything up."

CHAPTER SIXTEEN

TAYLOR'S FIRST FEW WEEKS AT THE ACADEMY WERE so busy that she almost forgot to be homesick.

After a meeting with Dr. Chen to assess where she stood academically, Taylor was given a full schedule of classes. She started every day with the brutal back-to-back of organic chemistry and trigonometry, two classes where she immediately felt overwhelmed. The teachers at the academy were different from the ones back home—faster talkers, sharp and enthusiastic, demanding.

Once her brain was appropriately mushed, Taylor finished her school day with European history and then classic literature. Taylor got into the habit of sitting in the back during history, keeping her head down where it was safe. Sometimes, there were objects literally flying around the room. With such a diverse population, class discussions often boiled over into intense debates. On her second day, Taylor witnessed a girl freeze her neighbor's hands to his desk during a shouting match about socialism.

Literature class Taylor actually enjoyed. She'd always liked that class best, but back home her classmates weren't such enthusiastic participators. At the Academy, most of the other kids always had something to say, although their book discussions were thankfully much mellower than their history ones.

"I remember Mrs. Reynolds used to have to call on people to get them to talk about *The Scarlet Letter*," Taylor told her father over the phone, reminiscing about her ninth-grade English teacher. "It was like pulling teeth. I used to feel embarrassed raising my hand so much."

"Shoot," her dad replied, his smile audible. "I used to keep my head down, pretend to be asleep until the teacher moved on. Although, in those days, they'd smack you with a ruler . . ."

"It's so different here," Taylor said. She lowered her voice, even though the corner of the student union with the shared phones was completely empty. "These kids all have so much to say. They have so many opinions. This one guy got into an argument with our teacher because he doesn't think Shakespeare actually existed. Nobody would ever come up with a crazy theory like that back in Turner, much less go at it with a teacher over it."

"So, wait," her dad said. "Shakespeare is real or no?"

"It's like they're all so sure of themselves," Taylor continued. "Like because they got Legacies, everything about them is suddenly marked for greatness."

"Well, you superpowered types are the chosen ones," her dad said. Taylor laughed. "Don't know why you're laughing, kiddo. You're one of 'em."

Taylor still couldn't believe that.

"You do know they record all those phone calls, yes?" Isabela scornfully said one night when Taylor returned from her nightly talk with her dad. "That is why we cannot have cell phones. There is no privacy. The internet, too. Think about the resources this Academy has, hmm? We should all have laptops. Two laptops! But we must go to the computer lab like third world people in the nineties. All so they can monitor us."

Throughout her rant, Isabela lounged on the couch in their common room, her legs draped across Lofton. During her few weeks at the Academy, Taylor had learned that he was something of a fixture around their suite. She'd begun to think of him as handsome furniture.

"Wait," Lofton said. "They keep track of our internet use?"

Isabela raised an eyebrow. "Why do you sound so concerned, hmm? What have you been looking at?"

"Nothing," he said quickly.

"Pervert," Isabela replied with a dismissive wave of her hand. "Do not touch me."

"Anyway," Taylor said, steering the conversation away from Lofton's browsing habits. "I'm just talking to my dad. I don't care if they listen in, if that's even true."

"Of course it is true!" Isbaela said. She quickly moved on. "Your dad's coming to visit soon, yes?"

"Next month," Taylor replied with a frown. The Academy allowed visits from family only once a month and she'd arrived just after the most recent Family Day. It'd been too long since she'd seen her dad face-to-face.

"Taylor's dad is a muscular farm man and a bachelor. I am very excited to meet him," Isabela explained to Lofton.

Taylor groaned. "You're disgusting. I've got homework."

And she did have homework. Essays and work sheets and lab reports, but also less mundane assignments. Every night, she was required to use her telekinesis to levitate grains of rice—not all at once, but one at a time—and keep count of how many she could manage before letting one drop. Telekinetic precision, Taylor soon learned, was much more difficult than blunt force. By the end of her second week, she was up to thirty-seven.

"Very good!" Kopano said enthusiastically when she told him. "I can only do twenty-nine. Rice! I would much rather cook and eat it."

Another day, another six hours of classes, followed by a few more hours of rigorous physical activity in the training center. Taylor and Kopano didn't have any classes together, so they often found each other during gym time. They trained their telekinesis by tossing objects back and forth, chatting about their days in this strange new place. Neither of them was allowed to run the obstacle course yet—a daunting gauntlet of ropes and barbed wire, pits and water traps, powered by a projectile-launching AI that adapted to their abilities. They watched from the sidelines as their classmates attempted the course and came back bruised and bloodied, never able to reach the off switch at the end of the run.

There was regular exercise, too, under the watchful eye of the Academy's staff of fitness professionals, who were all as impressively credentialed as the professors. Kopano chased Taylor around the track, huffing and puffing, unable to match her pace. In turn, Taylor looked on in awe as Kopano curled mammoth barbells.

Kopano winked at her. "My muscles are yawning," he told her as he effortlessly curled another 150-pound weight. "These weights, they must be broken. Or else I am the strongest boy here. That is probably it. They think my Legacy is Fortem, like Nicolas, but that mine is presenting in a much different way."

Taylor put her hands on her hips. "I saw Nicolas lifting way more than one fifty."

"I am just warming up!" Kopano replied. He switched hands and Taylor noticed the barbell remained suspended in the air.

She glared at him, catching on. "You're using your telekinesis, you cheater!"

"I am not," Kopano cried, offended. "Come see."

Taylor came over to put one of her hands on top of the dumbbell. She tried to force it down. Instead, she ended up rising off her feet along with the weight, lifted by Kopano's telekinesis.

"A new record from the mighty Kopano!" he shouted.

"Put me down!" Taylor laughed.

Another day, they had yoga class, but with a twist. Throughout the stretches, their instructor commanded that they keep an egg telekinetically hovering over their heads. Taylor found she was good at this exercise. She moved between stretches fluidly—from down dog to a back bend and then into a sustained tree pose. Her mind cleared and her gentle hold on the egg became second nature. She dropped her egg only when Kopano violently exploded his own during a bow pose—the fourth egg he'd broken—and she could no longer keep in the laughter.

"So, they still haven't figured out exactly how your Legacy works?" Taylor asked him after class. They'd been at the Academy more than a week.

Kopano scratched dried egg flakes out of his hair. "Not yet. They know that I am hard as steel when they try to poke me with their needles, but they do not know why it is so inconsistent or if I can control it." Kopano grinned. "Professor Nine wants to shoot me."

Taylor's eyes widened in alarm. "What? Kopano, that's insane!"

"I agree. Yet I am also strangely excited about it." He looked at her. "I kind of want to know what would happen."

Taylor squeezed his hand. "Kopano. Please. Don't let anyone shoot you, okay?"

Taylor had recently gotten firsthand experience with gunshot wounds. In order to train her healing Legacy, Taylor was allowed to leave campus one day per week. Accompanied by Dr. Goode and a team of stone-faced Peacekeepers with concealed weapons, she traveled to a hospital down in San Francisco. Under the guise of a "clinical study," Taylor saw a variety of patients with different types of injuries. When some of them realized what she was, they demanded a real doctor, but mostly the people she dealt with were sweet and eager to be well.

"I have some experience with Legacies like yours," Dr. Goode told her during their first visit, perhaps anticipating her nervousness. "I once sustained an extremely grievous wound that was healed by a Loric. The process does not hurt the patient and I've suffered no ill effects since. All that is to say—you can only do good here today, Taylor."

She looked down at her hands. "I'll . . . I'll do what I can, I guess."

"I also understand that your Legacy has limits, especially as a beginner. No one is expecting you to heal everyone in this hospital. Part of what we're trying to discover with these visits is just where your limits are and how far you can go beyond them," Dr. Goode continued. "As for the process itself, I believe it helps to visualize the body knitting and to . . . ah . . . push positive energy out of your body."

Taylor couldn't help but snort at "positive energy." The phrase sounded like something out of one of the New Age books her mom used to read before she bailed. However, when she focused on her first patient—a man in his twenties who had gashed his leg falling off a pier—she could feel the aura Dr. Goode spoke about come flowing out of her.

The cuts and bruises were the easiest to heal. She could visualize what the skin was supposed to look like, channel her warm energy through her hand and into the patient and the flesh would mend beneath her fingertips.

Broken bones were more difficult. The doctors observing her showed Taylor X-rays of where the fractures were. That helped a little. Taylor visualized filling in the shadowy crack in the bone and, slowly, her Legacy took over. It began to seem like Taylor could sense the injury. Visualization or not, her Legacy knew something was amiss and gave her the power to fix it. When a girl whose arm had been shattered in a car accident wrapped Taylor in a bear hug, she couldn't keep the giddy smile off her face.

Taylor met her match with a middle-aged cancer patient. The woman was frail, her head wrapped in colorful scarves, her eyes wet with hope. Lymphoma, the doctors said. The woman was no longer undergoing treatment; everything had failed. Taylor swallowed hard and pressed her palms against the woman's abdomen.

The healing energy poured out of Taylor, but was swallowed up by the sickness that grew inside the woman. Before, when she finished healing a person, Taylor felt a satisfying sense of reconnection—the patient's body was whole again, her Legacy snapped off in response. But now, with the cancer, her Legacy just asked for more and more energy, feeding it into the woman but making very little progress.

Dr. Goode stepped in. "Taylor, perhaps that is enough for today."

Taylor had gotten lost in the work. Five minutes had passed. She was sweaty, yet the back of her neck was cold. In fact, she was chilled all over.

"It's okay, sweetie," the woman said. She brushed a damp curl of hair out of Taylor's face. "I knew it was a long shot."

"I'll keep trying," she promised. "I'll get better. We'll both get better."

Later, Taylor sat in the dining hall and pored over an anatomy textbook. Maybe if she could better understand the human body, she could improve the potency of her healing.

"Look at this one, doing extra work," Kopano observed, sitting across from her. "Where is the girl of a few weeks ago who didn't even want to be here? Although, I suppose you did want boring and well—" Kopano squinted at a chart of the nervous system. "It appears you have found it."

"Don't make fun," Taylor replied. "This is serious. I felt like—like I really did some good today."

Kopano's expression immediately straightened out. "I did not mean to joke," he said. "You are a hero already in ways I have only dreamed of. You are changing lives. Isn't it amazing?"

"It's . . ." Taylor felt her face get hot. She couldn't help but agree. "It kind of was. Yes."

"Aha! At last, you admit it!" Kopano replied, his irrepressible grin breaking loose.

Taylor shook her head. "I just . . . I have to get better. It's hard to explain, but . . . I could feel the power inside me . . . and I could feel it start to weaken gradually, the more I used it."

"I know that feeling," Kopano said. "Like the headaches we get when we use too much telekinesis."

"I've never gotten one of those."

"No? Well, you have never floated your little brother around for eight hours."

"This feeling was different." Taylor searched for the right words. "My Legacy—it was like a sun existing inside me. And every time that I healed someone, it got a little dimmer, a little closer to setting. So, by the end of the day, I could still feel the warmth from my Legacy but . . . but it was like night, you know? I knew the sun would come back eventually, but I couldn't bring any more light. Does that make any sense?"

Kopano stared at her. "It does. It's like poetry."

"Yeah, yeah," Taylor said with a wave of her hand. "The point is, I need to figure out how to make that sun brighter."

"I have no doubt you will succeed," Kopano said firmly.

Lying in bed that night, Taylor realized that she was actually excited about the next morning. About her strange and sometimes unruly classes, her training, her friendships with Isabela and Kopano. She felt almost guilty when she thought about her father, because she was beginning to settle in.

So, of course, that was when the nightmares started.

In the dream, Taylor found herself back on her farm. The grass was overgrown and it swayed around her legs.

Something caught her eye—rivulets of blood on the emerald-green blades.

"Dad?" she called out.

Her farm looked decrepit. The walls were singed, the shutters hung crookedly from the windows, the roof sagged. There was something on the porch. In her father's rocking chair. Was that a body? A skeleton? Was that . . . ?

Someone behind her chuckled. Taylor whipped around. She saw the Harvester preacher in his vestments, a black bandanna covering the lower half of his face. He led something on a leash—a creature, gray-skinned and reptilian, but with the hulking appendages of a large gorilla. The thing salivated, licking its long, purple tongue across rows of razor-sharp teeth. It watched her hungrily through empty black eyes.

"Abomination!" the preacher shouted.

He dropped the leash. The beast charged her. Taylor tried to run, but . . .

Taylor woke with a barely stifled scream, out of breath, sweating.

Shaken, Taylor stumbled out of her room, still half asleep. In the common room, she padded over to their mini-fridge and grabbed a bottle of water. Her hands were shaking. She wanted to call her dad, but the student union would be closed at this time of night.

Instead, she knocked gently on Isabela's door. She remembered Isabela's policy on slumber party secret-sharing—we are not children!—but that wasn't what Taylor had in mind.

She needed the blustery Brazilian to tell her she was being stupid, to tell her to go back to her own bed. She needed to not be alone, just for a few minutes.

When Isabela didn't answer, Taylor gently nudged open her door. "Isabela? Are you awake?" she whispered.

Taylor managed to get the door open only about a foot before it knocked into something. A nightstand, pushed close to the door for some reason. And, when Taylor jostled it, a metal bell sitting atop it jingled sharply. It was as if Isabela had booby-trapped her room.

"Izz? What the hell?" Taylor whispered to herself, a moment before a dark shape lunged out of Isabela's bed.

For a moment, Taylor thought she was back in her nightmare. In the moonlight, through the narrowly cracked door, Taylor couldn't be sure exactly what she saw. The shape looked like Isabela—her slender body, her wild raven hair— but the face was twisted and wrong, scarred, like a horrible Halloween mask.

The apparition screamed at Taylor in a language she didn't understand. Was that Portuguese? With a violent telekinetic thrust, the door slammed in Taylor's face.

Taylor took a stunned step backwards.

"Is everything all right?"

Ran stood in the doorway to her room, hair tousled. In the weeks they'd been living together, Taylor hadn't interacted very much with Ran. The Japanese girl was polite and pleasant, but generally kept to herself and had little to say. Isabela told Taylor not to take it personally; Ran was like that with everyone. Well, everyone except for that rangy British boy Nigel.

Taylor glanced back at Isabela's closed door, uncertain what she just saw or how much to tell Ran. Eventually, she nodded, rubbing her eyes.

"Yeah, everything's fine. I just . . . had a bad dream. Sorry to wake you."

"I was already awake," Ran said.

"Okay. Well, good night."

Ran said nothing, but remained in her doorway. Feeling like she'd experienced enough weirdness for one night, Taylor trudged back to her room with her head down.

When Taylor was nearly at her door, Ran spoke quietly. "I also have nightmares."

Taylor turned back. "Really? You?"

Ran nodded. "Ever since the invasion. Why does that surprise you?"

"I don't know. You just seem so . . ." Taylor shrugged. "Tough, I guess."

Ran studied Taylor for a moment. Then, she stepped aside, gesturing into her room. "Would you like to talk about what you dreamed?"

"I . . ." The offer took Taylor aback, but after a moment's consideration she nodded. "Okay. Sure."

That night, huddled next to Ran on her bed, Taylor told her roommate about her farm, the Harvesters and the hideous creature that mauled her. Ran stayed quiet throughout the telling. At the end, Ran was still, her eyes closed. Taylor assumed she had fallen asleep. She yawned, her own eyes getting heavy.

"These dreams, they are creations of darkness," Ran whispered, without opening her eyes. "When we talk about them, we drag them into the light. We realize that they cannot hurt us anymore."

Taylor hoped that was true.

CHAPTER SEVENTEEN

RAN TAKEDA
THE HUMAN GARDE ACADEMY—POINT REYES, CALIFORNIA

THERE WERE NIGHTS WHEN THE ADVICE SHE'D given to Taylor rang hollow to Ran herself. Nights when no amount of meditation could quiet the echoes from her past— her brother's cries, the collapsing walls of her family's home, the explosions. Nights when, lying in bed, Ran felt pursued, like the Mogadorians who had nearly killed her at Patience Creek were still out there, chasing her.

On those nights, she ran.

Only a few nights after she'd consoled Taylor, Ran found herself jittery and anxious. She untangled herself from sweaty sheets and pulled on her workout clothes, slipping quietly out of her suite. The students had a midnight curfew, but it wasn't clear exactly when in the morning that was lifted. Anyway, it didn't matter to Ran. No one ever bothered her about her four a.m. runs. She wasn't sure anyone even noticed.

Ran first jogged around the dorms, picking up speed as she hit the path that led out to the woods. When she reached the tree line, she was in a full-on run. She turned—it was still too dark to go crashing through the woods—so she sped along the edge, her footfalls answering the steady buzz of crickets. In her uneasy state, she imagined the crooked shadows of tree branches as claws, reaching for her. She sprinted until her legs ached and her lungs burned, and then she pushed herself to go faster. If she went hard enough, maybe she could outrun the darkness at her back.

Eventually, her sweaty tank top cold against her spine, Ran doubled back for campus. The lights were on at the training center. That was unusual. Professor Nine sometimes held sessions before class, but not this early. Curious, Ran jogged in that direction.

As Ran drew close, she heard the clamor of the obstacle course in motion. Someone was making a run, which wasn't allowed without faculty and medical supervision.

That rule, obviously, didn't apply to Professor Nine.

Ran peeked into the gymnasium just as Nine stopped a burst of rubber shrapnel with his telekinesis and redirected the fragments so they would knock off course a sandbag swinging for his head. Nine wore only a pair of gym shorts and sneakers, so Ran could see where his prosthetic arm met the stump of his shoulder, the skin there red and upraised, run through with blackish scars.

As Ran watched, Nine leaped onto a balance beam and sprinted across it, dodging under a series of electrified wires. A piston-powered brick battering ram waited for Nine at the end of the beam. He put his shoulder into it, leaving cracks in the stone as he spun clear.

One of the course's wall-mounted cannons took aim at Nine, tracking his movement and firing bursts of rubber slugs faster than his telekinesis could work. Nine evaded them by running up the nearest wall, his antigravity Legacy kicking in. The computer adjusted and pieces of the wall began to leak grease under Nine's feet, making vertical progress difficult. He slowed down and the cannon fire began to catch up to him, so Nine leaped across the gym, towards the opposite wall, reaching out—

His fingers grazed the wall's surface, failed to stick and he fell. He landed in an awkward heap on the course's floor and was quickly peppered by rubber bullets. Ran grimaced.

Nine had tried to use his antigravity Legacy to go from wall to wall, but in the moment had forgotten about his prosthetic limb. His power didn't work through the metallic fingers.

Ran slipped away as Nine pounded the floor in frustration, not wanting to further invade the Loric's privacy.

Her stomach growled and so Ran headed for the dining hall. The doors were locked—the breakfast shift wouldn't begin for another couple of hours—but that posed no problem to Ran and her telekinesis. After popping the dead bolt, she paused briefly in front of the dining hall's bulletin board, reading the sign advertising the Academy's upcoming "Wargames" event. The students would be taking on the UN Peacekeepers in some sort of battle scenario with Earth Garde present to observe. She knew Nigel was excited about that, although also disappointed that they wouldn't be working as a team.

Ran tiptoed into the kitchen, liberated an egg from the refrigerator and headed out through the service exit. Cupping the egg in her hands, she walked down the path that led to the Academy's beach. It was cold by the water, but Ran didn't mind. She plopped down in the sand and waited for sunrise. She liked how the sun would come from behind her, heating the sand first and turning the water slowly purple.

Holding her egg, Ran used her Legacy. She'd sworn off exploding things, that was true, but no one needed to know about this silly trick, which wasn't even worth mentioning in Dr. Chen's seminar. She pushed just enough kinetic energy into the egg so that she could feel the molecules vibrating, let the egg sit in that agitated state for a few seconds and then sucked the energy back into herself. That process—retrieving the energy she produced—stung her palms and made Ran flinch.

The end result was a hardboiled egg. She cracked the shell with her fingernail and began to peel it away.

"Thought you'd given up your Legacy," said a voice from behind her.

Ran half turned. It was Professor Nine. She hadn't heard him hiking down—the big Loric was surprisingly stealthy.

Ran wondered if he knew she'd been watching him earlier. He sat down next to her, drying his sweat off with a towel.

"I had to file a report with Earth Garde about you," Nine continued when she didn't immediately respond. "Those dudes were pretty disappointed. I think they had a list of things for you to explode."

Ran popped a piece of egg into her mouth. "You may tell Earth Garde that I will use my Legacy for breakfast purposes only."

Nine snorted. He looked at Ran for a long moment and she could tell he wanted to say something. She waited in silence, looking out at the waves.

"Look, my job here is to make sure you and the others learn how to control your Legacies so you can go through life without hurting anybody. I mean, anybody you don't want to hurt." Nine paused. "After you graduate from here, you want to go be Earth Garde MVP, that's cool. You want to live some boring-ass life as a very specific chef, that's cool too."

"Hmm," Ran replied noncommittally.

"Point is, you don't want to use your Legacies for Earth Garde, that's fine with me. I don't know if those UN tools will be chill about it, but we'll cross that bridge when we get there. But what I gotta know, if I'm going to graduate you from the Academy, is that should push come to shove, if your life or someone else's life depends on it—I need to know you won't hesitate to drop all this pacifist horseshit and blow up some bad guys. Because whether you like it or not, you're a Garde, and situations like that tend to happen to us."

Ran considered Nine's words.

"I will not hesitate," she said quietly.

Nine nodded once, satisfied, and stood up. He laid his towel out in the sand and began the process of detaching his prosthetic limb. Ran realized he planned to go swimming.

"By the way," he said, "how's the new roommate?"

Ran tilted her head. "Taylor? She is fine. Adjusting, I think."

"Good," Nine replied, and set his arm down in the towel. "Keep an eye on her, yeah? You wouldn't think it, but healers got it worse than badass types like us. The whole savior thing, it can mess 'em up."

There was something in Nine's tone—almost like a warning, almost like he wasn't saying exactly what he meant. Before Ran could ask him any further questions, he jogged towards the water and dove into the waves.

CHAPTER EIGHTEEN

CALEB CRANE
THE HUMAN GARDE ACADEMY—POINT REYES, CALIFORNIA

"YOU KNOW WHAT YOUR PROBLEM IS, MAN?"

Caleb Crane shook his head. No. He did not know what his problem was.

"You don't have any balls. That's what your problem is."

Caleb's brow creased. He grew up with two older brothers and a drill instructor for a father. He was used to this kind of talk. That didn't mean he appreciated it.

"You like this Taylor girl, right? But it's been weeks and you haven't said anything to her. That's pathetic, man. I'm not even saying you should flirt with her. I'm not sure you're capable of that without embarrassing yourself."

Caleb rubbed the back of his neck. He sat on the foot of his bed, the door to his room closed. This lecture—on the topic of how huge a loser he was—had already been going on for some time.

"You could be like—'Hey, how are your classes going? What kind of music do you like? What are your favorite movies?' They call that small talk, you creep. I mean, if she asks you those questions back, you'll have to lie because your taste sucks and your life is lame, but whatever. Anyway, probably better to lie, just say you like what she likes. Always agree with her. That's a good strategy. How hard is that, dude?"

"It isn't really my style," Caleb replied. "To, um, be so manipulative."

"You don't have a style! Look, I know your confidence is shot because of, like, your brothers beating the shit out of you all the time and kids at school making fun of your big ears . . ."

This was true. Caleb had been mocked mercilessly in elementary school for his ears—which he had since grown into. His classmates would flop their arms in front of their faces like an elephant's trunk and make trumpet noises with their mouths. It had stuck with him.

". . . but you're good-looking now. I mean, you're okay. Your clothes suck. We can work on that. But listen, all you need to do is be nice, chat her up a little—and then, boom, you're her friend."

"The friend zone," Caleb said. "I heard that was bad."

"What? Did you read that in some ladies' magazine? Don't say 'friend zone.' Ever. Look, stupid, here's what a guy with your limited charms has to do. You get in tight. Buddy up. And then—well, school here is stressful. She's probably emotional. Most girls are. You wait for her to let her guard down, for her to need a good cry—and whose shoulder is she going to look for?"

"Mine?"

"Bingo!"

"But . . ." Caleb's brow furrowed. "The goal is to make her cry?"

"No! The goal is to take advantage of an emotional situation. God, you're a hopeless case. Why do I even bother?"

Caleb looked up at himself. A duplicate. Him . . . but different. A fast talker, mean, with highly questionable opinions about the opposite sex.

"I think it's time for you to go," Caleb said.

The duplicate held up his hands. "Whoa, hold on—"

Caleb stood up. He could reabsorb a duplicate without wrapping his hands around the duplicate's neck, but this one had really gotten on his nerves.

"Ack—! Stop!"

And then he was gone. The room was quiet. Caleb was alone.

Outside, in the common room, Caleb found Kopano watching a martial arts movie. The Nigerian smiled and waved.

"This part is good!" Kopano said. "You guys should come watch."

Caleb glanced over his shoulder. "It's just me."

"Oh," Kopano said, paying more attention to his movie than Caleb. "I thought I heard you talking to someone in there."

"No," Caleb said. He watched a few seconds of the movie, then headed for the door. "I've got Dr. Linda. See you later."

◇ ◇ ◇

Dr. Linda pushed her reading glasses up her nose and peered down at Caleb's file, thumbing through notes on his recent training activities. "I see here you were able to create nine duplicates this morning," she said. "A new personal best."

Caleb sat opposite Dr. Linda on her couch, back straight, hands on his thighs. "Yes," he affirmed.

"And did you have any issues with control?"

"No, ma'am," Caleb answered, then frowned. "Well, not during the training, anyway."

Dr. Linda looked up from his file. "What happened, Caleb?"

"Afterwards, in my room, I duplicated without realizing it," Caleb confessed. "One minute I was thinking about . . . I don't know. Stuff. And the next minute he was there. He was a jerk. Really mean to me."

Dr. Linda tapped her pen against her chin. "Are you angry with yourself, Caleb?"

"What? No."

"We've talked about this before, haven't we?"

"We have?"

"The duplicates are completely in your control," Dr. Linda said, standing up. "When one of them talks to you, when you talk back—this is you having a conversation with yourself."

Caleb shook his head. "The stuff this guy was saying—I wouldn't say anything like that."

Dr. Linda went to her filing cabinet. "No. You wouldn't. But your subconscious? Able to communicate without a filter? One can only imagine what kind of truths might tumble out. It seems pushing your powers can exacerbate these incidents. Tiredness, stress, strain—these conditions create adverse behavioral reactions in regular people. In someone with your Legacy, the problem is—no pun intended—multiplied."

Caleb crossed his arms. "It's not just me being tired. Or, if it is, it's because I keep them in check and then lose my grip. I swear, Dr. Linda, they have minds of their own."

"They literally do not."

Dr. Linda handed Caleb a slim file. He already knew the contents; she had shown it to him during their last session. A few weeks ago—spurred on by Caleb's continued insistence that the duplicates were their own people as well as the discussion of anatomy in one of his classes—Dr. Goode and the Academy's medical staff had given one of Caleb's clones an MRI. Not only was no brain activity detected, but the duplicate appeared to be made from a substance that only approximated human flesh. There was something not quite right in the molecules, but samples proved hard to examine because they kept being reabsorbed into Caleb. At the same time, the researchers gave Caleb his own MRI. They found that his brain responded whenever a duplicate acted or was stimulated.

Last session, the results had given Caleb pause. He'd had a week to think about them, though. He set the file down without looking at it.

"All due respect, Dr. Linda, because I sure do appreciate all you guys have tried to do to help me, but . . ." Caleb looked down at the floor. "Since we're dealing with, y'know, alien powers and stuff? Couldn't the science here be wrong? Maybe my duplicates think in a way that's beyond what your machines can register."

Dr. Linda narrowed her eyes a fraction. Caleb knew that look. He had disappointed her.

"In my opinion, and in the unanimous opinion of the doctors and scientists who work here, that is simply not the case."

Caleb nodded stiffly. That was his habit whenever an adult said something authoritative, even if he didn't necessarily agree.

"Maybe," Dr. Linda continued once it was clear Caleb wouldn't say anything else. "Maybe you could bring one of your duplicates to our next session. Do you think that might help you better express yourself?"

Caleb shook his head. "Oh no, I don't think so. With another one of them here, I don't think I'd get a word in edgewise."

✧ ✧ ✧

Back in his room, the duplicate wasn't happy with him.

"Talking shit about us to your therapist. That's real cool, bro."

It was the same duplicate as before—the aggressive one. He'd started to think of this one as Kyle, like his brother. The duplicate paced back and forth, agitated, while Caleb again sat on the foot of his bed.

"You've always been a tattletale," the duplicate growled. He shook his head in mock bewilderment. "Look. This is getting pathetic. You should let me take over for a while. Watch how much better I make your life. You'll love it."

"I don't know. I think Dr. Linda might be right," a second duplicate said. This one stood next to Caleb's bookshelves, perusing the small collection of paperback sci-fi novels he'd amassed. The reasonable one. He didn't show up too often. Caleb was glad for his presence.

"Dr. Linda's a goddamn quack," said Aggressive-Caleb, striding over to glare at his fellow duplicate.

"On the contrary," Reasonable-Caleb countered. "She seems like she knows what she's doing. I'd say there's a fair chance that we're simply figments of Caleb's imagination made manifest. Or aspects of his personality that he's repressed. You'll recall that his childhood—our childhood—didn't have a lot of room for expression." Reasonable-Caleb turned to smile gently at his counterpart. "Perhaps it would do you good, friend, to consider your own existence with a more open mind."

Aggressive-Caleb responded by punching the other

duplicate in the face.

And then they were brawling. The duplicates knocked over Caleb's books and went crashing into his desk. He couldn't tell which one was which anymore. Caleb sighed and stood up.

"Okay, enough," he said, concentrating briefly so that he could reabsorb the duplicates. "It's time for dinner."

✧ ✧ ✧

Caleb preferred to eat early, before the dining hall got too crowded. As soon as he sat down at a table in the back with his tray, he noticed Taylor across the room. Normally, she would eat with Isabela or Kopano, but tonight she was alone except for the huge textbook spread out in front of her.

Here was the opportunity Caleb had been waiting for. They were both alone and in a casual, no-pressure setting. Why shouldn't they eat dinner together? He could ask her all the questions he'd been cataloging in his head—what music did she like? What movies? What was it like growing up in South Dakota? Caleb's heart fluttered at the possibilities.

And then, he was sitting down across from her. He was actually doing it! Taylor smiled up at him—casual, relaxed, happy to see him—and he could smell her shampoo from across the table. She was like an oasis in this desert of foreign weirdos and mutant teenagers; a girl just like the ones from back home. The ones he never got up the nerve to talk with. But this was a new Caleb.

"Hey there," he said.

"Hi," she replied. "How's it going? Caleb, right?"

"That's me."

Except it wasn't.

Caleb watched as his duplicate settled in across from Taylor. He could see from the duplicate's eyes and hear through the duplicate's ears. Doing so created a disorienting echo effect, but Caleb had long ago gotten used to that.

"How you making out so far?" the duplicate asked Taylor. "Pretty big change from back home, huh?"

"Oh, that's right. You said you're from . . ."

"Nebraska."

"Right, right." Taylor closed her textbook and smiled at Caleb. "It's pretty nuts. A lot different than home, that's for sure."

"No kidding," the duplicate replied with a casual good humor that Caleb envied. "I'd never even been to Canada before this and now we're in like the world's biggest exchange student program."

Taylor chuckled. "I was really intimidated at first. I didn't want to be here at all. But I'm starting to get used to it."

A dinner tray thunked on the table in front of Caleb, startling him. Nigel took a seat with his usual cocky smile. Caleb blinked at him.

"Evening, my good man," Nigel said. "Up for a bit of roommate bonding?"

Caleb had noticed how lately Nigel seemed more social. The Brit was making a point to invite Caleb to watch movies with him and Kopano, or to eat together, or walk to class. Caleb suspected this was Dr. Linda's doing. If she'd gotten Nigel to finally forgive him for what happened on the island—what his uncle made him do—then that was a relief. But this was really bad timing.

"Um, I'd like to be alone, actually."

Taylor raised a confused eyebrow. "Ha—but you sat with me?"

Caleb squinted. The duplicate had spoken the words he intended for Nigel. Through his clone's eyes, Caleb could see Taylor now wore one of those weirded-out looks he was familiar with from back in Nebraska.

"Now isn't a good time," he told Nigel through gritted teeth.

"Sorry, I spaced out there," the duplicate said to Taylor, talking fast. "My roommate is always blasting this crazy death metal in our suite. I was just thinking about that. I've got two older brothers, so I'm used to sharing a living space but man, our dad would've never allowed us to listen to music at that volume."

"Oh. Got it," Taylor replied with a benefit-of-the-doubt smile. She shrugged. "I'm an only child and I actually don't mind the roommates, they—"

Caleb didn't hear the rest of what Taylor said. Nigel distracted him.

"Not a good time?" Nigel asked with a laugh. "Looks to me like you're sitting here by yourself having a wank. Of course it's a good time." When Caleb responded with silence, Nigel began looking around the dining hall. "Unless you're expecting somebody else . . . ?"

It took Nigel only a moment to notice Taylor and the duplicate engaged in conversation across the room. Slowly, he turned back to Caleb with an openmouthed look of bewilderment.

"The hell are you up to, Caleb? This like one'a them old TV shows where the bloke hides in the bushes feeding his mate lines?"

"Please, Nigel, just be quiet," Caleb pleaded.

"Some kinda weird hetero courtship ritual?" Nigel continued, laughing now. "You got your bloody clone over there talking you up? Is that it? He asking that bird—have you met my mate Caleb?"

Across the room, Taylor screamed, "I can see through you!"

At first, Caleb interpreted these words metaphorically—she'd spotted him and Nigel, discovered that he wasn't man enough to talk to her on his own. But no, Taylor spoke literally—his clone had gone transparent, ghostlike, as Caleb's concentration floundered. A moment later, the clone simply winked out of existence. Taylor screamed again.

"Uh-oh," Nigel said.

Everyone in the student union stared in Taylor's direction. Taylor, however, stared at Caleb, at last noticing him at his back table. Nigel worked a finger under the collar of his T-shirt and slid his chair innocently away from Caleb's table.

"What the hell was that?" Taylor shouted at Caleb.

In response, Caleb got up from his seat and fled.

✧ ✧ ✧

After dinner, as Nigel crossed the quad headed back to the dorms, the duplicate caught up with him.

"Hey! You really screwed that up for me, asshole!"

Before Nigel could turn around, the duplicate shoved him in the back. Caught off guard, Nigel stumbled a few feet and fell, landing hard on his hands and knees. He rolled over, skinny arms extended in defense, blood trickling from a scrape on his elbow.

"Oy! What the hell, Caleb?"

"I'm not Caleb, mate," the duplicate responded, unblinking eyes staring down at Nigel. The duplicate's fists clenched as he loomed over the scrawny Brit. "You like running your mouth. Maybe I should teach you—"

From out of nowhere, Caleb raced across the lawn and shoulder-blocked the duplicate to the ground. The duplicate bellowed as Caleb dove on top of him. Caleb began to pummel his mirror image, raining down punch after punch. The duplicate didn't bleed; but Caleb's fists left indentations in the thing's head like he was slamming his knuckles into clay. Nigel watched all this wide-eyed, crab-walking backwards.

Caleb's final punch thudded into the dirt. The duplicate went transparent and disappeared. Out of breath, he turned towards Nigel.

"I'm sorry about that," he said. "I . . . they've been out of control lately."

Caleb stood, then reached down to help Nigel up. Nigel

slapped away his hand and got up on his own, brushing himself off.

"You've lost the plot, mate," Nigel growled. "I been trying to let bygones be bygones but you're bloody mad, aren't you? Got it out for me."

"I don't. I don't have a problem with you. That—that wasn't me."

Nigel snorted. "Dr. Linda, she wants me to buddy up with you, thinks you need a friend. But you got friends, don't ya?" Caleb flinched as Nigel tapped on his own forehead. "Your friends are all up here, eh? Bloody nutter. They should commit you."

"I do, though," Caleb replied softly. "Need a friend, I mean."

Nigel's lips were curled in a sneer that slowly faded in the face of Caleb's abject piteousness. "Oh, for shit's sake, Caleb . . ."

"Ever since this happened, ever since I got my Legacies . . ." Caleb ran his fingers across his bloodied knuckles. His eyes were getting watery. "The stronger I get, the longer I stay here—they keep getting harder to control. I don't know who I am anymore. And those—those things. They just pop out of me. I don't mean them."

After a moment of reluctance, Nigel put a hand on Caleb's shoulder.

"Listen, I changed too, when I got my Legacies. I . . ." Nigel shook his head, trailing off. "We're all going through it, mate. We're all bloody damaged. Your damage is just showing more on account of how your powers work."

"I don't know what to do," Caleb said quietly.

"Here's what you do," Nigel replied. "The next time that asshole duplicate pops out, you come and get me, your friend Nigel, and I'll give him a spanking he won't forget."

CHAPTER NINETEEN

ISABELA SILVA
THE HUMAN GARDE ACADEMY—POINT REYES, CALIFORNIA

ISABELA PRESSED HER EAR TO THE DOOR OF HER room. She could hear them out there. Gossiping without her. That stung. Gossiping was one of her favorite pastimes.

"And then it turned out it was one of his, like, duplicates the entire time," Taylor said. "How weird is that?"

"Very strange indeed," Ran responded.

"Why would he do something like that?"

"I do not know," Ran replied after a long moment of quiet reflection.

Because he likes you! Isabela wanted to shout through the door. Instead, she huffed out a breath and continued to eavesdrop.

Hiding out in her room like some kind of dorky shut-in wasn't Isabela's style, but she'd been doing a lot of that since the incident a few nights ago. After Taylor's breach of Isabela's sanctuary—barging into her room in the middle of the night, the nerve!—Isabela had decided their friendship needed a brief cooling-down period. If Taylor thought she could just come traipsing into her room at all hours . . . no. Just no. Not okay. There needed to be boundaries.

Isabela did have to give Taylor some credit; she hadn't pressed Isabela since their midnight encounter. She kept her distance, gave Isabela space. So many of these Americans were like Dr. Linda. They always wanted to "talk things out." Isabela was glad that her roommate wasn't one of them.

Also, Isabela's eavesdropping led her to believe that Taylor hadn't said anything about the other night to Ran, even though the two of them were suddenly best buddies. That was a relief. The girl could keep a secret.

Isabela decided she would let Taylor apologize to her tonight. Just as soon as Ran went to bed.

In the meantime, Isabela checked her face in the mirror to make sure everything was where it should be. She tucked a curl of dark hair behind her ear and stuck out her chin. Was that little upraised bump a pimple? She shape-shifted just a little, smoothing her chin. She tilted her head to the side, then decided to lengthen her eyelashes as well.

These Legacies had their uses.

Stuck to the corner of Isabela's mirror was a picture of her family at the beach. The shot was taken two years ago—her beautiful mother, her potbellied father, her little sister who tried so hard to ape Isabela's disaffected pose and Isabela herself. Pretty, Isabela thought, looking at her younger self, but not as pretty as now.

She smiled at herself in the mirror. Oh, how the boys had been checking her out the other day. She had liked that.

After the incident the other night, Isabela had made an unscheduled trip to San Francisco. They weren't allowed to have locks on their bedroom doors at the Academy, but Isabela decided that policy didn't apply to her. As usual, she was able to sneak off campus by shape-shifting into one of the soldiers and simply signing a car out of the motor pool. In the city, she bought a dead bolt. And an iced coffee. They didn't get an allowance at the Academy, so she'd had to spend a little time disguised as an alluringly dirty-faced homeless woman, collecting singles from tech guys as they rushed off the BART.

Not a bad day, all in all. Helped take her mind off things.

Isabela felt much more comfortable now that there was a sturdy lock on her door. She didn't need to push her night-stand underneath the doorknob anymore.

"Maybe you should just be honest with the people in your life," Dr. Linda had suggested during their last session. "Remove all this need for secrecy."

Isabela scoffed at that. She had told Dr. Linda about the incident with Taylor, but left out the trip into the city that followed.

"If you gave me my own suite like I asked for, we wouldn't even be having this conversation," Isabela replied.

"Mm-hmm." Dr. Linda glanced down at her notes. "You know, I received another call from your parents. They say you haven't been responding to their letters. They'd very much like you to put them on the visitors list."

Isabela crossed her arms and looked at the clock. "Are we almost done here?"

Isabela shook her head. She'd spaced out staring at that picture of her family. They were good people. They loved her. And Isabela loved them. She even missed them, especially her sister.

But they did not know her now. They knew only the old Isabela. If they came, there would be too many questions.

The common room sounded quiet. That meant Ran was probably off to bed. Isabela brushed wrinkles out of her shirt, straightened her skirt and exited her room with a flourish.

Just as she'd hoped, Taylor was by herself, studying her anatomy textbook on the couch. She looked up at Isabela with a tentative smile.

"Hey, stranger."

"Hello," Isabela said with a flip of her hair.

Taylor closed her textbook. "So, I kind of feel like you've been avoiding me . . ."

"No. Obviously not," Isabela replied. She glided over to the mini-fridge and got herself a bottle of orange juice. "I am very busy. Lots of classes. You know."

"Yeah, I know how much time you spend on schoolwork," Taylor said dryly. "Anyway, um, I don't know if I overstepped or something, but I didn't mean to. I was just having a rough night and thought . . . I'm sorry if I, like, violated your privacy."

Isabela smiled brightly. "All is forgiven," she said magnanimously. "In the future, if you need me to hold your hand after a bad dream, please wait until morning. I am not myself when woken up by an American rhinoceros bursting into my room."

Taylor chuckled, shaking her head in disbelief. "You're so good at accepting apologies, Isabela."

"I know." She paused. "Oh, by the way, I listened to your conversation earlier. Allow me to illuminate the ways of the male mind for you. Caleb has a crush on you, pretty girl."

"Hmm." Taylor leaned back on the couch. "He's got a weird way of showing it."

"Yes, well, he is a weird boy, isn't he? Handsome, though, if you like them all clean-cut. You would make a good-looking couple."

"I don't know about that."

"They will put you two on the brochures for the Academy. Look at these nonthreatening Garde with their blond hair and smiles! Of course, Caleb is a secret freak, I think, but still. Everyone who goes here is strange in some way."

"No kidding," Taylor replied. "But you can stop with the matchmaking. I'm not interested in him like that."

Isabela shrugged happily. "It doesn't have to be forever! Maybe just a little fun. Loosen you up. You can be like me.

There's no harm in sampling."

Taylor laughed and covered her face with her hands. "I don't think I could ever be like you, Izzy."

Izzy. Her little sister called her that. Isabela felt a warm rush of affection and flopped down on the couch beside Taylor.

"Something to aspire to," Isabela replied. "If you don't want to discuss your love life, we can discuss mine. I have been dating Lofton for six weeks now. Getting bored. He graduates next week—good timing. Lofton goes away, no messy breakup and I find someone new."

"Uh-huh. And you have a list of candidates, I'm sure."

"I was thinking about your boyfriend's roommate, actually. The Nigerian guy."

Taylor's eyebrows shot up. "Kopano?"

"Yes. Big muscles on that one. Nice smile."

Isabela watched as Taylor ran a hand through her hair, her cheeks flushed. She bit her lip. They'd been talking so easily a moment ago, but now Taylor seemed to be struggling to find the words.

"Uh, yeah . . . ," Taylor said at last, her expression clouded. "He is nice."

Isabela smiled. So, she had learned something about her roommate tonight. The girl did have an interest in boys after all.

Isabela stood up and dusted off her hands as if she was done with the matter. "Eh. Never mind. I will choose someone else." She noted the look of relief on Taylor's face with some satisfaction. "Now, I need my beauty sleep," Isabela declared.

Taylor stopped Isabela before she could return to her room. "Hey, um . . ." The American's voice was quiet. "One more thing?"

"Yes?"

"I don't know . . . I don't know if I should say anything. But if you . . . if you ever want to talk about what I saw the other night—"

Isabela turned around slowly, one of her eyebrows arched, her lips a cold line. "What did you see, Taylor? What are you talking about?"

Taylor hesitated. Recognizing the tension in Isabela's words, she wisely backed off. "Nothing. Never mind. Good night."

Isabela nodded sharply. "Good night."

Back in her room, Isabela slid her newly installed dead bolt into place. She exhaled slowly. Taylor was sweet and kind; she wouldn't say anything about what she had seen. She'd leave it alone.

Talk about it. Pah. What was there to talk about?

As always, this late in the day, Isabela's face had begun to ache. It was like that tense sensation one gets from smiling too much. Her stamina had vastly improved in the months that she'd been at the Academy, but the constant Legacy use still drained her by nightfall. She took one last look at herself in the mirror, touched her smooth cheek and smiled wistfully.

Then, she turned off the lights.

With a sigh of relief, Isabela let her true face slide back into place.

CHAPTER TWENTY

KOPANO OKEKE
THE HUMAN GARDE ACADEMY—POINT REYES, CALIFORNIA

SIX A.M. THE FIRST RAYS OF SUN SHONE RED through the gym's wide windows. Kopano braced himself as he brushed by a series of thick ropes that hung from the ceiling. Cautiously, he made his way through the training center's deserted obstacle course. The program wasn't active at the moment—that meant no ball bearings or electric shocks would come shooting out at him. But still, there was danger. An attack would come. And soon.

Because Kopano was not alone.

"YAAAA!"

The scream alerted Kopano just seconds before Professor Nine dropped from the ceiling and landed on top of him. His knees crunched into Kopano's shoulders and knocked the wind out of him. In his one metallic hand, Nine held a savage combat knife. He plunged the blade down between Kopano's shoulder blades.

The weapon crumpled against Kopano's skin. With a grunt, Nine flung the ruined weapon away. Kopano rolled beneath him and socked Nine with a punch to the sternum. The older Garde went flying backwards.

Kopano's fists were as hard as bricks. Nine sucked in a breath as Kopano scrambled to his feet.

"Did I hurt you?" Kopano asked, grinning.

"Yeah," Nine replied. From the back waistband of his pants, Nine drew a pistol. "Same question."

Blam! Blam! Blam!

Kopano flung up his hands. One of the rubber bullets he managed to deflect with his telekinesis. The other two thudded into his chest. Kopano felt that now-familiar tightness in his skin as his flesh hardened to rebuff the impact. He wouldn't even be bruised.

"Painless!" he shouted at Nine gleefully. Then, he reached out with his telekinesis and yanked Nine's gun away.

Nine retreated. Kopano gave chase. His limbs always felt heavy right after his invincibility kicked in. Carefully, he hurdled a pile of logs, part of the obstacle course. His body got lighter, loosened up, and he picked up speed. These fights with Professor Nine had become part of his routine. Three times a week, bright and early. Nine pushed him, tried to hurt him and was rarely successful.

"Remember!" Nine shouted over his shoulder. "Control your Legacy! Think about what you're doing!"

Nine reached the sideline of the obstacle course, where a dented Dumpster usually served as cover for the projectile attacks launched by the system. With strength that still awed Kopano, Nine ripped a metal sheet off the side of the Dumpster and held it before him like a shield.

Kopano cocked his fist back, knowing his knuckles would harden as soon as he struck the metal. Sure enough—*wham!* He punched a dent into Nine's makeshift defense, nearly knocking the steel straight back into his professor's face.

Nine recovered quickly. He swung the metal at Kopano's head in a backhand motion. Kopano ducked, but the move was meant only to create space. Nine leaped on top of the Dumpster, escaping again. He held his hand up towards the catwalk that overlooked the training center.

"Weapon!" Nine called.

From above, something white fell down. Nine caught the object and sighed.

"Thanks a lot," he said dryly.

Kopano squinted as he climbed up after Nine, who now held out a pillow in front of him.

"Are you going back to bed, Professor?" Kopano asked with a grin as he squared up with Nine.

"Less talking, more hitting," Nine countered. He bounced from foot to foot on the Dumpster's creaky lid, swinging the pillow in front of him.

"As you wish," Kopano replied.

He should have known it was a trap.

Kopano swung a big right hook at Nine. The professor

raised the pillow to block. Kopano felt his knuckles strike the soft surface—and then his fingers cracked. He shouted in pain and surprise.

The pillow was filled with rocks. Worse yet, Kopano's Legacy hadn't kicked in to protect him.

"Hold! That's enough!" Dr. Goode called down from the catwalk.

Kopano thought a couple of his fingers were broken. He stomped down on the Dumpster, not so much in pain as frustration. This was the third time he'd been injured in practice, always because Professor Nine managed to somehow surprise him.

"You all right?" Nine asked. He tossed his loaded pillow away with a clatter.

"I'm fine," Kopano muttered, nursing his injured hand. He looked up at Nine with watery eyes. "Why doesn't it work? What good is being invincible only some of the time?"

"Clearly, you aren't invincible," Nine replied, and hopped down from the Dumpster. Kopano followed. "Or maybe you could be. But you're letting your instincts do the work for you instead of controlling the power."

"I have listened to all the lectures," Kopano replied, ashamed of the desperation in his voice. "About visualization and meditating on the energy within me. But there is nothing to visualize, Professor. And I do not feel any energy. It simply happens, or it does not."

"You aren't trying hard enough, kid," Nine responded brusquely.

Kopano frowned and began to pluck off the plastic sensors that Dr. Goode always affixed to his body before a session. Just then, the scientist made his way down from the catwalk, thumbing through results on his tablet.

"Anything to report, Malcolm?" Nine asked.

Dr. Goode stroked his chin and looked appraisingly at Kopano. "Actually, I did pick up an interesting reading," he said, and Kopano's heartbeat quickened. "When your Legacy successfully triggered, your weight momentarily increased. It went back to normal when you gave chase to Nine. Did you feel that, Kopano?"

Kopano nodded, remembering the heaviness in his bones when he first chased Nine. "Yes. That happens sometimes."

Nine snapped his fingers. "There you go, man. That's what I want you doing from now on. Thinking like you're fat."

Kopano frowned. Dr. Goode patted him on the shoulder.

"It'll come, Kopano," he said. "Go see Taylor about that hand."

As Kopano trudged off the obstacle course, Nine called after him, "Kopano! Show me something today, man. I'm counting on you."

Kopano nodded in response, then quickly turned away to hide his grin. Nine was counting on him! He didn't want the professor to see how giddy that made him. Had to be cool and macho, like Nine.

He'd show Nine something all right.

He'd win today's Wargames event even if he had to do it by himself.

✧ ✧ ✧

"How'd you do this?"

"I punched some rocks."

"That was dumb."

"They were hidden inside a pillow."

"Even dumber."

Kopano chuckled. Taylor held his hand, letting her warm healing energy flow into his fractured fingers. In a matter of moments, the swelling was gone and Kopano was able to flex his digits without pain. He bowed dramatically to Taylor.

"Thank you," he said.

"Yeah, yeah," she replied, shaking her head as she let his hand drop.

The two of them were part of a larger group on their way to the wooded area south of campus. Although participation in the Wargames event was entirely voluntary, all of the Academy's students were required to attend so they could at least watch. Many of the instructors were making their way to the woods as well. Students chatted excitedly, all of them discussing the possible challenge Professor Nine had designed in concert with Colonel Archibald and the Peacekeepers. The Garde got plenty of training time with each other and at the obstacle course, but today would mark the first time any of them faced outside opponents. The atmosphere reminded Kopano of when his school would face a rival in sports.

"You're actually excited about this, aren't you?" Taylor said. He hadn't realized she was watching him.

"Yes! Aren't you?"

"Not really." Taylor lowered her voice. "Even if it's just pretend, doesn't it strike you as weird that the people who are supposed to be protecting us would want to fight us?"

"Professor Nine says it's all to help us train," Kopano replied with a shrug. "Perhaps such violence goes against your natural instinct as a healer. I would understand that." Kopano punched his open palm. "But my natural instinct is to be a warrior!"

Taylor laughed and shook her head. "You got beat up by a pillow today, warrior."

They spotted Nigel and Ran in the crowd and went to stand by them.

"All right, big boy," Nigel said in greeting and squeezed Kopano's bicep. "Ready to kick some ass?"

Kopano grinned. He liked his roommate—both his roommates, actually, even if Caleb was a little strange—and always felt encouraged by Nigel's sharp and boisterous words.

"Oh, Kopano the mighty is ready," Taylor answered Nigel with a roll of her eyes. She looked to Ran. "Surprised to see you here."

Ran tilted her head. "It is required."

"She might be Legacy celibate, but that don't mean she'd miss a class," Nigel said.

Kopano shook his head. He'd heard the rumors about Ran swearing off her Legacies, just like he'd heard about what a total badass she supposedly was. He'd never gotten a chance to see her in action.

"How're you going to get better if you don't use your powers?" he asked Ran, baffled.

"Why would I need to get better at something that I do not intend to use?" Ran replied.

Kopano blinked. "But come on! Don't you think you got Legacies for a reason? Lorien picked us!"

"And perhaps that reason is past."

"But what if it's not?"

"Then I shall wait for a new reason to present itself," Ran said coolly.

Nigel flung his arms around the both of them. "Don't let her rain on your parade, mate. Ran and I, we been around a bit. She wants to take a holiday, I don't blame her."

Kopano frowned. "I should have been there. I should have answered John Smith's call."

Nigel and Ran's expressions both darkened.

"Brother, I'm not sure if that's true," Nigel said.

Before they could say anything else, a shrill whistle called them to attention. With the hundred or so students finally all gathered, Nine stood before them. Colonel Archibald joined him, red-faced from a close shave, his uniform immaculate. Nearby stood a man Kopano had never seen before—middle-aged but baby-faced, with slicked-back brown hair and a dapper suit. The newcomer held a tablet computer, jotting frequent notes with a stylus.

"Listen up!" Professor Nine shouted. He waved to the well-dressed man. "We've got a special guest for today's festivities. This is Greger Karlsson, an evaluator from Earth Garde. He's one of the dudes who will decide what kind of missions you're sent on once I decide you're ready to graduate. Make a good impression! He's Swedish and I hear he really likes it when you do that Muppet voice, right, Greger?"

Greger smiled politely at Nine and inclined his head towards the students, his gaze already appraising them. Kopano puffed out his chest.

"Now listen, I'm required by some law to tell you guys that this is a joint exercise between Earth Garde Academy enrollees and the United Nations Peacekeepers. Participation is absolutely optional. For those who do choose to participate, every precaution will be taken to ensure your safety, but safety can't be guaranteed. Ominous shit, right?" He glanced over his shoulder at Colonel Archibald. "Satisfactory, boss?"

Archibald nodded. Kopano looked around—the expressions of his classmates ranged from trepidation to excitement. He nudged Taylor.

"You might be busy today," he whispered.

She gave him a stern look. "You promised me boring, Kopano."

"Here's the situation," Professor Nine continued, pointing into the woods. "About a half mile into the trees, there's a cabin being held down by Peacekeepers. Your mission is to gain access to that cabin and rescue the hostage trapped inside. Our own Dr. Goode has volunteered to play the role of hostage, so, you know, if you don't rescue him, science class is going to be rough."

"The soldiers in the woods and guarding the cabin are all armed with nonlethal weaponry," Colonel Archibald spoke up. "My men and women would greatly appreciate that you take the same care with your powers that we're taking with our armaments."

"Yeah. Don't hurt 'em too bad," Nine said. "The point of this exercise isn't just to fight some soldiers. It's also to assess your teamwork and strategy skills. I could tell you the best way to take out these chumps, but I'm not going to do that. I could also break you into the most efficient teams possible, but I'm not going to do that either. That's all going to be on you. Anyone who's successful earns . . . hmm . . . let's say twenty hours of recreation time. That's three skip days."

As soon as Nine finished his explanation, the dozens of young Garde began chattering among themselves and breaking into teams. Kopano looked around eagerly. Most of the students with noncombat Legacies and the tweebs who hadn't yet developed their primary powers were already gathering at the edge of the woods to spectate, while the bolder Garde with more violent Legacies divided themselves up.

"Of course Professor Nine would give away such a good prize for brute strength," Isabela complained as she sauntered over to their little group. Simon followed along behind her, waving to everyone.

"There's literally no way I can participate in this," Simon

said. "Maybe next time the competition won't be so agro."

Taylor smiled. "You're welcome to come join us conscientious objectors."

"I want those recreation hours," Isabela muttered. "It isn't fair."

"Yes. And I want to show this Earth Garde man what I can do," Kopano added, looking around.

"You even figure out what that is yet?" Nigel asked.

"Well, not exactly," Kopano answered. "But I would still like to do it!"

Taylor bumped her shoulder against Ran, nodding discreetly towards Greger. "He's watching you."

Ran had already noticed how the Earth Garde representative was keeping an eye on her. She shrugged loosely. "He will be disappointed."

"Look at this group of badasses!" Lofton St. Croix said excitedly as he approached. Following behind him was Caleb, the fire-breathing Omar Azoulay, Nicolas Lambert the Belgian strongman and the speedy Maiken Megalos. "Ran and Nigel, c'mon, join Team Lofton."

Nigel snorted. "Look at this. You're just cherry-picking everybody from Dr. Chen's class."

Kopano felt a momentary flash of disappointment that he hadn't been selected for that seminar.

"Hell yeah I am," Lofton answered Nigel. "You know, I already got my call up to Earth Garde. I'm gone in like a week. If I get those twenty rec hours, I can take it easy until then."

Nigel glanced at Ran. She shook her head.

"Sorry, mate, but we're a package deal," Nigel told Lofton. "Ran sits out, so do I."

Lofton rolled his eyes. "Dude, your, like, singing powers hardly make the dream team cut anyway. What we really need is the hard-core chick who explodes things and once brought down a Mogadorian warship."

"It was only a Skimmer," Ran corrected.

"Seriously?" Kopano asked.

Ran nodded. "And I am not playing. Good luck, though."

Lofton sighed. Before he could express his disappointment, Isabela sidled up next to him.

"Don't worry, boyfriend. I'll be on your team."

Lofton laughed. He gave Isabela's butt a squeeze and kissed her on the forehead.

"Yeah, thanks for the offer, babe, but we're going for a full-frontal assault here. You're not exactly what we've got in mind."

"Great plan," Taylor said. Isabela crossed her arms and silently fumed.

"These army tools have never faced anything like us," Lofton said dismissively. "We're going to go right at them. They won't be ready."

Caleb spoke up for the first time, having spent the start of the conversation awkwardly avoiding looking at Taylor. "Actually, uh, I have some ideas we might—"

Lofton clapped Caleb on the shoulder, cutting him off. "It's cool, bro. You just make as many decoys as possible and beat some ass."

"May I join you?" Kopano asked.

Lofton raised an eyebrow and looked him over. "You're supposed to be bulletproof, right?"

"I may be invincible," Kopano said. "I also hit very hard."

"He's solid," Caleb said.

Lofton shrugged. "Well, at least we didn't come over here for nothing. You're in."

Kopano grinned. He turned to Taylor as the rest of Team Lofton made their way to the edge of the woods. "Wish me luck."

"Do not wish these sexist lunkheads luck," Isabela snapped.

"Good luck, warrior," Taylor said with a smile, ignoring her roommate. "I've got a feeling you might need it."

◇ ◇ ◇

They lined up at the edge of the woods. Kopano stood between Nicolas and one of Caleb's duplicates. With all the clones, there were a dozen of them, ready for battle. They were the first team to make a run.

"We head straight for the cabin," Lofton said. "Take out anything in our way. Nothing to it."

They all nodded in agreement. Kopano rubbed his hands together and focused. He searched for that feeling of heaviness that Dr. Goode mentioned, the sense of being weighted down. Nothing. He felt tragically normal. But Kopano was sure his Legacy would come when needed; it always did.

Professor Nine blew a whistle and they were off.

Team Lofton ran into the woods. For the first few hundred

yards, they saw no sign of soldiers. The trees became clumped closer together and they had to weave through them. Kopano felt a rush flow through him—he was on a mission, charging towards a target! This was the kind of heroic experience he'd envisioned.

Soon, the cabin came into view, only partially visible through a veil of vibrant green foliage. Kopano sensed movement in the windows, but didn't have a chance to examine that more closely.

"Hostiles!" Caleb shouted, his six clones echoing his words a moment later.

Three soldiers stepped out from behind trees. Kopano's group skidded to a stop with a good bit of distance still between them and their opponents. Each of the soldiers carried what looked like a traditional shotgun.

"Take them out!" Lofton yelled. The sharpened spines that grew from his skin on command burst through his shirt. He plucked a few of them and flung them at the soldiers.

The soldiers bolted for cover as Lofton's darts whistled by them, but not before they each fired a round into the air. Kopano extended his hands and threw up a barrier of telekinesis. His nearby classmates all did the same. It's what they were trained to do. None of them could reliably stop bullets on their own—not quite yet, at least—but together they were strong enough to slow to a crawl any projectiles coming at them.

Kopano's brow furrowed. He expected buckshot or rubber shrapnel like the kind Professor Nine had used on him that morning, but what hung in the air was much different. Each of the shotguns had discharged a metallic round about the size of a beanbag. They glowed and beeped with increasing frequency.

A countdown.

"Explosives!" Caleb shouted. At that moment, Kopano recalled how his roommate was what the Americans called an "army brat." He probably had experience with military tactics and exercises like this one.

Perhaps they should have planned better, but Lofton's bravado had been infectious and now it was too late.

The orbs burst apart with a piercing hiss. Each discharged a thick cloud of orange-tinted gas. Immediately, Kopano's throat tightened and his eyes burned. The fiery aroma of cayenne filled his lungs.

Lofton gagged. "We need to pull back!"

"No!" Caleb shouted. "We're committed! Push through! Maiken, use your speed, get a funnel going."

Caleb's duplicates didn't need to breathe. They barreled through the smoke cloud and began to pummel the soldiers. Meanwhile, Maiken, coughing raggedly, began to speed around in a circle, creating enough wind to blow the gas away from them.

That's when the rest of the soldiers struck from behind. In their haste to reach the cabin, Team Lofton had passed right by this squadron in hiding. They were surrounded.

Kopano heard a metallic twang. He turned just in time to see a soldier holding what looked to be a high-tech crossbow.

The weapon fired a metal circlet attached to a length of tensile wire. Eyes burning, Kopano couldn't get his telekinesis working fast enough. The circlet hit him right in the neck, opened on impact and snapped around his throat like a collar.

A charge went through the collar. An electric shock that drove Kopano to his knees.

With his telekinesis, Kopano tried to rip the electrified weapon away from the soldier. But just then, another Peacekeeper discharged an oddly shaped gun. The weapon looked like an old-fashioned blunderbuss and filled the air with hundreds of tiny projectiles, the harmless chaff spinning and flashing. The effect wreaked havoc on Kopano's telekinetic control.

A trio of darts—tranquilizers, probably—thudded into Kopano's chest. His Legacy kicked in, prevented the ammo from piercing his chest. A small victory.

All around him, his teammates were suffering similar attacks. Omar was down already, peppered with darts, and Lofton and Maiken had both fallen victim to collars like Kopano. Meanwhile, Nicolas had been locked into shackles around his wrists and ankles, the bonds magnetized together so that even his enhanced strength couldn't keep him from folding over. Only Caleb and his clones were left standing, and they were steadily losing ground to the soldiers.

"Oh, this is bad," Kopano grunted. He wrapped his hands around the wire that bound him to the soldier's electric crossbow, but the voltage running through his body only increased. It was too much.

As Kopano fell face-first into the dirt, he spotted Professor Nine, Greger and Colonel Archibald at the edge of the fray. Archibald smirked, Greger jotted notes in his tablet and Nine scowled.

Team Lofton never even got close to the cabin.

Show me something, Professor Nine had said.

The only thing Kopano showed the administrators was how gracefully he could be knocked unconscious.

CHAPTER TWENTY-ONE

PROFESSOR NINE STOMPED OUT OF THE WOODS, coming back to Colonel Archibald and Greger. Archibald's smile was infuriating. Greger, busy feeding notes and ratings into his tablet, glanced up.

"Where'd you go, Nine?" he asked.

"To take a leak," Nine grumbled. He glanced down and zipped up his fly.

"Are we about ready to wrap things up?" Archibald asked.

Nine glared at the military man. The day had not gone well for his students. After the first group of Garde had failed spectacularly to make it to the cabin—many of his most talented fighters among them—four more groups employing conservative tactics were similarly dismantled by Archibald's team of Peacekeepers and their high-tech weaponry. He'd made his disappointment with the Garde obvious, although his stream of insults had dried up about twenty minutes ago, morphing instead into stewing disappointment.

"I, for one, gathered some interesting insight," Greger said.

"Don't think of this as a failure, Nine," Colonel Archibald said smugly. "Think of it as a learning experience. Now you know how you can better hone your teaching methods."

Before Nine could respond, Nigel approached the edge of the woods. Behind him, the dejected student body sat in the grass, many of them nursing minor injuries. The scrawny Brit in his spiked-denim vest and combat boots didn't cut the most impressive figure, even as he cracked his knuckles and rolled his neck.

"Can I give it a go?" he asked.

Colonel Archibald raised an eyebrow. "Just you alone, son?"

"What can I say?" Nigel replied. "I believe in myself."

Nine crossed his arms and fixed Nigel with a stern look. "You're sure you can play by the rules, Nigel?"

"Aw, of course, boss."

"Nonlethal," Nine said firmly. "Remember. These soldiers have families. They're on our side. This is just a game."

Archibald and Greger both gave Nine a strange look. Nigel raised his hand in a solemn pledge.

"Swear I'll be gentle."

"All right," Nine said. "Let's see what you've got."

Without any sense of urgency, Nigel strolled into the forest. Like they'd done with all the other attempts on the cabin, Nine and the other observers followed behind at a safe distance. Out of the corner of his eye, Nine watched Greger pulling up the Earth Garde dossier on Nigel. He skimmed the file quickly, lips pursed.

"Pardon me, Professor," Greger began. "But why did you emphasize nonlethal activity with Mr. Barnaby? I have his powers down as sonic manipulation. I don't have any notes here about deadly applications."

Nine bit his lip. "Uh, well, it's something we just discovered. The kid reached a frequency the other day that caused aneurysms in rats."

Greger's mouth opened. "You're kidding."

"Nah," Nine replied. "Some of the research staff reported headaches afterwards, too. One of them had bleeding on the brain. Luckily, we caught it in time. Didn't Malcolm send out a memo on this?"

"No," Archibald said sharply. "He did not."

"Fascinating," Greger said, already making revisions to the file in his tablet.

"Yeah, well, it's not something he's been able to reproduce. Not that it's something we've been trying to reproduce, you know? Probably just a freak thing."

As Nigel continued into the forest, he fell into the same trap as all the other teams. He passed right by the first group of soldiers—camouflaged and hidden in trees—and they dropped down behind him. They could've picked him off then and there, but Archibald's men were under orders not to engage prematurely; they wanted the Garde boxed in. Soon, they formed an ever-tightening perimeter around him. Nigel didn't seem aware. Or, maybe more accurately, he didn't care.

When the cabin came into view, the group of soldiers guarding it stepped out to complete the trap. This was as far as anyone had made it.

Nigel held up his hands in surrender.

"All right, chaps, here's my strategy," he said. "I'm going to ask you nicely to release the hostage and let me win, yeah? Nobody's tried that yet. I'm thinking maybe this is one of those tests where we're supposed to fail, eh? Or look for a diplomatic and outside-the-box solution? What do ya say?"

Some of the soldiers exchanged glances and snickered.

Archibald was unamused. He spoke into his walkie-talkie. "Take him."

A soldier slightly behind Nigel fired a tranquilizer dart. Nigel managed to whip around just in time to deflect the projectile with his telekinesis. He wasn't able to turn back quickly enough to fend off another flanking soldier, this one launching one of those wire-attached shock collars. As soon as the collar was around Nigel's neck, the soldier depressed a button on his crossbow mechanism that sent a burst of high voltage cranking through Nigel.

Nigel's whole body contorted in pain. His head flew back and he let loose an eardrum-shattering howl.

Birds in the trees rose up in a squawking panic. Greger

dropped his tablet as he attempted too late to cover his ears. Colonel Archibald's chin went to his chest like he'd been struck, all his features tightening. Many of the soldiers cringed and tried to cover up. Some of them accidentally discharged their weapons into the dirt.

Despite the splitting pain in his own head, Nine charged forward. The scream rolled out of Nigel uncontrollably, loud as a tornado siren amplified by a megaphone. He lunged towards the boy and swiftly backhanded him with his metal hand. Nigel fell to the ground, the maddening scream at last cutting off.

"That was it, wasn't it?" Nine shouted, his ears ringing. "That was the frequency!"

Nigel stared up at Nine groggily, panic slowly creeping into his expression. "I don't know! I—the bloody prick was shocking me and—and I lost control!"

Greger took a halting step backwards. "Are we—were we exposed to something?"

"I don't know," growled Nine, looking around. Many of the soldiers had thrown off their helmets and were massaging their temples or pinching the bridges of their noses. Nine noticed one soldier who had been close to Nigel clean a bit of blood out of his ear.

"Christ," Archibald said, massaging the side of his head with the heel of his hand. "What's the protocol here?"

"Run back to the others," Nine snapped at one of the soldiers. "Get Taylor Cook up here. She's a healer." He looked up to the cabin, then back to Archibald. "Bring all your men in. Anyone who was in earshot needs to be checked." He surveyed the soldiers. "Anyone feeling dizzy? Nosebleeds?"

The soldiers, uneasy now and uncertain what to do, exchanged glances. One of them raised his hand. "I'm—uh, I'm feeling a little dizzy, sir."

"Me too," added another.

"Lads, I'm sure it's nothing," Nigel said pleadingly. "I, uh, the frequency only murdered some rodents the one time and I'm not even sure it was the same—"

"Stop talking," Nine snapped. "Shit. I knew this was a bad idea, Archibald."

"Don't put this on me because your students can't control themselves!" Archibald shouted back.

"What?" Greger asked, tilting his head to the side. "What? I literally can't hear what you two are saying."

Taylor jogged onto the scene along with the soldier who had gone to fetch her. Her eyes went wide when she saw Nigel on the ground, bleeding from the mouth, still attached to a shock collar. Nine snapped his fingers in her face.

"I need you to check all these men," he said.

"Check them? For what?"

"For, like, brain damage," Nine replied. "See if they need healing. Maybe we got lucky, but . . ." He urged her towards the soldiers. "Just put some healing into them. For safety."

"What's going on?" Dr. Goode asked as he ambled down from the cabin with the bored group of Peacekeepers who had spent their entire day guarding him without actually seeing any action. He glanced from the stricken Nigel to the busy Taylor, and finally to Nine. "Did something happen?"

"You didn't hear the shriek?" Nine asked.

"Of course we heard it, but—"

"That was the death frequency," Nine said grimly. "Nigel used his death frequency."

"Accidentally!" Nigel croaked. He rubbed his throat, freshly released from the shock collar.

"His—?" Dr. Goode stared blankly at Nine. "His what?"

Before Nine could answer, Taylor gasped and stepped back from one of the soldiers. He was a young guy—midtwenties with a baby face and a patchy red beard—and his eyes widened in alarm at Taylor's reaction.

"What—what's wrong?" the soldier asked.

Everyone went silent and stared. Taylor tentatively pressed her hands to the soldier's temples. Her eyes narrowed in concentration. She shook her head suddenly and spun to face Nine.

"He's—there's something wrong. His brain is—I don't know—it's like there's a darkness? A hemorrhage maybe? It's beyond what I can handle."

The soldier visibly paled. "But . . . but I feel okay. Ears are ringing a little."

"We need to get him back to campus," Nine said resolutely. "Everybody, let's go."

As a group, soldiers and Garde hustled back through the woods. Even though he was done screaming, everyone kept their distance from Nigel except for Taylor. She walked next to him, tending to the minor bruises he'd received during the skirmish. While the redheaded soldier seemed by all appearances to be fine, that didn't stop a couple of his buddies from hooking his arms over their shoulders and half carrying him out of the woods.

Dr. Goode quickly caught up with a speed-walking Nine.

"I'm sorry, Nine, but I don't understand what's happened," Malcolm said. "What is this business about a death frequency?"

"I'd like the healer to check me, if she's free . . ." Greger said nervously, glancing over his shoulder at Taylor.

"What is there to understand, Goode?" Archibald snapped. "You were supposed to send out a memo."

"A memo? Colonel, I have no idea what you're talking about," Malcolm protested. "Some kind of high-pitched noise capable of producing bleeding on the brain? It's—I hesitate to use the word 'preposterous,' but . . ." He looked again at the silent Nine. "Nine, what's going on?"

Slowly, a smirk spread across Nine's face.

Up ahead, the dejected student body came into view. Many of them stood up from the grass, surprised to see the Garde emerging from the woods with a full complement of shaken soldiers.

None of them were more surprised than Nine, who stood among the students, in the middle of giving Kopano a pep talk.

"What the hell!" Nine said in greeting. "You couldn't wait for me to finish pissing?" Nine was about to say more, but his mouth hung open in confusion. He was staring across the grass at himself.

Archibald, Greger, Goode and all the soldiers turned to stare at the Nine who had led them out of the woods. Only Nigel and Taylor didn't look surprised. In fact, they were grinning.

In a blur of motion, Nine's prosthetic arm turned back into flesh, the fingernails coated with bright pink polish. That hand closed around the handle of a tranquilizer pistol, yanked it free from a stunned soldier's belt and jammed the barrel under Colonel Archibald's chin. All this happened while her form was still transitioning—growing shorter, muscles diminishing, dark curls sprouting out of Nine's head.

Isabela stood with a gun on Archibald. Her other hand patted Malcolm on the shoulder.

"Hostage rescued," she declared. "And we also captured the enemy leader. I believe that should be worth an extra twenty hours of recreation time, yes?"

CHAPTER TWENTY-TWO

THE ESCAPISTS
THE HUMAN GARDE ACADEMY—POINT REYES, CALIFORNIA

RAN KNEW THE BRAZILIAN WAS UP TO SOMETHING the minute Lofton rejected her from his team. Ran recognized the spark in Isabela's eyes—part mischief, part vengeance.

She approved.

The plot hatched while Team Lofton was being picked apart by the Peacekeepers. Isabela would impersonate Professor Nine. With Nigel's help, she would concoct a story about the deadliness of his sonic powers. Taylor would pop up at the end and sell the entire ruse with her healing.

"We will win without even having to fight anyone," Isabela declared.

Nigel snorted. "Yeah. Except for me, right? Taking one for the bloody team."

"Stop complaining and act like a man," Isabela replied

with a dismissive wave.

"It's kind of like cheating, though, isn't it?" Taylor asked.

"No!" Isabela replied sharply. "I did not hear any rules. So how can it be cheating?"

Ran stayed silent throughout the discussion, at least until Nigel looked questioningly in her direction. Out of solidarity with her, Nigel had announced that he wouldn't be participating in the competition. He didn't know what to make of her renouncement of her Legacy—Nigel was trying to support her, but he still loved using his own powers. For all his put-on cynicism, he really wanted to be a hero. Last year, he'd been the first to volunteer to join the original Garde in the fight against the Mogadorians. Her own vow against using her Legacy aside, Ran would never deny her friend the opportunity to participate in Wargames—something he clearly itched to do.

Ran bowed her head to Nigel. "It is a good plan. You should do it."

They all grinned, especially Isabela, at her approval.

Now, all they had to do was wait for Professor Nine to separate from Archibald and Greger.

◇ ◇ ◇

When it became clear what Isabela and her team had pulled off, a cheer went up from the dejected student body, many of whom had spent the afternoon getting beaten down by the Peacekeepers. Colonel Archibald and his people loudly questioned the validity of the results.

"What were we supposed to do?" the soldier with the

red beard, the one who Taylor had convinced he was dying, complained. "Shoot at Professor Nine? He wasn't part of the exercise!"

Greger, the Earth Garde liaison, watched Isabela with new admiration. "I must say, it was an excellent ploy. True outside-the-box thinking is not easy to teach."

Professor Nine beamed, an entire day of losses forgotten. "I taught her that."

Isabela smirked, but didn't say anything in response to Nine taking the credit.

Archibald shook his head. "That would have never worked in a true battlefield scenario."

"Indeed?" Greger cocked his head. "In the chaos of a true battlefield, I think her technique would have been even more successful. She could have slipped in and out, undetected, as one of your own soldiers, Archibald . . ."

Isabela tuned out all the praise and commentary. She'd only wanted to show up Lofton and collect the recreation hours for herself. The beach called to her, classes did not. As they walked back to campus among their cheerful peers, Isabela hugged Taylor, and stroked the spot on Nigel's face where she'd punched him as Nine.

"Did I hurt you too bad, skinny boy?"

Nigel chuckled. "Don't flatter yourself, Izzy. I had to sell that punch like a professional wrestler, yeah? You got none of Nine's strength." He stroked his neck. "Those shock collars, though. Nasty bit of business."

"Yes. I did not enjoy those either," said Kopano. The

Nigerian's usual grin hadn't yet reappeared after his defeat by the Peacekeepers.

"There she is! The champion scammer!" Lofton swooped in and pulled Isabela into a hug, literally sweeping her off her feet. Her face remained expressionless while he spun her around. When, at last, he set her on the ground, Isabela put a hand on his face and shoved. Lofton stepped back, his features drawn in confusion.

"You mad at me, babe?" he asked.

"Bloke's good at picking out those subtle details, huh?" Nigel said in a loud aside to Ran, who nodded in agreement.

Isabela lifted her chin and rolled back her shoulders, her chest out, as she fixed Lofton with a withering stare. She had fully intended to let their relationship come to a painless close with his departure in a few days, but this morning's slight was too much to let slide.

"You boys, always mistaking boredom for anger," Isabela declared, her voice loud enough that the other students on their way back to campus couldn't help but overhear. "I am tired of your dumb face and soft brain. Good-bye forever, Lofton."

Isabela turned on her heel. Lofton, stunned, grabbed her arm.

"Whoa, wait! What about—?" He lowered his voice. "What about our plans for tonight?"

"Those plans are canceled," Isabela replied. She stuck her finger in his face. "You would be wise to forget they ever existed. Furthermore, I forbid you from thinking about me

219

in that way during your many lonely nights to come. Now, get off me."

Lofton let her go and Isabela resumed her walk to the dorms. Nigel and Kopano were both holding in laughter. Taylor came up alongside Isabela and hooked her arm through her roommate's.

"You okay?" Taylor asked.

"Why would I not be okay?"

"You just broke up with your boyfriend."

"Pfft. I have already forgotten him. My only disappointment is that we cannot . . ." Isabela trailed off. She'd been looking forward to her evening plans with Lofton. Just because he was out of the picture didn't mean those plans had to change. "Come," she said excitedly to Taylor. "We must celebrate our victory!"

✧ ✧ ✧

Back in their suite, Isabela pulled clothes out of her closet, trying to decide what she would wear for the night.

"You're crazy," Taylor said, leaning in her doorway. "I'm not sneaking out."

"No, I am not and yes, we are," Isabela replied. "Come on, Taylor! You will love San Francisco. I found a bar where they don't ID."

"I don't really drink."

"Ha. Well, whatever, we can get you some new clothes, at least. Have dinner. Sit in a restaurant like normal people. Check out some boys who lack delusions of grandeur." Isabela turned to face Taylor. "Does that not appeal to you?"

"When you said you could help me escape, I didn't think you were serious." Taylor shook her head, slightly in awe of her roommate's secret life as a jail-breaker. "How long have you been doing this?"

"I went for the first time a few weeks after I got here. Just to see if I could. And I could."

"How many times since?"

"Like, every other week?" Isabela pressed her hands together in a steeple pointed at Taylor. "Please, roommate! You must come! I am getting over a breakup. I cannot stand to sit around this dormitory and do nothing."

Taylor snorted. "Oh, now you're broken up about Lofton, huh?"

"I feel a deep emptiness yawning open beneath me and will surely sink down into it if you do not come with me to San Francisco," Isabela said with a straight face.

"I will go," Ran said.

Neither Taylor nor Isabela was aware that Ran had been listening to their whole conversation. Taylor turned with a small smile to look at Ran. Isabela's eyebrows shot up and she dropped a dress onto her bed.

"Eavesdropper!" Isabela yelled.

"I apologize," Ran replied. "But you are a very loud talker."

"You want to go?" Taylor asked, unable to keep the surprise out of her voice.

"Yes," Ran said. "I have been stuck on this campus since before it officially opened. I would like a break."

"You know we aren't going down there to do meditation,

right?" Isabela asked with a sternly arched brow. "We're going to party."

"Yes," Ran replied. "Good."

"Well, if you're both going, I can't just sit here by myself," Taylor relented. "You sure we won't get in trouble?"

"We will never be caught!" Isabela declared.

Ran turned to her. "I would like to invite Nigel."

Isabela stuck out her tongue. "Why don't we just invite the whole school?"

"Well, he was on our team today," Taylor said. "He should get to partake in the victory party."

"He enjoys drinking, like you," Ran observed to Isabela. Then, she cocked her head. "Unless it will be too difficult for you to sneak that many people out."

Isabela tossed her hair over her shoulder. "Of course not. I already know how I will do it."

"In that case," Taylor said, unable to keep the blush out of her cheeks, "could I invite someone, too?"

◇ ◇ ◇

Shirtless, Kopano stood on the common room couch and punched the air. "What was the name of this band?" he yelled to be heard over the music blasting from Nigel's iPod.

"The Dead Kennedys, mate," Nigel replied, already thumbing through his collection to choose the next song.

"I cannot understand anything they're saying!" Kopano shouted.

"I know! Isn't it great?"

"Yes! It makes me want to throw this couch out the window!"

The door to their suite banged open. Isabela entered with a flourish, dramatically covering her ears. Taylor and Ran followed behind her.

"Ugh, turn those terrible sounds off," Isabela complained.

With a smirk, Nigel released his Legacy's hold on the music. The screaming of the Dead Kennedys was reduced to a tinny buzz, emanating as it was from a pair of simple headphones. He slouched down in his chair and eyed the three girls. Meanwhile, Kopano hopped down from the couch and began to search for his shirt.

"Are we interrupting something?" Taylor asked with a smile.

"Not at all, not at all." Nigel winked at Ran. "It's a rare occasion for us to be graced by all three of the lovely ladies of room 308. To what do we owe the pleasure?"

"Oh, stop flirting when you don't mean it," Isabela said with a dismissive wave. She put her hands on her hips, surveying the boys' messy living environment. "It is truly disgusting in here."

"I was just going to clean up," Kopano said, unreasonably intimidated by the fiery shape-shifter. He began to gather up some loose clothes. Isabela slapped them out of his hands.

"Stop that!" she said. "Chores later. Tonight, we are going out."

Nigel leaned forward, bony elbows on his knees. "What's this, then?"

Isabela explained the plan to sneak away from the Academy. Her tone made it clear that the boys joining them was something of a foregone conclusion.

"My, my, my," Nigel said. He shot Ran a baffled look. "You're into this, even?"

Ran folded her arms. "We have been cooped up here too long, have we not?"

"Gods yes, I could use a pint," Nigel said, his smile crooked. "When do we leave?"

"Dark," Isabela said. "Obviously."

"I always wanted to see America," Kopano said dreamily. He finally found a shirt that was clean enough and tugged it on. "I thought they would show us more when we came to the Academy. There should be field trips."

"Yeah. Instead they bring in military guys to beat us up," Taylor added. "We deserve a night off after that ordeal today."

Kopano smiled at her. He liked the rebellious glint that he saw in Taylor's eye. He spoke to her in a tone of faux virtue. "It is my duty to warn you, Taylor, that this activity does not sound very boring."

She smiled at him. "Nope. It does not."

Just then, they all heard a loud bang from Caleb's room, followed by a pair of identical voices agitatedly whispering to each other. Everyone slowly turned towards Caleb's closed door. Except for Isabela. She whipped around to glare at Nigel.

"Your freak roommate is here? The whole time?"

Nigel ran a hand over his spiky hair, exchanging a look

with Kopano. "We, ah . . . we didn't check."

Isabela stomped her foot and yelled at the closed door, "Spy! Come out of there!"

Slowly, the door to Caleb's room creaked open and Caleb poked his head out.

"I didn't hear anything," he said.

Isabela groaned and flailed her arms. "This one! He is the ultimate tattletale. We must tie him up and gag him until we return."

Kopano laughed until Isabela turned to glare at him. "Wait. You are serious?"

Taylor watched Caleb warily, their weird encounter the week before not forgotten. Ran and Nigel, meanwhile, exchanged a subtle look. For his part, Caleb seemed to regret stumbling into the whole plan. He held up his hands.

"I won't say anything. I promise," he said.

"No. He cannot be trusted," countered Isabela.

Suddenly, Caleb stumbled forward. A duplicate hidden behind him had pushed Caleb out of his room. "Tell them you want to go, pansy," the duplicate hissed.

Nigel sighed and stepped forward. "Caleb, mate, what did we say about the duplicates?"

Caleb glanced over his shoulder, then absorbed the duplicate back into himself. Isabela shuddered.

"Sorry," Caleb said.

"Our roommate, he's got difficulties expressing himself proper like," Nigel declared, turning to face the rest of the group. "Bit of a weirdo, innit he? He owes it to his rigid upbringing and troubled childhood or some such."

"Um, we don't need to get into all that, thanks, Nigel," Caleb said quietly.

"I don't suppose any of us have similar back stories?" Nigel continued. "Or have had some trouble fitting in around this bloody Academy?"

"I am not a weirdo," Isabela declared.

Taylor smirked. "You aren't?"

Isabela shot Taylor a look. "No."

Kopano shrugged happily, like he'd missed most of the discussion. "You should come with us, Caleb. We are going to San Francisco!"

"I . . ." Caleb looked uncertainly at Isabela. "I mean, I would go if . . ."

"Six is too many," Isabela said, stomping her foot. "I cannot sneak out a small army."

"Yes, you can," Ran said, breaking her long silence.

Isabela glared at Ran. The Japanese girl stared back impassively. After a few seconds, Isabela relented with a toss of her hair.

"Fine," she said. "Fine. I will do it because my heart is so big and full of charity."

◇ ◇ ◇

The six of them waited until dark before they set out from the dorms. There were no rules about the students roaming the grounds at night—at least not before the midnight curfew—so they made their way towards the woods at a casual pace.

They hiked deep into the trees, until the fence that surrounded the Academy came into view. Isabela stopped them before they got too close.

"Do we climb over?" Kopano asked.

Isabela gave him a deadpan look. "I do not climb." She checked her watch. "We need to wait about seven more minutes."

"For what?" Caleb asked.

"Perimeter patrol."

Sure enough, seven minutes later, a Peacekeeper truck rumbled by on the dirt road that encircled the fence. As soon as the red taillights were out of sight, Isabela stepped out of hiding. The others followed, cautiously.

"First," she said, "we deal with the camera."

The others hadn't even noticed the little camera mounted on top of the fence. With a gentle nudge of her telekinesis, Isabela turned the device so it pointed in the other direction.

"Doesn't someone notice that?" Taylor asked.

"Of course they notice," Isabela replied. "But it is very windy out here. A technician will come out, turn the camera back around, tighten the screws. No big deal."

Next, Isabela stepped carefully back into the overgrown woods. She returned with a huge dead log, levitating the mossy debris with her telekinesis.

"It took me awhile to find one exactly the right size," she said. "I keep worrying that one night it will be gone, that the groundskeepers will clean it up."

Isabela propped the log up against the fence. She took off

her heels and gracefully scaled the improvised ramp. Lightly, she jumped down on the other side of the fence, dusted off the soles of her feet and put her shoes back on.

"Coming?" she asked the others through the fence.

One by one, they each ascended the ramp and jumped down. Kopano caught Taylor when she leaped down. Caleb watched them, biting his lip. When they were all on the other side, Isabela used her telekinesis to shove the log away from the fence.

"What happens now?" Nigel asked. "It's a long walk to San Francisco."

Isabela pointed across the dirt road. "Now, you wait here. There is a ditch over there. Hide in it until I return."

"Where are you going?" Taylor asked.

"You are all so nosy! Please. I know what I'm doing," Isabela complained. The others stared at her, so she threw up her hands resignedly. "Look, I am going to get us a car. Then, we drive off. Nothing to it. Get in your ditch so the patrols won't see you."

Isabela sauntered off into the darkness, leaving the others to hunker down in the grass on the side of the road. They stared up at the stars—blinking and visible out here in the middle of nowhere. They were nervous at first, but as the seconds turned into minutes, a peace settled over the five of them.

"This is kinda nice," Caleb said.

"Don't ruin the moment by talking about it," Nigel replied. Ran elbowed him.

They tensed up when another car rolled by, the headlight beams gliding right over their position. The patrol didn't even slow down.

"It'd be kind of funny if she just left us out here," Caleb said.

"She wouldn't do that," Taylor replied.

"I know . . . I'm just joking." Caleb shrugged. "We could camp out here. Worse comes to worst."

Kopano chuckled. "Sleeping outside on purpose. Something I will never understand about this wonderful country."

Another vehicle puttered up the dirt road. This time, it was a van. And this time, it slowed to a stop right above their ditch.

"Gotta be Isabela," Nigel said, standing up before Ran could stop him.

He was greeted by the face of the red-bearded soldier who he'd scared in the competition earlier, the man staring at him through his rolled-down window. "The hell are you doing out here, boy?"

Nigel tensed up. "Uh . . ."

In a blur of flesh that looked like melting clay, the soldier's face changed into Isabela's. She grinned at him. "Just kidding. Come on, get in!"

Laughing and excited, they scrambled out of the ditch and into the van. Taylor sat shotgun. There weren't any seats in the back—Isabela explained that the van was meant for doing supply runs, which was the pretense she used to sign it out from the vehicle pool, all under the identity of one of the many soldiers she'd memorized. The four others held on to leather cargo straps that dangled from the van's walls and ceiling.

"You're really something else," Taylor told Isabela.

"I know."

"In addition to something else, I hope you are also a good driver," Kopano said.

"Oh, I am," Isabela replied, setting off at a breakneck pace that jostled the four in the back. They were too amped up to complain, a game soon developing where they tried to keep their balance as Isabela zoomed through the curves of the patrol road. She slowed down when they reached a paved turnoff that led toward the Peacekeeper base proper and the final checkpoint before their exit.

"You should hide in the back. I need to put my face back on," Isabela told Taylor. The five of them all crouched in the shadows of the cargo area, holding in laughter, even Caleb giddy with the possibility of escape. "Are you ready?" Isabela asked. "Soon, there will be no turning back."

"We're ready," the others said in unison, not at all nervous as they approached the checkpoint. Isabela's confidence was contagious.

They were waved through without incident.

CHAPTER TWENTY-THREE

IN THE "FAMILY AREA" OF JIMBO'S MOTOR HOME, Einar ground his teeth until his jaw hurt. The room stunk—a mixture of body order and cigarette smoke. His legs ached from standing, but he refused to crowd in with the others around the faded dinette set. Not until Reverend Jimbo was done with his Bible study.

He hated Reverend Jimbo.

He hated his disgusting mobile home.

He hated the Americans.

In the background, Reverend Jimbo read a passage in his slow drawl. Einar watched the old man without listening—thick gray hair slicked halfway down the back of his neck, pockmarked face, the glistening eyes of a true believer. A group of Reverend Jimbo's followers crowded in around him, rapt, paying attention, although Einar figured the reverend could have read his flock anything—*The Lion, the Witch and the Wardrobe*, for instance, one of Einar's childhood favorites—and they would have taken it as gospel.

All of Jimbo's followers—bikers, ranchers, survivalists, burnouts—had the same stupid tattoo. A scythe slashing down on a serpent as it burst forth from a circle. The symbolism didn't require much unpacking.

Harvesters, they called themselves.

Einar glanced around the motor home. On the walls were pinned a jumble of newspaper stories about alien life, hand-drawn maps of UFO sightings and snatches of Scripture. Piled against one wall was a stack of rifles.

These people weren't professional. Compared to the research and resources of the Foundation, Jimbo's group was laughable.

Even though they often looked at him like a child, Einar missed the efficiency of Jarl and his Blackstone mercenaries. They were banned from operating on American soil, which made getting them into the United States for this operation too much of a risk. His employers had to use what resources were available. In this case, a grassroots cult that believed the Loric were devils made flesh and that any humans touched by them were irredeemably corrupted.

He and Rabiya were alone on this one. A calculated risk by the Foundation, Einar supposed. Even with the addition of the Italian Earth Garde healer, his employers still needed more healing power. Einar sensed the matter was becoming desperate.

If the Harvesters knew what Einar and Rabiya really were, they would certainly try to kill them. Einar sensed the way Jimbo and some of his brighter lights looked at him. They already had suspicions. But his presence had come with a generous contribution to the reverend's mobile church, both in money and weapons. Not to mention, Einar promised them violence, gave them a purpose. That kept the Harvesters from looking too hard at him and his partner. At least for now.

The weapons Einar provided were like nothing the Harvesters had seen before. They were designed specifically to fight the Garde and currently available only to select government agencies. Select government agencies and the Foundation. Einar and Rabiya were posing as representatives from Sydal Corp, the weapons manufacturer, spending time with the Harvesters so that they could field-test their anti-Garde technology. That made the Harvesters feel special.

"That's an honest-to-God multinational corporation, y'hear?" Reverend Jimbo had told his men when he introduced Einar. "We ain't just pissing in the wind out here. The powers-that-be, they're starting to take notice." That Einar and Rabiya were a little young to be representing a prominent weapons manufacturer like Sydal Corp didn't seem to occur to the Harvesters. That they were both obviously foreigners didn't raise any red flags either. Jimbo had stressed multinational, after all.

And what better place to test these weapons than out here, on the coast of California? They just had to wait for a suitable target to come along. A straggler. That's what Einar had told Jimbo and the others, anyway.

They didn't need to know that he and Rabiya were waiting for someone in particular.

Einar brushed a spot of lint off the front of his black button-down. The Harvesters favored what Einar considered silly postapocalyptic costumes—leather, gas masks, outlaw bandannas. He stuck out in their company by wearing a fine gray suit and wingtip shoes. Despite the preponderance of mildew in Reverend Jimbo's narrow motor home shower, Einar managed to stay immaculately clean. He kept his light brown hair rigidly parted from the side. There was not a speck of dirt under his fingernails.

He and Rabiya had been out here for a week. Living among the vermin. Waiting.

A walkie-talkie buzzed to life. "Got one coming your way," said the scratchy voice of a Harvester. Aside from the reverend, Einar hadn't bothered to learn any of their names. "White van. Looks like another supply run."

Einar quickly picked up his attaché. He turned to the reverend and his disciples, who had paused in their reading.

"I'll look into it," Einar said. "Ready yourselves."

"With the Lord's guidance, we are always ready," the

reverend responded. He motioned for one of the Harvesters—a muscular young man with slicked-back black hair—to join Einar. The reverend always had someone watching him.

Einar stepped outside, the cool night air a relief after the stuffy odors of the motor home. His escort followed him. Outside were a dozen more Harvesters and their motorcycles. They had skipped Bible study to drink beers and grill what were probably steaks but Einar imagined to be squirrels.

Their encampment was on a ridge that overlooked the Mar a Vista scenic roadway. In the decades before the Academy took over this piece of California, Mar a Vista was popular with tourists and surfers. Now, according to the Foundation's source inside the Academy, it was the route the Peacekeepers used when they wanted to travel unobserved. Unlike the nearby Shoreline Highway, this road was secluded. Usually without traffic. Perfect for discreet travel, but also ripe for a trap.

Thanks to their source, Einar knew exactly where the Academy's security checkpoints were located. The Harvesters had a handful of vagabond-looking bikers posted nearby there—far enough away to avoid detection but close enough to observe any comings and goings. That's who had radioed in.

In addition, there was a small team farther south on the highway, ready to spring a roadblock on Einar's command. Rabiya was down there, supervising that piece of the operation. If they were discovered as Garde and the Harvesters turned on them, it was better that Einar be with the bulk of the group. He could handle them.

Einar's source had assured the Foundation that the target made frequent visits to San Francisco, where she honed her skills at a local hospital. She would come this way. In all likelihood, she would be escorted by Peacekeepers and some Academy personnel. All expendable.

Whenever a vehicle left the Academy via Mar a Vista, they checked it. So far, there had been no sign of their target.

The Peacekeepers would detect their presence eventually. They couldn't camp out here forever without attracting attention. Every day, much to Einar's chagrin, the number of Harvesters increased. Word was spreading, a small army amassing. The atmosphere around the reverend's camp got more and more like a party. But Einar could tell the Harvesters were growing restless. Soon, they'd want some action, whether approved by Einar or not. He'd already overheard the idiots pondering an assault on the Academy. A lot of bold talk.

The operation would have to fold up if the Harvesters became too unruly. He hadn't been sent here for a pointless attack on the Academy.

The whole mission was riskier than Einar would've liked. Riskier, even, than kidnapping the sniveling Italian boy in the Philippines. Acting so close to the Academy; there would be consequences. His employers surely knew that. They'd likely run dozens of cost-benefit analyses.

Acquiring the target was worth the exposure.

And, if all went well, the whole operation would simply

be blamed on the Harvesters.

Three days ago was Einar's eighteenth birthday. He'd spent it among these sweat-stinking cretins. He hadn't told anyone, not even Rabiya.

As a belated gift, he hoped to see some of these Harvesters die.

Einar speed-walked towards the ridge with his Harvester escort. Once there, he crouched down in the grass, careful not to get any dirt on his suit. He opened his attaché and took out his goggles. They were bulky things and Einar tsked in annoyance as one of the straps caught on his ear.

"Here, let me help," said the Harvester. He straightened the strap on the back of Einar's head before Einar could stop him.

Einar turned to regard the Harvester. His eyes looked bulbous and huge with the goggles on.

"Thank you," said Einar coldly.

"No problem," the guy said. "That accent. You Russian or something? Been meaning to ask."

"Icelandic," Einar replied.

He turned to watch the road, waiting for the van to come into view. The goggles were not night vision. They did not magnify Einar's vision. He stared into the darkness.

If his target came down that road, he would know.

"Never met anyone from Iceland before," the Harvester continued. "That's cool."

"What is your name?" Einar asked.

"Silas."

"You are talkative, Silas," Einar observed. "Does the dark make you nervous?"

Silas laughed. "Hell no, man. I'm just making conversation."

Einar concentrated on this young man. Silas's palms began to sweat. His stomach turned over, clenched in a knot. His heart was pounding now. Was that movement in the grass? What were those shadows? Einar smiled thinly when he sensed Silas creep a little closer to him, as if for protection.

"Actually, it is a little freaky out here," Silas said, his voice cracking. "Shit, man. I'm weirded out."

"Be calm," Einar said, and released his hold on the Harvester. It was so easy to put the fear in people when they didn't know what was happening.

Headlights appeared in the distance. Einar turned his attention to the road below. The van approached . . .

"What . . . ?" Einar mumbled.

He struck the side of his goggles with the heel of his hand. What he saw didn't seem possible. He checked the diagnostic in the bottom-left corner of the display. Everything appeared normal; the goggle's batteries were fully charged.

The reading had to be correct.

Einar's lips quirked in a bemused smile. Through his goggles, he watched six vivid blue energy signatures pass by on the road.

He pulled his walkie-talkie from his hip. "Rabiya?"

His partner came back a moment later, her voice soft as always. "Yes, Einar?"

"There are six coming your way. Confirm the target is among them before engaging."

"Yes, Einar."

Calmly, Einar returned the goggles to his attaché. He felt Silas's eyes upon him, his mouth agape.

"You say six, fella?" Silas asked. "Six of—of those things down there in that van?"

"Yes. Six of them without an escort," Einar replied. He turned on his heel and headed back for camp. "Your men must arm themselves and prepare to engage."

CHAPTER TWENTY-FOUR

TAYLOR COOK
MAR A VISTA—CALIFORNIA

TAYLOR GOT AN UNEASY FEELING IN THE PIT OF her stomach as soon as the taillights came into view.

They were on a back road headed south from the Academy. Probably gorgeous in daylight, but empty and ominous at night. Taylor couldn't understand where her anxiety was coming from. She'd grown up in big, empty expanses like this. She'd never been unnerved by stretches of lonely country.

That was before the attack on her farm. Before the nightmares.

Isabela had the radio on. Bright pop music that seemed at odds with the night. Nigel agreed.

"Turn that rubbish off," he complained again and again.

"I am the driver," Isabela replied. "This means I choose the music."

"Bloody hell, let me drive then."

"No. You would kill us all. Drive on the wrong side of the road or something. Or poison our characters with your terrible punk rock."

"Aw, your character's already poisoned enough, darling."

"You should broaden your horizons, Isabela," Kopano said. "Nigel's music is awesome." Isabela shot him a withering look and he held up his hands. "What you're playing is fine, too."

Taylor looked over her shoulder. Ran sat cross-legged in the back, the bumpy riding not at all disturbing her meditation. Caleb sat next to her, his hand holding one of the cargo straps so he didn't slide across the van whenever Isabela took a turn too fast. He was watching her. Taylor still didn't know what to make of him. He had a crush on her? He was mentally disturbed? He was a sort of dorky boy from the Midwest? She caught his eye and immediately worried such a look would be misinterpreted.

"Everything okay?" Caleb asked her. He must have read the unease on her face.

"Yeah," she replied, and forced a smile.

"America is much bigger than I thought," Kopano observed cheerily. He'd wedged himself in between Isabela and Taylor, his butt on Isabela's armrest, his arm across the back of Taylor's chair. "Do you know I used to think one could drive from New York to California in a day?"

Taylor chuckled as she glanced up at him, relaxing a little. "Maybe if you drove like Isabela."

Isabela nodded firmly. "Yes. I could do that."

"Are we there yet?" Kopano asked.

"God, you are like a child," Isabela snapped. "It was an hour when you asked five minutes ago. Do the math, big boy."

"Don't make her turn the car around," Taylor said with a smirk.

"Look!" Kopano said, pointing through the windshield. "An accident?"

The taillights.

Kopano was the first one to spot them. Up ahead, a beat-up station wagon was parked across the center lane. The hood was popped, the headlights on, two silhouettes visible as they peered down at the engine. A curl of steam or smoke emanated from the open hood.

Immediately, Isabela stepped on the brakes. As the van slowed to a crawl, Isabela turned down the music.

"Looks like a breakdown," Caleb said.

"We should help," Kopano put in.

"I actually know a few things about cars," Caleb added. "Used to hang around with the base mechanics—"

"Should we really be stopping?" Taylor asked, embarrassed by the quaking unease in her voice. "We don't know these people."

Kopano gave her a surprised look. "Seriously? We just drive by them?"

"Need I remind you, we aren't supposed to be away from the Academy?" Isabela said sharply. "In San Francisco, we will blend into the crowd. But out here? What if that is someone from the school?"

Caleb squinted into the headlights as the van creaked closer to the breakdown. "If they're from the Academy, they'll probably recognize us anyway."

Nigel glanced at Ran. She peered through the windshield with an arched eyebrow, her lips pursed. He turned to the others. "If they aren't from the Academy, then what are they doing out here?"

"Driving," Kopano said with a laugh. "Going to the beach? Hiking? You guys are being paranoid."

"I would think it best if we avoid being seen this close to the Academy," Ran said.

That settled matters for Isabela. She leaned over the wheel. "Everyone duck down and I will drive us on the shoulder."

Before Isabela could do that, one of the people standing by the station wagon jogged into their headlights and waved. Taylor relaxed a bit when she saw it was just a girl, no more than a few years older than herself. The girl's pretty face was framed by a hijab, the dark fabric gaudily bedazzled. She wore a dress that covered her from neck to ankle, obviously expensive and fashionable. Completely normal, thought Taylor.

"Hey! Can you help us?" the girl yelled, standing right in their way.

Kopano laughed. "A stranded girl! And you cruel people

wanted to flee the scene."

Isabela put the van in park and rolled down her window. The girl hustled over, smiling sweetly as she got on her tiptoes and looked into the van.

"Thank you, thank you," she said breathlessly. "My dad and I have been stuck out here for like an hour. We just need a jump."

"I do not know what that is," Isabela said.

While they talked, Taylor found herself not looking at the girl but at the burly shape of her father. She couldn't see much of him besides that he had a tangled mane of curly hair. As he fiddled with the engine, his arms briefly came into the light. Taylor spotted a strange smudge of grease on his forearm. She leaned forward, trying to get a better look . . .

"Do you have cables?" Caleb asked. He got up and opened the back of the van. "Hang on. Let me come take a look."

As Caleb brushed by him, Nigel pressed up against the window. His head tilted. Something moved out there. He was sure of it. He cupped his hands around his eyes, trying to see through the glass into the dark.

"Oi, Ran . . . ," he said quietly.

The Japanese girl perked up and came to his side.

"Someone's out there," Nigel whispered.

Meanwhile, as Caleb climbed out of the back of the van, the girl waved to her father. "These are the ones, Dad! They're going to help us out!"

These are the ones. What a strange way to say that. The girl's words set off Isabela's finely tuned bullshit detector.

She shot a glance in Taylor's direction, but Taylor was too busy staring wide-eyed at the girl's "father" to notice.

The man had straightened up from his hunched position over the station wagon. He waved to his daughter and his arm came fully into the light. Taylor immediately recognized the symbol tattooed on the inside of his forearm.

Circle. Snake. Scythe.

"Isabela! We have to go!" Taylor screamed.

But it was too late.

As Taylor turned to Isabela, panicked, the other girl smoothly pulled a pistol from within the folds of her dress and shot Isabela in the neck.

CHAPTER TWENTY-FIVE

HIS ATTACHÉ IN HAND, EINAR WALKED SLOWLY down the dark road towards the sounds of chaos. Shouting, the roar of motorcycle engines, the electronic buzzing of the Inhibitor-2a's. Headlights from dozens of motorcycles flashed, creating a strobe-light effect in the otherwise peaceful night. Einar scratched his cheek thoughtfully.

Perhaps he should have waited for a more opportune moment to make his move.

The Academy Garde were trapped. They hunkered down around the van they'd been driving, fending off an assault from the first wave of Harvesters. Meanwhile, a dozen bikers rode in a circle around the area, fencing them in.

If he'd had the Blackstone Group out here instead of these half-witted trailer trash, this battle would already be over.

Reverend Jimbo had almost fifty men at his disposal. Einar had been worried about how their numbers had been growing.

Suddenly, they didn't seem like enough.

"I thought you said there were only six of them!" Reverend Jimbo yelled in his ear. The old man walked next to Einar, nervous but excited, brandishing a chrome-plated six-shooter. Silas stood on his other side, watching the fight with wide eyes.

Only. Einar sniffed. As if six Garde, even poorly trained ones, could ever be taken lightly. Oh well. It wouldn't be long now. One way or another, his mission to America was at an end. After tonight, he could wash his hands of the Harvesters and their ignorance.

"There are only six of them," Einar replied to the reverend.

"Then why do I see—?" The reverend squinted into the distance, trying to count. "A whole goddamn bunch?"

"One of them duplicates," Einar said.

"He does what?"

"He produces clones of himself."

"That's the unholiest thing I've heard yet."

Einar suppressed a sigh. He had read the file on Caleb Crane and found his Legacy to be an enviable one. According to his dossier, Caleb deferred to authority and followed instructions readily. Strange, then, to find him out here, apparently engaged in an attempt to escape from the Academy. Einar did recall some mention of instability with the boy. Possible multiple personality disorder. That would make sense, considering his Legacy.

"If your men can isolate the real duplicator and render him unconscious, the clones will disappear," Einar said.

"They'll do more than render that abomination unconscious," the reverend replied. He cocked his pistol.

Einar turned to glare at the reverend.

"I told you. No lethal weapons until I have what I'm after."

"Right, right. Your precious field test," Reverend Jimbo said with a snort. "Son, I'm grateful for the support and all, but I can't promise my boys won't get tired of batting these devils around with your little toys."

Einar took a step close to the reverend, focused his power and coaxed a feeling of fear out of the older man. Intimidation. If he pressed any harder, he could have the reverend on the ground praying to him. But there wasn't time for that.

With a shaky hand, Reverend Jimbo eased down the hammer on his pistol.

"I'll—I'll make sure my men don't fly off the handle," the reverend said meekly. He waved Silas and one of the other Harvesters towards the battle. "Sorry," he muttered to Einar, clearly unsure why he was apologizing.

"Mm," Einar replied noncommittally. He turned to watch a burly biker sneak up on a Caleb and fire an Inhibitor-2a leash at him.

The Inhibitor version 2a. One of Sydal Corp's finest creations. It then fired a collar made of a proprietary mercury-based alloy that snapped into place around the target's neck and self-welded shut. If knocked off course—say, by telekinesis—the weapon's sensors automatically recalibrated for the target's throat by homing in on the heat of the carotid artery. Once attached, the collar remained connected to the crossbow by high-strength tensile wire, delivering shocks on command to the target. The electric bursts were enough to disrupt any Legacies.

Einar would know; he had been on the receiving end many times during the weapon's testing. He remembered bitterly how an early version had nearly decapitated him.

The Inhibitor fired by the biker snapped around the Caleb's neck. He watched Caleb convulse from the shock. Then, the collar dropped uselessly to the ground; Caleb had disappeared. A clone, then. Not the real deal.

As the biker reeled his inhibitor back in, he was struck in the chest by a vicious punch to the sternum. The biker flew backwards, slammed into the van the Garde had been driving and lay still.

That was Kopano Okeke who threw the haymaker. Einar's intelligence on him was far from complete. The exact nature of the Nigerian's Legacies was unknown to the Academy, and thus unknown to Einar's employer. Einar didn't need reports to tell him that Kopano's strength was enhanced. He could see that for himself.

That would be useful.

Two more Harvesters armed with Sydal Corp tranquilizer guns fired at Kopano. The darts bounced harmlessly off him. A moment later, a glowing orb landed at the feet of the two Harvesters. They barely had a chance to register the projectile before it exploded, throwing the two bikers to the side of the road.

Ran Takeda. And if she was here, then it was likely Nigel Barnaby was as well. Skilled combatants, survivors of the massacre at Patience Creek. Einar might not have initiated this operation had he known they were present. The pair crouched for cover at the back of the van, using the doors for a shield. As Einar watched, Ran picked up a handful of gravel and charged it with her Legacy. She chucked the stones at another pack of Harvesters, the resulting concussive blast knocking them off their motorcycles. Word had reached the Foundation that Ran had sworn off using her Legacies. Apparently, she had chosen tonight to make an exception.

"My men are getting destroyed out there!" Reverend Jimbo screamed.

"Yes. They are very poorly trained," Einar replied as he continued to scan the battlefield.

There. Near the driver side door of the van, Einar could see a trio of three Calebs standing shoulder to shoulder. A human wall. They were protecting someone. Through their legs, Einar could see a body in the road, a second person crouching over it. An injured person and a healer.

"I see you, Taylor," Einar said to himself. He waited a moment for a Harvester on a motorcycle to pass, then darted through their snarling chopper perimeter and headed towards the battle.

"Where are you going?" Reverend Jimbo shouted.

"To finish this."

Time was of the essence. Already, the frustrated and frightened Harvesters were abandoning the nonlethal weapons he'd provided them with and were turning to more conventional, and deadlier, methods of assault. Although any injuries would surely be blamed on the Harvesters, a bunch of dead Garde would not be a welcome development. This mission would already bring too much attention.

A group of Harvesters armed with tire irons and baseball bats had descended upon Kopano. He blocked each of their attacks with a forearm or a shoulder or, in one case, his face. None of the blows hurt him. Einar watched as, one by one, Kopano knocked the Harvesters out with powerful uppercuts.

"Leave us alone!" the young man shouted, a note of fear in his voice despite his near invulnerability. "Leave us—!"

Kopano hesitated. He had spotted Einar walking towards him. A strange sight—a young man in a suit and tie, holding a briefcase, walking calmly through the fray.

Meanwhile, a Harvester advanced on Kopano from behind. He carried an old-fashioned sawed-off shotgun. Einar wondered if that would be enough to break Kopano's thick skin.

All of the Garde were occupied with other Harvesters. Einar sighed. He reached into his attaché, pulled out his blaster and fired a concentrated burst of energy. Kopano ducked as the red-tinged beam sizzled by his head and right into the Harvester's face.

Einar's weapon was far from nonlethal; the Harvester fell dead, his face a charred mess. The blaster was Mogadorian in origin, a little collector's item from the invasion. Einar relished any chance he got to use it.

"Who are—?" Kopano started to ask, his fists up.

"I'm your only friend," Einar said, getting closer. He reached out to Kopano with his Legacy and filled the boy with feelings of affection and trust.

"Right!" Kopano said. "Yes! Good to see you!"

"All these people want to hurt us. All of them," Einar said. "Hurt them before they can hurt us."

Anger. Einar made it flow through Kopano. It was a simple chemical reaction—lower the serotonin, pump up the adrenaline. Especially easy with males, actually. Kopano's eyes widened, his lips curled into a feral snarl, his fists clenched impossibly tight.

With a roar, Kopano whipped around and clotheslined the nearest Harvester. While that man gasped for breath in the dirt, Kopano lunged at a Caleb and punched the clone so hard that its head spun 180 degrees before it disappeared.

"Good boy," Einar said.

Emotional manipulation. It wasn't the flashiest Legacy, but it had its uses.

Kopano plowed through another pair of clones, then pummeled a fleeing Harvester. Everyone in the battle—Garde and Harvester—was now paying all their attention to the Nigerian.

Well, not everyone.

Einar took a moment too long admiring his handiwork. Something thudded at his feet. A glowing rock.

"Shit," he said.

He felt a yank on the back of his jacket and let his body go limp. Just as Ran's bomb exploded at his feet, Einar flew backwards on a telekinetic tether. He landed in the road, scraping his elbows. He'd been pulled backwards by Rabiya, who was hiding behind the tire of the broken-down station wagon they'd used as a roadblock. An unconscious Harvester was slumped next to her.

Einar cringed, fingering a tear in his jacket.

"I'm all dirty," he complained.

"Yes. But you aren't blown to pieces, so there's that," Rabiya scolded.

The two of them flinched as a motorcycle flew overhead, the bike obviously propelled by telekinesis and glowing with Ran's kinetic energy. It fell right in the midst of the Harvesters riding in circles around the fight and exploded, knocking a few of them off their bikes and driving others to retreat.

"This is going poorly," Rabiya observed. "We should have waited. It would've been easier to take her with the Peacekeepers than with these other Garde."

"Hindsight," Einar replied with a dismissive wave. "Besides, we don't know if she was planning to return to the Academy. They could have been running away."

Einar peeked out from behind the car. By the van, Kopano's berserk rampage was slowing down a bit. Normally, it took a few minutes for Einar's control to wear off, but the attack from Ran must have shaken his Legacy. He concentrated on Kopano and amped up his adrenaline, his rage, then smiled when the Nigerian smashed the heads of two Harvesters together with renewed ferocity.

"Kopano! Hey! What are you doing?"

That must be Caleb. The real Caleb. He stood in front of the larger boy, trying to calm him down. He couldn't have known what Einar had done to Kopano's mind, how it would take time for him to come down from the manipulations.

Kopano grabbed Caleb by the front of his shirt and flung him back-first into the windshield of the van. The glass crunched and spiderwebbed as Caleb bounced off it, tumbled over the hood and landed on the back of his head in the road. A moment later, the clones crowding the battlefield blinked out of existence.

"We make our move now," Einar told Rabiya. "Get our exit ready."

"Hurry, please," Rabiya said. She extended her hands. A blue glow started to emanate from her palms.

Einar slipped out from behind the car, blaster pointed ahead of him. With the clones gone, he could see Taylor leaning over one of her friends. Who was that? He couldn't tell and it didn't matter. She was unconscious or dead. Probably dead, based on the dark red scars that covered her face and neck. One of the damned Harvesters must have burned her up. Taylor was focused on pouring healing energy into her, but from Einar's perspective the effort seemed wasted.

As Einar scuttled towards Taylor, Nigel strode into the road and started to scream.

The decibel level was like nothing Einar had ever experienced. He doubled over and vomited, his head spinning. It felt like his eyes would bulge out of his head. The Harvesters who had remained standing during Kopano's assault now fell over, writhing and clutching their ears.

So did Kopano. In fact, he took the brunt of Nigel's scream. The attack seemed designed to bring him down.

Hand shaking, Einar managed to lift his blaster just high enough to shoot Nigel in the leg. The searing pain surprised him and cut off his scream. Nigel fell to his knees, but immediately started to get back up. Einar grabbed a rock with his telekinesis and flung it at Nigel's head. The blow wasn't enough to kill him, but it made certain that he wouldn't cause any more sonic disruptions for at least a few minutes.

Einar felt a tugging sensation across his knuckles. A second later, his blaster was ripped out of his hand. He glanced to his right and saw Ran Takeda. Unlike the Harvesters, she was still on her feet. Einar glanced around for Rabiya but didn't see her. She must have gone down when Nigel screamed. Einar struggled to his knees and watched as Ran stalked towards him.

Bang! Bang! Bang!

A bullet grazed Ran's shoulder. She dove for cover behind the van as Reverend Jimbo stepped onto the scene, his six-shooter blazing. He came with a small contingent of Harvesters. They seemed more concerned with gathering their injured than with pressing the fight against the Garde.

Thanks to the reverend's distraction, Einar was able to scramble to his feet. The way to Taylor was clear. She'd been affected by the scream, too, and was wiping her eyes, trying to gather herself so she could go back to unsuccessfully healing her dead friend.

Einar pulled a tranquilizer gun from his attaché and shot Taylor in the neck. She slumped over.

"Finally," Einar muttered.

Einar raised a hand, hoisting Taylor up with his telekinesis. Out of the corner of his eye, he saw Ran poke her head out from behind the van. He fired a dart in her direction, unsure whether it found its mark.

"Rabiya! Are you ready?" Einar yelled as he turned. He couldn't be sure she heard him. The ringing in his own ears was thunderous.

The girl was back on her feet at least. Her headscarves were a mess, blood dampening one side of them. She must have fallen and hit her head on the station wagon's bumper.

Rabiya extended her hands and focused. A stream of cobalt-blue energy flowed from her palms and struck the pavement. Slowly, the energy coalesced into a craggy pyramid of stone.

Loralite. Rabiya could produce the stuff at will. Now, all they had to do was envision the stone tucked away in Einar's backyard, touch the Loralite and they'd be out of this mess.

"Deceivers!" Reverend Jimbo shouted. Einar could hear his booming voice even through the intense ringing. "We have been infiltrated by the abominations!"

The reverend had seen Rabiya using her Legacy. He'd likely also surmised that Einar was the one floating Taylor through the air.

The reverend pointed his revolver at Einar. Quickly, Einar yanked Taylor to him so that he was carrying the girl over her shoulder.

The reverend squeezed off a shot. Einar brushed it aside with his telekinesis.

He started to fire again.

Einar gripped the man's arm with his telekinesis and twisted. The arm snapped at the elbow. Jimbo screamed. He still managed to pull the trigger.

But the gun was aimed under his own chin.

The leader of the Harvesters collapsed, his head blown apart. His men recoiled in terror.

Einar couldn't deny the satisfaction he felt at that.

He reached the stone just as Rabiya finished creating it. "Can we please get out of here?" she asked. She held out her hand to Einar. "Your place, right?"

The detached wheel of a motorcycle flung with telekinetic force struck Rabiya in the stomach. She doubled over and fell backwards. Einar glanced over his shoulder, saw Ran charging an object, saw Caleb stirring on the roadside, saw Nigel struggling back to his feet.

He looked down at Rabiya, catching her breath, now too far away from the stone. He started to reach out with his telekinesis.

A glowing rock floated in his direction.

One of the last Harvesters dove on top of Rabiya. He grabbed her and smashed her face into the pavement.

It was all happening too fast.

"I am sorry," Einar said to Rabiya, although he was sure she couldn't hear him. He touched the Loralite stone and, with Taylor, teleported himself to safety.

CHAPTER TWENTY-SIX

ISABELA SILVA
BIG BOX—STOCKTON, CALIFORNIA

ISABELA AWOKE SLOWLY, GROGGILY, LIKE SLIDING out from a pleasant dream. Her muscles were stiff, her back sore. It felt like she'd been sleeping for a long time. Where was she? In bed at the Academy? Back home? She smelled breakfast. Her mother must be cooking. She yawned luxuriously.

Someone gently shook her shoulders.

"Isabela. Isabela." Ran's voice. "Wake up, now. It is time to go."

Isabela snapped awake. This cold metal slab beneath her, it wasn't her bed. And she wasn't alone.

She sat up sharply, her back cracking, a rush of wooziness pumping through her head. Ran crouched in front of her. The Japanese girl's gaze was, as usual, completely inscrutable.

But Ran had seen her. Of that, Isabela could be certain.

"It is okay," Ran said. "You're safe."

Isabela touched her cheeks. She ran her fingers over leathery furrows, the patchwork border of skin grafts, puckered scar tissue. She brushed her hand over her scalp, the spiky bristles where her beautiful mane of hair once grew. Her eyes widened, locked on Ran, and she stifled a scream.

Then, she shape-shifted. Isabela put on her old face, the one from before the accident. The burn scars melted away, her skin smoothed out, her hair grew in. Ran watched with her head tilted, saying nothing. Isabela wondered if the other girl was capable of registering surprise.

"You saw me," Isabela said flatly.

"Yes."

"You weren't supposed to."

"The others, too," Ran said, glancing over her shoulder at the van's closed back door. "At first, we thought you had been injured . . ."

Isabela put her face in her hands. Months of keeping up appearances—literally and figuratively—wasted. They would talk and she would become an object of pity, undesirable, disgusting . . .

She peeked out through her fingers. Wait. There was something more happening here. They were in the back of the stolen Academy van, except it wasn't at all in the condition Isabela remembered. A warm wind blew in through the missing windshield. There were blood splatters on the floor.

She noticed that Ran's shoulder was wrapped in a fresh bandage.

"What . . . what happened?" Isabela asked.

"We were attacked," Ran said. "You were shot with a tranquilizer dart."

Isabela touched a sore spot on her neck. "Jesus Christ."

"A young man—we think he was Garde—took Taylor. Teleported her away somewhere using a Loralite stone."

Isabela's mouth dropped open. "No. That doesn't make any sense."

"We are trying to decide what to do now," Ran continued. "To begin with, we are getting rid of the van. That's why I woke you."

Isabela rubbed her eyes. "Where are we?"

"Stockton, California."

"Ugh. Why? If we were attacked, why don't we go back to the Academy?"

Ran reached past Isabela. From under the driver seat, she grabbed a broken weapon. A crossbow-looking rifle. The shock-collar thing. One of the guns the Peacekeepers had used against the Garde in the Wargames event.

"The people who attacked us had these," Ran said. "They could be working with the Peacekeepers. We don't know. Nigel and I do not feel safe going back there. And Caleb and Kopano . . . well. They want to go after Taylor."

Isabela brushed a hand through her hair. "Where are they?"

"Outside," Ran said. She nudged a plastic shopping bag in

Isabela's direction. "We got you a change of clothes."

Isabela looked down at the bright blue bag. The logo said Big Box—a huge chain of American stores that sold super-cheap versions of everything from underwear to guns. With great trepidation, she peered at the clothes within. A boring T-shirt and a terrible pair of mom jeans.

"These are awful."

"They were the best we could do."

Isabela sniffed. The cute and strappy dress she'd worn for their night out was ruined, smudged with grime and stained with blood. It was just one thing after another. She touched her wrist where, luckily, Simon's translator bracelet remained secure.

"Let me get changed," she said.

Ran nodded and turned to exit the van. She paused, half glancing over her shoulder.

"You are using your Legacy all the time," Ran said.

Isabela frowned. "I haven't figured out how to do it when I'm sleeping. Obviously."

"Don't you get tired?"

Isabela rubbed the scratchy fabric of her new T-shirt between her fingers. "Of course," she said. "My tolerance is getting better and better, though."

"It seems . . ." Ran paused. "I am sorry. It seems like it would be difficult."

"Walking around the way I am, the way I really am . . . that's harder than any amount of shape-shifting," Isabela said quietly.

Ran nodded once, opened the door and hopped out of the van.

Isabela exhaled slowly. She'd spent almost a year hiding her true self from her classmates, cultivating the image of the girl she was before the accident. Now, all her hard work had been unraveled.

Not to mention, Taylor, who Isabela begrudgingly had to admit was her closest friend, had been kidnapped by some psychopaths. This, too, was unacceptable. Taylor, who had seen her real face already—who had kept her secret and not judged. Taylor, who should be here now, who would know the right stupid positive thing to say to make Isabela feel better.

Dressed in her ugly Big Box clothes, Isabela emerged from the van. They were parked in a dingy alley behind a shopping center. Ran sat on the bumper of the van. Nigel stood a few feet away, a small bandage on his head and a larger one on his calf. It heartened Isabela to see that he'd been forced to abandon his punk rock attire for a pair of cargo shorts and a too-big Mickey Mouse T-shirt, which he had ripped the sleeves off of. Kopano stood at the end of the alley, keeping watch, his face as dour as she'd ever seen it. Isabela wrinkled her nose; the pungent aroma of warm trash emanated from a nearby Dumpster.

"Couldn't you have found a less disgusting place to hide out?" she asked.

"That's funny," Nigel said. He smiled at her in a way that she'd never seen before. Usually, his smiles were mocking or smug, but this one . . . it was as if he were smiling at a three-legged dog.

The pity. Already they were starting in with the pity. Kopano stared at her hard, like he was trying to see through her disguise, checking for seams. She snapped her fingers at him.

"Stop looking at me like that," Isabela snapped. "What do you think? That if you cross your eyes you will be able to see my real face? You already saw enough."

Kopano simply looked away. "Sorry."

Nigel cleared his throat. "Listen, love, you don't have to hide yourself from us, we're your fri—"

Isabela rounded on him. "Hide myself?" She gestured at her body. "You think this is for you? That I do this for your benefit? Pah." Isabela spit on the ground. "This is how I like to look. It's my choice."

Nigel held up his hands. "All right, all right."

"Did it happen during the invasion?" Ran asked.

Isabela threw her shoulders back and sighed. "This is the only time we will talk about this, okay? After this special bonding moment, you will never comment on my appearance again, unless it is to pay me a much-deserved compliment. Understand?"

They all nodded.

"It happened a month before the invasion," Isabela said. "I was at a warehouse party. Something caught fire. There were too many people. I was stuck and . . ." She shrugged. "When John Smith called us all to action, I was in a hospital bed, my body wrapped in bandages. I did not care about the invasion or what happened to the world. I only hoped that one of these aliens would come heal me. They did not. But I was given the next-best thing."

"Fate," Kopano said quietly. "You got exactly the Legacy you needed."

"Fate? Luck? Who cares?" Isabela tossed her hair. "Is that enough sharing? Do we not have more important things to worry about?"

"Yes," Kopano said. He looked down at his feet. It was strange to see the cheery Nigerian brooding. "We must find Taylor."

Isabela raised an eyebrow, turning to look at Ran. "You said she got kidnapped. Teleported?"

"Yes."

"They were Harvesters," Kopano said grimly. "Taylor must have told you about them coming to her farm."

Isabela nodded. "The whore who shot me didn't look like some religious nut."

"We think she came with the tosser who teleported away," Nigel said. "She created a Loralite stone. Her friend took Taylor, left her behind. Harvesters attacked her. Snatched her up while we was making our escape."

Isabela put her hands on her hips and looked at Ran. "Why didn't you just kill them all?"

Ran looked back at her, but said nothing. It was Kopano who grunted, shoving away from his spot on the wall. "We should go find Caleb. He's been gone too long."

"Where is he?" Isabela asked.

"Caleb is getting us a new car," Ran said.

"Him? Really?" Isabela asked.

"He knows cars," Nigel replied. "Figures he can get one started all telekinetically."

"Yes, but he is—what do the Americans call it? The little camper children."

"A Boy Scout," Nigel replied with a half smile.

"Not who I would put in charge of stealing a car," Isabela said with a shrug.

"Wasn't no Boy Scout last night. Lad fought like he was possessed. Might've turned those Harvesters away himself, if . . ."

Nigel trailed off, glancing gloomily in Kopano's direction. Kopano's frown deepened and he walked out of the alley. Isabela pursed her lips—she really had missed a lot.

"What's his problem?" she quietly asked Nigel as they walked, nodding in Kopano's direction.

"He bloody lost it last night," Nigel whispered. "We think the knob in the suit used some kind of mind control on him."

They made an odd-looking group as they emerged from the alley, but luckily the shopping center parking lot was uncrowded this early in the morning. Even so, Isabela felt exposed being out in the open. She'd been on numerous excursions since coming to the Academy, but none had ever spiraled out of control like this. At best, they were in deep trouble with the Academy. At worst, they were being hunted. For the first time since she'd come to the Academy, Isabela felt her confidence begin to waver.

"Shouldn't we at least call in to the Academy?" she asked. "Tell them that Taylor's been kidnapped."

"That lot's got to have noticed we're missing by now," Nigel said. "We give them a ring, they'll track us down."

"Would that . . . would that be so bad?"

"We don't know if we can trust them," Ran said. "I, for one, am not ready to go back yet."

"We can't go back without Taylor," Kopano said firmly. "I promised her . . . I promised I would protect her."

Isabela rolled her eyes at the macho posturing, but didn't say anything. Instead, she turned to Nigel and Ran.

"Taylor could be anywhere," she said. "Where would we even start?"

Nigel reached into one of his cargo pockets. "Took the liberty of searching a couple of bodies before we made our escape last night. One'a them wankers had this on him."

He handed Isabela a pamphlet. It looked like something hastily thrown together in Photoshop and then spit out from an ancient printer. Her eyes skimmed over the imagery—the Harvester logo, bulbous-headed green aliens, the devil, random Bible quotations. More importantly was the message, scrawled in Sharpie on the back. "Apache Jack's. 4866 Route 15. Gila. Outside Silver City. Ask for Jimbo."

"Where is this?" Isabela asked.

"Biker bar in bloody New Mexico," Nigel replied. "We think it's a spot where these Harvesters sharpen their pitchforks and grope their cousins."

"How do you know all this?"

Nigel pulled a cell from his pocket. "Nicked this from one of the bikers. Battery's all dead now, though. Found a bit of cash, too. How we afforded our lovely new wardrobe."

"That reminds me," Isabela said. With a bit of concentration, she changed the appearance of her clothes—made the jeans more formfitting and turned the T-shirt into a silky tunic.

Nigel scowled at her. "Not fair."

Isabela smirked. "So the plan is to track down these maniacs who already tried to murder us once and hope they will tell us how to find Taylor?"

"About sums it up," Nigel said. He looked to Ran. "Right?"

"Yes," she said. "Either they tell us, or perhaps we find the girl who creates Loralite. The Harvesters who survived took her when they were escaping."

"How did we escape?" Isabela thought to ask.

"The baddies hightailed it when their leader all of a sudden decided to off himself. Think the wanker in the suit played a part in that. Otherwise, don't make any sense," Nigel said. He glanced at Ran. "The ones who had a mind to keep fighting got their asses exploded."

Isabela eyed Ran. "You . . ."

She flexed her fingers, knuckles cracking. "I am not a very good pacifist. Especially when men are trying to kill me and my friends. We will find them. And they will talk."

Nigel smiled at Isabela. She realized he was actually having fun with this. "Going off half-cocked without official approval is the way Garde get things done," he said. "Or haven't you heard the stories, love?"

"Oh, I have heard. But you are no John Smi— Oof!"

Kopano stopped directly in front of Isabela and she bumped into the large boy's back. He didn't seem to notice.

"Uh . . . ," Kopano said. "This looks like a problem."

In the back row of the parking lot, Caleb stood with his hands on the hood of a minivan, not moving. Three other Calebs swarmed around him, all of them speaking over one another.

"We shouldn't be doing this," said one Caleb, this one rocking back and forth on his heels and hugging himself. "We shouldn't be doing any of this. We need to go back to the Academy. We need to tell the administrators everything and hope we aren't in trouble."

"Imagine how hot she's going to be for you when you bust in and rescue her," another Caleb said, this one strutting back and forth. "This is gonna be awesome, bro. Don't listen to these other shitheads."

The third duplicate stood a bit away from the others. He stroked his chin ponderously. "Has anyone considered the implications of a terrorist organization having access to the same weaponry as our government? Or the fact that there are Garde being used for violent acts against other Garde? I'm beginning to think we don't know as much about our situation as we should."

"We know exactly enough," whined the first duplicate. He tugged at the silent Caleb's arm—that one, Isabela surmised, must be the real Caleb, since these duplicates were all trying to coax him to action. "Please! Please can we go back?"

The strutting Caleb slapped his nervous counterpart hard across the face. "Shut up, man! Goddamn. You are pathetic."

Meanwhile, a Big Box worker pushing a train of shopping carts paused to stare at the arguing quadruplets. Isabela spotted him first and nudged Ran. "We're attracting attention."

All at once, the clones went silent, although their many mouths were still moving. Nigel had lowered their volume. He jogged forward, shoving through the duplicates to get at the real Caleb.

"You all right, mate?"

Caleb looked up. "Huh?" He stretched, the movement seeming painful. "Sorry. I spaced."

Nigel looked around, drawing Caleb's attention to his squabbling copies.

"Oh," Caleb said. "I didn't . . ."

"Quit listening to the voices, yeah?" Nigel said quietly. "We got work to do."

Caleb closed his eyes. In a blur of ghostly movement, the duplicates became incorporeal and flowed back into Caleb. Isabela shuddered. The Big Box store employee screamed and ran in the other direction.

"Oops," Caleb said.

With a burping sound, the engine of the minivan came to life. Caleb used his telekinesis to unlock the doors.

"We should probably go," he said.

"You think?" Isabela replied.

Caleb looked at her, surprise registering on his face. "You look . . . better."

Isabela groaned. "I'll tell you in the car, weirdo."

With that, they piled into the minivan and headed for New Mexico, the Harvesters and whatever waited beyond.

CHAPTER TWENTY-SEVEN

TAYLOR COOK
A ROOM WITH A VIEW—HOFN, ICELAND

THE HARVESTERS HAD COME FOR HER. THEY WERE going to finish what they started back in South Dakota.

That strange girl they had with them. She killed Isabela. Shot her right in the neck with some kind of poison that melted her face.

No. No . . . she was panicking. *Get it together, Taylor.*

Isabela wasn't dead, just knocked out. The scars on her face weren't from the girl's weapon; they were the same as what Taylor had seen that night in the dorms. They were what Isabela was trying to hide.

All that seemed so obvious now, as Taylor dreamily recollected it. Yet, in the moment, she had desperately pumped healing energy into Isabela. It was all she could think to do as chaos unfolded around her.

"I'll protect you," Caleb said, a trio of his duplicates surrounding her.

And then Kopano, frothing at the mouth, mad with anger, like nothing Taylor had seen before—he tossed Caleb into the windshield of the van. He was out of control.

A powerful shriek that made Taylor woozy. A sharp pain in the back of her neck. Was that a dart?

She floated up. Carried by telekinesis. Hard to keep her eyes open. A glowing stone in the middle of the road . . .

Taylor woke up screaming. Her temples throbbed. Woozily, she sat up in a bed that wasn't her own, shoving silk sheets off her body.

Wait. Silk sheets?

Taylor caught her breath and looked around. She was in a king-size bed, the dark blue sheets incredibly soft, the mattress more comfortable than anything she'd ever slept on. The room looked like a posh hotel suite. Directly across from her, a flat-screen television hung over a decorative fireplace. A bookcase stocked with classics; a writing desk; an expansive window with the curtains drawn. A stick of chamomile incense burned on the nightstand.

"What?" Taylor said aloud. "What the hell?"

This room didn't jibe with her idea of the Harvesters. They were bikers or rednecks or both. They didn't invest in hardback copies of the works of Albert Camus.

Cautiously, Taylor swung her feet out of bed. She wore a

pair of flannel pajama pants and a cotton T-shirt. Someone had taken the liberty of changing her. She shivered at the thought.

Across the room was a thick wooden door. Taylor went for it. Only when she stood right in front of it did she realize that there wasn't any doorknob or handle on her side.

She shoved against the door with her telekinesis. It didn't even shake. Must be reinforced somehow.

Taylor ran to the window and threw open the curtains. She gasped.

The view outside was otherworldly. Taylor's window overlooked a lake of the bluest water she had ever seen. Chunks of ice bobbed on the surface, steam rising up from between them, bending the landscape. Beyond that was an ice-covered mountain—a glacier? an icecap?—run through with cerulean veins that glowed in the hazy sunlight.

This was definitely not California.

Taylor pressed her face close to the window, looking down. She was on the second floor. Below, smooth obsidian pebbles fought a battle with stubborn patches of grass for control of the ground. There wasn't another house in sight. However, she did notice a small rowboat beached on the frozen lakeshore.

Taylor didn't know why she had been brought here or where here was. She didn't intend to stick around and find out.

She could jump. Find some place safe. Get home.

Taylor looked for a latch on the window. Like the door,

there was no way to open it.

Well, subtly sneaking away was out of the question. Time for a more direct approach.

Without further hesitation, Taylor picked up the writing desk with her telekinesis and smashed it against the window.

Not even a crack.

Taylor's eyes filled up with angry tears. The window was solid. Probably bulletproof. That didn't stop her from trying again. And again.

She bludgeoned the window with the desk until there was a small pile of wood on the floor at her feet. She ran her fingers across the window. Smooth as the sheets.

Maybe something sharper would do the trick?

As Taylor looked around, she heard a series of beeps from the other side of the door.

Someone was coming in.

Quickly, she grabbed one of the legs from the broken desk and gripped it like a club. She advanced on the door, fully intending to clobber whoever stepped through. She heard a hydraulic wheeze and then a metallic clanking as the steel pylons that reinforced the door gave way. Taylor cocked her arm back. The door slid open . . .

The little girl yelped when Taylor lunged at her. Taylor was just barely able to hold back from striking her. The girl nearly dropped the metal tray she carried.

"Don't hurt me!" the girl shouted. She stumbled back a few steps. Taylor, her teeth bared, brandishing the table leg, realized she must look like a total psychopath.

The girl couldn't be more than ten. She wore a white blouse tucked into a long black skirt and dark clogs. She was pale, dark-haired, her eyes almond-shaped and wide with fear. Upon her tray was a tall glass of water, a couple of Advil and a meticulously folded set of clothes.

"Who are you?" Even though she made an effort to calm herself, Taylor's voice was sharp. She lowered the club. "Where am I?"

The child swallowed hard, then tiptoed by Taylor. She stared at the destroyed desk for a moment, then set the tray down on the bed.

"I am Freyja," the child said nervously, her English accented. "You are in Iceland."

"Iceland?" Taylor exclaimed. "You mean, like . . . ?" She tried to picture where Iceland was on a map, imagining a jagged block of land hovering over Europe. "Iceland?" she repeated.

"Yes," Freyja said. "If your head hurts, I brought you medicine."

Taylor stared at the girl. Her head did hurt, but she wasn't about to ingest anything from this strange child standing guard on her posh prison cell.

"I also brought you a change of clothes," Freyja continued.

Freyja seemed as skittish as Taylor felt. Taylor took a closer look at her. The girl wore a choker with a bulbous red gemstone over the throat. The jewel flashed in the sunlight—or at least that's what Taylor thought at first.

Upon closer examination, Taylor realized there was a steady pulse happening within the stone, like the lights on a computer.

"Freyja, what am I doing here?" Taylor asked, her tone now under control.

The child looked away. "The man downstairs will explain. Also, there is breakfast."

Taylor glanced at the open door. Then, she went to kneel in front of the frightened girl.

"Are you in trouble?" Taylor asked. "Did they take you, too?"

Freyja gave a tug at her choker, which, Taylor realized, did not appear to have a release clasp. She nodded slowly, her watery gaze now fixed on Taylor.

"If you're good," Freyja whispered, "nothing bad will happen to me."

"If . . . I'm good?" Taylor's throat tightened. She stood up. "Yeah, that doesn't sound sinister at all."

Again clutching the broken table leg, Taylor left the frightened child behind to go see this "man downstairs." Outside her room, her surroundings became clearer. She was in a modernized log cabin, the hallway chicly decorated with paintings and sculptures. There were a couple of bedrooms identical to hers, their reinforced doors open. Their beds hadn't been slept in. At the end of the hall, by the stairs, was a bathroom with gilded fixtures, obsidian floor tiles and a Jacuzzi. There was a closed door kitty-corner to that, presumably the master bedroom.

Whoever the pervert was who lived here, he had fancy taste.

Taylor crept downstairs. She heard music—some eighties-sounding synth band played at a respectful volume. Her stomach growled; she smelled bacon and pancakes. The stairs led to a living area that featured a couple of lush sectionals and a tastefully large flat-screen television mounted above another fireplace. The whole downstairs was open. She could see into the kitchen—all glittering stainless steel and polished countertops.

The so-called man downstairs sat at the kitchen counter, reading a book and sipping a cup of coffee. He didn't look like much of a man to Taylor; the guy looked like a teenager like herself. He had soft features only slightly offset by his sternly slicked-over brown hair. He wore a cashmere turtleneck and immaculately pressed slacks.

Taylor didn't wait for him to notice her. She chucked the table leg at him.

He held up a hand and the chunk of wood stopped in midair. Telekinesis.

He was Garde. But if he was also a Harvester . . . that didn't make any sense.

Taylor didn't waste time thinking about it.

"Why the hell have you brought me here, you creepy asshole?" she shouted. At the same time, from the kitchen, she grabbed a trio of cast-iron skillets and a butcher knife with her telekinesis. She flung these objects at the boy, who hadn't been able to speak at all.

He deflected each of them except the butcher knife. The blade arced through his mug, shattering it, and spraying his off-white sweater with coffee. He frowned.

Something hit Taylor in the back of the legs. A sofa. He'd pulled it into her. She fell backwards, landed softly.

"Stop," the guy commanded.

She didn't. Again with her telekinesis, she picked up the shards of his mug. Soon, they were buzzing around his face like a swarm of porcelain hornets. The guy was having a difficult time fending them off.

Taylor heard a shriek and a thud. She turned in time to see Freyja come tumbling down the stairs. The small girl's body rag-dolled to the floor, her forehead hitting the bottom step with a sickening crack.

"No!" Taylor yelled and tried to get up from the sofa. Blood was already pooling beneath Freyja's head.

But Taylor couldn't get up. Or . . . she didn't want to. A deep sense of calm settled over her body. Moments ago she'd been tense, on the attack. Now, her muscles were relaxing, her heart rate slowing. She felt the way she did after an especially hot shower, like she could just melt.

Her head heavy, she looked to the guy at the kitchen counter. He stared at her. Focused on her. There was a spot of blood on his cheek from where she managed to cut him.

"What . . . are you doing to me?" Taylor asked sleepily.

"I am making you calm," he said, his accent similar to Freyja's. "My name is Einar. I am not here to hurt you. In fact, no matter what you do here, you will not be harmed."

He pointed across the room, towards Freyja's slumped little body. "She will be hurt instead."

Taylor blinked. Analytically, the threat on a child's life disgusted her, but the dire situation didn't quite penetrate her dreamy sense of tranquility. She just wanted to chill out and float away.

"I guess . . ." Taylor shrugged. "I guess I should heal her or something, right?"

Einar studied her. "I will let you do that in a moment, but first you need to accept the reality of your situation."

Taylor put her feet up on the couch. "Sure. I accept it."

Einar rolled his eyes. "I've calmed you too much. Hold on."

The mellow vibes that had washed over Taylor like a gentle wave receded, like a shark was suddenly in the water. Her adrenaline kicked back in, her heart raced. She shot off the couch, gave Einar a horrified look and raced to Freyja's side. The fact that she hadn't done this immediately appalled Taylor—how could she just sit there on the couch?

It wasn't her. This Einar guy had done something to her.

"She's just a little girl," Taylor said as she knelt down next to Freyja.

"Yes. She's just an ordinary little girl taken from a small fishing village up the coast. Her parents love her. They would like her returned. If you behave, that might be possible," Einar intoned. The speech sounded practiced.

"You're—you're an animal," Taylor said over her shoulder.

She took Freyja's head in her hands and healed a gash at the base of her skull. The girl, still unconscious, let out a tiny moan. Taylor looked her over quickly; she was bruised from her tumble down the stairs, but none of her other injuries seemed life threatening.

Taylor stood up and rounded on Einar. He had returned to the kitchen and was pouring himself another cup of coffee.

She stalked towards him. "I don't know what sick, psycho cult thing this is—"

Einar laughed. "You think I'm one of those Harvester idiots? That's . . . actually, that's quite insulting."

Taylor picked up a broken piece of Einar's mug. She brandished the shard like a knife.

"I don't care who you are," Taylor said. She made an effort to keep her voice steady, even though her knees were shaking. "I'm leaving and I'm taking the kid with me. If you try to stop us, I swear to God, I'll cut your throat."

"God, you Americans, always like something out of an action movie," Einar said. He picked a piece of his broken mug off a plate of pancakes and bacon, flicked it aside and slid the plate towards Taylor. "I made this for you. Eat and we can talk."

He was so calm; that both frightened and angered Taylor. "You aren't listening—"

"No. You aren't listening."

Taylor felt a sharp pressure on her chin and then her head was being whipped around. He had grabbed her with his telekinesis. He was strong—stronger than she was. With Einar controlling her head, Taylor had no choice but to swing her body around to follow. He forced her gaze upwards, to a corner of the room.

A security camera.

"I am not the one who hurts the girl," Einar said. "They are watching us. This place is wired. If they lose connection, if you misbehave, if you refuse their requests—they will kill her. Then, they will bring in someone else. Another powerless innocent. One after the next, until you comply. If the fate of strangers fails to compel you, they'll move on to people you do know." Einar's voice cracked. He paused, clearing his throat. "You don't want that on your conscience, do you, Taylor?"

Einar released his hold over her. Taylor let out a breath and slumped against the counter, her neck aching. She glared at him.

"Who—who are they?"

"The Foundation for a Better World," Einar said. "They are a private company that recruits people like us—Garde—whose powers can have a positive impact on society."

"You kidnapped me," Taylor seethed. "That's not recruitment."

"The current political climate forces the Foundation to operate using somewhat unorthodox methods," Einar said, almost like he was reading from a press release.

Taylor continued to stare at him. He was unflappable, almost robotic. She wanted to run, but sensed that would be considered misbehavior.

Einar watched her back. He picked up a piece of bacon

from the plate he'd prepared for her. "Do you mind?" he asked, before biting into it.

"What . . . what do they want from me?" Taylor asked quietly.

"That is the good news, Taylor," Einar said with a smile. "They only want you to do what you do best. What comes naturally. They want you to heal people."

CHAPTER TWENTY-EIGHT

KOPANO OKEKE • CALEB CRANE
FRESNO, CALIFORNIA

THEY HELD ON TO THE MINIVAN FOR ONLY A FEW hours.

"Someone will have reported this stolen," Isabela explained. "The Academy people are probably already looking for us. We don't want to add local cops, too. Not to mention, that nerd at the grocery store might have reported your little scene with the clones."

"I can get us another car," Caleb offered. He drove without taking his eyes off the road, always minding the speed limit. "It's no problem."

"Not just any car," Isabela said. "We need the right car. A car that nobody will miss."

Kopano thought the Brazilian sounded a lot like his father. A gifted scammer. Those two would get along. Imagine the grifts Udo could have pulled if Isabela were his daughter. He pictured the two of them working together, the daydream ending with short-tempered Isabela berating his father. On a different day, the thought would have made Kopano smile.

He stared out the window, still thinking about last night.

The guy in the shirt and tie had done something to him, of that Kopano had no doubt. Kopano had thought he was a friend—he'd wanted to take a break in the middle of the fight to hug this well-dressed stranger!—but now felt only emptiness towards him.

And then the anger. Reflecting on what he had done, it was as if he'd had an out-of-body experience. He remembered the violence felt like pressure building up inside him. It felt so good to unleash. Pummeling those Harvesters, smashing their faces with his rock-solid fists. When they weren't enough to sate him, he had turned on Caleb and his duplicates.

Whoever got close, he threw all his strength against. They tried to fight back, but in his rage he was unbreakable.

Kopano bit his lip. He had never thought of himself as a violent person. What he'd done last night . . . that was not heroic. The devil with his briefcase had forced him to act that way.

But the very fact that his Legacies made him capable of such acts . . . he could now understand why Ran had sworn off her powers for a time. What if someone made him do that again?

His companions had been looking at him differently.

Warily. Kopano had noticed.

Had he killed any of those men? He wasn't in control of his actions and they were certainly trying to kill him, but that didn't make him forget the bodies he'd left broken on the highway. It was self-defense. It was mind control. It was . . .

Kopano rubbed his knuckles. Tried not to think about it.

"There!" Isabela shouted, pointing at a highway sign for Fresno Yosemite International Airport. "That will be perfect!"

Caleb guided their minivan towards the exit. Isabela turned around in her seat and held out her hand to Nigel.

"I will need some money," she declared.

Nigel dug into his pocket and produced the wad of bills he'd stolen from one of the Harvesters. Kopano's frown deepened; his brutality had made that possible, his roommate looting the gravely injured.

"Not exactly rolling in it," Nigel said, counting through the wadded bills. "Need to make sure we got money for petrol if we want to make it to New Mexico."

Nigel set some of the cash aside and handed Isabela the rest. She counted through it.

"It'll do," she said.

"Heartened to hear it," Nigel replied.

They drove into the airport, where Caleb and Isabela got out. Kopano took over driving duties. He hadn't been behind the wheel since his days running illicit errands in Lagos. He navigated back towards the gas station they had just passed—the last one before the airport—where they had agreed to meet back up once Caleb and Isabela had acquired a new vehicle.

"She's good to have around, innit she?" Nigel said, referring to Isabela.

"Yes," Ran agreed. "We are lucky to have someone so . . . ethically flexible."

"Speaking of which, what'd you make of those two last night?" Nigel asked. "Fancy boy in the suit and his sidekick the Loralite grower."

Kopano's hands tightened on the wheel at the mention of the mind controller.

"Not Earth Garde," Ran said simply.

"Yeah, bloody obvious, that," Nigel replied. He itched the bandage on his calf. "But who, then? Free agents? Reckon that was a Mog blaster he shot me with."

"Yes," Ran agreed. "That was strange."

"I thought the Academy had all of us Legacy types rounded up," Nigel continued thoughtfully. "I know some countries didn't join the party but I figured our people at least had tabs on 'em. Spies or what have you. So is there some other group out there? Some shadow Academy we don't know about? One fulla ne'er-do-wells in dress-up?"

The picture Nigel painted—a murky one, where Garde did not all work together for the betterment of mankind—greatly disturbed Kopano. He parked alongside the gas station, thrusting the shifter into place with more force than was necessary. He sensed both Nigel and Ran watching him.

"I'm going inside," Kopano announced. Without waiting

for a response, he got out of the van and slammed the door.

He thought of the bodies in the road, of Taylor being carried off by a strange Garde with malicious intentions. Anger bubbled up inside him. Not the violent rage the mind controller had burned into him, but a righteous fury that such awful things could happen. This world was not as he'd imagined.

✧ ✧ ✧

"What's it like? Pretending to be someone you aren't?"

Isabela and Caleb wandered through Fresno International Airport's long-term parking lot. Just two travelers who had misplaced their car. Isabela had altered her features again. She appeared as a woman in her midthirties with tied-back black hair and glasses, wearing a professional if colorful pantsuit.

She shot him a glare when he asked his question, then quickened her pace so she could walk a few steps ahead of him.

"I already went over this with the others," she said, a note of exasperation in her voice. "I am not pretending to be anyone. That is me. At least, it is who I should be. Who I used to be."

"Oh, I don't mean that," Caleb explained hurriedly. "I mean like when you pretended to be Professor Nine or . . . or right now. How you're looking like, uh, an attractive Spanish teacher, I guess?"

Isabela smirked and raised an eyebrow at him. "Did you

have a crush on your Spanish teacher, Caleb?"

"I took German."

"Of course you did."

Caleb didn't know what that was supposed to mean, but he sensed it was an insult. Last night, he and his duplicates had stood over Isabela's prone body, protected her, while Taylor tried to heal her. But he didn't expect any special treatment from the Brazilian. What did his older brother used to call him? A magnet for mockery? That's just how it was.

"A middle-aged woman and her goofy son will draw less attention than two teenagers," Isabela said simply.

"Oh. Okay." Caleb frowned, but didn't dispute the goofy part.

They wandered down another row of cars. Isabela tapped her fingers on her chin, looking for the perfect vehicle. Caleb thought she was done talking, so was surprised when Isabela decided to elaborate.

"It is liberating, to be someone else," she said. "And it's enlightening. Seeing the world through different eyes. Seeing the way the world looks back at you, how it can be so different depending on which face you have on."

Caleb nodded, feeling a slight sense of jealousy. "Yeah. I imagine it'd be freeing."

She looked over her shoulder at him, an eyebrow raised. "What is it like to be able to physically confront the parts of yourself that you don't like, hmm?"

Caleb snorted. "What? I don't know."

"Of course you do. All those duplicates. Some of them mean, some of them geeky, some of them strange, some of them perverted." She smirked. "There are parts of me that I would like to slap across the face, if they would pop out of my brain for just a minute."

"Really?" Caleb smiled.

"No, I am perfect," Isabela replied sharply. She got up on her tiptoes and tapped Caleb on the forehead. "What is it like in there? Do they ever shut up?"

Caleb looked away. "No. Not really."

"Hmm. You know, I heard you before the Wargames started, telling Lofton your strategy ideas. He did not listen because he was stupid. But they were not bad ideas. Not as good as mine, of course, but not bad." She patted Caleb gently on the cheek. "I think you should practice being the loudest voice in the room. Or, at least, being the loudest voice in your own head. Yes?"

"Yeah," Caleb agreed. "Okay."

"Good," Isabela said, clapping her hands. She pointed out a shiny black Escalade. "Now, steal me that car."

◇ ◇ ◇

Inside the gas station, Kopano sullenly spun a rack of postcards. Fresno, Death Valley, Salt Lake City, Las Vegas, Reno—all these colorful places flipped past. He wanted to pick a couple out to send to his little brothers. He'd written to them every week, telling them about his days at the Academy. With every postcard, the details about Kopano's training started to seem, to him, to be mundane and routine.

But his brothers always wrote back with enthusiasm, eager for more details.

His mother and father were less forthcoming in their letters. A few sentences here and there. A detail about some distant cousin who had struck it rich or fallen ill. A prayer. Earth Garde had provided them with a new apartment on Victoria Island, a secure place where they would be protected. His mother only wrote that it was "too big."

Finally, Kopano had something exciting to tell his relatives. A story of adventure scrawled on a colorful postcard. An ambush on the road, a great battle.

But adventure in the real world—the ugly real world—it no longer seemed so glamorous.

He remembered how it was after he and his father were attacked in Lagos. How he'd wanted to just go home and sleep. He wished he could do that now.

Kopano jumped as Nigel clapped him on the back. He hadn't heard his roommate approach, so lost was he in his gloomy thoughts.

"You all right, mate?"

"No. I don't think I am."

"You want to cuddle up in my lap, have a chat about it?"

Kopano looked down at the much smaller Nigel, his frown unwavering.

"This is serious," he said.

"I'm just taking the piss," Nigel replied. He glanced over his shoulder. The gas station attendant—a very tan man in his fifties wearing a sweat-stained tank top—watched them with narrowed eyes. The two of them certainly made an odd pair. Nigel elbowed Kopano. "Come on. Let's retire to the privacy of the snack aisle."

Kopano gave the postcard rack one last spin, then followed Nigel. They were surrounded on all sides by colorful packages, greasy chips and candies. Kopano's stomach growled. He ignored it.

"My mom never wanted me to eat stuff like this. She said it was how my father got his fat belly," Kopano said, wistfully dragging his fingers across a package featuring a cartoon cheetah bathing in cheese dust.

"My mum was a health nut, too. Also an actual nutter, come to think of it." Nigel put his hands on his hips and looked up at Kopano. "You want some crisps? That what this is about?"

Kopano went on as if he hadn't heard Nigel. "When I first got my powers, my family was proud. All except for my mother. The way she looked at me changed. She saw me as . . . as an abomination. Something against God. Taylor told me about those Harvester men, about the things they preached. I think, if she had been born an American, my mom might have been one of them."

Nigel leaned against the shelves, the better to look at Kopano. "Brother, I doubt that. Those Harvester wankers don't raise upstanding young lads like yourself."

"I am starting to think . . ." Kopano hesitated. "I am starting to think maybe my mom was right to look at me like that. I thought the Academy would be like one of those superhero movies, you know? But now I see what I am capable of. Now I see how the world works. For the rest of our lives, we'll have to fight like we did last night."

Nigel bit the inside of his cheek, gathering his thoughts. "I know the look you're talking about, brother. The hairy eyeball. My parentals used to hit me with that before I even got Legacies. They couldn't understand me or didn't want to. Shipped me off to a private school with a bunch of hateful rich assholes."

Kopano slowly turned to look at Nigel. "That sucks."

Nigel nodded. "It did indeed. Couldn't wait to get outta that place. John Smith gives me a telepathic ring and I bust out of Pepperpont faster than an eye blink. I felt like you did—like it was the start of some grand bloody adventure and I was the main character. All those years of suffering were leading up to this." Nigel looked down at the floor. "Got my rude awakening during the invasion. Mogs came to our hideout, killed some of my new friends and a whole lot of soldiers. Brutal stuff. Grown men screaming and crying, dragging themselves about with missing limbs. Not like in the comic books, you know?"

"No," Kopano said quietly. "It's not like that at all."

Nigel gripped Kopano's shoulder with enough force that Kopano felt his Legacy almost trigger. "But listen, I stuck it out after that, nightmares and all. So did Ran."

"She swore off her Legacies."

"Oh, so it was some other quiet Japanese girl blowing shit up last night?" Nigel asked. "She did what she had to do, when it mattered. To save lives. The world ain't pretty like we hoped, mate, it's not sequined leotards and capes."

Kopano made a face. "I didn't imagine sequins."

"Makes one of us, eh?" Nigel smirked. "Point is, we don't have to fight ugly with ugly. We can be the change we want to see in the world. You know that fuckin' cliché? The Loric didn't make us monsters and they didn't make us heroes. They just gave us bloody Legacies and said have at it. We choose what happens next."

Kopano nodded along for most of Nigel's speech, but still couldn't shake the memory of the broken bodies he'd left in the middle of the highway. "I couldn't choose last night," he said quietly and ran a hand over his face. "If I can be made to do that . . . maybe my mom is right. Maybe we shouldn't have such power, maybe—"

"I been meaning to tell you," Nigel interrupted. "Those blokes you roughed up, they were all alive when we left 'em. I should know. I was the one with the foresight to nick what they had in their pockets."

Kopano's eyebrows rose. "Really? I didn't . . . ?"

"Nah, mate. Some of 'em might not be walking right for a while, but they're all still wasting space on our unhappy planet. Even Hulked out, your heart's still big enough to pull punches, ya bloody softie."

Outside, a car horn honked. Kopano poked his head out of the snack aisle and spotted Isabela sitting shotgun in an enormous SUV. An Escalade. His father used to talk about buying a car like that when he struck it rich. Isabela dangled her arm out the window. She caught Kopano looking at her, wiggled her fingers and winked.

For the first time that day, Kopano smiled.

He turned back to Nigel.

"Yes," Kopano said. "I am ready. Let's go rescue Taylor." He paused, then put his hand on his friend's shoulder. "Thank you, Nigel."

"Wasn't nothing, mate."

Kopano left the aisle, walking out to the SUV. Nigel lingered for a moment. Ran, who had been listening from the next aisle over, appeared quietly at his side.

"You lied to him," Ran observed. "Many of those men were surely dead."

Nigel's frown deepened. "You want to tell the big guy that?"

Ran shook her head. "Such knowledge would do him no good."

CHAPTER TWENTY-NINE

TAYLOR COOK
HOFN, ICELAND

ALL SHE HAD TO DO WAS HEAL WHO THEY TOLD HER to. That was the deal.

"In exchange," Einar explained, "you will be taken care of. Once you've proven yourself to the Foundation, they will build you a place like this. You'll want for nothing."

Taylor stood at the far end of the marble kitchen counter. She still held one of the stainless steel kitchen knives. It made her feel more comfortable and Einar didn't seem to mind. He sat on a stool and picked at the plate of food he'd prepared for her. Behind them, Freyja lay on the couch, tentatively rubbing the spot on her head that had been cracked open.

The flat-screen TV, the record player and speakers, the shelves of books ranging from pretentious literary novels to pulp detective stories, the massive collection of Blu-rays. The more Taylor looked around, the more she began to see this place as an extension of Einar—a dream house for a studious young loner.

"So they built this place for you?" she asked. "Because you proved yourself?"

He nodded. "They've treated me well."

"I guess they didn't kidnap you, then?"

He raised an eyebrow. "My recruitment was not painless either."

"But you gave in, so they hooked you up."

Einar didn't respond. He cut off a corner of cold pancake and swirled it around in a skinned-over pool of syrup.

"So if I play nice, they'll build me and my dad a five-hundred-acre farm in South Dakota? Let us live out there in peace except for when I need to go off to heal someone?"

Einar set down his fork. "I'm sure a farm could be arranged. But you will have to live somewhere outside the jurisdiction of Earth Garde."

"That's what? Iceland, China, Russia . . . the Middle East?"

"Venezuela," Einar offered. "Many other nations."

"Oh, so many enticing options," Taylor said dryly.

"Better than being a prisoner who is forced to fight shadow wars for a corrupt government agency," Einar replied.

Taylor raised an eyebrow. "Oh, you aren't a prisoner?"

"No. Not like you were."

Since Taylor had gotten ahold of herself, she'd been able to better survey her surroundings. There were more cameras than the one Einar had forced her to look at. There was at least one in every room. From her current position, Taylor could see the camera hanging over Einar's refrigerator, the one positioned beneath his television and the one tucked into the corner aimed at the front door and staircase. She suspected that the glowing gem on Freyja's choker was a camera as well.

"They must really trust you," she said. "To let you live all by yourself out here without supervision."

Einar followed Taylor's gaze to the camera. He sneered. "Please. As if you aren't under constant surveillance at the Academy."

Taylor's stomach twisted into a knot. Waking up here had been so disorienting, her short confrontation with Einar so infuriating, she hadn't paused for a moment to wonder about the fate of her friends.

"What happened . . . ?" Her fingers tightened on the knife's handle. "What happened to the people I was with?"

Einar shrugged. "I don't know."

"That's it?" Taylor asked. "That's all you can say? They're my friends."

"If it helps, those Harvester fools were very poorly trained," Einar said. "I'd wager that at least some of your friends survived."

Taylor fought back the urge to stab him by looking in Freyja's direction. The little girl had curled into a ball on the couch, staring off into space.

Another detail popped into Taylor's mind. Isabela with

the dart sticking out of her neck, courtesy of a girl in a hijab.

"What about your friend?" Taylor asked. "Where's she?"

Einar's expression darkened. She had hit a nerve.

"I don't know," Einar said evenly.

"Did you leave her behind?"

"She knew the mission parameters."

A tense silence hung over him. Einar picked up his fork again, but didn't eat anything. Taylor watched him, wondering how far she could push him. Further, she decided.

"Must get pretty lonely out here by yourself. Why don't these Foundation people kidnap you some friends?"

"I have friends," Einar said somewhat defensively. "There are others. We . . . occasionally socialize."

"Until you ditch them."

"Shut up. You were unconscious. You don't know the situation."

Taylor tried to make her voice as tender and understanding as possible. "You know, I was pretty weirded out by the Academy. I didn't want to go there. There's still some stuff about it that bothers me, like all the army-type training. But this? Getting kidnapped by some . . . charity? Corporation . . . ?"

"Group of private investors," Einar said stiffly.

"Whatever. I mean, this is gross." She glanced at Freyja. "The Academy never threatened any children to get me to go there."

"They didn't have to," Einar replied. "They simply arrested and incarcerated you. Forced you to sign your rights away."

"What about her rights?" Taylor waved in Freyja's direction, realized she was still holding the knife and finally set it down. "The Academy's never killed anyone."

Einar chuckled. "They haven't? What do you think all that combat training is for? Who do you think Earth Garde fights?"

Taylor thought of Kopano—the good he talked about doing, the imagined enemies he would one day bring to justice.

"Bad guys," she said, realizing how dumb the words sounded only once they were out of her mouth.

"That's such a meaningless term," Einar replied with another infuriating chuckle. "We Human Garde, we're all still young. What do you think will happen when we're older? Wars between countries will be fought between our kind, decided by our kind. Earth Garde hopes to get a monopoly on that."

"And your precious Foundation doesn't?"

Einar stood up, took the plate of food and dumped it into a tall garbage can.

"The Foundation only invests in Garde with nonviolent Legacies," he said, his back to her. "The others are viewed as threats to the human race."

"Invests," Taylor repeated with a shake of her head. She waited for Einar to turn back her way so she could study him. "Seriously, you're acting like this isn't insane and illegal. Did they brainwash you or something?"

"No," he replied curtly. "Feel free to make use of my home.

You know what will happen if you do anything stupid. I'm going to take a nap."

"A nap. You're going to take a nap?"

Einar nodded and went around the counter—taking the long way so he wouldn't come into stabbing range—and headed for the stairs. "We have an appointment later. Well, you do. You'll want to be rested, too."

◇ ◇ ◇

Taylor couldn't rest. Now that the effects of the tranquilizer had worn off, she felt too energetic. Instead, she explored Einar's Icelandic hideaway.

For all his movies and books and expensive gadgets, the first thing Taylor noticed was that the place lacked a computer. Maybe there was a laptop or something up in his bedroom, but Taylor suspected that wasn't the case. Just like the Academy regulated their internet use, so did this shadowy Foundation.

After a little poking around, Taylor went to the front door. Her hand hesitated over the handle. Was she allowed outside? She figured there would be a hydraulic lock like the one on her bedroom if the outdoors was off-limits. Taylor tested the knob. The door opened easily.

Cold air rushed in. After a few months in California, Taylor wasn't used to the chill. And she was still wearing the flannel pajamas she'd woken up in. She opened a nearby coat closet and found a pair of fur-lined moccasins and a heavy leather jacket. They were Einar's. She could smell his sandalwood cologne on the coat and it almost changed her mind about going outside. She took a breath, shrugged on the coat and stepped into the bracing air.

Oddly, the seclusion reminded Taylor of home. She looked around the rocky landscape as she stepped away from Einar's cabin—not another house in sight. There was a dark blue hatchback parked along the side of the house. She could make that her getaway vehicle if worse came to worst.

Taylor laughed bitterly. Wasn't this already the worst? When she developed her powers, she couldn't have imagined a more bizarre fate. She'd resented having to go to the Academy, but at least she was settling in there. The instructors were kind, she had friends, she was learning about herself. This . . . this Foundation situation, it was on a whole different level of strange and disturbing.

She heard footsteps crunch behind her. Little Freyja had followed her outside, snuggled up in a blanket.

A dark part of Taylor's mind reminded her that she hardly knew this girl. She could make a run for it. If she could live with Freyja on her conscience . . .

No. She couldn't. She would never be able to live with herself. Taylor glanced once more at the car. There wouldn't be any escape. Not if she couldn't figure out how to save the kid, too.

Taylor looked up at what she thought was Einar's window. She wondered how the Foundation had convinced him to join them. Did he have a Freyja, too? He was so cold, it seemed unlikely.

"Thank you," Freyja said quietly, arriving at her side. "For healing me."

"You're welcome," Taylor replied. "I'm sorry that you have to go through this."

"Me too," Freyja said. "Do you know when I'll get to go home?"

"No, I don't."

"When you give them what they want, right?"

"I guess so."

"Will that be soon?"

"I don't know."

The two lapsed into a melancholy silence. Taylor trudged towards the crystalline lake, Freyja following a few steps behind her. A chill wind swept in over the water, bobbing the chunks of vivid blue ice that floated on the surface. She could hear the ice crackling and shifting as the blocks bumped against each other.

"It's beautiful here, at least," Taylor said.

Freyja said nothing. Taylor looked over at her, saw that she was worming her index finger under the choker.

"It's cold on my skin," Freyja said with a sigh.

"Do you remember what happened before?" Taylor asked. "When you fell down the stairs?"

"This . . . this shocked me," Freyja said, dropping her hand away from the collar as if she were scared it would happen again. "I fainted."

"Jesus Christ," muttered Taylor. "This is demented."

Taylor turned away from the frozen lake and headed around the side of the house. She wanted to see the place from every angle.

"What're you doing?" Freyja asked, dutifully following behind her.

"Just looking around."

"For what?"

"I'm not sure yet."

On the back of the house, Taylor found a small wooden sunporch, the reddish timber coated in a thin layer of frost. The porch overlooked a rock garden. Polished stones were stacked atop of each other, some of them decorated with hardy vines. A small fountain stood in the middle of it all, although it was turned off at the moment.

At the back of the rock garden stood a high wooden fence. Taylor approached, walking the perimeter of the fence. It was a square, about twenty feet in each direction. On the side nearest the porch was a door with a keypad just like the one on Taylor's room.

"What's he got back there?" Taylor wondered aloud.

"I don't know," Freyja replied, her teeth chattering.

"If you're cold, you can go inside," Taylor said.

Freyja remained stubbornly nearby. Was she afraid that Taylor would try to escape if Freyja let her out of her sight? Taylor couldn't blame her.

With her telekinesis, Taylor knocked over one of the stone sculptures and floated a good-size block of granite over to the fence. Freyja jumped out of the way.

"What're you doing?" Freyja asked.

Taylor hopped up onto the stone. If she jumped from there, she could reach the top of the fence. "I want to see what's in there."

She leaped up, grasping the wooden barrier with both hands. She pulled herself the rest of the way, managed to swing one leg up so that she was straddling the fence.

Down below, inside the cube of fence, was just another rock.

But not just any rock. This one glittered cobalt blue, but in a shade different from the ice on the lake. The rock made something in Taylor vibrate. It called to her.

Loralite. That was Loralite.

Taylor knew the stories. All she had to do was hop down and touch the alien rock, visualize another stone's location and the Loralite would teleport her across the world. This must be how Einar brought her here.

Freyja let out a sharp cry. Taylor turned her head in time to see the wide-eyed girl clutch at her choker.

"It—it shocked me!" Freyja yelped.

With a frustrated grumble, Taylor climbed down from the fence. She landed next to Freyja and gently stroked the girl's shoulder.

"Sorry. Guess whoever's watching wanted to give me a warning."

Freyja said nothing. She rubbed her neck and stared sullenly at Taylor.

"Come on," Taylor said. "Let's go inside."

Halfway to the back porch, both of them stopped in their tracks. They heard the crackle of gravel and the purr of an engine.

Someone was driving up the solitary road.

Without stopping to think, Taylor ran around the side of the house, Freyja a few steps behind her. She wasn't sure what she was going to do, exactly. If this was some random Icelandic police officer or the mailman—she couldn't very well involve them without risking their life too. Still, she wanted to see who came to this remote location. Maybe it would give her an idea.

Taylor caught sight of the car coming down the road before she fully rounded the cabin's corner. Something about the vehicle gave her pause. It was a green Jeep, mud-splattered and dented from hard driving, with chains on the wheels. There were four men inside, but from her viewpoint Taylor could make out only the one sitting shotgun. He had reddish-brown hair, a thick beard and bulging neck muscles. Even at this distance, Taylor could see the fat scar that ran from his eye to the corner of his mouth.

These were not friendly neighbors.

The Jeep parked in front of the house. Taylor waited a few seconds, hidden around the corner, curious to see what they would do.

Nothing. The men just sat there. One of them rolled down a window to smoke a cigarette.

Freyja was at her side, one of her hands on Taylor's arm. "Who is it?" she whispered, then peeked around the corner to see for herself.

The girl nearly tripped over her own feet in her hurry to backpedal away. Freyja's face had gone ghostly white. She recognized them, Taylor realized. And she was terrified.

"Who are they?" Taylor asked.

"Those are the men," Freyja replied. "The men who took me."

CHAPTER THIRTY

ISABELA SILVA
OUTSIDE SILVER CITY, NEW MEXICO

IT WAS A FOURTEEN-HOUR DRIVE TO SILVER CITY. They bought a map from the gas station to help navigate.

"We want to stick to back roads, yeah?" said Nigel. "Don't want to be spotted."

Isabela drew a random pattern on the Escalade's tinted window. "No one will spot us. And no one will be looking for this car."

Caleb traced his finger east across the map. "There aren't really any back roads, anyway. Or it's all back roads. I can't tell." He held up the map so Nigel, driving, could see. "All the way through the desert."

Nigel nodded. "Lovely." He checked the gas gauge. "Could've nicked us something with a bit more fuel efficiency, Izzy."

She snorted. "That's what you're worried about?"

"Limited funds," Nigel said. "And a long bloody drive."

Ran reached out with her telekinesis and plucked the wad of bills from Nigel's cargo pocket. She counted through them. "I think we have enough," she announced.

"Hope so," Caleb said.

Isabela groaned. "God, we'll be fine. If we run out of money, we get more. No big deal."

"You mean steal more," Kopano said.

"Uh, yeah," Isabela replied. "Obviously."

Kopano was quiet for a moment. "We must find Taylor. That is the most important thing. But when that is done, we should make sure the cars we stole are returned to their owners. And that anything else we take is returned." He looked out the window. "I do not want to be a thief."

"Sure, mate," Nigel said. "We'll send 'em nice thank-you notes, too."

Soon, they had left the city behind and were cutting across the desert. Scrubby plants and cactus whipped by, whorls of reddish sand blown across the hot pavement. They passed through Joshua Tree, the fuzzy branches of the yucca trees reaching up like twisted alien arms. As they drove out of California and into Arizona the land became flat and burned, the view dotted by bursts of emerald palms that stood in opposition to the sun. For stretches, they could see for miles, but then the horizon would rise up and become mountainous. They navigated through chasms, the highway itself cut through the jagged sandstone mountains.

"I just saw a cattle skull on the side of the road," Caleb said as he peered out the window. "You know, with like the horns all bleached by the sun?"

"So?" Nigel replied.

Caleb shrugged. "Dunno. Thought that was just a thing they put in movies to make it seem hot out." He paused thoughtfully. "There's this game we could play. Roadkill bingo?"

"No," Isabela said sharply.

They all took turns behind the wheel. Whoever sat shotgun tried to keep the driver company. The others took turn dozing off, either sitting upright in the middle row or stretched out across the backseat.

Isabela was grateful that they'd found a blanket in the trunk. When she felt herself getting tired from all the sitting around and endless desert, she draped herself across the backseat and pulled the blanket over her. She turned to face the trunk, leaving a small gap in the blanket for air. This way, no one would be able to see her when she dozed off. None of the others commented on her huddled form.

When Isabela woke up, they were driving on the outskirts of Phoenix. It was sunset. The city glittered orange in the distance, an oasis of glass and life after hours of mountains. She shifted around under her blanket to get a look at the others. Nigel and Ran were both asleep, too, Nigel with his head resting on the Japanese girl's shoulder. Isabela smirked at that. In front, Caleb drove while Kopano kept him company.

The two of them were quietly talking about Taylor, going

over the events of the night before for the hundredth time. The guy who had taken her didn't seem like a Harvester. Unlike the cult, whoever he was, he wanted Taylor alive. Both Kopano and Caleb agreed that was a good thing. Well, as much as kidnapping could be a good thing.

"If he has hurt her in any way," Kopano declared, "I will have vengeance."

"Yeah," Caleb agreed. "Me too."

Under her blanket, Isabela rolled her eyes.

"I am sorry, by the way," Kopano said. "For throwing you through the windshield of that car."

Caleb rubbed the back of his neck, which was covered in small cuts and bruised up. Isabela noticed he had been sitting rigidly, but she'd thought that was just Caleb's normal posture. He was hurt, she realized. Ribs probably broken, but hiding it.

"No worries," Caleb told Kopano. "It wasn't you. That prick took control somehow."

Did either of the two would-be heroes know they both had a crush on Taylor? They were both oblivious and going out of their way to be nice, but Isabela figured they had to see each other as competition. All that macho talk, battling over who could promise revenge with the most gravitas. Dense boys. She couldn't wait to tell Taylor about this.

Weeks ago, Isabela realized, she would've been jealous of Taylor getting all this attention. But now, she missed her friend. She even felt a tinge of sadness for the two lovestruck meatheads in the front of the van, at least one of whom would surely be rejected.

Ugh. She was getting soft.

It took another couple of hours to reach New Mexico. By then, night had fallen and they were all awake.

They found Silver City and then Route 15. Caleb unfolded the map and studied it in the Escalade's yellowish dome light. Silver City's architecture was more modest than Phoenix, the buildings not as glittery and lower slung, man-made hunks of stone popping up from the desert.

"Did they want their town to look like a graveyard?" Isabela asked.

"The place we're looking for isn't really in town," Caleb said. "I think it's up north in the forest."

They passed along the edge of town and drove to Gila National Forest. According to the map, the area stretched over four thousand square miles. The rocky desert sloped upwards, gradually giving way to masses of thick, triangular pine trees. The grass grew taller here and didn't look as scorched; it appeared purple and wavy in the moonlight. They ascended via a series of switchbacks, the trees thickened and soon the dots of light from Silver City were swallowed up behind them.

For a while, there wasn't another car on the road. Nearby, a wolf howled.

"Bloody hell," Nigel said. "Of course they would set up in axe murderer country."

"I find it serene," Ran replied.

Nigel smirked at her. "See if you still think that when

312

some inbred bloke in a hockey mask is carving you up into little pieces."

Ran looked back at him. "I would like to see this bloke try."

Isabela chuckled, enjoying the banter. It helped ease the mood a bit. Kopano and Caleb were both wholly focused on the road ahead, ready for battle at any moment.

"Are we sure this is even the right way?" Isabela asked.

As if in answer, a pair of headlights appeared behind them. Kopano squinted into the rearview and slowed down a bit. The glowing headlamps behind them crisscrossed—not a car, but two motorcycles—the bikes soon careening by them up the road. They each carried the sort of leather-clad tough guy who had accosted the Garde last night.

"Want to bet those lads show us the way?" Nigel asked.

"Do not get too close to them," Ran warned.

Kopano let the motorcycles get out of sight, then continued up the winding road through the forest. Five minutes later, as they came around a bend, a wooden sign wreathed in Christmas lights came into view. Scrawled in chipped paint across the boards—*APACHE JACK'S.*

"My dad used to talk about places like this," Caleb said. "Dive bars off the beaten path. Used to brag about all the brawls he got into."

"Thanks for sharing," Isabela said.

A hundred years ago, Apache Jack's was probably a trading post. There was still a hitching rail outside the long brick building, but instead of horses there were now motorcycles parked in front. The gravel parking lot was also filled with trailers, pickup trucks and muscle cars, many of these decorated to look like postapocalyptic war machines. The whole scene was lit by neon beer signs in the bar windows and fire barrels in the parking lot. A couple dozen men milled around the vehicles or drank on the shaded porch. Half of them were armed with either shotguns or rifles.

Kopano slowed the Escalade, but Isabela snapped at him, "Keep going!"

"But . . . she could be in there."

"Does it look like we would belong in that parking lot?" Isabela asked. "I'm surprised they're not already shooting at us. Go, go, go!"

Kopano stepped on the gas and they zoomed by Apache Jack's. Some of the men in the parking lot tracked the Escalade with their eyes, but none of them made any move to follow. As they drove by, Isabela caught a glimpse of some kind of tall wooden structure behind the bar but couldn't make out any details.

They put a half mile of winding road between them and Apache Jack's to make sure they weren't followed. Eventually, Kopano pulled off to the side of the road and killed the engine.

"How are we going to do this?" he asked.

"We can hike in through the woods," Ran said. "Come at the place from the back."

"I should go in alone," Isabela said. "Do . . . what do you call it? Reconnaissance."

They turned around to look at Isabela and all of them jumped when they saw her new appearance.

She had taken on the look of a male midfifties biker. Hefty and hairy, with coarse salt-and-pepper hair tied in a sloppy ponytail. She wore an open leather vest that exposed her prodigious beer belly, a pair of scuffed-up jeans and cowboy boots.

"What do you think?" Isabela asked, her normal voice issuing from the biker's chapped lips.

"Your hottest look yet," Nigel said, staring at her.

"You want to make out with me?" Isabela asked, leering.

Ran reached back and poked Isabela's new belly. "Very good," she said.

Isabela grinned, the biker's teeth yellow and crooked. "Thank you."

"I could go in with you," Caleb offered. He looked around at the others. "No offense to you guys, but the rest of you wouldn't be able to pass for a Harvester."

"No offense taken, mate," Nigel said.

"But if there are any of them in there who were at the fight last night, they will definitely recognize you," Kopano said. "There were a bunch of you."

Caleb frowned. "I guess you're right."

"It'll be easy," Isabela said. "I'll sneak in there, find out if they've got Taylor or the little bitch who shot me and if not I'll ask a few questions. Find out what they know. You all watch from the woods. If I get in trouble, I'll send a signal."

"What kind of signal?" Ran asked.

Isabela shrugged. "I'll have to improvise. So, just keep an eye out."

"If you're gone too long, we'll come in looking for you," Caleb said.

Isabela stroked her blubbery man-belly in a way she hoped was disturbing. "Give me some time, cowboy. This is a slow-moving body I'm in."

Caleb chuckled and looked away.

"Ugh," Nigel added.

"We should try not to kill any of them," Kopano said suddenly. "These people should be brought to justice for what they've done . . ."

Ran and Nigel exchanged a look. Caleb said nothing, just stared out the window.

"Okay?" Kopano pressed.

"With any luck," Isabela said, "they will never know we're here."

The five of them left the Escalade behind and hiked downhill through the trees. They moved cautiously and Nigel used his Legacy to muffle the sounds of their approach. As the lights from Apache Jack's appeared, they realized their caution had been pointless. The Harvesters didn't have any guards posted. Most of them were too busy getting drunk. The Garde huddled in the shadowed cover of the trees and watched them.

"They must think this is a safe place for them," Ran observed.

"Well, the madmen don't lack for artillery," Nigel said,

pointing out a number of armed Harvesters milling around on the bar's back porch.

"These types of guys always carry guns with them," Caleb said. "It's their thing."

"What are they doing with that?" Kopano asked.

He pointed out the wooden structure that Isabela had noticed from the road. It was a twenty-foot-high snake in a ready-to-strike S shape, the thing made out of thin slats of clapboard and wicker. The snake sat atop a mound of sand. At its base—right at the snake's belly—there was a small door secured with a padlock. A few Harvesters milled around the snake, stuffing rags in between the wooden ribs. The wind picked up and carried the smell of gasoline to the Garde.

"That, my friends, is a good old-fashioned effigy," Nigel said. "The nutters are probably gonna light it up and dance around it naked before commencing the orgy." He glanced at Isabela. "Have fun with that."

Her biker's face contorted in a very uncharacteristic moue of disgust. "Nasty."

"That is a cell," Ran observed, pointing at the locked opening. "They are going to put someone in there."

"Our kind are the snakes in their stupid bloody metaphor," Nigel said.

"Taylor," Kopano whispered. "They would . . . they would burn her?"

"Still want to go easy on them, mate?" Nigel asked.

Kopano said nothing. The five of them remained still for a few more moments. Finally, Isabela stood up from her crouch, dramatically knuckling the broad back of her biker body.

"I'm going in," she announced, her voice now gruff enough to match her costume.

"Be careful," Caleb said.

Isabela strutted out of the woods. She walked the way she had seen some of the older men move around the Rio beaches; like her balls were too big for her pants and constantly getting in the way. Belly thrust forward, knees pointed out, shoulders back. When the first Harvester noticed her, she made a show of zipping up her fly as if she'd just returned from pissing in the woods.

Before leaving her friends, Isabela took the pamphlet that Nigel had swiped from one of the defeated Harvesters. If anyone questioned her slovenly alter ego, she planned to use that as her invitation. None of the Harvesters hanging around the back of Apache Jack's paid her any attention. Most of them were too busy putting the finishing touches on the effigy. A pair of scrawny college-age boys with matching sets of cauliflower ears nodded at her as she climbed the porch's rickety staircase.

"You ready for tonight, old-timer?" one of them asked.

"Hell yeah," Isabela replied.

"Can't wait until they light that bitch up," said the other, raising his beer bottle in Isabela's direction, then throwing back the contents.

Isabela grunted a response—that's how these types communicated—and made her way to the bar's back door.

A woman in her fifties sat on a stool next to the entrance, smoking a cigarette. She wore ill-fitting leather, her neck swimming in beads and charms.

"Haven't seen you before," the woman said as she tapped some ash off her cigarette.

"First time," Isabela said. She tried to move past the woman, but she wedged her foot against the screen door. Was this old hag flirting?

"Picked an interesting night to join the movement, honey."

Isabela paused. She sensed the two drunks behind her were now watching her exchange with the woman. She took the pamphlet out of her pocket and handed it over.

"Jimbo asked me to ride up here," she said in her scratchy voice. "Where's he at?"

Isabela detected something wrong immediately. An uneasy silence fell across the back patio. The older woman's face fell and she traded looks with the two men standing behind Isabela.

After a moment, the woman spoke. "You ain't heard?"

"Heard what?"

"Reverend Jimbo's dead," she said. "Killed by those abominations."

Oops, thought Isabela and stifled a smirk. Instead, she clenched her fists.

"When did that happen?" she growled. "How?"

"Last night," the woman replied. "Probably while you was making your way here." She shook her head. "We're going to pay them back, though. Promise you that."

Isabela nodded. "Who's in charge now?"

The woman jerked a thumb over her shoulder. "You want to talk to Darryl. Big guy. Skull tattoo."

Isabela grunted her thanks and was finally allowed to step inside. The smell of gasoline struck her immediately. The back hallway of Apache Jack's was cluttered with canisters of the stuff. Up ahead, she heard heavy metal blasting and men and women shouting at each other. She lumbered in the direction of the barroom.

She passed by a pair of bathrooms, the stink rolling out of them unacceptable. Isabela kept the disgust from registering on her face; she wasn't alone. Up ahead, two men with shotguns stood guard in front of a metal door. They were both thickly built, scarred up, with the Harvester symbol branded into their forearms. They weren't day-players like some of these people; they were real killers.

Isabela made note of them. Unusual to have a couple of badass dudes guarding the bar's freezer. She nodded as she walked by them. They nodded back.

She emerged into the bar proper. The screaming and thrashing music was worse than the garbage Nigel listened to. The room was crowded, nearly every seat filled. Mostly men, but a few women—an assortment of bikers and cowboy types, all of them with that same stupid tattoo. They guzzled beer and shouted at each other about conspiracy theories that Isabela couldn't make sense of—chem trails, sovereign citizens, Loric anal probes, blah blah blah.

A huge photo of a greasy old man sat on the bar

surrounded by wilted flowers and shell casings. The Harvesters kept coming over to dribble beer or liquor in front of it. She assumed that was the deceased reverend.

No one paid Isabela any undue attention. She bellied up to the bar and surveyed the crowd, looking for a skull tattoo. Finally, she noticed the bartender, the sleeves ripped off his flannel shirt, had a skull with a dagger plunged through the eyehole inked on his bicep. She waved him over.

"Everything's on the house," he said, "on account of the funeral."

"Get me a beer," she said.

The bartender went and came back with a frothy mug. Isabela resisted the urge to wrinkle her nose at the glass, which had smudges all over the rim.

"You Darryl?" she asked.

The bartender squinted at her. "Nah," he replied when Isabela simply stared back at him. He waved towards the guarded freezer. "If you want him, he's in with the creature."

The creature.

Isabela grunted her thanks and waited, not drinking any of the beer. Subterfuge was one thing, but she wasn't risking catching whatever contagious stupidity was circulating around this bar.

She sat on a stool and waited, keeping an eye on the cooler. After about five minutes, the door squealed open and a tall man wearing a black duster emerged. The man was bald, a complicated spiderweb tattooed across his skull. The woman outside had been being literal.

Darryl said something to the guards, then headed down the hall, into one of the smelly bathrooms. Casually, Isabela got up from her stool, walked past the two guards and followed him in.

Two stalls and two urinals, a sink with a cracked mirror, mold and mildew all over the broken floor tiles. Isabela paused just inside the doorway, observing it all. There was a Harvester at a urinal. Darryl stood at the sink, washing blood off his hands. Isabela checked the bathroom door. It had a dead bolt.

None of the men looked at each other. Isabela went to the other urinal and set her mug of beer on top of the cracked porcelain. She pretended to pee while waiting for the other Harvester to leave. He didn't wash his hands.

As soon as he walked out, she used her telekinesis to lock the bathroom's dead bolt. She turned around to look at Darryl.

"Heard you got one of those abominations," she said.

Darryl glanced over his shoulder and grunted. He continued scrubbing his hands. "Got the thing's blood on me. Don't want to catch some extraterrestrial plague."

"She still alive?"

"Of course. We going to burn the sin out of her proper, like Jimbo would've wanted." Darryl half turned, surprised to find Isabela standing right behind him. "Who are—?"

Isabela smashed her beer mug across his face.

Darryl reeled but didn't go down. Blood streamed down the side of his face, into one of his eyes. He took a swing at her, but Isabela ducked with agility that must have seemed supernatural for a fat biker. She thrust out with her telekinesis and slammed Darryl's face into the bathroom mirror.

He slumped over the sink, breathing heavily but not yet unconscious. Isabela leaped onto his back. She clenched her legs around his torso and looped her arm around his neck. Squeezed. She'd learned the chokehold at a self-defense class before she even came to the Academy.

Darryl's legs gave way. Isabela rode him to the floor, pleased with the sound his face made when it smacked against the tiles. He was out.

With her telekinesis, Isabela hoisted Darryl's body and shoved it into one of the empty stalls. She sat him on the toilet and studied his busted face.

Then, she shape-shifted into him.

Isabela stepped out of the stall and telekinetically locked it from the other side. She looked at her new appearance in the cracked bathroom mirror. Gross, but accurate.

Just then, someone tried to enter the bathroom, found it locked and pounded on the door.

Isabela as Darryl yanked the door open. She stared down at one of the boys from outside. He took an uneasy step back.

"What're . . . you looking at?" she asked, not meaning to pause so much. Isabela hesitated because she hadn't heard Darryl talk enough to perfectly mimic his voice. With the loud music, she hoped it wouldn't matter.

"Sorry, Darryl," the guy muttered.

Isabela shouldered by him.

She approached the freezer. The two guards stepped aside for her.

"Boys say the snake is ready," one of them said. "You want help bringing her outside?"

A fuzzy feeling came over Isabela as she tried to answer. For some reason, she was really struggling with Darryl's voice. This hadn't happened to her before. Nerves?

"I want . . . more minutes . . . ," Isabela grunted. "I'll bring her out . . . quick."

The guards eyed her, but they didn't make any move to stop her. They probably just assumed that Darryl had chugged some grain alcohol like all the other drunks in this freak show. Isabela unlatched the freezer, yanked open the door and stepped into the cold. She slammed the door behind her.

Isabela immediately had to swallow back a scream. A gutted deer carcass hung from a hook right in front of her. She carefully stepped around the animal, her breath misting in front of her.

The girl from the road, the one with the headscarves, hung by the arms behind the deer. Her headscarves were gone, her raven hair loose and greasy, blood clumping the curls together. The girl had been beaten savagely—her face was swollen, lips split, her clothes bloody tatters. Isabela's stomach turned over. Yes, this girl had made an enemy of her, but no one deserved this disgusting brutality.

At least they hadn't put her on a hook. Instead, the girl's hands were secured by a pair of the heavy-duty handcuffs the Peacekeepers had used against the Garde. The magnetized cuffs were attached to the corrugated-metal ceiling. Isabela also noticed a couple of strange objects attached to the girl's temples—triangular in shape, about the size of quarters, they looked like twin microchips. Some kind of Garde-fighting technology, surely, but not something she'd seen demonstrated back at the Academy.

Isabela approached the girl. Her breathing was ragged, her lips blue from spending so much time in the freezer. With a cautious glance over her shoulder, Isabela shape-shifted back into her normal form. She touched the girl gently on the chin, eliciting an exhausted moan.

"Please . . . ," the girl said, followed by words Isabela didn't understand.

"Stupid, open your eyes," Isabela snapped.

The girl did open her eyes at the sound of Isabela's voice. She gasped and strained against her bonds, babbling away in a language Isabela recognized but didn't understand. Isabela shook her.

"Stop talking," Isabela ordered, speaking quickly. "I will get you out of here, but only if you lead us to our friend who you kidnapped. Otherwise, you are useless and can stay here. They plan to set you on fire, so at least that will be a relief after this cold."

The girl stared at her. "English?" she asked. "English, please?"

Isabela stared back at her, brow furrowed. "I am speaking English, you stupid . . ."

She paused. The fuzzy feeling she'd felt before. The difficulty finding the right words for Darryl. It wasn't because she hadn't heard him speak enough . . .

Isabela looked down at her wrist. The bracelet. She tugged at it, looking for the one bead that should be emitting a faint glow. Brought her face close, cupped her hand against her wrist to see . . .

When was the last time she'd visited Simon for a recharge?

Slowly, it dawned on Isabela that she'd been speaking to this girl in Portuguese.

The bracelet was dark. Useless jewelry.

Her English was gone. Behind her, the door to the freezer clanked. Someone was coming in.

"Merda," Isabela said.

CHAPTER THIRTY-ONE

TAYLOR COOK
HOFN, ICELAND

AS TAYLOR CREPT BACK INTO THE HOUSE, SHE heard Einar's raised voice coming from upstairs. He was yelling at someone.

She took the stairs quickly, but as quietly as she could. Freyja stayed in the living room, furtively peeking through the curtains at the men in the Jeep.

At the end of the upstairs hallway, Einar's door was ajar. Taylor tiptoed forward. Through the crack, she saw Einar pacing back and forth, obviously agitated. The flat-screen TV on his wall was tuned to a video conference. Taylor could see only the lower-right corner of the screen—a woman, blond hair in a proper bob, a white dress shirt and pinstriped jacket, professional. Seeing only the woman's mouth and shoulders wouldn't be enough to identify her, if

Taylor was ever able to get out of here. She inched closer.

"Please explain to me why there's a team of Blackstone men parked outside my house," Einar growled.

"You know why," she replied with icy professionalism. Her accent was British. "There is concern your location is compromised."

"Nonsense."

"Rabiya knows how to get to you, does she not? You lost Rabiya. Therefore, your location is compromised. The Blackstone men are simply there as a precaution."

"If you'd let me take them on the mission instead of those moronic Harvesters, this never would've happened," Einar replied.

Taylor inched closer, trying to get a better look at the woman. A floorboard creaked under her foot.

"Now, Einar," the woman said, drowning out Taylor's misstep. "'Tis the poor craftsman who blames his tools. Rabiya is quite valuable to the Foundation. We've yet to catalog another Garde capable of producing Loralite."

"For weeks all you could talk about was acquiring another goddamn healer," Einar hissed. "I got her for you. If I hadn't—if I hadn't escaped when I did, all three of us would have been killed."

"So you said in your report," the woman replied dryly. "Nonetheless, it was sloppy work. Earth Garde is making inquiries. Thus, we are keeping the Blackstone men close by in the event we need to liquidate the Iceland side of our operation."

Taylor didn't like the sound of that. Creeping closer, she made out more details of the Foundation woman. A sharp blue eye, delicate wrinkles, maybe in her late forties or early fifties . . .

"Please, listen," Einar said beseechingly, obviously not liking the connotation of "liquidate" any more than Taylor. "You don't understand what it was like—"

"We've moved up your appointment. The others are teleporting in," the woman interrupted crisply. "Get your house in order, Einar. She is eavesdropping."

The screen went abruptly blank. Taylor glanced up, saw the hallway camera pointed in her direction and cursed under her breath. So, that was the woman on the other side of all this surveillance. She wished she had gotten a better look.

Einar stood in his doorway, glaring at her, his face a cold mask. He had changed out of his coffee-stained sweater and into an immaculately tailored gray suit. Taylor felt suddenly underdressed in her pajamas and borrowed leather coat.

"Are we going to prom?" she asked.

"Get dressed," he said simply. "We're leaving."

"Who was that woman? Your mean British nanny?"

"You may get to meet her one day, if things go well. She's a visionary."

"Oh, wow, do you promise?" Taylor replied with a snort. She locked eyes with Einar, probing for weaknesses like Isabela would. "You're in trouble, aren't you?"

"No."

"You screwed up in California. I heard her. Made a big mess. They're going to liquidate you."

"Not me," Einar replied with a meaningful look.

"Yeah, right. I'm a healer. Sounds like I'm more valuable than you." She made a point of addressing the camera overhead. "You'd rather have me than this fussy screwup, right?"

Einar took a sharp step towards her. "Stop it."

"They don't care about you," Taylor said quietly. "Or me. But the Academy could protect us. They'll be looking for me . . ."

Einar laughed in her face. She'd been close to getting a reaction out of him, but had pushed too hard in the wrong direction.

"I told you. Get dressed," Einar said through his teeth.

Taylor's muscles tensed. Her heart beat faster, stomach rolling over. She was suddenly afraid. Taylor took a step backwards, towards her room. She better do what he said or else—

No. She noticed the way Einar looked at her. Concentrated on her. This was his Legacy again. He was manipulating her emotions. Knowing that didn't make the fear any easier to resist.

"Stop—stop it," she said.

"Go," he ordered.

Taylor's palms started to sweat and her knees almost buckled. She gritted her teeth, but couldn't keep her body from reacting. With a yelp, she ran for her room, slamming the door behind her as if there were a monster on her heels.

In a way, she thought, there was.

The fear didn't subside until she began changing into the clothes Freyja had brought for her that morning. An austere peach-colored blouse and a long black skirt. The outfit was stuffy and didn't fit her exactly right. She had to roll up the sleeves. There was also a long sash of dark silk that she didn't know what to do with.

She came back out of her room and found Einar still waiting outside. The fear was gone now, resentment in its place.

"You're an asshole," she said.

Einar frowned. He held out his hand and took the silk from her. Then, before Taylor could stop him, he stepped in close and began loosely wrapping the scarf around her head. Taylor had to resist the urge to punch him in the mouth. Once her head was properly covered, Einar stepped back to appreciate his work.

"There's a dress code where we're going," he said.

"And where is that?"

"Abu Dhabi."

"What? Seriously?"

Einar headed downstairs, forcing Taylor to chase after him. Freyja was still wrapped in the curtains, keeping a close eye on the men parked outside. Taylor glanced in her direction and grimaced. Einar ignored the young girl completely, marching towards the back deck.

"What about her?" Taylor asked.

"Who?"

"Freyja. You know, your other prisoner."

"She stays here," he replied. "If you have an idea that you might do something stupid, imagine her dying gruesomely."

Einar shoved open the back door and strode across his frost-covered deck. Taylor hurried after him, grateful that Freyja was out of earshot.

"Isn't that going to happen anyway?" she asked. "I heard that Foundation lady use the word 'liquidate.'"

Einar paused and turned to look at her. "That isn't going to happen."

"But if it does . . ." Taylor waved towards the front yard. "Those guys outside will kill her, right?"

Before he responded, Einar glanced over Taylor's head at the camera mounted over his back door. It seemed to Taylor he wasn't sure how much he should say.

"That won't happen," Einar repeated. "We're too valuable."

He didn't sound entirely convinced.

Einar crossed through the rock garden and approached the wooden enclosure that contained the Loralite stone. Taylor watched over his shoulder as he punched in the four-digit access code, making no effort to hide it.

"All right," Taylor said resignedly. "So, what are we doing in Abu Dhabi?"

"You and the others will be healing the prince of one of the royal families," Einar replied, pushing the wooden gate open.

Taylor blinked. So many questions. "What others?" she asked first.

"You make the fourth healer the Foundation has acquired."

"Four," Taylor repeated. She was the only healer enrolled at the Academy. "You've kidnapped four . . ."

As they approached the Loralite, the chunk of cobalt stone pulsed in greeting, the glow coming and going like a heartbeat.

"The prince has leukemia," Einar continued matter-of-factly. "The others have so far been unsuccessful in healing him. Hopefully, the addition of your power will be enough." He put his hand on the Loralite stone, then hesitated, biting the inside of his cheek. "It has to be enough," he said, "or this entire operation will be judged a failure."

Liquidate. The word echoed in Taylor's mind and a sense of nervousness fluttered in her belly. She thought of the cancer patient who she had failed to heal back in California. Would failure here mean punishment? Death for Freyja? Some other unimaginable consequence? Her mind worked feverishly—she needed to save Freyja and escape—but she saw no outs. All she could do was continue to play this game.

Einar held out his hand impatiently. "Coming?"

Taylor made a face, wanting to be sure Einar saw her look of revulsion, before taking his hand.

The world spun and reality bent. Taylor had been unconscious when they last teleported, so this was her first experience with the alien process. It felt like her body dissolved—not in an unpleasant way—but a gentle coming apart, as if in a dream. The only thing she could still feel was Einar's hand, like an anchor that dragged her towards their destination. She felt dizzy, a speck of dirt blown in the wind. For a moment, her vision was filled with darkness penetrated by thousands of pinpricks of bright blue lights. Other Loralite stones, other locations. The cobalt fireflies swirled by her and then—

The heat hit Taylor all at once. That might have been the most disorienting part—to have the chill of Iceland wiped away so quickly, replaced with a dry heat that made Taylor immediately sweaty. It felt like she was baking. She shielded her eyes from the sun. Unlike the clouded-over Iceland, here the sun hung red and blistering in the sky. Taylor found herself surprisingly grateful for the scarf wrapped around her head.

She and Einar stood in the courtyard of a genuine palace. All around her were statues of lions and women, these gilded with what she assumed was real gold. A trio of burbling fountains flanked by fastidiously groomed palm trees complemented the cobblestone path in front of them. Taylor gazed up, slightly in awe, at the four-story building— blowing silk curtains from thrown-open windows, cupolas and crenellations covered in ancient-looking oil paintings, balconies filled with men holding machine guns.

The guards gave Taylor pause. There were dozens of them, both up high and along the edge of the courtyard, all identically dressed in long-sleeved white thobes and mirrored sunglasses. A small army. Taylor swallowed; she'd been around too many armed groups of men recently.

"They don't entirely trust our kind here," Einar said quietly, following Taylor's gaze. "The prince's father—"

"The king?" Taylor asked.

"Sheikh, actually," Einar replied. "He is a generous supporter of the Foundation. But not all of his brothers and nephews see our . . . utility." Einar adjusted his tie. "Behave. Remember Freyja."

Taylor sighed, looking around at all the guns. She glanced back at the Loralite stone. Making a move here would probably get her killed. She followed Einar down the cobblestone path, towards the palace entrance.

"About time."

A rail-thin Asian girl who had been hanging out in the shade of one of the palm trees smoking a cigarette from a sleek gold-plated holder cut them off before they could enter the palace. The guards eyeballed this girl in the same uneasy way as they did Einar and Taylor, which meant she must be Garde. Like Taylor, she wore a hijab, although hers was decorated with frolicking seahorses. The new arrival wore high heels that made Taylor's feet ache in sympathy, a half blazer and a sleek pencil skirt. Her nails were painted red and black to match her outfit. Although she looked only a year or two her senior, Taylor immediately felt like this girl was much older.

"Jiao," Einar said by way of greeting. When he attempted to walk around her, the girl simply fell into step with him. She completely ignored Taylor.

"We need to talk."

"Do we?"

"You told me, you promised me, that the Foundation would get my family out of Shenzhen."

"It'll happen," Einar said with a sigh. "You need to be patient."

Taylor got the feeling this wasn't the first time they'd had this conversation.

They entered the palace, Jiao's heels echoing loudly against the marble floors. The air was much cooler in here. Taylor tried to keep track of her surroundings—paintings that probably belonged in museums, dozens of rooms, more and more guards—while also listening to Einar and Jiao.

"It's been months," Jiao said sharply.

"Extractions take time," Einar replied. "I promise. I'll look into it."

"You'd better," Jiao said. "Tell that British gao bizi this is the last assignment I'm taking until they keep their end of the bargain."

Einar nodded stiffly and said nothing. Jiao flicked a glance over her shoulder, sizing Taylor up in a split second.

"This is the new girl? She's supposed to put us over the top?"

"Yes," Einar replied.

"Hmpf." Jiao gave Taylor another look, then turned back to Einar. "Where's Rabiya?"

"Couldn't make it."

Jiao studied Einar for a moment, obviously hoping he would elaborate. Taylor volunteered no information. If she was looking for an ally to help her escape, it wouldn't be this girl. She almost seemed like more of a shark than Einar.

"Wonderful conversation as always, Einar," Jiao said bitterly, then sped up her walk down the palace's domed hallway. She knew where she was going and didn't want to arrive at the same time as them.

After a moment, Taylor chuckled. Einar looked in her direction, lips pursed.

"I finally get it," Taylor said.

"Get what?"

"There used to be this clique in my school, the mean girls from a couple grades above me. They all worked in the same store at the mall. This—well, you probably don't have it in Iceland. It's like a popular store where they sell distressed jeans and sweatshirts with big store logos stitched into them."

Up ahead, Jiao pushed open a set of hand-carved double doors and entered the room at the end of the hall. Einar slowed down and then stopped, turning to face Taylor. The guards following them—herding them, really—stopped a respectable distance back.

"Please get to the point," Einar said.

"Okay. These girls were real tight until one of them got promoted to supervisor and then she got all serious, bossing the other ones around, basically acting like a huge tool. A little power went right to her head." She pointed at Einar. "That's you, man. You're like . . . an assistant manager. How lame is that?"

Einar closed his eyes for a moment, then reopened them. "Are you finished?"

"Well, the moral of the story is that the store went out of business and they all had to find new summer jobs, but their friendships were already totally ruined," Taylor said with a bright smile. "So, take that for what it's worth."

Einar took Taylor by the arm and led her towards the room Jiao had gone into. "These attempts to get under my skin won't get you anywhere," he said. "I'm not some silly bitch from your high school."

"I'm not trying to get under your skin," Taylor insisted. "I'm trying to make you see how dumb your situation is."

"Shut up, now," Einar commanded.

Einar ushered her through the double doors. It took Taylor's eyes a moment to adjust—the rest of the palace had been soaked through with sunlight, but this room was kept purposefully dim, all the curtains drawn, candles flickering in wall sconces. The room was huge, with a domed ceiling that featured a chipped mosaic of birds soaring through trees. Incense burned in one corner where a group of women were gathered, all of them covered head to toe, on their knees, foreheads to the ground in prayer. Spread out around the room were more guards with more guns. Taylor swallowed.

An older man with a thick white beard sat at a small table, a goblet of dark wine not far from his hand. He wore a robe of gold and white and Taylor could tell immediately that he was in charge here, the mood of the room seeming to bend around him. This must be the sheikh. He gave both her and

Einar a stern look when they entered, his fingers drumming on the table, but said nothing. At his side was an Arabian woman, not wearing the head-to-toe coverings of the group in the corner, but dressed in a hijab and lab coat. A doctor of the traditional variety. She crouched next to the older man and showed him a chart, explaining something in Arabic.

"We're late," Einar said quietly to Taylor.

"I got that impression."

Taylor's attention soon turned to the king-size canopy bed that dominated the center of the room. Laid up there was the sick prince. He looked like a younger and handsomer version of the sheikh. His beard and hair were clipped meticulously. Unlike the healthy olive bronze of his father and bodyguards, the prince's skin was ashen, his cheeks hollow, his body pointy and emaciated beneath the sheets. He was hooked up to an array of medical equipment, the steady beeps and hums creating a strange chorus with the prayers from the back of the room. If not for the slow rise and fall of his chest, Taylor would have thought the prince to be dead.

Jiao already stood at the prince's bedside. "Hurry up, new girl," she said.

There were two other young people around the prince's bedside. The first was a heavyset boy with a mane of curly hair. His eyes were red-rimmed, the side of his face discolored by recent bruises. He glanced up at Taylor skittishly, then quickly looked away. Another prisoner of the Foundation. Taylor remembered Isabela mentioning a healer who had graduated to Earth Garde, an Italian guy . . . could this be him? Vincent, she thought his name was.

Across from Vincent was an even younger boy with dusky skin, a shock of bright white hair and no legs. He sat in a wheelchair and seemed completely out of it—his head lolled from side to side, his eyes unfocused. A pair of strange-looking microchips were stuck to his temples. A conservatively dressed older woman stood behind the wheelchair, her hand resting gently on the boy's shoulder. Taylor found herself staring at this poor soul, sympathy mixing with apprehension.

"The Foundation is generous," Einar said in her ear, startling Taylor. "But, as you see, they can also be cruel."

He pushed her towards the prince's bedside. Taylor ending up standing at the foot of the bed, Jiao at the head, the two boys on either side. Taylor glanced nervously at the two traumatized boys, at least until Jiao snapped her fingers.

"Focus up," she barked. "Follow my energy."

Taylor's brow furrowed. "Follow your . . . I'm sorry. I've never done this with a group before."

She sensed the sheikh shift impatiently behind her, but ignored him.

Jiao rolled her eyes. "You'll know what to do once we get started." She gestured in the crippled boy's direction. "Even a vegetable can do it."

Paying no attention to Jiao's remark, the woman handling the wheelchair bent down and whispered something in the legless boy's ear. Robotically, he reached out and clasped the wrist of the sleeping prince. Vincent, still avoiding Taylor's gaze, did the same with the prince's other arm.

"See?" Jiao said, and set her hands on either side of the prince's face. She closed her eyes and went to work.

Taylor could sense all of them using their Legacies. The rest of the people in the room might have been blind to it, but to Taylor, the healing energy gave off a warm aura.

Carefully, she moved the sheet aside, and readied her hands over the prince's feet.

She sensed movement. The prince had opened his eyes. He stared, blinking, at Taylor, and a small smile formed on his lips. He looked almost peaceful. There was a kindness in his expression, a gentleness.

"Are you a good person?"

The words popped out before Taylor could stop them. She sensed a restless shifting from the many guards in the room and felt Einar step up behind her. Meanwhile, the sheikh's fingers suddenly stopped their drumming on the table.

The prince struggled to work moisture into his mouth. ". . . What?"

"Are you a good person?" Taylor repeated. "Because, you know, all of us were basically kidnapped to heal you. Some of us probably tortured. So, I want to know if you're, like, worth the trouble . . ."

Vincent trembled, but pretended not to hear, his eyes closed. The legless boy remained slumped over the prince, pouring his healing energy out. His handler glared daggers at Taylor. Jiao slowly opened her eyes, her lips curled in disdain.

The prince peered around Taylor, searching for his father. He looked confused. Something wordless passed between him and his father. Finally, he looked back at her and slowly shook his head.

"I . . . I cannot answer that," the prince said.

"Well, think about it when you're better," Taylor said. "Because this Foundation thing is totally fucked and somebody needs to do something about it."

With that, Taylor closed her eyes and clasped the prince's feet. She sensed the sickness lurking within him, just as she sensed three pulsing beacons of light trying to burn it away. She added her healing energy, giving as much as she could, as if her life and not the prince's depended upon it.

CHAPTER THIRTY-TWO

CALEB CRANE
APACHE JACK'S, NEW MEXICO

HIDDEN IN THE WOODS, THEY WATCHED APACHE Jack's in uneasy silence. The Harvesters appeared to have finished preparations on their snake effigy; a handful of them were gathered around the wooden structure, some holding torches, eager for whatever came next. Even more were hanging around on the bar's back deck.

Caleb remembered a scene from when he was fourteen and was called by his oldest brother to pick him up from one of the bars nearby the base. He wasn't even old enough to drive, but he'd snuck away regardless under threat of catching a beating if he didn't. The atmosphere there—drunk people looking for trouble—reminded him a lot of the one at Apache Jack's.

Isabela had been gone twenty minutes.

We shouldn't have let her go in there alone.

We should bail now. Call the Academy.

We can take them. This hiding is moronic.

Kill everyone down there.

Prove yourself.

They don't even like us. Run in the other direction. Leave them.

SHUT UP, Caleb insisted.

In the darkness, Caleb saw Nigel looking in his direction. He realized he was clenching his teeth, veins in his neck bulging. He forced himself to relax.

The muffled sound of gunfire erupted from inside the bar. The Garde all jumped and so did the Harvesters outside. They looked unsettled—some of them moved towards the building, others away from it. Those who had guns raised them.

"You heard that?" Caleb asked the others.

"Yes," Ran replied.

Seconds later, a fireball exploded through the back door of Apache Jack's. The force knocked the screen door right off its hinges and blew out the bar's back windows. Several Harvesters were knocked clear over the deck's railing, the others outside rushing to their aid. Fire crackled along the door frame and black smoke billowed into the night. A biker ran out the back door and tossed himself to the ground in an effort to put out the flames on his back.

"Bloody hell," Nigel remarked. "Imagine that's a distress signal, yeah?"

"We have to go in," Kopano said firmly, starting forward.

Caleb put a hand on his arm, stopping him. "Hold on. Let me go first." He paused. "I mean, let them go first."

A dozen duplicates slid out from Caleb. His three friends stepped back, giving him room as their patch of trees became suddenly crowded. Caleb was grateful for the opportunity to let his duplicates out; it quieted the voices in his head. Mentally, he commanded them to spread out. Keeping low— even though there was little chance the Harvesters would see them with all their attention on the fire—the duplicates fanned out into the woods.

"I'll attack them from all angles," Caleb said. "Keep them busy."

Ran hadn't taken her eyes off the chaos at the bar. She turned a pinecone over in her hand, a small pile of the things collected at her feet.

"I don't see her down there," Ran said. "I don't think the explosion was a diversion. Isabela might be trapped in there."

"I'll get eyes on her," Caleb said.

Nigel put a hand on his shoulder. "You can handle that many clones?"

Caleb nodded, although he wasn't entirely sure. A dozen at once was as many as he'd managed during the fight last night and that had left him feeling ripped apart, like his body had been stretched too far.

Hell with it. They needed to find Taylor.

He urged the clones forward. Focusing, he divided his

attention among the duplicates, making them move cautiously.

The duplicates spread out through the trees so they wouldn't give away Caleb and the others' position. Some of them looped around farther, towards the sides of Apache Jack's. The goal here was to locate Isabela and she could be anywhere within that bar. Caleb's vision blurred. Each duplicate's view of Apache Jack's was like a still frame from a movie made transparent and laid over the next angle. If Caleb concentrated, he could isolate one view at a time, but that meant losing some control over the other duplicates.

"I'm sending them in," he said through his teeth. Throughout the woods, the duplicates whispered his words.

"We've got your back, mate," Nigel said, sticking close.

A dozen Calebs charged towards Apache Jack's. The Harvesters didn't see them coming. They were too focused on the fire and whatever else was happening inside the bar. He hit the stragglers first, the ones closest to the woods. Two of the duplicates tackled one overweight biker and pummeled him into unconsciousness.

One of the nearby Harvesters—this one dressed like a cowboy and holding a shotgun—heard the commotion and spun about. A third duplicate was there when he turned and ripped the gun right out of his hands. The duplicate gracefully whipped the gun into a firing position and took aim.

This duplicate wanted to kill, but Kopano had encouraged them to limit their bloodshed. So Caleb took control. He smashed the Harvester across the face with the gun's butt and then tossed the weapon into the woods.

His duplicates scrambled onwards. They were like a wave, catching the Harvesters from behind and smashing them into the ground. A woman who'd been working on the effigy heard a muffled shout and turned just before one of the clones would've pounced on her. She thrust her torch in the duplicate's direction, burning his face. The pain didn't register with Caleb, only the vague sense that that particular duplicate was no longer fully whole.

"We're under attack!" the woman screamed.

A shirtless man who was trying to put out the fire turned at the woman's warning. He pulled a pistol from the back of his jeans and shot the burned clone right between the eyes.

No more element of surprise. But at least the clones had taken out a handful of Harvesters before they were discovered.

Caleb felt a jolt pass through him as the duplicate disintegrated and returned to him. Immediately, he gritted his teeth and manifested the clone again, sent it sprinting through the woods to take a new angle on the bar.

"The abominations have followed us, brothers and sisters!" shouted a scrawny Harvester cowering on the back deck. "Strike them down for Reverend Jim—!"

One of the clones clamored over the deck's railing and punched him in the mouth. Seconds later, a long-haired Harvester who looked like he'd spent the last five years living in the woods emerged from the smoke-filled back exit. He coughed raggedly but carried an automatic rifle.

The Harvester began to spray bullets wildly. He gunned down three clones and possibly a few of his own allies. The bullets even reached the trees. Ran and Kopano lunged for cover, while Nigel dragged the focused Caleb down to the ground.

With a sharp intake of breath, Caleb felt the clones return to him. He immediately set them loose, forcing them to charge back into battle.

"How long can you keep this up?" Nigel asked.

"Not sure," Caleb replied, a migraine tearing through his brain. He'd been wondering who would run out of ammunition first—him or the man on the back deck.

The Harvesters on the back deck took cover behind the broken wooden slats of the railing. They were pinned between the fire and the clones, but they were starting to get organized. They were picking off Caleb's clones faster than he could make them. Some of his duplicates grabbed weapons from fallen Harvesters and returned fire. The situation was too desperate to handle gently. They needed to find Isabela and get out of here.

In the darkness of the woods, Caleb couldn't see if Kopano wore a look of disapproval. Caleb switched views, looking through the eyes of a clone that had looped around to the side of Apache Jack's. He peered through a dirt-smudged window. Inside, a group of panicked Harvesters were getting the fire under control—it appeared to be localized around the back door, where Caleb could see charred and twisted hunks of what used to be fuel canisters. Other Harvesters had popped open a trapdoor beneath the bar that contained a stockpile of weapons, the bartender handing out rifles to whoever wanted one. Soon, they'd be in real trouble.

That's when Caleb noticed the freezer. Towards the back of the bar, near where the explosion had been, was a heavy steel door. A trio of menacing bikers in gas masks were taking turns whacking the door with axes, trying to break in.

Just then, one of the newly armed Harvesters came around the corner from the front of the bar, heading for the back. He spotted Caleb's duplicate and, without hesitation, shot him in the head.

Caleb gasped. "She's locked in a freezer," he announced breathlessly. He pointed towards the singed back entrance. "Right in there."

"You're sure?" Ran asked.

"Has to be," he said. "The Harvesters are trying to hack their way in."

"I'll get her," Kopano said, cracking his knuckles. "Their bullets cannot hurt me."

"I'm going with you," Ran replied.

Nigel put a hand on Caleb's shoulder. "You going to be okay back here, mate?"

Caleb nodded. In truth, he was beginning to feel ragged, like his body was sliding apart. All the same, he pushed another clone into existence and sent him towards the fray. "I'll keep the decoys coming as long . . . as long as I can," he said.

Nigel nodded and turned to Kopano. "Big man, let me and

Ran create a wee distraction before you go all juggernaut on 'em, yeah?"

The three of them started forward, sticking close to the shadows and the trees to avoid any stray bullets. At the moment, the Harvesters were too preoccupied with the remaining clones to notice their approach. Caleb kept his most recent duplicate with his three classmates, wanting to make sure he could see and hear what happened with them.

One of the Harvesters had dropped a lit torch in the grass. It was still burning. Ran or Nigel—he couldn't be sure who—used their telekinesis to pick up the torch and float it right to the effigy.

The gas-soaked wooden snake sculpture went up in flames with a mighty *whoosh!* Even back in the woods, Caleb could feel the heat. That Harvesters stopped their shooting for a moment, confused by this latest development.

Confusion turned to outright terror as the burning snake effigy levitated right off the ground. It must have taken Kopano, Ran and Nigel working together to accomplish the telekinetic feat, but soon the snake hovered over Apache Jack's deck, fireflies of burning wood drifting down on the Harvesters. A few of them pointlessly shot at the effigy.

"YOUR BULLETS CANNOT HARM ME, MORTALS!"

The booming voice erupted from the vicinity of the snake. It was Nigel, using his Legacy to throw his voice and make it as loud as possible. Desperate as the situation was, Caleb couldn't help but smirk.

"YOU WANKERS HAVE TAKEN MY NAME IN VAIN

TOO MANY TIMES!" the flaming snake bellowed. "NOW I'M GOING TO BELLY FLOP YOUR DAFT ASSES!"

Many of the Harvesters on the deck had already begun to scatter and the rest soon followed as the burning effigy crashed down on the back of Apache Jack's. Embers flew up into the air, burning wood breaking apart, small fires starting everywhere. The Harvesters dove aside, many winding up in the dirt, where Caleb's remaining clones could charge in and disarm them.

The Harvesters who managed to stay standing soon found glowing pinecones at their feet. The concussive explosions knocked them backwards.

Suddenly, there was a lull in the action and a clear path into Apache Jack's—well, clear except for all the smoke and burning chunks of wood.

Kopano barreled into that gap, knocking aside debris with his telekinesis. Nigel and Ran came in behind him, with Caleb's clone bringing up the rear. They kept low to avoid the smoke that was now everywhere. The heat from small fires made them all—except the clone—immediately begin sweating.

The trio of Harvesters in their gas masks had stopped trying to hack into the freezer and now stood at the ready. They saw Kopano and one of them charged. His axe clanged against Kopano's forearm and the Nigerian took him down with a well-placed right hook. A glowing pinecone exploded against the chest of a second Harvester, sending him and his axe tumbling over a nearby table. Nigel used his telekinesis to turn the gas mask around on the third. While the man yanked the mask's straps away from his eyes, Kopano put him down with a push kick to the sternum.

"Easy-peasy," Nigel remarked, glancing back at the clone. He banged on the severely dented freezer door. "Oi, Isabela! You in there?"

They heard a grinding sound on the other side of the door—something being pried loose. A moment later, the freezer swung open. Isabela stood hunched before them, her face blackened with ash, her side dark with blood. She said something in Portuguese.

"Huh?" Nigel replied.

Isabela groaned. She held up the bracelet that Simon had charged for her, waved it in Nigel's face and tossed it away.

"Her English is gone," Ran observed.

"Bloody great timing, that," Nigel said sarcastically.

Ran put her hand on Isabela's shoulder, peering at what looked like a gunshot wound on her side. "How bad are you hurt?"

Isabela glanced down, then tilted her hand back and forth, as if to say *so-so*. She pointed behind her, speaking rapidly in Portuguese.

Crumpled on the floor of the freezer was the girl from the road. She'd been beaten badly, but was conscious. A piece of metal ceiling that looked to have been recently ripped loose was attached to her wrists, stuck there by a pair of those magnetized shackles the Peacekeepers had used. She struggled to sit up.

Nigel and Ran went to the girl. Caleb kept his clone in the doorway, holding up Isabela. Kopano stood guard outside, watching for Harvesters.

"My, my, love. They did a number on you," Nigel observed as he grabbed the girl's arm and, with Ran's help, pulled her to her feet. "What's your name?"

"Rabiya," the girl croaked. A trickle of blood dribbled down her chin.

As they dragged her out of the freezer and into the smoke-filled remains of Apache Jack's, Nigel noticed the odd triangular microchips affixed to Rabiya's temples. "What're those?" he asked, tweaking one of them.

Rabiya pulled her hands up to touch the microchips and nearly struck herself in the face with the ceiling plate. "They . . . neurotransmitters. They scramble my telekinesis."

Nigel raised an eyebrow and exchanged a look with Ran. "Bet you'd like us to take those off, eh?"

"Yes."

"You know who we are, then?"

She nodded forlornly.

"You took our friend," Nigel continued. "About got us killed. But here we are, coming to your bloody rescue."

"Thank . . . thank you," Rabiya said.

"Don't thank me yet. You can make Loralite, yeah? That's your thing?" He paused to let Rabiya nod. "You know where that smartly dressed chum of yours took Taylor? You can bring us there?"

Rabiya's mouth opened as she searched for words. "They

are dangerous people."

As they picked their way across the burning debris of Apache Jack's back deck, a Harvester with a knife lunged at them. Kopano slapped the blade down with an open hand, then knocked the Harvester off his feet with an uppercut.

"We are dangerous people," Ran said coldly.

Rabiya glanced at Ran, her expression slowly hardening. "He was . . . they were supposed to be my friends," Rabiya said quietly. "Instead, they left me to die. We were supposed to take your friend to a safe house in Iceland. I can bring you there. But you have to free my hands."

Nigel looked at Ran. The Japanese girl shook her head stoically. She let go of one of Rabiya's arms and the girl almost sank to the ruined deck.

"I don't believe her," Ran said. "Leave her here. Let these animals finish her off."

Even through the clone's ears, Caleb could tell that Ran was bluffing. It was a classic case of good-cop-bad-cop. He had the clone glance down at Isabela, who he was still holding up. If she could understand English, Caleb was sure the Brazilian would appreciate this bit of subterfuge.

Rabiya bought it. "Please!" she yelled, her voice hoarse. "I never even wanted to join the Foundation! They forced me—they—!"

Ran grabbed Rabiya by the manacles. "This is going to hurt," she warned.

With a touch, Ran charged the manacles securing Rabiya's wrists. She didn't put as much energy into the metal as she normally did when making a grenade, but the high-tech restraints still exploded with enough force to throw Rabiya onto her back. She sat back up, rubbing wrists that were already swelling up.

"I think you broke my hand," she said quietly.

"Too bad you stole our healer," Nigel replied as he helped her to her feet.

Rabiya reached up to pick the microchips off her temples. Nigel slapped her hands down. "Nuh-uh. No telekinesis until you prove you're on the up-and-up."

She didn't argue, instead gesturing into grass beside the smoky deck. "Over there. The Loralite only grows from the ground."

At that moment, a gunshot rang out from inside the bar. The bullet bounced off Kopano, who returned fire by telekinetically lobbing a pair of chairs into the hallway behind them. The Harvesters were beginning to regroup. They'd fled to the front of the bar when the effigy came crashing down, but they were still armed and stupid. They'd strike again soon.

Kopano nervously rubbed the spot on his shoulder where the bullet had hit him. "Let's go!"

Caleb quickly switched views to one of his duplicates that was posted up around the side of the bar. He could see the Harvesters massing out front, steeling themselves for another attack.

"Quickly, quickly," his clone said, helping Isabela down from the deck. Nigel and Ran followed with Rabiya sandwiched in between them. Kopano came last, using his telekinesis to barricade the back door with furniture and debris.

Just then, an icy feeling came over Caleb.

It wasn't necessarily an unpleasant feeling. It was like a numbness, spreading through his legs. At first, he thought it was a sensation that he'd picked up from one of the clones. But no—this was happening to his actual body.

Something was wrong.

Caleb attempted a lurching step forward and fell onto his hands. His legs were heavy.

They were stone. Literally.

With a groan, Caleb rolled over. He sensed movement in the trees behind him and a glint of silver-tinged energy.

"Oh, what up, Caleb?"

Daniela.

He hadn't seen the girl for more than a year, not since she was sent directly to Earth Garde instead of the Academy. Daniela looked much the same except for her gear—she wore an armor-plated black bodysuit that hugged her lean sprinter's body, and her usually unruly braids were collected into a thick ponytail. She stood over Caleb, a team of Peacekeepers with night-vision goggles picking through the woods behind her.

"How—how'd you find us?" Caleb stammered.

"We didn't find you, we found them," Daniela replied conversationally, waving in the direction of Apache Jack's and the Harvesters. "Everyone's looking for you guys, glad you're in one piece. The others okay?"

Caleb didn't answer right away. Instead, he looked through his clone's eyes, stopping the duplicate in his tracks as his friends dragged Rabiya across the field towards the woods.

"Stop!" he had the clone yell. "Earth Garde's here! They've got me."

In the distance, the *whup-whup-whup* of helicopters became audible.

"Hell," Nigel said. He elbowed Rabiya. "Hurry up. Make the Loralite now."

Rabiya glanced nervously over her shoulder, worried the Harvesters might be on them at any moment. "Here—?"

Daniela shook Caleb's shoulder and he focused back on her. She'd crouched down beside him as the Peacekeeper soldiers continued on towards Apache Jack's.

"Hey, man, where'd you go?"

"Why'd you stone me?" Caleb replied. "I can help."

"Yeah, sorry about that," she replied. "Earth Garde's running this operation and you aren't authorized for combat. Can't let you get hurt." She touched a radio mounted on her shoulder and spoke into it. "I've got Caleb Crane down here . . ." She listened to a response, then smirked at Caleb. "Oh man, Professor Meathead isn't happy."

"Nine? Nine's here?"

The helicopters came into view. Three of them, all circling. Their spotlights swept across the wooded hillside around Apache Jack's.

Caleb checked in with his duplicate hiding at the front of the bar. Many of the Harvesters were bailing, scrambling for motorcycles and trucks and tearing down the road. Some of them took potshots up at the helicopters. They were quickly cut down by sniper fire.

"Harvesters retreating, Earth Garde closing in," Caleb reported through his clone.

A funnel of cobalt-blue energy rippled out from Rabiya's outstretched palms and struck the ground. With a groan from the earth, a craggy pile of Loralite slowly began to rise up.

The blue light caught the attention of one of the helicopter pilots. They swung the spotlight around, illuminating the group of Garde, and soon the chopper was almost right overhead.

"How much do you need to make?" Kopano asked Rabiya.

"Almost . . . ," she said tiredly. "Almost there."

"Que porra é essa?" Isabela said, pointing up at the helicopter.

Something had fallen out of the chopper's open bay door.

THOOM! Nine hit the ground with an explosion of dirt and broken bits of wood. He landed right in front of his students. All their eyes widened at the shallow crater he made and Rabiya yelped, cutting off her creation of the Loralite stone. Nine smirked as he straightened up.

"It's way after curfew, guys."

Nigel was the first to recover his wits. "Fancy meeting you here, teach."

Nine gave them the once-over, checking for injuries. Perhaps satisfied none of them were gravely wounded, he put his hands on his hips. His eyes widened a fraction when he noticed Rabiya and the steady pile of glowing stone at her feet.

"That's Loralite," Nine said, and they could all tell their professor's mind was working. "We found some at the spot where you guys were ambushed, been trying to figure out where . . ." He took a step towards Rabiya. "What's your name? Where'd you come from?"

Ran put herself between Nine and Rabiya. He stopped short, an eyebrow raised.

"Keep going," Ran said to Rabiya over her shoulder.

"We're going to find Taylor," Kopano told Nine.

"No, we're going to find Taylor," Nine insisted, gesturing around at the Peacekeepers and Earth Garde. There were sounds of a small firefight from in front of Apache Jack's. Meanwhile, Daniela led stone-booted Caleb out of the woods, her team of Peacekeepers fanning out. Caleb and his clone exchanged a look.

"Been doing a bang-up job of that, haven't ya?" Nigel asked.

Nine raised an eyebrow. "We found you, didn't we?"

"You stumbled onto us," Caleb had his clone say.

Nine waved this away. "Same difference."

"We know where she is," Kopano said. "She's in Iceland. We're going to get her."

"No. You're not."

Nine took another step forward. Or, at least, he attempted to. As one, Nigel, Ran and Kopano extended their hands, gently pushing Nine back with their telekinesis. Isabela, still holding her wounded side with one hand, joined them a second later.

"Oh, give me a break with this shit," Nine said. He dug his heels in and powered forward. Caleb watched with a growing tightness in his chest. Nine was strong. He could probably break their telekinesis if he wanted to.

"Stop, Professor," Kopano appealed. "We'll bring Taylor back. I promise."

"Like your lot never ran off half-cocked to save someone's life," Nigel added.

"I can't let you go," Nine replied, the words sounding hollow. "What you're doing isn't safe. I'm sure it's in violation of one of those stupid Garde bylaws, too."

"Nowhere is safe for us," Ran said. "That was proven at Patience Creek."

"That was during the war," Nine replied. "It's different now."

"Doesn't feel so bloody different," Nigel said. He glanced in the direction of the approaching Peacekeepers, noting that some of them were armed with the nonlethal weaponry that had been used during the Wargames. "You want to tell us how these wackjob Harvesters got hooked into the same weapons as your mates in the army?"

"I don't know," Nine replied. "We're looking into that."

"Yeah. Right. So, you keep doing that, behind your desk,"

Nigel replied. "We'll handle the hero shit."

Nine sneered and started to say something more, but Ran cut him off.

"You knew," she said suddenly, as if the fact had just dawned on her. "That night on the beach. You were warning me. Telling me to keep an eye on Taylor. You knew someone might be after her."

"I . . ." Nine glanced up at the helicopter circling above. "There's a lot going on you guys don't know about."

Rabiya took a breath and sagged against Nigel. The Loralite stone was done, the blue stone reflecting the small fires still burning at the bar.

"Mate, you can fill us in when we get back," Nigel said. "Who do you trust to go get Taylor? Us or these Earth Garde blokes?"

Nine sighed. Through his clone's eyes, Caleb saw something like nostalgia on the Loric's face. He was relenting.

Caleb tried to drag his feet, which wasn't difficult considering they were encased in stone. He wanted to slow up Daniela and the Peacekeepers, give the others a chance to convince Nine and escape.

"We'll come back," Kopano said solemnly, reading the hesitation in Nine's face. "We'll be safe."

"Yeah," Nigel added. "Just gonna pop on over to Iceland for a bit. No biggie. Things get hinky, you come pick us up."

Nine lowered his voice as he came to a decision. "At least make it look good." He jerked his chin in Isabela's direction. "And leave her. She's too hurt."

"Estou bem. Eu quero ajudar!" Isabela stomped her foot in frustration when the others simply stared at her, then wobbled and sagged against Caleb's clone. "Talvez não. Va, va . . ."

Ran nodded once to Nine, then gave Rabiya a shove. "Take us."

Rabiya reached for the Loralite. Ran had a vise grip on her arm. Nigel held Ran's hand, his other hand on Kopano's shoulder.

Nine made a dramatic lunge forward.

The Caleb duplicate tackled him.

Isabela stood there looking puzzled, holding her bloody side.

In a flash of vivid blue light, the other four teleported away.

CHAPTER THIRTY-THREE

NIGEL BARNABY
HOFN, ICELAND

NIGEL REMEMBERED THE SENSATION OF TELEPORT-ing well. He was the bloody pioneer champion of teleportation, for God's sake. He'd been the first Human Garde to use a Loralite stone back during the invasion. That dizzying feeling of getting flung halfway across the world toward adventure—he'd missed it.

This was what he always wanted. To make a difference. To take action. To do.

Like he'd told Kopano at the gas station, it wasn't always glamorous. Nigel still had flashbacks to the massacre at Patience Creek. He still got a bitter taste in his mouth when he thought about the bodies.

But the reality of the fight—against Mogadorians, against Harvesters, against snotty-looking Garde from frozen wasteland countries—it didn't scare Nigel off or make him second-guess his Legacies. The ugliness only made him want to fight more and fight harder. He'd spent so many years as a nobody, ignored by his parents, relentlessly picked on at Pepperpont—and now finally, finally he was going to take his rightful place in the world.

That's why, when they arrived in Iceland, Nigel was grinning.

The change was jarring. First, it was cold here, and Nigel's T-shirt was soaked through with sweat from the battle with the Harvesters. His breath misted in front of him and steam curled up from his narrow shoulders. It was also early morning. Even though the skies were clouded over and gray, the brightness stung his eyes. All the same, Nigel grinned.

Maybe it was Nigel's half-mad smile that caused the large man in body armor to hesitate bringing down his sledgehammer. Nigel liked to think so. But it was probably the four teenagers who manifested right in front of him that momentarily stunned the intimidating chap.

That was their welcoming committee. A badass-looking dude poised to bring his hammer down on the stone they'd teleported in on. He hesitated only a moment, then continued his downwards swing, not appearing to care that Nigel's head was now in the way.

Kopano caught the hammer in the palm of his hand with a metallic clang. Then, his fist heavy and hard, Kopano punched the guy square in the cheek. He slumped to the ground, unconscious, his jaw broken.

"He didn't look friendly," Kopano said.

Nigel patted him on the back. "He most certainly did not."

They stood in a small wooden enclosure. The gate was open, footprints in the frost leading from the house to the now-unconscious brute. The house was quaint and cute, a log cabin, with a rock garden outside. It looked entirely too peaceful.

Ran put her forearm under Rabiya's chin and slammed her up against the wall. "Where is this? Where did you bring us?"

Rabiya gagged, her eyes bugging out. Nigel touched Ran's shoulder and she let up on the pressure.

"I told you! Iceland!" Rabiya said hoarsely. "This is Einar's house. He took your friend." Her gaze drifted to the man Kopano had knocked out and her eyes widened.

Nigel kicked the unconscious man. "Who's this, then? You recognize him?"

"Blackstone," Rabiya said. "Mercenaries. If they're here, this place is burned. Your friend is gone or already dead. We should leave or they will kill us, too."

Nigel looked down at the unconscious mercenary. "This wanker won't even be able to eat solid foods in a dream, much less kill anyone."

"There will be more."

Ran half turned to look at Nigel and Kopano. "How should we—?"

The second Ran turned her attention away, Rabiya made a dive for the Loralite stone.

If she hadn't been so badly injured by the Harvesters, she might have made it. Her body moved too slowly, though, and Ran brought her elbow down on the back of Rabiya's neck. The girl slumped to the ground, her fingertips inches away from the Loralite stone.

"Damn," Kopano said.

"Coulda let her go," Nigel said with a shrug. "Poor thing's been through the ringer."

"The Academy does not know enough about these people," Ran said. She dragged Rabiya's body to the back of the enclosure and set her gently against the wall. "I am sure they will have questions."

"That shit she said about Taylor—," Nigel started to say.

"We must check," Kopano replied.

As soon as he stepped out of the enclosure, Kopano was greeted by a burst of machine-gun fire. He grunted as the bullets struck him in the center of the chest. They didn't penetrate, but his Legacy was slow to kick in. He would have bruises. Bad ones.

A second mercenary crouched behind a pile of rocks. When he saw that his bullets hadn't harmed Kopano, he dropped his rifle and took a different weapon from his belt. An energy weapon. Mogadorian.

"Where is Taylor?" Kopano roared.

He charged across the backyard before the mercenary could get a shot off. Kopano picked the man up in both hands, headbutted him and kept running with the man held out in front of him. He smashed through the house's back door using the mercenary's body as a battering ram.

"Not a lot of teamwork in his approach, but it's efficient," Nigel commented.

Ran's lips quirked in her almost-smile. "Let's go," she said.

The two of them emerged from the cover of the enclosure with a little more caution than Kopano had shown. They weren't bulletproof. From inside the house, they could hear the sounds of objects breaking and Kopano repeatedly shouting Taylor's name.

"This what you were expecting?" Nigel asked, looking over the cabin.

"Absolutely not," Ran replied.

"Me neither." Nigel nodded up at the wall above the back door. "See that?"

"Camera," Ran said.

Nigel wiggled his fingers. "Wonder who's watching."

It was a lucky thing. If Nigel hadn't called her attention to the camera, Ran might not have looked up and seen the glint of reflected light in an open upstairs window.

A scope. A sniper rifle.

"Watch out!" Ran yelled and shoved Nigel hard to the side.

Ffft! Ffft! Ffft!

The shots came like puffs of air, fired through a high-powered rifle's silenced muzzle. Chunks of dirt and ice struck Nigel's legs, one of the bullets hitting where he'd just been standing. He and Ran scrambled in opposite directions.

Nigel got close to the house and around the corner, while Ran dove behind a pile of discus-shaped stones.

"Ran! You good?"

"Yes," she replied, but Nigel heard a hitch of pain in her voice.

Ffft! Another shot exploded a rock near Ran's head.

"I'm pinned down," Ran yelled.

"On it!" Nigel replied.

From inside the house, Nigel heard the crash of a table being overturned. He peeked through a nearby window. Kopano was locked up against a large man with a thick beard and a scarred face, smashing through a fancy kitchen. Kopano punched the mercenary in the ribs, but his body armor absorbed the blow.

The man swung a combat knife for Kopano's throat and connected. The slice merely made a grinding sound, though, not breaking Kopano's impenetrable skin.

"Hah!" Kopano shouted, swinging again.

The knife attack was only a feint, though. With his free hand, the mercenary pulled a manacle from his belt. As he ducked Kopano's punch, the mercenary snapped the shackle around his wrist. Immediately, the bracelet emitted a humming vibration and Kopano was jerked downwards, his arm stuck to the side of the stainless steel fridge.

Kopano roared, trying to pull his arm free, failing, then trying to lift the fridge entirely and finding it too heavy. Quickly, the man drew a pistol from the holster attached to his thigh.

"Let's see if your eyes are bulletproof," he growled.

"Boo."

Nigel threw his voice so it sounded as if he were right behind the mercenary. He spun around, found no one there. Nigel took the opportunity to yank the gun out of his hand. The man got off one shot that harmlessly thudded into a couch.

Kopano took the opening to seize him by the scruff of his neck using the arm that wasn't pinned to the fridge. He slammed the guy's head down against the countertop, then hefted him using his telekinesis, rammed his back against the ceiling and finally let him fall to the floor.

While that was happening, Nigel clambered in through the window. He glanced out the back door—Ran was still huddled behind some rocks. As he watched, she used her telekinesis to fling a glowing stone at the second level of the cabin, aiming blindly for the sniper.

A small explosion soon followed. The air was still for a moment. Ran started to peek her head out—*ffft!*—and yelped when another bullet nearly took her head off. The shot grazed her cheek, opening a deep cut there.

"Sniper upstairs!" Nigel yelled to Kopano as he ran for the stairs.

"I'm stuck!"

"One bloody thing at a time, mate!"

Nigel bounded up the steps, taking them two at a time. His telekinesis tingled on his fingertips—ready to disarm the sniper as soon as he came into view. He raced down the hall, counting doorways to match the windows outside.

He burst into the room where the sniper should be. The window was empty.

"Where—"

Behind him. The sniper spun Nigel around and clocked him in the bridge of the nose with the butt of his rifle.

Nigel fell on his back with a cry, blood streaming down his face. The sniper spun his gun back around, smiled and took aim—

Nigel screamed. The sound was piercing and high-pitched enough that the glass on the rifle's scope shattered. The mercenary flinched and grabbed at his ears.

That was all the space Nigel needed. He yanked the rifle away from the mercenary with his telekinesis, grabbed it out of the air and pulled the trigger.

He shot the sniper right in the chest. The bullet cracked into his body armor and sent him flying backwards into the hall, where he slumped against the wall. Nigel got up, still holding the rifle, and stood over the man as he gasped for breath.

"Shouldn't go shooting at everyone who teleports into your backyard, mate," Nigel said as he chambered another round. "Maybe we were just coming by for a cup of sugar, eh? Guess you'll never know."

Nigel might have killed the mercenary—the guy had shot Ran and certainly would've done the same to Nigel if given the chance. But movement in the corner of his eye distracted him.

A little girl stood at the end of the hallway. Frightened and pale, she watched Nigel with wide eyes. Around her neck was a strange choker that she kept nervously tugging at.

Instead of shooting the mercenary, Nigel sighed and brought the rifle around and down like he was swinging a golf club. A swift blow to the temple knocked the sniper unconscious. Nigel then used his telekinesis to bend the muzzle of his gun into an unusable pretzel, a trick he'd picked up from Nine.

Finally, he turned to the girl. "Are you some kind of tiny assassin?"

"No . . . ," the girl replied with a shake of her head.

"Didn't think so."

"Are you here to rescue me?"

Nigel looked around. "Sure, love."

The girl approached him cautiously, still tugging at that weird collar. Nigel noted more cameras mounted along the hallway and in the rooms. What kind of weird shit went on in this Nordic cabin?

"How many of these guys were here?" he asked, nudging the unconscious mercenary with his foot.

"Four," the girl said.

Nigel made a quick count. "Right, then. Got them all." He crouched down to better look the girl in her face. "What's your name?"

"Freyja."

"Freyja, is there another girl hiding hereabouts? My age, American, pretty if that's your thing."

"Taylor," Freyja said, then shook her head. "She was here, but he took—"

A scream from downstairs distracted Nigel from the rest of Freyja's sentence. That didn't sound like Ran or Kopano.

It sounded like Taylor.

Regardless, screaming was a bad sign. "Stay here," he snapped at Freyja, then bolted back downstairs.

The first thing Nigel saw when he came down the steps was Kopano, still pinned by the wrist to the side of the fridge by that magnetized manacle. An uneasy feeling came over Nigel. There was fear in Kopano's eyes—not an emotion he'd seen on the big man before.

"Nigel Barnaby," said a smooth, accented voice.

The guy from the highway—Einar, Rabiya had called him—stood in the back door. He wore gray slacks and a white dress shirt, the latter spattered with fresh blood. He smiled at Nigel in a way that made his skin crawl.

"You have no idea how happy I am to see you."

CHAPTER THIRTY-FOUR

TAYLOR COOK
ABU DHABI, UNITED ARAB EMIRATES • HOFN, ICELAND

"TAYLOR," EINAR SAID, HIS VOICE SOFT BUT commanding. "Get up."

Taylor opened her eyes slowly. Her muscles felt tired, her fingertips and palms still tingling from the protracted use of her healing Legacy. Her mouth was dry, as were her nasal passages. She coughed scratchily, sitting up on the divan where she had passed out.

Einar handed her a glass of water. "You've been sleeping for almost six hours," he said. "I think that's long enough."

Taylor worked some moisture into her mouth. "You didn't do any healing. How would you know?"

Einar didn't reply. He simply grabbed her by the arm and helped her stand. They were in one of the palace's hundred guest bedrooms. This one was decorated with pictures of the sheikh—grim as he looked when Taylor first saw him—standing next to a variety of expensive cars. Taylor rubbed her eyes.

"What happens now?"

"We go home," Einar said.

Taylor gave him a look.

"Back to my home," Einar clarified.

"And then what? Wait around until this Foundation of yours picks another rich prick to have me heal?"

Einar raised an eyebrow. "Did you not enjoy it? Using your Legacy to save a life? To do the impossible?"

Taylor hesitated. She and the other healers—they had cured the prince's leukemia. Cleaned it right out of his body.

The cancer was deep in the prince's cells. She could feel it there. Alone, Taylor wouldn't have been able to produce enough healing energy to cure the sickness—but with the group, it was possible. Vincent had been of similar strength to Taylor; Jiao's healing energy was the most focused and precise; the crippled boy a font of raw power. After getting over her initial reservations, Taylor had thrown herself into the work, her energy commingling with the others, beating back the corruption that infested the prince's body.

The process had taken four hours. After, all of them were spent and ready to pass out. Oddly and despite the fact that they were strangers to her, now that she'd broken away from the other healers, she missed the warm feeling of their energy.

Taylor didn't tell any of this to Einar. "You know, the

Academy had me healing people too," she said instead. "They didn't pick special cases. They let me heal whoever was in need."

"The prince is a valuable ally. His family helps keep this region of the world stable."

"Who told you that? The Foundation?"

Einar said nothing, which Taylor took as a yes. He walked out of the guest room, forcing Taylor to follow him.

"These people you're working for, they get to decide who gets healed? They get to control the healing? Is that it?" Taylor pressed him.

"I'm sure we could arrange for you to do some kind of charity, if that makes you feel better," Einar said.

"It would make me feel better to not have some shadowy organization controlling my life."

Einar stopped, looking around. The hallways of the palace were clearer now than when they'd arrived; there didn't seem to be a squadron of guards assigned to them. There also weren't cameras mounted over every doorway.

"I liked what you said to the prince. 'Are you a good person?'" Einar chuckled quietly. "It does these people well to be reminded, once in a while, who really holds the power."

Taylor started to say something, but realized that Einar was being genuine. Opening up, even. She closed her mouth and let him keep talking.

"The Foundation, Earth Garde, the Academy. They are all just ways to control us," Einar said. "We are young now and not strong enough to make our own way. One day, though, we will be. In the meantime, we're forced to choose who we allow to exploit us. The Foundation . . ." Einar met her gaze. "They provide a good life. To fight against them, at this point, would be futile."

Einar resumed his walk down the hallway. Taylor followed after him, mulling over his words. So, he wasn't blindly loyal to the Foundation. But they'd corrupted him to the point where he'd do their bidding. She didn't agree with what Einar said about the Academy—that felt like home to her, which surprised her. Taylor hadn't wanted to go there in the first place, but now badly wanted to go back. She needed to find a way out. A way to free herself, and Freyja, from the grasp of these Foundation creeps.

As they entered the courtyard with the Loralite stone, Taylor had begun to remove her headscarves; they'd become annoyingly tangled while she was passed out. She and Einar stopped short. A dozen of the white thobe–wearing guards stood in the courtyard, blocking their path to the Loralite stone. All of them were armed and, while their weapons weren't raised, they all seemed ready for action.

Taylor swallowed hard. Maybe the sheikh hadn't appreciated her insolence.

"What is this?" Einar asked, apparently as surprised as Taylor to find their way barred.

Jiao emerged from the crowd of guards. She looked fresh and awake—a sharp contrast to how Taylor felt after their marathon healing session. The smartly dressed Chinese girl smiled at Taylor like they were old pals, then fixed Einar with an icy look.

"You can't leave, Einar," she said simply.

"Excuse me?" he replied. "What are you still doing here, Jiao?"

"The Foundation asked me to stay in case you got out of hand. But you'll be a good boy, won't you?" She wiggled her fingers in Taylor's direction. "Come on, darling. You're coming home with me."

"Um, what?" Taylor replied.

"Einar will remain as a guest of the sheikh," Jiao said.

Einar took a step forward and put a hand across Taylor, preventing her from going to Jiao. Not that she made a move in that direction anyway.

"I don't understand," Einar said flatly.

Jiao snorted. "Really, man? You lost Rabiya. Probably got her killed."

"I made healing the prince possible," Einar retorted.

"Yeah, and I assume that's why the sheikh hasn't already beheaded you," Jiao replied. "Doesn't mean he's happy that you threw his niece to the wolves."

"She belonged to the Foundation," Einar said sharply. "That was the deal. We heal his beloved son and we gain the services of his niece."

Jiao shrugged blithely. "Guess you should tell the sheikh that."

Slowly, Taylor put the pieces together. The girl with the headscarves from the road was related to the sheikh. Einar had lost her in the process of kidnapping Taylor. Now, he was in trouble. She remembered the conversation she'd eavesdropped on between Einar and the British woman.

Taylor ignored Jiao's outstretched hand, not making any effort to push by Einar. This was an opportunity to make a move, but whose side should she take? She was frozen.

"After everything I've done for the Foundation," Einar said bitterly. "One screwup and—"

"Oh, stop," Jiao said. "You know how it works."

Jiao made a gesture and two of the guards stepped forward. One of them carried a pair of manacles, the other held out two microchips like Taylor had seen attached to the crippled healer.

The two guards made it within five feet of Einar before they both began hysterically crying. They fell to their knees, clutching their faces, sobbing uncontrollably.

He was playing with their emotions.

"Einar—," Jiao started to say.

And then the shooting started.

It came from the two guards farthest at the back. Their weapons went off, shots firing into the dirt. Taylor noticed that they looked surprised. They hadn't pulled the triggers.

It was Einar.

The other guards spun around, startled, weapons coming up—and then Einar was telekinetically pulling all the triggers at once, a cross fire beginning, the sheikh's guards gunning each other down.

Jiao screamed. A bullet had struck her in the knee. She fell to the ground. Taylor remained rooted in place.

"I find this very disrespectful of my talents," Einar said. He lifted Jiao with his telekinesis and flung her through one of the second-story windows.

Then, he grabbed Taylor by the hair.

"Sorry," he said. "But you need to come with me."

Taylor was too stunned, staring at the bloody bodies of the murdered guards, to immediately react. Or maybe that was Einar, making her docile.

He dragged her to the Loralite stone and touched the cobalt surface.

The spinning sensation. Blinking blue lights. The sudden chill of Iceland.

Finally reacting, Taylor shoved away from Einar as soon as they were inside the wooden enclosure. He didn't seem to notice. Einar was too focused on the crumpled body propped up against the wall. She'd been so badly beaten, it took Taylor a moment to recognize Rabiya.

Einar laughed, looking down at the unconscious girl. "This is tremendously ironic."

"You asshole, what does this mean for—?" Taylor gasped. Outside the enclosure, Ran lay on her back, taking cover behind a pile of rocks. She was stunned to see her roommate there—and in rough shape. Ran had a gash along her cheek and a bullet wound in her thigh.

"Get down!" Ran shouted at her as Taylor made to run across the grass. "Sniper!"

Taylor ignored her friend's instructions, hopping over the unconscious body of one of those Blackstone mercenaries as she rushed to Ran's side. No bullets came from the upstairs window.

"You're hurt," Taylor said as she slid in next to Ran. "How did you . . . ?"

But then, it made sense. Rabiya. They'd gotten her to teleport them here.

"We came to rescue you," Ran said. She looked over Taylor's shoulder, tensing up when she saw Einar.

Einar edged out from the enclosure with more caution than Taylor, peering up at his cabin.

Quickly, Ran grabbed a stone, charged it with her explosive energy and sent it flying towards Einar.

He looked up just in time, swatting the rock away with his telekinesis. His lips curled in annoyance and he thrust a hand in Ran's direction.

Taylor recoiled as Ran's entire body began to vibrate. Veins in her neck bulged, all her muscles tight. Blood from her cheek flattened out against the side of her face. It looked like Ran was trying to sit up, but she couldn't. Her eyes were wide and bloodshot.

Einar was using his telekinesis to grind her into the ground.

"It's funny how the instinct is to use our telekinesis to throw things at our enemies," Einar said conversationally. "Even the Loric behave that way. You can see it in videos of them fighting during the invasion. They rip away guns, hurl around cars. But the body's an object, just like anything else.

My theory is, the Loric had an instinct bred into them, not to use their telekinesis on each other directly." Einar shrugged. "I've been trained a different way."

"Let her go!" Taylor shouted.

"How does that feel, Ran Takeda?" Einar asked. "Is it like Tokyo again? The feeling of being crushed?"

If Taylor thought there was some glimmer of humanity in Einar, she'd been woefully mistaken. He was insane. With her telekinesis, she grabbed a sledgehammer that lay near the Loralite stone and flung it at him.

The head of the hammer struck Einar right between the shoulder blades. He yelped and fell onto his hands, his grip on Ran broken. She grabbed her ribs, gasping for air.

Taylor plucked the sledgehammer out of the air. She stood over Einar and cocked her arms back.

"It's more satisfying to hit people with things," she said. "You'll see."

She almost brought the hammer down. But then a feeling of deep sympathy came over her. Who knows what the Foundation had done to this poor kid. He wasn't bad. He didn't want to hurt her. It was all just a misunderstanding.

No. That was Einar. Manipulating her.

By the time Taylor realized that, it was too late. Einar stood and ripped the sledgehammer out of her hands. He cracked Taylor across the face with the wooden handle, knocking her down.

"Hmm," Einar said. "You're right."

He raised the hammer and brought it down on Taylor's ankle. She screamed as the bones shattered, and nearly fainted.

"That should keep you busy," Einar said. He tossed the sledgehammer across the yard, stepped by Ran and walked into the house.

Tears stung Taylor's eyes. Warm blood trickled down the side of her face from a gash on her eyebrow. Her ankle felt as if there were broken glass under her skin.

"Tay . . . Taylor . . ."

That was Ran. She struggled to sit up, clutching at a nearby rock. Patches of mud and bits of ice clung to her shoulders where she'd been driven into the ground. She arched her back strangely and craned her head back, gulping air.

Or trying to, at least.

"I . . . can't . . . breathe . . . ," Ran said.

Einar must have broken one of her ribs or crushed a lung. Taylor looked at Ran dazedly, trying to focus through the immense pain and her spinning head.

"Hold on," Taylor said, her voice cracking.

As fast as she could manage, Taylor dragged herself across the yard towards Ran. Her lips were turning blue. Taylor needed to get there. Needed to heal her. Fight through it.

Meanwhile, from inside the house, Taylor became vaguely aware of Kopano shouting.

They'd come here to save her. All her friends.

And Einar was killing them.

CHAPTER THIRTY-FIVE

KOPANO OKEKKE
HOFN, ICELAND

KOPANO STOPPED TRYING TO YANK THE MAGNE-tized handcuff loose from the side of the refrigerator when he saw Einar enter. A feeling of dread washed over him as the young man trained his beady eyes on Kopano. He was relieved to be stuck.

If Kopano couldn't move, Einar couldn't make him hurt his friends.

Einar sized Kopano up briefly, concluded he was trapped and ignored him. He went into the living room and pulled an attaché case out from underneath the couch. With his case in hand, he started to leave out the back door.

That's when Nigel bounded down the steps from up-stairs.

Einar paused. He smiled slowly.

"Nigel Barnaby. You have no idea how happy I am to see you."

Nigel took a deep breath, filling his lungs with air, ready to unleash one of his sonic screams.

His mouth snapped shut, teeth clacking together hard. Einar had forced it closed with his telekinesis. Nigel's eyes were wide with surprise. Kopano could tell Nigel was struggling, but he couldn't break Einar's telepathic grip.

Kopano shoved Einar with his own telekinesis. Einar stumbled for a moment, but quickly regained his balance. A powerful telekinetic force overwhelmed his own and Kopano bounced back against the refrigerator.

"They need to teach better telekinetic control at that school of yours," Einar said.

Helplessly, Kopano watched as his index finger bent all the way back to his wrist. The bone popped. Kopano shouted in pain.

"Unbreakable skin, yes? But not unbreakable bones." Einar glared at Kopano. "Stay still or I'll rip you apart."

Fear clutched at Kopano's stomach. He held his injured hand close to his belly. His lip quivered as he watched Einar, unable to do anything else.

The anger had been bad. The fear was worse.

Einar glanced up at one of the room's cameras. "I hope you're watching," he said to whoever was on the other side. Then, he looped an arm around Nigel's shoulders.

The British boy, always so confident, possessed of so much swagger—his face crumpled into a mask of utter sadness.

His entire posture changed—shoulders slumped and turned inwards, chin to chest, eyes downcast and watery. To see his friend like this made no sense to Kopano.

"I want you to think about Pepperpont," Einar said softly. "All those years, without a single friend. Abandoned by your parents. A worthless piece of forgotten shit. Something the better-looking boys passed around like a toy, hmm? Do you remember those days, Nigel?"

Nigel shuddered, said nothing. Kopano stared. How did Einar know so much about Nigel?

"Will they hold you down in bed tonight and beat you? Will they lock you in a closet? Will they force you to take a shower with the water boiling hot?" Einar's lips were nearly against Nigel's ear. He led Nigel towards the door. "Better to end it, isn't it? Better to give up than endure another day?"

"No . . . ," Kopano croaked, the words hard to get out against the terror gripping him. He wanted to shrink back into himself, to get small . . . but he couldn't let this evil bastard get into Nigel's head. "Don't listen to him, Nigel! Don't listen!"

But Nigel didn't hear. Or, if he did, Kopano's shouts didn't penetrate the crushing depression that Einar was forcing Nigel to feel.

"It will be over quickly," Einar said. "Just walk out and let the cold take you."

He led Nigel out the front door. Kopano could hear their feet crunching across gravel.

There was an iced-over lake out there.

"Nigel!" Kopano shouted. "Ran! Someone!"

No answer. The backyard was quiet.

The fear disappeared. It turned off all at once, giving Kopano a nauseous feeling as the muscles in his abdomen unclenched. Einar must have gotten too far away from him. The effects of his control wore off.

The fear was replaced by desperation.

He had to save his friends.

With a bellow, Kopano used his telekinesis to lift the refrigerator. Food spilled out of it as the doors swung open—a glass bottle of milk shattered on the floor. Kopano crunched through the broken glass, carrying the appliance like an albatross, his wrist aching from the manacle still attached to the fridge's side.

Kopano charged across the living room. The refrigerator crashed against a chair, knocked it over. He smashed the base into a TV, shattering the screen and knocking it off the wall. Didn't matter. He maneuvered as best he could towards the front door.

He could see Nigel. Walking out on the ice. Like a zombie. Einar watched him from the edge of the lake with his arms crossed.

One second Nigel was there, the next second he was gone.

The ice cracked beneath Nigel's feet and the water sucked him down.

Kopano shouted. He tried to run through the front door, but the refrigerator became wedged in the doorway. He pulled against it, using both the strength left in his handcuffed arm and all the power he could muster from his telekinesis. The metal of the appliance squealed and bent; the wooden door chipped and broke.

But he was stuck. In the end, all Kopano's tugging did was get the refrigerator jammed worse. His wrist was a raw and bloody mess from where he'd pulled against the manacle.

Nigel had been under the water for thirty seconds.

He glanced warily around the lake's edge. Einar was gone. Out of sight.

Kopano had to get his arm free. Brute strength wasn't doing it. He tried to slip loose of the cuff, but it was fastened tight.

He pulled and pulled. The bracelet had to give. Or else, let it slice right through his arm. Take his hand right off. He could get to Nigel, save his friend, and worry about that later. Kopano snarled, bracing one of his feet against the fridge, ignoring the pain as he wrenched against the handcuff with all his might.

Kopano fell onto his back with a thud.

It gave. He was free.

His wrist was whole. The cuff was unbroken. It didn't make sense.

He didn't pause to think about it.

Nigel had been underwater for a minute. More, maybe.

Kopano sprinted towards the crystalline lake. During training, Dr. Goode had told Kopano to think of himself as heavy. That seemed to help him control his power—he often focused on that feeling, making his skin impenetrable and his hands hard as bricks. But he didn't want to be heavy now. He needed to be light. Nimble.

He hit the icy lake at a full sprint, the frigid water filling up his sneakers. The surface was already cracked where Nigel had walked on it. Kopano's long strides, his large body—he should've plummeted straight into the water.

He didn't. Somehow, Kopano's feet were light as feathers. He practically floated across the ice. Was he moving so fast that the ice didn't have a chance to break? Was it luck? Something else?

Kopano didn't care. He saw the dark and jagged hole where Nigel had fallen through. That was his goal.

He sucked in as deep a breath as he could and dove.

The water was so cold that it stunned Kopano and he nearly gasped. He steeled himself against the pinpricks and numbness, plunging deeper. He was never a strong swimmer and the water was dark. He couldn't see Nigel. He looked for bubbles but didn't see any.

Kopano needed to go deeper. He let himself get heavier, like Dr. Goode had taught him. He sunk farther down, his chest tightening.

Spinning, Kopano began to pull with his telekinesis. He didn't grab for anything in particular, he just made the water churn around him. He created a whirlpool with himself at the center.

Two minutes? Three minutes? How long had Nigel been down here? Kopano's lungs were beginning to burn.

A broken chunk of an old rowboat was pulled into

Kopano's whirlpool. A school of fish spun past him. Smooth black stones from the lakebed began to blur his vision.

There! It looked like a blond jellyfish waving back and forth, almost glowing in the dark water. Nigel's bleached mohawk.

Kopano reached down. The other boy wasn't moving, unconscious, his mouth open to the water. Kopano grabbed him by the back of the shirt.

Lighter, thought Kopano. *Be lighter. Up, up, up.*

Dragging Nigel with him, Kopano kicked his feet and sped towards the surface. He was surprised by how buoyant he was; it felt like the water itself was trying to shove him towards the surface.

A sheet of ice became visible above him. Kopano's heart beat harder, his lungs screaming for air. As a boy, he'd read adventure stories about a young man traveling the globe; always, when he was in cold climes, someone ended up trapped beneath some ice. His stinging eyes couldn't find the break in the ice that he'd jumped through.

Kopano reached out towards the ice with his free hand—his injured hand, the broken finger hanging loose, forgotten about in his rush to rescue Nigel. He prepared to thrust out with his telekinesis, ready to break the ice apart.

He didn't need to. Kopano's hand passed right through the ice, like he was a ghost. His eyes widened, uncertain what was happening. His whole body floated upwards, transparent, sliding through the frozen barrier. He could feel something happening within him—an opening sensation, like his body's cells were spreading apart to allow the ice to pass through. He glanced down and saw that Nigel had gone transparent too.

And then Kopano stood atop the ice again, his feet feeling light on the fragile surface. His Legacy—he'd unlocked something, figured something out in his desperation.

Kopano didn't have time to relish the milestone. Nigel wasn't breathing. His face was blue, his body limp and freezing.

Gulping in air, Kopano gathered the British boy in his arms and ran towards the shore.

"Kopano!"

The Nigerian let out a groan of relief when he saw Taylor and Ran running towards him from the house. Neither of them looked well—Ran's clothes were dark with fresh blood, Taylor was hobbling and bleeding from a head wound—but they were alive. They were alive and they would know what to do about Nigel.

Kopano set Nigel down on the rocky shore of the lake. His clothes were cold and heavy on his thick frame and he felt suddenly, unbearably heavy.

"He's—he's not breathing!" Kopano said. "That bastard made him . . . made him . . ."

Kopano couldn't bring himself to finish. He looked around wildly for Einar, his fists clenched.

Taylor went to her knees next to Nigel, immediately pressing her hands to his narrow chest. Ran caught Kopano's crazed look and put a weak hand on his arm.

"Einar's gone," she said. "He teleported away with Rabiya while Taylor was healing me."

Ran looked shaken and rough. She crouched next to Nigel and held his hand, rubbing it between her own. Kopano leaned in over her shoulder, staring between Nigel and Taylor.

"Can you . . . ?" He tried to catch his breath. "Can you heal him?"

Taylor didn't respond. She was concentrating on Nigel. There were dark bags forming under her eyes, her skin pale. She'd been overtaxed in the short time since her kidnapping. Kopano wondered how much healing she could manage.

A bubble formed on Nigel's lips. The water he'd swallowed slowly trickled out of his mouth, pushed out of his lungs by Taylor's healing Legacy. Kopano let out a sigh of relief.

But Taylor didn't look happy. She put her ear against Nigel's chest.

"He's not breathing," she said, her voice cracking. "His heart's not . . . I don't know how to heal this. It's not wounded, it's just . . . stopped."

Tears streaked down Taylor's cheeks. Nigel was still, no color returning to his cheeks.

"Step back," said Ran.

Taylor did as she was told. She stumbled to Kopano and he instinctively wrapped his arms around her, grateful for the warmth of her small body in his arms. His teeth were chattering.

"I didn't get to him quickly enough," Kopano said quietly.

"It's not your fault," Taylor replied.

Ran touched Nigel's cold cheek. Her shoulders shook. She bowed her head for a moment, whispering a prayer.

Then, she ripped open Nigel's shirt.

"Ran—?" Taylor said, startled.

Ran put her hand on Nigel's chest. She charged his sternum with her Legacy. He glowed. His body vibrated.

"Ran!" Taylor yelled, alarmed. "What are you doing?"

"Waking up . . . his body," Ran replied, her eyes flashing with energy. "Making . . . breakfast."

Kopano took a step back, bringing Taylor with him. Nigel's body pulsed with crimson energy. Kopano could see where Ran's energy surged out of Nigel's pores, out of his nostrils, his eyes.

And then, she pulled it all back into herself.

The force of yanking that much energy out of Nigel blew Ran backwards. Acting quickly, Kopano caught her with his telekinesis.

Nigel's whole body convulsed with the concussive force, bouncing against the rocks.

And then he screamed.

Coughing raggedly and holding his chest, Nigel rolled onto his side. Taylor clapped a hand over her mouth and Kopano let loose with a cheer. Color slowly blossomed in Nigel's cheeks. He shuddered, peering around at his friends with bleary eyes.

Ran grabbed him in a hug, squeezing him close. Her hands and forearms were already dark purple with bruises from where she'd pulled back the energy, but the pain didn't seem to bother her.

"I found a nonviolent use for my Legacy," she said.

"Fuckin' hell, Ran," Nigel said. "Tell me about it later, yeah?"

Then, he fainted.

CHAPTER THIRTY-SIX

THE SIX
THE HUMAN GARDE ACADEMY—POINT REYES, CALIFORNIA

FROM ICELAND, THEY TELEPORTED BACK TO NEW Mexico, where Isabela, Caleb and Professor Nine were still waiting. There was a lot of commotion over the amount of blood on their clothes, but Taylor had healed most of their injuries. She'd done a bad job mending her own broken ankle—had put only enough healing energy into the shattered bones to allow her to walk on it—so she needed to lean on Kopano for support.

He didn't mind.

They brought Freyja with them. Strangely, they found that the choker had simply fallen off her neck. The little girl claimed it "just happened." Taylor wondered what that meant. It seemed as if the Foundation had let them off the hook.

Freyja was turned over to the UN Peacekeepers. She'd have a long flight home, but they would reunite her with her family. She thanked Taylor and Nigel before the Peacekeepers took her away, but Taylor was disappointed to see fear in her eyes. The child was afraid of Garde. It was hard to blame her; the girl had seen firsthand what the worst of their kind could do.

Kopano offered to teleport the Peacekeepers and Earth Garde back to Iceland so they could apprehend the mercenaries and investigate Einar's house. It took them thirty minutes to get clearance for such an operation, but eventually they took him up on the offer.

But when they were ready, Kopano found he was unable. The Loralite stone in Einar's backyard was gone. Someone must have smashed it.

◇ ◇ ◇

The six of them returned to the Academy. They were allowed two days of rest and recovery. Then, the punishment kicked in. They were assigned training sessions at dawn five days a week, immediately followed with a shift serving breakfast in the dining hall, not to mention weekly sessions with Dr. Linda to deal with any psychological fallout.

Rumors about the six of them swirled around campus. They didn't talk about their adventure. Even Isabela refrained from bragging.

People started calling them the Fugitive Six.

As the weeks went by and things ostensibly returned to normal, the six of them had a hard time hanging out with other students around the Academy. The others—they hadn't seen what was out there. They hadn't really fought yet. They had Legacies, but they weren't yet Garde.

After one of their early-morning training sessions on Nine's brutal obstacle course, Caleb turned to the others as he toweled off.

"Do you guys ever get the feeling that this isn't exactly punishment?" he asked.

"No," Isabela groaned, rubbing her sore neck. "It is worse than punishment. It's torture."

"No, I mean . . ." Caleb shrugged. "I don't know. These team workouts, it's like . . ."

"We are being groomed," Ran said.

They all looked up at the catwalk that crossed over the training center.

Nine watched them from above.

✧ ✧ ✧

She might have hated the arduous physical training, but Isabela threw herself into her studies like never before. One subject in particular interested her. Almost every night, she would knock on Taylor or Ran's door.

"Flash cards?" Isabela would ask with a nervous smile.

They practiced her English for hours every night. Soon, she wouldn't need Simon's Legacy at all.

✧ ✧ ✧

"Can I show you something?" Caleb asked Nigel, about a month after they'd returned from Iceland.

"That question makes me nervous, mate," Nigel replied

with a smirk. "What is it?"

"It's upstairs."

Nigel followed Caleb up three floors to one of the unoccupied sections of the dorms. Technically, they weren't allowed up here, but even with the stricter security protocols that had been implemented since their little excursion, the dorms remained largely a free-for-all. The abandoned floors were a popular hookup spot if you had a prudish roommate.

"Caleb, man, you're a good lad and all, but I don't feel that way about you."

"What? No!" Caleb glanced over his shoulder at Nigel and blushed. "I'm not—I mean—it's okay that you are but I'm— um . . ."

"Relax, mate. I'm messing with you."

"I know," Caleb said, relaxing.

He stopped in front of a door at the end of the hall. Nigel noticed soundproofing pads had been stapled to the surface.

"Ready?" Caleb asked.

"I'm not sure that I am, brother."

Caleb swung the door open.

Inside was a garage band setup that warmed Nigel's heart. A five-piece drum kit, a bass guitar, a banged-up electric guitar and a keyboard. Each of the instruments and the soundboard that managed the volume were manned by one of Caleb's clones.

"Seriously?" Nigel said. "Clone band?"

"Hardly anyone ever uses the music room, so I liberated

some stuff and brought it here," Caleb explained. "It's our practice space."

"You can play all these instruments?"

Caleb shrugged. "I mean, not well. But we're learning. It helps that I can have each clone practice on their own."

Nigel raised an eyebrow at that. "Seriously?"

"Yeah." He walked farther into the room and grabbed the microphone stand. He tilted it in Nigel's direction. "Thing is, we need a front man."

Nigel grinned.

◇ ◇ ◇

"I'm afraid we've been going about your training all wrong," Dr. Goode told Kopano apologetically. He had the Nigerian young man hooked up to an array of machines that produced a variety of readings, all of them gibberish to Kopano.

"I don't know," Kopano said cheerily. "I think you've been doing a solid job."

Dr. Goode smiled. "Yes, well, you see, we believed your Legacy was a variation of Fortem that was tied to your skin. That you were somehow creating an impenetrable subdermal layer."

"But I'm not," Kopano replied. "Right?"

"No, it's much more amazing than that," Dr. Goode said. "Your Legacy is in your every cell, Kopano. In the atoms, in fact, that make up your cells. To put it simply, based on my preliminary findings, you can separate or contract your cells on a subatomic level. You can alter your density. You can become very heavy and hard or weightless to the point of transparency. Now, it's just a matter of learning how to control it."

Kopano looked down at his hands. "I haven't been able to do what I did since . . . since the ice."

"Oh, we're going to change that, big boy," Professor Nine said, striding into the room. In front of him, he floated a cube wrapped completely in barbed wire. He let the strange object bob in the air before Kopano.

"What's this?" Kopano asked.

"That's a box with a cupcake inside it," Nine said. "I wrapped it in razor wire. You want the cupcake, you gotta reach through the razors and into the box. Break apart your atoms and feast on deliciousness. Or slice your hand up. Come on. Try it."

Kopano eyed the box warily. "What kind of cupcake?"

It took Kopano weeks to finally master Nine's game with the barbed-wire box. When he finally did, he wrote home to his parents, describing the function of his Legacy.

He had yet to hear back.

◇ ◇ ◇

They weren't supposed to talk about what happened in New Mexico and Iceland, but that didn't extend to their weekly therapy sessions with Dr. Linda.

"Do you have those feelings often, Nigel?" Dr. Linda asked in her usual lilting way, Nigel spread out on the couch across from her. "The feelings that you felt when you walked out on the ice?"

"No."

"Are you being truthful?"

Nigel's lips curled. He scratched the back of his neck.

"Maybe I used to feel like that sometimes. Like a hopeless bloody case. But I haven't had that darkness in my life for a while. Not since I came here." His look turned dark as he thought about what happened in Iceland. "It was that wanker, the one I told you about. He put those feelings in me."

"I'd very much like to meet that young man," Dr. Linda replied. "His Legacy . . . it's quite interesting."

"Yeah. Quite," Nigel said dryly. "I'd like to see him again, too. Get some things off my chest."

"Now, Nigel, these thoughts of vengeance aren't healthy."

Nigel grinned crookedly. "I feel just fine, Doc. But you're right. They ain't healthy. For him."

"It's very unlikely you will ever get to act on these revenge fantasies," Dr. Linda said. "If you let them fester inside you . . ."

Nigel didn't reply. His cavalier smile gave nothing away.

But there was something Dr. Linda didn't know.

◇ ◇ ◇

Dr. Goode and Nine had personally driven their wayward students back from New Mexico to the Academy. They were all exhausted and injured, traumatized to varying degrees, but Taylor remembered how happy they were to be together. How close she felt to them all.

She told them everything. Einar, Iceland, the Foundation, Jiao, the sheikh, the healers, the strange British woman. Everything.

When she was done, Nine and Malcolm exchanged a look. Dr. Goode pulled over the car. Nine turned around to address his students. Behind them, the sun was just starting to rise.

"Listen, this might sound weird, but I think it's best if you keep most of the details of what happened between us," he said.

Taylor's brow had furrowed. "What? Why?"

"We think there are people within the Academy . . ." Dr. Goode hesitated. "We believe we've been compromised."

"A mole," Nigel said quietly.

"Like a spy movie," Kopano added.

"We've known about these Foundation assholes for a while, but we haven't had a name for them," Nine continued. "We just know that they're constantly trying to hack our system." Nine exchanged a look with Malcolm. "But we've got some brainy computer people of our own. We've been able to head them off, most of the time . . ."

"They knew things about me," Nigel said. "Things they shouldn't have known."

"Me too," Ran said.

Malcolm nodded. "Indeed. With their efforts to access our systems blocked, we think they've resulted to planting agents. Perhaps faculty. Perhaps students."

"Falta muito para chegar?" Isabela asked in Portuguese, looking around confusedly, not understanding the discussion.

"We're going to root these people out," Nine said evenly,

looking at each one of them in turn. "We're going to expose them. And you can help us."

"How?" Caleb asked.

"To start with, by keeping your mouths shut," Nine said.

Taylor thought about that conversation often in the weeks after their return to the Academy. She thought about all the things that she'd seen since becoming a Garde. The kindness and heroism of her friends; the ugliness of the Harvesters; the cruelty of the Foundation. The other Garde, both here at the Academy and spread around the world, all of them with desires and agendas, with the potential to shape the future.

When she first got her powers, she'd wanted to hide them. But now, Taylor knew that wasn't an option. She couldn't settle for a boring life. She needed to be here. She needed to be where she could make a difference.

A package arrived for her, filled with letters from the students at her old school. At least the ones who didn't think she was a freak. They were sweet—wishing her well, asking for details and gossip, wondering what John Smith was like in person. Taylor read each one of them, even if she felt like she didn't know these people anymore and, more important, like they couldn't possibly know her.

Slipped in among the letters from high schoolers was a piece of expensive stationery, thick and cream-colored, covered in a delicate cursive. Immediately, Taylor knew this letter didn't belong with the others.

Dear Taylor,

I hope this letter finds you well. Thank you for your assistance in Abu Dhabi and Iceland. I am truly sorry for the unpleasantness that transpired with your host. I fear that his bad example has created a poor impression for our organization. I hope, in the future, you will give us a second chance.

The world is a better place for your efforts. The prince sends his fond regards. A number of sizable donations have been made in your name to a variety of low-income hospitals in the region. By saving one life, you have saved thousands more.

I look forward to working with you again in the future, should you desire such an opportunity.

Sincerely yours,
B
The Foundation

The British woman she'd caught a glimpse of on Einar's screen. It had to be.

Taylor's teeth clenched. She nearly crumpled the letter in her hands.

Then, she marched straight to Professor Nine's office. He stood at his window, gazing out at the students walking from the dorms to the student center. Taylor tossed the letter onto his desk.

"They want me back," she said. The hardness and resolve Taylor heard in her own voice surprised her.

Nine picked up the letter, scanning it quickly.

"They've got moles here," Taylor said. "Maybe we should get some there."

EXCLUSIVE BONUS!

THIS IS A DELETED SCENE FROM THE DAY TAYLOR
AND KOPANO ARRIVE AT THE HUMAN GARDE ACADEMY.

NINE LIKED THE VIEW FROM HIS OFFICE. FROM here, he could look down on the open-air portion of the training facility. He watched a handful of Earth Garde trainees practicing their telekinesis down below, making mental notes of who was looking precise and who was looking sloppy. The precise ones he'd make a point to insult later; the struggling ones would get pulled aside for a pep talk.

Professor Nine had his methods down pat.

He rubbed the stump where his arm used to be and sighed. The phantom limb was especially achy today. He saw his reflection in the window and grimaced.

"My man. What the hell are you doing here?" Nine asked himself.

Truth be told, Nine never expected to live this long. He

never imagined a morning where he'd wake up in a cozy and familiar bed, walk to a private office, and be bored all day. He was only a few years older than the students he trained, but his life experience made him feel decades their senior. For so long he'd lived as a fugitive, as an alien refugee, constantly hunted by Mogadorians. And then, last week, while grabbing a meal in the cafeteria, Nine sat down with his back to the exit. A major oversight; any surprise attackers would get the drop on him. His own mentor—his Cêpan, Sandor—would've had his ass for that kind of careless behavior. Nine was getting soft.

Nine looked down at himself. His T-shirt looked a little tighter than it should. Was that a little pudge forming over his perfectly sculpted abdominals? The food was good here. And he'd been getting lazy. He shook his head.

Nine walked up the wall using his antigravity Legacy and began knocking out crunches while hanging from the ceiling. He was approaching one hundred when Dr. Malcolm Goode strolled into his office.

"Meeting time!" Malcolm announced happily. He glanced around, finally looked up. "Oh. You're up there."

Nine dropped from the ceiling, landed softly, and smiled at the older man. "Check it out. Not even out of breath."

"Very good," Malcolm said, setting down his coffee mug.

"We got two new ones in today, right?"

Malcolm nodded. "A healer from South Dakota and a young man from Lagos whose Legacy we aren't exactly sure of." Malcolm paused. "Lagos is in Nigeria, by the way."

"I know that," Nine lied.

Nine plopped down on the couch across from Malcolm. He never used the desk in his office; it made him feel too serious. The weekly meetings took place here; chairs for the Academy's highest-ranking administrators were arranged in front of the couch where Nine took his naps.

"So, what's the deal with this kid's Legacy?" Nine asked. "Why can't you figure it out?"

"Initial reports from the Nigerian field office described his skin as impenetrable. Apparently, he had a run-in with some street toughs and they broke a knife on him. But—"

"Wait." Nine's eyes narrowed. "Can he . . . ?"

"No," Malcolm answered quickly, detecting the edge in Nine's voice. "He isn't like our old friend Five. His skin doesn't change to match whatever substance he's in contact with. In fact, preliminary examinations and X-rays show that his skin hasn't changed at all. There needs to be negative stimulus—a knife or an injection—to trigger the hardening reaction."

"Huh," Nine said, leaning back. "Have we tried shooting him yet?"

"Not yet," Malcolm responded dryly. "We'll figure it out."

Nine nodded. Over the last year, he and Malcolm had developed a solid teamwork approach to identifying and improving Legacies. Nine preferred to field-test with physical activities while Malcolm took a more scientific approach. They'd yet to encounter a power that they couldn't crack.

Colonel Ray Archibald was next to arrive to the weekly

briefing. The middle-aged man was clean shaven, his uniform always crisply pressed.

"'Sup, Archie," Nine said as the colonel strode into the room.

Archibald responded with an icy smile and sat down. Nine had taken an immediate dislike to the man; he had his fill of ultraserious army types during the invasion. The feeling was apparently mutual. With the way the Academy was structured, Colonel Archibald was required to view the insolent young Nine as an equal. Thanks to his enhanced hearing, Nine had overheard Archibald refer to him as a "whelp" and a "sandbagger" multiple times.

"Have you given any more thought to my war games suggestion?" Archibald asked Nine, an eyebrow raised in challenge.

Nine smirked. The colonel was always trying to get him to agree to joint exercises between Nine's students and the Peacekeepers stationed there. Archibald argued it would be good for all involved, but Nine got the persistent feeling that Archibald wanted his men to practice killing Garde.

"Yeah, yeah. Still thinking about it," Nine replied. "We did finally get another healer in today, so your men wouldn't have to worry about all the broken bones."

"You sound confident, son," the colonel replied. "Are we on?"

"Once again, I must voice my dissent for this barbaric idea," said Dr. Linda Matheson, the school psychologist, as she joined the meeting.

"Aw, come on, Doc. Beating the shit out of army guys is like a rite of passage for Garde," Nine said with a wolfish grin.

"Not strictly true," Malcolm put in.

Following behind Dr. Linda was Dr. Susan Chen. The dean of academics tended to stay quiet during these meetings. Nine had sat in on some of her lectures, though, where she was a completely different person—lively and animated and supersmart. The students liked her and so did Nine. She'd almost managed to convince him to get his high school diploma.

"All you PhDs are pacifists," Colonel Archibald complained.

"Hmm," Dr. Linda replied. "You say that as if it were a bad thing."

"Are we revisiting the war games idea? Such an exercise would definitely be useful for me," said Greger Karlsson as he squeezed into the office with the others.

Greger was Swedish, with light brown hair that he kept immaculately slicked back. He reminded Nine of one of those pretty boy finance tycoons that always ended up getting hauled to jail huddled under their own suit coats. But Greger's background wasn't finance; it was politics. Before the invasion he was an ambassador. These days, he served as the Earth Garde's liaison to the Academy. Greger observed the various activities at the school, kept track of the enrollees, and filed reports back to his bosses at the UN on their progress and potential. When Nine's students were ready, they were turned over to Greger, a process that Nine still had doubts about. Entrusting Garde to the whims of a political organization, even one as diverse and well-meaning as the UN, made the hairs on the back of Nine's neck stand up. This was the world he lived in now though—instead of hostile aliens, he dealt with bureaucrats and administrators.

"As long as the safety of our young men and women could be guaranteed, I don't see the harm in a little friendly competition with the Peacekeepers," Greger continued as he pulled up a chair. "Could be fun."

"I've been running war games exercises since before the 'Professor' here was born," Colonel Archibald said with a wave in Nine's direction. "Never had a soldier come out with worse than some scuffs and bruises. They're more likely to get hurt in that maniac obstacle course we installed down there."

Nine reclined, feeling a sense of satisfaction. He had played a large part in designing the sadistic training facility the young Garde used to practice their powers, basing it in large part on the one his Cêpan once built for him.

"I don't mean to question your record, Colonel," Malcolm said, "but did any of your past exercises involve young people capable of breaking the laws of physics?"

The colonel gave Malcolm a withering look. "No. Obviously not."

"As long as it's properly supervised, I actually don't see a problem with such an exercise," Dr. Chen chimed in. "I guess I'm not such a pacifist, after all."

Dr. Linda raised her eyebrows. "Susan, I'm really surprised to hear that. . . ."

"I know we try to look at our students like any other teenagers," Dr. Chen continued, "but their lives are bound to be very different from those of the kids we're used to working with. We need to remember that. If we're being realists, self-defense is never *not* going to be a part of their lives. It's our job to properly prepare them for all aspects of being a member of Earth Garde."

"Well put," Greger said.

Dr. Linda shook her head. "I just worry that an exercise pitting non-powered humans against Garde will result in reduced empathy for all involved."

Colonel Archibald pinched the bridge of his nose. "Oh God. Here we go."

While Dr. Linda and Archibald went back and forth, Lexa entered the office. She took a seat on the couch next to Nine and opened her laptop. Lexa was probably as old as the other two women in the room, but she didn't show it—her dark skin was smooth and flawless, not a spot of gray in her short black hair. She was Loric like Nine; they didn't age at the same rate as humanity. Lexa was the oldest survivor of the Loric race and the only one that didn't possess the Legacies of a Garde. She'd spent years on Earth as a hacker, hiding out from the Mogadorians and trying to protect Nine and his friends without revealing herself. When the Garde became household names after the invasion,

Lexa's existence was kept mostly under the radar. Aside from Malcolm, no one in the room knew that she was Loric. To the humans working at the Academy, she was simply their cybersecurity expert.

"Nice of you to show up," Nine said with a grin.

Lexa gave him a look. "What did I miss?"

Nine yawned in response. These weekly meetings always went the same way. Each of the administrators would try to push the Academy toward their singular vision, they'd bicker about policy for a while, and Nine would zone out. Anything significant would go to a vote. With Nine, Malcolm, and Lexa always voting together, it was rare for an idea that they didn't approve to get through. The adult world was boring.

With everyone present, the meeting officially got underway. Colonel Archibald started with an assessment of recent threats to campus security. "The short version is: there aren't any," he said. "All's quiet."

"What's the long version?" asked Nine.

The colonel pursed his lips. "We got reports that those Harvester yahoos held a rally down in San Francisco. Poorly attended and broken up by local authorities. Still, something to keep an eye on."

"This is why the Academy should've been built in Europe. The rural death cult is a uniquely American problem," Greger said. That earned him a hard look from Archibald.

Next, Dr. Chen briefed the group on the students she thought were struggling academically. The list was short this week—just the usual offenders, like Isabela Silva and Lofton St. Croix.

"The two of them seem distracted with . . ." Malcolm cleared his throat. "Shall we say, extracurricular activities?"

Nine went on autopilot. He grunted his responses, raised his hand to vote "yes" whenever Malcolm did, let his thoughts wander into a daydream, and then . . .

Well, then, his office was empty. Meeting adjourned.

In his daydream, Nine had both his arms and was using them to take out Mogs. He sighed.

Nine reminded himself that he was doing good work here. Training the next generation. Sure, he had a desk now, but he didn't use it. He was still a badass.

Five minutes after the rest of the administrators filed out, Malcolm and Lexa returned. They closed the door behind them.

"All right," Nine said. "Now we can start the real meeting."

"You need to be careful about Colonel Archibald," Malcolm warned, retaking his seat across from Nine. "You egg him on too much."

"Yeah, yeah," Nine waved this off and looked to Lexa. "What have you got?"

Lexa sat down at Nine's desk, her laptop open in front of her. She shook her head. "Nothing good."

"These Harvesters that Archibald was talking about?"

"I wish. Those guys are a joke," Lexa replied. "There was an incident in Malaysia that they aren't telling us about."

The "they" in this case was the UN. Once students

graduated from the Academy, Nine and the others were pretty much out of the loop. That's why Nine had asked Lexa to hack into the UN's internal system and monitor the reports about Earth Garde. The new Garde might have graduated from his program, but that didn't mean Nine was done looking out for them.

"Earth Garde had a noncombat team there doing humanitarian work. Building houses, tending to the sick," Lexa continued. "They got hit by what's been described as a team of high-tech mercenaries."

Nine clenched his fist. "Casualties?"

"None, actually," Lexa replied. "These guys used nonlethal gear, all of it specifically designed to counteract the Legacies of the Earth Garde team."

"That is definitely concerning," Malcolm said. He went around Nine's desk to peer at the report over Lexa's shoulder. "It suggests a high level of preparation."

"It gets worse," Lexa continued. "You remember Vincent Iabruzzi?"

"Of course," Nine said. He could remember each one of the low-skill nerds that he whipped into shape and sent out into the world. "Vinnie Meatballs! Don't tell me something happened to Vinnie Meatballs, Lexa."

"They took him," Lexa said gravely. "It's the UN's opinion that the operation was specifically targeting him. They don't have any leads."

"Son of a bitch," Nine replied, pushing his hand through his hair in frustration. "What the hell are they doing out there?"

"Remind me what Legacies Vincent has?" Malcolm asked.

"He's a healer," Lexa replied. "You remember months back? That story we picked up on from the aborigines in Australia?"

Nine squinted. "There were rumors about a healer getting taken, weren't there?"

Lexa nodded. "No one could verify this healer actually existed. And there were so many false reports back then, we didn't look into it too hard. But then . . ."

"China," Malcolm said.

"Yep," Lexa replied. "A Chinese healer got scooped right out of Beijing. Well, allegedly. Since they aren't participating in Earth Garde, details are scarce."

"Didn't they blame us for that?" Nine asked.

"Yeah. But after they made their initial accusations and the UN denied involvement, the Chinese government put a lid on it. Pretended it never happened," Lexa said. "Regardless, if we assume there was some truth to the Australian story, that makes three healers taken within the last six months."

"And in increasingly brazen fashion," Malcolm said. "To strike against a team of Earth Garde . . ." He shook his head.

Nine crossed the room so he could look out the window. "Didn't we just get a healer in today?"

"Taylor Cook," Malcolm confirmed.

"We need to keep a close eye on her," Nine said.

Lexa made some rapid-fire keystrokes on her laptop. "There's something else."

"God," Nine groaned. "This is the good news, right?"

"Afraid not. We had another attempted hack last night."

Periodically, ever since the Academy got up and running, their databases had been getting probed by hackers. So far, no one had been able to penetrate Lexa's secure encryption. However, she hadn't been able to pinpoint where the hacks were coming from. It was a stalemate.

"They tried gaining access to the mousetrap database," Lexa continued.

Nine's eyes widened. "No shit."

Malcolm sighed, disappointed. "Then our suspicions were true."

Two weeks ago, at an administration meeting just like the one they had today, Lexa mentioned in passing that she would be transferring the bulk of the Academy's records to a new secure server. The announcement was innocuous and passed without comment.

It was also a lie.

Lexa set up a dummy account on the new server she'd mentioned, but never actually transferred any data. No one except the administrators present for the meeting knew about the server move. That was the mousetrap.

"We've got a mole," Nine declared. "Oh shit. I bet it's Archibald."

"Working for whom, though?" Malcolm asked. "And for what purpose?"

Nine leaned his arm against the window, gazing outside. There were still battles to be fought. Enemies lurking in the shadows, who wouldn't easily reveal themselves so he could punch their heads off.

"Dunno," Nine said through gritted teeth. "But we're damn sure gonna find out."

THE GREAT EASTERN

THE

GREAT EASTERN

A NOVEL

HOWARD A. RODMAN

MELVILLE HOUSE
BROOKLYN · LONDON

THE GREAT EASTERN

Melville House Publishing   and   Suite 2000
             46 John Street   16/18 Woodford Road
        Brooklyn, NY 11201   London E7 0HA

mhpbooks.com
@melvillehouse

Photographs by Robert Howlett, The Great Eastern:
Wheel and Chain Drum (England, 1857), frontis, *Isambard Kingdom
Brunel Standing Before the Launching Chains of the* Great Eastern (England, 1857).

ISBN: 978-1-61219-785-2
ISBN: 978-1-61219-786-9 (eBook)

Designed by Fritz Metsch

Library of Congress Cataloging-in-Publication Data

Names: Rodman, Howard, author.
Title: The Great Eastern / Howard Rodman.
Description: Brooklyn : Melville House, 2019.
Identifiers: LCCN 2019004681 (print) | LCCN 2019017259 (ebook) | ISBN
    9781612197869 (reflow able) | ISBN 9781612197852 (hardcover)
Subjects: LCSH: Brunel, Isambard Kingdom, 1806-1859--Fiction. |
    Engineers--Great Britain--Fiction. | Nemo, Captain (Fictitious
    character)--Fiction. | Ahab, Captain (Fictitious character)--Fiction. |
    GSAFD: Adventure stories | Science fiction
Classification: LCC PS3568.O34858 (ebook) | LCC PS3568.O34858 G74 2019
    (print) | DDC 813/.54--dc23
LC record available at https://lccn.loc.gov/2019004681

Printed in the United States of America

1 3 5 7 9 10 8 6 4 2

Cyrus Smith closed the eyes
of he who had been Prince Dakkar
and who was no longer even Captain Nemo.

—JULES VERNE, *The Mysterious Island*

He's a queer man, Captain Ahab—so some think—but a good
one. Oh, thou'lt like him well enough; no fear, no fear. He's a
grand, ungodly, god-like man, Captain Ahab; doesn't speak
much; but, when he does speak, then you may well listen. Mark
ye, be forewarned; Ahab's above the common; Ahab's been in
colleges, as well as 'mong the cannibals; been used to deeper
wonders than the waves; fixed his fiery lance in mightier,
stranger foes than whales. His lance! aye, the keenest and the
surest that out of all our isle! Oh! he ain't Captain Bildad; no,
and he ain't Captain Peleg; HE'S AHAB, boy; and Ahab of old,
thou knowest, was a crowned king!

—HERMAN MELVILLE, *Moby-Dick*

Which brings me to Isambard Kingdom Brunel. How many of
you know his name? How many even recognized the words as
identifying a person, rather than a tiny principality never
noticed in our atlas or stamp album? Yet one can make a good
argument—certainly in symbolic terms for the enterprise, if not
in actuality for his personal influence—that Isambard Kingdom
Brunel was the most important person in the entire nineteenth-
century history of Britain.

—STEPHEN JAY GOULD, "The *Great Western* and the Fighting *Temeraire*"

THE GREAT EASTERN

ONE

————————⚓————————

ON 20TH SEPTEMBER 1859—fifteen days after he suffered a grievous stroke on the foredeck of the *Great Eastern*, a steamship larger by
sixfold than any ever built, that he had designed and constructed;
thirteen days after that ship's launch from London's Isle of Dogs, embarked on a steam-driven crossing of an ocean; eleven days after a
massive boiler explosion shot through his *Great Eastern*, killing eight
stokers, catapulting the ship's nine-ton funnel into the air and dispatching her, now crippled, back to harbor; five days after his death
was announced to the world—the casket of Isambard Kingdom Brunel was lowered by winch into the family plot in Kensal Green.
There it would rest, parallel to that of his father, Sir Marc Isambard
Brunel, who had some ten years previous likewise passed away of
stroke. The tackle-blocks of the lowering winch were built on a machine designed by the elder Brunel, as were such blocks everywhere.
This was a family that knew how to make things, and how to make
things work.

Isambard Kingdom Brunel's funeral was attended by his friends;
his family; his collaborator John Scott Russell FRS, a legion of
dockworkers, and an army of trainmen—perhaps a thousand all
told—assembled to pay tribute to the man who, in addition to the
Great Eastern, had previously constructed the Thames Tunnel, the
Great Western Railway, the Hungerford Bridge, the pneumatic "atmospheric railway" from Exeter to Newton, and Paddington station, too.

The funeral oration was delivered by Sir Daniel Gooch, superin-
tendent of locomotive engines for the Great Western Railway, who
said in summation that "great things are not done by those who sit

down and count the cost of every thought and act." It was intended as tribute to Brunel, who had been, at his death, trembling on the very lip of accomplishing one of his grander dreams; and perhaps as a knowing rebuke to Scott Russell, Brunel's co-builder and financier, who had for seven years quarreled fiercely with Brunel over that dream's expense.

All funerals are sad, and to say one funeral is sadder than another is folly, as grief cannot be quantified. But this particular funeral had aspects that were uniquely dolourous. Brunel's stroke had cast a long pall on the launch two days subsequent. And now, on the 20th September, no one here on Kensal Green assembled could augur when Brunel's grand dream, the *Great Eastern*, would make her crossing. When, or even whether.

Sir Daniel's oration emphasized Brunel's earlier accomplishments—the Railway, the Station, the Bridge—to the neglect of his more recent, arduous, calamitous venture. And so the army of trainmen in attendance, who owed their livelihood in large part to Brunel, were pleased by the oration; as was Scott Russell, who had been bankrupted by the *Great Eastern* project, and was relieved that its failure, and his own, were not, that day, thrown in his face. What Brunel and Scott Russell had in 1851 envisaged as the work of one year became the work of eight. Those eight years had broken Scott Russell and, it was now being said, had killed Brunel. There had been no words from his frozen throat, no flicker of expression on his frozen face, still as arctic ice, when Brunel received the news of the explosion that had sent his creation back to its berth. But among the mourners in Kensal Green, it was assumed without serious dispute that had the news had broken his spirit. That his mind had willed his heart to cease. A decision from the bridge, transmitted by engine order telegraph, to pass from Dead Slow Ahead, to Stop.

An autumnal cumulus scudded across the sky. The oration ended, the casket was lowered, the graveside mound of dirt shoveled back in place. The crowd began to disperse. And if Brunel's death had, for a moment, brought them together as one, the distinctions of class, caste, occupation now separated the streams of departure. The family—Brunel's widow, Mary Elizabeth, in black bombazine; his two sons, Marc Henry and Isambard Junior; his daughter, Florence Mary; his sister Sophia and her husband, Benjamin Hawes—left the Green in Mary Elizabeth's carriage (the one lined in cream silk, which she deemed more suited to the occasion than the one bound in green). The financiers and Royal Society Fellows climbed into their cabriolets, while the foot attendants—pallbearers, feathermen, pages, and mutes—repaired to the nearest tavern to drink gin, and to smoke cheroots in the manner of the departed. A small river of carpenters, dockworkers, and trainmen departed by foot, through the Kensal Green gates, across Harrow Road, then south on Ladbroke Grove. Among them, unnoticed and unremarked upon, was a black-bearded man—a lascar, which is to say, a seaman or dockworker from the subcontinent. He wore the uniform of his profession: horizontally striped jersey under double-breasted coat of wool Melton. He did not call attention to himself nor did anyone call attention to him. Had they known certain facts they most certainly would have. To wit: the lascar had been present on 5th September when Brunel was stricken, and then had borne him to Mile End; had, on 7th September, attended the *Great Eastern*'s launch, and can be seen, in the photographs, holding Brunel upright; had, on 9th September, clamped shut the *Great Eastern*'s feedwater valves, causing the ship's boiler, one hour later, violently to explode; had, on 15th September, stood by Dr. Murdstone's side when the death was announced; and was now, on 20th September, near-invisible in the larger throng at the burial, his activities of the past fortnight lost to history.

The railmen and dockworkers walked down Ladbroke Grove, past Dissenters' Chapel, across the malodorous canal. The grand stream of mourners became a series of rivulets, then of rills. Soon the lascar could not be seen at all.

TWO

————— ⚓ —————

Young Shropham, a freethinker of peripatetic family, thirteen years of age, liked his job, or, to be more accurate, liked the liberty his job afforded. It paid enough to keep him in his apartments in Bow, and to eat sufficiently to keep his brain alive. He worked from sunset until dawn, and became, perforce, a day sleeper. It suited him. As the night clerk at Mile End Infirmary, he found he was not much bothered. The admissions were largely during the daylight hours when he was gone. The urgent night-timers, souls stricken under moon and stars, generally went to the Royal London, where the care was swifter and of better quality. Mile End catered to the residents of the adjacent workhouse, and to the sick poor among merchant seamen and dockworkers. You'd come here at night only if stabbed or shot in the proximate neighborhood. In broadest strokes, people did not come to Mile End to be cured. They came here to die.

Nor was Shropham's work difficult. Should there be an arrival, Shropham's job was to fetch—and, if need be, awaken—the physician. Shropham himself had no medical training, nor did he seek it. The frailties and mysteries of the body were of little concern to him. His delight was his music, which he composed in his head and then transcribed to ruled paper at his desk just inside the Mile End doors. On a good night he could work for hours without interruption. There'd be, of course, screams and wails and rantings and rales from down the corridor. But he tried not to hear them, or, if he heard, to weave them into his work.

On the night of 5th September he was composing a mournful Largo, the third movement of Shropham's Sonata Number Four, when he heard, from outside, the strike of hooves on cobbled stone, the scrape of wooden wheels— Followed soon by both doors swinging inward, as three lascars carried a makeshift litter fashioned of sailcloth. On the litter was a man in long coat and vest, about fifty years of age, with a leather cheroot case strapped to his chest. The man was not moving.

"Might you summon a physician?" The first lascar spoke politely, with a melodious, subcontinental lilt. But if his diction was proper, the urgency beneath was unconcealed.

"At once," said Shropham, and rang the surgery bell. He was apprehensive, no, terrified. Men of this class did not come to Mile End. The lungers, the mendicants, the ticket-of-leave apostles, yes—but not the kind of gentleman who now occupied the entry hall, borne aloft by lascars as if entering some distant royal city by palanquin. No good, Shropham knew, could come of this. If the gentleman died in Mile End's care there would be hell to pay.

Shropham ran down the corridor to the surgery of Dr. Murdstone, entered without preface, and there found the good doctor asleep, or, more precisely, near-comatose in his chair. He'd been imbibing. Shropham shook him, jostled him, called his name repeatedly. When Murdstone awoke he was more in that world than in this one. But he understood, immediately, the import of the situation: a man of high station, in grave condition, had come to Mile End to be resuscitated.

Where Shropham saw doom, Murdstone saw possibility: perhaps, with some luck, he could save the day. As a man of erudition, now fallen on hard times, exiled to the night shift of a wretched and sorrowful establishment on the wrong side of town, he was, when not numbing the awareness of his present station with gin, always mindful of the main chance. He awoke swiftly and completely. Perhaps he was not destined to spend the rest of his days with stethoscope and flask among the tubercular flotsam of Mile End. He smoothed his jacket, cleared his throat, pushed back his mouse-brown hair, rose to the occasion.

The visitor was brought to Murdstone's surgery. His name, they were told, was Isambard Kingdom Brunel, civil engineer, Fellow of the Royal Society. It was a name both Murdstone and Shropham knew from the popular press. Indeed, by all indicia Brunel was perfectly situated to fulfill Murdstone's dreams (or, perhaps, Shropham's fears). Murdstone took the man's pulse, listened to his breath, palpated his liver, shone focused gaslight on each pupil. It was, Murdstone essayed, a stroke.

"Does he smoke many of those?" said Murdstone, gesturing toward the leather box of cheroots.

"Some forty a day, sir, perhaps more when he is working or agitated." The first lascar's diction exhibited crisp consonants, long vowels, as if he were a Cantabrigian.

"And what were the circumstances under which he was stricken?"

"We had been summoned to the *Great Eastern*, sir, a steamship in Millward Slip, to pick up a set of drawings," said the lascar. "When we arrived, Mr. Brunel began to give us instructions, then lost, mid-sentence, the power of speech. The side of his face froze in rictus. He was then as you see him now. So we brought him here, that his life might be saved."

The doctor thought for a moment and said, "He is in good hands. You may leave him now."

The lascar smiled and nodded but made no move to go.

"There is nothing more to be done."

The lascar continued to smile. At such times, Shropham knew, there were questions that were invariably asked. A thousand questions, and they were all the same question: *Will he live?* But neither the first lascar nor his two associates asked anything. As if they did not care about the outcome. Or already knew it.

After a silence of several moments, interrupted only by distant tubercular paroxysms from the upper floors, Murdstone said, "I see you are a man of education. This allows me to speak frankly, and speak frankly with you I will. Some people come through these doors, and they are ill, but will be fine. It would make no sense for us to intervene, save the beneficial effects, more mental than physical, of perceiving some care. Such a case would be the common cold. Other people come through these doors and are doomed, willing nilling, no matter what we do, or do not do, or might do, or might not do. Such a case would be the Plague, as was experienced in 1665. Those two categories—the ultimately well, the ultimately doomed—represent by far the largest portion of the ill. In neither category does our intervention influence outcome. In between is not much. The broken finger, which can be splinted. The suppurating wound, which can be lanced, swabbed with

Courtois's iodine, suitably bandaged. The dislocated joint, relocated. Various ailments for which we prescribe various medicaments. So you see, the vast majority of our work is done for us, one way or the other way, by the Deity. And where we have agency, our work is simple." He paused to clear his throat, wipe a rheumy discharge from his nose, and, we might infer, congratulate himself on his clarity, which had come to him in the instant of need. "In the case of Mr. Brunel, let me state plainly the situation, the possible outcomes. He has suffered a cerebral hemorrhage—the cause of which, as Virchow has shown, is more likely to be mechanical than inflammatory."

The lascar nodded. And said one word. With a lilt at the end, as if it were a question: "Thromboembolism?"

Murdstone paused. The man to whom he was speaking was clearly no mere lascar but a man of education, including, it now seemed, specific medical education. It pleased him that he was now at liberty to discourse on the highest plane; excited him that perhaps this knowledgeable subcontinental might even become a patron, offering a ticket out of Mile End, and yet—it disturbed him. Who was this man? Who were his nocturnal retinue? Why were his dress and position so at odds with his rhetoric and diction? And why the incuriosity about the life-or-death prospects for Mr. Brunel in his current state?

Dr. Murdstone only said, "Indeed." And then, after some musing, decided once again to demonstrate that he, too, was a man at odds with his appearance: "I will not waste your time. If you know the etiology, you likely know the prognosis. Your Mr. Brunel will either recover, or he won't. The best we can do for him is to keep him horizontal, and to do what we can to reduce fever should fever occur. Should he not succumb, there is a spectrum of outcomes that range from full recovery to near-complete paralysis. He may not be able to walk. He may not be able to speak. His handwriting may become shrunken, readable only with a glass. That is, should he live. I say these words in front of him because though he cannot move, or talk, or even blink, he can hear every word, every sigh, every rustle; smell each medicinal; feel the comforting presence of a damp cloth on his forehead; taste the wood of the depressor I inserted into his mouth; and see, to the extent it falls within his field of vision, every person in this room. In short: his body has become a cage, and we none of us hold the key.

"And then, of course it is possible—not probable, but possible—
that he will snap to, sit up, smile broadly and symmetrically, walk
out of here tomorrow afternoon, fit as you or I, an abominable cheroot clenched between his teeth. And neither I nor anyone can tell
you, among those outcomes, which be the more likely. That, I will
tell you plainly, is, as referenced, in the hands of the Deity."

The lascar was very still. When he finally spoke his voice was
calm, dispassionate. "It may be, Dr. Murdstone, that you and I mean
different things when we say the word 'deity.' But that is of no material concern. I have read John Abercrombie's very fine *Pathological
and Practical Researches on Diseases of the Brain and Spinal Cord*, as well
as Creswell's *Pathological Anatomy*, and, of course, Cruveilhier. So I
understand your diagnosis, together with the prospects which may
greet us as we move forward. My only disagreement, Dr. Murdstone,
and it is not a grave one, is that I propose that his head be slightly elevated, as Lallemand would counsel. It will not harm, and there is a
small chance it might assist. I suggest this only because I have French,
and thus access to the Continental literature. I do not mean to claim
that my skills as diagnostician or as physician are superior to yours, as
they are demonstrably not in either case."

Young Shropham, who had abandoned his post at the receiving
desk to stand within listening range just outside the surgery, could
scarce believe what his ears were hearing, and could only imagine
the reaction of Dr. Murdstone within. Why had Brunel been brought
to Mile End, as opposed to the Royal London, or other establish-
ments more suitable to those of his station? Why would he have been
brought here by lascars, rather than by his manservants, his draughts-
men, his engineers? And who was this *babu* who knew, or seemed to
know, quite so much? This nighttime arrival had begun curiously but
was becoming, with reflection, more queer each moment to the next.

Most nights, when his compositions were interrupted, Shropham
found himself galled, annoyed, resentful; but this was less an interruption than, perhaps, an invitation. The opening of a door. But a
door to where? In his young life, Shropham knew only one kind of
door: the one that opens onto an abyss. He did not know the exact
nature of the calamity that was about to befall, but calamity, he was
certain, could be the only outcome.

MR. BRUNEL WAS SOON transported from the surgery to a room on
the first floor of which he was the sole resident—a lodging anomalous for Mile End, which, in the main, consisted of unwalled wards.
Brunel was attended to by his lascars, who would sleep on the floor.
When on occasion one of them would leave the other two would
remain, not leaving the bedside, even to visit the water closet. They
seemed to subsist on little save the small parcels of food, wrapped in
cloth, that one of the lascars would bring back with him from his
ventures outside.

The next morning news must have got round that Brunel was in
residence because deliverymen with flowers began to arrive in a near-
constant stream, and visitors would appear, clad in funereal black,
their faces grave, asking to be taken upstairs. Dr. Murdstone did indeed relish Mile End's new notoriety, which allowed him to function
not only as a physician but as a master of ceremonies. Both he and
Shropham stayed on past the official endpoints of their shifts, eager or
anxious, respectively, to see the day's developments.

Dr. Murdstone was a strict guardian of Brunel's apartment, allowing only one guest at a time (save, of course, the lascars). At ten in the
morning, Shropham overheard a heated discussion between Murdstone and one of the visitors, a lad older than himself yet still in his
teens, whom Shropham surmised to be Brunel's son. The lad—the
son?—wanted Brunel to be moved to another hospital where better
care might be provided. Dr. Murdstone was insistent that the dangers
concomitant with the transport far outweighed the benefit of a nicer
bed, a more capacious room, an airier view. Shropham heard Murdstone accuse the young man of selfishness, of wanting a locale more
convenient to the family's work and lodgings, not all the way out here,
near the docks, where the bells of St Mary-le-Bow could be heard. The
man, angered, said with some real vehemence that the conditions at
Mile End were insalubrious. The doctor replied that Mr. Brunel was
under his care and that in his best professional judgment the patient
should stay put. The conversation did not end in rapprochement.

Later that morning when young Shropham emerged from the
WC he caught glimpse of something he was, he strongly suspected,
never meant to see: the articulate lascar counting, into the doctor's

podgy hands, an unfathomably large number of gold coins, mostly sovereigns, but some older five-guinea pieces as well. When at noon the doctor introduced the lascars to the visiting John Scott Russell as his "staff," Shropham was less astonished than he'd otherwise might have been. The situation was clear: the lascars were masquerading as the doctor's servants. But there was sufficient pecuniary reason to believe that the relationship, in truth, was now vice versa.

The next morning, just before the end of his shift, Shropham heard loud thumping noises from upstairs, as if an armoire were being moved or a bed were being dropped. Then the creak of an opening door followed by the syncopated stutter of feet, many feet, on the staircase. Shropham turned his gaze to the hallway and saw, coming toward, a procession unimaginable: Brunel, in full dress, cheroot box, top hat, was strapped to a large wooden board, and was being borne, near-upright, by the lascars. It was a strange bookend to his arrival, two days previous, carried to Mile End on sailcloth by the same crew. The thoughts sprang to Shropham's brain: *You cannot remove him. The doctor will not allow*— But before those thoughts could become utterances, Shropham saw Dr. Murdstone, shaven and pomaded, bringing up the rear.

"I had thought he was too weak to be transported," said Shropham finally.

"In the larger sense, yes," said Murdstone. "But this is the launch of the *Great Eastern*, an endeavor upon which our Mr. Brunel has worked for the better part of a decade. Scott Russell thinks he should be there. The world thinks he should be there. And we—" Here he gestured to include the Lascars. "We concur." It was at that moment that a scrape of wheels and a clop of hooves confirmed the arrival of a carriage. And so Shropham stood silent while the great civil engineer was carried upright through the door. Silent, unmoving, paralyzed, but upright, silhouetted in the harsh East End light, bobbing sidewise, as if he were a cutout in a shadow play. Shropham watched the grim procession as it approached the carriage. Then opened his ruled notebook and turned back to his adagio.

THREE

BRUNEL HAD CONCEIVED of the *Great Eastern* in 1851 and on that same day did jot down some specifications:

> *A volume six times greater than any craft now extant. Six hundred eighty feet in length, with dimensions proportionate: beam of 83 feet and a draught of 58 feet. Cladding of plate iron, with sufficient overlap. Thirty thousand plates should suffice. Each plate 7/8 inch thick therefor third of a ton apiece. The hull to be doubled. All vertical joints to be butt joints and to be twice-riveted wherever required by the Engineer. Bulkheads to be at 60 feet intervals. No cast iron to be used anywhere except for slide valves and cocks without special permission of the Engineer.*

The *Great Eastern* could carry as much in one crossing as could smaller ships in half a dozen; and the cost of crewing one large ship, as opposed to six lesser, would in theory be similarly advantageous. To propel the craft Brunel had conceived of a screw but also twin paddle wheels, with auxiliary sail power. The wheels permitted a shallower draught which would, Brunel claimed, enable the *Great Eastern* to make port at the many-sided, smoky, magnificent city of Calcutta, a harbor that the Hooghly River would otherwise render inaccessible to a craft of this size.

To the end of constructing this floating city Brunel and Scott Russell were able, on the basis of Brunel's plans, to raise working capital of some £120,000. Yet the building of the ship was not without perils financial and technical, and what had been envisaged as the work of one year became nigh unto interminable. The keel was not laid until 1854 at Scott Russell's yard in Millward on the Isle of Dogs. One creditors' meeting in 1856 almost liquidated the enterprise entire; and the task of launching the ship, 680 feet in length and 12,000 tons of deadweight load, could not be accomplished in the traditional manner. The geometry—long ship, narrow river—required that the *Great Eastern* be built and slid into the Thames longitudinally. Thus Scott Russell was forced to purchase the property adjacent to his yard, and for no small sum.

There was also the need to recruit and train some 200 skilled men for the riveting gang. The first attempt to cast the crankshaft failed, as did the second, each attempt time consuming and ruinously expensive. When in November 1857 the *Great Eastern* was finally ready to be launched, her steam winches were insufficient to the task. Brunel, who'd been urging Scott Russell to purchase hydraulic rams (at no little expense), was livid. The next attempt, that December, attended by Prince Albert and the Prince of Wales, was no more successful than the first, and the blame was laid at the feet of Brunel: a correspondent to *The Spectator* opined that the friction of iron on iron was an unknown quantity, one which Brunel has grievously failed to take into account. A third attempt was made on 5th January 1858 but that too failed. A fourth try on 30th January, at last using rams sent down from the Tangye company in Birmingham, was canceled when the winds would not let up.

So you can readily understand that when on the following day—the hull well-oiled, the Birmingham hydraulics in place—Brunel's *Great Eastern* was finally eased into the River Thames, the mood on the dock was more one of relief than of exultation. Brunel would from that day forth ascribe the ardour and misery of the past several years to the frugality of Scott Russell, though the cost of the enterprise had now risen to £732,000—more than £1,000 per foot of ship—and Scott Russell now teetered on the very edge of bankruptcy.

The fitting out of the *Great Eastern* took another nineteen months. But now, on 9th September 1859, the *Great Eastern* was built, kitted out, set in the water, awaiting only ceremony before she was bound for Weymouth, Dorset, then to Holyhead, North Wales. Thence, after provisioning: to Portland, Maine, where the Grand Trunk Railway had already constructed a purpose-built jetty to accommodate the ship. *Holyhead to Portland, by steam!* A voyage that, when Brunel first conceived of it, would have been regarded as pipe dream. Yet here they were, on a crisp early-fall day, assembled to witness its origination.

Perhaps owing to the sheer number of departures scheduled, then canceled—and perhaps because Scott Russell, to increase his income in precarious times, had sold 3,000 tickets to the 1857 launch, a day filled with postponement, disappointment, yet no refund—the spectatorial crowd was far thinner this time. The Millward yard contained some 200 souls: relations of the workers and outfitters, who wanted to see what they had only heard described, and the parties of those embarking as passengers, who had been boarded earlier that morning.

There were some prominent personages, but no Prince Albert this time, no Prince of Wales either. On the platform before the bow were several members of the board of the ship's holding company; Scott Russell; Dr. Murdstone; the lascars; and, of course, Isambard Kingdom Brunel, tied ankle shoulder and waist to an oaken plank and elevated to 75 degrees. Brunel's eyes, mobile in a frozen face, tracked each stage: the waving of handkerchiefs from the deck; the singling of the immense chained-metal lines, each forged link the size of a man's chest, and far heavier; the raucous clatter and hiss of the steam engines, at first a cacophony, then a low rhythmic thrum as it reached speed; the dark oily plash of the grand wheels, turning now, scooping tons of river water with each revolution; the flap of the wide white foresails, now unfurled. Brunel watched the bottle of Champagne that Scott Russell banged thrice against the hull until at last it shattered. Now the ship's great low horn let out its mournful, triumphant bleat; now the platform crew sensed that slow and delirious drift: *are we moving backward? Is the ship moving forward?* Now a sudden and raucous cheer from the docks. And as Brunel's Leviathan, his double-clad floating city, began to glide down the Thames toward saltwater seas, a rivulet of salt-water tears began its slide down Brunel's rigid and unmoving cheek.

SPARE A MOMENT to contemplate the thoughts that his face, voice, body, could not at that instant express. To be surprised at your draughting table in the dead of night. Surrounded by lascars, injected with what foul paralytic. Brought to Hell's own infirmary and treated, if that word can even be used, by a doctor who cared not a whit for his patient. Then left to contemplate, in endless slow minutes within the body's frozen sarcophagus, that world and family must believe you to be deaf, mute, blind. And ne'er to return.

The ship slipped down the Thames, heading for the North Sea and thence the Channel. The workers and relations slipped away, headed home, or to tasks, or to their favorite local. The members of the ship's board repaired to their club. Scott Russell departed alone, letting his feet take him on a long peripheral ramble round the Isle of Dogs. Murdstone and the lascars—porting the planked corpus of Mr. Brunel—boarded the awaiting carriage. The sharp-eyed among the scattering crowd might have observed, had they been focused upon it, that Brunel had been carried to the platform by a crew of four lascars, but was carried from the platform by a crew of three. And when at last the carriage returned to Mile End, it most certainly did not escape young Shropham's notice that the lead lascar had not returned with them. Shropham was curious, of course, but the presentiment of doom, which had hung over his head all morning and which had infected his music with slow tempi and minor thirds, told him it would be far better not to ask. You can see them in Robert Howlett's photograph of the day. There's Scott Russell in three-piece suit with watch fob, trouser cuffs rolled against the dockside muck; Lord Derby in bow tie and double-breasted topcoat; Captain William Harrison in a practical coat of sailor's cloth with a sewn flap concealing the buttons; Brunel himself, in waistcoat, jacket, coat, each with its own lapels, and visible, strapped over the waistcoat, the inevitable cheroot case, bearing the imprint "I.K.B. *Athenaeum Club Pall Mall.*" And behind Brunel, heads tilted deferentially downward, holding the plank to which Brunel was affixed, the lascars. They are the only ones in the frame who do not wear top hats.

At some point after the photograph was taken but prior to the launch of the vessel itself—as we can see if we examine Howlett's photograph of the slip as the *Great Eastern* departed—Captain Harrison, having boarded, is no longer on the slip; and one of the lascars is no longer present, though which one in particular cannot be ascertained. (The grain of the photograph is larger than would permit the necessary scrutiny.) But we know now that the person absented from the second photograph is the lead lascar. And we know other things as well.

We know that the lead lascar slipped away from the platform and joined the boarding party queue. That he made his way up the wooden embarkation bridge, angling up to the ship at a tilt of perhaps 30 degrees. That with a nod to a fellow lascar he made his way belowdecks where he disappeared. He would not be seen again for the next forty-eight hours.

When he next made himself available to view it was on the morning of 9th September, emerging from the screw chamber in which he'd secreted himself into the larger hall that led to the engine room.

The engine room proper was fronted by nine massive boilers, larger than any seagoing boilers previously built, of double-joined iron sheets, close riveted. There were, on each shift, twelve stokers in two ranks, whose job consisted in shoveling coal into a furnace. The fire within was too bright to gaze upon direct; the harsh, heated light gave the coal-blacked faces upon whom it shone a hellish aspect. As one stoker scooped the coal the other fed the maw, and again, and again, powering the shafts for paddle and screw, night and day and night.

On either side of the boiler room were warrens of pipes, starting thick, branching thinner, conducting the steam where needed: to the pistons, whose up-and-down motion powered the revolution of the main crankshaft and of the smaller shafts that drove each of the paddle wheels; through the signaling system; and to the various other places where pressure was needed. Intertwined among them were the feedwater pipes, bringing water to the paddle furnaces and screw furnaces to be converted into steam. The lascar followed the course of the entangled, branching pipes, as difficult to parse as the tubes of the London Pneumatic Post. He moved swiftly, head down, consulting from time to time an ink-drawn sketch, written on foolscap, which seemed to be a rendering of the ship's steam system. (And, in fact: was.)

At last he reached the boiler antechamber, just the other side of the bulkhead from the hold where the stokers plied their backlit and exhausting trade. Among the pipes that branched out from the boiler's side was a feedwater that led to a 300-pound safety valve, which itself vented to the ship's exterior. Between the boiler and the valve was a pipe jointed to a stopcock. *A cock leading to a safety-valve!* The very existence of such an arrangement was barbarous. Yet it had been in Brunel's engineering diagrams, and those diagrams had been faithfully executed. *A cock leading to a safety-valve!* Even were the most extraordinary vigilance exercised, a feckless steamfitter, an ignorant stoker, had it in his power, by the simple shutting of a cock, to blow the ship from here to Kandahar.

It would take a man with a knowledge of Brunel's diagrams and a high general intelligence to understand the consequences of turning this stopcock. It would take a man with diabolical intent to turn it. Yet turn it the lascar did, exploiting the dark flaw in the *Great Eastern*'s design to which the engineer himself had been blind.

Then, swiftly and silently as he'd arrived, the lascar departed by different route, past the feedwater pipes, down the corridor, through the bulkhead door, up the gangway, onto the deck, over the bridge between the paddle boxes: and, gripping with hands and crossed feet, down the rope which held the compact steam chaloupe that served as the *Great Eastern*'s pilot boat. Once sheltered from the view of the deck he removed his pea jacket and shoes and trousers, and let them fall into the Channel— Then followed them, into the darkening evening sea.

He swam toward Hastings as the steamship was headed the other way. It was a fair distance and a lesser man would not have had the stamina. But the lascar had both strength and strength of purpose and so within the hour was onshore finding, and then donning, a cache of clothes along the bank that he, or a confederate, had previously secreted. He was headed by land back to London even as the feedwater pressure was building past its limit.

It was ten minutes to six when those on deck—mostly gathered under the forward bulwark for protection against the headwinds— suddenly heard a grand roar and crash, then turned to see the great forward funnel of the ship in two pieces, thirty feet in the air, rising up then sinking down in grand and terrifying slow motion, amidst a shower of splinters and pipes, obscured by dark, glowing columns of steam and smoke. Captain Harrison immediately ran belowdecks, knocking down stateroom doors behind one of which was his young daughter, unharmed. Mr. Comstock ordered his men to hurry up the afterforce pump. (His hope was to flood the boiler room with cooler water, checking the heat and condensing the steam.) Some of the passengers on deck scanned the waterline looking for signs that the ship was foundering; others made their way to the boats, and had begun to lower them into the chop, when one of the officers, brandishing a firearm, put a stop to that.

Belowdecks a volume of smoke and flame emerged not only from the chambers but from the furnace doors themselves, erupting down the corridor into the grand salon. Mr. Rawlinson, assistant adjuster of compasses, supervised the evacuation of the ladies from their apartments. The great struggle at present was to get out the miserable fire-men who were known to be scalding below, and whose terrible groans now reached the deck.

As soon as the smoke and steam had been sufficiently damped to render a descent if not safe then possible, several men at once volunteered to go down the shafts. In a few moments all the twelve fire-men on duty were brought up. One or two were not very seriously injured, and the worst injured seemed in the least pain, actually walking unaided. But the sight of them was heartrending. The scalp of one was hanging in strips from his head, the boiled flesh of another stripped from the bones of his hand. While removing his coat, another found his skin had peeled off with his clothing. The room designated as a hospital was more customarily used as a carpenter's shop and the floor was covered with shavings on which mattresses were hastily laid. Two ship's surgeons and a London physician—a passenger—at once set to work to alleviate the distress of the poor sufferers. Yet even had they been on shore, scarcely anything more could have been done.

The stricken were generally delirious and all seemed to be cold, begging to be covered up. In many ways their actual suffering was not extreme. But they had breathed the fatal steam and before long death, perhaps mercifully, had come to three of them, while at least five others were becoming quiet and unconscious in death's near approach.

Belowdecks—though the larger force of the explosion had been contained by the bulkheads, and though the ship's double hull had not failed—the consequences were well in evidence. The forepart of the salon was a pile of glittering rubbish, a confused mass of splinters and ornaments: the gilt castings broken and thrown down, the brass work ripped, the handsome cast-iron columns overturned and strewn about. Closer to the boilers, in a state sitting room for the ladies, every single thing was destroyed, the wooden flooring broken and wrenched-up. It was impossible to gaze upon the sequelae of the explosion's appalling force without profound gratitude to Providence that the explosion occurred at the only single moment when the grand salon was empty. What the consequences would have been had it taken place earlier, when the visitors had been in residence, is fearful to contemplate.

On deck the steam and smoke continued to rise. At the wheel Mr. Atkinson, the pilot, pulled his hat down to shield his face from the vapors, then proclaimed to anyone who might hear, "That's none of my business. I'm going to steer the ship as long as she is a ship." Gathered around the pilothouse the passengers were talking over the matter in view of their heaven-sent escape; others mused on the cause of the disaster, and not a few with reference to its commercial results. A vague apprehension of fresh terror—the sudden check to the great enterprise in the hour of its promise, together with a deep and universal sorrow at the fate of the dying, steam-struck men—gloomily ushered in the night.

By midday on 10th September the *Great Eastern* had put ashore at Portland Harbor, Dorset. The dead—and by then there were a full eight of them—were carried off; the remaining wounded were transported to hospital; the journalists rushed to file their stories. Chief Equerry and Clerk Marshal to the Queen Lord Alfred Paget stayed behind for some minutes to offer solace to Captain Harrison before setting off by carriage back to London. The cause of the explosion had yet to be ascertained but was attributed to accident. There would be no reason to think otherwise.

We know what they failed to know—that the turning of the cock was not without intent. We know as well that the lascar had some knowledge of probable consequence, otherwise he'd not have quit the ship, subjecting himself to harsh and perilous swim. But why?

What motive? What animus might a man bear 'gainst a ship? Why contrive an explosion when those most likely to be struck were those belowdecks: seafaring proletariat, stokers, fire-men, coalmen, who twelve hours a day stared into the fires of hell? Who would hate a hull of doubled iron? And who would want to delay the onset of progress, of the transport of men and goods from London to Delhi and Bombay? Such a man would have to lack moral sense. Either that or be deranged, so that night to him was day, and darkness light.

THIS LASCAR DID return to Mile End early on the morning of 10th September. He walked through the hospital doors without remarking upon his absence; and neither was it remarked upon by Dr. Murdstone or Shropham, both of whom observed his re-entry up the stairs and into the room set aside for Brunel. His sabbatical coincided with the explosion aboard the *Great Eastern* but neither the alcoholic physician nor the composer of tender age did speculate on the coincidence.

Returning to the Brunel room the Lascar spoke briefly with his two compatriots in a language Shropham had to no avail, over the past days, tried to comprehend. His best guess was that they were speaking Hindoo or one of its variants. The conversation was telegraphic, without to-do or palaver. Were they to have been overheard even by someone who spoke their dialect it would not have disclosed much at all.

The lascars continued their vigil for the next several days. On the evening of 14th September the lead lascar emerged from Brunel's sickroom and sought out Dr. Murdstone, who was red cheeked, perhaps from recent exposure to the sun, perhaps from gin. The two chatted amiably as they strode the corridors, Murdstone in the Kensington drawl he'd acquired in medical school, the lascar in fine Cantabrigian cadence. Shropham, who had been detailed to the supply room, could not help but overhear. And what he heard was a negotiation concerning money, which he, the lascar, would pay to him, the doctor, in two days' time. The doctor was wanting one hundred English pounds. The lascar he did agree.

To Shropham this was a harbinger of doom. What act was so consequential, illegal, or hideous as to command a payment of one hundred English pounds? He could scarcely contemplate the enormity of such a thing. And if the lascar had acquiesced to Murdstone's opening demand then something was very wrong. Either the lascar had been out-negotiated—something Shropham doubted to his core—or the lascar had no intention of making payment. There was a hedge maze of alternatives here, each more troubling than the next, none of them leading to sunlight.

The carriages began to arrive shortly after dawn. At first one by one, then, as the morning drew on, in pairs or even quartets. They delivered their passengers to Shropham's waiting room. Not the diseased or stricken, but rather journalists, from the *Times* and various publications of lesser repute. All Shropham had been given to tell them was that there would be an announcement round nine a.m.

At a quarter past, Dr. Murdstone—freshly shaven, coiffed, and in his very best suit—descended the stairs. He announced his name, spelled it. Limned a brief history of Mile End. Talked about its service to the community and the number of lives that had been saved. Alluded to three or four cases where there had been patients who entered in *gravis*, departed in the pink of health. (Young Shropham wondered if he chose these examples because they were the most illustrative, or because they were unique.)

Perhaps sensing the reporters' uneasiness, perhaps because he had run out of prefatory material, Dr. Murdstone then made his announcement: "At two minutes past midnight the gravely ill Isambard Kingdom Brunel slipped away. The great man, who will be remembered as long as there is an England, shall henceforth design railways, bridges, steamships only in the Better Place."

The assembled journalists, clearly expecting such an announcement, had but few questions. Some were medical, concerning the etiology of the disease, and these Dr. Murdstone answered in medical language that Shropham, if no one else, knew were word-for-word repetitions of the monologue delivered up by the lascar on the evening that Brunel was first brought to Mile End. Some were historical, concerning Brunel's achievements, and those Dr. Murdstone modestly declined to answer, referring them to Scott Russell or to the Brunel family. Still others were about funeral arrangements,

which Dr. Murdstone, reading from a folded piece of notepaper
veyed to them.

At length the journalists departed. The last of them had gone
Fleetstreetward when another carriage—longer, lower, and with
hoof steps more solemn—pulled up to the doors. The crew who came
with it were lower of class than the journalists and were dressed to
the man in dark overcoats. Pallbearers. Gravediggers. London's own
Charons, crossing the Thames in black cloth gone shiny with use.

Two lascars came down the stairs carrying a body on a hand-borne
stretcher. The body was covered head-to-foot with linen shroud.
Shropham strained for a glimpse but the shrouded body was borne
through the doors swiftly and without pause. All he saw was a toe,
peeking from beneath the shroud. The toe was dark in color, perhaps
as a result of *livor mortis*—but wouldn't that make the toe, elevated,
pale rather than dark? If what he was seeing were skin tone, this was
not the skin tone of a man from Portsmouth, even one, like Brunel,
of French extraction. And even more vexingly: the toe seemed to
clench, to pull in, as if it were aware of its exposure and sought shelter beneath the shroud. Shropham had never traveled more than five
miles from the street in which he'd been born but he'd seen his share
of death, both at Mile End and in other, darker corners of East London. And this did not seem like death.

Flowerets of unhealthy thought bloomed in the garden of young
Shropham's mind. Was this really Brunel's body? Was this perhaps
the body of one of the other two lascars, feigning death for reasons
unfathomable? That would explain the subcontinental darkness of
toe, and its movement as well. But this explication left in its wake
more mystery than it solved. Alternatively: might this be a real dead
body, of some darker someone from the upper wards? A lunger, a
mendicant, a ne'er-do-well? And even stretched out, the body with
the toe seemed normal height—something that Brunel, who courted
five foot flat, was not.

And if the figure between stretcher and shroud were not Isambard Kingdom Brunel, where was Brunel now? Young Shropham
was filled with curiosity, a curiosity soon overwhelmed by dread.
Much of him yearned to climb the stairs, to see, to investigate, to
know. But a larger part felt not thirst for that knowledge but terror

of it. Shropham stayed where he was. If there were a truth to be learned, and if he were to learn it: what possible good could come of that? He stood in the receiving room of Mile End pretending he'd seen nothing and hoping that no one had seen him see. Just another day at hospital with the sick ones carried in, the dead ones carried out. And if this particular dead man was the most prominent civil engineer in Great Britain; and if this particular dead man was perhaps not even dead— The thoughts along that path were morbid and frightful.

The thoughts spun, and swirled, one atop the next, in a paddle wheel of unhealthy mental excitement. Better not to think. Better to save the mind for the writing of the adagio.

DR. MURDSTONE WAS pleased, and pleased with himself. He had increased his notoriety in the press and had done it without suffering any concomitant scandal. As the attending physician to one of the Great Men of England he had improved his social standing overnight. And he was—for services rendered—now richer, to the tune of one hundred English pounds. All he had done, really, was to divert his eyes at crucial instants. He'd made sure not to see things that shouldn't have been seen. And where's the crime in that?

The evening of 20th September, after the body of Isambard Kingdom Brunel had left Mile End, and the mourners had gone off, and the press had dispersed, Dr. Murdstone, feeling more ambitious than he had in some time, and with the means to exercise that ambition, set out for his club. He'd have a joint and potatoes. And gin for starters, and some good claret to accompany the joint. Perhaps after dinner he'd enjoy a cheroot—he'd borrowed three or four from Brunel's leather case though without, truth be told, the intent of ever returning them. And after the cheroot it would be nice to find some female companionship. There was he'd been told a certain address in Marylebone where the original chevalet, the one devised and constructed by Theresa Berkley in 1828, might be found. Brunel had been an astonishingly inventive man to be sure. But, Dr. Murdstone now chuckled to himself: not all the great engineers of the nineteenth century were men. Yes, the chevalet. The Berkley Horse. Dr. Murdstone

smiled as he imaged it in his mind. That would be the perfect end to
a perfect evening: gin, joint, claret, cheroot, flogging.

The gin was cold and delightfully redolent of juniper. It brought
color to his cheeks and, for the moment, a sparkle to his eyes. He
imagined that the barman's greeting was warmer, the gazes of his fellow club-members more approving, since his recent bout with fame.
The joint was rare, as he liked it, and the potatoes that accompanied
well-buttered, garnished with parsley, too. A fellow physician nodded to him respectfully. Word had, he felt, gotten around. The claret,
from the Bordeaux region of France, was poured from a cut-glass decanter, and poured again, and then a third time. Dr. Murdstone now
repaired to the lounge for his cheroot where he could lean back in a
high-backed, well-stuffed chair, reclining against the antimacassar.
He savored each puff and waited for someone to enquire the maker or
origin of said cheroot. Because, of course, he had a tale to tell. The way
he'd prepared that tale, in his mind, Isambard Kingdom Brunel, FRS,
despite his inability to speak, had made clear his desire that Murdstone take several cheroots from his case as a way of giving thanks
for the extraordinary care he'd received at Mile End. As it turned out,
no one enquired; but Murdstone knew that, in time, someone would.

A hansom cabriolet brought him from the club to Marylebone, to
the particular address. He was quickly ushered upstairs to the private
apartments where he had an appointment with Emily, and with the
chevalet.

The chevalet was an instrument for allowing the body to be arrayed in such a fashion that it be optimally accessible to the whip.
Fashioned of wrought iron, there are warrens on the bottom for the
feet and apertures through which the buttocks and genitals can be
approached. Rings riveted to the chevalet permit the passage of rope
or leather thong, allowing the hands and feet to be bound, permitting
the kind of writhing that can to the supplicant be pleasurable, yet forbid escape. The angle of the upright can be adjusted and at 45 degrees
one may be flogged, simultaneously, front and back. This requires, of
course, two floggers, and at this establishment, costs twice as much.
(No discount offered.) But Dr. Murdstone, his pockets weighted with
gold, feels himself deserving of the extravagance. He asked for, paid
for, and received the full dorsal-ventral.

Following the session Dr. Murdstone bathed. Then slowly dressed, savoring the tingle. Then distributed gratuities. Then stepped outside into the Marylebone night air, feeling the sharp breeze against his hands and face. He strolled a while, flush with the lineaments of gratified desire. Then, in Bentinck Street, he stepped into a convenient hansom cabriolet and proceeded directly home.

Or so he'd commanded. The swift, low-slung cab seemed to be taking a route of its own design, one headed not to the warm precincts of Dr. Murdstone's apartments but rather to a colder and more forbidding destination down by the docks. He yelled for the driver but the driver perhaps did not hear him over the clatter of hooves on cobbled stone. He contemplated jumping off but the cab was moving too rapidly. The streets were narrow, ill lit, and the precincts not congenial, even to one who spent his working nights at Mile End. For several minutes he was wishing that the cabriolet would stop; and then, surveying the neighborhood, for a few more minutes was wishing that it would not.

At last the cab came to rest, dockside. Two men emerged, one from either side of the quay. They opened the cab's doors, did some work, departed. The driver decamped with them.

The streets were silent save the caw of terns, the slow lap of river water, and the occasional shout. The cab remained at rest until the morning when it would be approached by police, who claimed and ultimately identified the slain physician within, then returned the stolen cab to its rightful owner, after charging said owner for cleaning and storage.

There was an investigation, of course, as a physician cannot be slain without the social order demanding its due. An autopsy disclosed the presence of petechia with ruptured capillaries under the eyelids, upper airway edema, a fractured hyoid, all consistent with death by strangulation. It also disclosed the marks, front and back, of flagellation. But there were no witnesses to the crime and there was abundant motive: the physician had earlier that evening been seen flashing, with some ostentation, gold coins; and when the body was found, he was penniless. Simple robbery. The fact that the cabriolet had been stolen prior to the robbery did not figure in to that account so it was ignored. As was an eyewitness account of the speeding cab, which held that its driver was dark in hue. Had the police investigated further, they might have pondered the proleptic theft of the cab, the description of its driver, the particular dockside location where the cab and its passenger came to rest, and come to a conclusion other than random robbery and murder committed in that robbery's furtherance.

They might have looked into the identity and recent activity of the passenger and his role in ministering to the late Mr. Brunel. They might have made a connection between the lascars who brought Mr. Brunel to Mile End and the dark-complected driver. The fact that the slaying was committed by handkerchief, rather than by knife as was then the custom among the local footpads, would typically be viewed by the police as a sign of "Thuggee," or of "Dacoity" (words they used to ascribe to those with darker skin most any unsolved crime committed in worrisome precincts). But those words were not here invoked.

The constabulary might also have examined the gold sovereigns that Dr. Murdstone had been dispensing with such profligacy at his club and of course at the establishment in Marylebone. They might have found one that was an older five-guinea piece bearing the image of Queen Anne and the single word VIGO. The VIGO coins were re-minted from Spanish gold, the face of the jut-jawed Carlos II overstamped with the image of Queen Anne, and were limited in number to twenty. They have a specific history that we will not here convey. Even a cursory numismatic investigation would have raised the largest and most chilling questions about the source of Dr. Murdstone's recent windfall.

But as it was, the matter of the gold coins, as so much else, went unscrutinized. The physician was not a prominent member of his profession and it was widely whispered that he indulged in unsavory habits. (There were marks on his body consonant with such whispers.) Why lift that rock? We all know, all of us, what scurries beneath.

WHILE DR. MURDSTONE believed that "the Brunel episode," as he thought of it, could mean nothing but improvement in his station, an optimism that persisted until his untimely final breath, young

Shropham possessed, perhaps from birth, a different temperament. His assumption was that the worst that could happen would happen with the inevitability of an incoming tide. So when Brunel was admitted to Mile End, Shropham felt that no good could come of it; when he saw the financial arrangements between Murdstone and the lascar, he felt the presentiment of doom; and when he spied, despite himself, the errant toe emerging from the shroud, flexing, clenching, then pulling itself back beneath, he knew that he was done for. For Shropham, the only question was when.

Shropham attended Brunel's funeral out of curiosity, and also hoping that within a large throng, a large doom would have more difficulty finding him. He survived. Attendance at Dr. Murdstone's funeral was more obligatory, but owing to the vastly smaller number of mourners, far less safe. He survived that as well. A week later and Shropham found himself still alive and not yet ruined. Murdstone's replacement was a kindly older man, not particularly swift of wit but gentle, with an avuncular manner that comforted both patients and staff.

Shropham quickly settled into the new routine which was much like the old routine, before the irruption of the engineer, the lascars, the enquiring press. He missed the tumult to be sure but was also glad to have long dark evenings, without calamity or the prospect of chaos, in which to continue to indite his sonata. He was happy with the allegro but the scherzo needed work, so he went back to it. The largo wasn't working either but he decided to write the finale first and then, with his bookends intact, solve the architecture between them.

It was just after seven p.m. one evening in the month of October, and Shropham, composition book under his arm, coat buttoned against the sharp wind, had just rounded the corner off Bancroft Road and onto the loop that led to Mile End. As he was entering, others were departing. Two men, side by side, strode calmly through the hospital doors. They were lascars. The same lascars who had attended the stricken Brunel. The third lascar was absent: the one who spoke, the one who left and returned, the one who had dispensed the gold.

Shropham at once found himself shivering, as if the sharp wind had penetrated his coat. Did they come for him and, finding him not yet there, were they now walking the hospital paths, seeking a dark covert in which to lay wait? Had they got word of the night that Shropham, in his local, had quaffed perhaps too many ales and gone on a bit about the unshrouded toe?

He ducked behind a hedge and held his head low. Their footsteps approached, then receded, without the pause or hesitation that would have let Shropham know that he'd been spotted. The only thing that had paused or stuttered was his own heart.

When they were fully gone he entered Mile End, sat at his desk, tried to work on the finale, but the notes in front of him swirled and swarmed. They made no sense. He spent the evening and evenings subsequent imagining the arrival of his own death. Via kerchief garrote as it had come to Dr. Murdstone. Via migrating thromboembolism as it had come, it seems, to Brunel. Via chest stab during attempted robbery. A cornice piece of a tall building, choosing that exact moment to fall. The speeding carriage that veers, crashes, then disappears down the adjacent road. Shropham was a freethinker, a rationalist, and believed that neither he, nor any other man, could predict the future. (That was the province of second-sight merchants, sixth-sense apostles, psychics, mystics, clairvoyants, widow-fleecers, and Christians.) So, for Shropham, each death foreseen became, perforce, a death evaded.

By that week's end Shropham had catalogued well over a thousand images of his own demise, each distinct. The omelette filled with sage, onion, arsenic. The "accidental" nick, causing a commotion in the blood. The fire in his apartments, doors locked from the outside. No, they would not get him any of those ways. The more exhaustive the list, the more his mind began to clear, the melodies to recommence, the notes to snap into focus. Now the finale was done, and there were but a few passages of the largo to emend, the better to foreshadow the sweet progression of the finale's last chords.

When three days later death did come to Shropham—an ether'd rag to the face, then swift injection—it was all of a moment, and left him no time to thumb through his catalogue to ascertain whether he'd previously imaged it or not. His body was bound with nautical cordage, taken down to Scott Russell's slip, where the *Great Eastern* was being fitted with her new boiler funnel. The parcel was dropped, feet-first, through a small hatch on her foredeck. After a few muffled, reverberant clangs it came to rest, cradled by iron plates, in the space between outer and inner hulls. Shropham had few friends and his family assumed he'd simply up and gone, lit out, as his father and grandfather had done before him. The males of the Shropham family were not so good at sticking around. His composition book was never found, and it was assumed that wherever he'd gone, he'd taken it with him. Which was true.

By NOW YOU know, or have surmised with confidence, that the events surrounding the death of Isambard Kingdom Brunel were not as published in the daily press, or as have been purveyed to us in various encyclopaediae. But the glimpses you have heretofore gotten have been partial and obscure. It is time to lift the veil a bit and let you see the story as it would have been seen by its protagonists.

On the evening of 14th September the lead lascar, here simply called N.—but know that we will disclose more at the proper time—returned to London from Hastings and rejoined his crew at Mile End, where he told them that Brunel would die the following morning. At five a.m. on the 15th N. found Dr. Murdstone and informed him that Brunel had passed. Murdstone entered the solitary ward, listened for heartbeat, felt for pulse, bowed his head, then busied himself filling out the requisite documents, a supply of which Mile End always had at the ready. Murdstone was delegated to inform Mary Elizabeth, now the widow Brunel, and to make arrangements for the onslaught of journalists.

The morning proved chaotic—there were as is always the case some unanticipated moments—but in the main all went as N. had planned.

That afternoon two of N.'s crew bore, on cloth litter, a shrouded body out of Mile End. But the body was not Brunel's, nor was it lifeless. What was wanted was a show of transport even as Brunel himself continued his residence upstairs. Brunel's heart, which had for the examination and pronouncement been stopped via the administration of a careful dose of belladonna and other substances, was now, via the administration of a countervailing dose of pilocarpus, revivified. The effects of a specific subcontinental tincture that had, since the 5th, mimicked in Brunel the condition of an embolism-induced stroke, continued. His heart was beating, his breath would mist a mirror— Yet his death certificate had been signed, his "body" spirited away, his family thrown into full mourning.

That family, through a funeral establishment in Regent Park, had ordered a carved-wood coffin. It was as they had specified of dark walnut, clean of line, magisterially proportioned.

With a few acts of distraction and some significant bribery N. and his crew were able to weight the coffin with lead and have it sealed so that when it was conveyed to the Brunel home, thence to Kensal Green, thence sent down beneath the sod, no one among the large throng suspected that anything was amiss. Those who were by direct knowledge or surmise privy to the substitution were subsequently tidied up. That list would include, without limitation, the undertaker, two of his staff, Dr. Murdstone, and, sadly, young Shropham, who saw a thing he should not have seen, and had, concerning it, in his cups said a thing he should not have said.

You may now be asking: if Isambard Kingdom Brunel was not interred in Kensal Green; if the headstone bearing his name has no remains beneath; if the "death" induced was, subsequently, uninduced; if the stroke itself was perhaps not a stroke at all— What, then, became of Brunel himself? Of that we will have more to say. For now let us attend, simply, to questions of geographical coordinates.

From Mile End Infirmary the torpified body of Isambard Kingdom Brunel was under cover of night brought to an unlit warehouse on the Isle of Dogs. When it was clear they'd not been tracked or followed the crew proceeded from the warehouse down to a dark quay. A line of dank wooden steps brought them to a waiting chaloupe. The four lascars and the immobile Brunel boarded the boat, then two of the lascars took up oars and swiftly, silently pulled the boat into the Thames transverse, out around the bend to where the river widens. Through the light fog they now could see their goal: the riveted sheets of a conning tower, then, of a clad-iron deck. The lascars threw their lines and singled up to the hull. A hatch was opened. The lascars passed Brunel belowdecks, then followed, pulling the hatch shut behind them and securing it with several turns of the wheel.

And then the vessel disappeared: through the fog, into the night, below the Thames. For this was a sub-marine vessel, as remarkable in its own way as the *Great Eastern*. Remarkable, but flawed: limited in propulsion, scant of range, capable of attaining only shallow depth. The vessel's captain—again, we shall, for the moment, refer to him only as N.—wanted to repair and perfect his flawed, limited craft, and knew that there was but one man alive who possessed the *connaissance*. That man was Isambard Kingdom Brunel, and now you are sensing the purpose for which he'd been brought, and, as well, the motivation behind most of what you have just been told.

Yet there is a deeper, darker set of questions. Who, then, is N.? How did he come to be here? What cataclysm—accidental or malign—so extinguished the flames of conscience that kidnapping and murder were to him as means to an end? Hold to your thoughts, for those calls may soon find a response— E'en as our vessel, the *Neptune*, sinks beneath the gentle lap and plash of the River Thames.

FOUR

——————⚓——————

WE NOW TURN back the clock some thirty-one months, from late October of 1859 to late March of 1857: to an event (or, perhaps, occurrence) sufficiently large to have captured the notice of History. It was to have the most profound impact on the life of the man whom you know as N., but now, with a lift of the curtain, we shall refer to by the name he was given at birth, and by which he was known to his countrymen: Prince Dakkar.

Indeed, it might be said that this event set into motion the machineries that would cause Prince Dakkar to quit his homeland, renounce the terrestrial world entire, and become N. Resulting—nine years later and in the North Atlantic—in N.'s death at sea.

And what was this singular event? The spark which the prairie fire did light occurred in Barrackpore. That spark was struck by a sepoy, Mangal Pandey, whose name may be known to you. Mangal Pandey, whose visage now graces postage stamps, but who in March of 1857 was a soldier in the Bengal Native Infantry: a loyal sepoy taking orders from the British East India Company. Until one morning when he awoke otherwise and with vengeance in his heart.

Mangal Pandey's revolt was less a demand for redress than something more inchoate, and it might be ventured that not even Mangal Pandey himself fully understood his motivations. Mangal Pandey did not want: he needed. And what he needed was a world utterly unlike the one in which he found himself. That newer world could not be attained by dint of labor, nor even by dint of dream. To get there—if to get there were even possible—he would have to rend the fabric of the everyday, do it so dramatically and thoroughly that the real world might be glimpsed beyond the scrim. He was nothing and needed to be everything. But that was not the thought in his upper-most mind. Rather, it expressed itself to him as an impulse, one that could not be denied. He awoke knowing, with calm certainty, that he was going to kill the next white man he encountered.

What the sepoy Mangal Pandey staged the morning of 20th March was later referred to as "a one-man rebellion," but at the time it seemed less rebellion than an act, to use Rimbaud's locution, of "elegance, science, violence." Before leaving his quarters, Man-gal Pandey equipped himself with a *talwar*—a bowed sabre, whose honed edge made it more than ceremonial—and with a Jezail mus-ket whose stock was crescent carved. And so he quit his quarters a weapon in each hand, one for the longer range, the other more in-timate. The curve of the Jezail musket, the curve of the sabre, were as smiling moons. Mangal Pandey he was smiling too, but it was not a smile that rained warmth upon those who beheld it. There were those—disturbed by Mangal Pandey's affect, and the arms which he that morning bore—who went on to alert the command.

And so within moments of exiting his housing Mangal Pandey did see a British lieutenant on horseback. That man was Lieutenant Baugh, responding to reports of an armed and feral sepoy. Lieuten-ant Baugh, who'd donned a sword, and had strapped two pistols to his belt, rode in to examine at first-hand the behavior of this soldier-gone-wrong. Examine and, if necessary, put down. But Lieutenant Baugh had opportunity neither to examine nor to use his weapons—for even as he approached the sepoy houses, Mangal Pandey raised musket to his shoulder and fired.

The shot missed the lieutenant but found home in the flank of his horse—which cried, buckled, crumpled to ground. Before the lieu-tenant could fully comprehend that his mount had been shot out from under him, Mangal Pandey closed the distance between him-self and the officer. Lieutenant Baugh sought, and found, one of his pistols, then fired. Missed. Now Mangal Pandey, *talwar* in hand, was slashing at the lieutenant's head and chest. Mangal Pandey worked with a great ferocity but little skill—he had not done this kind of work before. Still he managed to inflict real injury and to shed a goodly quantity of the lieutenant's blood, before one Shaikh Paltu—who by caste was a Rajput but who in his own mind owed fealty to the Queen—did swarm and restrain Mangal Pandey. The other sepoy members of the quarter guard merely looked on. They were not—at least not in the moment—fierce like Mangal Pandey. Yet they were not of a mind to assist the British at the expense of one of their own.

As they watched, their Mangal Pandey—as if possessed—squirmed and flailed with the strength of ten. He handily evaded Shaikh Paltu's attempts to subdue him. An English sergeant major appeared on the scene, pushing through the sepoy crowd toward the end of quashing Mangal Pandey. Yet even as Shaikh Paltu still clung to his ankles, Mangal Pandey was able once more to load, and raise, and aim, and fire, his Jezail musket. The English sergeant major too went down, blood spurting from his leg.

Only later did more British officers arrive on scene, and only then was Mangal Pandey taken down. Pounded to the ground. Yet Mangal Pandey—with the determination of the mad—escaped long enough to retrieve the musket from the officer who'd taken it from him. As ten tried to restrain Mangal Pandey, he did his musket again reload and then, holding it at arm's length, did fire a shot into his own chest.

Mangal Pandey's attempt at self-slaughter was no more successful than his attempt at murder. The shot that Mangal Pandey inflicted upon himself passed through his chest, shattering bone and grazing the subclavian artery, even as the muzzle-burst set his garments afire. His captors, from whom he had just broken, stepped further back to watch him burn. Then someone—a fellow sepoy—stepped in with a thick blanket and wrapped it round Mangal Pandey, extinguishing the flames. By sunset Lieutenant Baugh's horse had been put down; the officers were in recuperation at Titagarh Hospital, in a high room with a view of the Hooghly; and Mangal Pandey, in wrist- and leg-irons bound, did lie on a dirt-floored cell in military prison. The guards who watched over that prison were, typically, sepoy. But not tonight.

It did not go unremarked that when Mangal Pandey was driven to rampage, but one of his fellow sepoys—the aforementioned Shaikh Paltu—thought to intervene on Empire's behalf. Perhaps the soldiers of the Bengal Native Infantry were cheered by the insurrection, however futile, of one of their own.

When on 8th April Mangal Pandey was hanged for his crimes the man who wove the noose, the man who fitted it round Mangal Pandey's head, the man who dropped the bottom from beneath Mangal Pandey's feet, and with that gesture dropped the bottom from Mangal Pandey's life— They were all of them English, all of them white. These hangings were typically done in public, as deterrent to future malefactors; but this one was done in closed courtyard, with no onlookers at all, or at least no witnesses of dusky hue. They wanted to make of Mangal Pandey an example, but they did not want him to become an exemplar.

In that endeavor, despite the precaution of a private hanging, they were not successful. Seemingly within moments the mad insurrection of Mangal Pandey became known throughout the subcontinent. Those events, among those seeking inspiration, did inspire. And thus did the morning of Mangal Pandey's hanging precipitate a rebellion the scale of which had not heretofore been seen, neither in the Princely States nor indeed anywhere else within the expanse of British Empire.

The news was carried by voice, by wire, by press, and thus in short order did reach our prince, Prince Dakkar, the prince of Bundelkhand. On his mother's side the descent was from the Garhwas, on his father's, from the Chandel Rajputs; one might say and with real justification that both reign and command were in the blood.

Prince Dakkar that spring possessed but twenty-seven years, an age where we find remnants of the boldness of youth, yet this was tempered by the wisdom of a well-traveled life. And so upon hearing the news our prince—who had studied the classics at Trinity College, Cambridge, but also the arts military at Sandhurst—pulled together his best soldiers and his wisest advisors, that he might ready himself and his men.

The prince a large and detailed map of Hindoostan did lay out upon his palace table. Troop movements and strengths were upon that map indicated with blocks of colored wood. With each new dispatch concerning their number and disposition the blocks were shifted round. Dakkar paced round the map considering the terrain from every angle, and considering, too, his terrain interior, where even now the colored blocks were shifting.

The causes of any given national rebellion, revolt, mutiny are multivalent; there likely are as many interpretations as there are interpreters. Thus of the Sepoy Rebellion (as we herein will call it), there is much to say by way of explication. But what of the mutiny internal? What of the rebellions and revolts that occur inside the soul, and chart not the course of nations but the destiny of a man? What is the congeries of thought and feeling, within the mind and heart of a prince, as he ponders his future?

Let us acknowledge, then, that we will never know what "caused" Prince Dakkar to take up arms, leave his home, and pursue the Company's army to Cawnpore, any more than we will ever know what "caused" the Sepoy Rebellion. Nor can we fully know the moment when Dakkar did say goodbye to Madhya—his wife and his princess, his love and his treasure, his anchor and his polestar—knowing that it was likely, nay, far more than likely, that the two would not in this lifetime meet again.

Another wife might have gone at him with a dagger, so that if his death were certain, it would at least be here, rather than on some distant plain; intimate, rather than random; and with certainty, rather than with the agony of waiting for the news that must one day arrive. Another might have accepted her fate, as wives for millennia have accepted theirs, when their men go off to war. And our Madhya? If we do not know her thoughts, or his, we do know what transpired when other eyes were present: she stood still, and thin, on the palace balcony, in a sari of purest orange. Her eyes met those of her husband—now on horseback—and did not look away. Nor did his. He was as fully in love as in the first instant he had ever set sight upon her: the years in between vanished like dust in the air and he was once again a schoolboy, seeking the most impossibly lovely young woman. Madhya. He had known her all his life, before he had ever met her, and he would carry her with him, until the moment of his death. Perhaps beyond. Madhya. Dust, and the cry of horses, as his men waited for the call to set forth. How can a man forsake family for country, love for slaughter? It is not a question unique to the story of Prince Dakkar; and it is not a question to which we know, or have ever known, an answer.

With his men behind him, his country before him, a long *tal-*

war draped from his belt—a *talwar* that had never heretofore seen blood—Dakkar looked at Madhya for the longest moment in the world. She looked back without trembling, and if there had been tears before, there were none now. She lifted her arm in salute, ending the moment, allowing her prince to pull on his stallion's reins, to turn his mount to the right and, at the head of a column of his loyal and prepared men, ride into the east, shielding, when they could, their eyes from the morning sun.

Dakkar did not turn back. He thought of his men, whom he was now leading into battle. He thought of Madhya, of course, and of his children. Rani. Hanuman. And he thought of something else, too, a story from childhood: the tale of the Mussulman of Gwalior, his name lost to time across the intervening years, who'd woken one morning with an image—*a dream, a wish, a premonition?*—of a boat that sailed beneath the waves. The Mussulman of Gwalior had sketched his dream on vellum in blackest ink. The vellum, it was long gone, and the story, if you were to examine it, was scarcely a story at all. A man has a dream, wakes up, tries to capture in daylight what he'd seen with his eyes closed. Why would such a tale persist? Why would an amah tell it to the young boy, and why would that young boy ask to hear it, again and again?

PRINCE DAKKAR AND his men—a band of perhaps eighty, including among their number his most treasured mentor Mr. V. K. Singh, a practitioner in his youth of what the English call Dacoity but who had through self-education become learned, and who was the young prince's tutor in math, chess, and much else; the Brahman Mohan and his inseparable companion Feringheea; the outlaw Sikh Daku Jagga; and the French tutor Thomy-Thiérry—did then leave Orchha Palace. They made their way from Bundelkhand to Cawnpore where, it was said, rebels of the Bengal Native Infantry sepoys had taken hold of the city entire.

The grasp of the sepoys upon Cawnpore was wide but shallow, and although they had the goodwill of the citizenry, they were from a military standpoint spread thin. It was far easier to take the city than to defend it. Dakkar reasoned thus: if he could bring his men to

Cawnpore—engage, and weaken, the British Cawnpore regiment—
he could gain time for the sepoys to consolidate their grip.

Dakkar and his men slept by day, traveled by night. Past Parichha,
where the road parallels the river, then on to Chiragaon, Moth, Orai.
It was here that they began to hear more of the rebellion that the mad
strike of Mangal Pandey, the fire-arrow assault upon the telegraph
office at Barrackpore, and the mutinous BNI soldiers of Meerut had
unleashed upon the land. "Devil's wind," the British called it. And
the British would not countenance what to them was disobedience,
breach of command, betrayal. To make an example, the officers of
the Honourable Company took sepoy mutineers, lashed them one
by one to cannon, such that they were bent backward over the muz-
zles. They then fired, cannon after cannon, so that each sepoy was
in turn scattered to the wind in a coarse amalgam of dust and body
parts—the cannon balls then recovered, to be used again.

They rode past Kalpi, forded the Yamuna at Daulatpore, followed
the railway bed through Chaunrah, where they met, engaged in battle, and defeated a British section out on reconnaissance. It was the
first time Prince Dakkar had taken life or seen life taken. He did not
reflect much upon it. It was, to him, like the Yamuna: a river now
forded.

The contingent from Orchha then resumed their march, through
Jalpura and Bhoganipore, past Pukhrayan and Hansemau. Just outside Hansemau they came upon a company of British infantrymen.
Dakkar, recalling the tactical lessons he learned at Sandhurst, divided his men into columns, surprising the British from all points
of the compass under cover of darkness. The battle was bloody and
extended over the course of three days. Dakkar's troop emerged victorious though at the cost of perhaps thirty of their own number.
Among them was the dear and incomparable Daku Jagga. Sent, with
one bullet, from this life to the next.

The day after the fighting at Hansemau had ended they came
upon an elderly man, his right eye clouded over, dressed in the simple cloths of a mendicant. He told them of something he had seen.
It was an elephant, but no ordinary elephant was this. An elephant
made of iron, held together by rivets; and plumes of steam did hiss
and stutter from its trunk. An armored pachyderm? asked one of

Dakkar's men. No, replied the mendicant. This was a machine, and made the noise of a machine, and had the smell of a machine.

On the elephant's back was a tall octagonal *hauda*, whose glistening gold-leaf surface contrasted with the elephant's dull metal. The *hauda* was topped with a *shikhara*, or tower, dome shaped, and *stupi*, or finials, in the colors of a UK flag. (Not only was this elephant mechanical: it was British.)

This clattering and steamy beast was making its way through central India. When the mendicant had seen it the "elephant" was headed north, toward the Himalayas; but it was just as likely, he said, to turn south, and become an instrument of war. "Your bullets cannot pierce its hide," he said, "because it is not made of skin. Your bullets cannot still its heart, because its heart is made of iron. When you hear it approach—and hear it you will, because the steam and engine make a fine havoc—I suggest you move from its path, disappear from its sight. The men in the *hauda* have guns and it is far easier for them to shoot down upon you than for you to shoot up at them."

Some of Dakkar's men believed the mendicant, word for word; others were more skeptic. (How can one believe visual descriptions rendered by a blind man?) But in a land where rebels were by Englishmen tied backward to cannon—then dispatched, one by one, to the wheel of samsara—the notion of credibility was already stretched to limit. Dakkar and his men had been on a march, weary of limb, scarred by battle, exhausted from constant vigilance. And so it was hard to know what was fact and what not; what was reportage, and what was fiction; what was reverie, what was dream; what danced and trembled before rather than behind one's eyes.

Dakkar and his men reached the outskirts of Cawnpore just past nightfall. Once in the city proper the British garrison with its crenellated walls was not difficult to locate. Dakkar dispatched three of his most silent and cunning men to surveille and reconnoiter. They returned with news that the garrison was perhaps as deep as it was wide—no mere encampment but a city within a city, housing the British soldiers, their families too, civilians of various trades and positions: in short, all those who comprised the Anglo-European community in Cawnpore. Though the wall was well-fortified there was, in addition to the main gate a small portal on the far side, presumably for the ingress of victuals and supplies. If it were not heavily guarded on the interior it should be possible to breach the supply portal and disarm the sentries before they might raise alarm.

Dakkar was, in his raid, aided by the clear and moonless night. They were able to reach the garrison wall in full force without attracting notice, and, by means of stealthy crabwise locomotion—too near to the wall to be observed by any atop it—they massed on the far side of the garrison by the supply portal on either side of its reinforced doors. Had they scaling ladders, Dakkar would have sent the eldest and most respected of Thugs, their *jemadar* Mohan, to top the wall, descend by rope, then open the portal from the inside—a maneuver Dakkar had been taught, had practiced, had mastered, at Sandhurst. But they'd not brought such ladders, nor was there anything on site from which they might fashion them.

Dakkar then sent his men to build a ram, and that they did, a makeshift ram of uprooted shesam, substantial in length and breadth, and with enough weight to lend good momentum to their task. While all others bent low against attack—for once they commenced to ram, there would be no more pretense of secrecy—the ramming crew gathered in position and then, at the quiet count of three, commenced. They slammed once, and twice, shearing the hinges; and on the third attempt broke through.

They had assumed that they would be attacked, met with a fusillade of bullets, and were prepared to respond in kind. But there was no fusillade. There was not a single shot. Still, they made their way into the garrisoned city with caution. It appeared to be unguarded. But Dakkar and his men knew that the high point of danger was the moment you assumed yourself to be safe.

Dakkar sent scouts left and right, past the barracks to the west and the civilian housing to the east, and another set of scouts down what was, in effect, the main thoroughfare. None drew any fire. Each returned, each reported much the same news: the garrison city seemed to be deserted. No smoke from cook-fires, no sound of movement. The city, they told him, was a labyrinth with nothing at its center.

What could not escape their notice: the odor, the awful pungent odor of rot that hit them the moment they were through the walls, and never left, and which seemed only to intensify as they advanced upon the city center. Secure—or reasonably secure—that they had not entered a trap, they advanced toward that center. At the head of the column was Dakkar, a warrior Diogenes: sword in one hand, lantern in the other.

The silence was in its own way more frightening than the noise of armed defense, and the lack of human habitation in its own way more terrifying than would have been a brigade of armed troops. Had the British already departed for Lucknow? And if they had: where were the wives, the children, the merchants, the bootmakers, the pandits?

As Dakkar swung his lantern the light caught, now and then, a darker spatter upon the walls. Dakkar wet a finger and rubbed it along the stain. Not new blood but not, in any case, all that old. *Something had happened here.* In the shifting lantern light under moonless skies shapes appeared, danced, vanished. Ghost armies leapt out at them then disappeared into the shadows. The quiet had put their nerves on edge, and the smell of rot more so, that with every step they fully expected to meet their death. By silent massed British fusiliers, or by whatever demon had devoured all that was living in Cawnpore garrison and left it dry.

Now Dakkar's lantern shed its light on a wall more darkened—not just streaks but blots, a fresco of bloody handprints: the indexical traces of men, women, in the throes of their death. Some of the handprints quite small, and low-to-ground. It was hard to come up with explication, other than that these were children, or had been. The walls also bore indentations, scars, sabre-cuts. From high down to low. As if the victims had crouched to avoid the blows.

On the ground were objects yet more disturbing: a row of children's shoes; a man's index finger; a foot, severed at the ankle. There was a yard-long lock of thick black hair. Dakkar did not want to look at the proximal end, for it seemed to have been ripped from a head, taking scalp and skin along with it.

He moved forward with his men in darkness, the dirt path increasingly muddy, the stench ratcheting up with each new step. A courtyard now, where the walls were dense with drying blood. If they were alive, how had they escaped? If they were dead, where were the bodies? Dakkar's men tied bandannas over mouth and nose. The way to find the victims was but to follow the stench.

Some fifty feet east of this courtyard was the well that served the garrison. It was perhaps five-foot wide and deep enough to reach groundwater. The shaft of the well, glimpsed in Dakkar's flickering lantern, was brick-inlaid. But what they saw within was not water: no other way to describe it other than "remains"—severed and inert fractions of what once had been human. What once had lived, walked, worked, slept, dreamed, loved.

Dakkar's lantern guttered, casting intermittent shadows. He lost certainty as to what he had seen, what had been imagined. But in the lantern's lambent light they came to discern that they were gazing at sundered limbs, at heads cut off from bodies, the eyes sightless and gazing up. Dakkar looked away and then looked back. The well was perhaps some fifty feet deep. The bodies filled the well.

Dakkar did what he could to keep thoughts focused on the present moment: *were there British troops hidden, lying in wait?* But the mind, however trained in dispassion, cannot gaze straight down to that abyss without wanting to flee.

He now knew what had happened: the regiment had never left Cawnpore. Instead an overwhelming force of sepoy had breached the gates or, more likely, the walls. Had been shot at by the British, had been slashed at, had been slain. For three days the British held them off, and for those three days the mutineers were hung, were eviscerated, were draped over the mouths of cannon by the British militia. But for each sepoy slaughtered, ten o'ertopped the wall. The magma of a thousand sleights, over a hundred years, oozed up, then burst. Imagine, if you can, a battalion of Mangal Pandeys, gone wild simultaneous. An army of the mad cannot be defeated. And so victorious they were, over the regiment, yes, then over every English being within their sight. Man, yes, but also woman, and also child. Pursued, slain, hacked up. Dakkar could hear their screams over the moonless silence. They echoed still, if not within the walls of the garrison, then within the walls of his head.

Perhaps there were someone alive, someone who could tell the tale. But that seemed scarcely to matter: the tale was here, told on the walls, told in the alluvium through which they'd walked— And told in the well, which reached down past groundwater, through densest rock, layer upon layer, down past imagining, to the dark, hot, center of the world.

At the same time that he tried to breathe, and with his mind tried to reconstruct what had occurred from what he had seen, he knew with certainty that he, and his men, were as of this moment marked for death. The Company would think that they had committed these acts, or that they were with these acts associated. There were British soldiers to be avenged. And women, and children. Dakkar knew he would be hunted to the ends of the earth, and until the end of time. That he would be slain on sight; that his family would not be spared; that onward down the years no relative or offspring of Prince Dakkar would be allowed by them to tread the earth. And who, asked Dakkar, could to that vengeance assign anything like blame? *They killed ours, and we will now kill every last one of theirs.* It is an impulse deeply human if not, in any other sense, possessed of humanity.

Yet even as he knew that he was already dead—and even as his mind, thinking of the walls and of the well, did not cease imagining what could never fully be imagined—there was also an inundation of energy. Of freedom. A sense of possibility opening up more rapidly than he could grasp. A blossom, a bloom, in each and every direction. For if he were already condemned: in the house of the dead there were no shackles. What, now, might constrain him from thought or act? The fear of consequence? There was no more consequence to be had here. He was Dakkar and he was dead and he was a prince of men but he was also no man. He had no future and so all futures now opened up before him for whatever time he'd been allotted.

He'd long had no regard for the British. Now, gazing down and away and back down the well, Dakkar had at once lost regard for the race of man. He was not a subject, and he was not a brother. He was a free man, free of compassion, free of the ties that bind, a sodality of one.

He would disband his small troop. Allow them to pursue whatever course they now saw fit. He would make his way alone—on horseback, or should that be too conspicuous, on foot—back to Bundelkhand. To spend his remaining moments within the walls where he'd been born, and with those whom fate had allowed him to love:

his amah, his children, his wife. If by venturing within the gates of Cawnpore, by leaving his footprints in garrison muck, he'd sealed Madhya's fate along with his own, he wanted to be with her before that fate came due, to make her remaining moments joyous, free from all care. Until whatever came after, no matter how brutal or final, were as mere footnote to a thousand-page text. Let her know that I love her. Then I can die, and my death will have been earned, and my life not without purpose in this world.

And so he gave over command to his wisest lieutenant, and gave his men autonomy to pursue the fight wherever it would lead. They chose to head northeast, toward Lucknow, where there were, perhaps, battles to be waged, comrades to be supported, a people to be freed. Dakkar would go west-southwest to Bundelkhand. To Orchha Palace. To home.

They went their separate ways at dawn. The sun was coming up and the full weight of what they had by lanternlight witnessed could now fully be seen. The sepoy massacred by the British. The British savaged by the sepoy. The sword marks low on the walls. The blood in spatters, then streaks, then pools. The thick, gelatinous smears on walls and on branches—what could only be the brain matter of those, sepoy and British alike, whose skulls had been crushed, shattered. With the rising sun came rising heat, and with rising heat, rising stench. You didn't want to take a breath deeper than your throat.

Dakkar embraced his lieutenant, left shoulder–right shoulder, ceremonially, as if awarding a medal. Took him close to his breast, held him. Then:

Dakkar: "You will be victorious."

His men, behind him, nodded. It was not a time, or a place, for cheers.

Lieutenant: "Travel well."

Dakkar bent his head down briefly. Turned his back on his men. Took one step, then another, through unspeakable Cawnpore muck, toward the gate, thence toward home.

He went on foot—to travel by horse seemed the surest way to raise attention. Not in uniform or in finery but in the simplest garb, a cream-colored *dhoti* frayed and paled by time. Two days out, near Chapar Ghata, where the river for a brief stretch runs parallel to the road, he encountered a section of Campbell's skirmishers, patrolling the road to Lucknow to assure that the main force of Campbell's men were not attacked from the rear. But Dakkar had neither arms nor the garb of a soldier and he walked so humbly along the path that there was no reason to suspect him an enemy. They stopped him, made him turn round, patted him for weapons. What they saw: a man whose beard was rimed with dust, whose hair and skin had not been washed for long time, whose teeth and gums were red stained from chewing *paan*, whose feet were bare and callused and cracked. They made him lift his *dhoti* and patted him again. When they were satisfied he could do them no harm they let him go on his way. The next man they stopped was not as fortunate. The man had, in the folds of his *kurta salwar*, a small crescent-shaped *kris*. They confiscated it, let him free; but then, as he was walking away, shot him twice in the back and in the head. He fell to the ground and lay still. Dakkar heard this, knew what fate had befallen the other man— But did not turn around. He did not want to look, and did not want to be seen looking. He kept his head down, his feet close to earth. Through Sachendi to Rania; Nagin Jasi to Todarpore; back across the Yamuna; via the Kalpi Railway Bridge; past Shahjahanpore and Osargav and Okasa and Chamari; around Orai (there was too much danger of encountering British there, so Dakkar circumnavigated); then through Alt, where he labored for three days mucking the stables for one of the local men of good fortune in exchange for water and food. But with head down, always with head down.

Then, roughly paralleling the river down through Moth and Semri, Chiragaon and Parichha and Baragaon and Goramachhiya, past Karguan, where lived a man he knew he could trust. The man gave him a horse, his best, and asked nothing in return. Dakkar asked the man how he might thank him. The man replied that Dakkar already had.

It was on that horse that Dakkar rode through Shivaji Naggar, past the British cemetery on Gwalior Road, then up to Orchha. To home. Dakkar's heart was not light—*how could it be, given where he had been, what he had seen?*—but the thought of returning to Madhya filled his spirit with a sense of light, of possibility.

The first presentiment that something had gone wrong came with the first man he saw. It was Achyuta who ran the kitchen staff, as did his father before him. Achyuta looked up. But instead of breaking out into that broad and contagious grin, as he had on so many encounters previous, he just looked down.

The second man Dakkar saw—the stable keeper Revant—did the same.

Now Dakkar was close enough to see the amahs, on the balconies, beating rugs with dusters. (When were the amahs *not* shaking pieces of cloth in daylight?) When they saw Dakkar and recognized him they cried, shrieked, keened. It was an unearthly sound. Still others recoiled, ran back into the palace, leaving their dusty rugs to hang in the now-still air. Ran back, as if they'd seen a ghost. Seen a *bhoot*: a perturbed and restless soul, condemned by some flaw or failure of this life to be interdicted from moving on to the next.

It was not until he had dismounted, was on the steps of Orchha Palace, with the amahs peering out through slits and windows, that anyone came to look him in the eye. Pashupati, who worked with Revant to mind the horses and other animals, came through the door. Stared at his prince from foot to eye. Finally: "Welcome home." But in saying it he did not evince joy. Then he pulled the prince to him, close, something he'd not in thirty years done, or was likely ever to do again. The amahs, much of the staff were now near-certain that what they saw was a man not returned from the dead but rather from long travel.

"Where is Madhya?" said the prince, and in the faces of those assembled found his answer. They brought him inside, unwound his dhoti, and bathed him, and brought scented flowers into the chamber, and soaked his feet in salt and essential oils. His hair and beard were washed and soaped and combed until all the dust of travel had been washed away.

In this he was looked after by Devi, who had been his amah when he was in swaddling cloth and who swaddled him now: she wrapped the prince in cloth that clung to his damp skin and made it dry. And as she soaked him and rubbed him and combed him and dried him and wrapped him and soothed his skin with sweet oil, she also spoke to him. Told him what his heart could not bear to know. That his daughter was gone, that his son was gone, lost to British knives; and that Madhya too was gone, lost to grief, lost to *sati*, when the men from Oudh—liars, traitors, merchants of grief, with deceit in their souls and British coin in their pockets—delivered to Madhya news of Dakkar's death. One was a Sikh; another a bellied, jovial merchant's son from Pondicherry. They did not seem like agents of empire but it was for that, and that alone, they had been chosen. They knew what effect their words would have. It is why they were by the British Empire paid to utter those words.

When Dakkar was clean, was dry, his servants helped him into his trousers, his tunic; then wound a turban round his head. A turban with upright feather. His best and oldest *talwar*, slow curved and honed, was strapped to a jeweled belt round his waist. He did visit, and for long moments, his room, their room, the one he had shared with Madhya—gone large and small and dark.

Then they went with him, one at each elbow, through the doors and out, blinking in sunlight. They took him to the pyre and they let him see what was there. It was not anything he did not already know but now he knew it in a different way, by image, by smell, and then, as he sifted cinders through his fingers, by touch. The taste of dry ash was in his mouth now. And would be, forever.

He stayed in the palace for three days. Long enough to send back the horse to the good man of Karguan, together with a small sack of gold coins. Long enough to make sure that every thing he had done as prince could be done by others in his absence.

On the third day he walked to the river Ken where it makes its canyon. The walls of the canyon were of pure crystalline granite in shades that ranged from pink to red to gray. He walked alone, a bamboo stick over his back and a small sack on the end of the stick. The Ken had been running for aeons, longer than man could measure or even fathom: the canyon ran some three miles and was a hundred feet deep. Then he reached the end of the canyon: Raneh Falls. It was there that the waters dropped long and low. The noise comforted his ears.

He put down his stick and untied the corners of the sack. Inside were the ashes of his wife, and of his children Rani and Hanuman, commingled. He took them up in his hand and let them fall through his fingers to the river just above the falls. He did this again and again until all the ashes were gone, down the falls; and the souls of his wife and children had gone to their next place.

His eyes were dry and there was some ash on his face from where the ash had blown but he did not make to wipe it off. He just turned, retraced his steps, walked back—it took him some time—to Orchha. He stayed in the palace overnight. Then he left. An odd quartet—his treasured mentor Singh, his aging French tutor Thomy-Thiérry, his Brahman Thugs Mohan and Feringheea, all now back from Lucknow—followed at a distance. The Prince did not speak to them, nor they to him. He wished no more to have truck with the society of men.

It was then that the prince recalled what he'd never forgotten: the dream of the Mussulman of Gwalior. A dream of a boat that sailed not upon the waves but beneath them. But to the prince: a dream of a life not lived upon this earth. A dream that called to him more loudly with each step. The waters of the Ken drowned out the sound of the land, until all that was left was the echo of his footsteps. Step by step he entered the old dream. Dakkar of Bundelkhand was now the Mussulman of Gwalior, and also no man, and also every man who had ever been given more than the heart can endure. He knew, now, his task. The earth was his home but it was time to leave.

He would wander the lands of the earth until he reached their edge, and then he would roam the waters of the earth, and when he could he would dive down into those waters and there find another home. The prince would become as the nameless Mussulman of Gwalior: He would fashion a sub-marine vessel, to be called the *Neptune*, honoring the lord of the sea whose dominion subtended two-thirds of the globe. The prince would be no man. In Latin: *nemo*. And thus did the Prince become Captain, and thus did Dakkar become Nemo.

And as Nemo he would live within the *Neptune* and live there beneath the waves. He would help the Candiotes in their rebellion, yes; he would disrupt the larger plans of empire, yes; he would sever the filaments that linked London to its empire, yes. And of course: he would put paid to each and every British man-of-war that dared to sail upon the seven seas.

He would live beneath the waves as a child beneath a blanket, reading by scant light creating worlds of his own. And there beneath the waves our Nemo would live until his time was done. Until a bullet from a large-bore rifle should find its way to and through his heart.

WE HAVE SEEN, now, the concatenation of events—some world-historical, some small as a mote of Cawnpore dust—that did to our Nemo give birth. And we shall most certainly return to our Nemo's saga at the proper time. But for the moment let us lift the curtain more fully to introduce another of our tale's dramatis personae, a man whose life will intersect with Nemo's in ways that are neither casual nor without consequence.

As was the case with Nemo, this man may also be known to you. He is John Ahab, out of Nantucket. These two men, they are as like and as opposite as South Pole and North. You know of Nemo as a man who lives beneath the sea, and hates all upon it. John Ahab he lives upon the waves and hates, with equal fervor, all beneath. When the two of them are pitched 'gainst each other—and this they will—'tis likely that neither will survive. What we know to a certainty: at battle's end, when smoke and mist do clear, not more than one of them shall remain alive.

FIVE

————— ✧ —————

No one would be faulted for believing the Captain Ahab to be dead. The tale of his dénouement has been ably recounted elsewhere, and seemed to leave our Ahab no means of egress save the path that o'erlooks paradise, or the other, so similar in appearance, that gives upon perdition. (Most would assume, given what they'd been told, he'd walked the latter.) There are, to be sure, deaths that bring a life to its full stop. Yet there are those deaths, particularly among the legendary, that punctuate more lightly.

Here is what we know with more certainty: Within a year or two of said captain's demise, a traveling entertainment did mount and tour through the towns and cities of our Republic. It was billed: *I AM AHAB: A ONE-MAN SHOW*. The first recorded appearance was in Indianapolis, where there was enough business for a run of three weeks' duration; it then moved on to Louisville. From Louisville to Nashville, from Nashville darting into Florida, then across Alabama and Mississippi and Arkansas, up the river to Illinois then over to Indiana to start the circuit anew.

The show was less a play than a series of tableaux. In the first a young and strapping Ahab ascended the gangway, off to sea for the first time. In the second the young man told of his love of the sea, recited oceanic paeans in blank verse, sang a chantey. Then this boy of eighteen, this apprentice harpooneer, found his ship capsized and himself attacked by a whale. There was a brief intermission during which refreshments were sold. The show recommenced forty years later, with Ahab gaunt and aged and with hair more salt than pepper. He had but one question, which he asked of all: "Hast thou seen the White Whale?" In the following scene, unaccompanied by dialogue, he nailed a gold coin—an Ecuadorian eight escudos doubloon—to the mast. A long silent moment, one with fine resonance for those who already knew the tale. And on that moment: the curtain fell.

The curtain rose again. Now Ahab stood on deck, aimed his harpoon, let fly. Hit his mark. The rope wrapped itself around him: He was enmeshed. Dragged down by it. Dragged overboard by it. Entombed by it. Curtain.

Then the curtain rose for the final time. An exhausted Ahab, hair now gone white as driven snow, addressed the audience directly. "And I only am escaped alone to tell thee." Thumped his ivory leg against the boards of the stage to induce generosity as the tall hat was passed among the spectators. As he moved from city to city, north to south and back, he adjusted the cadences of his speech to the rhythms of his audience. Cut some scenes. Elongated others. Continued his tour. Was offered a residence in Michigan but did not like that state. A state should be contiguous, he thought, and the idea of two disparate land masses with one name disturbed him.

It all came to an end, as many things do, in Philadelphia, where a young reporter, less canny than persistent, did by his research discover that whereas all documentation of the *Pequod* and its captain showed it was the captain's right leg that had been savaged, the Ahab of the dramatic tableau was absent his left. Worse, word of the reporter's article reached far beyond the newspaper's circulation, traveling by telegraph, from mouth to ear. Within weeks there was nowhere in Indianapolis or Louisville or Nashville or Atlanta or Decatur where this John Ahab might ply his trade. He did then return to his hometown of Weehawken, to incubate other schemes by which a man missing a leg might make his way in the world without reliance upon alms. He stayed first with his mother and then, when that lodging grew to be insalubrious, in a small rooming house hard by the river, where a sextet of one-roomers, day-drinkers, isolatoes— most cast off by their wives—insisted to anyone who would hear them out that their billet was only temporary.

His third night there he woke abruptly from his dreams. Something had come down hard on the small of his back. He heard, then felt, the bones of his ribs crack asunder. The pain, when it arrived a brief moment later, was like unto hellfire.

"Jabez."

A voice spoke the name he was given at birth. A name no one had uttered for almost a decade. In his mind, as if incited by the pain, is a song, sung by a choir he heard in Mississippi in a white clapboard church in a darker neighborhood; it comes back in this room now, surprising and unbidden and in full force.

You better get ready for judgment,
You better get ready for judgment morning.
You better get ready for judgment
My God it's coming down.

Jabez opened his eyes and what he saw was as terrible as the most terrible dream. What he saw was a man standing impossibly tall, in black trousers and black coat. In the large dark man's hand was a thick ivory club. It was an object with which Jabez was more than familiar: It was his own leg. Unstrapped in preparation for bed, left casually on the coiled rug, raised high. And now descending again with great and terrible force.

Better get ready for judgment
'Cause God is coming down.

Who is this man? In Jabez's mind this is the man he played onstage and off. This is the man who died at sea and whose legend was his sustenance and provision. In Indiana, in Tennessee, in Alabama, across the South and up the Mississippi River, Jabez had taken the role of this man, safe in the knowledge that the impersonation would go uncontested. The man was dead. Is dead. How could he be here in this room? How could he now come through the door to enact his own drama of vengeance before this terrified and trembling house?

Jabez stared up at his assailant; a red mist descended before his eyes. The image of the large black-suited man shifted in and out of focus but the face remained still and clear. Jabez is staring at himself: a larger, more terrible image of himself. Jabez is staring into a demonic glass, all his faults, all lapses of faith reflected large in front of him even as the long club descended once more, hitting the side of his head, fracturing his left orbital socket, the hum in his ears, and the song louder—

> *Better put on your morning garment*
> *And get your staff in your hand*
> *'Cause Jesus coming that morning*
> *He's coming unaware to man.*

—and now, only now, does unconsciousness blissfully descend. Somewhere downstairs a grandfather clock ticks the slow seconds. Somewhere down the hall an isolato hacks and coughs. Jabez has the breath for just one word:

"Why?"

The large dark man gave no response. Laid down the bloodied club on the bed: the sheet-white Jabez, the red-soaked sheets. The man turned, presenting his broad and black-cloaked back. Took a step toward the door. And left without giving answer.

JABEZ'S KILLER HE made for the river. His route was direct, not the route of a man bent on evasion—as if he were running not away but toward. He encountered no one on the narrow streets. There were lights in some of the windows but he kept his eyes fixed ahead, not knowing or caring whether he was spotted along his line of march. The air grew more saline. His shoulders rose as if with each step toward the river a burden were being lifted.

At the edge of the Hudson was a wood-frame building, a shack really, with a rusted hasp that would prevent no one, let alone a large man, from gaining entrance. The door creaked on rusted hinges. The large man went through, from gloom to darkness, descended two wooden flights, debouched through the rear door—smaller, but no more secure than the other—onto a brief jetty. Tied to the jetty was a skiff. He climbed in, bad leg first, unhitched the hawser, grabbed the oars, shoved off. His face was pointed toward the fine shore of New Jersey but the craft made straight in the direction opposite, toward the isle of the Manhattoes, where fireworks burst in air and infernos could even now be seen glimmering on the far banks. 'Twas the cable that was being celebrated, the telegraphic cable, a single length of wire 'cross the North Atlantic, with words exchanged in mere moments between President and Queen—about which, more anon!

The shore receded stroke by stroke. He was on water. There had been a man making sport of him, earning his living by pretense, adopting his own name and history as a means of livelihood. This had to end and now it had ended. At the hand of John Ahab, the real.

Ahab now he glides, stroke by stroke, into the future, eyes fixed on the past, but in no sense lingering there. That is land. He is on water. He is heading toward an island. He does not like land but an island is, to him, tolerable, on account of what surrounds it. He would live, if he had to, on Martha's Vineyard. He would live, were he compelled, on a cay in the Caribbean. But right now, neither on land nor on island, he is not here, he is not there. Which is why he is at home. At home but rowing, now, toward the light. Toward the flames. Toward the fireworks. A fête incited by, and in celebration of, Telegraphy. Telegraphy! The thread that runs like unbroken filament of ductile and conductive copper through the lives of our three protagonists.

SIX

————⚓————

AFTER TWO FALSE starts, four failed expeditions—and more breaks, snaps, bankruptcies, failures, and disasters than anyone might have contemplated—it was done: a braid of cable, packed in gutta-percha, unspooled by the ship *Agamemnon* and the ship *Niagara* upon the bed of the North Atlantic, now stretched from Valentia Harbor to Trinity Bay! A rope of copper—conductive, continuous—from Foilhummerum to Heart's Content, Ireland to Newfoundland, Europe to the Americas. That world and this one were now joined, by strands of lightning under water.

The circuit had been completed at 1:45 a.m. on 5th August. The enterprise's director—the paper and dry goods magnate Cyrus Field, out of Stockbridge—had run ashore in Newfoundland and awakened the local telegraph operators proclaiming, "The cable is lain!" The first official message was then sent by the Company directors in London to their fellow directors in New York. Transmitted in Morse's code, it read as follows:

. ..- .. -- .—. / . -. -.. / .—. .-. .. .. .-. .- / . .- .. / .. .- .. -. . -.. / .—- .-
/ - . .-.. . —. .. .- —. —. -. .- /—- -- .—. / —. .-.. -- -. .- / .-- / —.
—- -.. / .. .-. / . —. . / —. .. —. -. . —- / .-. —— .- / -- -. / .- .-. .-
—. / . —. . -. . / .-. -. -——- .- / —. .— -- -.. .- .- ... .-.. -.. / . -- .- .-.
-.—/—. -. /—- -- .—. / . . .- -.. .. ... - /

Or, in plaintext:

EUROPE AND AMERICA ARE UNITED BY TELEGRAPHY STOP GLORY TO GOD IN THE HIGHEST COMMA ON

EARTH PEACE COMMA GOODWILL TOWARDS MEN
STOP ENDIT

The next exchange was even more exalted—to wit, a missive
from Queen Victoria to the President himself:

*The Queen desires to congratulate the President upon the successful
completion of this great international work, in which the Queen
has taken the deepest interest. The Queen is convinced that the
President will join with her in fervently hoping that the electric
cable, which now connects Great Britain with the United States,
will prove an additional link between the two places whose friendship is founded upon their common interests and reciprocal esteem.
The Queen has much pleasure in thus directly communicating with
the President, and in renewing to him her best wishes for the
prosperity of the United States.*

To which our President Buchanan did respond:

*The President cordially reciprocates the congratulations of her
Majesty the Queen, on the success of the great international
enterprise accomplished by the science, skill and indomitable
energy of the two countries. It is a triumph more glorious, because
far more useful to mankind, than was ever won by conqueror on the
field of battle. May the Atlantic telegraph, under the blessings of
heaven, prove to be a bond of perpetual peace and friendship
between the kindred nations, and an instrument destined by Divine
Providence to diffuse religion, civilization, liberty and law throughout the world. In this view, will not all nations of Christendom
spontaneously unite in the declaration that it shall be forever
neutral, and that its communications shall be held sacred in passing
to their places of destination, even in the midst of hostilities?*

And with those words, thus did celebrations begin that night on
both sides of the Atlantic. These revels were as is ofttimes the case
accompanied by the imprudent consumption of alcohol. There were
poems of many stanzas indited to commemorate the occasion. The

attorney and lapsed pianist William Winter was so moved by the
event that he reverted to his former métier and wrote the following,
to the air of "Hail, Columbia":

> Grand with feeling, sweet and strong,
> Swell to-night the choral song!
> For the noble work is done;
> And the precious prize is won;
> And the raptured nations stand
> Face to face and hand in hand.

Even for a city renowned for its refusal to call it a night, a visitor
to the island of the Manhattoes would see what spirit looked like
when fully loosed. The roister was cumulative, crest adding to crest,
trough canceling out trough, each night a recapitulation of the night
previous and then more on top of it. A flaming rag for every broken
heart on Broadway. Were there sufficient barrels of kerosene and
rum to fuel these torches, these bellies? It seems that there are. Have
the songs all been sung? Well then, add another verse.

> While Thought's winged couriers sweep
> Through the oozy dungeons deep!
> Honor those who sowed the seed—
> Noble thought and noble deed!

> For the rainbow arch sublime,
> Rises o'er the sea of Time;
> And the starry lights presage
> Triumphs of the golden age.

The incomparable Liliendahl organized a pyrotechnic display
for the Crystal Palace, and as word spread all of Reservoir Square
was filled cheek-to-jowl. Other, lesser pyrotechnicians laid claim to
other monuments, began packing their powder. Come nightfall all
down the Stem, for a distance of three miles: fires of oil and wood
and cloth and paper, the flames sprinkled with copper sulfate, with
arsenic, with elemental salts, to render the flames blue and crimson

and green, deep oceanic green, and purple too, the color that appears when you press your knuckles into your eyes. As if the flames were not sufficient the revelers projected large transparencies onto every hotel and many private dwellings. Down Broadway each storefront became a canvas for the epigrammatic and laudatory phrase, projected bright and flickering onto the glass and stone. It was night, but in Times Square now it was as bright as day, the colors and hues gone tropic and riotous.

Yet even as songs were sung, fires were lit, and glories were offered unto God, there was a hollow at the center of the jamboree: by 7th August Mr. Field—now repatriated to New York—learned that the cable, having carried a few fine and select messages, had flickered. Guttered. Was now: extinguished. And with it, the imagination of a trans-Atlantic future. Up and down the streets of Manhatto, thousands of celebrants were paying loud, intoxicated tribute to light from a star that had already been extinguished.

Mr. Field kept the knowledge close to his chest, as a religious man might travel with a Bible stuffed into his breast pocket, protecting his heart. Mr. Field he was a straightforward man from Massachusetts. The dreaming he left to others while himself tending to the practicalities. So even as the banked flames of panic flared up within his gut his mind focused on three distinct tasks, and three only:

The first, to keep the news contained. Were the word to leak out among the community of capital, among his investors, Mr. Field's livelihood and even freedom would be upon the rack. And were the word to spread more precipitously, one can only imagine how the streets' fierce inebriates, wild carousers, and hopped-up celebrants might respond to what they would likely see as fraud, if not betrayal.

The second, to gather capital for yet another expedition, that the sundered cable be re-joined. There were no funds from the previous venture left over. The paradox faced by Mr. Field was not a new one: there would be investors only for a successful cable, but if the cable needed repair, it was no longer successful. The money men—whether they be merchants, or the solons of the US Congress—would not associate themselves, or their funds, with anything redolent of failure.

The third, and perhaps most difficult: it had become clear to Mr. Field that the problem was not in the laying of the cable—that had been done, and done well, on several voyages—but rather the protection of the cable 'gainst whatever had snapped it. Mr. Field was a God-fearing man, and believed, as did many Massachusetts Christians, that the good fortune visited upon his family was but a sign of God's blessing upon it. His brother Stephen—whom he hated—had just been appointed to the California Supreme Court. His brother Henry, the doctor of divinity, was the editor and publisher of *The Evangelist*, devoted to spreading the word of God in a Protestant way. The New York State Code of Civil Procedure was known as the Field Code, as it was instigated and written by his third brother, David. So clearly: the breaks in the cable were not expressions toward the family Field of disappointment on the part of the Almighty.

It was possible that the slow settling of the cable into the ocean-floor sediment might be the prime cause—yet if that be the case, how to explain the way the breaks seemed timed, as if with exquisite precision, to raise hopes, and then to dash them down?

After a morning spent in contemplation and prayer, Mr. Field came to the conclusion that his cable's nemesis was neither God- nor Nature-driven, but was rather the work of active agency. Of consciousness. Having eliminated what, to him, were all other possibilities, what remained was the one both simplest and most terrifying: a sea-creature, of malevolent will and unimaginable might. And who might combat this oceanic Leviathan? Who in our Republic would have the knowledge to find him, the instinct to track him, the desire to slay him?

'Twas not a long list. 'Twas not even the fingers of one hand.

SEVEN

————— ⚓ —————

LATER THAT MORNING, after Mr. Field to himself had admitted he was in need of a knight to slay a sea-dragon, he did make some discreet enquiries. But his ideal candidate—you will by now have surmised, of course, that we are referring to our Ahab—was not someone who basked in the public gaze. He was said, by all, to be peripatetic, but was also said, by all, to return again and again to the island of the Manhattoes: living low, somewhere by the battery's great south wheel, even after the voyage that was held by the crowd to have been his last.

It was thus on the recommendation of some fellow members of his club that Mr. Field did that afternoon hire a Manhattan native, one James Fearnley, a lapsed or recovering detective, late of the Municipal Police, to locate the captain, and having located him, retrieve him. It was Mr. Field's hope that Fearnley, by repute an able and practiced rooter, might flush him out.

What he asked of Fearnley was to bring John Ahab to his apartments in Gramercy Park. It would then be Mr. Field's task to make the offer sufficiently rewarding that Ahab would have no alternative but to assent. Should Ahab not be found? Or should he refuse, once found, to join with Mr. Field? Field sighed to think of it—for then the cable scheme would, like the cable itself, be buried in the silt of time; the rainbow arch sublime would be left for another generation of dreamers and doers; and those gathered at his memorial would sing the praises of Cyrus W. Field, paper merchant, of Stockbridge, Lee, and Westfield Massachusetts, brother of, brother of.

HAVING BEEN THUS commissioned, Fearnley paid visit to the sa-
loons into which his beloved Municipals had burrowed to console
their decommissioning. He paid similar visit to a distinct and separate set of drinking houses where the hated Metropolitans—who by
upstate subterfuge had replaced the Municipals earlier that year—
would repair after, and at times during, their working day. He spent
an evening at a brawling, roiling Tammany beefsteak, where four
hundred men devoured three times as many pounds of grilled cow.
He went high, he went low; he walked up as far as Haarlem and
down as far as Castle Clinton, making enquiries, leaving word: *Has
anyone seen a large man, one good leg, who, if past be prologue, would
gravitate toward the shore?*

Fearnley's employer, Mr. Field, was in possession of a secret large
enough to bring ruination, and did not share with his hired man
anything that his man had not a need to know. Hence: nothing of
the cable, nothing of its prospects, nothing of Ahab's importance to
the venture going forward. This was, from what Fearnley had been
told, a simple find-and-retrieve. Fearnley assumed, by experience if
not by direct instruction, that news of the quarry's death would be
as equally welcome as the retrieval of the quarry itself. In Fearnley's
time with the Municipals he had learned that of the two alternatives,
the former was safer, easier, more prone to please one's commander.
He'd been a policeman for some twelve years during which it was
the live ones who gave him trouble, never the other kind.

And so Fearnley ventured forth with a pair of handcuffs retained from his previous employment. Handcuffs, yes, but also
with his pistol.

AS WITH MUCH detective work, enquiries went unanswered, prom-
ising leads yielded up little, informants demanded compensation but
as quid pro quo gave forth with legend rather than fact. And though
there was a small per diem, Fearnley's payoff would come only with
completion of the task. He decided, on 17th of August, to cease for
the evening his pursuit. It would be impossible, in the midst of the
unending celebration—which had built up, and grown more fierce,

night by night—to contemplate forward progress. So he gave in to the larger thrall, let himself be carried to Reservoir Square on Forty-Second Street where his employer was making yet another magnificent public speech to a crowd numbering in the thousands. Brother could not find brother here. Fearnley was spent, off-the-clock, in the midst of this densest throng. Limpid in the August heat. Yet what was that? Over there! What was that? At the far edge of the mob? What was that? A tingle *felt* before *seen*: a large dark man with syncopated gait—

Who just might be his Ahab. Or just might be a wish-apparition: the chimerical upshot of too many days spent in pursuit of elusive goal.

Fearnley worked his way through the sea of his fellow humans, fellow New Yorkers. After the loss of his job, the prospect of an uncertain future, might for once a beneficent god be smiling upon him? There was a smile upon his own face, even as he trained his eyes on the large and distant man, reached down for the one-shot pistol lodged in the waistband of his trousers. Behind him, fireworks turned the sky red, then blue. Then: turned the sky white as the arctic continent.

EIGHT

———————✼———————

INTO THIS THEATER of light strode our Ahab. With each uneven step he found the crowd more thick, the smoke more dense, yet he plowed forward—escaping, by fugitive's habit, evading whatever pursuers from Weehawken might be on his scent, yes, but moving to-ward, not merely from. He wanted to disappear in that crowd, as a hunted sea animal disappears beneath the waves.

The torches crazed his vision. Transparencies bobbed and weaved upon the side of thick buildings, like the shadow puppets he had seen in Bali. But that was another voyage, and a long time past. That was when he was young. He did not at this moment feel young. He felt old, and tired, and full of spent vengeance. But he was not ready to lie down.

He found himself in Reservoir Square, depending south from Forty-Second Street and extending from Sixth Avenue to Fifth, a plot of greensward rendered mud by the pressure of so many boots in so confined a space. At the far end of the greensward was Carstensen & Gildmeister's Crystal Palace, their massive, delicate monument to fenestration: all wrought iron and rolled glass, illumined now by hundreds of tiny flames and a few large ones.

Tonight, in front of the palace, on a purpose-built wood-plank platform, Ahab beheld a bearded orator, Mr. Cyrus W. Field, speaking into a horn so large it was borne by two. When the horn was aimed toward him he could hear, quite clearly, the words of the night; and when Mr. Field democratically turned his mechanism to other parts of the Square, he heard nothing but the cheer and echo of eight thousand souls.

"—the applicability of "electricity to the communication of intelligence—"

Our Ahab looked repeatedly over his shoulder. The crowd had filled in behind him. He was for the moment lost; he was for the moment safe. He shifted his weight from bad leg to good.

"—the nations of the world conjoined, its peoples as one people—"

Ahab spat upon the ground. The men on either side shifted, giving him more room at the expense of their own.

"—so that our great country America may once again be reunited with her twin—"

Abruptly—and it was the work of an instant—a *change* grew over him. Ahab's eyes, which had been fixed on the stage, or, alternatively, had been darting, furtively, over his left shoulder, now went all soft, lustrous, effulgent. Staring not at the crowd, the speaker, the Crystal Palace, but to some wide vista beyond. It was as if he were gazing less through space than through time. And as if he were seeking not the horizon where the water meets the sky, but rather the horizon inside. The one, as we all know, that is farther away.

He is seeing, now, his sister. Seeing: though he has no real image of her, no true memory of her voice. She has been with him since before his birth and has never really left.

There is, two states north and an equal ways east, in Nantucket, a small shallow hill on a larger flat of green, latticed with large stones and larger mausolea. It is the Quaker graveyard. And on that shallow hill are two markers, side by side. The first marker has, as is customary, a date of birth, a date of death. They are but six days apart. The marker bears a name:

ANNABEL.

The second marker shares with the first the date of birth. Yet below that first date is but stone, blank stone. Smooth, featureless, polished, like a crystal ball in which no image has yet formed. This stone, too, bears a name:

JOHN.

He sees it. His name. His stone. The stone of his beloved sister. The small shallow hill where, after all ports of call, he will come to rest. Next to Annabel's small sad coffin. Her home, and in time a home for him.

She is half of him. More than half. And the farther he roams—through city, over sea, atop peak, within isolate isle—the nearer she stays. In anger, in alcohol, in densest crowd, she can always find him. She is here now in Reservoir Square. He can see her and feel her. He cannot touch her. He knew her before she was born and for the shortest time afterwards. Her loss was the first of every loss and the only loss. She is his rock: but not, he knows, his salvation. He was with her in the womb and soon, he knows, will be with her again, beneath the loam of that small sad shallow hill. And because of her: death held no dominion over him. Death, to Ahab, would be a return. A reunion.

Mr. Field droned on, an orator before a crowd of thousands hailing a triumph that he alone knew to be a defeat. His voice was at once amplified and made hollow by the outsized horn. He was speaking of the unity of Man. Ahab spat once more upon the muddy soil of Reservoir Square, threaded his way through the crowd toward Broadway, transparent illuminated Broadway, a rampage of song and dance and flame.

From the far end of Reservoir Square, a city block and some eight thousand densely packed humans away, a former policeman with a pistol in his trousers struggled to keep sight of him.

Fearnley was on the trace. Wherever there was dirt, or mud, or sod, the dot-dash footprints confirmed not only identity but direction. The signature stutter of his gait was heard even by those with no direct line of sight. And even along stretches where there were neither prints nor witnesses, Fearnley had discovered the trajectory. Ahab he was following Broadway, the river Broadway, coursing thick and diagonal across the island of Manhatto, until, round Ninth Street, it snaps to grid, heading down, always down, relentlessly down.

Revelry was everywhere, not just on the Squares (Longacre, Madison, Union) but between them, continuous. With each southward step the celebration mounted. If on Forty-Second Street they had sung the glories of the Transatlantic cable, by Twenty-Sixth they were raising thick-bottomed glasses to the World United, by Fourteenth, all pretext abandoned, each toast saluted nothing save the toast previous. Houston Street was a crosswise river of torches; Canal, barely navigable. Following the spoor of his large dark man who, perhaps only moments before, had strode, with trademark syncopation, toward the bottom of the island, where Manhatto widened out, the grid of the city giving way to the angled grid of the waterfront.

Below Canal now. Lispenard. Walker, White. Franklin, Leonard, Worth. But it was not until Thomas that Fearnley finally caught clear sight of what appeared to be his quarry: a large, dark man, three blocks ahead, almost at Chambers Street.

Fearnley quickened his pace, taking three steps for his man's every two. Soon he could see with clarity the man's broad wool-clad shoulders gliding steadily south, even as the legs beneath those shoulders slid and stuck, slid and stuck. There was no doubt in Fearnley's mind that he had found his bounty.

When he came within fifty yards Fearnley extracted, from his waistband, the percussion pistol. He rested his forefinger against the Lovell washer, pulled back the hammer with his other hand. The pistol's load was a dense .57 ball that at this range could smash through a man's gut, or depose a man's head from its spiny pedestal. All of which Fearnley contemplated even as he focused his eyes on the vertical seam that bisected Ahab's large dark coat.

Fearnley wished he'd had his revolver, an 1851 Colt with fine octagonal barrel. The Colt would afford a chance second, a chance third, etc., should the first shot fail to find its mark. But the revolver had been turned in—some might say confiscated—when he'd been decommissioned. If it weren't for the freelance employment offered by Mr. Field and others, he'd soon have to leave his rooming-house in Turtle Bay and find less costly accommodations. But, he thought: tonight, should I meet with success, there might even be an opportunity for employment permanent on the staff of one of the wealthiest men of Manhatto.

He was very far south. All was tohubohu now. Fearnley stared through that crowd at his backlit quarry twenty yards ahead. But now the man turned! Turned left! Leaving Broadway for the first time in more than fifty blocks, heading east. Fearnley shoved his weapon into his waistband once more, the barrel dug into his groin even as he ran, ran, ran, following his prey to the three-sided park that fronts City Hall.

But what a City Hall it was tonight! It was a City Hall as neither Fearnley nor anyone else on Manhatto had e'er seen it. Each aperture was illumined eerie and majestic from within. The effect was that of some enormous jack-o'-lantern with windows for eyes, and the large outsized portal its mouth. The windows were of differing hues depending on the light behind them: the blue flicker of the gas lamps, the redder flames of whale-oil candles— The warm yellow glow of wood and paper, heaped into galvanized cans and buckets, now set aflame.

More: the flames interior were but prelude to the fireworks above. The ringmaster of those fireworks, visible now in silhouette atop the Hall, brought torch to fuse. Even from down here you could see that his eyes had the gleam of the autodidact. Contracted neither by the city nor by anyone else, this low-rent Liliendahl lacked the cadence and subtlety of the master but sought to obscure that and any other deficit via quantity— And now, as the main fuse sputtered, transmitting spark to the secondaries, which then split, and split again, each line finer and more specific, this self-appointed pyrotechnician performed a small jig of triumph, of victory, of celebration, his steps as rapid, jittery, stuttering as the gunpowder sparks he'd just incited.

James Fearnley was a mean little man. And when he'd had a bit to drink, as in tonight, or was tired, as in tonight, why that meanness would come to the fore. He contemplated the labor involved in sidling up to his prey, surprising him, persuading him (with his .57 pistol), restraining him (with his pair of Tower Bottom-Key Handcuffs). Minding him the rest of the night, until an hour of morning decent enough to remand him to the custody of Mr. Field. Which now to Fearnley—in the full bloom of his smallness, his meanness—seemed a bridge too far.

In all his years with the Metropolitans, *bring him in* was but half a sentence, the other half of which: *alive if possible*. Inebriated, exhausted, Fearnley he was no longer interested in the possible. He was interested in a drink, and then home, or perhaps a stop or two before home, his celebrations fueled by the anticipation of the payday that would soon be his. A payday and then: a job, a proper job, a job in Gramercy Park. The waltz internal grew louder, drowning out now the cacophony of the park.

Avenging and bright fall the swift sword of Erin
On him who the brave sons of Usna betray'd!
For every fond eye he hath waken'd a tear in
A drop from his heart-wounds shall weep o'er her blade.

And so Fearnley he extended his right arm. Used his left to brace his right. Stared down his arm, along the barrel, continuing that line straight direct as if down a taut string, to the back of Ahab's large dark head. In an instant the large dark man would meet his maker and he, Fearnley, would be the hero of his own dreams. *Pull the trigger softly toward you*, his instructor had said, *as you would stroke a woman's neck.*

Atop City Hall the nameless pyrotechnician continued his victory jig as his fuse lines, consumed in spark, transmitted flame to destination. Then, in one struck and blinding instant—a moment too short for rational thought, but not, alas, too short for awful, gut-plummeting realization—the intent of the artist became terrifyingly apparent. This was not pyrotechnics as a time-based art but rather the all-in-one, the eggs-in-a-basket, the *tout mange*. It might, in some technical sense, still be called *son et lumière*, but the *son* was that of one large explosion, and the *lumière*, in the blink of an eye, that of City Hall entire convulsed in flames. Projectile flames, shooting out and down to the park below.

What happened next happened too quickly for Fearnley to comprehend. There was no sense of past or future, only a present, sliding slow and inexorable from now to now to now. He is taking aim. He is squeezing the trigger. He is thinking of the promotion that will be his, the hero's welcome. City Hall is exploding. A projectile is launched from its roof. The projectile is larger, sputtering flame and spark behind. The projectile is larger still, but in the same place in his field of vision. Now he can see it no longer. There is a pain in his chest and everywhere. Then there is blackness.

Twenty yards forward, the large dark man Ahab shields his eyes. He has just been in a race with Death and he has won, yet of this victory he is unaware. To Fearnley, everything has changed; to the man, nothing is different, save the awful cataclysm which, one minute previous, had been the administrative seat of the municipal government of the most wondrous and important city of the Republic. Of, many would hold, the world.

Ahab watched as up on the roof the man who had set those flames in motion, his name now lost to history, disappeared into his own fires, flickered, and was gone, as if he himself were the grand finale. Ahab listened as behind him one screamed, then several. He did not turn around but rather kept his gaze on the pyrotechnician, burning now like a night-marcher's torch, his bones the wood, his flesh the oil-soaked rags. Ahab owed the man the largest debt of gratitude. But it was a debt of which he would never become aware.

The revelers jammed up against each other as they made their exit from the park. Boisterous, sullen, mid-song and mid-silence. If it were possible Ahab he would dispatch them all: not in grand fury but with deliberation. He wanted the larger justice. In all rooms, streets, avenues, boulevards. On broad ways, in alleyways, in all the streets, large and small, of this city, of every city, and all who there inhabit. And all in the dark forest, too, and all in ships upon the black and roiling sea.

He stood in the triangular park, the one side snapped to the grid of the city, the other to the grid of the waterfront, the third a hypotenuse between them. He regarded the fleeing crowd. There were hundreds, perhaps more. There was among them no single soul whose life our Ahab would, at this moment, spare. They were, to him, automata, no more deserving of life than a stave of wood, a mass of forged iron, a sedimentary brick. Were they to trample each other into the drunken mud he would not mourn, eulogize, linger. Our Ahab stood fast as others fled. He was a tall dark stanchion in a dark roiled sea. It appeared that he was staring at the fire, and, later, when the fire department made its arrival, at the comic and frenzied activity of the pumpers. But he was gazing further, past City Hall, across the East River, up through the woods of New York and Connecticut, up to New England, to a certain hill marked with two adjacent stones.

Behind him, outside the range of his gaze, the former policeman Fearnley leaked blood and life into the muddy ground. The ebbing of consciousness went slow as the present shut down while older memories remained intact. Fearnley recalled the candles on his birthday cake when he was young, arrayed at the points of a star, he must have been five years old. He recalled Matilda, of the same age, but the other sex, who visited the outhouse and neglected to close the door. Had she done this in haste? With obliviousness? Did she know he was in the yard? When he could image no more he recalled his father, or the scent of his father, who applied each morning to his fresh-shaven face a homemade tincture, one part witch hazel, one part bay rum. The scent was old and comforting, far more than the high reek of gunpowder that had stung his nose and sinus, just moments before, when he had been alive. He floated out on that scent, on a river of bay rum, downstream, past unseen fronds of green and fragrant Hamamelis along the shore.

Fearnley went unnoticed, regarded, if at all, as one of a common many: that legion of revelers, still drunk with glee at the cable's completion, who'd ginned up beyond capacity and were now sleeping it off. It would not be until the dawn that anyone would see that he did not rouse.

Even as Fearnley he did bleed out our Ahab walked on. Further south, toward the lower tip of the island. The Customs House. The Battery. Breathing in the salted breeze that carried with it thin and compelling scent of the places he had been, the places he had never been, the places heard about in taverns, glimpsed on old charts, sung about in chanteys. It was time, he knew, for him to single his lines. He was not walking but pacing back and forth, as if Manhatto were the yard of his prison.

He could see, behind him now, the full flames of City Hall, lighting up the sky, dense clouds of black smoke against the black sky, clouds—bulging, orange, ominous—growing bigger each time he looked. Let the first to go form a pyre for those above. Let it grow higher, consuming the fire-men in the flames they sought to quench. Let it spread. Zipping uptown, along the diagonal of Broadway. With each step Ahab he saw the largest wave, coming in from the sea, engulfing the island entire, from the Battery upwards; and with each step Ahab he saw the firestorm, spreading outward from the park.

NINE

—————❦—————

ON A BRIGHT morning some months later Mr. Field was dictating
his morning correspondence. His amanuensis, Ulysses Taylor, was
able to keep pace even when Mr. Field spoke with great rapidity.
Mr. Field was seeking to donate some of the Andes paintings of Fred-
eric Church whose expedition he had financed. The paintings had
been commissioned to make the Andes seem beautiful and to encourage investors in one of Mr. Field's development schemes; and
now, having served that purpose admirably, Mr. Field wanted them
properly recognized as art.

After lunch at his club a few doors down Mr. Field walked to the
offices of the American Telegraph Company, which he had founded,
and which, at the moment, was perhaps the nation's premiere corporation for telegraphy (though the Western Union would likely de-
mur). Field made enquiries as to the volume of telegraphic traffic,
and listened to a proposal for additional western trunk lines, perused
diagrams for a revised, and improved, relay—a Barclay Box rather
than the more standard Morse. But the cost of replacing the extant
relays across the system was not negligible, and he was not certain
that the improvement would generate improved revenues or lower
the expense of operation.

He also requested, as if in afterthought, an update on the price
of his company's shares on the London market: truth be told no
afterthought but rather the *punctum* of the day. The Company's
shares were originally offered at £340, but upon the news in August
that the cable was complete and had carried a message, the shares
had shot up to £600, then £800, then on to comfortably inhabit a
range between £880 and £920. In late August, though, word had

somehow gotten round that the signal had deteriorated since the initial triumphant exchange between President and Queen, and the shares plummeted to £350. The position of the Company was dependent, far more precariously than Field would wish, upon the valuation of the London shares, and if they slipped below £300, the Company would sunder. And as the cable was no longer carrying words from London, there was no way to get news of the consequences of its own failure. Word of the shares' price could travel no faster than a ship could carry it. Field might be boom, he might be bust but he would not know until many days from now whether he were dead today.

Field left his office, repaired once more to his club, ate supper, enjoyed a seated cigar, then lit a walking cigar and went home. The air was damp, the fragrance pleasing to the nose. The sun was setting. Had it been blotted out from the sky this very moment Field and all else in Gramercy Park would still bask in its warm and slanting rays for another eight minutes.

He dressed for bed and joined his wife Mary, already there installed. They had been married since he was twenty and she had borne him seven children. They were still amorous. They were, in fact, in matrimonial conversation when Mr. Field heard a syncopated noise, *th-TUMP, th-TUMP*, that increased in volume—as if something were approaching. It seemed, at first, to originate in the children's wing, but now, *th-TUMP, th-TUMP*, it was clearly coming from downstairs. And heading his way.

Mr. Field pushed his wife under the bedsheets, grabbed the curtain rod, shook off the curtains. He took the rod in both hands. He was standing there, naked, thick brass rod held crosswise, when the door to his bedroom was flung open. Silhouetted in the doorframe was a tall man in black. One of his legs was not a leg. He did not brandish a gun or seem armed in any way. And he did not speak.

"I have in my hands an instrument capable of bashing in your skull. You will lie face down on the carpet while I summon the police."

The man just waited.

Mr. Field took a step forward. "I meant what I said."

"Had thou meant what thou sayest, thou would by now have

done that thing." The man's voice was low, calm, as if he were in the middle of a conversation, not the beginning of one. As if he hadn't just broken into the house of the man to whom he was speaking.

"One hath heard, on highways and in low places, that thou didst send yer man to summon me." And when Mr. Field made no reply: "Thou hast a task. Nautical. Murderous. Elsewise thou wouldst look for someone else. But thou seekest me."

Extending his hand:

"John Ahab."

Mr. Field said nothing. Then took the extended hand.

A brief silence, now broken by the visitor: "Pays well I'll take it. I'll go downstairs. You think. Not too long. Thou cometh down, we shall set a price. Thou stayest up, then I am gone. And know thee well: that after Ahab's departure thou shalt have need of a glazier. Ha. Locksmith too."

With that he turned, out of the bedroom and down the stairs, *th-TUMP, th-TUMP*. Mr. Field surveyed the room: the damask curtains pooled on the floor, the covers still pulled over his wife's head and body.

"Everything will be all right," he said to her. It was the work of a few moments to rethread the rod through the curtains and hoist them back into place. Then he stroked the shrouded head of his wife. At length she peeled back some of the sheet, allowing her eyes to look out.

"He's gone," said Mr. Field.

"He's still here," said Mrs. Field.

"Never you worry. He's safely downstairs."

"He broke into our house," said Mrs. Field.

"That he did," said Mr. Field. "But you are safe now, and you were never in true harm's way, and the children slumber on, peacefully, as they should."

"Are you leaving me?" asked Mrs. Field.

"Only to go downstairs for a conversation," said Mr. Field. "I shall be back." In the children's floor of Mr. Field's townhouse, there were four boys, three girls. One of them—one of the boys—heard, faintly, the crash of glass, the opening of the door, the bedroom conversation, the stark *th-TUMP, th-TUMP*— And in his dream, the syncopated tattoo was the wheel of a railway carriage carrying him away from home, farther than he'd ever been, and with no way back.

"SOME THINGS ARE best experienced freshly, in the going-forward, without preconception," Mr. Field said, "but in this matter past is prologue." They were seated in the parlor, two chairs flanking the unlit fireplace. "What I want to talk about is the laying of the cable. Are you familiar—"

Ahab cut him off: "Some."

"Do you know the ships then?"

"*Agamemnon*. And the other."

"The *Agamemnon* and the *Niagara* then. Yes. Meeting in the middle. Paying out cable. The *Agamemnon* heading to Valentia, the *Niagara* to make port on this side. And as you may have heard the weather was not of the best, and the enterprise was in many ways problematical. But it was not just the weather. The cable snapped or, and listen to me carefully—" Here Mr. Field took a long pull on his cigar. "—was severed."

When his visitor said nothing he continued. "The core consists of four copper wires of Number 16 Birmingham Wire Gauge, each individually coated with two layers of gutta-percha to two-gauge, then twisted together and the spaces between packed with tarred hemp, the whole being covered in another layer of gutta-percha, wrapped in tarred hemp followed by twelve nine-gauge armoring wires. This is not a fragile reed.

"The *Agamemnon* put out from Valentia on 5th August of last year and the first break occurred not three days later. It was said to be due to a fault in the descent limiter but I do not think this to be the case. Three hundred eighty miles out the cable failed, spooled to the ocean floor. We had to return to port. Had to make an additional 700 miles of cable. At no small additional cost, including of time."

"Expense," said Ahab.

"Of course. Which is why our next foray was not until the subsequent June. And with new method—rather than meet in the middle we would start there, then pay out the cable in both directions simultaneous. We stocked with 3,000 nautical miles of cable. On 10th

June the ships set out to rendezvous mid-ocean at latitude 53°17′; longitude 33°18′. On the day they left Plymouth the sea was calm, as it was the day following. On 12th June the wind started to pick up and on board *Agamemnon* the screws were lifted out of the water and the fires raked out; she continued under royals and studding sails. The weather got worse and by the 20th a full storm was blowing. The *Niagara* began to give us a very wide berth, and, as darkness increased, it was a case of each ship for herself. The *Agamemnon*, rolling many degrees, looked to be breaking up. The next day the barometric glass was lower, the wind and sea were even higher than the day before.

"What was told to the press was that due to the storm, the cable broke on board the *Niagara*, overriding and departing the pulley that led onto the machine. What I shall tell you now: the cause was not mechanical. There was something beneath."

At length Ahab said, "Beast."

"So you know," said Mr. Field.

"Yes," said Ahab.

"Again the ships met, and again we made a splice, putting a silver shilling into the splice for good luck. This time they managed nearly forty miles before it broke. Again, the break was from below. Marking the fourth time we'd been severed."

"Ah," said Ahab.

"We do not undertake tasks of this magnitude without knowing that it is more likely than not that we should fail. You of all men will know the truth of what I speak. We were beating against the wind and then: another break. The fifth.

"I took my electricians from the *Niagara* and came on board the *Agamemnon*. A comparison of logs showed the painful and mysterious fact that each vessel's line sustained a complete fracture, at the very bottom of the ocean, and within fifteen minutes of each other! Though human skill and science can lay the wire down, there may be obstacles—"

"Ye did then summon Ahab."

"Yes," Mr. Field continued. "It is possible that there are, after all, sharp-pointed rocks lying on the plateau of Maury, Berryman, and Dayman. But there is another possibility."

"Tell," said Ahab.

"You know that we re-spliced, continued, and even though our supply of cable ran perilously low, were able to make it to our respective shores. You know of the messages sent in August, and you know of the celebration."

"Ahab was there."

"But what you do not know is this: that within a day—"

Ahab interrupted: "Line went dead." He went on. "Leviathan. I do knoweth him. Knoweth him head to head. Thou might say soul to soul. He's smart. Has power." Ahab's pegged leg tapped against the floor. "Of all men: yer Ahab he knoweth this."

Mr. Field offered him a cheroot, which he waved away.

At length, Mr. Field began once more to speak. "If Louis the Great boasted that, owing to his statesmanship, the Pyrenees existed no longer, we can truly say that there is no longer an Atlantic. More wars are occasioned by blundering or designing ambassadors than by real grievances, and in this light the cable may be the Great Peacemaker between the two chief nations on the globe. And so as a charitable gesture, in the interests of peace in the midst of a bellicose century, I am mounting—"

"Dung," said Ahab. "Thy shares ain't worth shit now. Thou art in ruin. How doth Ahab know this? William of Ockham. *Lex parsimoniae.* To wit: no one looks for Ahab. No one save the law. Not ever. 'Cept: when all's gone down the hole. Then do they come a'calling." He tapped the leg that was not one. "Then and only then."

Mr. Field said nothing.

"Thou'rt facing a monster, Mr. Field. Canst he be slain? Ahab will not promise. But no man be more capable of it. Or who more—" And here he again tapped his ivory leg. "—wants more to see him dead."

"Yes," said Mr. Field.

"One thousand dollars. In coin. Tomorrow. Fifty bucks a day. Additional. Set of Maury's hydrographic charts. Hark ye: Ahab does not suffer fools. The man Whiteman whom ye hired—"

"Dr. Whitehouse."

"A dolt. Ahab will not serve under or with him. Nor with the turd Everett. There is one God that is Lord o'er the earth, and one Captain that is lord o'er the ship. Not beholden to other men. Not beholden to thee. Care not for thy profits. Care not for thy peace of mind. Care for one thing. And ye know what that be." Then: "And what boat do ye propose yer Ahab to guide?"

Here, Mr. Field allowed himself to smile. He exhaled, a small cloud of cigar smoke meant to be illustrative of his thoughts. Then said, "I think, sir, that you will be pleased beyond imagining by the boat I have for this venture procured. It is the noblest craft by far that you, nay, anyone has captained. She carried passengers white-gloved and noble she did. Then freight, of which she was the best and most capacious. And now—'tis a near-miracle, Mr. Ahab—I have managed to obtain her services for this historic task. I refer, of course, to the last and best masterpiece of Mr. Brunel, the *Great Eastern*."

But if Mr. Field thought his guest might display joy, pride, anticipation, he quickly came to understand elsewise. Ahab's face, no masque of delight in the best of hours, became more graven, more somber still, if such a thing be possible.

"'Tis not a ship," said Ahab.

"I do not understand."

"Ship's a thing of wood. Thy *Great Eastern*'s a thing of iron. Thou hast seen trees float downstream: thou hast not seen, nor e'er will, yer iron drift downstream. Ship's a thing with sails. Thy *Great Eastern*, her sails be like unto parlor curtains: pleasing to the ladies, but of no utility beyond the decorative. Thy *Great Eastern* she runs by steam, which is an abomination 'gainst the gods, and an albatross round the neck of each and every good sailor who must stoke her. No. Thy Ahab will not ride such a beast. Let yer *Great Eastern* pay out the cable. Yer Ahab will captain his own.

"No cable-payers on Ahab's boat. No electricians. A first-shelf crew devoid of simpletons. North Atlantic. Storms out of nowhere. Then gone. Leave you wrecked, wracked, drowned. So. Give thy captain what thy captain needs."

Mr. Field said nothing. Considered what had been proposed to him. Was calculating the expense of boat, of crew, the rest of Ahab's requisites. It would be costly, and though the cost would ultimately be borne by the shareholders the cash would have to come out of pocket. Those pockets were not as deep as once they were. Nor: as full.

"One last. A lawman 'cross the Hudson wants to jail Ahab. Charge him. Try him. Never mind why. Simple. Ahab in jail is Ahab not on the seas. Ye of all knowest the order of things. The lower pay heed to the higher. A word from thee will do it. Ahab needs to walk. Eyes ahead. Not o'er his shoulder. 'Til we put out to sea."

Mr. Field considered the glowing stub-end of his cheroot. Then said, huskily, "I will do what I can."

Ahab stood, turned his head toward the entry hall as if he were about to depart. And then, as afterthought: "Log show yer last wire got cut two places, separate by ten miles, within the quarter hour. So thy logs be shit. Or Leviathan has a friend. A brother.

"'Gainst one Leviathan, the war's more hard than any on land or sea. But. If there be two?

"Then heaven help thy cable, 'twill always be cut. Heaven help thy Company, 'twill go bust three times for every time revived. And heaven help this poor soul, for yer Ahab he shall be slain in the pursuit."

With that Ahab turned, nodded, walked toward the inner door, whose lock he had picked; through it and toward the outer door, whose glass he had shattered. And without further word he went out into the night of Gramercy Park, his syncopated footsteps echoing loudly, then faintly, then not at all.

In the eye of his mind he witnessed once more the grand conflagration, the inferno that spreads without cease and consumes the island entire. He saw, as well, the grand flood, as high and massive waves top the Battery, washing all away, until the East River and the Hudson were one. This was no place for a man to stand. He was glad, and heartened, and spirited, and relieved, to know in his soles and gut and mind and heart that he'd soon be shipping out.

Did Mr. Field know the nature of the nemesis? The answer, to near-certainty, was no. Did Ahab know? Ahab he had both experience and certain kinds of *connaissance*. But you who read these words, knowing what you do of the dream of Gwalior, and of the way that dream did possess an Indian prince; knowing what you know of said prince's enmity toward the civilized world, its intentions and activities—

Then you have intimation— More than your cable magnate, more than his nocturnal visitor— Of what might ensue.

Let us move then from land to sea, from the company of John Ahab to the sub-marine vessel commanded by our Captain Nemo. Conveying within its pressurized hull a certain British civil engineer whom you have previously met, and whose sad and glorious tale will now recommence.

TEN

THE CABIN IN which I am imprisoned is such that with extended arms I can touch both walls simultaneous. But it is larger than the cell of my body, in which I had been imprisoned by the administration of what fiendish paralytic, then made to watch the launch of my ship. A day that I had for years awaited, but could in no ways celebrate. Nor even fashion a smile.

There is within these confines a lamp, which glows by electricity, a bunk, a chair, an outjutting that may serve as a desk, albeit one without appointments. The throb of engines and the reverberant clang of work elsewhere makes dedicated concentration difficult, when it does not make it impossible. The air is foetid. I have not taken a full breath since inhabiting these foul apartments.

The captain today provided me with a Hawkins journal, and ink derived from squid, and a pen with which to write: the scrimshaw'd bone of some marine mammal. His expressed wish was that I should use this journal to capture, before they evanesce, those Inspirations and practical insights that will visit the waking (or, indeed, sleeping) engineer. But I will here use them to another purpose: to express the thoughts uppermost in my mind. I will try not to succumb to melancholy, nor to dwell unduly upon the continuing conditions of my captivity in a sub-marine vessel whose pilot and crew are members of a dusky race, and whose language, habits, and e'en motives at each and every moment elude the comprehension of this Englishman.

We have left London en route to one of Cook's islands, where the captain he has a harbor nigh unto himself, unknown to the seafaring charts of civilized nations. I suspect we shall follow the clipper route round the Cape of Good Hope. Were we motivated by sail we could run the easting down, aided by those zephyrs that men of the sea call the Roaring Forties. I doubt that our craft, sans sails, will benefit from those beneficent westerlies.

I wish to present myself as I am, that you who fashion history may judge me with more accuracy than you otherwise might. I am not pleading my case before the large bar. Still I would want to bring the facts to light, so that you will see the man who wrote these words neither grander than he was nor more diminished. You will notice that I use the past tense. I cannot conceive of a circumstance in which these words be read yet I am still alive.

What I wish to here set down is a brief account of my days and nights aboard this accursèd craft: all that has transpired following my "death" in London, and how I have comported myself in this, my unwilled afterlife.

I THINK IT fitting to commence with my first morning below, and a greeting from the man who had been on land my savage captor— and was still that, to be sure!—but now was also my captain.

"Welcome to the *Neptune*," he said. "I hope the accommodations are congenial. And of course if there is anything that would make you more comfortable, within the limitations of what might be available on a craft this small, you must let me know." He was a brown subcontinental, yet his elocution was that of an Oxonian or, perhaps, a Cantabrigian.

"I thank you for the water, for the food," I said. "But what I want is neither drink nor sustenance but swift return to London. To my work. And to my life. I have, as you know, a wife, and children, and—"

"They have already mourned," he said. And then: "I know that this to you must seem criminal. But I assure you it was of the essence. And that were there any other way of accomplishing goals of necessity I'd not have put you, or your loved ones, through any of this."

There was a dire lack of connection between the elegance of his diction, the courtesy of his address, and the impossibility of the situation at hand: I had been wrenched from my life and was now forbidden to rejoin it. You will understand if I withheld gratitude.

"Let us begin anew," he said, "as if we were just now encountering each other. I am Captain Nemo and this is my craft. The *Neptune* is iron hulled, a mode of construction whose virtues you yourself have so ably championed. There are details of its build that would be of interest to you and I shall share them with you at a later time.

"The *Neptune* travels on the water and beneath it. It is unlike any other ship built or imagined. You, M. Brunel, are the brightest and most practical man in Great Britain. I have studied your work and found much inspiration in it. The visionary leap of the atmospheric railway, the first of your feats to come to my attention. The wisdom of the shield for tunneling beneath a river, a feat never before tried, yet alone accomplished—and the fortitude with which that tunneling was carried out. The careful laying out of the route of the Great Western Railway, and then the bridges and tunnels, sturdy and of surpassing elegance, which that route necessitated. The *Great Western*, whose design inspired that of the craft that now bears us both. And of course the *Great Eastern*, whose destruction I attempted, and whose ability to sail unaided back to port is a tribute only to the strength and wisdom of your design."

I had for more than a week been reeling due to the course of events, but now my head spun even more. This man, this captain, was reminding me once more—perhaps less reminding than boasting—that he had attempted to destroy my ship! And in the process had killed several good and innocent men. Nor was this a confession extracted under duress: this was a voluntary dissemination, retailed in a tone matter-of-fact as if he were letting me know that my shirts had been freshly laundered.

"You will go to hell, Captain," I said when at length I had regained my voice. "You have murdered those fire-men whose only crime was hard and thankless work."

"Yes," he said, "there were eight dead. No more than the number of dead in your Rotherhithe Tunnel when it suffered a breach. The digging, the stoking, these are not easy jobs, and they are not purveyed as safe. Those who take them up are decently rewarded, and part of that reward is compensation for the knowledge, freely dispensed, that at any instant the tunnel might cave, the furnace blow."

"You cannot make the comparison between the two," I said. "The one was an accident. The other? A planned and deliberate act of war."

"It was not a war I myself declared," said the captain. "Rather one waged upon me, and my family, and my city. A war in which I sustained the most grievous of losses: the lives of those who mattered to me more than all else. But that is prologue, and I wish to speak of the future.

"M. Brunel. You have wisdom and knowledge unparalleled, and in so many realms." (I here made note of the fact that he used the French "monsieur," a nod to my heritage and schooling, but in defiance of my nationality.) "You are now a passenger aboard an example of engineering as advanced as you will find anywhere on the globe. It was built by the late H. Lal of Bombay and by me. Yet even our *Neptune* has limitations, ones which if truth be told are significant. The system for scrubbing the air is haphazard and precludes the longer stays beneath the seas. The auxiliaries are powered by batteries designed and built by these hands, but the span of their utility is short. And the main motive power is steam, a mechanism not ideally suited for the underwater purpose. The hull is well-wrought but for it to withstand the pressures of the depths to which I would like to take this craft it needs to be sturdier still—without added weight I might add. The propellers, following your designs, have real strengths. But I believe in my heart that there are far more efficient means of undersea propulsion. Which will be to the screw propeller as that propeller was to the wooden oar.

"So you see, M. Brunel: these are problems which are sufficiently knotty to engage a mind the calibre of your own. And should we find solutions—practical and elegant, as has been the Brunel hallmark—why then together we shall make history."

Again it took a while to regain speech, due not to paralytic drug this time but rather to astonishment. "Our work together"? I would sooner open my wrists and let the blood flow out than assist this murderer, these blasphemous ambitions. And on top of it all, something worse: the presumption that "we" had something in common other than the rope of hatred that together binds captor and captive. My reply, therefore, was short, and meant to cease conversation rather than encourage it.

"No."

He went on as if I'd said nothing at all: "It is only natural that you should feel the way you do now. I would have no respect for a man whose inner fibers were so limp that he bent this-way, that-way, acceding to each and every argument. But in the course of time, when you have taken pause to consider the situation, and to consider the contribution you might make to enterprise and human progress, I have hope, indeed, I have every faith, that you will reconsider.

"In the meanwhile know that from this minute forth you have the run of the ship. You are my guest here. And there are discoveries that I have made, mighty ones, I wish to share with you. I see the protest in your eyes and the sadness as well. Believe with all your heart, that if there had been an alternative way of securing your collaboration, I would have availed myself of it. As it is—"

"And this vessel which you have commissioned. In which I am entombed," I interrupted. "Why was it built? And to what foul end do you traverse the seas?"

"Toward the realization of human freedom."

"Even as you keep me enslaved."

The captain made no response. It became clear, via his silence, that the contradiction weighed more heavily upon me than upon him.

"Where are we?" I then asked.

"We are beneath the Thames. Within our limitations—and those limitations are severe, or we'd not have summoned you—we are seaworthy. Though most of the journey will be made upon the surface rather than below it we have the ability to get from here to there. Now I must go and attend to other matters. In the interim please make your needs known. I shall close the door for your own privacy. But I shall not lock it." Then: "In some fifteen minutes there is something I would like to show you, and unless I am quite mistaken, it is something you, M. Brunel, would be uniquely interested to see." And with that he was gone.

I heard his departing footsteps, boots echoing against the metal gangway then growing more faint, 'til all I could hear were the sounds of the ship. The thrum and clang of the engine, the susurration of steam through pipe, the movings about of the crew. Then I heard, echoing down the metal corridors, an organ, a pipe organ!

The opening phrase of a toccata by Bach! Tentative steps, octave-doubled, descending. A low note established, built upon. Resolving into D-minor chord. Then up and down in a trail of sixteenth-notes, as if illustrating the ascent and descent of a sub-marine craft.

And as the music unfolded—up and down, single notes and clusters, flurries and sostenutos, discords and resolutions—my thoughts once again focused on the extraordinary concatenation of circumstances that had become my life.

I spent a quarter of an hour alone with my thoughts while the organ played on—who but a madman, working within the drastically confined spaces of a sub-marine vessel, situates at its center a pipe organ? And enveloped in that music I allowed myself to shed tears, at first slowly, then in a great onrush. I felt ashamed and undignified, relieved only that my unmanliness could not here been seen or made note of. By the time the captain knocked on my door my eyes were dry and my cheeks free of trace. "You will accompany me," he said. It was almost—not quite—an invitation. My thoughts turned from the contemplation of my own mortality to a kind of curiosity about the thing, person, or event the captain wished me to see.

We turned right, walked down the narrow gangway which debouched onto a suite of rooms. The salon was filled with roll'd-up charts, a variety of sextants, an astrolabe. Lined up across the shelves all manner of tomes on oceana, ichthyology, atmospheric studies could be seen, as well as works of philosophy and classic literature. They seemed to be alphabetized by author without respect to language which led me to believe that our captain was polyglot, conversant not only in English, but also French, Greek, and Latin, and perhaps even Arabic. There were a surpassing number of books in Hindi, reinforcing my sense of the subcontinental origins of the captain and those who followed his directives. I was not surprised to see the complete works of Arago, but there was also much from the experimentalist Faraday, and from Léon Foucault, whose work on the rotation of the earth, and with the gyroscope, would of course be of interest here. I was vaguely surprised and to a small degree disturbed to find so many books (down here) that were identical to those I kept in my own library (up there).

The adjacent chamber contained the pipe organ, surprisingly

large in size. "Do you see those pipes?" said the captain. "They were wrought in collaboration with the extraordinary Aristide Cavaillé-Coll, whose habitual impecuniosity rendered him susceptible to my patronage. They are crafted not from any of the traditional materials but rather from the horns of sea mammals. Cavaillé-Coll and I have constructed those manuals I most treasure: the Aeoline, the Lieblichgedeckt, the Chalumeau, the Bearded Gamba. The Vox Humana. And, of course: the Clarín de Mar.

"I aim to want nothing that the sea fails to provide. The surface of the globe is far more of water than of land, as you know, by a proportion of some three to one. Yet as a resource the seas are monstrously untapped. The keys of my little device are of sea-ivory and they are as felicitous to the touch as anything made from the tusks of elephants."

Particularly in a sub-marine craft, where each cubic foot of mass displaces similar quantity of air, it is strange to find that which is not strictly necessary. I could only assume that he was sustained by these objects in ways that overruled the intellect.

On the wall opposite hung several paintings, the only one of which I recognized was a portrait of the writer Baudelaire, done by Gustave Courbet. In full confession I know this only because I saw that very portrait in a salon in Paris to which I was taken by Mary Elizabeth on holiday when she wanted to make some visitings on the Continent. I endeavored to slip away because I wanted to be alone with my own thoughts and in particular to revisit by foot and in no one's company the streets of l'île du Palais and other loci connected in my mind to great sentiment. But the schedule that Mary Elizabeth fashioned for us did not admit of this possibility. My mind was elsewhere when I toured with her yet still I believe that the portrait that I saw on the captain's wall was either the same painting—or perhaps one much like it with the same subject and by the same hand.

Also in the salon was a chess table and cabinet, the pieces arrayed mid-game, with a ceramic figure whose arm, slid along by pantograph, seemed poised to make the next move. I had read of this—the "Mechanical Turk"—yet had never seen, let alone this closely, such a fine clockwork automaton.

Perhaps even more extraordinary was a clock—large, freestanding, ornate—what is called in horological circles a bracket clock, four-sided with feet at the bottom: solid brass cubes topped with wood topped with a dark marbled rock as if it were less a timepiece than a palace. Set into the side walls of this chrono-palace were two additional timepieces, one lunar, one sidereal. And atop all of them was Earth, the planet Earth, seemingly afloat without support within brass circles horizontal and vertical, in the manner of an orrery.

I stared at it for the longest time (enough to register the movement of the hands). Here was the planet Earth, its continents of gold, its seas and oceans of blue stone. And on the outer ring of this orrery: a tiny ivory ball, representing the Moon. I found myself increasingly entranced, 'til I could scarce look away, at that moon, that tiny ivory ball. It had a whited translucence which I have in no other context seen, as if one were looking *through* as much as *at*. It was etched in finest filigree, a scrimshaw allowing glimpse of the still-smaller sphere within—and, perhaps, the smaller-still within the sphere within. The pull of that Moon on my inner tides was substantial—if uninterrupted I might have stared upon that Moon for a full lunar month as it circumnavigated its beautifully wrought Earth.

"You're wanting to know something of the clock's origins, and of how it came to rest within the *Neptune*." It was not, as he phrased it, a question.

"I am an engineer and as such never incurious," I replied.

"It was a gift," he said, "from the nation of France to the Ottoman Empire, a thank-you for the Ottoman troops seconded to the French during the Crimean War. And so it was borne by carriage from Paris to Kostantiniyye where it was received by the Ottoman Sultan Abdülmecid. As you know, I do not believe in the artificial demarcation of nation-states and so the gift from one 'state' to another was not by me recognized. By means of a substitution there is a now a replica in residence at Topkapi, and the real one before us now."

He gestured to the clock, said "it is time," then gestured away from it toward a circular concavity set into the wall. It was covered with thin, overlapping metal blades. The captain pushed a button inlaid into the wall carving and at once there was a mechanical *whirr*—electrical motors?—and the curved thin blades slid as if anchored at individual pivots yet ganged so as to move in concord. The effect was that of an opening up, as the iris of the human eye when finding itself in conditions of darkness expands to admit more light: an outspreading circle of vision, from a pinpoint in the center to a circular window perhaps five feet in diameter. On the other side of the aperture was a convex window of glass with brass mullions. And beyond the glass: the inky-black water of the river beneath whose surface we at the moment were gliding.

"You have been in a diving bell, am I not right, M. Brunel?"

"I have."

"And when you were in that bell, what were you able to see of the sub-marine world outside?"

I thought, and decided it best to give the answer straightforward. "Little, or nothing."

The captain seemed almost to smile. "That is only natural. The diving bell was designed for its specific purpose, which was to maintain air pressure within a vessel so that humans could be lowered beneath the surface of a river or sea. The *Neptune* is designed for a purpose different: that of exploration. How do we obtain knowledge? By the five senses, the most useful of which for these purposes is sight. So let me say to you, fiat lux." And with that he pressed a second button held in the indented position by latch. Immediately there was the snap and sputter of a carbon arc—and the sea outside the viewing glass was illuminated, as bright as the day! Though the murk of the water was substantial, and undissolved solids swarmed about in the swath of light occluding long-range sight, there was the ability to see *into* the depths as hypnotic as it was to me unprecedented. Looking downward I saw the murky bottom of the river, and then a hump, a rise, near-circular in its shape, as if we were gazing at some fantastic immobile eel. As we drew closer I could make out regular patterns upon its back—scales?—and irregularly placed lumps along its spine. I did not know whether to gaze upon it in awe or with real fright.

The dilemma was resolved as I drew closer and saw that what I'd imaged as scales were really bricks; what I'd seen as spiny lumps were sandbags; and that what I looked upon was no monstrous sleeping eel, nay, but rather the tunnel of my own crafting! It was the Rotherhithe-Wapping tunnel, as seen from the outside!

"I had thought," said the captain, "that you would want to see this." And despite my despair—and the abject nature of my circumstance—and criminal nature of my confinement—and the large distress that I can only imagine my burial had created in the hearts of my family—I was, in the moment, content. To be at that specific vantage, viewing what I'd heretofore only imagined.

I gazed for a small eternity, examining the way the bricks of the tunnel were laid into the river-bottom silt. The curvature which the Shield system of construction allowed. The fortuity of the location of the sandbags, having landed more-or-less where we—placing them blindly and without visual confirmation—had intended. And then, around the tunnel, the varieties of flora that had already attached themselves to the tunnel wall in a manner that would create, in time, a seal tighter than any we could by hand of man have constructed. All enveloped by the thick and impenetrable Thames, conduit for all manner of human jetsam, the detritus of a large and swarming city, of its motley inhabitants, its mills and manufactories, the discards, castoffs, and wastes shat out once the beast that is London has been fed. You cannot comprehend—'less you have seen it—that slow balletic dance: the beauty, unearthly and sublime, that lives above the bed of our river, and below its surface smooth.

After the longest while I became aware of the captain's hand on my shoulder. "You have had, M. Brunel, a day longer than the hours it contains, and experiences deeper than one can fathom. There is so much more that I would wish to show you—the mechanisms of the *Neptune*, its tanks and its ballasts, its propulsive systems in need of re-imagining. But these are better left for the morn." He pressed a button and the arc was extinguished.

"I beg you as you rest to consider your situation with a level head as to the alternatives. Know that I will not return you to your former life—that life has ceased to exist; and even as we speak, your family has begun to reconcile itself to your absence from it.

"No, M. Brunel: you can be my honored guest as I travel the world in pursuit of my goals. But as honored as you would be, you would be chained to my itinerary. My hazards would become yours—for if the English, in pursuit of me, should bring me down, and the *Neptune* with it, you would not be spared. You will eat as we eat, venture as we venture— But you would be, if sans shackles, a prisoner.

"Yet there is another way, M. Brunel, have you the courage to see it. You can be my partner in imagination, in invention. The good merchants of Bristol, flush with money from the sale of human chattel, were happy to have you connect them to market; and the good burghers of London were happy that you created for them a less costly way of exporting their goods and of importing what they required from distant ports. All of what you have done, however well-wrought, was but labor for a set of masters: in this case, the wealthy merchant class of the United Kingdom. You know the disdain of the upper classes for those who work for them yet were not to their manner born. They appreciate nothing save the profit that your work will allow them to accrue.

"What I treasure is the work itself. The elegance of it, the science, at times, the violence—all these are characteristics treasured for themselves. And what I offer you is work in service not of commerce, or of empire, but in service of human possibility. I will even say it: human freedom. Right now the British Empire is clinging with its fingernails to its far-flung holdings. I saw with my own eyes the sepoy rebellion and I know both the savagery of empire and its fragility. I know that history is not on the side of that empire. It is with the larger march of time, and toward the fragility of empire, that I aim my craft.

"Unless I miss my mark, your eye can see the difference between works for hire and what the soul, freed of constraint, can accomplish.

"The perfection of a sub-marine vessel, to be sure, would be the first of our tasks. But it would be only the first. From there we are limited only by the reach and power of your dreams. Know that we will have the world as our canvas, and the loyalty of an army of craftsmen as good as any you would find in London.

"So in briefest form, these are your choices: to go mute and idle while we combat a savage empire, or to join with us. Your work has already made swifter, more rational, grander, and more efficient, the way that world performs its tasks. But the world has stayed the same. Now is your chance to change it."

Another button and the ganged metal blades of the iris began to push in, narrowing the field of view until it was but a pinhole, then gone. Without my being aware of signal of summons, and without approaching sound, the second mate Feringheea now appeared.

"You will take Huzoor to his cabin," said the captain. And with that the captain without so much as a fare-thee-well he walked off prow-ward while I was led aft. To my confines.

My sleep that night was anything but pacific. It was not so much the bedding, which was of a utilitarian quality—I have in my life slept in rougher surrounds, and am in general inclined to agree with Aristotle, that to conflate *the good* with *pleasure* is to prefer a life suitable for beasts. No, 'twas the far more troubling sense that the track of my life had forked, had doubled. On the one track was the life known to the world: Isambard Kingdom Brunel suffered a stroke at age fifty-three and—died shortly thereafter due to the sequelae of that stroke. Was mourned by family friends and the larger community then laid to rest in Kensal Green, side-by side with his late father. On the other, the one onto which I was so abruptly and unreasonably diverted: Isambard Kingdom Brunel was imprisoned in a sub-marine vessel, subject to the whim and command of its captain, a murderous if well-educated *julab-sahib* whose diction and manners did not conceal the fact that he would stop at nothing to attain his goals. 'Twas as if he had pitched himself against all notions of human progress save his own.

In my mind thoughts spun and churned 'til all I could think upon was the moment when someone had pulled the switch lever—taking me off the one rail and shunting me onto the other.

And as I roiled I realized that there was yet a track the third! One in which I was neither buried on land nor incarcerated sub-sea— but one in which I lived on, worked on, for the rest of the century and even, with some fine luck, beyond. One in which I was there to see the transatlantic voyage of the *Great Eastern*; and there to see the construction of the Clifton Bridge; and there to see my children grow into adulthood. At once I was seized by the most violent and abstract feeling! That this life, the one in which I found myself, *was the dream*—and the one to which I had no access *was the reality*. A vertiginous spin, a topsy-turvy, a mal de mer of the soul.

How could I waken from this dream, from this nightmarish world, into my real life? Into the serenity of sun slanting through my own window—Duke Street, off Manchester Square, in my very own West London?

I have noticed, of late, that there is, in the realm of my dreams, another figure who looms. He was not in my dreams for the longest time, yet he is onstage here near-nightly. And that is my Father. How odd that he should choose to visit me now.

When I was in the flush of life, having rounded thirty but not yet reached forty, I did experience a moment, one of those life's moments that occurs in an instant and then is never gone. I had been performing a magical feat for the amusement of my children involving a half-sovereign coin, which was meant to disappear from my closed fist, then re-appear behind their ears, or perhaps, even more remarkably, in their pockets. I will not here record the mechanism of this sleight. Let it suffice to say that in the course of this performance I found myself inhaling one of the half-sovereigns which immediately lodged itself in my windpipe. My cries for help were hoarse, inarticulate, desperate. I feared for my life, feared even more that I would expire in front of my family! And all for legerdemain!!!

Professional help was summoned and our rancid local physician slid a pair of narrow forceps down my trachea. Needless to say the discomfort provoked by the coin was only amplified by the attempt to dislodge it. I could breathe but only with wild effort, and the awful wheeze of air circulating round the coin quickly scared my children back to their chambers, whence they peeked through the curtains down at the awful events unfolding on the garden.

My father then came round and suggested that I be turned upside down. To this end he—and his neighbors, who now were gathered round him—affixed me with coarse sisal rope to a wooden upright. So: up-right was soon up-wronged with my boots in the air, toes pointed to the heavens, head depending low to the ground. I coughed sans cesse for long minutes and then, even as the pain, the lack of oxygen, the vertiginous rush of blood to the inverted head, were about to o'ercome me, the half-sovereign tumbled out. Dropping quietly to the grass, as if it had gone for an adventure but had now tired of it. I was up-righted and then slapped, far too heartily, in congratulation.

That afternoon was always and subsequently referred to as the time that my life was almost brought to stop, yet re-started by the swift intervention and mechanical cunning of Brunel père. I always felt that interpretation to be far too coarse. (I had some agency in this, as did the coin.) But looking back I do not know why it is now, only now, I realize that in two different sets of circumstance, separated by a wide span of years, my life was stopped, and started up again, while bound with rope to wooden plank. What to make of this?

ELEVEN

————— ⚓ —————

I AM NOT sure how long I have just slept—perhaps four hours, most certainly fewer than eight. My dreams were expansive, of lakes and trees and woodland paths and music, beautiful music everywhere. But when I awoke I found myself in the same small metal room, the air malodorous, rank, and foul. This is the mausoleum in which I have been interred.

I'd here had the intention to set down in these pages other memories from the distant land of childhood. But I today at breakfast learned news that disturbs the soul and that takes precedence over other tasks. Put in its most simple form: our captain is taking us east, not west; north, not south. Which is to say that since we have left London we have been heading not down the channel to the Celtic Sea and beyond, but rather up the channel, to the North Sea (where we are at this moment), and then the Norwegian. Have we changed our destination? We have not. Our captain has succumbed to an idée fixe: that the best route from northern Europe to the South Pacific runs not round the Cape but o'er the Pole.

Were travel by sea as simple and direct as stretching a length of twine over a globe 'twould make sense. But 'tis not. The route polar is encrusted with ice: it demands a vessel capable of diving beneath. Neither the *Neptune*, nor anything yet constructed by man, has that capacity. Let me, then, make best use of my delimited time, a few days at most, before our icy captain consigns us to our frozen grave.

DUSK IS FALLING quickly. It is just after seven p.m., and the month is October. On our portside now, the Faroe Islands. To our starboard soon will be Tromsø, then Murmansk as we continue heading north. Then the Barents Sea, which upon encountering we shall dive under.

By my simple calculations, the *Neptune's* hull—assuming it was fashioned of plates as thick as those of the *Great Eastern*, and assuming, too, similar care and skill used in the welds and rivets—will withstand pressures as deep as thirty feet. From what I know of polar ice, one must dive some fifty feet or more to find one's way below it. If I can ascertain as much, working from imprecise figures, then surely the captain knows this too and with greater certainty.

I endeavor to keep myself awake—what use to apportion hours to sleep when there may be so few of them left to me?—by all manner of device, such as pressing fingernails into palms, &c.

WE ARE SURROUNDED by water colder than water, the pressure down here keeping it liquid when anywhere else it would be ice. Before we went below the *Neptune* did navigate by stars, yet there be no stars here, only walls of ice on either side and a vault of ice above. Should the walls of ice converge all shall die as if never were, yet that possibility does not for our captain seem to hold terror. Others among the Crew—from what I am able to understand of their language, and from one or two remarks directed discreetly toward me—are of different mind.

One of the captain's men—Mr. V. K. Singh, a small, rotund, mutton-chopped man who had been to the captain a tutor since childhood—came earlier to speak with me. His English is quite good, if spoken in that odd and grating singsong endemic to the dusky race. Sotto voce he let me know that he, too, sees the captain's itinerary as one that can only lead to extinction. He is of the opinion that the only voice to which the captain might pay heed is mine. He, and his comrades, who have been with the captain through campaigns unimaginable e'en before they put to sea, will petition him to speak with me.

I am moved and find it in no small ways odd that one of my gaolers would now want to work in concert. Captor and captive together. It is not without precedent that the nearness of death does encourage alliances otherwise unlikely.

Our captain has since yesterday afternoon been ensconced in his study behind locked bulkhead, manipulating air: ten fingers, three manuals, thirty-two stops. It is a piece by Bach, after Vivaldi, in the key of A-minor.

Many years ago, centuries perhaps, masses of ice met, abutted, pressed together, slid beneath other, subduction. Over time the great walls of ice thrust downward, and it is these walls that guide our *Neptune* but also do confine her. A labyrinth without minotaur, but also without escape.

WHAT WAS SURMISED and what did occur were one and the same. Mr. Singh and I were told that the captain would receive us. Accordingly we approached the forward hatchway. At Mr. Singh's knock: "You may enter, Mr. Singh. And you may bring your M. Brunel with you." The fugue that had flowed mellifluous and thick now quieted. No longer the rush and roar of full raging sea, but a threnody written and sung by one lone heart. We entered. The captain had his back to us and neither turned nor ceased to play.

"We are on a path of doom, sir," said Mr. Singh. "And most assuredly will die. The course you have set for us is a course of madness, leading only to the grave."

Mr. Singh indicated that I should speak, and I did so.

"Allow me, Captain, to talk of physical limits. The hull is, I am told, three-quarters of an inch at its thinnest. We are aided by the pressure of interior air, which is now 1.5 times that of surface. But already there is seepage at the welds and it is only a matter of time before the exhaust pipes become inlets and water fouls the engine."

I awaited the captain's attention. Did not receive it. "Should we not turn around the water inside, and water without, will attain equilibrium."

Mr. Singh then took up where I had left off: "The crew are loyal and will follow a sailor from hemisphere to hemisphere. But they will not follow a madman. Should you not relent, they will take control of *Neptune*, guide her back to safe harbor."

The captain responded only in A-minor.

"I report only what I see and hear without embellishment of any sort," said Mr. Singh. "The crew are as one, poised on a fulcrum with the sharpest of edge. When I say crew, I mean all."

Now the music stopped. Now the fingers lifted from the keyboard. Now the captain's round, threaded seat performed half a revolution. His back had been toward his audience. Now he faced us.

"We cannot go back. Neither will we." There was a drop of water, then another. The water accumulated at the ceiling's top seams, gathered, then, as weight overtook tension, dropped. The captain noticed this, as did all, but if we felt alarm, and more than a small sense of urgency, the captain it seemed did not. "Behind us is the past," he continued, his tone unwavering. "Behind us is death. In front of us? Merely the future."

With that he lifted from its setting the voice receptor that led, via crenellated metal tube, down to the engine room. "Steady as she goes. Maintain three-quarter speed ahead." Abruptly he rose, quitting the salon by the forward door, disappearing through the passage that led to his private quarters, thence, by narrow stair, to the wheelhouse.

Mr. Singh turned to me. "Let us pray," he said. "You to your god, me to mine." I stood there for a long moment, collecting the thoughts. If I were to have but minutes before the curtain descended, how would I wish to spend those moments? Immersed in what thoughts? What actions? I repaired to my room to set down this account.

If these words survive me, and you come to read them, please do not judge me harshly. And if by some miraculous and uncanny stroke of fortune I should outlive them—know that the larger part of me would wish not to.

TWELVE

————— ⚓ —————

SOMETHING I HAVE known since birth, a lesson taught neither by amahs at Orchha nor by my dons at Cambridge: when the world spins, there is always one small, still point about which all else revolves. It is of use to know this.

The contemplation of sailing beneath the Pole induces chaos within our mentation. But there is a still point: the center of the earth. The molten core, an inferno beyond imagining. Magma travels up from that core, and even after a journey of some 1,300 leagues, retains sufficient heat to erupt and bury cities. Think only of Pompeii. Of Atlantis.

The lower we descend, the closer we approach that core. Counter to intuition but not counter to science, there will come a point in our descent where the sea—which had, 'til that point, gotten colder—becomes warmer. The temperature at which impassible ice becomes, perforce, navigable water.

Accordingly, I commanded that *Neptune* make a descent to the depth of six atmospheres. And at that depth, there is nothing but water, liquid water, from here to the Bering Sea. The capable M. Brunel, who was not present at *Neptune's* construction, but who possesses perhaps the world's keenest mind with respect to naval architecture, calculated that our hull would not withstand six atmospheres, and made his calculations known to me. He concluded his analysis by maintaining, with some clarity and force, that at any greater depth than the one we were maintaining at present, this craft will break.

I proposed, by way of response, that we compensate by increasing the air pressure within. He countered that "the Almighty," as he referred to his deity, built our lungs for one atmosphere, not for six. That capillaries bleed out at any pressure more than three. He also dispatiated upon the difficulties, once pressurized, of returning to surface. His argument: in the decompression any gas in the bloodstream becomes a bubble, as if the blood itself were boiling. That bubble makes its way to the brain which it then proceeds, in simple and predictable fashion, to destroy. He gave examples from his experience during the construction of the Rotherhithe Tunnel.

I did hear, of course, what M. Brunel had to say. But there is a still point within me that knows what he does not.

To wit: like many dreams, the dream of a submersible preceded the dreamer. It floated on tides of aether the way we now float in sea. When the gods think of us—bipedal, earthbound, mortal— they take pity. So they fashion for us a pair of dreams. The one is of flight, into the air, as if we were hawks or ravens. The other is of submersion, beneath the waves, as if we were whales or dolphins.

The dream of flight exists in each newborn. From time to time the dream finds a dreamer who can image it in ways more specific. Hence Leonardo, whose sketches for a flying machine provide in enchantment what they lack in practicality.

But the dream of submersion is equally strong, equally pervasive. It was captured in a net of ink and paper, perhaps for the first time, by a nameless Mussulman in Gwalior: a man who had been born and died without ever having seen the ocean.

The man from Gwalior died but the dream did not. The submersion machine found its next dreamer in Archimedes, who envisioned both a craft and that craft's propulsion by means of the spiral water screw. The dream left Archimedes, moved on, gathering force and detail as it went. During the siege of Tyre, Alexander the Great descended below the Mediterranean in "a very fine barrel made entirely of white glass." The dream passed through Bourne, Drebbel, and Mersenne; through Borelli, Papin, and Bushnell; through the American Robert Fulton. Through me, most certainly, when I was on the boat that took me from my parents' land across the sea to England. Six weeks above the waves, which time I passed by imagining six weeks beneath them.

Most recently the dream first glimpsed in Gwalior possessed a

Bombay shipbuilder, H. Lal, who in opiated reverie saw it in fine specificity. I woke him from that reverie as if I were the person from Porlock but he remembered enough of it to sketch it down. I fear there was more in his head, but it scattered as images on the surface of a pond into which a stone has been cast. Hence I summoned Mr. Brunel: to ink in the lacunae left blank by the abruptness of H. Lal's awakening.

The dream first glimpsed in Gwalior is wrapped around us. It was made of aether and now, thanks to much labor, of thick metal plates. But neither I nor anyone who lives and dies can be said to own the dream.

If we perish, if the craft implode, we will have been a link in a chain. And the next dreamer, in Reykjavík or Samarqand, will glimpse a vessel faster, sleeker, more robust: a vessel that will be, for its century, what this one is for ours. The chain cannot be broken; our place upon that chain is not for us to decide. Hence I say, with oceanic calm: full rudder down.

THIRTEEN

————— ⚓ —————

BEFORE THE DAMP rag of sleep is passed over the slate board of memory, I wish to set down in this Hawkins journal an account of the *Neptune* as its possessed and accursèd captain did give the order to descend.

Mr. Singh and I stared through the iris'd window. Outside of us were walls of ice, throwing back in wild iridescence the arclight that *Neptune* hurled at them. A green almost indigo in its intensity, a blue more deep hued, a yellow more intense, a salmon so pink that it rends the heart. The colors became for me sounds as if the play of light were the play of fingers on the keyboard of a Cavaillé-Coll organ. Thus the ice sang to me, each color accompanied by its synaesthetic tone. What symphonies resided in that refraction! What grand musical narratives, heard now by eye and ear! Whether this be due to the wildly increased atmospheric pressure, or the nearness to death, or the Mesmeric effect of the play of colors, can not be ascertained.

I was not dreaming—but now, with a grand shudder, found myself awakened! There was a terrible low scream of metal against ice, a bursting high-orange scraping sound, the yellow of ammonia high in the nostrils. I could hear screams through the speaking tube and, distant, from the other side of the bulkhead. Something had been breached.

I looked up to the captain but he was not there. He was already through the hatch, moving toward the back of the craft even as it continued its forward motion. I followed.

The sound became louder as we moved sternward. Water, rushing, not a drip but something more continuous. My feet and trousers were wet, water well over my ankles. Ahead was the captain, traversing, with long strides, the chart room, the dining hall, the crew's quarters.

Through the next bulkhead and the water was deeper still. This was the engine room. A half-dozen men at a half-dozen pumps forcing the water out. They pushed and pulled, bent and straightened, each 30 degrees out of phase with the next, pumping seawater back out into the sea as if they were pistons in a giant Otto engine. I found myself captivated by their taut, synchronous *ballet mécanique*.

But then remembered why I was here: I could see the breach. And something more than seepage, further aft. The pumpers were working methodically and well, but the waters coming through exceeded their ability to evacuate them.

"Mister Mohan," said the captain to his first mate. "Will you go to the machine room? We have need, as you can see, of increasing the air pressure." His voice was calm and he spoke as if discoursing upon Boyle's law before some royal academy.

I placed myself between the captain and his mate, and the captain, to his credit, did meet my eye. To him directly I then did say, "Sufficient pressure to force the water from the craft would be more than sufficient to force the air from our lungs. You would have a craft from which the water had been expelled. But also: the life."

"Then we will put the pressure in one section, the humans in another. Were not these bulkheads devised to contain such pressure?"

I calculated in my head. Then: "We would have to pressure everything from here aft. But we'd lose the capacity to expel ballast. And your engines will full stop under more atmosphere. You would lose all motive power."

Even as I spoke I registered the use of the second-person pronoun. But there was no time to self-recriminate.

"What if we reversed the ballast pumps?" asked the captain. "That their pressure be directed toward the interior of the craft, not the outside. Would not that expel the water from the aft sections?"

I considered for less than a second. "That it would. But—"

"Done." The captain did not try to shout over the roar of waters. Rather, he raised and lowered his hands as if conducting an orchestra: with his left, telling the pumpers to halt their work, to walk, in a rapid but orderly fashion, amidships; with his right, telling his first mate Mohan to prepare the hatch.

"The switch. The junction. The one that activates the pumps."

Mohan spoke with the calm, even tone with which first mates the world round greet disaster. "That switch be aft of the hatch you now presume to close."

"Would there be no way to route the leads to this side?" asked the captain.

"Had we a day or two."

The captain looked down at the accumulation of water. The inrush of cold ocean. Then turned his gaze back to Mohan.

"Our time is now," said the captain. Mohan nodded gravely, as if in full awareness of the impossibility of the choice he had with those four words been assigned.

"I shall, sir," said Mohan. The ease, near-reflexive, with which he offered up his own life was not lost on me.

"You are needed here," replied the captain. A long silence followed. Finally Mohan did speak:

"There is a man," he said, "whom I love more than life itself. But if there is to be one who gives for all he would be the one. He is my cousin and he is your second mate."

They were both of them now gazing at that second mate: Feringheea, who by countenance and demeanor displayed full recognition of the request about to be uttered. It was not really a request. And at this juncture, did not really have to be uttered.

Feringheea—it was the work of seconds—wrapped his arms around each of his mates, Mohan last. Then without speaking went directly, six long strides, through the aft bulkhead. Turned home the hatchlock, noon to three to six to nine on his side, while before us the wheel spun nine to six to three.

The hatch between us and the *Neptune*'s aft was now firmly secured. The hatch rearward—the one that separated Feringheea from the ballast hold and the sea beyond—was about to be opened. E'en at the expense of the life of any who would that hatch open.

Now we saw Mohan slap his flat palm on the hatch door. Once, twice, three times. There was a long, low, hollow peal. A knell.

Feringheea, on the other side, did knock back thrice. And even before the last reverberation damped out there was another sound: a whoosh unimaginable, a torrent, an expulsion, as the unseen Feringheea brought the ballast pumps to speed.

Without word or thought we rushed all of us at once out of the chamber at full speed, now amidships, now fore-ward toward the salon—to the iris'd window, *Neptune*'s umbilicus, giving view. The ice was white, as if glowing from within; the water had astonishing clarity. And as we looked out we saw the perturbance as our ballast—treasure from the Bay of Vigo, as gold has no worth down here save for its weight—rushed out of us and into the sea. It glinted in the eerie and sputtering light, a slow rich dance, a kaleidoscope of poise, of beauty.

And within the billow of gold: the mortal remains of he who had been the second mate but was now but human-sized mass, tumbling random, sinuous amidst the onrush of treasure.

And with this wild expulsion the *Neptune* lurched its way upward. We looked down now to the panorama below. The ballast, jetting out in smooth, slow convulsions, as a squid expelling ink. Ever more distant as we moved forward, as we rose, heading toward surface, heading toward the Pole, heading toward the collision with ice that would likely kill us all. We all of us gazed, rapt, at the surge and flow of treasure. Second mate Feringheea, borne to icy grave within a pall of gold.

Yet now I espied a second body! Near-lost among the glitter and gush yet unmistakable. Tumbling in slow glycerin motion through the arc-lit sea beneath rising *Neptune*. A second body. That of the treasured Mr. Singh.

How did he get there? He had been here, in the sealed portion of the craft. Had he somehow, unnoticed by all, gone aft to assist Feringheea in his noble, doom-struck task? I gazed out through the glass as if in Mesmeric trance. And watched the captain as he came to understand that his best tutor, his most trusted friend, his wisest companion, his solver of all problems was now in permanent residence beneath the Pole.

I studied our captain. If the loss of these two lives induced in him any quantity of melancholy or e'en regret, those thoughts could in

no ways on his face be discerned. Then we heard—felt—a low reverberant thud as the tower of *Neptune* hit something solid, the top layer
of ice atop the cold and unfathomable sea. We hit it and—

Went through.

It was scarce short of miraculous: the sacrifice of Feringheea, of
Mr. Singh, had in this cold and astonishing place allowed us to find
our deliverance.

Now we had fully broken surface. We stared out. The layer of ice
here was as thin as the rime on a windowpane. We'd broken it with
no more difficulty than that of an Englishman, at breakfast, tapping
the shell of his four-minute egg.

For the longest moment no one moved or e'en breathed. Then
Mohan he climbed the cramped metal ladder to the tower. Spun the
hatch lock. Pushed upward. For the first time in four days there was
fresh, dry air, and so we breathed deep into our lungs. He clambered
on deck, followed by, followed by. The sky was white, a translucent
shallow dome lit uniformly from behind. The sun was low in the sky
and it was white, the same white. The ground: flat white ice, all the
way toward the horizon. It would not be hard to imagine spheres
within spheres, the whole borne on the back of a giant tortoise.

We were at the Pole now. Could see it. Feel it. The still point
round which all else revolves. Nine crewmen silhouetted, backlit,
stark black against the glowing white world.

The captain he surveyed. Hand to forehead, shading his eyes as
if posing for an heroic gravure. What he espied, shiny white 'gainst
matte white: a thin river, lightly rimed with ice, leading from here
to there.

The line of liquid between solid floes, out to the Chukchi Sea,
the Bering straits, thence to Mr. Cook's islands. The Almighty will
forgive if I shouted a hallelujah.

Clambering. Clanging. More crewmen emerged from the hatch.
Stretched. Breathed air. Looked out across the sheet of ice under the
glowing dome of sky. Everywhere they looked was south. The heat
from *Neptune* warmed the air where they stood, steam rising from
the deck and from each face as they exhaled.

Now, without being led or commanded, they found themselves
in song. A few, then all. It was a song of air, of breath, of life, after

the possibility of life had been abandoned. They sang in their native tongue. But every now and then I could discern a verse in English: for English is the language of the sea.

It's round the pole we've got to go
Go down, ye blood red roses, go down
To find the line 'tween ice and snow
Go down, ye blood red roses, go down

The song it had many verses. (Melody and rhyme are mnemonic devices, enabling the memorization of long text otherwise without discerning feature.)

It's one more pull and that will do
Go down, ye blood red roses, go down
For we're the mates to kick her through
Go down, ye blood red roses, go down

They sang their song for a full quarter hour, each verse different, each chorus the same. It was a saga of life on land, life at sea, then life on land once more.

My dear old mother said to me
Go down, ye blood red roses, go down
My dearest son, come home from sea
Go down, ye blood red roses, go down.

There were many adventures, told in specific order, with recurrent themes including, but not limited to, the elements; fellow sailors; piracy; creatures of the sea; demigods; exotic locales; ecstatic sexual congress.

Oh you pinks and posies
Go down, ye blood red roses
Go down.

E'en the captain, whose face now bore the sorrow of Feringheea's loss, and more, that of his beloved Mr. Singh, could be seen to join the chorus. I alone did not celebrate salvation.

And so we breathed the Polar air, and looked up at the ice-colored sky, and across at the sky-colored ice, and down from the top of the world. Everything—the world entire—now spun round our axis. It was a moment that had some magnificence in it, and more than a touch of the Sublime.

But e'en as time and rotation did seem to cease, I knew this was pause, not full stop. And that within a very few moments we would be back inside the *Neptune*, headed for the captain's preferred atoll in the South Pacific, where he would repair and improve his ship before recommencing his career of evil.

I know some of this intent from our conversations; and I know additional from remarks made by his dusky crew when they for one reason or another did English speak. He meant to fix his machine, and, once fixed, to kill once more. Striking out at England, indeed at civilization itself. And in this latter war there were for him no innocents, no civilians. We were, all of us who lived and breathed the air of freedom, *la chair à canon* for his submersible cannon.

All of this was, to him, certain—the only matter left undetermined was where, or what, he would strike next. I fear the fate of English merchantmen, and e'en of English passenger ships, whose lookout is to the waves themselves, and not to whate'er malignity might lie below.

Go down, ye blood red roses.

Go down.

FOURTEEN

———— ⚓ ————

The Great Eastern.

THE MANAGERS OF the *Great Eastern* seem determined to play with the public impatience to the last. Either they have no settled and matured plan of operations, or they are determined that the world at large shall not know what it is. The London journal received by the *Niagara* all announced that the great steamer would positively sail on the 9th, the day advertised. The *Times*, on the morning of the 2d, the day of the *Niagara*'s departure, said: "The *Great Eastern* will proceed to sea on the day appointed, whatever may be her internal condition as regards general accommodation." These assurances, in which all the other papers concur, must evidently have emanated from the management: yet we now receive from Messrs. GRINNELL, MINITURN & Co., her New-York consignees, the following official announcement that her day of sailing has been again postponed:

"THE GREAT EASTERN.—Owing to the delay in procuring reports from the Surveyors of the Board of Trade, which must precede the clearance of a ship with passengers, and also with the view of arriving off Sandy Hook at the period of spring tides, it has been determined that the departure of the *Great Eastern* from England shall be postponed until about the 23d inst."

This note came by the *Niagara*, and bears, of course, the same date with the newspaper announcements, that she would sail on the 9th. The reasons assigned for the delay are not especially satisfactory. The date of the spring tides could have been ascertained six months ago as well as now, and it is scarcely conceivable that the time of departure should have been fixed originally without any reference to these tides. This reason, therefore, very possibly covers the real cause of a delay which the owners may not care about accounting for more definitely. This is the more probable, that the Assistant Secretary of the Company, in a note to the *Times* of June 4, gives "delay in the completion of the vessel" as the ground for deferring her departure.

It has also been related, though with no official imprimatur, that the *Great Eastern* may not be carrying passengers on this voyage, but rather, will be freighted with common cargo. This would represent a humiliation for The Great Eastern Company, who in all of their statements did purvey the craft as the pinnacle of luxury.

The whole career of this gigantic ship seems to have been one gigantic blunder. The most culpable mismanagement appears to have marked every step of her progress. Her cost has been enormously beyond the estimates: the time consumed in getting her ready for sea has been twice as long as was anticipated:—she is not well fitted for the service for which she has been built, and there are very grave suspicions that, in spite of all that has been said of her performances on her trial trips, she is really not seaworthy. Yet should she set sail, on "about the 23rd" or on some subsequent date, all luck and grace is wished to her.

—*The New York Times*
18th June.

FIFTEEN

———⚓———

IN WISHING THAT you understand my captivity, forgive me if I now—as promised at the commencement of this journal, but postponed until this instant—limn some moments lived by the younger Isambard, moments that have marked and haunted all the hours since. Events from childhood too small and interior to have been caught in the skein of history, ne'er having been conveyed to another soul, & hence would perish with me were I not to transcribe them here, on this page, in this ink derived from the blackness a cephalopod does throw out when needing to protect itself from imminent threat.

I was born in Portsmouth, the very name of which denotes shipping lanes and the might of English sea power. My father though was French, and when he'd saved up enough to do so sent me back to his homeland for, as he put it, proper education. I had then fourteen years of age and did not want to leave, nor did my mother see the necessity. The decision was neither mine nor hers. As to why my father wished to exile me, your speculation will likely be no more informed than mine own. I do know that he loved his native land but had left, in ruin, when contracted to manufacture some 80,000 boots by the military, for which boots, after Waterloo, there was no demand. He sought a new life first in New York, then London, then Portsmouth, supplying the Royal Navy with pulley blocks of his own design. There was money in it, enough to send me away.

Thus, following a sea-roiled, bilious trip across the Channel (my first experience upon the waves), did I report to the Lycée Henri-IV in the rue Clovis, hard by the Panthéon in the heart of the Quartier

Latin. I'd brought what they'd packed for me: a small trunk full of clothes and a Hadley's quadrant of ebony and brass (would that it were with me now! or I with it!) that my father had fashioned, by hand, while a naval cadet in the West Indies. It was my father's hope that I would matriculate to one of the Grandes Écoles, thence to sea. It was not a hope I shared.

On the rare free afternoon at the Lycée, I would walk to the Seine, up the rue Saint-Jacques and over the pont au Double to l'île du Palais. It was the custom in our circle to eat bread and cold meat on the very tip of the island, past the municipal buildings, past the somewhat disreputable Place Dauphine, at the apex of an acute triangle that represented, in a sense, the phantom extensions of the Île's quai de l'Horloge—where I was boarding at number 79 with the Breguets—and the quai des Orfèvres. The river flowed by on either side, then met up with itself. There was a tree under whose boughs one might sit and eat and contemplate. Under that tree, on the tip of that island (and here I summon the courage to set down these words) I had never felt more desolated or alone, in need of home, and of my mother. The absence would grow within me until the void was larger than my chest could contain. I would pull my shoulders down, knees in, so that none of this would be visible, while everyone else laughed or sang or played odd games with chalk. I would imagine myself not on the point of an island but rather the prow of a ship.

Yet if for a moment I was able to transform my solitude into captaincy, know that the moment did neither linger nor persist. Within three or four breaths, ten or twelve beats of the heart, I was aware once more of the prison that kept me apart from human commerce, and apart from my dreams.

I did not know that my life was not my real life until V_____e walked by. To set a line between what was past and all that was to become. I was fourteen years of age when in one stopped moment I had—with all the suddenness of a tunnel flood—a past. And because I had a past I now had something I before had not: a future. I hope these words can be comprehended by anyone who has seen, as I have, the person walking by who changes all.

When she left down Place Dauphine toward the rue de Harley I had fears larger and more pressing than all the fears of my life: to

wit, that I would never see her again. 'Twas not a vague and loom-
ing fear such as low thick clouds on the horizon of an otherwise
clear sky. Rather: a stab in the chest. Let me make my admission
here, and to the person who reads these words, that V_____e, or,
rather, thoughts of V_____e, have been, over the years, my château d'Espagne!

When I saw V_____e that morning on the place Dauphine
I knew she would be in my mind that moment and each moment
and every moment afterward. How is it even possible I knew so
much in one instant? An instant now become worn, polished, as
rock smoothed and rounded by the currents of time. I wonder now
whether my last thoughts will be of that moment on the île du Palais. And I suspect, or even know, that they shall be (just as they
were when for the first time I approached my death, tunneling from
Rotherhithe to Wapping, beneath the Thames).

May I speak of that now? You know of the public triumph; yet
that tunnel for me had been an enterprise of continuous dread. The
sewage'd water seeping in from the river without, it ferried with it
the methane gas from which my father took ill, and which rendered
his frame-maker hors de combat. I was pressed into service.

It was again not a decision to which my own sentiments were a
contributing factor. Might one imagine a more dread-filled occupation than to descend each morning beneath the river, with nothing
separating Me from It save a Shield designed by my father? Muck and
gas and constant muffled noise; the stink of the river mud that ne'er
went away. And the pressure, of which we were never for an instant
unawares, of the river, seeking by every means and at each instant
to crush those beneath it. There was nothing to do but push back.
Twelve feet in a good week, eight feet on a bad one. The pushing was
always a matter of inches. I was twenty-one years old.

On 12th January 1828, a cold and dispiriting morning, the river
did come at us. The moment was like an onrushing doom, sensed
before felt, felt before heard, heard before seen, seen before hit. And
what a hit! In chest full force as if by wooden ram. My head snapped
forward then back as rib and gut pummeled, my whole body tossed
upside down. Then: the slowing of time, the second hand moving
with the deliberation of an hour hand. And in that distended instant

I did see V_____e walking on the rue Dauphine as if for the first time and with clarity that lacked all blur of memory. It was happening at that very moment. But I was also clubb'd by water and I was also dying. Is there explication, other than Fate—or, perhaps, V_____e as angel guardian—for the fact that I was carried by that fierce cataract to a place I could lay hold of the rail rope? And thence, salvation? I used the rail rope to head back down, hand over hand, and was able to grab two of my diggers, assist them back to land. Others they were not so fortunate.

But now the light in my room, via the luminescence of a glass bulb, has dimmed. I shall recommence in the morning, or whatever passes for such in our sunless realm. We are heading south now, down from the Pole, through the Bering Sea. The ocean will be Pacific; my thoughts far less so. As the giddy energy concomitant with finding oneself alive ebbs out, what is left is the dullness, and dread, and the ongoing captivity. Perhaps there is a devil's bargain to be made: I do his bidding, assist with his infernal tasks, rebuild his sub-marine ship on some lost south sea atoll. And in return he sets me free.

E'en that seems chimera. I have never been farther from home.

SIXTEEN

————— ⚓ —————

The Great Eastern *and the Atlantic Cable.*

WE ARE AUTHORIZED by Mr. CYRUS W. FIELD to state that the announcement which has appeared in print, that the steamship *Great Eastern* has been sold to the French Government, is untrue. The *Great Eastern* was sold by auction for £25,000, her purchasers being Messrs. GOOCH, BARBER, BRASSEY and others, who have formed a company under the title of the "Great Ship Company." This Company have chartered her to lay the Atlantic cable before the 31st of December, and if the cable is successfully laid, they are to receive £50,000 in shares of the Atlantic Telegraph Company.

Soon after the purchase of the *Great Eastern*, her present owners were addressed by a French firm, as to what terms she could be purchased for by the French Government. The response was that, after the Atlantic cable was laid, the steamer could be purchased for £25,000, since when nothing further had been received from the French Government at the time Mr. FIELD left England.

—*The New York Times*

22nd May.

SEVENTEEN

———— ⚓ ————

I DID NOT know, at the time, that the thing was a *Regalecus glesne*. That taxonomy came later, when we were afforded the leisure to consult the books in the captain's study. In the moment, though, there was less knowledge than confusion, and no small portion of the fright-unto-death. Let me recount in the order in which the events themselves did unfold.

It was my second summer aboard *Neptune*. I was up on deck as is my custom. (The *Neptune*, though outfitted as a sub-marine vessel, spends most of her time riding atop the waves, for reasons herein previously recounted regarding capability, issues of engineering, including but not limited to motive force, the crisis of dead air, &c.) The sky was a relentless blue with wispy Cirrus clouds if clouds at all, and so the various deckmen were bent to their tasks without disparity from the days before.

And yet is it not with this kind of unremarked and unremarkable routine that all tales of terror commence? Then there was a noise, a clamor, a loud *Pop* like the burst of a balloon: it was aft, near the engine quarters. But that *Pop* was but the getter of attention, 'cause once all eyes were turned, there was a far louder Burst from the aft boilers, and with *son* came also *lumière*, in the form of a piercing flash of light from the aft. And at the same instant one of the claddings, a ferrous plate perhaps two foot square, lifted into the air. Even as it did I was in some far part of mind calculating the force necessary to raise said mass such distance, a force legibly of substantial magnitude, if one take into account the necessary shearing of the rivets. It was clear that something had gone Quite Wrong.

I was put in mind, even as the raised iron cladding commenced its downward arc, of the breach, and collapse, when the tunnel 'neath the Thames commenced its flood. And as in that influx (though I was then a far younger man than at present) I ran toward, rather than from. So without meditation I made my way astern, but even to say, "made my way" implies consciousness, when in the instant there was none. Better to say: that I.K.B. *found himself* at the *Neptune*'s aftmost deck, gazing through the steam at the place where the section of cladding had moments before been integrally fastened— And beyond it, to the waters abaft.

Much happened in a period of time far shorter than it now takes to set down here the description. Among the thoughts or near-thoughts that passed through my uppermost mind in that instant: we were witnessing a catastrophe. It would be revealed, likely between the tick and its subsequent tock, if this moment be the *Neptune*'s last—and correspondingly, ours. So my gaze was in part involuntary—in the way one stares into the abîme—yet in other ways diagnostic, in using the perceptive powers and those senses available to ascertain the cause of the failure, and then, on the basis of that knowledge, to plot a course of action that might save us from extinction.

In this half-second it was the engineer, not the man or the prisoner, who commandeered the wheelhouse internal.

Now that all accounts have been collated, I believe that Engineer Brunel was the first to espy the efficient cause of our disaster. Because as my gaze moved laterally from deck to rent cladding to sea, I espied a fish, nay, a school of fish, following (as fish at times do) the *Neptune*'s course, swimming in the wake, perhaps accepting *Neptune*—despite its inorganic nature and composition—as the lead fish, or perhaps merely drawn, by the movement of current and variation in the underwater pressure, into the backwash.

Nor were these fish of the kind we customarily in that wake observed: the small pilot-fish, the sardines, the occasional dolphin. No, these were long things, more eel-like than fish-like. Sea-snakes. Snakes that were somehow ocean-borne rather than wriggling sidewise on desert land, or emerging vertical from the basket of your subcontinental flautist. I now know these to be *Regalecus glesne*, more commonly called, "oarfish." But in the moment, on the stern of the *Neptune*, I did know only three things:

- That there was a school of inordinately, nay, unimaginably long fish trailing our craft;
- That one of those fish, adjudging from the way its latter half protruded from the starboard aftward intake pipe, had clogged said pipe, preventing the ingress of air, and perhaps in doing so had provided the efficient cause of the explosion; and
- That further, and more pressingly, another of these unfathomably long fish was heading, either by its own main force or by the suction that the intake pipe did generate, into the main aft intake; and that its girth would be sufficient to clog the larger pipe, thence bringing about an explosion far larger than that which had attracted our attention in the first place!

Again what happened happened, with the action preceding the thought and absent any decision on the part of myself. I immediately (to use once again that mystifying and inadequate phrase) *found myself* in the water! With yet no memory or sense impression of having jumped! The one instant I was perceiving the fish, the pipe, the disaster-to-come; and in the next I was fully clothed in the equatorial Pacific, and swimming arm-over-arm astern (in this aided by the still-forward momentum of the *Neptune*). And in that next instant (for this was not a narrative, but rather a succession of moments! an archipelago of mind!) I was headed for, and then grabbing, the fish.

- My arms were round it, embracing.
- My full being engaged in tightening that embrace, that I might prevent its hindquarters from going where its forequarters had already gone, viz., into the pipe.
- A saline tang in the nose, salt and sharpness ascending to brain and illuming the traceries therein.
- It was not just the tide I was fighting, no, the fish, too, worked to free itself from my grasp, as if it possessed intellect, and as if, more, that intellect were pointed toward the full destruction of the *Neptune* and all those aboard.
- Now a glimpse of firmament, radiant, saturated, numinous. A full azure from here to the heavens. Discerned in that long mo-

ment with more clarity than in my life up to that point I had known, or known to be possible.

I was in true danger of being the drowned man, yet in the instant was of that unaware, or, if aware, unminding. And then I was pulling, at first by inch, then by foot, the long and (in this circumstance) deadly creature from the pipe in which it had become lodged. I braced feet against the hull while my arms with scant leverage did the grasping and pulling. I do not know how I did this and then it was done.

There was a noise of anti-suction as the head were freed; and another noise, from the deck, of the day crew, cheering me, and applauding me, and the captain too, though he were not clapping as were some of the others, yet gazing down with beneficence and, I took it, gratitude. It was clear that they had grasped what had in front of their eyes occurred with a perception that exceeded in those rapid moments mine own. Next I knew I was once again aboard the *Neptune* (did they haul me up? did I climb of my own strength and accord? was I from drowning saved, or did I from drowning save myself?) and being wrapped in coarse wool blanketry, and rubbed, and brought belowdecks that I might be dried and warmed.

As they performed these acts of rescue and remediation the crew referred to me, as were their custom, as "Huzoor"—a word that in their language means, quite simply, The Presence, but which is most customarily employed with reference to Englishmen. But in that appellation, where in my time aboard *Neptune* was only the stigma of difference, was now, were I hearing correctly, some measure of respect. As if in their eyes they had this day discovered that being English, and being a man of courage, were not in their entirety exclusive. By dint of birth I was, it is clear, their enemy; but by dint of behavior, a fellow sailor.

Thus: when they enwrapped me in wool, and rubbed it to erase the chill of the dark water in which I had been dipt, 'twas not merely the efficacy of sound practice but also the affection that one man of the sea to another will display. It is not remarked, or mentioned, or anywhere writ down, yet I have seen it among dockhands, among welders. And I did today see it manifested from the crew of the *Nep-*

tune toward its prisoner, despite the lack of common language, save the one which the sea to all who sail upon her provides.

After I was warmed and did myself rest there was a *rat-tat* at the door and I was summoned to the table of our captain. The table was draped in white cloth, with finer napery than I had to that moment seen aboard this craft. And the tableware were silver, and the knife at each plate (it were the two of us, and the two of us only) handled of horn or, I presumed, sea ivory, in keeping with the predilection of the captain to obtain his viand and accouterment from the oceans on and beneath which he sailed. The iris opened full; and even though the craft was sailing as ship rather than as sub-marine, it was still possible to see through the captain's Large Glass the wash and glide of particles below the waterline. Our meal commenced with circles of white meat, pleasantly resistant to the chew yet tasty. I nodded (in thanks, in satisfaction) and asked, "Octopus?"

"Squid," he responded. "The octopus is a creature of true intelligence—more than that of the human in some aspects. I would not capture or kill it. It would be the victory of might over intellect, and in that there be no triumph."

I wondered, but did not state, the contradiction evident—here was a person who showed little hesitation before, nor compunction in the moment, nor remorse afterward, in my kidnapping, and in the deliberated murder of his fellow man. And yet would not (or so he proclaimed) place an octopus (such as I had eaten at the Athenaeum, and in other fine residences of London) upon his plate. That in his ethics the captain drew the line in ways jagged, curved, was not to me a revelation; yet with each example his redistricting of the moral map grew more confounding.

The knife, the ivory-handled knife in front of me, was no butter knife, no. It was pointed, and sharp, and if it was well-equipt for dispatching viand, it was also equally well-wrought for mayhem. A plunge of that knife would penetrate a man's chest and a subsequent twist dispatch him to his doom. Why would our captain provide me, so close at hand, with the means by which I might, should I choose, send him to his Acheron?

I contemplated this question in the abstract and in the practical. It was clear that were I to avail myself of the opportunity for vengeance it would be of little use as the crew would to their deceased captain maintain loyalty, and would of Huzoor make short work. (I here did recall the instantaneity and utter lack of hesitation with which Mohan had, in moment of crisis, offered up his life.)

No, the captain would be dead but his craft would sail on, and his malignity would itself perpetuate, across the seas and down the years.

I gazed out the glass into the sea where plankton and other forms of life swayed this way and that, as they had since the oceans' begetting, and would, long after we and all that we have begat are long gone. And I wondered—and I have to take into account, that I was tired, and weary, and had without intervening sleep experienced shock, and near-death—why, when faced with the opportunity to destroy the craft, or at least do it major and perhaps irreparable damage, I chose, instead: to save it.

The captain as if following my thoughts did now offer me a cheroot and with it a lighter of flint and glass. "Whale oil," he said by way of explanation. And I did that flint make spark, and when the oiled wick was aflame, did apply that flame to the tip of the cheroot.

Said the captain, "I do hope you enjoy its pleasures."

The taste was not like the cheroots that typically I carried with me in my leather case but exotic, more equatorial.

"Are these leaves from your homeland?" I asked.

"No, and yes," he replied. "The tobacco is not from my native country. Nor is it tobacco. It is from the weeds of the sea, though 'weeds' connotes the ragtag and unwilled intrusion into an orderly garden, while these sea-weeds are neither intrusive nor undesirable. After some experimentation I have ascertained that these, the flat leaves from the coastal regions near a certain isle in the Indian Ocean, make for the best smoking. It is in one sense a substitute for land-grown tobacco, but in others, it is less an imitation than a satisfaction in its own right."

He went on. "When I said 'no, and yes,' I meant that these were not leaves from the land of my birth. But they are leaves from the sea, which is now my home—" He only now took for himself a sea-cheroot, lit it with the same flint-and-crystal mechanism. "—and will be my home, for the rest of my years."

He placed his hand now upon my sleeve, looked at me with an intensity of gaze that did not allow me to look away.

"Those years might have come to end this morning, were it not for your instinctive courage. And though the reward may not be in any way commensurate with the deed, I wanted to offer up the pleasures of my table, if I might, and to join you in the confraternity of smoke."

"Much obliged," I heard myself to say.

And even as my mouth those genial words did pronounce, my mind in uppermost were occupied with thoughts not genial in the extreme. Viz., how did I come to be held captive beneath the waves? And to dine with this dusky murderer? We were smoking cheroots, this man and I—how had we come so far from home, that we had lost not only sense of time, and place, of long. and lat., but also that the moral compass was so skewed, as if the iron will of the man across the table had attracted, misaligned the floating needle.

While I inhaled the thoughts danced in my head even as the smoke danced without. The three men inside me linked arms and danced a gavotte, but 'twas a gavotte of struggle for which but one would emerge victor: The Engineer, Father of Paddington, blessed with the extraordinary ability to all problems solve; the captive, the Prisoner, Huzoor, who strained against his shackles and spent each waking hour in the contemplation of escape if not revenge; and the remaining member of this triumvirate whom we shall, with simplicity and compassion, call Isambard. Isambard, the babe in his mother's arms; Isambard, the schoolboy at the prow of the île du Palais; Isambard, who in the berth of family and home did find harbor. Which one of these three men pulled the lever as I spoke I do not know, and may never.

"There is an imbalance, Captain, I wish to address. Let me pose it in its simplest terms. The *Great Eastern* was over a span of years imagined, designed, constructed by myself. A ship of ambition and accomplishment. That ship you did destroy, or did attempt to destroy. In turning that stopcock you knew, indeed, hoped, that there would be conflagration and loss of life and limb—yet you did it regardless. One might even say that for you the loss of life was not incidental, but rather the objective and aspiration.

"Now contrast your behavior—if behavior we can even term it—with that of mine own, with respect to this vessel. Where mine was on course, you sought and destroyed; where yours was endangered, I did what I could to steer her from harm's way. Our comportments were as antipodes.

"I am not trying to paint myself a saint, for I am nothing of the sort. But it is not unfair to state that you are a sinner. 'Gainst God, and 'gainst your fellow man, for whom you seem to have no care, or compassion, save the ways in which he can further your ends. It is almost as if you held yourself to be another species above that of humanity, and that to you the scurrying of humans on the planet mean no more than the scurrying of ants round the rotting stump. And this human: do you intend to keep him captive for the remainder of his allotted days? Or merely until your captive has outlived his usefulness, then to be dispatched to a watery grave?"

There were a pause, quite long in duration, during which could be heard the whine of the *Neptune*'s turbine, the coming-going of the crew, the occasional thud, an impact of something 'gainst hull generating sonics propagating through air and through iron, yet at differing speeds, and by distinct routes, direct and circuitous: *THRUMbum bum bum, THRUMbum bum*, damping out slow over the course of several seconds.

"Are you quite done," asked the captain finally, with what might be perceived as a trace of impatience. He gazed at me—stared, really—as if he were taking my measure. And then commenced to speak. I was of course exhausted, and spent, from the events of the day; and as I write this now I know that I am not transcribing *verbatim*. But I set this down now, prior to what I hope will be a long and pacific night in the arms of Morpheus, as I do not wish (have stated before?) the pungency & tang of immediate memory to be unsharped. Thus here is what the captain he said as best I can set it down—and if his words do not seem directly responsive to my questions, this is neither an act of elision nor an error of transcription.

"As you may have previously learned, or perhaps surmised," he said, "I did not achieve command but was born to it. I was a prince, in Bundelkhand, in the mountains of what you call India. By English map it is one of the Princely States, yet to us it is simply our land.

Bundelkhand. Of which I was, from the moment of first cry, Prince. As was my father before me, and his before him, as was, as was, going back further than any European or Englishman can count or imagine.

"I state this flat: you do not know what it is like to be the prince of Bundelkhand. You do not know. Perhaps the best analogy might be, 'tis like being the captain of a ship, but the ship be land, near-infinite land, all that the eye can survey. And as puissant as the powers of a ship's captain might be, that of the Prince are ten- or hundred-fold. My wants, even as a child, were unquestioned. Were I to make to sit a chair would appear beneath me before my rump hit bottom. No one entered a chamber in which I was present without bowing, low, so that forehead touched earth.

"Nor was I raised by my parents as, I suspect, you were by yours, and to good effect, given the training and *connaissance* in engineering which your father to you did bequeath. No, I was raised by a succession of amahs, such that I had neither companions nor rivals nor figures of masculine authority over me. I was the prince of Bundelkhand. And Bundelkhand was the world.

"My word was law from the instant I could utter. Even as a babe in arms the lives of others were dependent upon my wishes. And that power only increased as I came of age. So you speak of the fire-men aboard the *Great Eastern* who perished, with a quarter-turn of my wrist. Yes, their lives are on my account. But the lives of thousands, nay tens of thousands, have been on my account since before I could stand on two legs. I am not saying this as self-absolution, for the totality of my actions in this lifetime will certainly be taken into account when the deities consign me to the next. But I am saying, M. Brunel, that you cannot *imagine*—" And here his wide-set eyes bore into me, full, with an unblinking intensity. "—you *cannot* imagine."

It was impossible to interject.

"And though I reject the notion of the double-entry ledger," he went on, "of that-which-is-done-to-me-I-shall-now-to-others-in-same-measure-do, I want to lay out for you, not as justification, but let us say as context, my history with the English race." Here he fired up another cheroot (taking care to offer one across the table which, owing to my habits, I accepted, without fully thinking of the moral obligation thus incurred) and continued his tale.

"It was a given that the young prince of Bundelkhand should be given the finest raiment, the swiftest horse, the most glistening of jewels; and among those jewels was, of course, education. For it was not sufficient for me to be *powerful*. I was shipped o'erseas to become *knowledgeable*, with the understanding that I would upon completion of my formal education return to Bundelkhand, there to become *wise*.

"I was thus dispatched to Trinity College, Cambridge. It consists, and I am sure you know this, of a great court, round which is a wall. As if the learning and tradition contained within be subject to siege, or might want from the confines of Cambridge to escape.

"I was not like the others: this was a given. I did not expect to be liked. Yet there is a tradition in certain colleges—as Trinity, as Oxford's Magdalen—that encompasses those such as myself. Which is to say, princely figures from what they call the subcontinent—and why 'sub,' as it is larger than the British Isles by a factor of ten? We have come to these places for hundreds of years so I was neither the first nor the last to cross the gate, enter the court, porters carrying my bags behind and a turban wrapp'd round the head. Even as I gazed up at the intaglio'd device, carved into that stone wall—Trinity, meaning, of course, the father, son, and ghost of what to me is a Johnny Newcome faith—I expected to within those walls find, if not compassion, at least acceptance. I already knew, as a matter of cultural difference, that there would be some difficulty among the Cantabrigians in matters of ritual and language. Would they, for instance, grasp the properispomena of my native tongue?

"What I found, though, was different in kind as well as degree. It was as night turned day—or, more accurately, day turned night. Whereas in Bundelkhand I was unquestioned master, here I was regarded as some dark-hued bottom boy, beneath the baby lords, and the viscount's son, beneath, in their eyes, the porters who swept their rooms, the laundresses who each week scrubbed from bedsheets the signs of their decadence. In their book the highest prince from Bundelkhand ranked beneath the lowliest Englishman. It was as if, by dint of birth, I had already a crime committed before my first sigh.

"My chamber-fellow, a corpulent badger named Ffoulkes, at first would not meet my gaze. And when it became clear that I was both more intelligent, and had more capacity for learning, than Ffoulkes and his ale-swilling pals— His diffidence turned to enmity active. I will not enumerate for you the thousands of slights, all of similar intent: to let the dusky creature know that he was not, and never would become, fit to polish their boots.

"Both as a representative, however unwilling, of my caste, and because it was how I was by Devi and my amahs raised, I was slow to anger. Nay: I did not allow myself that emotion to feel. I did not retort, reply, respond. When they re-made my bed so that the one sheet were doubled and there be no room for my feet I simply slept curled. When they jostled my plate in the common room that evening I ate not. There were incidents of this nature every day, and every day I kept my silence. And with it, my honor.

"Now I had brought with me from Bundelkhand few possessions. There were some treasured books, of course. And some personal correspondence, of which I will not speak here. I allowed myself but one extravagance. It was an object. An object small yet perfectly wrought. Do you know, M. Brunel, what is: an armillary sphere?"

"Indeed."

"Then I need not lay out for you the intricacies of brass and wood that go into the crafting of such an object. In my case, the wood was shesam, and the brass forged by the masters of New Delhi. The sun at the center of the sphere was of yellow ceramic that seemed somehow to glow from within. The planets were extraordinarily detailed. Our earth, for example, was depicted with the aid of jewels of varying hues—emeralds, rubies, but also tourmaline, and beryl—the oceans deep celeste, the mountain peaks nacarat. And of course with diamonds, inset, representing the significant cities of the world. The mechanism of the sphere was so well-wrought as to be nearly without friction, so that once the handle were turned, the planets would commence their circling of the earth and not stop for the longest while, or until a human tired of the cosmos and intervened by hand.

"This armillary sphere was given to me by the wisest man I have ever known. It is nothing short of a blessing that you had the occasion to know him. Mr. Singh was my tutor, but he was more. Though it makes no logical sense for a prince to say this of a subject: he was my master. It was from him that I learned the calculus; from him that I learned the interactions of elements which constitute the chemistry; it was Mr. Singh who inhabited the mechanical Turk and was responsible for all of the Turk's victories. It was from Mr. Singh that I learned language, or, to be more accurate, languages plural; but more. It was from him that I learned that the world was not sad: the world was large. A notion of which I have tried to keep hold since his wrenching and untimely death.

"I can only imagine the cost, on a tutor's wages, of this object. Was it something for which he set aside, each month, the larger moiety of his salary, that he and his own did without? Was it, perhaps, his sole inheritance, passed on now, not to his son, but to me? Can one even fathom the degree of sacrifice, the depth of generosity behind this gift? There is no parallel in my life nor, I suspect, in yours. And in giving it to me on the eve of my departure, he was teaching me a final lesson. A lesson in dignity, a lesson in heart. And, of course, a lesson about our planetary system, with the sun at its center: not the planet on which we reside, as many for centuries had assumed, and some still do.

"I do not, M. Brunel, place great store in objects. In books, yes, as you can see. In charts. But I am not a sentimental man, and the rigors of living in these confines teach a certain economy. I have retained nothing of childhood. Yet this mechanical representation of our planetary system meant the world to me. It was something that could be held in two hands and yet it was the universe."

He stared out through the large glass, then returned his wide-set and relentless gaze to his Huzoor. "One afternoon, toward the beginning of winter, I left my chambers to take advantage of decanal hours. As I left it was raining. When I returned the sun was low in the sky, rays slanting and painful as they are when we near the winter solstice. The rain had turned to sleet. I tell you this to set the scene, to let you know the weather exterior that was soon was to become a winter in my soul. Because when I returned to my room, there was my bed, my books; there was the squat and porcine Ffoulkes. But what was not there: the sphere, the armillary sphere, the axis round which my inner life revolved.

"I immediately demanded of Ffoulkes, 'Where is it?' And he said, 'Where is what?' I realized that this was less a response than a taunt, and his mirth was ill-concealed 'neath his placid dropsied face. And then, when he felt he'd be able to speak without laughter, he said, 'And I believe that in these precincts, Prince, it is I who ask the questions and you who supply the answers.'

"I realized that he was not malign—that he had not hid the sphere solely with injurious intent. Rather he was righting a balance. He had been forced to share a chamber with someone not of his class, someone whom nonetheless was in the larger sense less his inferior than his better. And so his resentment festered until his oedematous brain devised a scheme: he would take from me all that mattered, that we by that act would somehow be more equalized.

"I realized that further interrogation would yield naught. Thus I returned to my customary demeanor: 'I seem,' I told him, 'to have misplaced my armillary sphere. If your eye should fall upon it, would you be so kind as to let me know?' He did not know if I was mocking him or admitting defeat. His reply, in a voice I can only describe as redolent with Ffoulkesian condescension, was but this: 'Of course, Your Highness.'

"I made three vows in one instant. The first, that I would recover the sphere, no matter the cost to my standing, my studies, or to the détente which between myself and my fellow students had heretofore prevailed. The second, that Ffoulkes would die well before his allotted time. The third—and this came of the realization that the problem was not Ffoulkes, but the larger group of Ffoulkeses, which is to say, England—that I would direct my education to the end of protecting myself, and all of Bundelkhand, from their depredations.

"None of these was an easy task.

"The first took some doing. I did not report the loss to the College or to the Cambridge constabulary, knowing that this would be futile and would only expose me to a more protracted ridicule. But each night after Ffoulkes was asleep—and I can still hear his loathsome and indolent snore—I quit my chambers and, attired in black, padded silently to the Great Court. I knew, from tales injudiciously revealed by Ffoulkes and his ilk in ale-induced candor that they often used certain spots in that Court as carnary grounds for that which they sought to conceal. With a metal probe I poked at the dirt looking for hollow or for full stop. I was methodical, devoting each night to a different sector, as if blacking out boxes on a quadrant-ruled sheet. My course of action subtended sixty-four nights. And it was on the fifty-second of these that I found, not what I was looking for, but a fragment.

"I dug more, and found: more fragments. In the end, most of the sphere was recovered by me, and hidden in my locked chest—even as my emotions were hidden deeper, in the locked chest of my person.

"It had been smashed as if with a sledge, 'til the dark, rapturous wood had been reduced to splinters and picks. The brass had been bent, hammered, torched. (The inorganic cannot scream, of course—but I could imagine the cry of those pieces, as they were subjected to the full weight of Ffoulkes and his cohort, taking pliers and tongs to the sphere, as they would have done, I'm sure, to the sphere's owner, were there not, even for their class, certain prohibitions concerning homicide.)

In short: it was not susceptible to repair. The ceramic shattered, the jewels pried out. There was not a one of them left. And in taking them, they had taken my heart.

"I continued of course to explore, square by square, the Great Court. And on the penultimate night—number sixty-three, if you are counting with me—I was digging under the chandratap of a gibbous moon and came upon something they'd forgot to take. 'Twas not a jewel, and so, I suspect, they thought it not of value. It was the small ball of ivory which in the departed and vanquished sphere had represented the Earth's moon. A gift from my wife's father on the night before I was wed, and in the intricacies of these things, my acceptance of that ivory ball was in and of itself the marriage vow. When I had received the armillary sphere from Mr. Singh I was filled with the largest gratitude; when I saw that Mr. Singh had made that ivory ball the moon of my Earth, my heart o'erflowed.

"I pocketed the sphere. My work at Trinity was done.

"I will not go into detail as to the second promise I made to myself. Let us simply say that in a state of inebriation Ffoulkes one night did decide to go riding. That his mount was more spirited than he had anticipated, and less susceptible to command than he did wish. That he was thrown, it is said, many feet in the air, then descended, legs splayed, onto a sharp whited fence. It pierced him in the sacks of his manhood and he from that wound exsanguinated. One can imagine the final scream. I did not attend the memorial service, but I did permit myself the indulgence of reading, for pleasure, the coroner's certificate.

"Now you may recall the third of my vows. And to that end: studies completed, I departed Cambridge, yet I did not immediately return to Bundelkhand. Rather, I matriculated at Sandhurst, an institute for another kind of education: military, and those arts pertaining to war. It was during this era that the East India Company commenced a series of annexations under a peculiar doctrine that proclaimed the Company's right to take over a princely state, should the head of state be declared by them to be incompetent, or should he die without leaving any heirs. This annexation did they practice in Satara, in Jaitpore and Sambalpore, in Nagpore and Jhansi, in Tanjore and Arcot, finally in our neighboring state of Oudh. I feared for my own life, and for the life of my children. Rani. Hanuman. Would the Company find the world more convenient should they not be alive?

"At Sandhurst I was—and by stating this flatly I mean no arrogance—as good a student in arts sanguinary as I had been, at Trinity, in the arts philosophical.

"I did not take my military training with aggression in mind. Rather, I knew, from my own land, the power of the British army; and I knew, from my time at Trinity, something of the true feelings that the Englishman, in his heart, harbors toward the subcontinental. I knew that the full power of British force might someday be unleashed 'gainst my own, and I wanted for that day to be prepared. You might say that I was prescient, but truly, M. Brunel, the thoughts in my mind were no different than those in the minds of hundreds, thousands, in Bundelkhand and other of the Princely States, who had seen the Englishman in puttees and with rifle raised at close range. The only difference between me and my fellows was that, as a prince, I had the resources that enabled me to learn from the Briton himself the arts of war. Would you care for a Madeira?"

He brought from a cabinet a cut-glass decanter and without waiting for reply poured two small glasses. In that moment I was again cognizant, as I had been at many moments previous, of a certain disparity. The captain was my junior by well over a decade—by the looks of him, by a decade and a half. Yet he acted not simply as the commander of the vessel within which I was captive but in all ways as my senior. As if it were he who had lived the full life, and I were on life just now embarking.

"Like many raised within the Empire, I was of course brought up that the Claret be the best accompaniment to viand," he said, "and that after dinner, why a man must want of Port. But if truth be told I do believe that the popularity of Port has much to do with Port's residual sugar. Your Englishman he likes his sweets. And in his postprandials, while he may not tell his butler to bring him the crème anglaise, the Montélimar, the floating island—as if he were a man of moderation—he will command his servitor to bring him a Port.

"As for myself I always found it too cloying. And then I discovered Madeira. The complexity is there, to be sure, but the sweetness, it is not. The best of Madeiras, they are put into large casks and sent round the world. For education, if you will. It is said that no butt of Madeira is complete that has not the equator twice-crossed. It is in this voyage that evaporation concentrates the wine, and oxidation matures it. The best Madeira, then, carries within it the tang of the seven seas. Let us drink."

It had been the longest of days, and, though the captain seemed at full throttle, I myself was weary beyond my capabilities to stay 'wake. I knew I would not often have the opportunity to hear the captain in this voluble—and, dare I say, self-revealing—a mode, yet the thought of bed (even if said bed were a cot!) had charm and attraction that were at that moment outweighing all else. And now that the conversation—or monologue, really, for the true conversation of necessity entails the exchange between parties—had seemed to reach a natural pause I thought it best to avail myself of the opportunity to quit the study and to walk aft-ward (even as the craft pressed fore-ward) to my room. To my gaol, but also to my dreams, in which from this captivity I find release.

"I can see, M. Brunel, that you are weary. It has indeed been the long day for you. But I beg your indulgence for one additional moment."

Here I interrupted, in a way that was not characteristic for a man of my temperament—and for that I blame the strenuous nature of my morning "swim," and the lateness of the hour, and the torpor induced by a full meal, and the Madeira. But also the conditions of my confinement, which will after time induce emotions that may spring out uncontained.

"You beg my indulgence, Captain, as if I had any choice in the matter. This is your ship, your demesne. I had no agency in the decision to enter your realm, and I have no agency should I wish your realm to depart—none save the possibility of self-slaughter. So for you to speak of granting, or not granting, 'indulgence,' while you speak on— Why this be a travesty and a bitter one at that. It is as if you were offering the condemned man the choice of a last meal where there has been no crime, no indictment, no trial, no jury, no sentence."

I fully expected to be yelled at, or worse; but that was not to be the case. Instead, he buried his head in his hands. And when he spoke it was without looking up.

"I can put myself in your shoes, M. Brunel. Your position must be nigh unto untenable. That is why I have given you a cabin more capacious than that of my first mate and that is why I have given you run of the ship. If I were to tell you that the captivity you experience at my hands pales before the captivity experienced by Bundelkhand at the hand of the British, you would, I suspect, find the comparison meretricious. Yet here we are.

"I will not, given the lateness of the hour, bore you with details concerning the savagery of the Englishman during the sepoy rebellion, and how my training at Sandhurst was put to use. And you would perceive it to be a mere play for your sympathy were I to tell you of the death of my children by their hand, and of my wife as a consequence direct of their actions. That has shaped my character to a degree greater than any you might imagine. But you too, sir, are no stranger to the wrench and wrack when one is separated from family."

I could not help but interject: "You say 'is separated' as if this were some passive event in which only fate played a part. Yet there was a cause to my misery as there is to thine own. And if the British were the effective cause of your desolation, the cause of mine is here, in this room. It is you, Captain. And all that has been done to you does not give you the right to do in turn. Even should you hate my government, my land, I am not their representative. I am—"

Now it was he who interrupted. "You are an engineer, a citizen of the world. On board the *Neptune* not as a representative of your country, but rather as the recipient of a grand opportunity. Perhaps the greatest challenge—"

"Poppycock."

"Then I put it to you simply. I ask not for your understanding or for your agreement since that apparently is not forthcoming. So let us do this as an exchange, an act of commerce. You do this for me— and by this I mean apply your skills toward the task of making this ship truly seaworthy, above and below—you do this for me and I will give you the only thing that matters: your freedom. I will repatriate you to your native land, that your liberty be restored, and you may reunite with those you love.

"I ask not your conversion to our cause. I ask not that you endorse my program, which must seem to you savage at best. I ask not that you engage, as I do and will, in the slaughter of empire and of that empire's satraps. I ask only that you make the practical man's sound decision: To seize the possibility to live again on land, and in the cities of your own choosing, and to raise your children, and to see those children give you grandchildren to cherish. And, in the fullness of time, constrained only by the mortality that dogs us all, to be laid down in that grave which has already been prepared—but with a final date, carved in marble, several decades beyond than the one it bears now.

"Know that this is not a plea, M. Brunel. Rather: a proposition. You may sleep upon it. And while you sleep, dream on this. The *Neptune* has but limited range, inefficient propulsion, and no ability to sustain itself undersea for any real length of time. Its hull and cladding of wootz iron are first-rate, and we have made many innovations. But a ship is not mere hull and lights. It is engine, and range, and, in a sub-marine craft, depth. These are the challenges to which you must put your mind—and I say, without flattery, that it is the finest mind of our century. That is why you, and you alone, are here. Apply your best intelligence and you will be home within three years at the most. I give you my word as a captain, as a prince. —And as a fellow scientist, though one not nearly of your rank."

He seemed about to continue but he did not. Rather: stood abruptly, nodded, walked out. Though he did not utter a sentence in summation, his meaning had it been writ out on parchment could not have been more clear: *the choice is yours.* But of course 'twas not a choice at all.

E'en as I knew that to aid him would be to aid a murderer—e'en as those crimes committed by a perfected version of this ship would be on my conscience, for now, and for forever—still, I thought of my room in London, and the things I had in that room dreamed up, and might dream up again, were I reestablished there. And I thought of Mary Elizabeth, who would be liberated from her grief, who could shed the black bombazine and don once more her preferred creamier hues. And of my children (Isambard Junior! Henry Marc! Florence Mary!) who by now had got used to a world without me in it and would have to get used to a world in which I was again the master of the house. And, unaccountably, I thought of V_____e, whom I had not seen since childhood, and would likely ne'er see again.

This man, he meant without remorse to slaughter the caretakers of our empire—more, whomever among the white race might earn his displeasure. Were I to throw in my lot with this madman, 'twould be the blackest mark upon my soul. I could convince myself that I was doing this for Mary Elizabeth, or for the good of my country: the tunnels yet to be dug, the bridges yet to be built, the rivers and seas yet to be spanned; still, in my uppermost mind, I knew those arguments to be mere casuistry. This was not about what comfort I might provide to my wife or what glory to my queen. It was not even about the gifts to Mankind.

Alone in the Captain's chambers, I peripatated in circles counterclockwise. Gazed out through the open iris into the darkling sea, illumed by the arcing light of the captain's device. Looked—without really seeing—at the portrait of Baudelaire. Stared at the Turk, whose mechanical gestures imitated life but did not equal it. (Should I throw in my lot with the captain and his cause, would I become that Turk, winning game after game, a marvel of the Intellect, yet without a Soul?) And, finally, at the ivory ball, the captain's moon, and the planetary system round it. I spent, now, several long minutes gazing at closest range at its traceries and mechanisms—

And now saw something I'd not previously seen. It was small, and at the base of the thing, where the horizontal of the pediment met the curve of the legs. It were a signature intaglio'd into the brass. A signature I knew well:

Breguet et Fils

And there was, after the signature, a date:

1849.

There it was. Not a clock commissioned to commemorate (and appreciate) assistance during the Crimean War, which did not begin until some four years after the Clock it were crafted! Not something purloined from Abdülmecid! Not a gift—or if a gift, a gift to and from himself. A man whose life was as much a self-creation as the story he retailed of the criminal substitution of clock for replica at Beylerbeyi Palace. The captain he did openly confess to all manner of crime and atrocity—so why would he make up a tale about the clock, when said tale could be contravened by evidence plain? Among those with who I am familiar, such deceits are in largest part occasioned by matters of the heart. But can our captain be said to possess one? Thus I cannot declare with any reasonable assurance the facts of this matter. Still: allow me to tell the tale that mind and imagination here propose:

After his time at Trinity and at Sandhurst the prince returned to his native land—not without first making a stop in Paris where I propose that he there asked, who makes the best clocks? And the answer he'd been given would be the same I or anyone would have proffered: Breguet. And this young prince, perhaps nineteen years of age, he would have gone to Breguet and he would have said: build me a clock. One that will display the hours of the day and, as well, the circulation of moon and planets. And here he would have handed M. Breguet a tiny ivory ball—sole surviving artifact of the (ravaged; beloved) armillary sphere. And in handing it to him, would have said, *"la lune."*

Breguet (and this I know) would have replied: Monsieur, this is beyond me. And then (I had seen this, time and again) he would have said: *mais laissez-moi réfléchir.* And then: *c'est possible.*

So (and this I do imagine, rather than know) after some many

weeks' labour, Breguet would have sent message to the young prince
that he should return to the quai de l'Horloge. The young prince
would have walked the same quai with the same fine tang of river
Seine that I myself had walked some twenty-seven years before. And
he would have walked up that half-flight of stairs to the workshop of
Breguet, the workshop at whose bench I myself learned such large
portion of what now I know. (Ah, Breguet! With your beard perhaps
now turned to snow! What debts I owe to your fine care! How much
I long to see you!)

The Prince would then have stood, silent, while Breguet gestured
him to stand before an object covered in velveted cloth (so well I
know that cloth! purple, near-black! And of such texture that to
touch it would almost be to taste!). Breguet would then take a corner
of that cloth and via gentle tug the object itself undrape. And there
would be the clock, more intricate and fine than e'en the Prince
might have imagined, with its face, and its gears, and springs, and
regulators, and escapements—and its Solar System. And round the
beauteous azure Earth, the most exquisite small Moon.

Of ivory.

And did that prince then take that clock down that half flight of
stairs? Did he take in the air of the Seine, redolent of rot and stone
and wonder? Did he see the fishermen down there, on the lower quai
with their thin rods and thinner creels? Did he see the glorious tree
at the very tip of l'île du Palais, nobly spreading her branches as if
she were the flag of some yet-to-be-discovered land? Did he feel himself aboard a ship? And did he then see V_____e, now all grown,
but no less extraordinary for the passage of years? Or did he see a
V_____e of his own, not mine but alike in power of enchantment?

And what else do we have, I now thought (gazing out through the
captain's Large Glass before closing the iris and retiring at last to my
own bed, my own sleep, my own dreams) save those moments where
scurry and motion do cease— Where Time itself does take its stop—
Where between tock, and subsequent tick, might lie sweet eternity?

OUR ISAMBARD HE did here break off his journal entry, falling after
longest day without resistance into the arms of Morpheus. We do

not know, and never will, what dreams flowed and flickered within as Isambard in his cabin slept. Still, let us posit that on his sea of dreams did float the *Great Eastern*: his pride and his obsession, his buoy and his deadweight, the double-hulled embodiment of all to which his soul aspired. In his dreams, the man and his ship were once again united.

And oddly, meaning not oddly at all: even as *Great Eastern's* creator slept, the Almighty was already mapping their reunion. First, though, we shall offer up some details as to *Neptune's* resurrection. A tale of the islands, of kidnapping-en-masse, of pursuit-at-sea. Concluding with some hopes raised high, and then, as can happen in these realms: some hopes dashed beyond repair.

EIGHTEEN

—⚓—

Upon opening the Hawkins journal I see that it has been a goodly length of time since the last entry. To you who read this—if readers there ever be—know that I have been immersed in the tasks of each day. Were I to attempt here to set down or e'en recapitulate my travails since last I wrote 'twould be laborious to the writer and would likely prove tedious to the reader. Allow me rather to Skip Over, and indite here the simplest facts: that the captain has brought his craft, and me within it, to his island. I do not know if it appears on the Charts, or if so, under what name; but those who this island do inhabit call it Erromango. They call themselves Sye, but to us they are Canaques: that is our name for them and I have yet to learn if they in turn have a name for us. The Canaques are a sturdy people, and under my guidance have proven to be the most industrious of workers. Dare I say, more than the Englishmen of a certain class that one finds by the docks in London? We have been at work upon the *Neptune*, improving it in each aspect. Or had been, until the events of last night, which were so shattering and extraordinary that they caused me after long lapse to once again set pen to paper. To wit: the wholesale kidnapping of our Canaques by a ship of sea pirates.

The good fortune—if within the grievousness and calamity of last night's occurrence I may have the temerity e'en to use that phrase—was that these blackbirders did thieve our Canaques as we were so near to finishing our work, rather than, say, ten months ago, when the devastation would have been more complete, the blow to my emotions more profound. What is left can be enumerated simply on a list and that list confined to a single piece of paper. To wit: the sintering of the starboard batteries. The fabrication of six new plates to match the extant wootz, so that the former exhaust tubes might be removed and the lacunae replaced with solid hull. And less crucially: the replacement of the interior filament lamps, which consume electricity with a rapacity that takes away from our reserve, with other lamps that the captain and myself had together designed, in which the electricity is used not to heat a wire to its glow-point, but rather, to stimulate a light-emitting admixture of chemicals as in nature does the firefly.

I was in the midst of contemplating the work that remained, and how I might martial the resources necessary for its completion, when the captain did my thoughts interrupt. "We shall get them," he said, "before they reach Queensland."

I did not follow his line of argument, and did tell him so.

"The winds are low, near-still," he said. "The blackbirders' ship be dependent on those winds, and when the winds are becalmed, they can do naught but sit and wait for them again to start up. Let us say that they can average, over time, five knots. And let us say that we can be at the ready in ten days' time, and that we are capable of fifty knots. It is clear that we shall reach them before they are safe home." Here his disturbingly wide-set eyes left mine and gazed out. Toward the sea, toward the blackbirders, thence toward the future.

"Think upon it, M. Brunel. They are burdened with their cargo—I make it, what, perhaps sixty Canaques? Even should they have the fortune of weather, that will slow them further still. So we will finish our work here and set out in pursuit."

I could not help but apply our chosen mission to another set of circumstances, viz., mine own. Yet e'en in this access of pity for myself I knew at the self-same moment and with the larger and uppermost portion of my mind that we had work at hand. When that work was done, he would set sail in the newer, better *Neptune* and free the Canaques (and later on further freeing, lest we forget, M. Brunel). It was the liberty that the captain had pledged to me; and in the years during which we had kept company neither I nor anyone among the crew had e'er seen him fail to honor his word, regardless in matters small or large.

The final sintering—fusing mineral dust into Plates for our batteries—would have been difficult were we fully manned, and as it was, with so many hands gone in the night, there was no quick start to the day. Those that had been trained in the laying-out of powder trails into the mold were nowhere to be found, so the laying-out fell to myself. I worked swiftly as I could consonant with good result. I tried to keep the mind in present, dwelling neither on the dreadful events of the past night, the thieving of souls from the adjacent village; nor of the reward—the unlocking of my manacles—that awaited me upon completion of the build. I put my mind only to the pouring, through sieve and funnel, of powder upon flat plate. And even while I poured, the remaining welder-men were setting up the tower, and the burning glass, that my lacy traceries be fixed, for longtime, into solid (if to the eye translucent) mesh. The rays thus converged—collimated by the outer ring of Reflectors, then through the Glass, crenellated, in the manner of the Cordouan Lighthouse at the mouth of the Gironde, and following the practice of Condorcet and Fresnel—down toward the sintering plate where I did so carefully array the powder. The rays, their power multiplied by the convergence, were not to be trifled with.

All this meant that the arm providing the powder's distribution—the arm, in the present instant, of one M. Brunel—must lay it down quick, then be out of the path of the Ray. Too fast and the metals separated out; too slow and the arm was sintered along with the grid. And those burns of the sun were not like those obtained by the city dweller who with his family decides upon a day at the shore. No. Given the reach of the reflectors, and the precision of the crenellated *lentille* (as designed and executed by M. Brunel) the collimated ray was, at its point of convergence, hotter than the heat of the boiler of the largest steam ship yet built (and that, too, by M. Brunel). Nay, was hotter than anything this side of the sun, which is what makes the sintering of such disparate metals possible, but also what makes the apparatus, no matter how well-built, not without its own danger. It might be said that those Canaques—from Erromango, from 'Ata, from Kiribati, from the more southern of the Caledonies—who were so recently scooped up in dead of night, and slapped in chains, and taken in captivity, and shipped off, by desperate and unscrupulous blackbirders, who cared only to keep them alive until they could in bulk be sold— That in some sense there were among them those who were fortunate to be on a ship at this moment rather than beneath the Glass, whose ferocious focus could reduce arm to nub in a single instant, faster than the power of nerves to react. It was work for which the Canaques—exhibiting in all aspects the nobility of the wild man, the cloudless mien of the savage—were so well suited to it that they might have been to that purpose built.

But now I was sole builder of this infernal machine—infernal here used as description, rather than as moral judgment—and as such were there an arm or a head to be sacrificed, why then it would be mine. *Isambard Kingdom Brunel, him what built that what kilt him. Buried at Kensal Green and now again in the New Hebrides, so far from any place called home.* But this is mere imagination and pity of self: for the final sintering it was done, and done in a day.

Next: the tanks would be prepared. The solution of pure'd water and electrolytes mixed and poured. The sintered lacy plates lowered down 'til they were full beneath the liquid surface, like a descending sub-marine. That when all that had been done, as the Engineer had designed and decreed, the potential it was measured at the two output wires. Then there would be from those sintered plates, from those batteries beyond compare, sufficient voltage to power the vessel entire. Its lights, its instruments, its motive force. Pumps for air and pumps for ballast. So that the ship might rise and fall, by electricity. So that those within might inhale and exhale, by electricity. So that if the captain wished his craft to ascend or descend; or should said captain wish to consult his magnificent clock, or play chess with his Turk; or should his engineer, held (but not for long, not for long!!) in his cabin, wish an old and treasured book to read—

All would be possible, by electricity. All of this, and what worlds to come.

AT THE RISK of appearing as if I have no mettle, I want to state what must be stated: that the focused sunlight, it does hurt. That the eyes, in gazing upon it, are darkened by after-shadows for the longest time. So that today spots swim in and out of my field of vision, and already there are thin white peels of skin on forehead (why did I not wear a hat?) and forearms, and the odor of sintering metal remains in the nares. This is not work for a man of my age or station. That I did it is testament to my love of the invention, a love so large that it o'erlaps its bounds.

Still: there are larger and weightier matters at hand. The exterior work has gone well, and the metal plates that we have fabricated are fully as sound as the wootz with which they enjamb. The alloys are not identical, which can lead, in longer run, to rust, and in shorter run, to electrical potential. And the air-pumps, which I have fashioned from Archimedean cylinders, have yet to be laid in place. But I distract myself from course. Let me now lay down the large events of tomorrow, and of today.

Let us commence with the *tomorrow*. Having completed the work as related above, the ship—as the captain had imagined, and now realized by the work of the engineer—she will launch! Will slide, on skids formed of native island trees, from her dry-docking up above the beach, across the sands, into waters shallow then deep. She is a handsome craft, just shy of 230 foot long, with a displacement of 1,500 tons. She was built double-hulled—the inspiration, the captain has acknowledged, was my own work—but now the outer hull is, via my own methods, stronger by a factor of three (and by the same factor better able to withstand the pressures of the deep). Her prow is rather sharp, in the manner of, say, a narwhal, with serrations top and bottom; and there is a raised section just abaft of the prow within which the captain's chair resides. Though not built on the customary ten-to-one ratio, she is nonetheless sufficiently well-formed to allow her to part the seas when above, glide through them when below.

There will of course not be the portent or ceremony that attended, say, the launch of the *Great Eastern* (or shall we say launches, plural, with respect to the grand gathering at her official launch, which I attended on an upright board to which I had by the captain and his lascars been strapped). No royalty nor ministers of state, but rather the remaining Canaques, still in throes of grief for their brothers, swept up and carried off.

Also *today*: there is a change of nomenclature which must be noted. You will note that heretofore in this entry I referred to the craft not by name, as I have on all days previous, but rather as "the ship." For you who read this: I wished to withhold, until now—with a flourish of trumpets, or their Erromangorian equivalent—the following fact: that the captain, in tribute to my work, the invention and the craft, did tell me that perforce, she is not the same ship. What tomorrow would set sail is not that which months back did here arrive. So she arrived as *Neptune*; but as she departs, she is H. Lal's *Neptune* no longer. Rather: she is I. K. Brunel's *Nautilus*!

If she were named for distant planet (reminder of the loftiness of her aspiration) and for god of the sea (in the mythos of the Greeks), now she were named for a sea-creature herself. And in doing so she is no longer a stranger in sea-waters, but one among its denizens: no longer god with trident, but shelled, chambered *dweller*. Less that which *commanded*—than that which *belonged*. And in honor of this: beneath the name *Nautilus*, which was now lettered out in rivets along her starboard prow, were also an insignia, a device: a circle (without commencement, without end) around which were writ the words MOBILIS IN MOBILI. Moving within that which moves. Is there a better way to describe a sub-marine vessel, whose life is to be spent beneath the oceans of the Earth? Our azure sphere, far more wet than dry, around which orbits her serene and ivory moon.

And so, with the rising of the sun in the eastern skies we will watch as our much-reduced force of Canaques lay out a path of horizontal trees to act as bearings while (and now I can say her name!) the *Nautilus* is rolled carefully down to sea, the sub-marine craft departing in better shape and spirits than when she had arrived.

And what of I.K.B.? Was he departing in better shape and spirit than when he himself arrived? In ways of body, not entirely: the portions of the beard given o'er to whiteness were significantly larger, a glacier spreading south in long winter. Yet the sun had given color to I.K.B.'s cheeks, and the manual labor a tone to his arms and chest. Might we even say a sunniness to his disposition? That would be too much to ask, or, if asked, to answer.

THE DIFFERENCES BETWEEN *Neptune* and *Nautilus* are, if I may say, sufficiently wide-ranging as to merit the rechristening. Perhaps the most dramatic is the transition in motive force, from that of steam to that of electricity. Gone the soot from the coal; gone the whoosh and thump of steam through pipe.

In their place: silence, and a far quieter revolution as batteries directly power the shaft that turns the screw. And that screw does turn with vastly increased torque, that the resistance of the water impinge far less upon its abilities.

Then there is the air. Using an exchange system—alike in kind, but more sophisticated in structure, to that which we in the construction of the Thames Tunnel did employ—the air is no longer fouled. And at the same time that air can now be brought to higher pressure, that the pressure of air within compensate and countervail the pressure of water without, enabling us to seek deeper currents and for longer periods of time.

To speak only in terms of the engineering: is the *Nautilus* as grand an achievement as my beloved *Great Eastern*? 'Tis is somewise more advanced, as it must cope with conditions below as well as above. Yet if truth be told: is also a lesser achievement, in that the *Great Eastern* she were built from naught but imagination and steel, while *Nautilus* she was and improvement upon that what others dreamed and made. Still, I will not castigate myself for pride in this work, the first—will there be more?—of my ships made to sail beneath the waves. And of the Fracture of Life, and the Captivity, and Grief of Family? Do they outweigh aforementioned Pride? These measurements are not for me to make, or, perhaps, were better made from a vantage, after sufficient ticks of the clock that the immediate emotions have given way to a more measured reflection.

I do observe, and set down as well, what I see to be other changes from N. to N.: less questions of equipment than of the shift in mood and consciousness amongst the crew that our improvements may have in some smallwise induced. No longer did it feel as if we were below (and mostly above) the seas in some floating experiment, audacious in aspiration yet everywhere constrained in design. Now we were in a true ship and in every visage that increased sense of pride it were reflected. The word "Huzoor" now being used with real deference, the way one might, for instance, say "captain."

OUR FIRST TASK in *Nautilus*: the o'ertaking of the blackbirder's ship and the liberation of its human cargo before that cargo be sold in Queensland to the highest bidder. To that end we have set a course WSW across the Coral Sea, toward Airlie Beach, near Bowen and Proserpine, the most likely dockings for freight of this kind. In our chase we were aided by our new ability to spend long hours beneath, that when the weather above become inclement we surged forward unperturbed. It is astonishing that rain, even in copious amounts, and squall, and whitecap wash, do the surface of the waters disturb, but that disturbance does not deeply penetrate, so that when one is but thirty feet below the blast and flurry is aboard *Nautilus* nowhere felt.

And so we pressed on, toward the ship (name not known to us) whose captain and crew had the Canaques abducted. Yet, for all the enthusiasm which welled up from my gut for the chase, I was brought up short when in contemplation of the victory. The Canaques were of sufficient number that we could not take them aboard the *Nautilus*—we lacked, plain and simple, the capacity. Perhaps we might improvise rafts and laboriously tug them abovesea back to Erromango. But by far the more economical method, and the one most consonant with what I know of my captain, would be to jettison the ship's commanders and give dominion to the cargo. Then the Canaques could make their way home, by their own speed and in enjoyment of real freedom, while we of the *Nautilus* would proceed efficient and direct to the next task, that of my repatriation and the freedom that back in London I would once again obtain.

And what would be the fate of the blackbirders at the hands of those whom they had taken with the goal to sell? It would not be a lovely destiny. And though 'twas no less than their conduct and disposition merited, one could say that—in putting shoulder to wheel, in so efficiently executing the final transformation of *Neptune*-to-*Nautilus*, and in doing it to a timetable that enabled the chase—I had been accessory to the savaging and death of fellow humans. Miscreants, yes; lawbreakers to be sure—would my freedom be accomplished at the expense of their lives?

"We all of us die," said the captain. "And those that enslave oth-

ers but shorten their expectancy." These contemplations made for
scantly-eaten dinner, and an overuse of Madeira, and a sleep more
troubled than not.

How quickly dreams flee as if insects exposed to sudden light!
And so without further preface let me set down the images and dis-
quietudes of last night's dreams—before they are fully retrieved by
the dream world, thus rendered inaccessible to the waking mind.

In the dream there was a grand and enormous Wave. It stood the
full height of a tall house and one could see it from the window of
my lodgings in Duke Street. The Wave—and here I lend it capitaliza-
tion to emphasize its size and force as well as the terror it induced—
was neither preceded nor followed by other Waves, but loomed on its
own. Now that I think on it—and this was not a thought I had in the
dream but a thought that comes as I write—it may have been what
Scott Russell would call a Soliton.

The Wave approached and I could see it as it submerged everything on the south bank. (In real life I cannot from Duke Street see
more than Manchester Square but in the dream from my window I
could see the city entire.) Then it began to break, and the resultant
floods and eddies—on a scale too massive for words to convey—
upended everything. Cast the city itself adrift. Some houses were
reduced to shards and flotsam as I watched; others taken whole and
floated off. What surprises me now as I recall the dream was that
there was no accompanying anxiety—no sense of dread—as the
Wave approached. The waters were inexorable yet the dreamer calm.
What pieces of the city floated by! Life itself uprooted, displayed now
separate from its customary moorings. I saw (and will no longer comment upon scale or perspective of viewing) a woman walking her
dog in the Square only now both were afloat. Various Fellows of the
Royal Society bobbed up and down then were swept aside as they
gathered round a large oaken table. Good old Bill Gravatt, my man,
my best right hand, smiling and waving to me above the waters and
below them—above and below in rhythm stately—he too not at all
afflicted with panick—he looked at me as he disappeared. The hospital at Mile End—being built of cheap material and rotted at that—
collapsed into dust—or particles too small to see—all at once!

And in recalling that image now there is much pleasure—as my time spent in that building was nothing but pain—but in the dream the pulverization was equable and unperturbing—as was my good man Gravatt bobbing up and down—or the Fellows at their table—

And then through what feat of dreamer's logic I saw myself! I was bound to a plank propped upright on the deck of the *Great Eastern*—perhaps my darkest hour. And then by the sort of effortless transition of dream I was not regarding myself but rather was within myself looking out, unable to move as much as eyelid as the Wave approached. As it neared it became taller yet the breadth of the base was invariant. I knew as I watched it would topple—the ratio too steep to permit otherwise. And it was then that I began to feel the fear—that I would die and nothing to be done about it—that I would in a matter of moments become entombed in water—my least favorite imagining of my own demise now come to pass. (Why is it that in dreams the worst fear becomes actualized—and repeatedly at that?) And so my heart pounded thick and fierce within my chest even as my chest was about to be trapped beneath how many imperial tons of water.

I watched as the highest and most acute peak of the Wave began to topple forward, momentum o'ercoming structural coherence. Moving forward but also downward now with terrible force. There was no impediment to the slow but certain breaking and the cascade of death soon to come. I felt my heart pound with e'en more rapidity, more force than it would seem my chest could bear. I was about to die and did not want to die!

Then the Wave broke upon me just like that. I breathed and what I breathed was not air but water. Stinging throat and lungs. Salty like blood or like the sea. Sharp intake of breath. And then I was dead.

In all dreams previous that I can recall, my death in the dream was succeeded, and immediately so, by wakening, such that the death in the dream was the birth into consciousness.

But in last night's dream—and it flees from me even as I write, *hélas!*—there was no wakening. I was dead and swept up into the Wave now careening now submerging now tossed now pulled along. Yet though dead I was able to see, and also perceive sounds!

And so the light filtered through the water in ways that had some beauty in them. The sounds were all low—muffled—slowed down. And the panic which I have here described was replaced by a calm.

As if—being dead—I had been relieved of the obligation to fear. Nothing could harm me now. I was past all concern, all dread, all anticipation. Content to be flotsam, carried along, carried under.

At some length the random to-ings and fro-ings of the Wave coalesced into motion counterclockwise. A swirl, a vortex, wide at the top, but with a downward spiral, so that with each revolution I was be carried down into a circle e'er smaller, deeper, more swift. I knew somehow that this was my Passage—from Death into some After-life. There was no vertigo but a slow, protracted calm, deepening with each turn of the funnel. And then I saw her! On the opposite side of the funnel: miles away yet sharp as if above ground and in brightest daylight. Not Mary Elizabeth but V_____e and she was there and she was spinning with synchronous velocity that we were always opposite and though all moved we were of constant aspect with respect to each other and in fact approaching—becoming closer—with each turn of the funnel. But always out of reach. It is like the first time I saw her, on île du Palais, walking back from the "prow" of my island ship—

Abruptly I was awake in my chamber aboard the *Nautilus*, the ship beneath the sea and the sea beneath tropic sun, nary a cloud or so I imagine from zenith to horizon. The dream—as I had hoped or in some ways feared—did in that instant fade.

But I recall V_____e's face— And the weight of years, taken by the spiral of time, and from time's maelström ne'er to be reclaimed.

WE HAVE CHARTED, this time round, a route to the North Atlantic far more sane that the one that brought us here. We shall follow the path of the Roaring Forties (would that we moved by sail, and could take advantage), round Cape Horn, up past Trinidad, across the Equator (enriching, of course, the captain's butts of Madeira), up the North Atlantic, then home.

As I write we have rounded the Cape without incident and are hugging the shore of the South American continent. To our port are Salvador, Recife. The captain brought us as close to Rio as he could without risking our being sighted, then put himself near shore via skiff, as a one-man boat, a lascar at its helm, met him in mid-harbor, laden with periodicals and certain provisions. The captain wanted to reacquaint himself with the things of the world, the news of the world without touching land, without lingering any longer than was absolute necessary, that the stain of civilization not spread to his hands.

I do know that I in this journal wrote more regularly, and at greater length, in times of catastrophe, or when in the slough of despond. And I still vow to write when occasion merits. Now, though, I am being summoned to dine with the captain, to be followed, as has become our custom, with Verdelho, then sea-cheroot. Then to bed, knowing that even in my sleep each minute brings me closer to my home. And to that moment when my life, and my afterlife, having split violent and tragic in the fall of 1859, once again converge. As the Seine meets itself at the tip of the Île. As a cask of Sercial, having crossed the Equator twice, returns now, matured and ready, to Madeira.

I realize now that I have neglected to set down any record of our encounter with the blackbirders. (Perhaps neglected, viz., because not wanting it to be memorialized?) Of all the hours of my life, 'tis not the one I'd want to recall when preparing for my quietus. Yet if this journal is for uppermost thoughts, I cannot escape the obligation to here set down some words.

In naval battle, such as the world has heretofore known, the attacks they were made at night, with the advantage thereby of surprise. But now, for the first time in history as I know it or have seen it recorded, we were able to approach unnoticed in sunlight, under clear skies, as we were underneath and could not be seen from above. When we became visible, when we ascended, we were already lying abeam. The wootz of the prow and of the tower did engage with the wood of their ship, not piercing it, but conjoining our ships so that they were now, in effect, one. I stayed below, in the captain's study, while the sturdier among the crew, and some who with the captain had served in the rebellion of the sepoy, made their way out the top hatch, up the hawsers of the pirate vessel, some armed with sword, others with pistol. If the truth were to be told, I did not see them climb the hawsers, daggers clenched between teeth. But I did hear it, and I did imagine the image that would be in concordance with the sounds I did at that moment hear, of bodies on metal, bodies on wood.

What I find I have neglected to say, and do say now: that the captain was the first through the hatch and, I do believe, the first to board the thieving ship. As I am not a young man, and have no training in the military arts, or e'en fisticuffs, I remained with *Nautilus* along with a small number of sailors: a skeleton crew if you will. I was alone in the study. The iris'd window was full open, but as we were at right angles to that other ship, could see but naught.

A quarter hour or so did pass (I know this by the clock, not by sense of time internal, as time will dilate when one is in moments of love and battle). Then I heard footsteps o'erhead, and the shouts triumphant of the crew as they commenced to return. I wanted to know many details and moments of the fight on that ship as I remained safe in this one. And also: did not want to know.

Then came through the hatchway a sailor. I knew in the instant, by clothes and skin, he was not one of ours. I had thought that we had boarded their craft: were they now boarding ours? These thoughts were superseded by one more specific and pressing, viz., the sailor I had never seen had a long knife in his left hand, and was headed toward me. He then did lunge, and slash. Without reflection I did hold my arm in front of my chest to protect it and thus was my hand that was cut and not the body's core. A slash, long and deep, across the flat of my palm.

The sailor he raised his arm on high to slash anew when the expression on his visage it did change. From combatant's rage to something else. A look of odd surprise. Then within the instant he was face-down on the floor of the captain's study, and only then did I see the knife protruding from his back. And behind him, framed in the hatchway: the captain himself. Who had saved my life. E'en as the shouts from abovedeck, in subcontinental lilt and cadence, assured me that the battle was over and had been won.

Captain Nemo he did bind my wound himself, but before doing so did something that then, and now, I do find remarkable. He took self-same knife that he used to retire the man who attacked me, wiped it clean upon his waistcoat, and then did slash his own palm and held it to mine, that my blood (or small portion thereof) did now run in his veins, and an equal portion of his did now run in mine: the Captain's dusky blood in the body of your Engineer. I do not know how to think of this, or of what effect it may have, upon my thoughts and actions, as I continue to live out the days that have been given to me, the beats my heart has been allotted.

NINETEEN

————✧————

I LOOK BACK on those words above that I preprandially indited, the ink scarce dry, with a dark and bitter laugh. What madness on my part, or what stupidity (and the determination of which seems little to matter) that I did believe I was headed to port! It is enough to create in me a fury at my capacity for delusion of the self. How had I come to take his word as his bond?

The captain it seems did in Rio come by some newspapers (in Portuguese!). And in reading those periodicals did come across mention of a certain Cyrus Field, American. A magnate of telegraphy, having presided o'er the major cables of the United States, and now, with the backing of his government (the legislators thereof being, it is said, in his pocket) commencing to set down, upon the ocean's floor, a copper line between England and her former colony.

I had been previously apprised of the captain's enmity toward entities telegraphic. The cables in and among the Princely States of India were, the captain did on more than one occasion maintain, the greatest military advantage held by the British, enabling their forces to communicate in ways that the rebels could not, with the resultant victory of Crown over sepoy insurrectionaries. (Mindful of the captain's personal journey, what with loss of wife and family, I did ne'er bring up the subject of the Mutiny, and always trod lightly when he brought it up himself.) Still: the enterprise of Mr. Field seemed at far remove from any conceivable theater of engagement.

"Are you at war with the United States," I asked him.

"They—and all of civilization, to use the term they arrogate to themselves—are at war with me." He exhaled, the smoke from his sea-cheroot sucked upward toward the *Nautilus*'s much-improved ventilation. "They have made two attempts at laying such cable, and those attempts have failed. This is for them the do-or-die, and I am determined that it be the latter."

My glass drained, my sea-cheroot nearer stern than stem, I was about to excuse myself when the captain he commenced to take a chart-on-a-pole from the rack, smooth it out upon the table, and explain. "We are here. The cable runs, or will attempt to run, here: from County Kerry to Newfoundland. The ship that pays out the cable, the one that has just now left Ireland, that is the one we want."

"When I've reclaimed my life," I said to him, "you may pursue your château d'Espagne, much as I shall pursue mine."

"There isn't time," he said.

And I knew, in that instant, that I would be, will-I nill-I, subjected to any and all catastrophe the captain wished to wreak, before e'er again—as promised, as so long promised—finding home.

Outside it had begun to rain, at first lightly, then with real intensity. The captain picked up the speaking tube, issued orders for this craft—this *Nautilus*—to dive beneath.

TWENTY

————⚓————

WE WENT DEEP, sufficiently so that the storms above would not perturb. (The squall lent a fine, stippled texture to the surface of the sea as seen from below—a surface that, in other atmospheric circumstance, would be as a gentle and silvered mirror.)

But if the *Nautilus* beneath those storms was gently sleeping, I.K.B. was not. The tempests above were heard, and felt, with full threat and disturbance. Isambard Kingdom Brunel, who writes these lines, wished to curl up, become a chambered mollusk, safe within his carapace, where roil could neither penetrate nor suffuse. But these were storms within, and from that there be no shelter.

When I woke this morning I saw that something had been slipped under my door. It was a periodical, printed on thin and shiny paper, and in a language I took to be Portuguese. But if the words were for the most part beyond my ken, the meaning was not. It was the saga of the steamship they called *o Grande Oriental*, and as such was not difficult to decipher. It told her story in chapters, each complemented by appropriate gravure; and while some of these incidents were known to me in their larger contours, having been previously related third- or fourth-hand, their appearance here, in chronological order, and in a narrative designed to give to the *navio magnifico* the weight of history, could not to me have been more troubling.

- The *Great Eastern's* great sidewise launch on 3rd November 1857 (failed), on 19th November (failed), on 28th November (failed), grand crowds assembled to attend the one embarrassment after the

next—though the penury of Scott Russell, the cause of said embar-
rassments is, sadly, nowhere mentioned.

- The explosion on her maiden outing, September 1858, the details of
  which need not be dwelled upon here.
- A mutiny shortly thereafter, stemming from dispute about holystoning on Sunday. (The holystoners, as you would imagine,
  wished to honor the Lord's day of rest; the captain he did not.) The
  mutiny was put down with two months' hard labor for the ring-
  leader, two weeks in the quarry for the rest.
- Her maiden transatlantic passage in June of 1860, ten days long (not
  bad! not bad!) yet with only thirty-five paying passengers. As I did
  read this paragraph, I worked to contain choler, because the management of this ship was in no ways commensurate with the dignity of the ship herself.
- A subsequent passage from Liverpool carrying a large freight of
  fish oil, and the resultant stink when the tanks split in rough
  weather, soaking the hold with extract of cods' livers, and the seep
  through all the timbers of the ship, which was, in some respects,
  good for the wood, but whose odor did with time turn only more
  pestilential. (A good laugh, despite myself.)
- A docking in New York in 1861, where the ship's owners hoped that
  its sheer size and reputation would attract paying sight-seers, and
  drinkers too (the ship's bar, in the sixty-two-foot-long salon, was to
  be the locus of profit). Perhaps due to the *Great Eastern's* novelty
  having been exploited the year previous, and perhaps due to the
  distraction of the great Civil War, scarcely a soul, drunk or sober,
  set foot upon her decks. (Again, the choler rose, as she was built to
  transport, not to be gawked at; and the bar was there to service her
  passengers, not city dwellers in search of floating inebriation.)
- A mutiny in early 1862 when, what with most able-bodied men having been conscripted in America's war, a crew of undesirables was
  crimped into service—with predictable results once the ship left
  the Americas, and a passenger committee hastily formed to protect
  the women aboard from the black gang, less interested in stoking
  than in breaking into the liquor stores.
- The captaincy of Walter Paton, a "passenger's man" charming to

the gentlemen and even more to their ladies, who with silk tongue did the travelers enchant, but whose inability to anticipate and navigate round a squall resulted in the ship's being left without screw, paddle, rudder, helpless in the becalmed North Atlantic, and at length limping by sail back to dock in Queenstown, County Cork.

- The fitment in Queenstown of new steering tackle, and new paddlewheels—four foot smaller in diameter than the ones original to her! (And wished that droit morale, which in France gives painters perpetual say over their art, applied to those whose artistic medium is the steamship!)

- Her encounter with a submerged and unseen rock while rounding the Long Island of New York; and the subsequent heroic repair— via evacuated caisson! below the waterline!—as due to its size, no drydock was possible for her. (The rock, formerly unnamed, is now called Great Eastern, in honor of the vessel she quite nearly sank.)

Throughout all of these, and in accounts interstitial, it was possible to trace a history of *Great Eastern* after she and I did part ways. 'Twas not the history I would have imagined. Her fall from grandeur seemed at once steady and precipitous: from Miracle to Anomaly, stopping, en route, at the ports of call Grand Steamliner; Notsogrand Steamliner; Nearempty Vessel; Common Cargo Carrier; Old & Patched-Up; Laughingstock.

And I wondered if my life—had my life been allowed to continue as planned—might have sailed a parallel course. Would I now be seen as Isambard Kingdom Dunderhead, father of the Washed-Up Leviathan? Would I by now be a figure in my own wax museum, gesturing toward the gangway of a ship that no longer sailed, but was instead some double-hulled public house, serving up whiskey-by-paddlewheel?

But my musings as to what humiliations might have been in store for I.K.B. had the reputations of I.K.B. and his ship been for the past five years yoked together were soon put to abrupt halt. I followed the article to an interior page, set in finer type, and read—inasmuch as I do not have Portuguese—that my *Great Eastern*, her grand paddlewheel replaced by one of random diameter, her grand salon hacked out to accommodate cargo, had fallen yet again. Was now no longer liner nor merchant ship but worse: *a cable-layer*. And engaged in that task was about to set out from Foilhummerum, Valentia, Ireland. Massive spools of twisted copper in tow. On a mission to lay on the sea's bed a line between old world and new at the behest of Mr. Field.

It did not take an excess of empathy to feel for the ship, given the depredations to which it had been subjected. It did not take an excess of imagination to realize—nay, to *know*—that we were now en route to destroy Mr. Field's cable. Knowing the captain's disregard for innocent life, it would not be large leap to say that he would have no hesitation in deploying Isambard Kingdom Brunel's *Nautilus* to engage Isambard Kingdom Brunel's *Great Eastern* in sea-battle. My mightiest creation, and my most ingenious one, set upon one another. I know, now, why the captain had given me this sheaf of Portuguese newsprint to read. It fills my heart with no little sadness, and more dread than the soul can carry.

If the *Nautilus* were to be pitched against the *Great Eastern*, 'tis an engagement I cannot imagine this craft—perhaps one-hundredth the mass of my great iron ship—to survive.

And if I know one thing to a certainty, it is that Isambard Kingdom Brunel, at yesterday morning's sunrise a man with liberty within his grasp, will ne'er again find home. If in sea-battle the *Great Eastern* were to make short work of a sub-marine attacker I would be deprived of my life. But also: would be made free.

LET US NOW close our engineer's journal, leaving its pages to rest within their buckram binding, and bid for the moment an au revoir to our Mr. Brunel: his dilemma at this juncture neatly stated, deeply felt.

Let us take up our story, then, from another vantage: that of our sea captain Mr. John Ahab, as he steers unknowingly into battle with his nemesis, recently re-christened: outfitted by our Engineer; captained by our Prince.

We have reached the point where the destination is closer than the departed port. There is no harbor here, no turning back. The horizon is flat all round with neither shore nor human construction to offer hope, shelter, salvation. Out here there is naught save the voice of John Ahab, lone and only, John Ahab, whom now we shall allow to speak.

TWENTY-ONE

A.

Ye heard me: *A.*

First letter of the God-damned alphabet. *A.* No letter before it. First one. When they only needed one, it was *A.* Quick, mates: who's the first man? Adam. And what's his first letter? *A.* Mine the same. *A*-hab. Accent on the first. Not a-HAB, like ye were making to sneeze. No, not that. *A*-hab. Starts with the first letter, which is A. Are ye getting me? Are ye getting what Ahab is saying to ye about First Things? Later we can talk about Last Things. But that be later. And maybe we won't talk about them at all. For now just say the name, will ye? Ahab! There ye go. John Ahab! Ye might make it yet. Ha! Ye might not.

Say my name and be gone with ye. But say it right, man, or ye'll be taking a stick and I'll be jamming it up yer bunghole. And ye'll be whining like the stuck pig and Ahab will yawp. Big and loud. Like an A-merican (*no accident there!*). When they only needed one letter the letter was A. Eons pass. Then BCD. Then all the other woman letters. Letters weak with blub. With bla. With blab. With the blabble of women at a table. Ye don't need words if ye've got yer *A.* Ahab. Adam. America. What more needs be said? Do not mess with an American lest ye be reamed. Remember that all thy days and thou shalt not go wrong. But make the missed step or defy Ahab's word or mock yer Ahab in his person then Ahab he doth say

Ha! He doth say

Aha! He doth say

Ahab!

And ye, as ye mewl, can say it too. Ahab. Where the death wind meets the sea.

IF YE KNOW yer Ahab, Captain John Ahab, captain now of the ship *Valparaiso*, escort to the Great Iron Boat, if ye know him at all ye know then that he absented himself from the public foofaraw round the arrival and departure of said Great Iron Boat in Foilhummerum. Yer Ahab, he joined the mission but later, at the Splice. Field, he'd wanted Ahab to be with them in Foilhummerum to participate in celebration abysmal. Parade of dignitaries. Perorations as the sundial sweeps. Hosannas of civic pride. Solemn, ragged parades of specta-tors. Here massed, here missing, juts and gaps, a sailor's scurvy'd smile. Tents made of old sails. Pipers and fiddlers, so help me God. Itinerant gamesters doing good business with the Spoil-Five. And the marks upon whom they preyed, eyes turned away from the game toward the horizon.

Why so turned? Why so gathered? To see the *Great Eastern*! Not to see but to have seen. Stories for the grandchildren: Once I saw a giant ugly iron paddlewheel railway-built floating contrivance right here in Foilhummerum Bay I did I did. Did you really Grandfather? Yes I really. May I then adore you Grandfather? Yes you may—and will you sit upon your grandfather's lap, little girl little girl?

Why Ahab would want to witness such a foul corrupted gathering is a question so fathomless as to have no bottom. As ye know: Ahab he does not want to be on land. Accordingly Ahab told one thing and did another. Ahab will see, Mr. Field, if Ahab can join thee. That's what Ahab said. That's not what Ahab did. To Mr. Field the pomp and vulgarity were as precious ambergris. To Ahab, as whale vomit.

So I'll not tell ye of the festivities at Berehaven where the un-gainly Leviathan first made land. Of the screw-steamer *Caroline* she had in tow. Of how the tow-rope broke, and how the *Caroline* had to make her own way to Valentia under strong gale winds and upon a heavy sea. Nor of the laying of the earth cable and its labori-ous attachment to the ass-end of the sea cable on the cliffs above the tedious town whose name we have repeated so often it will not again be mentioned. Nor of the paying out of the cable from the prow of one ship to the stern of the next, from the *Caroline* to her sister steam-screw ship the *Hawk*, up to the instrument house. Nor of the mindless, endless round of Orations, odes upon the Greatness of the Occasion, culminating in the valedictory of the Knight of Kerry, whose unbounded salute to the Queen and to the President of the United States lent nothing to the enterprise, yet subtracted mightily from the store of human contentment.

No, these ye will not hear from Ahab as Ahab was not present. No fool, Ahab. He met them, rather, at the Splice, some miles out from Foilhummerum, where he needn't have waking hours or sea-borne dreams troubled by lubbers in antic array. No, it was not until the hip-heavy Leviathan made the Splice, her cable to the one hauled from Ireland in relay by the steam-screws aforementioned, 51°50', N., Long 11°2'20" W., watched on by the *Hawk*; by Her Majesty's sloop-of-war the *Sphinx*; by the *Terrible*, whose state of repair echoed its name; and of course mine own ship, mine own. So damn many escorts, so little yield! The town wallflower taken to the ball by a sextet of lolly'd-up gents, each more eager than the next to quit the premises. The combined folly of Mr. Brunel and Her Majesty's government knows no equal in the world contemporary, or e'en in the world historic. Ahab is an American and as an American he laughs at them, he laughs upon rising, he laughs yet again just before embracing the arms of Morpheus. Nor doth he conceal his laughter. Ahab is from the New World, father, and if his manners be crude, his way of speaking rough, his stride long, his reverence lacking, why then, come at us again! And see if ye fare better this time round.

Capt. Anderson of the *Great Misshapen* said that there was eating and drinking to be done and so dispensed the hospitalities of his ship in a kind and genial way. This too was an evening at which Ahab was not in attendance. Ahab was not hired to be social nor to befriend the captain of that large and accursèd craft. He was hired to protect the cable from the Leviathan—and so the obligation was to the enterprise, not to any of its associated ships and crew.

Ahab is the captain of but one ship, this one. His task is to stand vigilant, then to strike. His other task: to protect his own crew. Doth ye hear me, mates? Ahab will not let ye be harmed. Unless there is no choice. But in circumstances that dark, that dire, we are all of us done for. Will ye see Ahab pulling from the heavy seas the bodies of crew aboard the G____ E_____? Not until his own men are first secured. Every man jack, down to yer holystoner.

And what did they eat aboard the iron-hulled sea-sloth? It was not salt that they ate. Not pemmican, not bacalao, not any of the sad and tawdry victuals that we seamen eat, no. They ate lamb! Lamb from Ireland, though it was July! They ate pheasant! Pheasant fresh-killed, neither salted nor iced, slide yer finger boys between gum and teeth to extract the lead shot. They ate salmon, not the smoked variety beloved by the Russians and the Jews, not the brined variety beloved by the Laplanders, no, it was salmon, boys, fresh from the sea, and scaled, and boned, and tossed over a fire, and ate just like that. Later they had fancy French dessert consisting of meringue (the white of the egg, no yolks at all whipped then baked); and caramel (that's burnt sugar, me boyos!). All shaped and fancied and set down on a bed of crème anglaise. (That's English cream and fuck ye all.)

What did they drink with the meal just described? Why they drank wine! They drank Bord'eaux, which in the manner of the creamy English they called Claret. The captain Anderson, he being a man of refined taste don't ye know, he pulled from his store some red Burgundies. And then they drank Madeira, from butts and casks that had twice crossed the equator. There was a Malmsey, yes, and a Bual, too. And of course the liberal application of Grog, because yer sailor, don't ye know, likes nothing better than to be bathed in Rum. Why the Rum? Because it comes from Barbados, and the islands nearby, where they were given it, in exchange for African cargo. Ye get the Africans, we get the Rum!

That's commerce, lads. Who makes that commerce possible? Sailors we! Who makes the profit! There are many answers to that one, lads, but among them is not thee. Nor thee. Nor Ahab. The elaborated dance of freight doth cross the seas of the globe, and in London and New York they celebrate with the proceeds while we sail on. 'Tis the way. And woe to he that questions why, or lifts up the lid to see what lies beneath.

And now ye be wondering: Ahab, he says he stayed aboard his own ship, no venturing onto that of Capt. Anderson—yet he doth seem to know, and know in some detail, what was et and what was drunk. How can that be? Doth he have telescopes so full of power that they see through doubled-iron hull? Can he tell just by sound, by the scrape of fork 'gainst china, what be the victual emitting such frequency? No, and no. Or if he can, Ahab not be telling ye, that is for sure and certain. If Ahab have the Powers, Ahab be saving that knowledge for his Self.

No, Ahab knows on 'count of Ahab sent his crew. Ahab will not dine with electricians aboard a floating railway car. But he treasures his afterguard almost above himself. So when the skiff came he saw them aboard it, each of them and every last man Jack, so that they might eat, and drink, and celebrate the Splice. He sent the sturdy, honest Evander Jaques, a first mate as was his father before him, out of New Bedford. He sent Ed and Vin and Jonesy Jones, his bowline-pullers. He sent his carpenter, named Chips. (Was he called Chips because he was a carpenter, or did he become a carpenter because his name was Chips? The mysteries of the sea!) He sent his boatsteerers, his swabbers, his polishers. (Yes they have names, but Ahab shall not here name them.) He sent his binnacle man and his sheet man. (Like-wise.) He even sent Langhorne, his chanteyman, who otherwise would have stayed on the *Valparaiso*, the better to entertain his Ahab with mellifluous song.

Reuben was no sailor,
Ranzo, boys, Ranzo
Reuben was a tailor;
Ranzo, boys, Ranzo

Ranzo joined The Beauty,
Ranzo, boys, Ranzo
And did not know his duty:
Ranzo, boys, Ranzo

They called Ranzo a lubber,
Ranzo, boys, Ranzo
And made him eat whale blubber;
Ranzo, boys, Ranzo

The Beauty *was a whaler,*
Ranzo, boys, Ranzo

Ranzo was no sailor;
Ranzo, boys, Ranzo

They set him holy stoning,
Ranzo, boys, Ranzo
And cared not for his groaning;
Ranzo, boys, Ranzo

So: four mates, four boatsteerers, carpenter, cooper, steward, chanteyman, and cook. But Ahab he stayed alone, as was his custom and wont, dining on salted meat, or was it meated salt. And did without song, save the borborygmus of his own guts and entrails. And did without fun, save the satisfactions of solitude.

True, after his repast he came abovedecks, and considered at length the moon, waning gibbous, and those stars whose view the northern latitudes do afford. They shone down upon him, distant, white, remote, uncaring, arraying themselves in ways that meant much to the Ancients, and to Ahab not a thing at all. They mayswell have been crystals of salt spilled atop a black tablecloth.

And so at ten post meridiem, Greenwich time, Sunday, 3rd July, after a dinner aboard the *Ate Greasetern* of which he did not partake, and well-made wine he did not drink, yer captain watched as the crew of that ship, bellies full, heads aswim in good Madeira and bad Grog, payed out the cable, discharging it slow and deliberate over the stern of the ship. From tight coil to long lazy strand, metal dipped in gutta-percha, arcing low, into the sea, then beneath it, to lay against the bottom of the sea, where it would ne'er be disturbed. Not until the very end of Time. To which Ahab doth say, and ye say with him: ha!

NOW THERE'S HAWSER-LAID rope. The kind ye know, likely as not. (Though, upon thought, ye may know nothing.) The hawser, it's three strand, meaning three ropes coiled into one. Now the three ropes can be coiled in a pair of ways. There's with the clock and against it. The turn to the right and the turn to the left. When yer with the clock what do we call that? We call that coiled with the sun.

Because that is the way of the sun across the sky. When yer anti-clock what do we call that? We do not call it anything, ye royal termagant! Why? Because we only coil with the sun. We are sailors and we do things the way they are done.

Four strand, now that's a thicker rope. What do we call it? We call it shroud-laid. Also with the sun, because and &c. But with four.

Shroud is what we use to wrap the dead. But yer shroud rope ain't about death. Least not always. 'Tis a thicker rope for the harder tasks. Sheets. Tacks. Rigging. Do we call it a shroud-laid rope? We do not. Do we call it a plain rope? Nope. We don't call it a rope, be it three strand or four, coiled with the sun or contra. A rope to us is: a line. We don't care what it's of. Just what it does. From Manila that's all well and good but we don't want yer history yer stories yer palaver-blahver about the bent-over brown men who gather the strands— When we need to pull a sail 'gainst the wind we need a line. That's all. Line. Four letters describing the short path between two points. That's a line to Euclid and it's a line to any Argonaut. Didn't think yer Ahab knew his Classics? Well jam the pole in yer own sad self!

Then there's cable-laid. That's for cables, ha. And cables is why we're here. Ahab and all who serve Ahab. The ship that carries 'em. The other ships that escort it. All here because of cables. Cable-laid cable. And what do we mean? Children, what do we mean? Cable-laid means more than four. Could be five. Could be six. Could be an orang-utan for all the fuck we care. More than four is cable-laid and shut yer gaping hole.

The cable here is made of copper. Wound into ropes and then the ropes wound together. But then: wrapped in gutta-percha. From Malay. Sap of a tree what grows there. A liquid and then it's not. Electricity won't go through it. Fish won't eat it. Bends when it has to. Man named Chatterton mixed it with tar. Stockholm tar! Some rosin, too, who knows what else. Then called it his own: Chatterton's compound! Well hell and baloo! We know what it is. Gutta-percha, plain and simple, with some shit mixed in. Chatterton we don't need thee! Stop sticking thy name where it doth not belong. Ahab says: When they write in history's book they'll be calling it gutta-percha. *Yer gone, Chatterton!* And not coming back as long as some tree in Malay has the thick sweet sap.

The thing out here is water. Have to be blind not to see it. Deaf not to hear it. The other thing out here is the salt. Ye can smell it and ye can taste it. Can ye hear salt? Mayhaps! Ahab he doth hear it in the water, one tiny piece of salt bumping up against its brother. Ahab hears all.

Also: can taste it. Because without the salt: the rot. What is pemmican? It's the meat with all the wet drained out of it. Drained by what? Drained by salt. Keeps forever. Maggots won't eat it. We eat it. Because we're sailors we are. Surrounded by salt water and they make us eat salt! Where's the logic in that? 'Tis the logic of the insane. The boot in the face. Whose boot? Their boot. Whose face? Our face. No. Yer face. My face is here, laughing at ye, ye orang-utan pemmican eater! Ye muncher of bacalao! Any civilized country, anywhere on land, bacalao they soak it first. For hours. For days. We, we chew it dried. We feast on desiccated shit.

But we do it for a reason.

Reason is, there's this cable. Cable-laid! Of copper! Of gutta-percha and shut up, Chatterface! And it breaks. Because things break. Because of currents. Because who knows what's at the bottom of the sea. Currents, there is nil ye can do anent. Breakage random—again, there is nil ye can do anent. The unknown bottom of the North Atlantic? Well we don't know, do we? And if we don't know— Ye got it this time. Sing along with me: there is nil ye can do anent.

But maybe— Just maybe— Because of the Leviathan. Can ye do against the Leviathan? Is there agency, against the Leviathan? Mayhaps. And if there be anyone who can, why then, it's Ahab. Aha! And so Ahab helms the ship next to the ship that lays the cable. And ye be here with me, only belowdecks, and eating pemmican. I've smelled it down there. Smells like shit. No. Smells like salt. Here e'en shit smells like salt. Heaven save us all.

As to the Why of this ye already know. Yer Ahab has been paid. He hath been compensated to be yer captain. Yes, compensated! Dost thou think thy Ahab labors for the emolument of his own joy? Dip thy wick in a vat of lye. He is paid to watch for Leviathans and when seen to kill them. So that the outward tranquility of the cable-laid cable, and the electric turbulence within, shall continue unperturbed. That an eructation in Ireland will by electricity be known in Newfoundland e'en before the smell leaves the room.

And so we sail, and so we labor, and so we watch. And so we breathe the salted air and eat the salted meat, cracking our teeth and drying our souls, 'til we are as dry inside as wet out. And so we take a thick portion of our God-given days and hand them over to Mr. Field. Those of us whose home is on land, we yearn for home; and those of us of no fixed abode, why then, we curse the sea. We quarrel over matters small and ne'er speak of matters large. We haul the lines and trim the sails and watch the northern sun dip below the rim of the gray sea as each sundown follows the one before. And if we are so fortunate as to encounter the Leviathan why then we all shall die. And all in service of a fart in Foilhummerum.

Let us now review. Should it be the random fault— Should it be the currents— Should it be the bottom of the sea— Then we're here for naught. The cable, it'll hold, it'll hold not. Matters not what we say. Matters not what we do. But! Should it be the whale, the white whale, the great white whale— Then we all shall fight it to the death. So. We be without purpose, without use, taking the time allotted to us and pouring it down the sinkhole. Or. We be with purpose and be doomed. Those be yer choices. End of first day's lesson, ha!

Now let's eat some salt and shit some salt. Have ye e'er drank blood? Yer own blood, or the blood of others? Blood of others is sweeter of course. But what does blood taste like? Like salt. Like salt water. Like the sea. What is a body, what is a human body? A nice little boat made out of ocean. Once ye know that— Aha. Ye know all.

Ahab lied. When Ahab said we all would die? Ahab lied. Well in a way Ahab did not lie. Because we're all going to die. Hell we're dying now. Each breath is one subtracted from the number granted. Each beat of the heart one less before that poor muscle says *no mas*. (Yes and Ahab he doth speak Spanish too ye landbound blubberwub!) So that's been settled afore we were born.

But the lie— The lie was this. I said that should Leviathan be out there we would all perish. Yes and no. Most of us will perish. Die in bad ways. Salt water in the lungs. 'Til ye be dead of thirst in the middle of an ocean. But not all of us will die. Exempli gratia: Ahab shall not. Ahab shall not perish. Twice before Ahab hath met this beast. Twice before the beast almost got the best of Ahab. Note that word. Almost. Denotes what? Triumph! Had the Leviathan triumphed would ye be hearing these words? No ye would not. Unless this conversation be conducted in Hell.

So: ye may die but Ahab will endure. 'Tis what Ahab does. And this time mayhaps Ahab shall stab the Leviathan in the head and pull the blade down and across and up and across and down again. 'Til oil and life come gushing out and flooding out and slicking the sea with oil and blood and entrails. Until the Leviathan troubles the waters of the earth no more— And Ahab sails home.

But!

Home hath Ahab not!

So we sayeth instead: *And Ahab sails on.*

TWENTY-TWO

―――――⚓―――――

THE CAPTAIN NEMO he was in his salon among his things. The purpose-built organ (on which he had, just moments ago, been playing Bach's *Pastoral in F-Major*); a Niépce photoplate, coated with bitumen of Judea, on which one might, in certain lights, see an etched depiction of a woman with her children, one boy, one girl: positive, now negative, floating just above the polished surface, all that remained of family. The iris'd window; the mechanical Turk; the clock whose orrery contained a specific ivory moon, one that had traveled long to arrive at this place, and to whose microscopic crenellations adhered a lifetime of emotion.

What occupied him now were the charts upon his chart table, each on a long wooden stick, unrolled now near-flat. The *Nautilus* was in the North Atlantic and the charts reflected that. They were detailed in latitude and longitude, marked on by hand with the deeper currents, with outcroppings of rock and coral. Nemo's own charts were now augmented by plots that laid out the more common shipping routes; several Lists of Lights, giving the locations of known lighthouses; tide tables, and a tidal stream atlas; and various ephemerides, as an aid to celestial navigation (including the Alfonsine Tables, and the Prutenic Tables that succeeded them).

His most prized chart was by the king's hydrographer, a position established after Admiral Cloudesley Shovell died off the Scilly Isles in October of 1707 following the collision of his ship with a hitherto-uncharted reef. The King decreed that such a loss would never again occur, appointed a Hydrographer Royal. And to this day the United

Kingdom Hydrographic Office charts the seas and what lies beneath them with unparalleled precision and reach.

As Nemo pored and perused he was animated by a sole desire: to extrapolate from what was known the present position of the cable ship; to chart a course intersecting; to sever what cable payed out behind, so that the current endeavor, like so many before it, would be declared failure; and, if possible, to sever the cable in deeper seas, beyond the coastal shelf, so that any subsequent attempts at salvage would come to naught. It would be preferable to sever the cable and have the ship return home in defeat; if that not be possible, Nemo would then prevent the ship from returning.

He knew even as he studied the plots and tables that were he to sink the cable ship he would be causing loss of life and not in insignificant measure. But this was not a factor in his calculations, nor did it trouble his moral sense. The murder of his children, the death of his wife, the annexation of his state, the slaughter of his countrymen, all of them weighed so heavily upon his balance that no matter where the fulcrum were placed a few English or American lives could scarcely cause disequilibrium. A life, a hundred lives, a thousand lives, were as the twinkling of distant celestial bodies, had all the weight of starlight. He was determined that the cable enterprise fail, and with such resonance fail that it would be attempted ne'er again.

His first encounter with the world of telegraphy was one of cryptographic tenderness: a message from Madhya, encoded from prying or intervening eyes via the Hoe & Co. telegraph chart, of which chart more shall be said anon. Later, when the Prince was in Cambridge, he did again correspond with Madhya via telegraph, using other shorthands of their own devise. His missives would be taken to a telegraph office and from there transmitted in turn to London, to Paris, thence by rail and other conveyances overland to Geneva, Milan, Zagreb, Plovdiv, Ankara, Baghdad, Tehran, Karachi. They would take weeks or even months to arrive, and at times the missives would, due to the travails of the transit, be lost in entirety. Other times the transit would be by sea, from London to Bombay, thence by train or carriage. This was a more certain route but could

be delayed by vagaries in the weather, and by stops en route necessitated by commerce.

To the young Prince the telegraph was an instrument for conveying, over long distance, love's exquisite sentiments, its longings, its
gratifications. The idea that the telegraph might be purposed as an
instrument of commerce, empire, dominion occurred to him sec-
ondarily, if at all.

The full force of telegraphy would hit him only later, in the
1850s, when the Honourable Company began its annexations. It was
as much conquest by wire as by militia—an insight rendered acute
when, in 1857, the Company offered £20,000 a year for a cable, spanning the Red Sea, from London to India. The prince realized that
with one swift clip he could do as much damage to empire as with a
regiment of fusiliers. Accordingly, when the *Neptune* departed Bombay on her maiden voyage, she headed west into the Erythraean
Sea, across Sindhu Sagar, around Aden, and up into the Red Sea.
The cable, he had been told by sympathetic lascars, ran from Suez
to Kossier to Suakin to Aden, with a supplementary run from
Aden to Karachi via Hallani and Muscat. The undersea run from
Suakin to Aden was not the shortest or most direct route across the
Red Sea route but was the one, given the colors of the map, deemed
by the Company the most geopolitically feasible. It was not hard
for *Neptune*—even within her limited capabilities—to submerge,
approach the cable underwater, and then, with pantograph arm, in
several places to sever it.

The proposition seemed simple to him. Wherever the spider of
empire sought to weave her web Nemo would snap it. Wherever
news was conveyed more quickly than a man could carry it, Nemo
would slow it down. He knew from the battles in his own land, he
knew from efforts of the Candiotes against Ottoman rule, that rapid
communication could only aid the overlord. If you kill an Englishman, another grows in his place. But if you keep the Englishman
here from making known his wish to the Englishman there, you've
won a battle without shot being fired.

In Nemo's mind, there was even more to it. What made Bundelkhand its own world was its distance from other realms. His palace was not just nine miles from Jhansi, it was three hours. Jhansi

was not just 650 miles from Bombay, it was nine days if you did not for a moment cease your walking, two or three times that if you paused for rest and sustenance. Imagine, Nemo thought, if the news (good for the Habsburg Netherlands, bad for Spain) appeared at Aix the very moment it transpired in Ghent— The rebellion would have been over before it had scarce begun.

And if the Atlantic were no longer barrier between there and here? If the Pacific could be spanned in moments? If each toll of the Lutine Bell were heard not only in the Underwriting Room of Lloyd's, but all over London, and the Continent, and down to Bombay, and across to Boston, and in Peking and Djakarta, and Osaka and Auckland, the second toll rung before the first had ceased to echo?

That would be a world in which empire would ne'er again be defeated. Worse: a world in which all habit, custom, distinction, cuisine, language, visage, sport, pleasure, devotion— Musical scales, decorative jars, the clouds that scud, the clouds that linger— The feel of sisal fibres on the rug that leads to the bedroom— The sound the Betwa river makes when its banks o'erflow, and the sound the Betwa river makes in drought, when it is all but dry— The high musk that seeps from beneath various bedchamber doors, only years later associated with sex— The dull clang of large pots as they are being washed just outside the Palace walls— The hot and foetid breath of the cow when it yawns— The Jermyn Street cologne worn by officers of the Company, designed to convince them they'd not left home, when every sight and smell and sound that hypothesis would contradict— The place visited with a trusted childhood friend, small and dark and damp, that was known to no one else, and never would be, under oath and on pain of death— The aroma of your amah's kitchen, which is all we know of home.

Could ne'er again be sacred.

These were Dakkar's memories but surely each of us holds on to a thought, a notion, a thing—a badge of time and place—whose meaning would be lost were it to be worldly shared. Whatever, for you, be the flower that only in the Andes blooms, and even there but once in each fifteen years— In this world we have tiger here, and lion there; the elephant here, and rhinoceros there— But in the telegrapher's kingdom all beasts would be Company beasts; all places would be

Company places; and all time, too— Until noon in San Francisco were as midnight in Bombay.

And soon all of it, rolled up in one large tarpaulin, as big as a map of the world, as big as the world itself; and all people places things bound up in it, and the whole thing tied together—tight, knotted, inescapable—with thick winds of copper cable. No. That was not the world Dakkar grew up in and not, were he to have a say in it, the world that would inherit this one.

The depredations of his own time were bad enough. He'd make it his ambition—his life, really—that when the sun set upon this century and rose upon the next, there would be as much spirit, variety and distance as there were in it this very evening, here, beneath the waves of the unanimous sea: the sea that separates, better than all else, that land from this one. He knew, our Prince and Captain did, and knew deep: that where missionaries landed, soon would come rum merchants, and soon after the slave traders. Let them ply their evil if they might. But let them do it in person, where they'd not be immune to slaughter or revolt. They should not have the ability to enslave by wire.

And so when Nemo's time on this planet came to end, when he was laid down in his watery grave—for there was nowhere, not e'en the Betwa River where it flows beneath the Orchha Palace in Bundelkhand, that he could now call home—he wanted to descend in peace, knowing that what was cooked by amahs in the palace of his childhood gave out tastes and smells that were, in their precise mix and pungency, elsewhere unknown. That to eat the food of Devi's kitchen one would have to journey by sea and rail and horse and foot. And that once eaten, the tastes and smells, they would be transported, if at all, by memory alone. The traceries of mind within the cerebella of those who'd had the good fortune that unique ambrosia to eat. And if you had not been there, all you would know would be the fine and distant song, passed from mouth to ear to mouth to ear, o'er space and yes, over time— The way it should be. And the way it would remain, as long as *Nautilus* sailed, as long as Nemo were alive.

The mechanics of Nemo's quest for the cable were neither abstruse nor difficult—a matter of applying compass and straightedge, then some basic calculations. This is where the telegraphic cable has been, is; therefore, this is where it will be. This is where *Nautilus* is now, and this is where it needs to go in order to be where the cable boat will be then.

His thoughts now turned to what he thought of as the Other Question—should the large ship not be deterred, how to take her down. Can the *Nautilus*'s serrated prow pierce the *Great Eastern*'s underbelly? What are the weaknesses of that craft, the ways in which, by odd design or by time's depredations, she might be vulnerable? What are the strengths of the ship—and how can those strengths be used 'gainst her?

In most questions of engineering the captain would of course consult Huzoor, whose mind was more nimble in these aspects than that of anyone on the waves, or e'en, perhaps, the planet entire. Nemo had conversed with Huzoor in the past, once Huzoor had got past the willed silence of captivity. E'er since *Nautilus* was *Nautilus*, Huzoor had been of invaluable assistance in matters nautical, and, on one or two occasions, matters tactical. (The captain did believe that he'd even got Huzoor to remember that his own heritage, and a vital chunk of his youth, were not English but French. And for a Parisian to take up 'gainst an Englishman—why that was not a unique occurrence.)

But there was an added difficulty here. That being: they were not, here, engaged in abstract aid to the Candiotes rebels. They were not, here, plundering some ship anonymous on high seas. The cable-layer in this instance was no broke-down tramp of little name and less distinction. Rather it was the *Great Eastern*. The captain did not spend overmuch time taking into consideration the feelings of other men. But he could certainly see how Huzoor might be reluctant to assist in any attack upon that large and ferrous masterwork.

TWENTY-THREE

———⚓———

THERE'S A BOAT and there's a ship. Boat's a little thing. Ye could sit in it. Stand up in it have ye the balance. What do boats do? They rock. Pitch. Yaw. Boat floats on the sea. Sea gets troubled, boat is troubled. Sea is calm and boat just glides. But! More likely yer former. Why? 'Cause the sea's the sea.

Boats are what we lower from a ship.

What's a ship? Ye ask twenty men ye get forty different answers. But ye asked me, so ye will get my answer: Ship floats on the water and is propelled by the wind. That's a ship. Doesn't float? Then: not a ship! Not propelled by wind? Then: not a ship. This case is closed.

But— But— What to do about this ship? Not the one Ahab is on, the *Valparaiso*. Ahab did not build her. Ahab did not name her. Had Ahab named her she would have had another name. But they built her in Chile and named her after the city where she were built. Tant piss.

Is the *Valparaiso* a ship of greatness? That she is not. She has a stern that could as well be a prow, a prow that could well be a stern— She's a seafaring palindrome. Masts straight up. Deck flat from stem to stern, or stern to stem as case may be. Wheel fixed by shaft to the tiller, that the helm itself slides, side-to-side, as the captain wills his ship. Ye know not how to ride the wheel, ye'll be leaving great lazy *Ss* in yer wake.

Is this the once-great *Valparaiso*, now on in years, and slowly gliding toward her final dry dock? No, she not be that. Yer *Valparaiso*, she was rot-bucket built and rot-bucket remains— And rot-bucket will be until the seas dry up and Mankind, what's left of it, walks on dry cracked kelp. *Valparaiso*'s pumperman works around the clock to keep her from taking on more water than he can expel. A ship fit for Ahab? Ahab he doth want to hear the chorus of no, he doth want to hear it loud and uniform, no and no and no, all in cadence, with harmony if ye will, but above all, no. And if there be among ye one who is silent on this question, let me have thy tongue, that thou shalt be silent evermore.

The ship that *Valparaiso* escorts— Why that ain't really a ship, is it? It is big, we will give her this. Ye could fit six, eight, ten *Valparaisos* in her hold. Her *boats*, as big as my *ship*. But is yer *Great Eastern* as big as the Leviathan itself? The answer is no. Nothing is as big as the Leviathan itself. But! This ship was called the *Leviathan*. When they were building it. Not no more. Now she sails as *Great Eastern*. No improvement if ye ask yer Ahab.

The *Great Eastern* she was a passenger ship. And she never sunk, we'll give her that. Ye are waiting for the caveat because ye be smart. And here is the caveat. The *Great Eastern* not a ship! Not if ye go by Ahab's definition. What be a ship? Floats on water propelled by wind. Yer *Great Eastern* floats, yes, on water, yes, propelled by wind— Some of the time! Other of the time, by paddle! So it can be a ship but ain't always, at least as Ahab calls 'em.

Great Eastern is a sea-going vessel. Used to haul passengers. Doth ye recall the glory? Were ye there in 1860 when the President and "Miss Lane" (the first lady in all but conjugality, and about that, we ponder, we ponder) traveled by rail from the capitol to Annapolis? Went out on the screw-tender Anacostia a full five miles out, where the *Great Eastern* lay at anchor? When aforesaid Anacostia did salute her with guns one-and-twenty? Those were, me lads, the days. Then ha! And bang! And boom! Dost ye hear the explosion, reverberating through the years? The explosion of gold coins, flying out from the investor's coffers, up in the air, 'til the skies be rainbowed with reflective coin? What do they say in France? They say, waouah! And Ahab says with them, waouah! And ye can now say with me: waouah!

So: yer *Great Eastern*, bought on the cheap. Just like Ahab? No not just like Ahab. Ahab be in his prime. For what Ahab doeth? Ahab be just the right age. What doth Ahab do? He kills. Do ye want yer young killer, gone all simple with the spree of it? Ye do not. Do ye want yer killer in the midst of life, shaken and quaken with the remorse? Ye do not. Or do ye want yer Ahab? Knows the art. Does it. Receives no pleasure from it. That's what ye want. Yer practiced and unsmiling killer. And that's what ye have. Ahab would kill ye. Not for the fun of it, for killin' ain't fun. Because he can.

And kill a whale as soon as look at it. More than just because. On account of leg &c don't ye know. For what's better than a practiced killer? A killer practiced and motivated!

So back to the Q: why paddle wheels? To move when the sea is becalmed. The other way— The true ship's way— Is to wait for yer wind to come up. Which it does. Always does. We ain't yet been in a place where the wind don't move forever. Sometimes the wind it takes a nap. But what's that?

The other reason for the paddles is paddles don't need much draft. So yer *Great Eastern* could go up the Hooghly. That was the idea. But she ain't never gone up the Hooghly and now she's a broke-down cable tramp. Built for Calcutta and never seen it. Ahab's seen Calcutta. Seen enough of it. Building a ship just so that ship could go to Calcutta? Ahab will not even utter his opinion. Reason 'cause: ye knows it already.

Also: a ship, like a man, must needs make up its mind! 'Tis the one, or 'tis t'other. But choose, man! Make a selection and stick to it. Sails or engines, both have their place. But! On the same ship? Let me ask. Do ye know the French? Of course ye do. Do ye know what they mean when they say *à voile et à vapeur*? (Didn't know Ahab spoke French? Well Ahab can speak any language on the face of the Earth. The dead ones, too. That's why he's Ahab.) When they say that of a man. When they say *à voile et à vapeur*? They mean, he travels by sail and by steam. And what do they mean, "he travels by sail and by steam"? Here be a hint: ye don't have to know yer French, ye just have to know yer men!

Is this all Ahab has to say about the *Great Eastern*? No, 'tis not. 'Twould be enough! But that ain't all. For when one speaks of the *Great Eastern*, there be ONE MORE MATTER worthy of discourse— And that be the matter of celestial grace.

We all of us knows Proportion when we see it. To some it is the Euclidean solids: the cube, the sphere, the tetrahedron—and the interplay amongst 'em when engaged in dance of beauty. Crystals of salt! The sun and the pyramid! &c &c!

To others, it be the Golden Mean. The ratio at the end of the Fibonacci rainbow. Three is to five, five is to eight, eight is to thirteen, thirteen to twenty one, twenty one— A is to B as A + B is to A! And after a while ye get yer Leonardo, ye get yer art, ye get yer beauty! So of what is beauty born? The mathematics of the stars! And what exhibits this beauty? The undulations of the coral reef. When we say sinuous, we mean sine! The proportions of the sea creature, from the bulge of the head to the incurved waist through the scoop and efflorescence of the tail. The beauty of the night sky, reflected in the mathematics of fish! Though ye may think him daft, Ahab doth tell ye that Proportion is at the center of all Beauty; and that Beauty ain't mere whim but the heart of Essence— And recto verso: Beauty be the essence of the Heart.

Now gaze upon yer *Great Eastern*. Dost thou see Proportion? Dost thou see Ratio, in ways that pay tribute to the Night Array of Stars? To the crystal of salt, to the diamond discovered in dark mine, to the pyramid and the sun above it? The *Great Eastern*, do her curves quicken the heart? The honest man would say: no, and no, and no, and no, and no. What one sees is this: the usual array of sails, but proportioned in ungainly fashion, with the jib too far forward and the mainsail too far back— Why? Because they cared more about the Engine than about the sail. Why? Because the man what built the *Great Eastern* was not a sailor. No he was not. He was not a man of the sea. No he was not. He was a civil engineer! We'll say it again, all five syllables sticking in this sailor's parched throat: civil engineer! A man of—

Railroads!

As if: by constructing that which rides on tracks of iron, thou then knowest how to build that which rides on no tracks at all. As if: by understanding the iron and invariant Way from Here to There, ye somehow understand the undulations of the sea, the elegance of its To and Fro, the geometry of the Tack, the persistence necessary to FORGE ONE'S OWN WAY WITHOUT PATH LAID DOWN AFOREHAND. The rail is as much preparation for the ship as—

Well: ye may know how to board a sleeping car, yet by that token, dost ye know how to swim?

So the *Great Eastern*, paddles neither poised gracefully amidships nor lending thrust and power to her stern— With its iron prow parting the seas that her chugging iron engine show its might— This be not a Ship! And more, this be not a thing that pleaseth the eye. Or heart. Or soul.

When a man giveth himself over to the ocean he begins to know of beauty and of his own heart; but when a man decideth, of will and iron, to conquer that ocean his efforts be all mechanical, and out-of-sorts with the ways of the sea.

Ye know that a ship goes from port to port. Yer merchant, yer capitalist, all he sees is the port. To him what is a ship? A conveyance! All boiled down to grim utility! A ship is that which moves the goods from the one port to t'other.

Now ye know—Ahab knows—any sailor knows—that the port is the least of it. The goods and pieces and ladings and cargoes so beloved to yer merchant class? That's just what allows yer ships be built. What allows 'em to sail. But the punctum— Ah me lads, the punctum is elsewhere. On the oceans of the planet and the waters of the world. The ship comes first, and what it hauls mere— Mechanism! Device! Excuse! Palaver!

The difference in price 'tween cargo here, and cargo there, lets ships be built and launched. Which is to the good. But it is not the Point. Money be just—ha!—a ship's way of building another ship. And a ship is an ocean's way of saying: thou art small. Thou art without will or command or purpose in my realm. On my waves I raise thee and plunge thee at my will or whim. Says ocean: shall thee cross? I care not! I am indifferent! The ocean, she spends as much in thought about the *Valparaiso*, about the *Great Eastern*, as the lung spends in considering the molecule of air it sucks in, then expels. So when the ocean destroys us—and in the end, the ocean will have us all—'twill be without malice, without sorrow, without triumph. To the ocean the ship does not exist. But to the ship? The ocean is all it knows. Ocean is to ship as the fluid amniotic is to us! As we float, curved inward, little beans, little human beans, curled up knees to chest, head to knees, thumbs brought up to our mouths— As we suck on ourselves in fine contentment of dark and wet— Head-to-toe, toe-to-head, in cosy loving company with Annabel don't ye know— Until that bright and terrible day we find ourselves expelled, and slapped, and forced to breathe. Now where was we?

TWENTY-FOUR

—————⚓—————

NEMO MOVED ROUND to the omni-scope, lifted the valve that the hydraulics might raise the scope's objective above the water. What he saw accorded with what he'd been told: a ship so large as to dwarf imagining, with paddle wheels, and a screw, and six masts, too. The sails were reefed 'gainst high wind, the wheels stilled, so Nemo surmised it was pulling along by screw. The cable behind, like black excrescence from some oiled iron cloaca, draped as it sank from ship to wave. There were other ships, too: escort ships. Three of them. As if something that size, and made of iron, needed anything other than its own massive self.

"Ahead three-quarters," said Nemo into the speaking tube. It was best, he knew, to sever the cable on the ocean floor itself, where the depth make it hard to retrieve, and the silt cover it up, and the corals grow around it.

"Dive," said Nemo into the speaking tube. All the while watching the iron ship, large as a city, grow closer.

TWENTY-FIVE

———— ⚓ ————

PERHAPS TIME FOR Ahab to lay to rest, once and for all time, a popular slander. It says this and this sole thing: that Ahab wants revenge only. That the sailing, the ship, the crew all mean naught to him. That what Ahab he seeks is the white whale all else be damned. That the cable matters not to him. That the well-being of his employer matters not to him. That his ship matters not. That his crew could all drown in the icy North Atlantic and Ahab shed not a tear.

Whereas yer Ahab, yer veritable Ahab, *le vrai* Ahab, is a man of peace. His being is as placid as soft forgotten isle. What drives him? What constitutes his motive force? His drives, his motors, are those of charity and of compassion. To how many sailors under his command has he given additional emolument?

They gave him lashes twenty,
Ranzo, boys, Ranzo
Nineteen more than plenty—
Ranzo, boys, Ranzo

Then the skipper did forgive him,
Ranzo, boys, Ranzo
And went down-cabin with him,
Ranzo, boys, Ranzo

He gave Ranzo cake and whisky,
Ranzo, boys, Ranzo
And then skipper he got frisky;
Ranzo, boys, Ranzo

With rum the skipper plied him
Ranzo, boys, Ranzo
Then skipper occupied him
Ranzo, boys, Ranzo

Gave Ranzo education
Ranzo, boys, Ranzo
And taught him navigation
Ranzo, boys, Ranzo

He made him his best sailor,
Ranzo, boys, Ranzo
Sailing on that whaler;
Ranzo, boys, Ranzo

Now Ranzo is a skipper,
Ranzo, boys, Ranzo
Of his own China clipper;
Ranzo, boys, Ranzo!

So Ahab is, and so, like any man, wishes to be perceived. To be taken for who he is. To see his good works find purchase in this world; and by that to be acknowledged— Though this be not his motivation. No! Ahab, careth he for fame? Doth Ahab harbor the wish to be cherished? *Nein, nein, mein Lieber Segler!* Ahab he wish only to do what is right. And if that is recognized, so be it, and rewarded, so be it, &c &c. And if not, those winds they will moan and howl, west to east, as they did before he arrived, and will do long after he and any who knew him have long since gone beneath. But Ahab he knows, the *deed* is the thing: in itself, and of itself. That be the wine and the viand. The rest is as Persian sherbet.

Ye can see, canst ye, the full measure of Ahab's generosity? To take a lubber under his wing? And give him care? And give him cake? And make him a sailor? As Ahab hath done with Langhorne? And others far too numerous to count?

For Ahab knows the true law of the sea: that for every skipper there is a Ranzo, yes, and for every Ranzo there is a skipper. But more, me lads, more: yer skipper was once himself a Ranzo! He did not know his duty! He was, dare we admit, a lubber! And on board his first ship, did he find his sea legs? He did not! And was he the object of ridicule from the mizzenmast on back? Why yes he was! Ahab himself, though ye'd not see it now were ye to gaze upon this countenance— that time has staled Ahab, yes, he did his holy stoning! And had his lashes, he did, and his back with oil was painted!

Let me tell ye, lads, where the charity lays and where the grace resides: when the sun hath swept the dial, and the clock hath chimed and chimed again, and the pages of the calendar flip and float and fly as numbered butterflies in unrelenting wind— When back in Nantucket what once was grass now is hay, and when the man stained by time wants once more to chew with colt's teeth— He doth it now with memory. And a sense of the larger wheel.

Ahab is nothing now but a man of that larger wheel.

As that wheel did turneth, so did Ahab become the master of his ship. But Ahab, he doth recall, even now, a time when even he was subject to the law of others. So if there is blood, why there is cake, too, for the sailor. And rum. And the lullaby, sweet lullaby of major chords, and more verses than fingers and toes can count, to smooth the furrowed brow and soothe away the care.

In this way did Ahab sing to Langhorne, and now Langhorne, in voice deeper and more sonorous, sings to us. His black skin invisible under this month's new moon, but his voice ringing out o'er the deck, that every last man Jack can hear, and o'er the sea, too, that the men of the G_____ E_____, and those who escort it, can share, too, in the magnificence of his instrument, and the power of his melody, and the incantatory thrall of those very old words, ne'er written, just handed down, and handed down again, and now with us, as we prepare to hand them down to the next.

And aboard that other, larger boat, as they hear the deep and perfect voice from our *Valparaiso*— On that other ship, Mr. Field's ship— Well on that ship the cable-men make their splice and the percha men apply their tarry liniment and the winch men pay it out and the electricians watch as their magnets move, all while the glass-men scan the horizon for lowering skies, and the sextant man eyes the sun and takes his fix (know ye, that on this ship, yer Ahab does his own fix, each morn, and none but he knows for sure just where we are, or have been, or will go)— And as aboard the iron boat the panics come and panics go— And when they are afeared of a break, why then, they summon Ahab; and when they ascertain that t'aint a break at all, why they dismiss him, skiff him back to his own ship— And the day passes into night into day once more, and each fix shows a latitude e'er more western. We are off the coastal shelf now. What's down there is ocean floor. What's down there is the vasty deep.

The shorter rendition, the one-verse-no-chorus of it: as of an hour ago we are in that place where Leviathan he likes to swim. And play. And wreak his havoc. Destroy the lives of the innocent. And the not-so innocent. But in the eyes of the Man Upstairs: is that any less a crime?

Those that come at Ahab do so at their full peril. And whatever response to threat Ahab be compelled to unleash, why that not be on Ahab's ledger. No. That be on the tabulation of Leviathan, and, should Ahab prevail, on the balance sheet of the Almighty.

TWENTY-SIX

———⚓———

THE CAPTAIN IN his wheelhouse now, hands perched above the levers and contacts and gauges and switches, as curved and expectant as if he were about to play the toccata. The silence before the attack. Then Nemo did move his hands rapidly among the controls and conveyances before him. And through the round wheelhouse glass could see the pantograph extend from its housing just below *Nautilus*'s prow. Powered first by steam and now—and for this we tip our hat to the Engineer—by electricity.

The pantograph was designed to extend downward, to ocean's bed, to seize objects from that bed and retrieve them for examination. Your unexpected coral. Your anemone where none heretofore'd been seen. But the pantograph, along its far end, had blades that were sharp, that could cut as well as grasp.

The Captain he kept his breath low and regular as he turned the rheostats that fired and banked the motors that pulled the pantograph this way and that. The work required the dexterity and patience of a surgeon and down here, two thousand fathoms down, he was guided as much by instinct as by sight. When his heart got fast he counted his breaths 'til his heart was slow again. When at last the pantograph reached the cable he could see that it was black with pitch. Insulation. Nemo positioned the blades—concave, curved—round the cable and pressed home the single-pole switch. It did not bite the first time, nor the second. But then it did. The motors were geared down, a hundred turns of the shaft to an inch of movement at the far end of the pantograph. The blades pressed the cable and then, at once, met. As Nemo watched, the lower length of the cable made its bed slow and silent, on the bottom of the sea, even as the upper length—tension now released—snapped, recoiled. Spun and writhed. Aboard that iron ship, they would know that all was not right. Eighty-three counted breaths. He watched as they began to reel in the cable, then he spoke through the speaking tube to Mohan. Said a phrase in the language they shared, a phrase which in English is best rendered thusly:

"It is done."

Then Nemo spun the hatch on the wheelhouse bulkhead, descended the eighteen spiral steps to his salon for a tot of Madeira and to think about the cable-laying ship, which was infinitely larger in size and sturdier of hull than any he'd yet taken down.

TWENTY-SEVEN

—————✤—————

YER AHAB STAYED as logic and prudence would dictate aboard his *Valparaiso*. Yet news from the *Grand Excrescence* did not escape yer Ahab's grasp: the paying out had gone—as e'en Mr. Field would wish—smoothly, with the cable emerging slow and deliberate from its wheel; with the G_____ E_____ picking up speed; and with the depth lowering as she headed west—

And in that a tale. Now yer Ahab, can he tell a tale straightforward, without the bellowing, the rodomontade, the perorations, the puffery, the repetitions, the perambulations, the phrases circumlocutory, the tangent and from there the tangent again, the roundabout sans exit? Why yes he can, as ye shall now see. For when the telling requires a certain precision—as in this case it must—why yer Ahab in that is the equal of any man, and the better of most. As the man he sayeth: list' me now!

Our motley fleet were some four days out from Foilhummerum and the cable lay some two-and-a-half miles beneath us. The day it had broke thick and hazy then became more warm and with better seeing. The sea was calm, her whitecaps small and now more widely spaced, and in response, the arrogant and misbegotten G_____ E_____ decided to show the world what she could do by way of steaming. And so the stokers and fire-men bent low to their task, feeding coal into the maws of the furnaces, unseen of course by yer Ahab who was, let us recall, upon another ship. Yet Ahab he knoweth that the furnaces burned bright; and that the black soot adhered to the stokers' faces, affixed there by the sweat of their labor.

The *Terrible* could not keep up, nor could the *Sphinx*. The *Ter-*

rible, as signal, sent down her top-gallant masts— But the signal either went unseen by the G_____ E_____'s master, or, if 'twere seen, went unheeded. Mine own *Valparaiso*, powered as it was by wind and not by steam, lagged as well. The *Valparaiso* was content to watch the paddle-wheeled railway car go as fast as she might wish, gain as much distance as she might want. To refresh the memory: the G_____ E_____ was more in need of us than we of her. Let her outpace by fire what the rest of us by nature's gusty motivants might accomplish. Let her be self-proud and alone, unaccompanied by her protectors. We not be paid to worry on her behalf.

Our course was NW½w.; the wind NNW. She moved forward and, as we watched, payed out backward. All seemed well until—it was the work of an instant—all did not. The snap was not audible from here but it was visible indeed as the lazy downward arc of the cable concatenated and the cable now dipped, straight down, from the V wheel at the G_____ E_____'s stern, down to the grey and choppy sea. Clear and apparent to all: the cable, she had snapped.

The large double-hulled craft cut her engines allowing first her escorts, the *Terrible* and the *Sphinx*, more nearly to approach, port and starboard respectively. The *Valparaiso* brought up the rear, but even as our ship was approaching the iron maiden she had put out a skiff whose oarsmen were making straight for us. Ahab he was being summoned.

The greeting by the large craft's captain, Anderson by name, 'twas perfunctory, and Mr. Field, presumably somewhere aboard, was in that instant nowhere to be seen. Ahab was escorted downdeck to the cable hold. The room was dominated by a V wheel, the speed of which was regulated by a friction bearing on the same shaft. Around the bearing were thick leather straps weighted by levers and running on tanks full of water to keep the cable taut to the drum. Between the repeater drum and the driving pulleys were Appold brakes, and then, between them and a stern wheel, a dynamometer. It would tell you the speed at which the cable was being payed out. Right now its red needle was to the left of the zero. The pay-out, as much else, had clearly ceased; and the large spindle, larger than any other e'er made, was winding counter-clock. The sailors in the room stood about, features immobile, lips compressed.

"Hast ye hauled back the cable, that we might examine the break?" said yer Ahab.

"That we do now," said the officer, hands holding one another, tight, behind his coat. The screech of straps and bearings, never pleasant while paying out, became, on reverse, louder and more sad, as if the middle note of a chord had been lowered half a step, the resultant triad now shifted into minor.

"How much left to go," asked yer Ahab.

"We were more than two thousand in depth," said the officer. "By my lights we've recovered some half of that."

"Was there a pull, or—"

"Just— A stop."

Ahab watched as the spindle pulled back the cable that it had, not so long before, far more happily dispensed. It had taken the better part of an hour for the skiff to reach Ahab, for Ahab to board, for Ahab to be led here. It would be something like that before we would reach the cable's fag end. Ahab he motioned for some grog to be brought, sat down upon an up-ended cask, watched the sad reverse spinning, smelt the intake of salted sea, listened to the mournful threnody of spindles ne'er meant to turn 'gainst the clock.

Now the cable, stinking of the depths from which it had been retrieved, returned to spool. 'Twas a task monotonous to watch yet with its own Mesmeric tension. With each revolve of the wheel would we reach the break? And what, once seen, would that break tell us, about its Cause?

As yer Ahab drank the grog he knew it was that question, that question alone, he had here been brought to answer. And as yer Ahab waited he saw in the mind's theater various wise in which the cable might be sundered. Roughly, as if exploded, with strands as wild as Medusa's hair; raggedly, as rope cut by dull knife—

The musings of yer Ahab were then brought up sharp as, with great screech and commotion, the spooling up ceased and the dynamometer needle sprang to center, holding fast at the zero. The task it were done. In a matter of moments we would gaze upon the break as if, from what remained, we might narrate what had transpired. To gaze into the wound and by doing so: divine our disease.

The officers gathered round and it was Captain Anderson who

widened the circle, making room for Ahab. And as we pulled close, the cable-man went at it with a deck swab, rubbing off the glut and grime, residuum of the cable's stay upon the ocean floor. Gutta-percha was coated with sea-bottom muck all the way to the break. No one among us spoke, but 'twas clear to yer Ahab that all among us knew, at once, the significance of what we'd seen: that the break occurred not near-surface, not mid-depth, but all the way down at the bottom of the sea: two and a half miles down. Whatever had rent the cable had no difficulty at depths that would crush a human, implode him, crack his skull as if 'twere the shell of an egg.

The cableman stroked and swabbed, debriding the gutta-percha yet retaining the spent rags that they might be of use to us for purposes diagnostic. When the muck proved too resilient he applied a solvent, taking care not to touch the last yard where the secrets, if any, would reside.

At last it was before us, laid out on a carpenter's bench. The gutta-percha intact, sans corrosion or rot. And at the end of the cable: no fray, no lap, no tendril, no wild coil of individual strand, no hair of the Gorgon, no wounded frenzy. Just a cut. The cable coming to abrupt end— And with it, all our notions of futurity.

"Let me through," came a voice from the back. It was Mr. Field's science-man Everett and he came with a satchel. Opened it. Produced his set of lenses.

"I need more light," he said, and we stepped aside so as not to block what weak sunlight suffused via the aftward gate.

He bent close, holding lens to the cable. From time to time he could be heard to speak, yet without words— Sounds of satisfaction, bemusement, puzzlement, sounds of wonder and dismay. Grunts such as one might hear from a lover yet there was no love to it. The small noises they did quiet. Then he said: "Look here."

We pulled close, yers truly at the fore (there is no one steps in front of Ahab, be it upon a ship Ahab himself commands or any other). Peered through the glass. Saw the shear in all its perpendicularity, its smoothness. One polished slice, save a small lip at the lower end of the braid. The cut gleamed in the light. It was not a gleam that offered comfort to head or heart or gut.

"Can you opine?" Captain Anderson asked.

"Here is what there is to say," replied the science-man Everett. "This be cut. Not snapped, or nibbled at, or corroded, or rusted, or decayed. Cut. Rent. Nor was it tugged or snapped. This be not yer tension snap. This be not yer concatenation of frays. Third, no defect in the manufacture. This was made right, wove right— Then: cut right. And more: whatever done cut this, cut it swift. No residue of hesitation. Nor was it a sawing motion, the back and the forth, as that leaves trace, and of such trace there be none. No hack, no hew. This were done in one."

There was a silence what enveloped the hold broken only by the creak of deck above, the lap of waters below. Neither shift of weight, nor murmur of phlegm—

"With what force?" asked the Captain.

"Enough to pass through annealed copper with the ease of knife through a drunkard's belly."

"And what done it?" said the Captain.

"A jaw," said science-man Everett. "'Tis a question of lever and fulcrum."

"To what," asked the Captain, "does that jaw belong?"

"Hard to say."

There were again some moments of silence. Then the silence parted, making room for Ahab to speak, and so did Ahab speak, and none interrupted.

"Hath anyone a flame? A flame with some heat to it? Ahab would like to put the end in flame and see how it burns. How it glows. With what colors, with what intensity. Why we know that there is copper, and copper will burn with a flame now blue, now green. It is a distinct hue, and one that many here will recognize. Other elements have, each of them, their own insignia. We know, thanks to the work of yon science-man Everett, something of the force with which the cable was rent. We know magnitude. What we seek now is to know something of mechanism. We need to know, and know without delay, the contours of our nemesis."

Captain Anderson, recognizing wisdom when he heard it, nodded gravely and in assent. And so made his reply, that reply consisting of but one word: "Furnace."

A moment of silence, then the clang and scurry of motion, grand motion, as the Cableman took hold of the end of the thing, and the Brakeman took the straps off the spool, and we all of us grabbed ahold, and marched, from the very aft of the ship, through the hold, up onto the deck, toward the mizzenmast, then down again, past the mid-axis, down toward the firehold, and all the while the cable snaking out behind. Pulling and tugging and marching up and marching across and marching down, yer Ahab with his Aaron's rod marking time.

> *Hey don't yer see that black cloud a-risin'?*
> *'Way haul away, we'll haul away Joe!*
> *Hey don't yer see that black cloud a-risin'?*
> *'Way haul away, we'll haul away Joe!*

'Tis like the sailor to strike up the chant. Ye might call 'em sailors who sing, ye might call 'em singers who sail. So much of our work is heave and rest, heave and rest, so we find our way to song. And the song keeps shoulder to wheel, lifts the spirits when they are down, sets the beat for the labor.

> *We loaded for the homeward run, all hands so free an' aisy,*
> *'Way haul away, we'll haul away Joe!*
> *And in his galley sat the doc, a-makin' plum-duff graisy.*
> *'Way haul away, we'll haul away Joe!*

Now yer narrator not be sayin' we sang as we hauled. We do, of course, at times, as we have told ye, and laid out for ye, and explained to ye that even the slowest among ye might understand. But this be not be one of those times. We were too much in the shock of things to make use of the throat-and-bellow. Still, as we hauled the cable-laid wires, ONE-two, ONE-two, it'd be strange did we not hear, in the mind's ear of each and every head, the lilt of a chantey. And since we was hauling: a haulin' chantey.

> *Yiz call yerself a second mate an' cannot tie a bowline,*
> *Way haul away, we'll haul away Joe!*
> *Ye cannot even stand up straight when the packet she's a-rollin'.*
> *'Way haul away, we'll haul away Joe!*

And what with thoughts of shear and severance all agog in our noggins, we of course were put in mind of this next verse, the most *à propos* to our task of the moment, and of course, as ye might have imagined, the personal favorite of yers truly:

King Louis wuz the King o' France, afore the revolution,
'Way haul away, we'll haul away Joe!
But the people cut his big head orf an' spoiled his constitution.

All together now:

'Way haul away, we'll haul away Joe!

So we hauled, and so we sang in silence, as we bore the severed neck of our serpent from aft to fore, dragging all behind—

And then we reached the fire hold.

Where the stokers stoked, dispatching shovel after shovel of black coal, not a gleaming black but a dull and unreflective black, not light but its opposite, aha! Flinging it into the maw that was nothing but light, light so bright it stabbed, hurting the eyes e'en before ye were close enough to get beat back by the heat. It was like gazing into the sun if sans the satisfactions thereof. It'd not blind ye, nay— Just bright enough that ye could stare into it, day after day, and have just enough sight left to do yer job. Which was the day in, and the day out, from the first watch at midnight round to the blessed eight bells, feeding the impossible bright beast with chunks of darkness, chunks that served not to blot the flame but to feed its increase. This be the infernal paradox of yer stoker. Ye needs be small of brain to become a fire-man, and if ye not be small of brain when ye signed on, ye will be soon, lads, ye will be soon. 'Tis the most thankless task aboard a ship and the most wearying. Should ye take any task aboard a sail-ship, there be more humanity in it than in the feeding of the furnace in yer steam-driven vessel! The G_____E_____'s furnaces, larger than any seagoing hellboxes yet been built, and by a factor not of two or three but of six, said furnaces were a feat of engineering for that railway man, yes, but 'twas a life sentence for those whose job it is to make 'em run. Mr. Isambard Railway Man, did he think of that, did he, at his table in some tonier part of London, when he set down the plans? Ahab was not there, in Isambard Railway Man's study, and Ahab was not there, inside Isambard Railway Man's head— Yet he knows the answer, and that answer is no, a resounding no, a haul-away no. Follow yer logic: had Isambard Railway Man given it the thought, he'd not that way have built it.

So now we was in the fire hold and the stokers parting before us, making way for the men and the cable. As all this be Ahab's fine idea in the first place, yer Captain Anderson did to Ahab defer, and so Ahab walked into the flame— *No he did not, are ye paying attention?* Ahab he walked up to the flame, he walked up to the fiery maw of the boiler belly but he took no step further. No, ye lads, no; no, ye lassies, no. What he did do, Ahab did: he took his arm, his harpoon arm, the mightiest and truest arm in all the North Atlantic, and some would say well beyond— He took his harpoon arm and with it picked up the cable. Held that cable high, as if it were his weapon, a fierce rending barb ready to plunge into the tenderest parts of mortal foe. Ahab held that cable, that cable-laid cable, that braid of copper and gutta-percha, he held it up high, and while he so held it, there was not an exhalation of breath aboard the G____ E_____ entire, not in the boiler hold, not nowhere else neither. Nor did a clock tick, nor did the sun's gnomon shadow move 'cross the dial. The waves themselves paused, some in peak, some in trough. Drops and droplets of sea water churned by those waves held, mid-air. Then, after that eternity—*and how dost thou measure an eternity?*—Ahab with his arm did lunge, and the churn of life recommenced, while the boiler hold crew looked on, rapt— As yer one and onlie captain thrust cable into fire.

The flames they did leap up. Oh did they leap. Fierce and terrible, with a heat beyond imagining, and for one short moment it seemed as if the boiler hold itself would be consumed. *In girum imus nocte et consumimur igni!* That's Latin for, *in the middle of the night we turn and are consumed by flame!* And what's more: 'tis the same backward as 'tis forward! Aha!

After the initial flare that threatened to consume the world, but did not, the flame did settle back as if cowed by Ahab's unremitting gaze. And then the flames did part, enough to render visible the sheared edge of the cable. And from it: the hues they did arise. There was in background the yellow-hot flame of the coal furnace, to be sure, but now other colors, too, dancing rapid, ethereal.

There was of course the blue-green of copper, a verdigris, but purer and more intense. A haunting tone, and lovely to cast eyes upon: no dull glaucous earthbound green but a blue-green that spoke of less of corporeal satisfactions than of what lies beyond. But that was not the only color, no! There was entwined with that fine blue-green a yellow glow, less pure and of less intensity— A pale and evanescent yellow, the signature yellow of yer sodium chloride.

So there be copper, and there be salt. Both known, both expected. But what other colors danced essential in the maw's revealing heat? Was there yellow-red? The fine and mellow yellow-red of calcium? For if there were, we might know, or reasonably infer, that yer cable, she were chomped by teeth-and-bone, by the hard and calciferous mandible of some deep-dwelling creation— So deep as to ne'er have been seen by human eye! Whose origins go back before recorded time! That hast lived in briny depths e'er since! Yet even as Ahab stared—and, if we may remind, 'twas like staring into the heart of the sun—he saw no yellow-red.

What he saw was gold.

A gleaming gold, not the baser gold of worn and tarnished coins, but an altogether purer hue, translucent, diaphanous, fugitive, a gold that was barely there before the eye and gold ye might see clear through, a slight and light and evanescent gold, the gown of some Scheherazade. And as he saw that gold yer Ahab froze in place. Of the men in the boiler hold only Ahab—and yes, perhaps the science-man Everett, who was trained in sun-fixing, and in mathematicks, and in the allied sciences—knew the meaning of that gold.

'Twas not the signature of the element gold, counter as that might be to the intuition. No, 'twas not gold. 'Twas the *carte de visite* of— Iron.

TWENTY-EIGHT

———————✧———————

WHAT COULD BE seen through the iris, through Nemo's Large Glass: the swirl of deep anemone; the seabed flora; the end of the cable where, in one leveraged slice, the pantograph had neatly severed it.

Now Nemo's curiosity turned to what was upon the waves rather than beneath them. Accordingly Nemo he quit the salon by its foreward hatch, climbed the eighteen wrought-iron steps that spiral'd up to wheelhouse. The omni-scope could, on bright days and when *Nautilus* was at shallow depth, project image onto ground glass, the image as sharp as real life, in the manner of a camera obscura. When *Nautilus* was at depth there be not sufficient illumination, but the omni-scope could still offer up a view of the above, via an ocular. Nemo put his right eye to the lens. Up there was the *Great Eastern*, and he needed to see her. To ascertain whether she would turn tail or instead— Do something else.

If departing Foilhummerum with an unspooling cable had been *Great Eastern*'s P to K's 4th, severing said cable was *Nautilus*'s P to K's 4th response. At some point—and Nemo hoped it would be soon—*Great Eastern* would topple its own king, concede the loss, Nemo master of the board. But until *Great Eastern* scuttled her task and made her grand defeated turn, Nemo would maintain vigilance.

Would this be a four-knights game? A Ruy Lopez (always Mr. Singh's favorite, and hence, the Turk's)? He watched intently as the cable, which had been paying out in a lazy catenary arc from the V of the ship's stern, now reeled back in. Then began the gathering of the *Great Eastern*'s escorts—they'd been substantially in her wake, but were now, with the lead ship stilled, catching up; and he could see, too, a smaller wake, that of a chaloupe, from one of the subsidiary wooden crafts to the larger iron one. Supplies, or a specific piece of kit that needed to be brought to *Great Eastern*? A specialist, called in for consultation?

As Nemo's eye adjusted to the vista, the dance of thoughts within his head fell into synchrony with the dance of severed cable. It rose, yes, as it was being hauled back in. But also undulated, a long slow sine, as beauteous in its own way as eel or sea-snake. The line became shorter, the oscillations more rapid as it was wound back to berth. Nemo was not a man prone to the wager, but he set store in experience, and he knew that each time previous that the cable had broke or been severed the cable-ship it had returned to port. And if so, *Nautilus* she would play in North Atlantic currents until she received that the cable scheme had been abandoned; and then set out for sunnier climes.

Thus it was with more than a little curiosity that the *Nautilus*'s captain did drink his elixir: steam, pressured up to nine atmospheres, forced through ground roasted coffee (as finely pulverized as it would be for the Turkish preparation). Nemo had spent long months experimenting with different varietals, different methods of extraction. He loved his Malabar but these raw beans came from Harar in the east of Ethiopia then brought by land to the straits where the Red Sea empties out into the Erythraean. He'd brought them aboard in their green state, stored them in the ballast hold, roasted them in small quantities. They kept well in the green state, but once roasted the oils did, in short order, become acrid.

As he sipped he listened to Bach (on an organ to all other ears, save his own, silent: the toccata internal, played on the stop *Vox Intus Vero*). And all the while keeping eye affixed to ocular, awaiting the moment that the *Great Eastern* would make her slow, wide turn, from compass point WNE round to ESW, back to harbor, there to await the next chapter of her sad decline. When the *Great Eastern* had beat its retreat Nemo would summon Brunel to the salon, let him know that his old iron ship was no longer in jeopardy, that repatriation was at hand. And that the next port of call for him would be Home.

Then again: if the *Great Eastern*'s response to the severing were somehow different—not the expected B to N's 5th but something more outré—Nemo would counter. With elegance, science, violence, until the final *shāh māt*.

TWENTY-NINE

———————✤———————

Now ponder me this, ye lads and mates. Yer calcium, why that would tell a tale, a tale of sea-creature from the vasty deep. But yer iron, she tell a different tale. All fish known and all fish ne'er seen, hath jaws and teeth of bone. Not iron. And yer cetacean mammal, that cetacean mammal hath jaws and teeth of bone. Not iron. And yer cephalopod, why he be deadly, yet that cephalopod have tentacles and suckers of squidly flesh. Not iron. What's made of iron? Why yer G____ E_____ be made of iron. Yer Isambard Railway Man's railway be made of iron. Dost thou sense the thing-in-common? What unique property be held by all of these? There be a tell-tale word, and that word be *made*.

Things of iron were ne'er born, no: they were wrought. Thus here we were gazing into the fiery maw of Isambard's ship's boiler. Peering rapt and painful into what ungodly light. Staring fixedly at the end of a grand copper snake that yer Ahab had with his magnificent harpoon arm thrust into that light. And seeing in the flames that danced from cable's edge a light and golden flame: gold, here meaning iron. And iron meaning, removed from the world of the natural and thrust hard into the realm of the made-by-man, yer cause, yer motive. Yer intent. No, the cable did not snap. Something, someone wanted the cable snapped. And so: snapped it. With shears of iron.

Mechanical beast. Pneumatical sledge. Steely automaton. What devil's concatenation of hard, shiny, malleable, fusible, ductile metal— Of gear, clockwork, escapement— Of slow-turning wheel and pinion rod— Of riveted skin and ridged metallic jaw— Ahab, he imagined all manner of infernal machine, and in his imagination he saw a sub-marine railway, the triumph of the engineer o'er the seaman, gleaming iron rails stretching from the one continent to t'other, and upon those rails a dark and ferrous train, belching white steam black smoke into the dark northern seas, thick plumes rising up through viscous dark toward yer moon or sun above. A ferrous train dispatching all in its path, tossing each and every obstacle up and away with the ease of cowcatcher dispatching cow. First a rumble, then a roar— Then the Cyclopean headlamp piercing lower ocean depths, fixing ye in its beam, 'til ye were torn beneath its wheel, as inexorable as the dream gone bad.

Yer Ahab he saw that ferrous train in the eye of his mind, saw it in massive and terrible detail, bearing down on him, and no way of stopping its forward push nor of stepping aside from the rail-ordained path. Yet even as that headlamp caught his gaze, Ahab he returned it and stared into the maw: man versus machine so far beneath the surface of the sea that the waves were as cirrus clouds in a distant night sky. And he refused, yer captain did, to yield! He would meet it full on, and we shall see who be the more stalwart. For Ahab hath what no machine doth possess, which be this one thing: the intellect, which no iron engine e'er could match. Confronted with the *connaissance* of iron, Ahab did not flail and weep, no he did not. Instead: he thought. And as with many Ahabean thoughts, the thought took the form of a question, and the question it was this: What made of iron lies so far beneath the sea? Why a piece of iron wrought on land and brought down low! And what might it be, and how had it been brought so low?

At one instant Ahab, he did not know; and in the instant next, he knew. Said iron was a sharpened spear, wrought in New Bedford by Thad Samuelson, ironmonger. Bound with coiled hemp to a length of round-turned teak by yer Ahab himself. A harpoon! A lance from the past! A harpoon hurled, ye may recall, swift and accurate by yer Ahab, into the maw of Leviathan, and lodged there like an iron tooth! Lodged in that jaw long after hemp and wood hath rotted away!

And so when Leviathan encountered Mr. Field's cable, paying out from the stern of yer *G____ E_____*, swaying slow and sinuous beneath Atlantic North— Why Leviathan he see that cable and

Leviathan he think, this be eel! This be coelacanth! Morsel for the maw! And so without regard for the this or for the that yer Leviathan swam toward— And when the eel be within reach, raised his lower jaw, clamping down, clamping down. And the piece of jaw what hit the eel first, why that would be the most protruding tooth: in this case, by history now we know, the tooth of iron! The harpoon tooth! The ferrous dentition that near-killed Leviathan, but was now fully part of him!

And so the pale gold what Ahab saw in the terrible furnace was the gleam of American iron, of Thaddeus Samuelson, of Ahab, of a story from long ago come back to haunt.

The mystery posed and solved!

'Twas, for Ahab, great and grand relief. But also: old and awful fear. And swift upon the heels of that fear: a command. What Ahab had given soul and leg to do, first time round, must now be done again, and with finality. 'Til one or both were dead.

Ahab he can be the quietest of men, when he is stepping behind ye three paces, unheard, until he loops his hands round yer neck. When justice is on his side he will mete out his vengeance, and that he will do swift and direct. A messenger from the future when yer future is all spent.

But he can also be a man of peace yer Ahab can. When the ship runs steady, and the hands on deck all acquit themselves with diligence and honor, and the holy stoners sing of holystoning and the haulers sing of hauling, and all have accepted Ahab's morning fix and all work in fine concord to moving the ship in the direction Ahab himself hath determined, and the serene unblinking sun doth shine down on the pacific seas, and the sun slideth down behind them if they are sailing east, or in front if they are sailing west, and the sky goeth salmon at the rim, then red, presaging clear night ahead and the prospect of a morning not unlike the morning previous: why then Ahab be an ocean of contentment, an ivory-legged apostle of calm.

So before ye jump to yer conclusion, the simple and base conclusion, that Ahab he was in it for the Great White— Before ye think that of all the wild plumage of human emotion, the sole ambition belonging to Ahab were the one quill marked "vengeance"— Before ye think that Ahab were in it only fer Ahab— Consider two things if ye might:

The first thing, that be the word of Ahab. He were hired, and paid, to escort Captain Anderson's iron beast from Foilhummerum to Heart's Content, to keep it safe from harm. So in fixing on the Leviathan, was not Ahab simply honoring his word, and the conditions of his employ?

And there be the second thing that Ahab he doth beg ye, lads, to take into yer fine consideration. What doth Ahab hold high, above the roil of self? What doth he place before him, and above him, with every waking thought, and equally in dream? Why the life and livelihood of those under his command! Ahab, he be but one man (though a grand man, to be sure). But what be the life of one man, compared to the many lives of the crew entire? So many paths, so many histories— Each as variegated as Ahab's own. He thought now, Ahab he did, of Langhorne, his chanteyman. How could he allow Langhorne to fall into harm's way? And if Leviathan, will-he nill-he, were to harm his chanteyman, and had Ahab not done all in his power to prevent it, well then could Ahab sleep? Ye all know the answer: no, he could not sleep. He would not rest. He would wander the surface of the seas for an eternity, racked with remorse, mind occupied to fullness with thoughts of that other world receding from his grasp like jetsam thrown into the wake, that other world where Ahab was brave and Langhorne he lived on.

So before ye think that Ahab only wanted what Ahab wanted, without regard for the honor of his word, or his obligation toward those in his fine care— Before ye do, consider yer thoughts. And gaze, lads and mates, not upon yer captain, but the other way, inward, toward the depths of yer own souls should ye have 'em.

And so yer Ahab sayeth, to all those aboard the *Valparaiso*, be they sheet men or rope men or carpenters or swabbers, be they boatsteerers or stewards or cooks or coopers or chanteyman, be they rats in the hold or maggots in the meat: look in, look in. And question not the spots upon Ahab's soul, but upon yer own.

THIRTY

———————✥———————

YET E'EN AS Ahab gazed into the fiery furnace, and there saw the tell-tale flames, Captain Anderson he gazed into Ahab's face, and there saw the flames interior.

At that moment, in the boiler-hold, though no words were in that place exchanged, we all of us, save the stokers and fire-men bent upon their ceaseless and wretched task, we all the rest of us exited the hold, going back out the way we'd come in, and pulling the cable with us, which unseen and accommodating hands re-wound on the large capstan, that by the time we reached the stern-hold the cable were all snug, and wound up tight on its bobbin.

Then Captain Anderson did nod his chin, and at that Ahab followed him. It were just the two, as all else waited, and the two—the captain of this awful iron tub and the captain of the awful wooden *Valparaiso*—went fore again, Anderson in the lead, forward to the foc'sle, then down, into the salon, the chairs that were once excellent now frayed, and the papered walls, in Zuber murals depicting Hindoos and Éléphants, torn and marked by time. Where the gilded elect once had dined and danced, where then the commerce of nations and not a few butts of Madeira had crossed the seven seas, was now but grand abandoned space, the celebration having ceased or, more simply, having moved on. Into this hollowed hallowed hall was yer Ahab now granted admission.

Yer Captains Ahab and Anderson, we sat down now in that ruined salon, and in that gold and tattered space we were there joined by Mr. Field, whom Ahab had first met in New York, in Mr. Field's apartments off Gramercy Park, and who was now Ahab's employer.

As if anyone could Ahab employ! But Anderson, sad to say, was an owner's man, and his crew they knew it, and they disrespected him on
account of it. Now a sailor who will "show willing," that sailor is of
value, for he will not slack, and he will not moan, and he will do the
task assigned, and not quit 'til either it is done, or he is.

But a *captain* who will "show willing," that is another story. For
if he doeth what be asked by the owner, and pays not attention to
those beneath, why they will wait until he is equidistant from port
and home, then there will be maggots in his coffee, bugs in his crib,
alum in his biscuits, 'til his shit run warm and thin down the back of
his legs, and him trying to keep the dignity of command, while all
around him the stench.

So the three of us we sat, and Mr. Field to Captain Anderson did
say, "Report." And Anderson, who knew enough to know what he
did not know, did in turn gesture to yer Ahab (and in this, if nothing
else, did show a fine intelligence).

Thus freed to speak yer Ahab did tell his employer what Ahab hath
already disclosed to ye, anent the nature of the shear, the colors of the
flames. And yer Ahab, possessed of native wit and acumen, and with a
lifetime of experience in dealing with the owner class, yer Ahab, rather
than belabor the point, he left it to Mr. Field to draw the conclusions.

"So you tell me, Captain, that some metal monster lives beneath
the sea, with crafted pair of claws, and intent malign toward my
enterprise?"

"Ahab presents what Ahab saw, Mr. Field, and extracts no meaning from it. But if ye ask, Mr. Field, and with respect, the opinion
Ahab holds is this: that a metal monster would seem to be the least
likely of explications for what were done to yer cable."

"Are you telling me, Captain, that though the jaws or claws bore
ferrous signature, there was no human agency behind today's set-
back?"

"I can only say, Mr. Field, with William of Occam, that the simpler explication be the more likely."

"And can you tell me, Captain, what you believe to be that simpler explication?"

Here Ahab he paused, as if full of reflection. And spoke slowly,
as if the thoughts were formed in the mouth, conclusions emerging

only at the instant of need. "I would propose, Mr. Field, that the iron were the remnant of an old harpoon, lodged fast within the jaw of yer sea creature."

The elephants they did from the wallpaper stare down at us.

"And yer sea-creature, Ahab he knows it better than any man on earth. It was the self-same Leviathan what took Ahab's leg. 'Twas the self-same Leviathan that, upon second encounter, near unto took yer Ahab's life. Did take it, if ye place your faith in the popular press. Now the fates have brought us together for the third and final time. For yer Ahab he will kill the beast, kill it and slay it, kill it and slay it 'til it float lifeless upon the surface of the sea. And then yer cable will be safe, for then and ever more, and the cables you lay on other seas, they will be safe, long after we have all of us been dispatched to heaven."

Mr. Field lit a wood-and-sulphur match, held the flame to the maw of his pipe, circled it round that the tobacco be evenly lit. Took a long and reflective pull. Exhaled smoke. Then shook his head.

"I have built grand consortiums, have held them together, and when they fell, have built them up again. It takes skill, as you would know, to bear the weight of command. Skill and fortitude. Some might say: resolve."

"Aye, sir," said the craven Anderson, who knew not how to do other than to agree.

Mr. Field went on. "I have earned that resolve by trusting in my mind, and trusting in my gut, and mediating, between the two, at times casting caution to the winds, and at other times hanging back.

"To move now, from the general to the specific at hand: you tell me, Mr. Ahab, that the flames danced gold. But this I did not see myself, and the event was too fleeting to allow for corroboration. And even if we shall cede that there were flickers of gold in those flames, I am not certain that iron be the only element that might yield up that particular hue. E'en if we say, for the sake of argument, that what we glimpsed was the unique signature of iron, why then, there are other explications than that of a harpooned Leviathan."

He took another pull upon his pipe and continued to speak, gazing neither at Captain A nor Captain A-prime, but upward at the great vaulted ceiling where once had been chandelier and now naught save battered filigree.

"But the question is less of causation than of consequence. If, for the sake of argument, we grant that a lance-jawed Leviathan inhabits the seas beneath our ship, what then? Can said Leviathan, harpoon-in-jaw or no, rend us asunder? Well, no. We ourselves are made of iron, and of thickest gauge, and double-hulled at that. So even if your extrapolations, Captain Ahab, be grounded, they do not to me indicate that we should behave any differently than we would were the flame that you saw one of purple, or crimson, or jade green, or pure sky blue. You are following, are you not? While I do not dismiss your speculations, they are of no weight to me in determining the course of future action."

In case yer Ahab were dense, he then payed out the same thought, but in different dressing: "I speak not to cause but only to itinerary. The where-we-go-from-here. All else is history or speculation."

Mr. Field he then turned to the paid-and-bought Anderson. "Is there any means or mechanism by which we might retrieve the water end of the cable, haul her up, make a splice?"

"The splice, she be easy," said Anderson. "The haul-up, that be hard. We are now beyond the Shelf, and when we fixed depth this morning, we were at just shy of two thousand, two hundred fathoms. 'Tis a long ways down. There be far more ocean-bottom than there be cable, and the distinction between the two be impossible to make from our vantage up here. Descent with the grappling hook or grapnel is possible, and we've on occasions previous retrieved cable from that depth or better. But the course of our work be trial, and error, and trial again."

"Indeed," said Mr. Field. "So without regard to what is past, or passing: what, for us is to come?" He looked not at Ahab, who had some distinct thoughts on the matter, but rather to Anderson the Miserable. Who replied in a manner that will surprise no one who hath been following this tale.

"I recommend," said Captain Anderson, "that we return to Foilhummerum. Begin anew. I put it to you that our time best be spent in transit, rather than in efforts toward recovery. Which efforts will be dispiriting at best, futile at worst, with the latter outcome far more likely."

"And how long to return?" asked Mr. Field.

"Four days. Perhaps five," said Captain Anderson.

"And to make the new splice?"

"It is the work of a morning," said the captain.

"And to set out again, 'til we get to the place we are now?"

"Four days, if the seas be with us," said the captain.

"Nine or ten days, to set this right?"

"Nine or ten days," said the captain. "Shall I give the command to turn round?"

Mr. Field held up his hand and puffed again upon his pipe. He did not speak for the longest moment, during which we heard the sounds of the sea lapping against our doubled hull, the sounds of the crew going about their work. Somewhere on deck a binnacle was being polished, teak was being swabbed, lines were inspected for fray, pulleys oiled. Down here, just Mr. Field and his lucubrations.

And then he spoke.

"We will deploy the grapnel and we will do so until we have retrieved the severed end. Then the wire-man shall splice it together, each strand to corresponding strand. And when the two cables are one again, we shall pack it with perch, lower it gently back to its rightful place upon the floor of the North Atlantic. And 'twill be the stronger for it, like a bone broke then knit.

"This is, beyond all question, the best way now to economize the affairs of all the companies embarked in this. If the prospect of success is, as Captain Anderson has said, but fair, to return to shore would incite a chain of events that would cause failure catastrophic. And I dare say were we to return, we would not, given the circumstances, again have the wherewithal to depart.

"Convey then the message that Mr. Field is buoyant and hopeful. We shall at once go at the picking up. We shall start now, and we shall persist."

"Sir," said the awful Anderson. And gave a nod of acknowledgement, assent, obeisance.

Mr. Field did now turn his gaze to yer Ahab who, it must be said, had sat silent and uninterrupting through his employer's disquisition. "You will return now to the *Valparaiso* and make your crew available to Captain Anderson should he need assistance with the grappling."

Now yer Ahab is a man who keeps his silence, to be sure; but yer

Ahab is also not a man who holds his tongue. He will contradict the mighty as oft as he will the weak. He payeth no heed to rank, only to his god, his one ecstatic deity: the truth. So ye who know Ahab know that he could not leave that tatterdemalion ballroom without voicing what needed be voiced.

"Sir," said yer Ahab.

"Yes?" said Mr. Field.

"Yer logic with respect to yer financial partners is impeccable; still 'tis all for naught or worse. For if we stay in place, unmoving, while the grapnel we lower and raise and lower and raise, perhaps for weeks— Why we make of ourselves a fat target for the Leviathan beneath.

"And let us speak of Leviathan. Ahab he doth know him as ye do not. By floating in one place, bobbing up and down, becalmed, we will give him the opportunity. Yer backers may flourish but we shall die. To pursue the course which ye propose— 'Tis *selbstmord*, plain and simple. Our main chance, and our only one: to search out the Leviathan: and the Leviathan to destroy."

Mr. Field now looked at Ahab direct. "I have some knowledge of your history. It is a history of passion and pursuit and there is courage in it. It was because of said history, rather than in spite of it, that I took you on for this task. Were it clear to me that we were under attack there be no other man on land or sea to whom I'd entrust the task of safe passage. You have the hand, you have the eye, but more, you have the stuffing, to meet all foes and having met, vanquish.

"Yet there are three factors in my calculus. Bear with me, Captain, and do me the courtesy of considering what I here have to say, even while being mindful, of course, of your obligation to do what I say regardless. Are we clear?"

Yer Ahab he said naught. There were a shift of his chin, down and up, that might be interpreted as assent. And might be not.

However Mr. Field took the response, or lack thereof, he went on. "The first is, despite your knowledgeable and perhaps imaginative extrapolation, from gold-hued flame to sub-surface monster, I am not convinced that the evidence is singular or that the chain of logic is ineluctable. You may disagree, but I think as well you can fathom how other eyes might see different. I am familiar with your Occam of Orange and, if I may indulge in metaphor, it is with his razor that I shave most mornings. Yet I do not see how the harpoon-jawed monster with a taste for eel to be the simplest and most elegant explication for what has befallen our enterprise.

"The second factor be one of engineering. I know that you have grand and tragic experience with what the maw of a sea mammal can do to wood-staved boat. But this is not your boat of yore. Our hull is made of iron, a material so sturdy you yourself use it to tip your weapons. The *Great Eastern*, she were built by Brunel to have not one hull but two, independent, so that if the first be breached, the second will still hold. And we have a choice of motive power, the sail and the steam, so that if we need move, and move rapidly, we are not dependent—as you have been for most if not all of your seafaring life—on the vagaries of wind and current. Were there—and I use the subjunctive, condition contrary to fact—were there a meeting of ship and monster, why 'tis the mandible that would break and not the hull. And should it come to a chase, why we can move as swiftly upon the waves as any creature can beneath them.

"The third is a question of economics, as simple as it is pure. Our enterprise is subvented by a consortium of investors. They knowingly take on risk that they may share in reward. Yet as you know money is not silent. Even where it has no expertise it has opinion. If money is anxious it will seek calm, and money that is panicked will seek safe harbor. This construction of this ship itself was started, stopped, commenced again, having less to do with the ocean's tides than with the influx and outflow of capital. So as with the previous attempts to lay this cable, were we to encounter a monster we might be damaged. But were the investors to lose confidence, we would be sunk.

"This voyage be the last, best essay at achieving the dream. A dream of mine longstanding, but truly, a dream for all. Dreamed by the century itself, with me the servant or vessel. A dream of poetry by wire, of the ability to trade the thought as well as the crate. To move the product east to west, and the capital west to east, without dock, crane, boat, storm, boat, crane, dock. A movement instantaneous with joy spreading in the moment from there to here, and capital, too, flowing back and forth without the barrier of time.

"You have seen a feather drift downward in a column of air, wafting beautiful and slow; and perhaps you have seen, too, that feather in a column from which the air has been evacuated. It falls with the same rapidity as a ball of lead shot. What we are doing with this cable, Captain—" And here he addressed solely yer Ahab, as if the craven Anderson were not even in the room. "—is to remove the air. And by doing so: to eliminate friction between worlds old and new. That weighty commerce, and feather-light philosophy, might travel without bruise or chance or impediment. What leaves there, arrives here, and in an instant, sans damage, sans loss— Direct. As face-to-face as two men speaking chair-to-chair."

Did he wait for yer Ahab to be converted by what he held to be the compelling truth of his words? He did. Was yer Ahab by those words converted? Listen, me lads, and ye will soon know (ye that do not, from yer *connaissance* of Ahab, know already!). Are ye following the mind of Ahab, even as he takes in the three-pronged stab of Mr. Field's argumentation? Good. Then sit ye down, for yer Ahab is about to reply.

"No," said Ahab.

"Are you telling me you will not agree, Captain?" Field held pipe in hand. "Or are you telling me you will not obey?"

Yer Ahab he thought long before making his response. Yet by the beat of the clock in that great ruined room, 'twas but tick and no tock. Inside was yer grand and leisurely lucubration; outside, as seen by Mr. Field's eyes, Ahab's words were the work of an instant.

"I am yers," said Ahab. "That is the way of command. Yer holy stoner answer to yer watch-men, yer watch-men to yer officer, yer officer to me, and me to thee. And if thou in turn answer to capital, that be neither my business nor my concern. Thou hast outlined a plan by which we work at every hour to retrieve the cable's fag end. And Ahab, he will work with thee, without shirk or slack, and those whom Ahab commands, why those men will work with thee, too, strong of shoulder and singular of mind."

Mr. Field allowed a small cumulus of smoke from his pipe to rise, to float, to disperse. Then, as if to prove that he, too, could be laconic when the occasion suited, said but one word. Ye know the word, but Ahab he doth set it down here that there be no ponderments, nor scratchings of the head.

"Good," said Mr. Field.

With that yer Ahab he did then arise from his chair, and yer Monkey-See Anderson he did likewise. And so did the three men quit the chamber, Mr. Field to return to his stateroom, his charts, above all, his ledgers; Captain Anderson to the foredeck of the *Grand Excrescence*. Where the sit-in-the-water waste-o'-time follies were soon to commence.

And so yer Ahab he watched, and listened, as the fixes were made, and the calculations run, the commands given, the commands received. The *Ferrous Folly*'s navigator placed the ship in lat. 51°25', long. 39°6', course 765 S, 25 W. She'd run 1,062 miles from Foilhummerum, and were now just 606 from Heart's Content. (*So near and yet so far!* said Ahab, but not, ye know, aloud.) Nothing could be more beautiful than the weather or more favorable for carrying out Mr. Field's (misguided, forlorn, delirious) hope.

THIRTY-ONE

———————⚓———————

NEMO, AT HIS table, among his treasured objects, his large glass iris'd full open, did now ponder, aided by the thick coffee he'd himself concocted. He'd spent three cups in contemplation of the iron steamship and what might be transpiring among its command. By now they had certainly ascertained that the cable had been severed. Were there any aboard of enquiring bent, they could in short order ascertain that the cable had been sheared rather than snapped. But it was not clear to Nemo how this would dictate their tactics as they proceeded.

Nemo knew full well that the laying of this cable was a commercial venture, and as such, those who laid it were less concerned with the elegance of the thing, or the science of it, than with its capacity for generating revenue. Hence they'd be balancing the time and expense of returning to Foilhummerum versus what might be gained by yet another expedition. Nemo thought it likely that after all these failures they'd turn west-to-east and seek port. These were not men of principle. These were businessmen and as such were subject to prediction. Their greed could at all times be turned against them.

The alternative would be to lower the grapnel and attempt to retrieve the sea-bed line, that it might be raised and spliced. Still, even if the grapnel yielded naught, and they turned tail in failure, Nemo felt it provided him with better outcome to sink the large ship in its entirety rather than simply scupper this particular mission. He wanted to put paid to this voyage, of course, but also to any voyage subsequent. Not just this length of severed cable, but the ambition itself should be left to rest on sea-bed, there to gather silt. Lost to rust, lost to decay, fed on by *Semibalanus balanoides*, hidden by sea anemones, crusted with *cirripedia*—until the very notion itself was gone, elided from memory and imagination, ne'er again to cross the mind of man.

THIRTY-TWO

——————⚓——————

THE GRAPNEL—AN ANCHOR, cast of iron, man-tall, weighing three cwt. or more, with five very strong flukes—was brought up from the stores and bent onto the wire rope (of which they had a supply of five miles on board) as yer Ahab watched and worked to restrain his tongue. The G____ E_____, under nominal command of the captain Anderson, now steamed to the place where, far as could be surmised, the cable parted. The grapnel was let go at 2.20 ship's time on its deep-sea fool's errand. Her small engine was set going, her wheels and drums revolved at a terrific pace as the wire rope went down, buckets of water thrown on the drums to keep them cool. Yer hissing clouds of steam arose.

Down, down went the wire rope, and one began to realize at every turn of the drum what a grandeur there be in the depth of this mighty ocean. At five p.m., intimation was given that the strain was becoming gradually less; and, in a few minutes more, the man-high grapnel had arrived below, two thousand two hundred fathoms, having taken just shy of three hours in its journey from North Atlantic sunshine to the inky depths.

From five until quite dark the cablemen, with able-bodied assists from the deck crew, vigorously engaged in getting one of the huge buoys over the port bow. The lower-and-grasp it were reminiscent of the carnival game, in which young children are parted from their money in quest of the gaudy bauble, which always lies just out of reach or insusceptible to the claw.

THIRTY-THREE

⚓

MOHAN FOUND NEMO in his chamber and alerted him that the large ship was attempting to raise the severed end of the cable. In hypnopompic state, where dreams were fleeing the grapnel of consciousness but were not yet altogether irretrievable, Nemo was in Orchha Palace, where he had spent the night. It shimmered, danced, before his eyes— Then was gone. Nemo was awake.

"Let me suit up," he said. And then: "Prepare a suit as well—"

"For myself?" asked Mohan.

"Not at this moment," replied the captain. "This is something," he said, "I would like Huzoor to see."

And so Huzoor was summoned; and so did Nemo explain to him that they would be making an excursion. And so were they wrapped and fastened into suits of waxed canvas and brass; and so were forty pounds of gold coinage from the ship's ballast placed into purpose-sewn pockets to weight them down; and so were the round helmets, with thick re-enforced glass, lowered o'er their heads and clamped in tight; and so were the cocks at the neck of the suits' tanks of air turned from stop to go; and so were the two men escorted to the hatch; and so was the hatch fully battened behind them— And so were Captain Nemo, born Prince Dakkar, and Huzoor, born Isambard Kingdom Brunel, in water submerged.

It was hard for Brunel to see, to feel the rise of water in the chamber's narrow confines and not be brought back, in gut as well as mind, to the Thames tunnel. In this world he was in an enclosure that led from *Nautilus* to the sea; but in every other aspect he felt 'neath the Thames between Wapping and Rotherhithe. He recalled when that tunnel collapsed, leaving him stunned by the influx of water, crushed by its weight, left with scant ability to breathe. Now the chamber within was full of water from without, and so the hatch was opened. Nothing between Brunel and the sea. He took his first step into the realm beneath the sea, illumed by *Nautilus's* arc lights. At once he saw the full awe of the ocean-beneath, nothing between him, and it, but the faceplate of his diving suit. He felt a moment of full awe; yet even within that moment, that he was once more one swift *tick* away from his own death. The rhythm of his heart was loud in his ears, displacing all other sound.

His breathing was slow, tempered—*Would this breath be his last? This one? This one?*—but soon found a less conscious tempo. To glide within the water and yet by that water not be drowned or crushed was something of a revelation. But the shock of underwater mobility was nothing compared to what came next. There was the cable: lying down on the floor, an undeviating line (with some small sinuosity here and there) leading straight back, one must assume, to Foilhummerum. There was the end of the cable, severed, by the Captain or one of his men. There was the grapnel, lowering now from the cable-ship, seeking—blindly, as there was no method for those lowering, up there, to see their grapnel, down here—the cable, to grasp it, hold it, bring it back to surface. But then there was— The mass. The round, elongated mass, floating dark. Only one ship that big. Only one ship, in all the oceans of the world.

He knew it: oh yes he did. He knew the stem and the stern, the port and starboard of it. He knew the plates and knew the rivets. The paddles he knew, and the screw, and the boilers that drove the paddles and screw. He knew her draught and all below; he knew her waterline and all above. It was his ship and it was a magnificent ship and it was his *Great Eastern*.

He thought of his children, and what their faces might look like, and where they'd been schooled, and what were their ambitions for life. And whether his son, like his father, and his father's father before him, would take up the profession. And whether the Hadley's quadrant that his father had so precociously and accurately constructed, which had been handed from Marc to Isambard just before the Thames Tunnel project, and last seen in his office in London—

Whether that quadrant would now be on his son's desk, gazed at, forgotten, rediscovered, touched, held in hand, the weight of the ebony wood, and the weight, too, of his heritage. *Would the lad remember his father?*

And all of these thoughts in the instant between systole and diastole, as, encased in undersea suit, moving beneath the North Atlantic, he gazed up at the belly of the ship that once he'd built, and whose launch he'd wordlessly attended, and whose current rack and ruin—*a cable layer!*—mirrored perhaps too closely that of its creator.

Now the two of them—the iron ship, and the man who'd built it—were, after seven years in which they sailed on separate seas, brought once more together. He was close enough that he could swim to her; and if there were not the water and the glass between them, he could smell her. He could see the fairings of her paddles, now reduced in diameter, to the large patch of thinner plates on her belly, where she'd been scraped and repaired to standards less stringent than he himself would e'er have allowed.

And even as the Captain did with a touch of his metal-encased hand guide the grapnel away from its intended target, Brunel he thought, *but if she wants the cable, why shouldn't she have it? How can I deny her anything?* The grapnel now was raised up slow and empty. They gazed for a while at the reflective trembling underside of the sea.

Nemo beckoned and the two of them swam back toward the *Nautilus's* forward outer hatch. Nemo opened the hatch, ushered Brunel through, but stayed outside the craft, shutting tight the hatch from the outside. Swam swift and elegant back toward the cable. Brunel was in the chamber—neither boat nor ocean but passage between the two. When the water drained he would re-enter the ship that had been, to him, home for the longest time, and which he had part-constructed, and which bore a new name—*Nautilus!*—in tribute to his work. Yet he wished he were aboard that other, grander boat, the one above, the one bigger than any other ever built, forever tied to the name of Isambard Kingdom Brunel.

The water now did drain out, displaced by pumped-in air. But Brunel's thoughts remained intact. Even as the helmet was removed, and the air-tank stopcock turned 90 degrees, and the sea-suit peeled

off, and as he made his way back to his room, he could not stop
thinking about what he had seen, and about the life of the ship he'd
not seen for seven years, and about his own life, which for the same
seven years had been removed from sight. And thought, also: *My
father was Sir Marc Isambard Brunel. Knighted. As I shall never be.*

Passing through the salon, the iris full open, he saw, outside *Nautilus*, its captain, more than two thousand fathoms beneath, gazing
up at the grapnel as it descended one more time. Pulling the grapnel's iron teeth to the side. It was impossible to see his face, but Brunel could imagine his expression as the grapnel once more failed,
with Nemo's intervention, to find purchase.

If he were to compare his life now, to the life that was his in
London, Isambard Kingdom Brunel could certainly see it as a series of subtractions. His wife and family were gone; the comforts of
home and office, gone; the familiarity of the old streets and circles
and parks, all gone. Would he e'er again would he have a joint of
lamb and claret at his club, or fire up what had been his favorite cheroot, or discuss the shaping of lasts with his bootmaker? He recalled
one particularly beautiful spring day on a family visit to London in
Green Park—*or was it Saint James?*—when he had been five years old
and the world, grayed and drearied by winter, had suddenly, as if
overnight, been reborn.

If one were to make entries in the ledger, one would start with
Isambard Kingdom Brunel in the fullness of his fifty-three years,
and then begin to take away, and take away again, until you could,
should you wish, find the subtotal that would be writ in red.

But the ledger is double columned. The pleasures of the draughting table, which had been so central to his landed life, continued here
at sea, and the conundrums in whose solution the Captain had asked
him to participate were no less challenging or worthy than those offered up in his former existence. He'd had to devise a way to tunnel
'neath a river; now he was living in a moving tunnel 'neath the sea.
In Brunel's former life, not all of his designs had been built immediately, or even built at all—one recalls the years of travail, mounting
almost to a decade, that went into the *Great Eastern*, and the long
saga of the Clifton Suspension Bridge, designed in 1831, yet not e'en
begun at the time of his departure.

Here, when he sketched out something for the captain, why the captain then brought into play his carpenters, his metal-men, his lifters and carriers, his welders, his hammer-men: who worked without cease 'til the thing were built.

And in the way that what arrives as shock can depart as habit, many of the accouterments of his new life appealed. We might, in our catalogue, include the sights afforded by continuous oceanic travel; the freedom from the obligations of the larger social comity: and perhaps, though any of us would be loath to admit it aloud, the freedom from the obligations of commerce, routine, family. So for almost each red entry in the left of the ledger, there was a companion entry, in black, on the other side of the line.

Though it would be as useless as it would be futile to seek one moment in which the stimulations of the new life overcame the sense of that new life's cost, if there were such a moment, it likely occurred during the design of what would come to be christened the *Nautilus*. Brunel at first was frustrated, then triumphant, in devising a method to use the differential between the water temperature near the surface of the sea, and that of the deep below, to generate electricity, and with said electricity recharge the *Nautilus*'s batteries without the need to make landfall.

And as the *Nautilus* continued her voyages, Brunel became more and more committed to her perfection. Circulating interior air through a bed of charcoal to filter out odiferous gasses. Reconfiguring the seals on the Marié-Davy scope that it could be turned 360 degrees without incurring water's entry. (Often Brunel, with the Captain's permission, would press his eyes to the ocular, then move round the pole, a circle-dance of sort, while above-sea the objective synchronously did swivel. And pausing to track the flight of a gull, or to inspect what might be a plume of smoke on the horizon.)

Perhaps more crucially, to an extent that Brunel did not himself acknowledge, his social views were in the midst of their own circle-dance. The London Brunel, an Englishman by birth and acclaim, would have assumed that his country was in all ways bringing enlightenment to the darker places of the world. The oceanic Brunel began to consider other points of view. It might be said that his good character had been rusted by his captivity, but 'twas more complex than that.

In London he had read, in his morning *Times*, of the glories of the British Empire, narrated in the triumphal voice of those in whose gloved and powerful hands were held that Empire's reins. Yet in Erromango, in the Candiotes, and in the Aden Settlement of British India, he had seen the other end of the strap: those who by the United Kingdom were cast off, or passed over, sapped for their utility without remuneration for it. Those who had been brought enlightenment yet at the expense of their freedom.

It was not a pretty sight, and the fact that most Englishmen were unaware of the source of their well-being accounted, in Brunel's mind, for their tranquility in accepting the gift. He was unwilling to entertain the darker supposition: that were the general English populace to know of the suffering at the other end of empire, a suffering that had been kept from their view, they would not merely accept it as a cost but would endorse it, even with enthusiasm. Brunel recalled the way his French-born father was accepted in his newfound land, his accent and Continental table habits notwithstanding. And the English had, both in legend and in practice, a fondness for eccentricity. But the tolerance, the fondness, perhaps did not extend to the darker races, or to the map's outer verge.

Still, Brunel retained his full enthusiasm for technology. As regards the cable, it must be remembered that Brunel chaired those sessions of the Institution of Civil Engineers at which sub-marine telegraphy was first, and at some great length, discussed. All his life Brunel had put shoulder to wheel in service of Progress, which in his case meant bringing far places together. He and his father, with great labor and no little bodily jeopardy, drew and then built a tunnel to connect the Londons on either bank of the Thames. Brunel took grand pride in designing and implementing a railway system to make possible the rapid conveyance of people and goods among the various towns of the West of England. And of course the Clifton bridge was meant to re-unite two banks, separated across the years only by water and time.

If the Captain Nemo approached the cable as instrument of empire, as avatar of a future that was bound to benefit with wild disproportion that empire, Brunel's reaction was more complex. He saw the consequence, but he also saw—in the gleam of copper, the sinuous braid, the thick, satisfying pack of gutta-percha, the lazy arc as the cable draped down from ship to sea-bed—a beauty and symmetry that appealed. It was the Way of the Engineer: in the cable he discerned the elegance of a unitary solution to so many interlaced challenges. The way it was wound, and packed, and laid—a hundred small decisions, all of them made with imagination and sound mind, each of them the residue of a ninety-nine choices inferior abandoned along the way.

And if far places could be brought together not by physical conveyance but by electricity coursing through wire—what man alive could deny the triumph? This was something he believed.

Yet here he was, aboard the craft *Nautilus* that he himself had perfected and built, a craft whose mission was to sever rather than to connect. How to reconcile? Within the cavern interior, the electrified cables that crossed Brunel chasm were, at this moment, beginning to touch, to short, to spark.

THIRTY-FOUR

———— ⚓ ————

Now and then, as yer Ahab bore witness, there was a sense that the grapnel it had got hold of something, and one bite sufficiently strong as to induce the hauler-men to pull up and see what had been caught. About a quarter to seven (Greenwich time) the pick-up engine was put in motion and to aid its feeble efforts the rope was passed round the capstan close by. It came up kindly at first, and by eight p.m., 1,500 fathoms were on board. The dynamometer, which had been registering as high a strain as 70 cwt., suddenly indicated an increase to 75 cwt., and it was clear to all that the flukes of the grapnel had at last got hold of something! Even the most skeptical aboard admitted that, if 'twere anything, 'twas the cable.

About eight and a quarter of the clock, just as the mirthless sun it were setting low and orange in the west, one of the wheels of the picking-up gear began to complain and very short afterward broke. Thus the work of the haul was thrown to the cable staff, pulling by hand, and singing a short-drag chantey as they pulled.

In the Black Ball Line I served my time
To me way-aye-aye, hurray-ah
And that's the line where you can shine
Hurrah for the Black Ball Line

At Liverpool docks we bid adieu
To me way-aye-aye, hurray-ah
To Poll and Bet and lovely Sue
Hurrah for the Black Ball Line

This were not easy work, nor without jeopardy, as the line could without forewarning spring with such force as to imperil the lives of those who were near it. Now did: the wire snarled and flailed two men—unknown to yer Ahab but they were fellow seamen, and in that they were yer Ahab's brothers—received serious blows, and were taken amidships to receive the care of Dr. Ward, a man for whom rum were the ultimate medicament, and best applied to doctor before patient.

> *And now we're bound for New York Town*
> *To me way-aye-aye, hurray-ah*
> *It's there we'll drink, and sorrow drown*
> *Hurrah for the Black Ball Line*

And so the night did fall, and the air o'er the seas thickened with nocturnal haze— Yet yer Craven Anderson (despite the dark, and gloom, and without respect to the injuries already sustained by his men) pressed on, pressed on. The crew worked on, t'other captain's spirits did rise with each fathom of the rope coiled over the drum. But, then! Of a sudden, and in one bound, the rope she sprang into air with a ringing noise, while the drum, no tension on it now, spun mad and cacophonous as if 'twere some demonic top. And before its revolutions could be arrested by the cable staff or the hempen stops, the sea-end of the thing slipped away from them and darted down. Down, 2,200 fathoms to the Atlantic seabed.

The break, the sudden snap, 'twere a mystery to the Andersons and Fields of the world, but 'twere plain as yer fist in daylight to Ahab, yes! (And to repeat the phrase of which ye have begun to recite along with yer Ahab: *ye already knew that.*) Ahab alone were in possession of insight as to the motive cause, both of the cable's severance, and the setbacks (ha! ha! and ha! again) encountered in the attempts at retrieval. If his deductive reasonings as to first cause needed any confirmation further, his reasonings their confirmations received with the grapnel's every failure. And so as the officers and hands departed the gloomed foredeck, heads bent low in defeat, so did Ahab, his head bent low as well, but for reasons different. Yer Ahab, he were studying the rope-and-cable, and where it dipped into the sea, and with what support it remained fastened to the large drum. He made sure that the drum were fixed, jammed, by long staves, into unmoving state. (Why did he do this? Ye shall soon know! And ye know far better than to ask, ye pouchless marsupial! With patience all will be revealed. All, save that which cannot by human senses be perceived, or by human intellect fathomed.)

There were then a mournful party in the grand salon. One by one the dank and dour celebrants dropped away from the table, each to the privacy of his cabin, 'cept yer Ahab, who made his way amidships, climbing the gangway ladder, striding the deck, surmounting its rail— And into one of the chaloupes did himself catapult.

"Ahab needs be taken back to the *Valparaiso*," he said and the mates, not waiting for confirmation from their own Captain—for they knew, in Ahab, a man of the sea when they saw one—freed up the oars, even as others worked the winch to lower by ropes the wooden boat.

It met the water gently and with quick moves the oarsmen freed the winch ropes from their belaying cleats. Ahab did point to the *Valparaiso*, the clumsy *Valparaiso*, laid out as if by the yard and sawed to length, with her stern-like prow and her prow-like stern. And then mates did as mates worldover have done: they put their back into it, and with each and every parcel of strength did commit the craft to the direction that Ahab did point.

And as the chaloupe made its way 'cross calm Atlantic from the Thing That Was Not A Ship to the wooden Coming-Or-Going, as Ahab scanned the horizon from where the sun rose to where it set, as he scanned the sea for perturbation in the normal lap and flow, as he reviewed in his mind the conversation with Mr. Field, he now thought to himself those words he had, within the confines of his head, formulated, words that he knew better than to pronounce. And the things he could have said but did not were these:

"Ahab was brought on for the job: the job of finding what hath sundered yer cable, and once found, dispatching it, to hell or watery grave. Should we spend our time in lowering the grapnel that chance be lost. We make ourself ripe for plunder when we should be thin and swift. Leviathan is near. We must give chase without hesitation, and then, once he is within our sight, pursue without cease."

And in the theater of Ahab's mind, where *I Am Ahab* played nightly, with matinees on Wednesday and Saturday, Mr. Field did thus reply:

"The *Valparaiso* accompanies the *Great Eastern*. And the *Great Eastern* shall remain in place 'til the cable be retrieved, spliced, perched, re-laid. If you are holding me up for money you may as well stop now. Your compensation shall not be revisited—especially not on account of an act of God."

"What cut yer wire, that were no God," said Ahab, staring less at the Owner than outward, through the wall invisible, toward the Audience, and thus garnering its applause. Ahab stood, tapping his Aaron's rod 'gainst the floorboards, doing so with vim and momentum, that the stage quiver and the deep dark note reverberate throughout the hall. When the sound and its reflections were damped, and the Audience be as quiet as a choir of churchmice, dead churchmice at that— Then and only then did Ahab continue:

"There is something, Mr. Field, what hath wrought yer damage. 'Tis the Great White come round again, no other. Nothing else will fit the facts.

"Now, ye knew yer Ahab when ye first sought him out. Ye sought him out because ye thought him of a single mind, and if ye be honest ye'd admit this. Well yer Ahab hath no thoughts preconceived, no agenda what preexists. Yer Ahab hath but one motive, one drive, one line of action: to find what sheared the cable and dispense with it. Ahab will not rest 'til that be done. He shan't turn back e'en if ye do. He goeth forward. To find the nemesis. To cleanse the seas. 'Til there be nothing beneath those seas than what God there meant to be. And nothing upon the surface of those seas save the blood of those who would defy us."

Again the crowd gave up its applause, longer and heartier, as they bent their emotions to the emotion of the man on stage. Then the crowd waited, to hear what "Mr. Field" could say, or do, in response to logic so passionately delivered, ideas so compellingly drawn.

"You were bought and paid for," said Mr. Field, now rising, now pacing back and forth, upstage from our Captain. Were there a note of bonhomie in his voice previous, that note were now gone. It were all business, all command. "That mission consist of following *Great Eastern* where'er she shall go, whether to hell or Foilhummerum. And if you continue to object why then we shall seize the *Valparaiso*; and if you attempt to fight us off why then we shall ram the wood-hulled *Valparaiso* with our iron-laid prow 'til she break up. Nor shall we offer assistance to the human flotsam from that break-up, no. Your mates, your boatsteerers, your swabbers, your carpenter, your cooper, your cook, and yes, your chanteyman, they will perish, and their mortal souls we be on your account. And when we make land in Nova Scotia we will there tell the saddest tale: of the sudden storm that did you in."

Here he turned to the third figure on our stage, a bit-part player of no real distinction, whose role consisted in sitting there, without distraction to the leads (and in that he did well, did well). "Am I correct, Captain Anderson?"

And here yer "Captain Anderson," knowing well that this was his Moment, the lime lights upon him, here did he show in his countenance the wrack and dilemma of a weak man, a pitiful man, a man whose integrity had been up for sale, then purchased. It were the task of this actor to show his bravery be o'ertaken by his cowardice. Thus did the character "Captain Anderson" cast downward his eyes, in such a way that no observer could read anything other than assent, and obeisance, and the moral failing that would, in longer run, condemn his soul to the fire.

"I give ye both one hour," said Ahab, commanding the stage, "in which to re-consider." And with that he strode, by boot and Aaron's rod, offstage, to applause thunderous, while the curtain were lowered, legg hitting the stage with deep low thump, making manifest the end of Act One.

And as the audience in Ahab's Theatre took their break, and drank their drinks, lit their tobaccos; and as Ahab in his dressing room breathed deep, preparing for the ardors of the Second Act; while all this transpired *within*, here, *without*, on the chilly North Atlantic, under lowering skies, did Ahab's chaloupe approach yer *Valparaiso*, on whose decks even now the ropes were being lowered in anticipation of Captain Returned. Thus did Ahab, the applause of the Audience still echoing within his head, look up to see the faces—expectant, grateful, solemn, profound—of his men. Of his boatsteerers and binnacle men, swabber and cook, his chips and yes, his chanteyman.

THIRTY-FIVE

———————✥———————

AS THE ROPES were lowered, fastened to the cleats of the chaloupe, raised up again— As the men of the *Valparaiso* pulled the ropes and pulled again— As Ahab ascended from sea to deck, rising up, as if from the terrestrial to the heavenly— The *Valparaiso*'s remaining hands gathered to welcome, more, to await news. For Ahab had to the iron boat been summoned, Ahab had been told, and now they wanted Ahab to relay to them the news. Conveyed not by pulses through wire but from mouth to ear, the way news has always been conveyed, and always should be, and amen. Thus when all were on deck, and quieted by the solemnity of the occasion (notwithstanding their jubilation at their captain's return), Ahab did look from one to the next, meeting their gazes and returning same. He mounted the foredeck that all could equally hear and from that perch did issue his report.

"The cable hath been severed. The *Great Eastern*'s Captain Anderson, having neither mind nor motive of his own, doth in this matter as in all else defer to capital, in the person of Mr. Field, who speaks for the monied consortium. The investors, hence Mr. Field, hence Captain Anderson, sees only cost and benefit, the ink black and the ink red. From that perspective they weigh and decide. And what they have decided is to spend the days as needed, up to ten of those days, in lowering and lifting the grapnel, to retrieve the cable from the ocean floor, some two thousand fathoms deep."

The crew they were silent but in their countenances Ahab he could hear their boos, and their hisses, fully as loud as the boos and hisses he had heard, moments ago, in the Theater of Ahab. "Be the grappling successful they plan to splice, repack, re-lay, then continue 'cross the Atlantic, paying out the cable as if no thing had transpired. But should the grappling take too long—which is to say, should its cost exceed the cost of failure—why then they plan to return to Foilhummerum, hat in hand, and there beg the moneymen to back yet another try.

"In this they did not take into account, let alone heed, the observations and recommendations of yer Captain. On this deck, with ears more open to logic and the truth, let me lay out for ye what yer Ahab hath seen; what, having seen, he knows. And what, having known, he does. That the cable it were severed by the jaw of the Leviathan, so mighty it could us swallow, should it wish, *Valparaiso* in a single bite. It could drown us by malice, it could, or with neither thought nor intention, by a wave of its fluke. We'd all be interred en masse in the North Atlantic. Ye, holystoner! What wouldst they know of ye in Nantucket? None but that ye went to sea, and were presumed there to have died. And if ye have a wife—do ye, holystoner?—she'd be the Widow Uncertain, mourning thy death without the comfort of laying thee to rest, each step of her life haunted by the possibility that ye might wash up one day, ragged and transformed, upon the doorstep. I want now each of ye to think of yer connection on land, the piece of yer heart ye left behind— And what would become of it should we meet our end here at the hand of Leviathan.

"For all the obfuscations of power, the truth of our situation be dead simple. Should we follow the command of capital, come down from the consortium, as conveyed through its satraps and plenipotentiaries, through Mr. Field, to Captains such as Anderson— We would sit here, bobbing like discarded wine cork, until Leviathan wake and we sailors drown.

"But should we instead follow the command of common sense we should pursue Leviathan, and slay it, that it harm *neither* us *nor* others, nevermore. Until it belch plumes of blood so thick as to be beyond the reach of the capacity of yer human to imagine. As it descends slow inexorable to its grave, near two thousand fathoms below.

"Are ye with me?"

There was nary a voice raised in dissent. Did they share the desire to fight, or share it in the measure that their Ahab was by that urge possessed? This we do not know. But we do know this: that none among them wished to die.

And so, having been dismissed, they returned to their sea-borne tasks while Ahab went belowdecks and, accompanied only by his chanteyman, did think, and plan. For the work at hand best be done in full darkness. The moon tonight would be near-new, less orb than scimitar, and thus would cast scant illumination. This was, to yer Ahab, a sign that his intentions had been blessed by fortuity.

THIRTY-SIX

————— ✦ —————

IF YE GAZE up at the moon under the clearest skies, on a night when said moon be full, ye might notice a place bluer than the rest, above the moon's equator, nearer to the pole, and a hairsbreadth to the right of central longitude. That be yer *Mare Serenitatis*, sea of serenity: and that be yer Ahab. And to the right and below, another patch shifted a jot toward the blue: *Mare Tranquillitatis*. That be yer sea of tranquility, and that be yer Ahab, too. A temperament as sunny as the moon. As he walks, serene and tranquil, from the stern of his ship, past mizzenmast, all the way to prow. With a smile on his—

No, lads. Yer Ahab doth not smile. Yet he can radiate a calm, he can, and when he doth so, the days that emanate from his soul spread out 360 degrees, becalming all within range, 'til the crew entire, and yes, the rats in the hold, and yes, the maggots in the meat, all creatures aship be as content as the babe just woken from dreams of womb and pleasure, eyes still closed in that instant before acknowledging the day.

And so I caution ye, do not think ye know yer captain. He can be a *Mare Serenitatis*, yes, and a *Mare Tranquillitatis*, yes— But neither friend nor foe would think to call him *Mare Cognitum*: sea that has become known.

I say this to thee, lest thou Jumpest to Conclusion— Lest ye think that Ahab care naught about all save Leviathan— Know that the course of action he was about to undertake were undertook for reasons calm and beneficent. And that his temperament, as he embarked upon those actions soon to be revealed, that temperament be as pacific and as tranquil as pale blue seas on the lambent moon.

And so when clouds hid both that moon and most of yer stars surrounding, when the largest number of the crew of yer *Grand Excrescence* would be in dreamland, save those on watch or cursèd with insomnia— When 'twas late enough that all those conditions be met, then did a chaloupe set out from yer *Valparaiso*.

The tholes were well-greased with tallow and the oars wrapped in rag that the rowing might be accomplished in silence. And those who pulled those oars pulled them with tact and care, blade meeting sea at the most acute of angles, that the plash of wood 'gainst water be kept to its minimum. The crew had been provided with coffee beans which they chewed and sucked, it being Ahab's belief that coffee doth enhance the awareness, and aid in the ability to pass a long night with less fatigue.

The chaloupe passed the marking buoy, the surface indication of just where the cable lay beneath, and the grapnel wire, cool now, its work paused for the night. The chaloupe it were dark, were silent as it glided forth, and tis a tribute to the men under Ahab's command that the chaloupe did reach the G____ E_____, it did, without a soul aboard the latter aware of its arrival.

To clamp the chaloupe to pulley lines, thence to raise it deckward, would have caused commotion unsuitable to the tasks at hand. And so the crew of the *Valparaiso* shimmied up the grapnel line—can ye understand now, me mates, why Ahab had took the time to study that line before sun had set? Why he had secured the drum with staves? 'Twas in preparation for this moment. Ahab acts in the instant, to be sure. But Ahab, he will also plan ahead. Thus did our chaloupians shimmy strong and noiseless, working with deft hand and crossed ankle, as if nocturnal *Cercopithecidae*, up the grapnel line, onto the darkness-within-darkness that were the *Great Eastern*.

And so Ahab, clad in black (like all the Valparaisans this unanimous night), and bare of foot (one wants not clomp of shoe on deck, not even the smallest squeak of leather, on a night like this)—and with his Aaron's rod encased in muffling cloth, padded at the tip, so that his gait be silent if asymmetric—shinn'd up the rope, then vaulted o'er the iron rail onto the wooden deck. Without the customary shoe on his left leg, and with the added height of padding on the carved prosthesis on t'other side (carved from the jawbone of a sperm whale, don't ye know!), yer Ahab he listed to port.

Which now, as he made his way back, was the boat's starboard. He were bent low, yer Ahab were, that he not be seen neither by yer fore-watchman nor yer aft-watchman, 'til he found the staircase amidships that debouched out to the grand corridor. And while his crew waited patient, silent, Ahab did round the entrance to the Grand Ballroom, 'til he reached the cabin he knew belonged to the captain.

The door be locked from the inside, and yer Ahab, he did not knock, no. He did something different he did, he slipped from his pocket a well-greased master key and inserted it into the lock. Turned it left to right, as a clock would turn, until the bolt retreated back into its pocket. He slathered more tallow upon the hinges so that when he did what he was about to do—*id est*, open inward the door to the Captain's apartments—there would be a minimum of noise to herald his arrival.

Through the scant light that filtered through the porthole Ahab made out the recumbent body of the captain of this large and awful boat, lying on his side, yet snoring. (Yer Ahab, he believed, from long experience in close quarters with his fellow seamen, that a man will snore whilst on his back, yet will silence once turned to his side. Hola: here was the exception.) Yer Ahab did then silently approach, or as silently as muffled peg would allow. And when he was bedside, listing over the surprisingly wide mattress (*wide for a stateroom! e'en for the stateroom of a captain! but then yer Anderson he were no ordinary captain!*)— Thus listing, Ahab did with his left hand cover the mouth of the Snoring Captain, and with his right did thrust a blade—a curved iron blade, forged and tempered, obtained in Stamboul, whose contours mimicked the crescent of tonight's near-new moon—did thrust that blade 'tween Anderson's back ribs. Thrust and turn. It is a fact, not familiar to the general yet well-known by yer Ahab, that if ye stick a man between his ribs that the lung be pierced, and if ye give said knife a quarter-turn clockwise, then the passage from lung to back be well and fully pioneered— Such that, when said man goes to scream, the air will emerge from rent and not from throat. For air, like water, like so much else, it prefer the path of resistance least. And so did Anderson give up his last, endeavoring to make known his alarm, but in doing so he did make as much noise as in the eating of a piece of cheese. E'en as air hissed from the fast-deflating lung, and blood guttered from the wound (the scimitar having severed the aorta or something akin), the loudest noise in the Captain's stateroom were the tick-tock of the ship's chronometer. Keeping the Greenwich Mean Time, no matter where boat may roam.

Anderson he were still heaving and guttering like a spiked fish on the deck of a trawler but Ahab did not linger, no. In one version of this tale yer Ahab would have communed with the dying man, and taken note of the flight of his consciousness, and espied the very moment that his soul ascended heavenward as his mortal remains heaved their last. In another there be a piece of eternal wisdom uttered by the dying man heard only by his killer. In yet a third, Ahab did take his Aaron's rod and establish dominion o'er the dying man.

But those be yer sea-stories, handed down from mate to mate. Those be yer sentimentalist's way-of-seeing, and to that faith yer Ahab did not subscribe. To commune, to receive wisdom, to bugger: there were no need. Ahab had killed him, quick and sans fuss, and having done so, quit the stateroom and turned to the task next at hand.

And so Ahab he walked on down the hall seeking his Mr. Field.

His purpose with Mr. Field it were different, of course, as yer Mr. Field were different in vital respects from yer Captain Anderson. With the Captain, 'twere necessary to remove from the minds of all aboard the G____ E_____ any doubt as to who was now in command. (Ye sever the head and the body it may squirm, and shudder, but in the fullness of time 'twill cease its rictus.) With Mr. Field, on yer other hand, 'twere sufficient to contain him, lest he spew his ideology and infect the crew (who, Ahab knew, would rather take their orders from seaman than from landlub).

If Mr. Field's door were opened with equal silence, the subsequent motions they differed. Here, in this stateroom, with the even-wider mattress, among the filigree and the wainscoting and the emblems of empire, did Ahab say, "Awake, and with yer hands in front." And yer Mr. Field, without fully shaking off the dream, did comply. It may

have been that he understood the voice of command, or, more pro-
saically, that the sight of Ahab's scimitar, stained with blood not yet
dry, were the Compelling Thing. Ahab did then by means of hand
signals prearranged summon his chips and his swabber, who bound
Mr. Field to one of his stately chairs, using three-strand hawser-laid
on the wrists and chest, and sturdier four-strand shroud-laid on the
ankles. It were not necessary to insert a gag as Mr. Field, quickly
discerning the calculus of the situation, knew that his only ally on
board, Bumboy Anderson, was no more, else Ahab would not be
roaming the boat with such impunity. So Mr. Field he accepted his
bonds if not his fate. Knowing that if Ahab had spared his life, 'twas
no act of beneficence, no, 'twas but the cunning of a mutineer who
might later have need of certain knowledge inside his head. And that
Mr. Field's lease on life, nowhere writ down, could be revoked at any
instant for reason good, reason bad, reason none at all.

Meanwhile (*and ain't that the grandest of words!*) even as Ahab and
his trusted men secured the financier's quarters, other of the *Valparaiso* crew were dispersing, each to his own specific task as per prear-
rangement. (Thou thinkest that yer Ahab would take this iron tub
without a Plan? Then thou art even more a cretin than Ahab thinks
thou art!) The navigator would be, at this moment, in the fire hold,
telling the stokers that, as of this moment, they no longer needed
to feed the maw. (The G____ E_____ may be a huge and ungainly
thing, and made of metal where wood would be the better fit—but
from this day on, the G____ E_____ by wind will go, and not by
vapor! There were, in all this mass, somewhere a Ship. And yer Ahab
determined that Ship to find, or, failing, to create . . .)

And even while the agent of capital was suitably restrained, and
the fire-men relieved of their ungodly task (and know ye well, that in
being told to put down their shovels, and to let the fires damp, they
offered up no resistance, only the exhalations of relief and, in one or
two cases, voiced and audible huzzahs)— While all that were coming to pass, the watch crew on deck were being informed of Captain
Exsanguinated's new status; the navigator of the G____ E_____
was informed by the navigator of yer V_____ that there would
be a new course set with the morning fix; and the cook he were told
to make a mess for all hands, as there would be a summonsing of

the crew entire, at first light, and it would be only prudent to feed 'em. (That be yer Ahab's strategy, now can be told: to use force to assert command unambiguous; to bring relief to those engaged in hellish work; to reach out from the small ship to the large, navigator-to-navigator, cook-to-cook, that each member of the crew be full of Sailor's Fellowship; and finally, that all be fed, so that a night of terror be followed by a full-bellied morn. Ahab deploys the fear of death, the deep and bowel-clenching fear— But then, he doth feed, he doth nurture, he doth reassure. There may be other ways to take o'er a ship but when the small force must conquer the large, and when the crew to be subdued have the advantage of Home Territory, well it pays, don't it lads, to be smart. So the scimitar and the mess pot too.)

With the first light all hands they were on deck. The men of the *Great Eastern* entire, save Anderson (deceased), Field (belowdecks)— And absent three souls, valiant and foolish in equal measure, who sought the night before to repel what to them was perceived as an attack. It were tribute to Ahab's men that in each of those encounters they were victors rather than vanquished, and sustained injuries only minor. (One swabber he were stabbed in the calf, yet when the cloths were applied and tightened the bleeding it were stanched.)

Yer Ahab waited in the wheelhouse for all to assemble— Better, ye know, to make an Entrance, than to stand there like a fool waiting for the hall to fill. (In his own mind this were still *I Am Ahab*, and the curtain it had just rose on the triumphant Act the Third.) And there were the aromas of new-steamed beans, and the biscuits too, so that the sailors they knew, that after church there be the meal— First ethics, then grub, as the wise man he once said.

So picture, me lads, this new tableau. An iron vessel, scaled to a size scarce imaginable, well out from Ireland, yet not within sight of Nova Scotia. In latitudes where the sun it sets late (and in some seasons not at all). Thin, slanting, northern light. And hands on deck, and the shadows of those hands—navigators and brass men, stokers and swabbers, those who spent their lives before the mast, and those who were aft of it— All of them, casting shadows long, thin, westerly along the flat ungainly deck.

And now onto that deck here come Ahab. With shoe returned to its rightful place on leg the left, and the padding now gone from t'other, so that the list of Ahab were no more perceptible than the list of the ship. Comes Ahab, with a *thud* and a *thump*, a *thud* and a *thump*, and all souls on deck quieted to hear it. Ahab he stood in front of the sun, backlit, that as day commenced, and the orange orb rose in the skies, it be his dark power they would see, not the features on his face. The mass of Ahab, and the Ahab voice— Those were what yer Ahab did his new crew wish to see and hear.

And when all did settle, when the loudest noise were that of the rising sun; when Ahab were surrounded by his trusted men (his chips and yes, his chanteyman); when the waft of bean and biscuit promised contentment to come, and coffee too; when the black-rimmed stokers blinked their eyes in unaccustomed daylight— Then did Ahab give his first command.

"I am Ahab. And yer Ahab doth tell ye: raise the mainsail. We now cease our steaming. It is time for us to sail." His voice it were calm but left no doubt that he were the man on this new and untrod day, where the sense of possible were still before us, yet to be un-rolled.

And so the deckmen and the ropemen they did snap to, and all on deck saw the raising of the mainsail, and saw it billow in the easy morning breeze. It were the work of perhaps ten minutes, yet when it were done, all of them saw in that sail the flag of a new nation. And knew that the best days of the G____E_____ were not, all of them, in the past.

"Afore we continue: three good men were last night killed. They were fighting on the wrong side, but they were loyal to their ship. They were sailors. And so I have told my chips to craft three coffins, of good wood, and of brass fittings, that their mortal remains be returned to family, should they have family, to home should they have home, when next we make port. They were casualties but they were not mine en-emy. We owe the three good men the honor of their action. Let us be silent, and for those of us who are godly men, let us pray."

With that Ahab did his head bow down, and left it down for three minutes full, that there be no doubt of his respect. He were quiet 'til the silence lost its comfort, and then some. When at last he spoke all were relieved to have that silence broke.

"Nor do we forget yer Captain Anderson. Ye can say this, and ye can say that, yet he were a man of the sea. To the oceans of the world he did consecrate his life. And in doing so did see more of the world than any landlub can scarce imagine. Across those seas in weather fine and weather fierce, through waves and icy floes, did Anderson his ships command without the loss of any. So we remand his body to the waters in tribute to a life spent upon them."

Cued by Ahab's words two swabbers did emerge from belowdecks, carrying with them the muslin-swathed body of the late Captain. With all eyes upon them they did march, slow and solemn, from near-prow to near-stern, and then did mount the iron tower, where the cable it had been payed out. With one at head and one at foot they heaved their load off-deck, into the sea, where it hit the water with low plash, then slowly sank beneath, even as the *Great Eastern*, powered now by wind, left all in its wake.

"'Tis the sailor's lot to do, and not to ask. Yet even without the voicing of it, ye may be wondering what necessitated this change of command. Was not a whim and was not arbitrary. The life of us all did on this change of course depend.

"All of ye know that the cable she had been cut, and cut, and cut again. And now yer Ahab he will tell ye the why of it. There lives below us, in depths unfathomable, a Leviathan whose bulk and power be to the sea creature as the *Great Eastern* be to yer sailboat. His jaw can slice through metal the way a scimitar will slice through yielding flesh. While Leviathan lives, at any moment we may die.

"Yer investors told yer Mr. Field, and Mr. Field he told yer Captain, and yer Captain he told ye, to stay in one dead spot, while the grapnel were lowered and raised, lowered and raised. But to stay in one spot is to be prey. To be morsel. Our only way forward, our only way to see land once more: to seek and to kill and to destroy.

"The men of the *Valparaiso*, they will tell ye: at those tasks yer Ahab be adept."

Ahab let there be a silence, while the words traveled through the clear air of North Atlantic dawn, from the foredeck to those massed below. And when he was certain all understood, only then did he say this:

"We will meet our Leviathan, and our Leviathan will we defeat. And in that moment yer *Great Eastern*, she shall once more be great.

As great as the day when she were launched, the onliest, biggest, proudest ship on this sea or any other. That were our past, and that be our future. All we need is the mettle to sail into it. And I know that all of ye are sailors, and all of ye have the gut.

"So we will again pay out the cable. We will let the cable sink from the stern of our ship down to the depths of the sea. Think of it, men, as fishing, but with stouter line. What do we know about the Leviathan? That though its breakfast consist of krill, and lunch of sardine, yer Leviathan likes to feast, on special days, upon copper. He hath done it once, twice, thrice, and will do it again.

"Yer Captain Anderson, the good Captain Anderson, were under orders from Mr. Field, to cease the pay of cable. Mr. Field, all that concerns him, be utility and cost. Once the cable had been severed, then it must be repaired, or abandoned. That is the way a cable-man sees the world. I am a sailor and so I see it different.

"To me, the cable is our main chance.

"If we sit here for weeks with the grapnel and the whatnot, we bob up and down while Leviathan stares at our belly from beneath and waits for us to sleep.

"Listen up. I hide my notions from no man. Here is what we do: we pay the cable. And should there be a tug, meaning the Leviathan hath grabbed it in his terrible jaw— Why then we come about and go at it. With everything we have. We glide silent—by sail! by sail!—to where he on copper wire feasts.

"And we come up on him. And we come down on him. And with every strength in my strong right arm— And with every sight in my sharp right eye— I stare down upon him. And fix, in my mind and heart, the spot between his eyes, where the skin is most soft, the skull most thin. A foot to the side and ye might as well try and pierce a wall of rock. A foot below and yer lance is consumed up to the hand-end with no damage done at all. There is that spot that few men know well, and Ahab he know best of all. The spot within his skull that day and night thinks of the spot within the skull of the Leviathan. It is the place within the skull of Ahab where Leviathan lives, and the place corresponding within the skull of Leviathan where Leviathan will die. The two are connected by a line sturdier than hemp or copper. It is a line of thought and of will.

"Ye may think me mad. Ahab asks not for yer faith, but for yer cognition. For what choice, really, hath the Almighty given us? To sit and bob upon the gentle waves, soon to be slain. To churn back toward shore, knowing the Leviathan will kill so many more, on so many other days. Or to pay out behind us the thing he cannot forgo. To wait for his moment of triumph and delight. And in that moment, a stroke of blood and surprise, of iron and of justice, as the lance be correctly placed, and the line between Ahab and Leviathan be charged as if with electricity. The 'poon plunges. The Leviathan he thrashes, the way a fish will thrash when dumped on deck, he will thrash his flukes bigger than most ships. But 'twill be the thrash of death.

"And then the line between yer captain, and yer beast, that line shall be severed. For good. And yer captain he can return to land to live out his simple days. And all of ye: ye can return to sea, knowing that the winds may foul yer sails, and the ice may seize yer toes and fingers, and ye may in the horse latitudes find yerself becalmed and die there of thirst and of sun. But those are the deaths of a sailor. Not to be killed before ye are awake by that white and demonic beast. Because the beast will be on the bottom of the sea, where he will feed a multitude of krill, and sardine— What once he ate, now will eat him. And all of ye will feast by day, sleep sound by night.

"Even now I feel the throb. Even now I know he grows near. The line that connects us, it has that pulse, it has that tug. I spin—" And here Ahab did spin, upon his fixed leg, and did spin round thrice. "—until that line is taut. And the tug and the glow tell Ahab that he hast found he true compass."

Ahab he did look out upon his crew, and upon the crew of the Great Eastern, and then o'er their heads to the stern of the ship, and then o'er that to the ship's long and V-shaped wake, where soon the cable she'd once more be paying out.

"He is astern. He is nearing."

There were a hush, as if all had their breath inhaled, but had not yet thought to let it out. A blanket of damped sound, where even the lap of waves be quieted. And at length Ahab did that silence break, with a brief remark as he did rest his case:

"If ye have the gut: the Great Eastern she will have the grace. And we, all of us, shall prevail."

With that yer Ahab turned, and paused, allowing them to see his coat, his legs, his silhouette 'gainst the rising sun, then Ahab he went belowdecks, to the stateroom that had been that of Captain Anderson, and now belonged to the other, stronger captain. While on deck, my navigator, my chips, my swabbers, and yes, my chantey-man, were left above: to let them know who John Ahab was on this unanimous morn.

So if the Leviathan he had the advantage of speed— Yer Ahab would have to rely on his best skill: the harpoon. He'd not have to outrun it, or o'erpower it: just place the lance—large to yer Ahab, small to Leviathan—in the locus of harm. Above the eye, through the orbital lobe, there to unleash the roar of blood within the skull. Drown Leviathan's brain in a sea of its own ichor. Sever the vessels and let the beast's own heart do the work of flooding the cranium, from eye to occiput. And then, once they were thus paralyzed—

Peel the skin (and this must be done quick: *have ye any idea of the heat generated by yer decomposing whale?*). Hack the blubber into rough cubes. Lash them, secure them—or let them float out to sea. (The *Great Eastern*, she was no whaler, and the profit from whale oil, why that be of no interest to her.) And when the skin was scored and parted, the blubber hacked away, the oil saved or spent— There would be the whale, still alive, still sentient, knowing, without being able to flee or prevent, that it was skinned alive, peeled alive, being taken apart, ton by ton, 'til there would be nothing left save bone and sinew and teeth and skull and blood and viscera.

And still yer Ahab will not let it die. Let that come later, and slow, let the beast realize all the harm it had done, and let the beast feel the judgment, the pound of humanity's gavel. Let the sentence be en-graved by harpoon and by knife. A scrimshaw, only whilst the ivory were still alive, and could know how it were being knived.

THIRTY-SEVEN

————— ⚓ —————

IN THE LARGE iron ship there was a wheelhouse, and within that a wheel, and at that wheel a captain. And within the large and terrible whale there must be a wheelhouse, and within that a wheel, and at that wheel a captain of sorts: the part of the brain that takes all in, then wishes, decides, performs. Would this whale of all seas know, e'en as the red curtain descended, that his executioner be from America?

He would be made to know it.

Let Leviathan come. And if in this fight yer Ahab were himself killed, if he gave up his life in this way: he would know that all those years had toted up, and that the sum rendered worthwhile all that had come before. The years at sea, the years on land, all the two-bit *Valparaisos*, the taverns of New Bedford, the chilly nights on Manhatto when he felt he would die of cold, all would be seen as preface. As that what led him here, drenched in blood and oil, harpoon in one hand knife in the other, all the air his lungs would hold expelled in one long, sharp cry.

As other fishermen seeking other kinds of fish did let out a line, Ahab did also cast. Yer Ahab he had told his men to pull the staves, un-fast the clamps, lift up the wood-and-leather brake and let the large wheel turn, paying copper cable—no signal upon it but no matter, no matter—out her stern, into the sea and down, where the scent of gutta-percha would spread out into the North Atlantic. And one of those fragrant molecules would reach the Leviathan. It would sense direction, trajectory— Then set out in pursuit. Little knowing that it was less pursuing than pursued, and that in its quest to sever cable it would sever, instead, the line of its own life.

Let us watch. We have some tales to tell.

THIRTY-EIGHT

———— ⚓ ————

THE CHANTEYMAN LANGHORNE was a child of the islands, of the West Indies, as they are called, a name applied by the British in a time of geographical confusion. He was born on the sugar colony of Tobago. His history was inseparable from the history, on that island, of slavery in its various forms.

The trade in human slaves (though not slavery itself) was abolished in 1807. This took from the islands' plantation owners (who were, as might be imagined, neither desirous nor capable of tending their own cane fields) their stream of unsalaried labor. The owners campaigned for compensation and nine years later were granted it. In August 1816 some 700 former slaves from the US South who had escaped to the British lines during the War of 1812 were freed from bondage and with the same stroke conscripted into the Royal Marines. Then, as reward for their service to the British Crown, demobbed to the islands.

Among them was Langhorne's father, who had survived both cotton slavery and maritime battle to find himself at least by definition a free man. But if he was liberated from bondage, he was not liberated from the necessity of subsisting and thus like so many of his brothers found employment on the plantations of Tobago. There was a wage, to be sure, and there were no shackles, least not of iron; but in other aspects the life was not so different than that which he'd known back in the United States as chattel.

On 1st August 1838 the fuller emancipation of slaves on the island became a reality; and again the cane field owners pleaded for the importation of workers on favorable terms. This they received. On 30th May 1845 the British brought several ship-holds of indentured servants from East India to Trinidad. Among them was Langhorne's mother, Saraswati Ramroop, who met Langhorne's father the day she arrived. Who was in love with him by sunrise the next, and before the anniversary of their meeting had given him a son.

Langhorne was born in the fields and when he was old enough to hold a machete he worked in the fields. Where else to go? Langhorne cut cane. What else to cut? The days were long, the work hard, the company good. They'd start from the northeast corner, work forward around and back 'til all was cut. Then on to the next field. There were many fields all owned by the same man. By the time you finished with the last one it was time to cut the first again. They sang as they worked, old songs, songs from nowhere— Received, handed down, sung again.

If you want to have a fill
Of kingfish or of mackerel
Just come down the hill
To Charlotteville

Though they worked the fields, the songs they sang were often sea songs, the ones their fathers and grandfathers sang.

I'm going to stand on a sea of glass
Hold the wind! Don't let it blow!
I'm going to stand on a sea of glass
Hold the wind! Don't let it blow!

Sometimes when they'd sing they'd sing in parts, with a low melody in baritone, holding down the bottom of the song, and a tenor in harmony. Langhorne found he could without effort find a path between, a fine sweet strain a major third above the baritone, or a minor third, or a fourth or even something flatted, all without having to think: he sang and the song was with him. Or, the way it felt: the song found its way through him, without him having to do much other than open his heart and lungs.

And then I had a Baltimore girl and when she took the notion
She'd rise and fall as steady as the waves upon the ocean.

Langhorne's right arm—the one that held the machete—was strong like that of Hercules. And so he swung his arm back and forth, and walked the fields forth and back. The seasons came and went. One day a ship came down Rockley Bay to harbor at Scarborough and when it left Langhorne was on it. He did not know for what port it might be bound and he did not care. It wasn't that he'd decided to leave. He just found himself on board, as easy and true as following the line of a song.

Langhorne worked hard and they liked that. And when they sang hauling songs he hauled with them and sang with them in a voice so sweet it broke their hearts, a voice that would break the heart of a mermaid, too, were any in the sea and happening to swim nearby.

A dollar a day is fisherman's pay.
Oh yes it is.
Sail all night and fish all day.
Oh yes, oh yes it is.

He was fourteen years old when he stepped on his first ship and nineteen when he first saw New York. It was late October. The news of John Brown's raid on Harper's Ferry had come up by rumor and by wire: in certain precincts of Manhattan some revelry was set loose. It was late at night or early morning in an alehouse a short step from Cooper Union that Langhorne met the man who would, from that day forth, be his captain. They were the only seafarers in a saloon otherwise frequented by landlubs. Two men of the world, surrounded by men whose lives were narrow and circumscribed. Brought together as if by divine magnet. The conversation was easy, it continued until closing, then well past it.

The man was Ahab and so Langhorne left the crew with which he'd arrived. Ahab soon had a ship and Langhorne was his chanteyman. The men of the ship liked a song while they worked. It lifted the spirit, lightened the load. They chanteyman did the hauling, too, but he was by virtue of his song the first among them. And by night he was Ahab's chanteyman, lulling him to sleep with melodies from heaven. They sailed together on ships too numerous to count.

When Ahab was given the *Valparaiso* Langhorne did go with him. And when Ahab came to understand that he was called to take command of the *Great Eastern*, Langhorne did go with him. Had *Great Eastern*'s crew been American they might have taken issue with a black man among their number; but they were English and Langhorne's father had been in the Royal Marines and that was enough. They taught him some tunes which he sang beautifully and thus won their hearts. He told them stories of Tobago, of the luminescent fish that swam in Man O' War Bay and would light up the waters with a pale green glow.

Within a few hours of Ahab's command of the *Great Eastern*—and with the assistance of several jugs of distilled fermented cane, passed generously round—Langhorne, who the previous night had boarded their ship as a pirate, was now accepted as fellow sailor. So, too, were the rest of *Valparaiso*'s swabbers, line-pullers, welcomed to the fold.

The routine of those before the mast is not likely, on any given day, to be affected by the composition and identity of those behind it. The men had in their seafaring lives labored under captains generous, captains cruel; captains competent, captains in all ways at sea; captains who oversaw every detail and captains who ventured only upon occasion from stateroom. And under all of these had survived: a sailor's work is, largely, a sailor's work, without regard to whose hand be on the Wheel. The binnacle man he polishes the binnacle, whene'er it needs polishing (and oft when it does not); the sheet man he minds the sheets on days fair and days foul; the holystoners the decks do scrub, from stem to stern, and when that is done, from stern to stem again. As is said on land: regardless of fluctuations in the price of beef, the sacrifice remains constant for the ox.

As Langhorne was quick to learn, this perspective was not shared by the officer class. They had seen their Captain Anderson dispatched (from the ship, and from life itself). Anderson had been, like them, a Londoner, and this new man, this Ahab, was an American: a murderer, a mutineer, a thief. He was a man of the colonies in command of Englishmen. His manners were abrupt and his language wrong. Though they let the cable unspool as he commanded, it remained to be seen in the longer run if they were his men or the *Great Eastern's*.

And they were not comprehending why a commander of the *Great Eastern*—whose holds contained a full 1,500 tons of coal, whose boilers were fiercer than the flames of Hades, whose screw was as the blade bone of some huge pre-Adamite beast, whose paddles were as large and implacable as the Wheel of Fate itself—had chosen to forgo all in favor of the sheet.

But before the mast it was understood. They were sailors and they forgot not their name. Sailors: those who live, and die, by the sail. And so they again unreefed the sails, back-to-front, starting with the jigger-mast: the jigger-mast lower, the jigger topmast, the jigger top gallant. Then to the mizzenmast, where Ahab had stood; then the mainmast in all its glory. Once the mainsail was set the trysail no longer had use, so it was reefed. Then the foresails, and finally the bowsprit.

And as they hauled line they sang, and as they sang one voice rang out clear and true among them and it was Langhorne's. It was a voice to lift the spirit and to calm it, and it made of many, one.

And once they were ahead full sail; once Ahab knew that the *Great Eastern* was tight under his command; once it was clear that his men had been recognized by the *Great Eastern's* crew as fellow men of the sea; once he was assured by his men that he need not focus an abundance of his attention on questions of disobedience; once the cable were again being payed out in a languorous sag from the rear of the ship (the better to attract the Leviathan, whose unseen presence beneath the Atlantic had become the sole occupant of Ahab's thoughts)— Only then did Ahab feel freer of spirit, and was thus able to divert his attention from the larger life of the *Great Eastern* to other pursuits.

The *Great Eastern*, he knew, would never be his. He was a ship's captain and, try as he might, this was—to Ahab—no ship. But it did not have to be. Its purpose was, to Ahab, well-defined, and limited to tasks. One: not to sink. Two: to deploy the cable that to the Leviathan was as glittering prize. Three: to let Ahab work his lance.

Should they return home in good stead that would be fine. Should they slaughter the beast and from its oil make profit, that would be fine. Should Ahab be considered hero, and borne on the shoulders of his countrymen, and hailed down Broadway, and heralded by fireworks, and celebrated in popular song, that would be fine.

But none of those things were necessary. To ensure his being, the sole requisites were the one, the two, the three. All else was dross. Not even the clear and ringing song of his chanteyman, a voice that all ails might cure, could bring him peace, or lead him to quit.

It was as if he and the Leviathan were twins in the ocean's womb. One of them would die and the other be born: there was not room for two. So either Ahab be delivered into this world and the great white die— Or the recto-verso, and Ahab would die and the Leviathan rule all and forever.

That shall not happen, Ahab said. To himself, to Langhorne, to whomever sufficiently close to hear him mutter, sufficiently keen to read his mind. His life up until tonight, all of it—the cold winters in New York, the years at sea, the men dispatched to the next life without e'en a fare-thee-well, all of it—was to take him to this moment. The moment where Leviathan dies, that Ahab might, for the first time in his long and awful life, be born.

THIRTY-NINE

———————✦———————

"Why have we stopped? Is the ship—"

"There is nothing wrong with *Nautilus*," said the captain. "Its engines are full stop because I gave the command that they do so. We are presented with a conundrum, M. Brunel, and while I pondered, and in mind weighed alternative explications, I wished for us to be still. And so we are."

It was the Engineer who broke the silence. "Might I ask, Captain, on what you are thinking?"

"Once I have made known to you the subject of my thoughts, you will understand why I sought to summon you. I have, as you have yourself seen, severed the cable which, had I not intervened, likely would have spanned the Atlantic. And yet, though the cable be severed, I now can see that the cable is again being laid."

"Was the grapnel successful," asked Brunel. "Were they—"

"No." Nemo's word reverberated in the ship's new silence.

"They lowered the grapnel repeatedly and each time failed to grasp. They spent the night without activity. Then, this morning, they commenced paying out again. I will let you see." With that he actuated the switch that caused the metal iris to widen; and through the glass saw indeed what the Captain had described. Cable—percha-clad copper cable—draped from the stern of the large iron ship.

"Is it possible that they were unaware of the break?"

"Had they been unaware they'd not have lowered the grapnel."

Brunel had no real wish to assist the Captain in his present goal. Yet it was difficult not to share the Captain's ponder: *A ship lays cable. That cable snaps. And yet she lays cable again as if nothing had been sundered.*

"I would have thought," said the captain, "that they'd return to Foilhummerum, take on board another spool of copper. Either that or—and this was my hope—abandon the project. Yet here they follow another path, one that begs comprehension."

"Is it possible," said Brunel, "that for reasons of contract it is necessary for them to complete the voyage, break or no?"

"It is possible," replied the captain, "but scarce likely. What kind of contract would prescribe a crossing, yet care not if the mission of that crossing were accomplished?"

Brunel found himself seated at the captain's chart table. The captain joined him, pulling from a drawer a pair of sea-cheroots. They fired up and leaned back, following the lazy drift of smoke—blue from the tip, brown from the tail—toward the cabin's coffered ceiling. At length the captain continued to speak. "To solve the mystery of the severed yet continued cable, we are obliged to follow her. This causes me no end of displeasure."

Brunel sensed he was waiting for an interjection: *why so, Captain?* Instead Brunel waited to see what thoughts might form in the captain's mind. He waited for a full minute and then the captain did again commence to speak.

"I am a man of the sea and by sea I mean the sea entire: the Atlantic, yes, but also my beloved Indian Ocean, which itself encompasses perhaps a fifth of the waters of the world. And the Pacific where, as you know, I have found solace and restoration. And the icy seas of the Poles, above and below. In the years that are left to me I want to explore those seas. Yet here we are in a fool's circle.

"Now they are acting in a manner that is not by any standard a rational one, and again we are drawn into the cable's web. The most effective means at my disposal to end this dismal cycle is clear. If I cause the iron ship to drown 'tis unlikely they'll be dispatching another.

"Were there an alternative I'd seize upon it. But I do not see one. Thus: I must put paid to her. I only ask that you hear me out.

"I have, as you know, scuppered many a vessel. I have caused loss of life. But no more so than in any war. The English did against me and my land declare war. That war ended as far as they were concerned but it did not end for us. There are the personal matters here, as you well know. But this goes beyond.

"We are engaged in a battle for the soul of the century itself. You either will understand implicitly, and to the depths of your intellect, or you will not understand at all. You know that I will not argue 'gainst fixed opinion. There is never any profit to it.

"And so while she wags her black tail at us—taunting us, mocking us, begging us to follow—'tis our duty—"

Brunel interrupted, something he'd rarely done, and an act for which the captain had no tolerance. But he needed to say what was in his mind, and the thought pushed out with such pressure that it escaped past the sentries of reason.

"Let go of it, Captain. Let go. You have already won. The cable you hate will not be lain—the break assures it. Let the ship sail where it will. She is no threat to you. If you wish to visit Reykjavik, or return to Erromango, or traverse once more beneath Pole north or south, why then do so. The cable is as dead as a severed snake—it may, for a while, twitch, but there is no motive force left in it, nor can current pass through it. I pray you Captain: let go of it."

The captain looked off, as if he were considering the words of Mr. Brunel. Then the captain he spoke:

"What I am about to ask, you may accept or reject. I will, in fact, not expect a reply at this instant, but rather expect you to contemplate it in your own quarters, removed from my importuning or influence. And the question I pose is this:

"What are your *Great Eastern*'s weakest attributes? Where is she less than fully sound? Seven years ago I was able almost to destroy her by means of a quarter turn on an ill-placed stopcock. Could I gain access to the ship I suspect I could, without grand fuss, find similar imperfections. But for that I would need an accomplice aboard *Great Eastern*, to haul me aboard; and I readily admit to you that I have no such accomplice.

"So I ask you— If you were a small submersible craft, such as *Nautilus*; and if you were up 'gainst far larger craft, double-hulled with metal plate— Where would you strike?"

He paused for several long moments. With the engines silenced Brunel could hear, distinctly, the tick and tock of the extraordinary cabinet clock, the one crafted and fashioned by Breguet, case of ormolu, moon of ivory. He wondered whether the captain were aware, as he spoke, of the enormity of the question he had asked. He could hear the click and sigh of the pipe organ's bellows and pumps, still breathing though no fingers were as of this moment on the keys. Brunel was being asked to assist in slaughter, of machine and of men, by a man who had yanked him from his proper life and now proposed that he destroy what was, in essence, the culmination of a life's work. Through the iris'd window he could see—as he had over the course of his captivity aboard *Nautilus* become accustomed to seeing—a sea-creature of extraordinary aspect. This one was as a billowing sheet, curling in on itself and extending out, then waving, like a flag in the wind—*of what unknown nation?*—but slowed to the point of languor. There was a mouth or cloaca near the top, and the skin—though skin seems far too mundane a word to describe the roll and undulation of what he was glimpsing—was of pristine white, with glowing veins, some golden in hue, and some with purplish cast, spread across the creature's surface, forming skeins in vaguely hexagonal array. The veins shifted and vanished and reappeared and reformed like sunlight on a windblown ocean. Brunel's thoughts went deep, even as within *Nautilus*'s salon he gazed at it, rapt, through the iris'd window, and could have gazed out at it for the longest while, perhaps forever.

"I know that it is difficult," the captain was saying, "to choose among your children." And with that two of the *Nautilus*'s mates appeared in the hatchway escorting their Huzoor sternward, back to his quarters. When he was returned to his room they closed the door behind themselves and fastened it from the outside. What had been, ab ovo, a cell, and had for the better part of a decade become a cabin, was cell once more. Into which he'd been tossed, until he either assisted the captain in the destruction of *Great Eastern*, or, he supposed, perished within the confines of his sub-sea gaol.

The captain had a conundrum he could not solve: why would *Great Eastern* continue to pay out a cable that to which nothing did, or could, connect? And the engineer had one no more susceptible to solution: why would the captain wish to destroy a ship that no longer possessed the capacity to do him harm?

Now the engines of the sub-marine craft started up again. All of the small sounds—silverware in the galley, footfalls along the gangways, the scrape of metal and the low squeak of leather—were swallowed up. Brunel could feel the ship list, then turn: Nemo had commanded *Nautilus* three-quarters ahead, and on a path toward *Great Eastern*. The small sounds were gone, and with them were the small thoughts inside his head. There were only large sounds now, large thoughts, and all of them concerning doom. The destruction of dreams, and of lives.

FORTY

—————⚓—————

NEMO HE WAS in his salon, eyes clamped to the omni-scope. Its objective lens was above the water, the *Nautilus* below. Yet there was no water seeping in, nary a drop: Brunel's design of the nesting rubber gaskets was intelligent and precise.

What Nemo through the omni-scope saw: the stern of the *Great Eastern*. It was sailing along at no great speed, paying out cable behind. And *Nautilus* the *Great Eastern* did now follow, keeping pace, neither gaining nor losing ground. The hours passed and the new-moon skies grew darker still.

Then Nemo saw, on the stern of the *Great Eastern*, a glint— And then another. It was the objective lens of a telescope and it was trained on the *Nautilus*. He was staring at the large iron ship and it was staring back.

The locked gaze was held for the longest time and while Nemo stared at the ship-that-stared-back he fell into thought, and as reverie internal replaced what the senses did perceive, the ship in front of his eyes slow became another ship, pale, translucent, a darker gray among clouds of dark gray fog, a mystery ship, a ghost ship, a ship whose hold contained all the troubles of the world. He saw in his mind a map of the seas with lines wherever British freighters and cargo ships and men-o'-war had crossed. From London out to India, to be sure; but also to the Americas, north and south; and to Australia; and to the ports of Asia and the islands of the Pacific— A web of lines, parallel and crossing, a weave that held the world in its skein. And he saw, too, the privation, the suffering, inflicted causally or with no motive or even without the awareness it had been inflicted. The raw materials taken for little compensation or none at all. Those strapped to cannon and gut-shot with lead balls large as a man's head. Those dead of scurvy in service of the queen. The humans extracted from their lives and pressed into service. Those packed into ships and taken from their homeland and brought somewhere else to harvest for someone else, without pay or prospect or liberty. Those whose languages were lost and forgotten with scant fare-thee-well as English became the mother tongue. Those whose souls were sucked dry by the double-ledgers of English accountants. Those killed in wars fought for lines on a map. Those who were as butterflies broken on the English wheel.

How to end it? How to take the march of civilization and turn it round? How to put a stop-point to history? How to reclaim the lives spent and discarded for naught? How to avenge the deaths of so many whose only crime was to live on a piece of land thought propitious by Company or Crown? How to reclaim agency—and some small piece of dignity—for the lost children of empire?

There was no path to it. There was no one thing one man could do. Even Mangal Pandey—what had he done? His homeland no longer in chains of iron, but still in no ways free— Nemo thought of Mangal Pandey and thought of the slaughter of Rani and Hanuman by English sappers, come in the night and departed, bloodied knives wiped clean on Orchha sheets; and he thought of Madhya, told by traitorous satraps that he himself was dead, so that she went to cinder (and ash, and smoke) by own desire.

The *Nautilus* she had a pointed prow, well-serrated, fashioned of wootz, capable of inflicting fatal damage on wooden-hulled ships. It had done in the *Governor Higginson*; it had rent a hole in the port side of the *Cristóbal-Colón*, from which the *Cristóbal-Colón* did not recover; and similarly with the *Helvetia*; and, as well, with the *Shannon*. The *Péreire*, the *Etna*, the *Lord-Clyde*, all of them pierced by the wootz-clad prow, and all of them by it brought down. The *Castillan*, the *Constitutional*: same. The *Moravian*: gone.

The cable beckoned. The *why* of the cable beckoned even more brightly. Of the mystery: there was no tar, no pitch, no gutta-percha, to matte its gleam. He knew now what he had to do. He would take the *Great Eastern* and slit her side. It was nothing: it was the loss of one ship in a sea of a thousand ships. But it was something.

He fastened his eyes to the omni-scope's ocular and fixed the stern of the Leviathan in its field, dead-center. He watched it for the longest while in silence. It would be better, he thought, to have the benefit of M. Brunel's wisdom at this hour. Preferable. But perhaps—

Not necessary.

"Full speed ahead," said Captain Nemo into his speaking-tube.

In the engine hold the dynamo man did receive the command and, accordingly, pulled the long brass lever rightward as far as it would go. Then Nemo he quit his salon without glance backward at his Cavaillé-Coll organ, his mechanical Turk, his library of books, his table of charts, his Courbet portrait of Baudelaire, his Niépce heliograph with its faint, faded commemoration of his wife and his children. All of this he left behind sans regard. But he did, before he left, take the small ivory ball from its socket in Breguet's orrery and place it in his pocket. Only then did he ascend the spiral steps that led from salon to wheelhouse.

FORTY-ONE

————— ⚓ —————

LANGHORNE DID NOT speak so much: when he opened his mouth it was far more often to sing than to converse. But in spite of his habitual silence—perhaps because of it—he was a keen observer of his fellow man. This, too, was an inheritance from his father, who'd picked cotton in Virginia, cut cane in Tobago: work hard, say little, be mindful of the master. By day Langhorne hauled, and by his singing helped the other men with their hauling. By night he would lie with the captain who would fall asleep almost immediately, though never for very long or in any consistent manner. But Langhorne could tell by the manner in which his captain's body would sway, list, and keel in the night, and the grunts and moans emitted in sleep, all that the captain would never share if awake.

Here is what Langhorne he knew: that the captain was in the slough of disquiet between two periods of certitude. That once he was reacquainted with his own resolve—such as he was, when he decided it was of necessity that they board the *Great Eastern* and overcome its captain—he would again sleep through the night. But until then: the tossings and the turnings only intensified, as if demons within were themselves struggling for command, mutineering 'gainst the captain in which they lived.

When the seeing wasn't good the captain would spend long hours peering into the mist. He'd climb up the mizzen under lowering glass when any sensible person would be climbing down. All Ahab could do was wait: inviting—begging, really—the Leviathan to pursue him. And then, with the *Great Eastern*'s steam-powered chaloupes at the ready, and his lance well-honed, Ahab would do now what he'd failed to do then. One of the more reliable of human motivations, thought Langhorne— And one of the more foolish. Except that if Ahab were right, he'd take down not only himself, but the crew entire down with him.

And if Ahab were wrong, he'd fall into the blackest mood, one from which he might not his self be able to extricate. That would cause sadness in the Captain and in those who cared for him. But at least they all would live. Langhorne found himself in the odd corner: wishing failure and defeat to one he held dear.

On the night of the new moon Ahab was sleeping with un-characteristic depth, his breaths slow and widely spaced, the sound and image of a man at rest, when abrupt from nowhere he was up, eyes wide, limbs tense— Within moments was dressed and out the cabin door.

Langhorne heard his syncopated step as he strode up the gang-way to abovedecks, followed him discreetly. What Langhorne from the doorway saw: Ahab, pacing fast from his cabin to the stern of the ship, a distance of perhaps six hundred feet— *T-THUMP, T-THUMP, T-THUMP*— A tattoo that would wake the dead. And all the while Ahab yelling at the very top of his lungs: "She's here! She's here!" Until all on board were waked, and all on board (save Mr. Field, still in confines) were (sleep-eyed, confused, and in mot-ley variety of nightdress) trailing in Ahab's wake.

"She's here," said Ahab, more softly now. His voice was low, intimate yet all heard; and when he pointed astern, they now all saw what he saw: a faint luminescence, two symmetrical orbs—*like eyes! like eyes!*—trailing the ship at a distance of perhaps a quar-ter mile. They kept pace with the *Great Eastern* and never veered more than a degree or two from her wake. "Right half rudder," said Ahab, and the wheelman called to his men, and his men pulled the rudder chain, and the sail-men trimmed in accord—

And as the *Great Eastern* turned, the lights turned with it.

The crew—all awake now, all gathered, and someone making coffee in an iron pot, and someone dragging the telescope astern— stared. The phosphorescent globes stared back. The fog, the wake, the eyes that followed them at steady pace and without remit.

The sailors on board the *Great Eastern* had, in the course of their lives at sea, seen extraordinary things. They had seen the sheer cliff of the Antarctic shelf; they had seen ships swallowed up whole by a maelström that five minutes before was nowhere to be seen and five minutes later was gone. They had seen fires off the Isle of Dogs flickering in wild and eerie semaphore. They had seen hapax legomena: sea-creatures that existed in no taxonomy, that had ne'er been seen before and ne'er would be again. And they of course had seen all manner of human behavior, from acts of wild and generous self-sacrifice to cannibalism, the food still shuddering on the knife.

But none of them, o'er the course of the hour that they stared at the willful and persistent phosphorescence, had e'er attended a moment more unsettling, and a long moment it was, and quiet, too, under the clouded sky. All men on board were filled with awe and wonderment and not a little fright: *what was this?*

Langhorne he had a deeper ponder: how did Ahab know, in deepest sleep, that there was—*something*—astern? How did the distant phosphorescence penetrate the water, the iron hull, the cabin wall, to make its way into his dreams? Or was there something that by the laws of nature could not be explained— Only by the laws of the sea, which cleave to a different contour.

"Ahab wants the steam-chaloupe fired up, and Ahab wants it done quick; and when it has pressure then my men—we of the *Valparaiso*—shall board, and ye shall lower us down." This is what Ahab said and the crew they did snap to.

Langhorne did not want to be lowered down. But his captain had spoken. What use is a chanteyman on dangerous seas? Could his high and clear song protect them from harm? What use is a human voice, no matter how pure its tone, no matter how jubilant or mournful its melody, 'gainst the glowing uncanny?

Langhorne knew in that instant: he did not want to die. He was not sure if the captain, in the depth of his soul, felt similar. Yet he was yoked to the captain, even as the captain was yoked to the creature astern. At once Langhorne knew that what followed Ahab was Ahab. Langhorne did not know how this be possible but he did know that this be true. He knew that Ahab and the creature they were doublegoers; that if the creature were to die Ahab would

die with it. And so would Langhorne. And so would they all, because they were tied to their captain, and the captain needed to
kill—*something*. In stabbing the creature, the other end of the lance
would pierce Ahab's own heart. And the blood would gutter out,
soaking them all, and draining down to the sea, the sea so deep
and vast and wide that all the blood of all the dead of all the world
could be mingled with it and the sea still blue, a deep and tranquil
blue.

The hiss and sputter of the steam-chaloupe, readied now. Hauled
up to deck for boarding. Ahab and his chips and his swabbers and
his holystoners and his line-men and his navigator and his wheelman and his chanteyman, all queued up, and Ahab he was about to
swing his good left leg o'er the gunwale when from the man with
the telescope came sharp cry. One word:

"Approaching!"

And the phosphorescent orbs that had for the past ninety minutes haunted from fixed distance now were coming up upon them.
With great and ferocious rapidity: *how can it move so fast?* The lights
streamed up on them and then— Went out. The sea as black as
the moonless sky. Where had it gone? But that question was answered soon enough: with a clang and a crash and a terrible groan
of metal. And the grand ship pitching around its midline. And from
belowdecks, from the cable-hold, an awful cry:

"We are hit!"

Langhorne looked to Ahab, half o'er the rail, who clutched at
his chest and belly as if the pain of the ship were reflected in his
body, and by locating the hurt he could thereby know how the
Great Eastern she had been compromised.

And e'en in this shocked and terrible moment the *Great Eastern*
officers, Englishmen all, could be heard to speak among themselves.
The words were muffled but the meaning was clear. Had Anderson
been captain, this would never have happened. Had *Great Eastern's*
grand boilers been ablaze, had the screw and paddles been turning,
they could have outrun it. But with this madman, this American—

Then Ahab spoke with a clean and cool voice, no tremor in the
voice, nothing but the sure and calm voice of command.

"Cable and boiler crew, scout and report. If we are taking on

water Ahab will remain with his ship. If 'tis just the outer hull Ahab
will board the chaloupe and do the monster in."

The men were silent as Ahab spoke. Langhorne could see the
change at once: in affect, in posture— Ahab was their captain now,
and if he were giving orders why they would follow them.

"Bring her about," said Ahab, and the deck-men flew to action,
hauling in the boom, while below the rudder-men pulled in concert.

"Look!" said the mate with the telescope.

Within a moment Ahab's eye was at the ocular. Langhorne, beside him, even without the aid of glasswork, could see what the
mate saw: the two rounded phosphorescent eyes, now fleeing the
Great Eastern off its starboard side with a speed wild and nigh-
unimaginable for so large a creature. The small ones, thought Langhorne, were fast, and the big ones slow, but this one was large, and
fast— And as frightening in departure as it had been in approach.

"Fire up the boilers below and when we have a north heading,
full speed ahead," said Ahab. The English officers exchanged the
briefest of nods and glances. Then Ahab turned from the officers to
the sea, and to the ocean he spoke.

"Ye cannot attack us with impunity. Ye can only attack us and
die." And with that Ahab turned his back, that we saw his billowing shirt as he descended, *T-THUMP, T-THUMP,* down to the boiler
hold. The stokers followed. Soon they would be shoveling coal into
the fiery maw as they'd not done since Ahab took the helm. Soon it
would be a blazing hell down there. Soon the *Great Eastern* would
be churning, prow pointed toward the northern pole in rapid pursuit.

There was no way of knowing how this would end. But Langhorne knew. And deep in his heart was a sadness, the sadness of
predestined fate. It was the sadness his father felt, born a slave and
knowing he would for the rest of his life a slave remain. In the
Royal Marines he was a slave (to the Crown); and on Tobago he
was a slave (to the work)— And on his deathbed (and on his deathbed he was not old) he told his son Langhorne that there was nothing more a man could do, nothing better a man could do, than to
be free.

He had tried, Langhorne had, to be free. But that path had led him here, to this doom-struck ship, on an errand of death. His only uncertainty was this one: as to whether he would die of shipwreck, drowned in the icy sea; or die of cold, wandering the ice floes of the pole, looking for shelter, looking for food, finding neither. His mad Ahab pursued his Leviathan—even as his Leviathan, in turn, followed the drinking gourd, north, ever north.

FORTY-TWO

———————✧———————

THE FIRST BRUNEL knew of it was the acceleration—that moment, more felt than seen, more sensed than felt, when the captain did change the *Nautilus*'s speed from follow-at-a-distance to full-pursue. And he could hear the treble-clef whine of the electric motors as they went into higher range. He knew those motors, he'd designed them, he'd wound the armatures by hand. And they were soon pitched as high as he'd ever heard them.

He tried the door of his chambers. Still locked. The captain had asked him to reflect. But—and this now had the clarity of crystal or of bell—the captain would do what he would do, will-he, nill-he. It was the first time—at least since the perilous voyage 'neath polar ice—that Brunel wondered whether he, or anyone else aboard, would survive.

He wished for something to hold—a rosary (though he was not Catholic or even, in any abiding sense, religious). Or, better, the Hadley's quadrant that Marc Brunel had fashioned from ebony, handed down to him and which, last seen, resided in place of honor upon his desk in London. A desk that—like all else—would ne'er be seen again, 'cept in mind's eye, where Brunel saw it now with grand clarity, as if each object were glimpsed through convex glass, and outlined in black so as to stand out from its surround.

Brunel again tried to quit his room. He pounded on the door with real force and yelled at the top of his voice phrases in the odd language of *Nautilus*'s crew. There was no response. If he were going to perish he did not want to do so alone.

He was pounding on the door when he felt the shock, the deceleration more brutal than any he could recall, from full-speed-ahead to— Full-stop. He was not braced 'gainst anything and his body was tossed a full yard back from the doorway. Books flew from the rear shelf as if by their own devise. A drinking glass on the nightstand took to the air, soared, hovered, stood mid-air for the longest moment as if frozen in time— Then at once dropped to the cabin floor, hitting bottom, glass shattering, water blooming up and out and down in thick drops and sheets.

Then there was the noise, the noise, the thick and awful noise, louder than any he'd yet heard undersea, and lower too, with a frequency that shook the bones and loosed the bowels, a low and terrifying groan octaves below any orchestra's lowest note. It wrenched and tore and would not cease. It was, Brunel thought, as if he'd been strapped to the clapper of some enormous bell, high up in a cathedral's tower, and now some masked demonic madman were pulling on the rope with insane force, and the clapper—Brunel with it— were slammed and slammed again into the side of that bell, which, once struck, emitted tones loud, low, unearthly. And blood did spatter now too. He tasted salt in his mouth. Was he bleeding? He took his hand to his forehead. Yes, he was bleeding. Yet he had no recollection of having hit his head. Odd. And then the ferocious groan of metal, the *Nautilus* entire shaking in low subsonic tremor.

They'd hit something.

With what had they collided? There was at this latitude the occasional iceberg, but *Nautilus*, beneath the waves, would be able to see any iceberg long before any possible collision. There were rocks that jutted up from the ocean floor, but none that were so high as to violate the shallow depths at which *Nautilus* was now cruising.

Yet this was but idle mental speculation for in his gut and, were he to admit it, in his head, Brunel knew exactly what had happened. It was the *Great Eastern*. And the hit was deliberate. The captain had pointed *Nautilus* toward the grand iron ship, had given the order for full speed. And his crew, his strange crew, the crew that spoke an other-worldly tongue, the crew to whom Nemo's word was command, and whose command was as edict from the gods, would not have demurred, or e'en voiced hesitation. Nemo says full ahead, then— Full ahead.

Brunel's stomach—or what was left of it following the crash, the gut-shaking, the terrible low roar that even now continued—dropped out on him. It was as if he'd been tossed from a high bridge. The captain: Was he mad enough to think he with *Nautilus* might sink *Great Eastern*—the largest ship afloat, the grandest, of iron, and double hulled, too? It could not be done. Or— Could be done, just as a man with a harpoon can take down a whale. But would be folly to attempt, and would cost countless lives; and it would be toward ends that could by no rational mind be fathomed.

It was now perhaps five full seconds after the collision. The awful low ringing had not yet damped out. In his mind Brunel now reviewed the events, which all had seemed near-simultaneous, tried to see them with clarity, place them along a line: the ahead-full-speed; the crash; the wild deceleration; the ring and low scream of tortured metal—

And now the ringing abruptly ceased. Leaving silence— Not silence so much as an onrush of ear pressure, as if the very atmosphere were collapsing around him. Brunel now wondered where on *Great Eastern* they had hit and what damage they had caused.

Scant seconds later Brunel heard the dynamos wind up again and there was another jerk. The last book dropped from the sternward shelf. Brunel by this knew that the ship she was now running backward. Full-speed astern. This was accompanied by another low and terrible ringing, the screech of metal 'gainst metal. He only now noticed that in the collision the door to his chamber had unlocked, had flung itself open.

Without premeditation or thought Brunel rushed through that door, down the gangway and up the metal stairs to the captain's salon. There were books strewn everywhere, and the Breguet clock lay on its side, its delicate ormolu hands bent up and ruined, the case cracked along its length. Books, clocks, charts, all mix'd round as if in aftermath of a maelström— But no captain. *In the wheelhouse? Likely.*

The salon's large glass was iris'd open and though it Brunel could see, if he looked through it sidewise, what in his mind's eye he had already imagined: the sharpened prow of *Nautilus*, retreating from *Great Eastern*'s belly. But the image in life was worse than any he'd in imagination envisioned. He could see with terrible clarity the long length of thinner plates where *Great Eastern* she'd been repaired, and the prow of *Nautilus* pulling back from the center of that scar where she'd struck upward as a knife to the gut. Already—and the lighted plankton gave clear picture—the waters were rushing round the wound and into the maw of the grand iron ship.

Had the second bulkhead been pierced? From here it was hard to tell. Brunel knew, with true precision, the kinds of impact that *Great Eastern* had been built to withstand. But he did not know what had happened to his ship in the interim, the ways she'd been repaired, degraded, jerry-rigged, kept afloat on the cheap.

Brunel watched as *Nautilus* now fully retreated from the wound it had itself opened, her serrated prow catching on a plate of half-inch metal, taking it with her as she departed, tearing it as if it were no more substantial than a leaf of paper in a diary or journal. The retreat was accompanied by another low and terrible wail, of metal, this one less the rattling sub-sonics of the first attack, but more a cry, an oddly human cry: a babe-in-arms, high, piercing, in wild distress.

As Brunel watched, *Nautilus* she retreated from the wound and the water with increasing force and volume did rush into the gap. Now *Nautilus* was a full three hundred yards back and from this distance Brunel could for the first time see the *Great Eastern* entire, and see the belly, and see the wound. Brunel felt a pain in his own gut. Sharp and wrenching and pulsing with each systole.

Now the image in the glass fixed, all still, as if it were a Nièpce plate. Full stop. And time it seemed to stop with it. The long, precarious moment where any future were possible. Followed by—

Full speed ahead.

They were headed north. Toward the pole. For what reason Brunel could only surmise, though the most simplest one—Occam!—be the most likely: that having wounded *Great Eastern*, *Nautilus* wanted her to give chase. To make her expend resources on the pursuit, not on the repair.

And so *Nautilus*, barely sub-surface, she ran full North. And just visible through the aftward edge of the iris'd glass: the grand and damaged *Great Eastern*, perhaps a mile behind. By the high whine of the dynamos Brunel knew that *Nautilus* was at her full speed. Yet *Great Eastern*—incomparably larger—she kept up.

Abruptly Brunel found himself hurled to the port side of the salon. Looking out the Glass he could see clearly what was now transpiring. *Nautilus* was making a sharp right full rudder. Where moments before she was polar-bound, now she was charted for the tropics. The *Great Eastern* had the speed, but nowhere near the mobility. And in an instant Brunel understood. There was no other way to image it, no other account to propose. The madman Nemo had brought *Nautilus* round, and was taking her in for another strike!

What Brunel then did was not without art but it was without conscious thought—a reaction instinctive, his hands moving before his mind instructed them to do so. What those hands in sequence did:

- Reach down, and seize from the debris strewn along the salon floor a substantial metal dinner plate.
- Raise up, and with that dinner plate smash the glass ampoule of the salon's electrical bulb.

Shards rained down, one of them lodging in Brunel's right eye. The pain was sharp, immediate. Above, the electrical filament nova'd out in sudden exposure to oxygen—bright flash then all gone dark. Through pain and blindness Brunel reached down and tore off one of the filigreed ormolu hands—already twisted at sharp angle— from the fallen Breguet clock. He took the ormolu hand—*did time stop?*—and shoved it up against the fixture. His vision was still occluded by the shard that had pierced his right eye, and half-dimmed from the flash, the world a throbbing rhodopsin purple— But as he raised the clock-hand to the overhead fixture and lodged it home he could sense the sparks and feel the buzz of voltage shooting up fingers to wrist to forearm to shoulder to heart.

The spasm ran through him and he fell to the floor convulsed. But in the long instant he'd held the metal to the fixture he'd shorted out *Nautilus's* electrical system, burning to ruin the thin wire that was round the armatures so carefully wrapped. That the dynamo-turbines, and the ship they powered, were now—

Dead stop.

Brunel on the salon floor: surrounded by shards and clock and books and charts, convulsing in wild spasm even though the electricity was no longer in circuit with his body. He arched and flipped like some large fish dumped from net onto the deck of a trawler. And as he did he saw so many images, not in sequence but in simultaneity, each and all of them at once, projected before him like Balinese puppet-shadows, but sharper, and with a clarity far exceeding that of memory. Some of the images had sound, and odor too.

There was his father, dressed up for the evening before going to the Athenaeum, ascot knotted carefully so as to look as if done without fuss or care, and the smell of his father's shaving lotion, the fragrance done up for him by J. Floris, perfumer, of Jermyn Street. (Marc Brunel felt it made him smell like an English gentleman, a status to which—having been born low, and in France—he could only aspire.) Musk, stephanotis, bergamot. There was his own desk in London, a still-life now, with of course the Hadley's quadrant set apart from all else as if backlit. There was the moment of terror as when beneath the Thames the tunnel gave way: the inrush of water certain but not yet arrived, and all was for a moment silent and calm, but the next instant high sharp river water in his nostrils, and no ability to breathe without breathing liquid, and tossed about into the side of the tunnel and around and out with no thought save that of his own doom. There was the grandeur of Paddington Station, its tracks parallel all the way to the horizon, the day it was complete, a week before the ceremonies and the crowds, before the stink of coal and steam, before the pressing mass of people coming to London from afar, before the stain and tarnish of time, when the station itself—for that moment—resembled nothing so much as his imagination of it. There was Mary Elizabeth's hand, which he took in his own in a carriage in Leicester Square, her small and damp hand, trembling now as he asked her if she'd be willing to become his wife, and knowing that this was one of life's grand moments, yet knowing it more than feeling it, and a part of him on the upper right corner of the carriage, looking down at Isambard and Mary engaged in this strange and distant dance. There was the smell of oiled metal—that, too, was a smell of his father—and an image of thick linked chains, each one wider than a man's waist, all rolled up dockside as *Great Eastern* readied for her first aborted launch. There was an evening in

Erromango when he'd eaten a fruit whose name he never learned, together with the charred meat of waterfowl. And felt in mouth and nose and belly as if he were in paradise. There was the song his mother sang to him in cradle—*yet how could he remember this? Babes-in-arms recall nothing of those years!*—with its high, reedy melody and verses that went from one to the next and after each three a chorus: disturbing in lyric, reassuring in melody. There was the horror of standing, paralyzed, on the *Great Eastern*'s deck on her proudest day, unable to move trunk or limb, tears coursing down his cheeks, body made still by some terrible drug, and every atom of his being wanting to cry out, *my captors, they are standing here, seize them, imprison them, and set me free!*, while the speeches droned on, and Scott Russell strutted back and forth like a man who is sure what is true. He could not move then—

And he could not move now. Yet there was within him now a satisfaction. That of the choice made right. If he were dying, heart stopped by the application of electricity, it was to save the life of his grandest and best creation. And in that there was pleasure amidst the pain.

When Brunel had left his room he'd by reflex strapped on his cheroot case, his leather cheroot case, the one inscribed "*I.K.B. Athenaeum Club Pall Mall*," and which now contained only sea-cheroots. It was wedged beneath his back in a way that was sharp and painful but he could not reach it or even reach its strap and he had no means to dislodge it. As he convulsed now on the salon's dense Amritsar carpet, blood coursing from his forehead and the fluid leaking from his right eye, and the sharp line of nerves from hand to arm to shoulder to heart each a thin taut line of flame, as his brain shut down and the screen became white, blank, all-surrounding, as if by the billowing sea-creature he'd been wrapped and shrouded, as if he were being lowered down slow into his grave, his one last thought placed him on the very tip of l'île du Palais. Where the Seine splits in two, on the point of the island like the prow of a ship, under the shade of an old and spreading tree, then turning his head to see the young woman of his life. He knew her name—*how did he know her name?*—and it echoed in his head, until the white shroud went whiter still, with hexagons of pulsing yellow and lines of deep optic purple dancing along its surface, now opening up a path, beckoning, down a white-lined tunnel, beneath some other Thames, taking him to a place where there was nothing to trouble the waters, and all his pains were gone, and all memory too, and ahead nothing, save the floating city of his dreams. Cloaking him, floating him, out and up and away.

FORTY-THREE

---✧---

WHAT HAD TORN *Great Eastern*—what had bilged her amidships, with water now flooding in between her two hulls as fast as her pumps could void it—sped away fullspeed. Vanished in the distance. Langhorne—whose vision, unsuited for close work, was naturally inclined toward the longer distances—did gaze at that spot where the phosphorescent eyes had disappeared. Thus he was the first, e'en before the glass-man, to see those luminous eyes reappear. Larger. Brighter. Heading swift and sharp and silent toward the *Great Eastern*.

Until the eyes they stopped. In place. Glowing. Staring.

Langhorne he called over to the glass-man and then together they summoned the captain. All gathered. And within moments the phosphorescent orbs, no longer retreating, were the object of every pair of eyes on *Great Eastern*'s deck. "She be stuck," said Ahab. Then the men they turned from sea to ship to attend to what next he might say.

"And we are not."

One of the English officers—his name unknown to Langhorne, one of those who'd been slow to accept the new command—now spoke to Ahab. If there had been resistance in his demeanor the day preceding there was none in evidence now. He was ship's crew, the ship had been attacked— And now the one and only thing that mattered was pursuit and slaughter. The name, origin, nationality of the captain were, compared to that, as the beatings of the wings of flies.

"Shall I steer the chaloupe?"

Ahab did fix him with a stare. It was clear he was looking straight through to the Englishman's heart to ascertain his loyalty, his commitment, but more— To see if he possessed the belly and the wit to take on such a task.

"How many years hast thou at her wheel?"

"The full seven, sir. There be no one on board more accomplished."

"Sailor?"

"Sir."

"Let us board."

And so did the chaloupe crew make for the gunwales and o'er them climb. The officer went first, then the various men in his command. Ahab he beckoned toward Langhorne and thus Langhorne did come. Before the chaloupe was by rope lowered down into the sea the Captain did turn back toward *Great Eastern*, on whose starboard deck had now assembled most all of the hands on board. And to them he did speak.

"Ahab knoweth not—and it cannot yet be known—what body, what motive force, lies behind those eyes. We do not know the cause of its present stillness. Whether it plays dead, lying in wait for our arrival. But what cannot be known cannot be known. Ahab will not by speculation be constrained.

"He will venture toward our Leviathan, knowing that whate'er he finds there he will conquer. The manner of that conquering is not known to him but of the outcome Ahab he is certain. Nor does he need for you, aloud, to say it. Each and every one of ye knoweth, too, who in this battle will survive. Ye have only to look at yer Captain— who hath been shot at, who hath been part-devoured, who hath been attacked by savages and pursued by the forces of law. Who hath dispatched to the mortuary five men larger than himself when they, in an alehouse in Manhattan, did make the mistake of being disagreeable. And as ye know, as ye know: who hath pierced the largest whale—the white—that e'er these seas have harbored.

"Yet though the outcome be certain, keep yer eyes fixed on the northern horizon, and keep yer Captain in yer minds and prayers— Until next we meet, on this very deck, assembled in vict'ry." And then, as he turned:

"Who among ye will hand Ahab his lance?"

A scullery boy, scarce more than twelve years of age, did come up with it first, taking it from its tie-down in the wheelhouse, where

Ahab had secured, carrying it to the gunwale, handing it o'er to the Captain. Who took it from him, giving quick nod of acknowledgement. And with that Ahab he disappeared o'er the rail, and those on deck heard the *T-THUMP* of his feet on the wooden floor of the chaloupe and those in the boat did welcome him. Now the rope-men on *Great Eastern*'s deck did lower the chaloupe, from level with the deck 'til she was dipped into the sea. Langhorne, seated near the bow of the chaloupe, watched as the deck receded, the ocean approached. When the Captain did give command the pulley-hooks they were slid out. The steam-chaloupe had been fast and now she was loosed, even as Ahab with whetted stone did sharpen his harpoon.

FORTY-FOUR

───────✤───────

THERE WERE SIX of us in the boat. The man at the wheel was English from the old *Great Eastern* crew. He said his name and now we all knew it. His name was Redmayne. Some men in his command. All rest of us from *Valparaiso*. Chips was here e'en with no carpentry in sight. Me, I was a hauler and a song-man. There was no hauling to be done here, and why would we want to sing?

We were good sailors all. To be again in a boat-sized boat was just the thing. It had a steam engine but not like the fires of hell on the *Great Eastern*.

We were in fog. From the stern you could not see the prow. Redmayne stood at the cutwater and stared ahead. Staring into the fog. I have heard men call it sea smoke. My father he called it sea smoke. But it is none like smoke to me. Smoke will rise and will float off. Fog piles in on itself. We were all in our coats but the fog was on our face and hands. We plowed through it.

Behind Redmayne was Ahab. Ahab was lacing straps round his right leg and then through the boat. Leather straps. Through eyes and tholes. Now he was fast to the boat. Fast to the boat so if come a tug on the lance-rope he would not be pulled into the sea. I knowed his story. That he had once been pulled. And I knowed Ahab. He would not again be at the mercy. Of this Leviathan or any other.

We moved forward through the fog, dark summer fog. From up on the *Great Eastern* the water had looked to be light chop. Down here: What my father would call under heavy sail. Ups and downs. We were looking for a pair of eyes. Glowing. We saw them from the deck of *Great Eastern* but lower to the water the fog was more thick.

More deep. We did not see the eyes. Maybe we don't see the eyes until we be nigh unto atop them.

Redmayne he just looks ahead steers ahead. I watch my Ahab. Tied to the boat. I cannot see my Ahab's eyes. Like Redmayne he looks ahead, only looks ahead. His right hand holds the lance and the rope from the lance pools on the floor of the boat. Wrapped round a cleat. Then wrapped round Ahab. When he throws his lance he wants to be at one end of the rope and Leviathan at the other. He wants to be connected to it, by rope.

Then through the fog we see them again: the eyes. The eyes in the sea. Round and glowing. Half-mile away? Redmayne calls out and we correct course. We had been heading ten degrees starboard of them but now they are dead ahead. Yes, half-mile ahead.

Now the things happen fast. So fast it seem all at once. The fog it lifts. Like that. Was fog then no fog. Clear to horizon. Then: chop gone. Just gone. Sea smooth as glass. Poured glass. Flat and shiny sea. All the way to horizon.

Those two things sudden but what happened next more sudden. Sea— Sucked out. We fall maybe six feet maybe ten. Like all the water rushing out through a hole at the bottom of the sea. Maybe twelve feet maybe more. And because fog it had gone we now see it, port astern: a wall of water. All the water what was sucked out from 'neath us, mounted high. A wave that does not break. Maybe a mile away. And coming toward.

I had heard of this in tales and songs. The water sucked out, then up. But when it happens to you then you do not sing. The air in your chest is sucked out and then you forget to breathe. I look at my Ahab. He does not see. He looks only at the eyes, the glowing eyes. Everyone else, we look round. Now Redmayne says, "Captain!" Ahab he does not hear. Or hears but does not act. His harpoon sharp and tight in his fist his raised right fist. "Captain!" As if when the water drop he did not feel or see. "Captain!" third time and now Ahab he turns. And sees a wall, a wall of water. And nothing with which to kill it save his lance raised on high.

FORTY-FIVE

————— ✤ —————

ON THE AFTERNOON of 12th July a magnitude 7.5 earthquake struck the Anegada Trough between the islands of St. Croix and St. Thomas. These shocks generated a pair of tidal waves.

The first struck the town of Charlotte Amalie on the island of St. Thomas and ten minutes later the second wave did hit. Both waves struck the harbor at Charlotte Amalie first as a large recession of water, followed by a tall, hollow bore, which eyewitness accounts describe as a fifteen- to twenty-foot wall of water.

At the southern point of Water Island, two-and-a-half miles from Charlotte Amalie, the bore was reportedly forty feet high. The wave destroyed a score of small boats anchored in the harbor, leveled the town's iron wharf, and flooded out all buildings along the waterfront area. The waters reached 250 feet inland.

Frederiksted St. Croix was then struck. The US Navy ship *Monongahela* was beached and her sister, the *De Soto*, sustained damage to her keel. Five people on St. Croix were killed, some of them 300 feet inland when the wave struck. The greatest damage occurred at Gallows Bay, Christiansted, where twenty houses were in one instant destroyed.

The sub-sea quake and subsequent landslide produced waves that worked southward toward the islands, northward into the Atlantic. The northbound wave propagated with some rapidity into the sea and did not diminish in strength as it did so. It was in this sense what is called a wave of translation: a solitary wave. Or as Scott Russell termed it: a Soliton.

Scott Russell, who was the *Great Eastern's* financier and, as you may recall, a scientist, too, was the first to observe and document the phenomenon. He'd been observing the motion of a boat that was being rapidly drawn along the Union Canal at Hermiston by a pair of horses when the boat suddenly stopped—but not so the mass of water in the channel which the boat had put in motion.

The water mass that had accumulated round the prow of the vessel in a state of violent agitation at once departed, rolling forward with great velocity, assuming the form of a large solitary elevation, a rounded, smooth, and well-defined heap of water that continued its course along the Canal with neither change of form nor diminution of speed. Scott Russell followed it on horseback and overtook it still rolling on at a rate of some eight or nine miles an hour, preserving its original figure some thirty feet long and a foot to a foot and a half in height. After pursuing it for one or two miles Scott Russell lost it in the windings of the Canal. You may here pause to contemplate the image of the man, on horseback, chasing a perturbation.

According Scott Russell, a Soliton will propagate in accordance with the following basic precepts:

- The wave is stable and can travel over very large distances (normal waves tend to either flatten out or steepen and topple over).
- The speed depends on the size of the wave, and its width on the depth of water.
- If a wave is too big for the depth of water, it will split into two, one big and one small.

It is now thought that the pair of waves that hit Charlotte Amalie and Frederiksted was in fact a single Soliton that, due to the shallowness of the water, had split in two; but that the wave that propagated in the northerly direction, where the sea was far deeper, stayed as one— One solitary wave, as high as the two that struck Charlotte Amalie combined. A wave whose height and force were undiminished as it traveled—fifty foot tall, stately, imperturbable— into the North Atlantic. It is left to your imagination to contemplate just where in the North Atlantic our Soliton might be headed.

FORTY-SIX

————— ⚓ —————

THE EXTENT OF the ruin perpetrated by M. Brunel was troubling enough; the thought that he would do this to the *Nautilus* of his own volition was of course more than disturbing. But those who waste their time in shock, or who become waylaid with thoughts of might-have-been, do not in times of crisis fare decently.

My first perception of Brunel's attack was the dimming, then brightening, then extinguishing of the lights, followed immediately by the deceleration of *Nautilus*'s motors.

I knew at once that the electrical system had been compromised. My first impulse was to summon Mr. Brunel, who had planned and built that system; but before I could summon him I was alerted by one of my men to M. Brunel's convulsed and unmoving presence on the floor of my salon, surrounded by shards of the glass ampoule he had himself shattered. There was a double anger: at M. Brunel for having caused this ruin, and at M. Brunel for being hors de combat with respect to any present or future efforts at repair.

But there was, as I have indicated, no time for anger at his misdeed, nor for lamentation of his current state; no time, indeed, for anything save swift assessment, swift restoration. I did not allot these next moments to a consideration of the life of a great man, who had nobility and courage in him, yet in the past few moments had extinguished the life force of *Nautilus*, and perhaps of himself.

My officers reported to me that while we were not taking in water we were at present without motive force. Neither had we the power to acquire ballast or expel it. We were thus rendered immobile without the ability to move forward, backward, up, or down.

Given the damage we had done to *Great Eastern* it was likely that the ship, or a boat by that ship dispatched, would soon be engaged in our pursuit. My motor-man informed me that it would be a matter of days, if not weeks, before the shorted, burnt-out armature wires could be isolated and replaced. In the immediate future, escape via forward propulsion would not be at our disposal.

Since the options of moving in the lateral plane were for the moment denied us, I considered ascent and descent. We were now visible and powerless upon the surface of the sea in a manner that left us at tactical disadvantage.

Our only recourse then would be the manual flooding of the ballast tanks. This could not be accomplished from within *Nautilus*. Accordingly I alerted the crew via speaking tube of my intent: then made for the exterior hatch assembly and there did, rapidly and over the clothes I was at the time wearing, dress myself in full diving habiliment. I was aware even as I quit the ship that re-entry via the customary hatch would be difficult, as without power the water in the egress lock must needs be expelled by hand, if such expulsion could be accomplished at all. Once having left *Nautilus* I might very well be without means to return. But that was not the problem confronting me in this moment and so I put it out of mind.

The undersea was calm now, without the roil or perturbation that can at times be found there. I made my way aft and inspected the exterior intake pipe for the port ballast. The valve was inset a good distance and was not favorably placed for external control. It was perhaps twelve inches within the ship; the pipe was narrow and would not admit my hand or wrist; and my wrench was not sufficiently long. Still, if I were willing to damage the pipe seals and surrounds I might be able to access the valve, to allow water to flood the ballast tank that we might, thus weighted, descend. What repair these actions might necessitate could be performed later, whereas the damage that would accrue from remaining on the surface would be by far the greater. I went at it.

At last there was enough of an aperture to permit me to find, then using the leverage of my body entire to turn, the port ballast inlet valve. The inrush of water was slower than one might wish but steady. The ship listed to side as the water filled the port ballast.

Without waiting for completion I went round the bottom of *Nau-tilus* to the starboard side to perform the same task there. Having done it once it should be more expeditiously accomplished, because I now had some experience in the external operation of the ballast valves and would not be hindered by the trial-and-error. I will not say that the work was pleasurable, as there is never any pleasure in taking a harsh and damaging wrench to one's own creation. But it proceeded decently and in good time. E'en as I worked I was aware that I was under the sea, enveloped by the waters of the world, able to see the flora and fauna of which the terrestrial world was so largely unawares. This was a source of pleasure and comfort as I continued the work.

Within some moments both aftward tanks were taking in water with the resultant rear-tipping of *Nautilus*. Thus I went to work on the fore-tanks. That work was straightforward. I knew of course that the expulsion of water from the tanks would require the restoration of *Nautilus*'s motive power, and that without the ability to expel ballast *Nautilus* would only sink and ne'er again rise. Our large dynamic armatures, now shorted to ruin by the impulsive act of the engineer, could scarcely be repaired absent long weeks in drydock. More easily accomplished might be the repair of the far-smaller ballast pumps. That would be the hope (a word that I of course detest). But for now we were deeper beneath, even as a ship and a boat—the *Great Eastern* and one of her chaloupes—were bearing toward us. Only depth would afford us some protection from their gaze, and, should they find us, their attack. It was better to be down here, facing uncertain future, than up there, immobile, facing certain death.

Even as I worked the fore-tanks and watched from beneath the approach of the pursuers, I felt a downward pressure startling and instantaneous. This pressure, this fall, was not a matter of inches but of feet, and not of few feet but of many. I adjudged that I, and *Nautilus*, and everything else in these environs, sunk (in tandem) a distance of perhaps thirty feet. And did so in abrupt and sudden manner.

The swiftness, depth, and power of the drop was confounding. The catalogue of possible causes was not a thick one. Was this some weapon deployed by the chaloupe? Unlikely, unless it were invisible, and without the percussive effects that in my experience most always accompany the explosive device. Was this the result of the motion of the tail and flukes of some Leviathan? There was none visible in any quadrant (and the seeing at this depth was unmurked by sediment). My first surmise was that this was the result of some undersea quake that by coincidence of timing I was experiencing even as I was external to *Nautilus*. I tried to be as observant as possible that I might add an entry to my log upon my return.

Events with precedent offer more comfort, but events not previously experienced are far more conducive to the accumulation of knowledge. And so I watched with as much openness of mind as might be possible under these circumstances as I dropped, *Nautilus* dropped, the chaloupe dropped, the *Great Eastern* dropped, a descent of perhaps thirty feet, all in parallel, so that in relation to each other we remained unchanged.

Having noted as much as I could, and with the problem of ballast intake having been solved I turned my attention to the chaloupe, and pondered what might be done to destroy her; and then, chaloupe having been scuttled, what might be done to bring the larger ship to naught. I was engaged in those useful ponderments when the water, which had as I described receded with astonishing rapidity, now seemed to be returning with a swiftness equal to or greater than that of its departure, and with immediate increase in pressure. I looked up to see, heading toward, what seemed the underside of a wave whose height and propagation were of unknowably large size and proportion.

Might it be possible that the damage we'd inflicted upon *Great Eastern* was larger than we'd supposed, and that she was foundering, and that this was the residue of her massive demise? But substantial as *Great Eastern* was—and I knew full well there were ne'er larger built—this wave was far more immense, far more vast than might be caused by the sinking of any ship, even the one at hand. And a glance to the south disclosed the presence of *Great Eastern*, fully afloat, and under her own power, not all that far behind her own chaloupe.

My next thesis was the ascription of the conditions I was experiencing to an event meteorological. I had often seen, on land and on sea, things seem to *drop* from the sky— Which is to say, dramatic and even murderous changes in weather, the occurrence of which was without herald or foreshadow. I think of the flash floods in Uttarakhand during one of the Junes of my childhood, a flood that appeared as if from nowhere, killed upward of a thousand, left thrice that many without home. The river Alaknanda overflowed its banks in an instant and—if one may ascribe emotion to the motiveless—with great anger. "It was as if Lord Shiva were doing his *Tandav*," said one of my amahs. She was speaking of the Hindoo god Shiva, who, it is written, performs his divine dance to destroy a weary universe.

Many sailors have seen this or worse as they plied their routes. There is much I myself have with my own eyes seen that to recount would beg credulity. A cataract of dense ash that damped visibility even as it turned the water to weak thin milk. Fog or mist so thick as to deny admittance, opening up before one's eyes, then closing just behind. Ferocious and unremitting storms, gone as quickly as they'd appeared, leaving o'erturned ships in their wake, upside-down beneath what was now sudden sunlight—clear blue skies, presenting to anyone who wished to fathom the Mystery of the O'erturned Ships no evidence, no trace, no origin, no author.

What, then, was now occurring? What was the etiology of this event, and what would be the effect upon a massive iron ship, a steam-chaloupe, a sub-marine vessel? On a man beneath the waves in waxed-canvas diving suit weighted against buoyancy by gold bullion? Even as the—*wave?*—came nearer, memories of every sort were pressing in upon my head. I was diligent and effective in keeping them at bay.

What mattered to me now was the rapid movement—decompression, compression—of water molecules. With an abundance of curiosity I observed the wave's approach and awaited the arrival of disaster. Show me one thing here on Earth which has begun well and not ended badly. This downfall constitutes the heart's drama, and the negative meaning of history.

FORTY-SEVEN

————·⚓·————

MR. FIELD WAS NOT a happy man, but truth be told he had rarely if ever been a happy man. His current circumstance—in chains, confined to the ruined salon of an iron ship, watched over by burly seamen in shifts of three, not allowed to relieve himself save under surveillance—did not suit him in any aspect.

Still he was bothered less by the imprisonment than by the death of the one thing that to him mattered: the cable. The length of wire, or wires, strung from there to here through which limitless news and information might be conveyed. It began as a dream and had it stayed vaporous, evanescent, the current situation might have been less painful. But he had put his will to the task, raised capital, persuaded solons, worked toward the solution of insoluble technical obstacles; and after some error and much trial had succeeded. In 1859 he saw his dream in the world, and there were songs and celebrations, there were proclamations and conflagrations—*New York City Hall!*—it was as if he had been borne on a palanquin on the back of an elephant into a holy city. Presidents and queens conversed across seas and via wire and all due to Mr. Field, all hail Mr. Field, and all bow down.

And Mr. Field he did not gloat, nor conduct himself in self-congratulatory or unseemly manner. No, he was content to have built what he had set out to build. And warmed by the prospect of repaying his investors and then, in perpetuity, reaping the royalty from each wired transmission. And then—

It ceased. For reasons unfathomable. And not in a stroke, either. The conveyance of electricity became slower, and the text more garbled, the dots and dashes less distinguishable from one another, until they began to tail off. And thirty-six hours after the initial triumphant missive there was naught but silence. Or, to be accurate: static so loud that all message was lost within it. The greeting sent by president to queen was just a memory now. Telegraphy across the cable faded, then vanished, a dream that upon waking one tries fiercely to recall.

The failed attempts, the setbacks, the hopes raised and dashed, the fortunes lost and borrowed and lost again, will not here be recounted. Put simply the years 1857–1865 were not fashioned of gold. But this last voyage, with one large spool of wire aboard one large ship, had held such large promise. Some bank their hopes against the possibility that those hopes be dashed. Others fire up their hopes, full-bellow, with the rise of the sun each morning: they are less afraid of hope than of failure. To men like Mr. Field, being thought a fool is of no real consequence. There is only the prize and the getting of it.

Now, even as he was held captive in what had once been a gilded silk-draped floating palace, Mr. Field was contemplating the next expedition. Enumerating, in his mind: the manufactory from which he would source the cable; the investors from whom he would raise capital; the ship he would hire to pay it out.

He liked to learn from failure, but the current circumstances could not be classified as failure. Yes, the cable had snapped. Yes, the ship was o'errun by a brigand he himself had hired. Yes, he was in chains and the cable was at present being payed uselessly out to sea, connected at neither end. But the technical concepts remained sound, and the projected return on investment still sufficiently large to call forth the venturesome. Now that the War and its distractions were receding there would be, Mr. Field felt a new spirit o'er the land, a spirit of exploration and of ambition on the largest scale. In the current mood, the coming mood, one could be no better situated. In terms world-historical: was there e'er a better time to be Wire King?

Mr. Field's thoughts were thus of triumph when the bottom dropped out of his belly. It was as if the entire salon had—and quite abruptly—no underpinnings. He felt himself rise up even as the chains kept him in place. The chandelier leapt up, banged against the coffered ceiling. Silverware lifted, floated in air. Ascended to the ceiling as all else dropped. And this dropping did not stop, for what seemed a full five seconds. Then it was very quiet.

Now Mr. Field, and the salon, and the *Great Eastern*, rose almost as rapidly as they had descended. It did not feel to Mr. Field as if this were equilibrium returned. No, this was a trip up fully as awful as the one down. Only this time: accompanied by screams from the foredeck. What happenstance or emergent thing would make a merchant seaman scream?

Then he heard the noise louder than anything he'd ever heard, a low and harsh and terrible noise, as if a giant had taken the planet itself in his mouth. The crash, when it came, was of a magnitude neither Mr. Field nor anyone else on board had e'er experienced or e'en imagined.

As Mr. Field in the ruined salon could only guess, but to the rest of the crew was all too evident: this was no mere wave. They had all of them known bores, been near-capsized, been pummeled by the squalls of the North Atlantic— No, this was something of a different nature. A wall of water taller than the topmast, twice as tall, three times as tall, taking *Great Eastern* in its grasp as if she were a balsa boat in a child's pond in a private park. The great iron ship listed a full thirty degrees in three seconds, and the howl of metal plate would have been impossible to bear had not that and all else been drowned out by the wall of sea.

As the masts snapped like sugar canes, as the once-taut sails ripped into a thousand rags, as the coffered roof came down in pieces, as the binnacle pulled free from its stanchion and slid into the sea— As men on deck were tossed off the edge as so many crumbs off a white tablecloth, as rivets and welds popped and parted, as Chips was drowned still standing up— As ribcages were crushed and heads staved in, as the gleam of day was replaced by a liquid ebony that seemed to suck up all and every light—

If there were any solace at the heart of this maelström, any shard on which to cling, it was that the wave, the wall, the bore—*whatever it was*—was larger, and more powerful, than human motive could combat or impede. It would do what it would, and the men knew that they would die, and if they did not die it would not be through any agency of their own. The *thing* cared not if you were resourceful or witless, rapid or somnolent, had led a life of rank depravity or one of impeccable grace. It continued to lift and hurl and break, implacable, without malice or design. And it was not over in a minute, the longest minute of the world.

Men on deck—first to starboard, then to port—most of them went overboard. Men belowdecks most of them were trapped, speared, broken up. The stokers were tossed against, and into, their infernos. Still there were those aboard the *Great Eastern* who by happenstance survived. In retrospect, Mr. Field would come to understand that it was only the links and cleats and chains securing him to the salon's floor and wall—*'twas only those!*—what saved his life.

Yet even as wreck and ruin unimaginable were being visited upon the *Great Eastern*, Mr. Field did not think of final things. He had never before thought—and in that moment did not begin to think—that his own death were possible. Instead his mind was filled with images of the telegraphic cable, a single singing span, undersea from Foilhummerum to Heart's Content, thence overland in either direction far beyond. It would be thought of, now and forever, as Mr. Field's cable.

All of the untoward events—up to, and including, the rack and devastation to which the cable ship was even now being subjected— none of these had availed to bend the iron will of Mr. Field, whose triumph, as he would later tell it, was that of mental energy in the application of science.

FORTY-EIGHT

———— ⚓ ————

THEN WE WERE raised on high. We were lifted up on a wall of glass. A curved wall with a smooth curve. Taller than any thing. No bump or jerk. Just smooth rise from the level of the sea up into the sky. Pulled up smooth into the sky.

Up here you could see everything. Above us the sky was blue and the clouds were near. Quite near, low and fluffed. The white of an egg dropped into low-boil water. The blue sky was a dome we could almost touch. And the higher we were raised the farther we could see. The edge of the dome grew wider as we grew nearer the heavens. Below was the ship, yes, the ocean, yes, but we could see too how the Earth she were curved. Edge sharp and clear. Ice, blue-white ice, across the top.

Time it was slow. Was slowed. Was it the work of a minute to be lifted atop? Did that minute take an hour? How many chimes of the clock between each beat of the heart?

We were none of us thrown off. Or e'en thrown to the side. Just the long slow glide up. On a wall of water so smooth as to be glass. Smooth and curved as a wave of frozen ice. I looked to my Ahab. He was still with straps from him to the gunwale, and wrapped round cleats, and the lance in his right hand. Raised right hand. Against the wave, the lance was as mosquito to Behemoth. Everything we had e'er done, were doing, would e'er do, was as a mote of dust in the eye of god.

Ahab's face was tight with cheek and lips pulled back. *I'm going to stand in a sea of glass. Hold the wind! Don't let it blow!* In a state of high excitement he was. But also a calm in the eyes. He was looking out, looking down, and he could see the world or half of it. Down there the *Great Eastern* was small. Small against the sea. Against the angry sea and on it she was as jetsam. Tossed and turned and wrecked and wracked. Expelled. It were hard to tell if Ahab he grin in fear or triumph. But I know him well and I think was not the one or the other. I think he knew his time had come round. And in that found some solace. I had often tried to smooth his brow, to grant him calm. This I tried and could not do. Perhaps Langhorne was not the man who could do it. Perhaps it could not be done. But here at the top of the world I believe he found some peace. After long and wracked life, some peace at the top of the sea.

Then the heart beat and we did commence to descend. Slow at first then fast. Now it was as if we had been dropped from on high. The wall was curved and we had been on the edge of that curve. Precipice. The wall was curved away. At its edge there was naught below save air, and way down low, the sea. *Hold the wind! Don't let it blow!* And as we screamed we fell.

The drop was fierce and it was the work of a moment. We were up there and now did plummet. Hats flew off. Men flew off. Ahab floating above the chaloupe. (The leather straps they strained and snapped, just like that.) And me I was floating too. Did not know it until I looked down and saw my feet. Standing on no thing. When we were on top of the wall, looking down at the oceans of the world, and for the longest time, there was no noise. There was no sound. Just the high lullaby of lofty winds. Now as we were dashed down we could hear only roar. The loudest roar. The tortured souls of all the world and they were singing to us in chains. Each voice low but together loud. Drowning loud. And then we hit. Were smashed and were shattered. The staves of the steam-chaloupe splitting and tossed apart. The furnace up then down into the high-chop sea. Me I reached for Ahab. But he was already in the air. Out of reach from these arms or any other. Dispatched by the sea and in long arc. A rainbow. One end here in the chaloupe. (What was left of the chaloupe.) The other end at *Great Eastern*, now listing on her side. Forty-five, fifty degrees. I clung to a stave. Other men were dead. Already gone and I do not know, and cannot speak, as to why I was not among them.

Then Ahab hit the sea, right up against *Great Eastern*'s great wheel. On the port side. And it was still turning oh yes. Scooping up water and scooping up air. And now scooping up my Ahab. Once more he was raised on high, not by sea, no, but by the work and craft of man.

And behind the sidewheel, at the aft of the ship, where the cable she payed out, the cable was taut now. Not the long and low and lazy loop, nay: a straight line. From the back of the ship to the sea and into the sea. Pulled, as if from below. Because now the stern of the ship she was pulled into the sea, and the prow did lift. She was a heavy ship, heavier than any ship built by hand of man. Of men. And yet her prow did lift.

FORTY-NINE

—————✧—————

IT WAS OF some interest to observe the effects, beneath the surface, of the perturbation on and above it. It is self-evident that when a large solitary wave—a mountain of water, in effect—is raised high above the sea, the water comes from *somewhere*; and logically the only source is by siphoning—borrowing, if you will—the waters of the deep. Thus, while the wave presented to viewers on the surface an extraordinary sight as it proceeded on its path across the Atlantic, the disturbance below was equally profound, and extended as deeply below the surface as the wave extended above it.

The currents of water, greater in magnitude and speed than those typically found, induced a variety of effects. The *Nautilus* and *Great Eastern*, which before the wave's advent had been perhaps three-quarters of a mile apart, were, with the evacuation of the intervening seas, abruptly shoved up near-'gainst each other. And the steam-chaloupe, which had been between them, was—with equal abruptness—nowhere to be seen. Either plunged swiftly down to a depth below what was from here visible; or, alternatively, lifted up upon water's wall.

The cable that depended from *Great Eastern*'s stern, braided and with gutta-percha packed, not in most circumstances possessed of any great flexibility, did now blow and thrash and twist like hair in the wind. From here—and I was now some hundred yards from my craft—I watched as the loose and dangling end of the cable did whip *Nautilus*, lashing at and around—and, within moments, had coiled herself about *Nautilus* thrice. Thus there was a line of cable, the one end round *Nautilus* wrapt, the other wound tight round a spool within *Great Eastern*.

As the rush and eddy pushed the ships further apart the line grew
e'er more taut. The up- and down-drafts surrounding me were fierce
and I possessed—if compared to either the sub-marine vessel or the
iron ship—comparatively little mass. Hence it was impossible to
keep from being tossed this-way-that-way, and difficult to keep my
orientation toward the ships. But with rapid motions of my arms
and legs, and some astute countercurrent maneuvering, I was able to
keep the ships largely in view. What I saw was, in essence, a tug and
a battle. The wilder currents were drawing *Nautilus* deeper down,
toward the bottom; and with the Medusa cable snared around her
she thus pulled on *Great Eastern* with considerable force. I saw the
prow of *Great Eastern* raise up, out from the waves, as the line pulled
steadily and forcefully at her stern.

If you consider the force—mass times acceleration—necessary to
cause so large a displacement in so massive a ship, then you will have
some idea of the strength of the currents pulling *Nautilus* downward,
ever downward.

You know that I have seen much in this life, upon land and sea;
you know that I am a man of equanimity, to whom little is "remarkable"; and you know, as well, that I am not prone to the lie or the
exaggeration. With that in mind, I must now tell you that what I saw
was something I did not—nay, could not—expect to see. Yet this was
the product of neither savage poetry nor opiated dream: what I am
about to relate is that which could empirically be observed, by these
eyes, and through the glass port of my undersea helmet.

The first event was a tearing-away of the metal plates surrounding the *Great Eastern*'s cable hold. Though water be a denser medium
than air for the propagation of sound waves, and though I was encased in suit and helmet, nonetheless I could hear—or, more accurately, feel—the low and wrenching sounds as the tug of the cable
did pull—something—'gainst the cable-hold plates. The question
that at first presented itself was this: given the mass of the plates, the
sturdiness of the welds, why were the plates loosing, rather than the
cable simply breaking off? The answer, I think, lay in the braided and
coiled construction of the cable itself, lending it significant tensile
strength, especially along its longitude.

As the plates continued to be pulled outward I could now from my vantage point see what was from the inside pressing upon them. It was the spool of cable. A large, nay, gigantic spool, most certainly the largest e'er constructed on land or sea: for it had to have the capacity to contain a single strand of cable capable of stretching transoceanic from Foilhummerum to Heart's Content. Thus some 1,900 miles of cable were girdled round the spool—perhaps more if they had made prudent allowance for play and drop, minus what length had already been spent.

One can only imagine the spool, with Herculean hub, and flange as wide as the ship would accommodate. The full mass of that spool, together with the mass of an oceansworth of cable, did now lean and press against the rearmost plates. The more the cable was tugged upon the more the ship did tip; and the more the ship did tip, the more gravity did align with the spool to increase the pressure on the plates from within.

There was a fascination in the watching of it, to see such large and terrible damage playing out in slow deliberate cadence. Then at once all changed. The spool it had breached the hull, and with loudest reverberation—a sad and deafening noise even within the helmet—began its descent to the bottom of the sea.

The plummet of reel-and-cable was extraordinary to behold. One wanted to look away but one could not. The spool was as wide as the *Great Eastern*'s beam, and the *Great Eastern*'s breadth was larger than most ships' length. From where I observed the spool looked to be some eighty-foot in diameter. I began to calculate the weight of wood, the weight of metal, but was distracted from my figuring by the impossible spectacle of the spool's descent. The fall in water is nowhere near as rapid as the fall in air; and as we go deeper beneath the waves the pressure perforce does increase, increasing with it the density of the water and the resistance it offers to a falling object. Thus a projectile falling from the sky—a shot from a cannon let us say—will ramp up in momentum as it nears the earth. But a projectile falling from ocean's surface to the bottom will, owing to the resistance above cited, fall at a far steadier pace, her acceleration well-damped.

Thus the eighty-foot spool of cable did descend slow and torpid to the ocean floor. That languor will at times seem oneiric, for where else do we see such unhurried and deliberate descent save in our dreams?

One might expect the cable to unreel as the spool she sunk. But it did not. Accordingly, to the observer the spectacle of the cable was as thus:

- The wrenching exit of the spool from the rear of the *Great Eastern*, as if the ship itself had given birth;
- The slow descent, in the initial phases of which the taut cable became slack;
- The moment where the spool was of the same depth as Nautilus, and the umbilical connecting them low and curled;
- The spool's continuing descent, pulling at the cable, and rendering it once more taut; and then the movement which I should have anticipated but in all honesty did not, whether due to failure of intellect or the Mesmeric qualities of the sub-marine ballet unfolding before my eyes—
- The spool, descending, pulling *Nautilus* down with it.

I watched: in awe, in horror, and with shock's odd detachment. As the enormous reel—tethered to my vessel by a length of telegraphic cable—took my *Nautilus* to the bottom of the sea.

As she fell I saw, through the water's shimmer, tableaux that will stay with me for as long as I shall breathe. The slow rock, stem-to-stern, of *Nautilus* as she settled down. The implosion of the Large Glass, as the water pressure became too great for the iris'd structure to withstand. The compression of her hull, denting and caving as if it were a tube of paint in the hands of a profligate artist.

Objects from *Nautilus* were now expelled—some sinking with her, some rising as jetsam to the surface. I saw the Turk, that marvel of gears and rods and escapements, float out and away, his porcelain face turned toward me, nodding in lifeless farewell. (And was reminded, too, of Mr. V. K. Singh, without whom all the Turk's movements were but mechanical. Singh! We are close now, very close.) The books of course, the books of my beloved library, each volume now splayed, pages ruffling slow in the deliberate sea, swaying like *Hexacorallia actiniaria anenthemonae*. The navigational charts, billowing out wide and thin in the manner of deep-sea mantas. The device I fashioned for the extraction-by-steam of roasted-coffee elixir. The Courbet portrait of Baudelaire. The musical notations that had been perched on the lid of my Cavaillé-Coll organ, now mutely exiting, never again to guide these fingers into ecstatic or mournful dance.

And I am compelled to state that among those objects were human bodies. Souls, now floating free of *Nautilus*, commingled with the objects of my salon, exiting through the aperture where moments before the glass had all outside forces contained. I saw my lascars—my Hindoos and my Sikhs and my Mussulmen, my Dacoits, my Thugs. Men whose fathers had served my fathers in Orchha Palace. Men with whom I had gone into battle gainst the Company in Jhansi and Satara, in Jaitpore and Sambalpore, in Nagpore and Tanjore, in Arcot and Oudh. Men who stood at my side as together we pondered the bloody frescos of Cawnpore. Men who in Bombay did labor day and night in *Neptune's* build, and men who with equal diligence did of our *Neptune* fashion our *Nautilus*. Men with whom I had descended beneath and through the Pole; men with whom I had sailed on and below the seven seas of the world. Men with whom I had idly conversed, whose lives and families were shared in story and song.

And of course M. Brunel who, for all his panic and treachery, remained an architect of ideas unparalleled in imagination and grasp. In the eye of my mind M. Brunel and I were again sharing Madeira and sea-cheroot. And before me, not in memory but beneath the very real sea, I watched the mortal remains of the Engineer, shrouded now by one of those ghost-white creatures. One of those ghost-white creatures with purple veins, which had now wrapped itself around him, like a leaf round the filler of a cigar. Thus wrapped he did float upward toward the sun. Did these creatures, ghost-white and golden, have their own sentience, agency, mission? Brunel he was floated slow upward even as *Nautilus* she went the other way. I saw it all with the clarity of a dream, yet was in no way asleep. Ah Brunel! Ah *Nautilus*!

Looking below, I did now recall my sub-marine's ballast: of bullion, of gold coins from the Bay of Vigo. They were meant for the rebels of the Candiotes, fighting against the Ottoman Empire, and of course for those in India still engaged 'gainst the British. Gold coins to buy iron guns, iron guns to shoot lead bullets. But now the Vigo gold taken from the bed of the sea was to the bed of the sea returned.

The last object to free itself of my beloved *Nautilus* as she was pulled down was the cabinet clock. *Nautilus* tipped on her side and the clock slid out, then fell—*upright!*—to her new home on the sea-bed. Where her one remaining bent and mangled hand would continue to tell the time, her orrery chart the movements of heavenly bodies, until that moment where there was *tick*— But no *tock*. A bowed my head in farewell to Breguet's masterpiece. I alone knew its origin, its link to my younger self: a tale held dear and close, when I did return to India, and when I did go to sea. Even a prince has the right to a secret.

It was only as the clock she settled into the silt that I recalled the ivory ball, no longer the moon to Breguet's Earth but rather in my pocket, abstracted from the clock before I left the salon, taken without real consciousness but as odd reflex. I was glad that it was with me— e'en as I watched my objects, my men, my ship, my memories—it was a wonder that I be still alive. What use if any to make of that fact was beyond my capacity to ponder, imagine, desire.

As I ascended toward the surface I could now see through the faceplate of my suit, the sea-bed entire. There was the eighty-foot spool of cable canted in to the sea-bottom silt. There would be neither grapnel nor salvage nor recovery and in that there was some satisfaction. Curling outward from the spool was a length of cable, now tangled and sinuous, extending from spool to *Nautilus*, around which the end of the cable was still thrice-wrapt. *Nautilus* her glass was staved in, her metal crushed, her rooms and gangways and cabins filled with sea. What began as a dream of a nameless Mussulman in Gwalior was now lying in repose, on the sea-bed, well-nestled into the silt.

I waved farewell to my life's work, all dead and in ruin. Then I moved my arms and legs, not knowing if their propulsion would be sufficient to enable me to reach surface. Or, if it were, what I might find there, on smooth seas under a sunlit sky, after the wave had passed and with it taken all possibility of future.

FIFTY

——————✥——————

THE WAVE IT raised us up and took us back down. It took us far then brought us back near. Now again we were by *Great Eastern*. The iron ship and her chaloupe, close enough to swim. But we were not brought back the same. Chaloupe she was in ruin. Chips gone. Others gone. Ahab gone too, tossed up and down, all the way to the *Great Eastern* wheel. He did hate that wheel when he was captain and now that he was just Ahab he held to it. He held to it and it lifted him up. No. He did not hold. He was caught up in it. Jammed between the vanes. He could no more hold to it than he could let go. His clothes and his straps and his good left leg all caught up in it. The wheel took him up and took him down. Now the wheel took him down from air to water, pulled him down there, beneath the waves down there. I did take my breath. Then my Ahab was by the wheel brought up again. I let the air out from my lungs and commenced again to breathe. On the wheel Ahab's arm did move and his hand did move. He had been drowned by the wheel but he was not dead. My Ahab he was not dead.

He was taken up again and at the top of the wheel I heard him cry out. I had never seen him cry out in pain. No one had. I heard him in my ears or in my mind I do not know where. But I did hear him. The *Great Eastern* she were half on her side, half-foundered, yet still the great wheel did turn. *How did that wheel still turn?* Then Ahab he was brought down again, and the wheel once more did take him down there. Down there where no air to breathe. Only water, dark and salty water.

Then lo! he was bought up again. And lo! he did still move as he was brought up. His chest it did heave. Cough and rack and heave. Still he was fixed to the wheel. Carried round and up. A prisoner of the wheel whose turning had no cease. Then he was taken low again, and plunged once more to dark cold sea down there.

I could do naught but watch the wheel turn. And it turned and turned and came round time and again but when it came up from down there Ahab was not upon it. He had been fast to the wheel and now somehow was loose. Loose beneath the waves. Nowhere to be seen by me. Nowhere to be seen. I cried out for my Johnnie Ahab and I sang for him too.

The sea so deep and blind
The club the wheel the mind

My singing did not bring him comfort. My singing did not bring him back. All my singing did not bring him back up again.

I sang loud and I sang all day, I sang all day and sang all night. The chaloupe it rode the waves as I sang but my Ahab he heard no song he heard no voice he heard no thing. He would hear no thing see no thing touch no thing no more— E'en as *Great Eastern* kept turning round. *How did that wheel still turn?* And lo! my Ahab was lost to me and lost for all time. From this moment now until the last days of the Earth.

Who's that writing?
John the Revelator
Who's that writing?
Take him up to the highest high.

The wave took him to heaven but heaven did not want him. (Why would heaven want Ahab?) The wave took him and tossed him and sent him back to the iron ship. Ahab despised that ship: hated her iron and hated her motive force, hated her size and hated her form, hated her screw and hated her wheels. Who says the ocean she has no wit? The ocean set John Ahab down upon the wheel he so despised. Quite rightly! The wheel he so despised.

Tell me who's that writing, John the Revelator
Tell me who's that writing, John the Revelator
Tell me who's that writing, John the Revelator
Wrote the book of the seven seas.

FIFTY-ONE

————❦————

AND THE WHEEL did what the wave had done, but did it small: the wheel raised him heavenward, but not to heaven, no. It raised him far as *Great Eastern*'s deck, that far and no more, then it took him down. The *Great Eastern* was built with side-wheels to have a better draft, that she might ford the Hooghly. But there were no Hooghly here, just Ahab and the deep blue sea. Deep black sea. Beneath that sea he was taken, once and again and again. Then the wheel it spun him out.

His head face-down, his arms thrust up, his legs splayed out—*left leg long, right leg short*—like a man who'd been dropped from the skies. He breathed out and his breath made bubbles down there. But there was no air and when he breathed he breathed dark and salty water. Ocean blood. The bubbles went up and he went down. Slow, trembling, but down, always down. Then he saw the spool, the eighty-foot spool, Mr. Field's dream of cable spool, as it sank down to the bottom. And he saw her wire.

And he saw the Leviathan. He could see it was no fish, no it was not. He could see it was no sea-going mammal. No narwhal, no Great White. No work of nature. A machine built by man to sail upon the seas and sail beneath them. A machine of iron. And it set his mind on fire, and in that fire were flames of a gleaming gold—*not the baser gold of worn and tarnished coins, but an altogether purer hue, translucent, diaphanous, fugitive, a gold that was barely there before the eye and gold you might see clear through, a slight and light and evanescent gold, the gown of some Scheherazade*—and as in his mind he saw that gold yer Ahab knew that he had been right, in the furnace-room of the *Great Eastern*, where the stokers they had built the flame and Ahab did the cable's severed end thrust into that flame. He had seen a flame of gold that none other in the room had seen. The signature of iron. And there it was, the iron Leviathan, below him, and closer with every untaken breath.

Somewhere—*on the chaloupe? in the air? on the wheel?*—he had let go his harpoon. He held his right fist tight. In his mind he still had his lance, and in his mind his lance he did hurl. And in his mind the lance did all metal pierce, through the skin of it, and into the guts of it, and it did pierce again, through the heart of it. Until the iron submarine Leviathan bled out into the sea and would menace no ship no more and would menace no man no more. He saw it roll, belly to the side. He saw it shake, the last shake of dying beast, then it shook no more. Now all grew dark. But before the curtain to the stage did fall, Ahab did know that he had signed on to find the Leviathan and he had found it. He had signed on to kill the Leviathan and he had killed it. There was the matter of his leg, his right leg, and now that debt was paid. And in this moment now all debts were paid.

Well what's John writing? Ask the Revelator.
What's John writing? Ask the Revelator.
What's John writing? Ask the Revelator.
A book of the seven seas.

The legg of the curtain did now bump the boards, and somewhere—the other side of the curtain—there was applause. And if there was applause enough, maybe someone would raise the curtain up again, and Ahab he might take a bow, a final bow, one last bow, before his lungs fill up with the water of the sea, and his body does fall down there to the bed of the sea, and he lies in the bed of the sea, and dreams the dreams of Ahab, ne'er again to wake nor to rise from the ocean floor.

The last thought to occupy his mind was of his sister who died a lifetime ago. He'd always meant to join her in Nantucket, their kingdom by the sea: the grave marked JOHN next to the one marked ANNABEL. To be with her again was his life's work. But now he was floating in the dark wet sea as he and Annabel had floated, together—entwinned, entwined—'fore being hurled into the world. Her face which he had never seen was before him now.

In time the silt will cover him up. He lies there, a man of the sea buried at sea. He lies between a spool of cable, eighty foot wide, the dream of Mr. Field, and a sub-marine vessel, now crushed, the dream of he who was born Prince Dakkar, but now was not even Captain Nemo. In time the silt will cover them all. As all our dreams are buried, lost, with no salvage save the powers of memory, care, and human labor—which, from time to time, can resurrect the dead.

FIFTY-TWO

———————✧———————

THOSE OF US who walk upon the land, or sail upon the surface of the sea, will never know the truth that lies beneath. We have at best our grand surmise. But we also have a tale to tell, and cannot be deterred by our lack of certitude. Accordingly: when science and history have done their able best and moved on, we will work with what is left behind, what cannot exactly be verified—the loamy residuum of what we know in our hearts to be true, even if we cannot with straightedge and compass offer proof.

This we do know: Ahab was cast off by the wheel, tossed down, plunged deep, buried in silt. This we do know: Nemo, in waxed-cotton diving suit and metal helmet, was cut free from crushed and solemn *Nautilus* with no means of return. And this we can but conjecture: that the ocean, in majesty serene, in wisdom infinite, did the two of them bring together. Not back-to-back, no, nor oblique, no: but *face-à-face*, that one captain he could gaze at the other, and the other, he could gaze back. Are the dead able to see? Are the dead even dead? If the currents electrical within the skull persist after the heart has given forth its final shudder, who among us can deny this as mentation? And if the two men were by the ocean placed near each other, toward each other, heads moving slow forth and back in the undulant wake of our Soliton, well then: is that not recognition? Or even: conversation?

Yer Ahab, he did not know the name our Indian prince was given at birth, nor did he know the name our prince did adopt at sea. What he saw was but brass helmet, thick glass faceplate protected by metal bar, and behind: black beard, black as the ink of India, two wide-set eyes of equal blackness. In turn our Nemo, though a man of erudition profound, was in darkness as to the identity of this American harpooneer. What he saw was long beard gone white with time and trauma, eyes the color of a cloudless sky on a Nantucket midsummer afternoon.

Both sets of eyes disclosed, full-on, the panoply within. All that had been lost. By slaughter, storm, and fire; by murder, by devastation; by beast, by man; by ambition unchecked; and by failure in the simplest duties of love.

We here posit a moment—no more than that—before the bodies were by oceanic currents parted. When the two men did see each other. Did gaze through water into the other's eyes. Did then understand that they were not strangers, and in most ways never had been. Did they, in that stilled moment, acknowledge their twinned fates? And did they in that last moment—one above, one below—yet share a common vantage on the ways of humankind, a view most oft reserved for the moon, planets, stars, other objects in the firmament, as they look down upon us from the night-time skies? Again: we have at best our grand surmise.

They did not fear death. But we can mourn their passing. Those among us who cannot cry spend their lives in salt water.

FIFTY-THREE

———————⚓———————

LANGHORNE, WHOSE VOICE could make the toes of the ocean curl, was rescued from the sea by the crew of *Great Eastern* and allowed to stay aboard her as she limped to the new world. They would land in Nova Scotia. From there he caught another ship, the *Athabasca*. She was a whaler and she plied the seas of the South Pacific. The skies were magnificent and the seas congenial yet he did not find his contentment there. When *Athabasca* she stopped at Erromango Langhorne did leave ship. In Erromango Langhorne found the memories of happier times but found nothing save those memories. He exchanged his labor for passage on a freighter bound for Shanghai, then San Francisco. He left the freighter and spent a year in that fine American city. Though he took his pleasures there when the seasons turned it was time to move on. By an assortment of railroads he headed east.

> *And now we're bound for New York Town*
> *To me way-aye-aye, hurray-ah*
> *It's there we'll drink, and sorrow drown*
> *Hurrah for the Black Ball Line*

In New York he found a sense of freedom that had been lacking most of his life. And so he settled there on the insular city of the Manhattoes where he let a room on Ludlow Street, losing himself contentedly among the people there. He was a man of the crowd. He belonged to no one and his time was his own. He worked for some years at 488 Broadway, his hand on the lever of a passenger elevator.

He took them up and down. There was no one who could stop the floor of the elevator car more level with the floor of the building. It was often remarked upon, and it became, in its own way, a source of pride.

When some years later the noise and compression of Ludlow Street became too much for him Langhorne he set out for Brooklyn where he lived in a variety of rooming houses, the last of which was situated by Coney Island Creek, now called Sheepshead Bay. The brine of the Creek would hit his nostrils each morning in a way that was familiar, was comforting. But he grew tired of the Creek and what passed for conversation there. After a year, perhaps two, Langhorne quit his Brooklyn lodgings to seek once more a room on his adopted isle of Manhatto. He found one in Depeyster Street between Front Street and Water Street, a block or so in from the East River, and not far from those precincts in whose streets and taverns John Ahab had spent some time, awaiting the ships that would take him back to sea.

In his latter years it occurred to Langhorne that he might want to die in Tobago. But he did not want to make the journey. And although he longed for the smells and tastes of his childhood, he recalled that in Tobago he had never felt free, and that on the island of Manhatto he did most always feel free.

His death, when it came, was of consumption. It came quickly and it was only a matter of a week or two between the onset of his infection and his death, in his sleep, among his dreams. His songs and his wanderings came to their full stop.

Yet our larger story is not done. It continues, in another place, and at another time, in a city of light, among the precincts of the dead, with some dramatis personae new to us, and others more familiar.

FIFTY-FOUR

————————✤————————

ON 23RD MAY 1871—sixty-two days after the government of Adolphe Thiers retreated to Versailles; sixty days after execution of generals Lecomte and Clément-Thomas in Montmartre lit the fuse of revolt; fifty-eight days after the proclamation of the Commune of Paris before a crowd of a 100,000 or more; two days after the Republican troops, regrouped and strengthened, attacked the Commune, penetrating Paris by the Port de Saint-Cloud— The city of Paris was in smoke, in chaos, riddled with bullets and stopped-up with barricades.

It was Tuesday of *la semaine sanglante*. On that day the fighting was fierce and deadly. Jaroslaw Dombrowski, a commander of the Commune's *fédérés*, was killed by a fusillade of government bullets in the rue Myrha while defending the city's northern arrondisse-ments. The Opera and the Chausée-d'Antin, the Ministry of War, the caserne in Bellechasse, the hotel of the Legion of Honor all fell to the Republican troops. The Commune's Committee for Public Safety, wishing to prevent the inhabitants of the great bourgeois houses from assisting in the assault upon the Communards, issued a proclamation. Article I ordered that all blinds, curtains, and shut-ters shall remain open. Article II ordered that any house from which emanated a single shot or aggression against the Communards shall be burned to the ground.

Many of them were. Word spread quickly—or was spread, by the government troops and their sympathizers—of "pétroleuses," young women who were said to be torching systematically the great houses of Paris. For men to kill other men in the course of war was considered normal. For women to engage in combat was considered

an act of savagery, as if the Commune were unleashing an unspeakable force of nature. For every conflagration the pétroleuses were,
rightly or wrongly, consigned blame. The Republicans themselves
burned down the home of the novelist Prosper Mérimée in the rue
de Lille, wanting to destroy some incriminating papers which in that
house resided. (Perhaps these involved Mérimée's activities as a spy;
perhaps they involved a certain Italian scandal memorialized in the
letters of M. Panizzi. We may never know.)

But it was, undisputedly, the communards themselves who
torched the Tuileries. The old world was dying, and the new could
not yet be born. In the interim a great variety of morbid symptoms
appeared.

Céline Carbonnel, who was seventeen—the same age as Arthur
Rimbaud, who would arrive in Paris later that year to bedevil and
enchant—lived in the 5th, which on that Tuesday had not yet been
attacked by the men from Versailles. It was the district of the Uni-
versity, to be sure, but also of the narrow and winding streets behind
which immigrants, and men and women of the working classes,
made their home. Céline was the second-oldest of five in the Carbon-
nels' small apartment in the rue du Pot de Fer off the rue Mouffetard.
Their street changed its name every few blocks as if trying to evade
the authorities.

Céline quit her apartment that Tuesday to join her friend Sophie
Grasset who lived not far in rue de l'Épée du Bois. They would, most
days of the week, market together, at the bottom of rue Mouffetard
where it crosses rue Jean Calvin. There was a seller of vegetables,
and a fishmonger, and, their favorite, a man who in season made
potato galettes, fragrant with onion and cheese.

"How is your mother doing?" asked Céline.

"Her health has not been assisted by the events," said Sophie.

"Understood," said Céline.

There were peas and late-season asparagus. Haricots verts were
not yet in evidence.

The first sign that the world of the previous week was no longer
present occurred at the fishmonger, who was turning away custom-
ers. "No paper," he cried. "No paper." By which he meant: no printed
Francs. "Only gold," he cried, "only gold." And so Céline and Sophie

headed for their respective homes carrying in their sacks only vegetables. And when they reached the bottom of the street the Galette Man was not there. Perhaps it was a week too early for potatoes; more likely he was engaged, elsewhere in Paris, in activities of a more pressing nature.

The following morning, Wednesday 24th May, did not begin auspiciously: the barricades at the square Montholon, at the Bank of France, and at the Louvre, were dispersed at bayonet-point by the troops from Versailles. The Committee for Public Safety took refuge in the city hall of the 11th arrondissement. That afternoon the Hôtel de Ville was set afire. By midnight the communards held only the 11th, 12th, 19th, and 20th arrondissements, and parts of the 3rd, 5th, and 8th.

The streets deep in the 5th where Céline and Sophie made their home had not yet been penetrated by the Republican onslaught. But the Communards were everywhere in retreat and now the wounded were being brought to the Hôpital Misericorde, just above Sophie's apartment. The skies were filled with smoke and even here there was no real escape from the battle. The hands of the clock were being turned back and the future would soon no longer exist. Just soldiers, and the government, and the world as it had been.

The next morning, Thursday 25th May, Céline and Sophie debated whether they could safely make the walk to the Halle aux Vins between the rue St. Victor and the quai St. Bernard. But there were already flames rising from the quai and a woman heading across the rue told them that the Versailles troops had come down the St.-Michel bridge, which the *fédérés* for lack of ammunition could not hold. Then down the boulevard St.-Michel via the rues Racine and De l'Ecole-de-Médecine, which women had defended. She told them: the Panthéon fell almost without a struggle. She told them: forty prisoners were shot one after the other in the rue St. Jacques, under the eyes and by the orders of a colonel.

It stood to reason that the Versailles troops would seize the early opportunity to sack the hall of wine. Céline and Sophie instead ventured south, a direction for the moment safe, to the markets they knew. The Versailles troops would, it stood to reason, soon mount an assault on the caserne on the rue de l'Oursine, so it would be best to leave, and return, early.

Near-all of the shops were shuttered and perhaps three-quarters of the market vendors were dark. The four-seasons vegetable man was there, as well as a few others; but this morning no one was accepting paper. The crowds were thick with women, all of whom wanted to bring home food for their families, none of whom had currency that the merchants would accept.

There was a knot, and a clamor, at the center of the street. Céline made her way toward it. At its heart was a man, head bent low, who was giving gold coins to all he passed. He was offered currency in return but refused with a polite flex of the wrist, an open raised palm. "No thank you," he seemed to say though he did not utter a word. It was one of the small mercies of the days of the Commune, of which there were hundreds if not thousands.

The coins were not French coins but they were gold: undoubtedly and indisputably. Some of the merchants tested the edge of those coins with their teeth and were pleased with the softness of the metal. Gold, near-pure. You could buy vegetables, you could buy meat. The coins bore the face of Carlos II, the jut-jawed Spanish king. When the man who did not speak had given away all he had he disappeared into the crowd. Disappeared, heading north, toward this morning's barricades.

The 3rd and 11th arrondissements had fallen and by midnight Céline and Sophie's 5th as well. In the heart of the 5th the Lycée Henri-IV, at which the young Isambard Kingdom Brunel had matriculated some forty-nine years previous, was taken over as barracks and supply depot for the Republican troops. Friday morning was relatively calm but at noon the forces from Versailles were once again in full attack. Mid-afternoon the Bastille was in Republican hands.

By nightfall the lines of battle were well-delineated. The Communards were holding a perimeter ascending from Faubourg St.-Antoine, along boulevard Richard-Lenoir, up the canal de l'Ourcq, to the bassin de la Villette. Although history, written by victors, ascribes to the Communards's compound acts of savagery and bloody slaughter, atrocities beyond compare, it is worth remembering that the number of those killed at the hands of the Commune was at most a hundred, and that the number of those killed by the Versailles troops was, by all accounts, between 20,000 and 30,000. (And this in an era before automatic weaponry.)

But we are not here to make a case for the relative politesse of the Communards. They were fighting for the future of human relations and for the possibilities of the imagination. The soldiers were fighting, as soldiers largely do, to maintain order. But the order that they strove to maintain was old, corrupt, murderous, and consigned the majority of the populace to lives of scarcity, failure, confinement, futility, and dread.

On Saturday 27th May, despite fierce resistance in the 19th and 20th, the Place des Fêtes and the church of Belleville were seized and occupied by government troops. The city hall of the 20th defended itself nobly, a resistance organized by Ferré, Varlin, Ranvier, and Jourde. (We cite, here, those names that have not been lost to history; but we acknowledge that there were thousands, or hundreds of thousands, whose deeds were equally valiant, but whose names were not recorded.)

Yet even while the 20th stood its ground, Marshal MacMahon, commander of the Versailles Republican forces, issued a general proclamation: "To the inhabitants of Paris: the French army has come to save you. Paris is freed! At four o'clock our soldiers took the last insurgent position. Today the fight is over. Order, work, and security will be reborn."

Céline did not consult with her family. Her father would, she knew, have counseled caution. But the presence of soldiers in the 5th, in her beloved quartier, seemed wrong beyond compare. She could not live while those bayonets were raised. And so she left for market but did not market; she left to meet Sophie but did not meet Sophie. Rather she made her way down St.-Geneviève and the rue des Postes, turning right on the rue de l'Arbaletre, working her way down and over to the rue d'Enfer, down to where it meets boulevard Saint-Jacques. There is, on that square, a stone kiosk with a wooden door. A sign above that wooden door says, *Arrête! C'est ici l'empire de la Mort.* Stop: here is the empire of death.

It is the door to the catacombs, where the bones and skulls of countless, nameless men and women are interred, arrayed along the walls in meticulous stacks and patterns, a Braille of remains. It can be reached by a spiral staircase that descends for the longest time. It is not pleasant down here and there is no light. But Céline was hoping to find a realm beneath the dominion of the soldiers from Versailles— And she was hoping, too, that without having to return aboveground, she might find a route beneath the 14th, the 5th, under the Seine, through the 4th, under the Bastille, across the 11th, and up to the 20th, where liberty was still said to exist. She carried a torch of sorts—a rag-wrapped stick that had been dipped in oil—and tried to make her peace with the eyes, or eye sockets, that stared back at her. In life limbs were strewn this way and that. In death they were stacked with the precision of carbon atoms in a diamond.

Nor was she alone down there. Other Communards, escaping, and Versailles soldiers, pursuing, were attempting the same journey. Up ahead: bones scattered on the floor of the catacombs in wild disarray. She did not have the time to replace them as they had been as she ran, forward, into the progressively confined and lightless passage.

Then she found herself in a taller, wider room, which—though she could see no source of illumination—seemed to be awash in a faint moonlit glow. Along the left wall was the customary patterned stack of crossed bones, skulls-in-a-row. But along the other side, engraved on the smooth rock of the passage, was a large-scaled image of an Indian palace. The piece was intricate and detailed, in the manner of scrimshaw. A labor of love in the hall of the dead. Who had drawn it, and why had he (or, perhaps, she) spent so much time— weeks, most likely—in this small and dismal space, that stank of death, that offered no comfort or reward?

She wanted to examine it more closely but there was no time. Then she realized she was not alone in the room. She turned to see the man who had, two days before—*two days, and it might as well have been two decades*—given away gold coins in the rue Mouffetard. In the dark of the catacombs by the flicker of torchlight she could barely see his face.

"You may follow me," he said.

He warned her that the Versailles soldiers had made their approach from the south of the city, and that a regiment was now working its way up the catacombs from the plain of Montsouris. "Come," he said.

He was from— Somewhere. His French was impeccable but his accent bore the trace of another land, far from here. His beard was deep, impenetrable black, the black of India ink. Then—speaking more to himself than to her—he took a backward glance at the meticulously intaglio'd palace. Said, "Orchha." She was not sure what he'd uttered but was certain that it had meaning to him. But what meaning—even what language—was beyond her ability to fathom.

He led the way with his torch. She followed for a while but then could not keep up and lost him around a bend in the narrow ossuary. It was dark and damp and quiet.

Then in the next moment all was different. Ahead of her were soldiers, a line of soldiers, and they were shooting ahead, blindly, clearing the passage of anyone who might be fleeing their dominion. There were perhaps eight of the Versailles soldiers. They would fire, reload, fire again. She turned around and attempted to retrace her steps but the way was blocked with fallen bones. Céline had been searching for those remaining few square miles where dreams had not yet been extinguished, where the future had not yet been recuperated by the past. Céline wanted to find that place, needed to find that place, more than she needed to live. But now that the soldiers were firing at her—were trying to kill her—she understood that she had wanted to be free but that she had not wanted, and did not want, to die.

There was no light down here save the occasional flash of a soldier's torch and that provided by the muzzle-flare of their rifles. Bullets would lodge in skulls that had been dead for centuries. (There were six million remains down here, perhaps seven million. The living of Paris did not outnumber the dead.) Now a Republican bullet hit her in the arm. She pulled into a declivity where she hoped the soldiers—shooting blindly now—could not find her.

"Here," said a voice, and it was again the voice of the man whose beard was inky black. He saw that she was bleeding and tore a piece of cloth from his blouse and wrapped it around her upper arm, knotted it tight. The soldiers shot off another volley. "Where are you headed?" he asked.

"To the 20th," she said. "Where freedom—"

"The 20th is fallen," he said. "Belleville. Menilmontant. Fallen. All of it: fallen."

"Where—" she began to ask.

"Nowhere," said the man. "The *fédérés* all rounded up. In Père-Lachaise now. Without possibility of rescue or escape."

They shared a silent moment in which each considered the import of what was just said, what was just heard. And then he said: "You are wounded. You want to go home."

"Here," he said, and showed her something she'd not noticed: behind a neat stack of bones were rungs of bent iron sunk into the rock. A ladder of sorts. Which could only lead— Above. Away from here. Out from the empire of death. "Here," he said a third and final time, pressing something into her hand. "It will bring you good." It was a small object wrapped in cloth. She put it into her pocket.

The man then lifted her up, helped her find purchase on the rungs of the inset iron ladder. The soldiers fired yet again and by the sound of it from closer range. She climbed up perhaps ten or fifteen feet then looked back, expecting that the man would be following her. He was not. She did not understand why he would help her to escape yet not seize the opportunity for himself. When she looked back down into the darkness of the catacombs she could see, by faintest light, the man's back as he was quitting the chamber with the small palace. He was heading north. Not toward home, or safety, but toward the cemetery, where the *fédérés* had already been sentenced and condemned. He was walking, at a steady pace, not away from the firing squad, but into it. *Why would a man*, Céline thought, *walk toward death?* And then in an instant she knew. *He was walking toward freedom.* And if in doing so he had sealed his own fate, that was of lesser consequence.

It was not a decision she could emulate. But it was one, given the events of the week, she could well understand.

Aboveground the Versailles soldiers had opened a breach in the wall of Père-Lachaise where some hundreds of Communards had taken refuge. Combat was intimate, with *fédérés* concealing themselves within catafalques or leaping from behind tombstones to knife those soldiers who strayed from formation. The quarters were too close for rifle work and thus the Versailles soldiers removed their bayonets from their rifles and went in by hand.

The moon had been new on the 19th and now, on the night of

27 May, was only in its first quarter. With scant light one did not know who was friend, who was combatant, who was ghost. The blood of *fédérés* soaked into the ground, surrounding with warm fluid the cold dry caskets of those who had died before them.

By sunrise on the morning of Sunday, 28th May, all combat in Père-Lachaise had ceased. The *fédérés* who had been there surrounded, the Versailles soldiers who had with gun and bayonet secured the perimeter, all for the moment exhausted, silent, or, in many cases, dead. Throughout the city—in public gardens, in prisons, in streets, in catacombs—thousands of men, women, and children were being executed without charge or trial for the crime of being Parisians. Many of them would soon be brought here, Père-Lachaise, to share a common grave.

As the sun rose in the sky the Versailles soldiers now rounded up those left within Père-Lachaise. Some 147 of them were lined up against the stone cemetery wall, above the rue de Charonne, near the cemetery's southeast corner. There were soldiers who had fought with the *fédérés* and Communards who had brandished no weapons; there were Parisians who were guilty of living in the wrong quartier or of working in undignified occupations; and there were women, too, because any among them might be a pétroleuse.

And so they were lined up and shot on command. Ready, aim, fire. And then again as necessary, until all those who had been lined up were dead on the ground. Once they were dead, once they were no longer the enemy, the soldiers from Versailles obeyed the basic precepts of civil dignity and placed the bodies in simple wood coffins, one to each. If you were to examine them you would find a man with an untamed red beard covering his mouth and chin; a man with a mustache clutching his own elbow; a clean-shaven man with hands crossed, smiling. Adjacent to him you would find a man with head tilted oddly to the side—*had he been strangled?*—and next to him, a man with his chin raised, arms beneath him, frozen in a rictus of contempt for those who had shot him.

They bore, all of them, simple numbers, written on small scraps of paper and placed on their chests. They had no names but the army of Versailles was in need of something to record, to enter in their ledger books before quitting these precincts.

I. 2. 3. 5. 6. 7. 8. II. 19. 23. 46. 52. 53. 68. 74. 79. 80. 81. 92. 93. 101. 112. 117. 118. 123. 127. 135. 138. 140. 141. 147.

Number 93 had a piece of cloth wrapped round his head, a cloth wrapped round his body, but otherwise seemed to be wearing no clothes. Number 1 clutched a wreath. Number 129 had a white cotton cloth loosely draped around each arm so that from above he resembled an angel. Number 20 was a very young man, a child really, and barely filled his coffin. Number 6 had impossibly wide-set eyes, a beard of inky black, and the look of a man who had spent much of his life at sea. He had crossed Paris beneath the ground—a feat impossible, as the catacombs of the left and right banks are not thought to be contiguous, yet he had done it—in order to find freedom, dignity, and now, peace. As he had read, etched into catacomb rock beneath a hand-wrought palace the previous night: *Has ultra metas requiescunt beatam spem expectantes.* Beyond these limits they rest in the hope of eternal happiness. Unlike the others his eyelids had not been slid shut, and even in death it was clear that he saw everything.

Though it has at times been a conceit of popular fiction, we cannot examine the eyes of a dead man and find, fixed there, the last image he was to see before all seeing ceased. Likewise, we do not have the means to know what M. le 6—he of the inky beard, the wide-set eyes—was thinking in those final moments. But we can posit that even as he was in a walled cemetery in a northeast quartier of Paris, he was also elsewhere. When last we met him, if you may recall, he had uttered a single word, at once an escaping breath and an aspiration: *Orchha.* The palace of his birth and now, of his final dreams.

PÈRE-LACHAISE WAS BUILT in 1804 when the other Parisian cemeteries were at capacity. (Paris has never had adequate space for its permanent residents.) It was called *cimetière de l'est* to distinguish it from the cemeteries in the south (Montparnasse) and north (Montmartre). The first person buried there was a five-year-old girl. Her name was Adélaïde Pailliard de Villeneuve and she was the daughter of a bell boy. Napoléon, who had been named emperor three days previous, proclaimed, "Every citizen has the right to be buried regardless of race or religion." The word missing from that sentence is, of course, "class."

Père-Lachaise grew slowly, perhaps because of its distance from the nine central arrondissements, perhaps due to the fact that it was not, to the Church, holy ground. In 1806 and 1807 there was at most one burial a week. In 1817 someone wise in what was not yet the art of marketing had the remains of Abelard and Héloïse transferred to Père-Lachaise and placed in an ornate crypt. Lovers flocked to the eastern cemetery and the deceased followed.

Over the years there were, following Abelard and Heloïse, any number of significant Parisians who made their home there; but in the larger sense, perhaps osmotically influenced by its location in the working-class 20th, Père-Lachaise was to become home to those Parisians who in life had not been emperors or bankers or even shop-keepers. It is a city now of perhaps a million residents. If you were to include the remains stored in the ossuary, called *Aux Morts*, that census would increase to two or three million. You'll never be alone in the bone orchard.

In 1871 Père-Lachaise did not yet have a wait-list, and citizens of all kinds—*pace*, Napoléon—were embraced in its loamy arms. The 147 Communards who were, on the final day of *la semaine sanglante*, shot against the wall there, were buried there, not far from where they had been executed. (You can visit them now, and many do.) But let us now be exact: of the 147 slain *fédérés*, 146 of them made their final home in Père-Lachaise. One of their number did not. And that would be number 6.

Sometime in the very early hours of Monday, 29th May, three dark-hued men in sailors' attire—had this been London, they would have been referred to as lascars—took advantage of the fact that most Parisians were elsewise occupied and slipped into the eastern cemetery. They departed with a body in a muslin sack, leaving be-hind an empty casket. They assumed that no one would care and in that they were correct.

The men—we will, for the sake of convenience, continue to call them lascars, though it may be noted that none among them have made previous appearance in our tale—had been given a set of in-structions, uttered in vivo, now executed posthumously. He had told them he was not to be buried in Père-Lachaise, no. There was another journey yet to make. To his wife, with whom he wished to be reunited.

Accordingly they took the body of number 6 to a slaughterhouse in La Villette. There it was carried to the furnace. They stood round it, heads lowered, as the body was reduced to ash, and as the smoke rose toward the skies.

It is of course unclear what transpires after death as none of us here have been to that land. But let us assume that the smoke bearing the spirit of our prince, our captain, our number 6, ascended. And that in some sky or sea unknowably high above the earth, the prince's smoke and spirit found its companion: his bride, who had long ago herself been rendered as smoke and ash. Some fourteen years before, and in faraway land.

FIFTY-FIVE

————— ✤ —————

THE SKY SPREADS out before her like the blue sunlit cloudless sky of Zuber wallpaper. (Hand-blocked, panoramic, the motif called *L'Hindoustan*.) The flames ripple the air, a disturbance in the field of vision. The flames are impossibly hot; they cannot be endured. But on the other side of this moment, an eternity: her children, her husband, and all the time in the world. Even as the flames grow higher, the fires hotter, the pain now in excess of what can be borne.

The images in her mind are not those of the present. What she sees when she closes her eyes are nighttime flames: long wooden sticks, wrapped tightly at the top with rags, dipped in oil, set afire. Hundreds of them, lighting up the village. The night before she and her prince are to be joined in marriage. She sees it now, spread out before her in panorama, as if she were watching her own life from distant vantage.

Full moonlight. There were to be a thousand in attendance but there are sevenfold that number now on the vast lawn behind Orchha Palace. Some brought with them sweets of boiled milk; others—when the food provided by the palace was gone—purchased fried noodles served in small cups made of leaves.

Closer, on the vast lawn on either side of the Orchha Palace gates, are the special guests of the Political Agent. Here each plate is heaped up beyond demand. Fruit from Bombay, cakes from Delhi, beans from Allahabad, tinned foods from elsewhere. There are small fish with silver scales, caught on the high seas, preserved in oil, tinned in Iberia, now somehow here, in Bundelkhand, prized open for their benefit.

The Agent has mounted a small raised platform, no more than a foot high, and he is speaking to the assembled guests: "Every man is pleased when his rights are regarded." Just beyond the palace a larger crowd, awaiting debris, remains, jetsam. Jostling, now shoving, their sweeper trays thrust out before them, singing, speaking— Then silent. All pausing now, for the arrival of the Procession.

At the head of the Procession are State officials, men all, older all, in long silk robes and bright-colored turbans. There are many of them. Even in rows of three it takes the longest while for them to pass.

As they advance through the village the flare and flicker of the torches is augmented by Chinese rockets; and the noise of men and horse and crowd supplemented, too, by trumpet voluntary.

Now from the western road come the elephants, their hides gone silver in the moon's blue light. They swing their great trunks side to side. There are five of them. They are draped with tapestries of silver and of gold, and on their backs *haudas* of silver and ivory, *haudas* within which men, dressed in satin, hold parasols and feathery fans. On the great feet of the elephants are silver anklets, bells that tinkle lightly with each heavy step.

The last *hauda* is vacant. The elephant has no rider save his mahout, cross-legged on the gray beast's head, guiding it with sharp metal rod. The elephant is a gift to the prince and no one may ride it but the prince himself. Madhya watches from the crosshatched window. The prince is elsewhere. But soon: here.

She steps forward, allowing her face to be glimpsed behind the lattice. It is her night. The State and the men and women of Bundelkhand have come to pay her their respects. Yesterday she was a daughter and tomorrow she will be a bride. On this night alone she casts her own shadow.

The camels and their riders now arrive from the eastern road. They are the final converging column and they take their time, knowing nothing can transpire until they are in place.

The horses, the elephants, the camels, all still now. There is no sound but there is light from a carpet of flaming torches. The low, earthy scent of animals, the high acrid scent of combusting oil, carried up by air and heat to the window behind which Madhya is contained— , silent, solitary, amidst a city of thousands convened to behold her.

The first avatar is the sound, the distant sound of breath, many breaths in synchrony, 3,000 breaths, 6,000 lungs from the throng at the far end of the central road. Intake and hold. Now *there*, now *there*, now *there*, now *here*.

In the inhaled silence Madhya can hear the hooves on packed dirt. The other beasts—the horses, the elephants, the camels—had arrived in cohorts. This one is alone.

A stallion, a black Arabian stallion trapped with silver. It has a rider. The rider is a *Tikka Raja*, is a prince, is Prince Dakkar of Bundelkhand.

His garment is cut in the traditional way: long, double-breasted, with a bib set into the front. It is trimmed in gold. His crown is six pounds of pure gold. The royal device, intaglio'd into the soft gold, is a circle atop a circle, the smaller perched atop the larger. The ratio of the two circles is 3:11, that of the diameter of the Moon to the diameter of the Earth. Three divided by eleven is 27.3, which is the length, in days, of the lunar cycle. These are things Prince Dakkar knows. These are things Prince Dakkar keeps in his head. The crown circles his head, a planet orbiting its sun.

Now the great doors swing open, all inhale, and in that still moment between heartbeats the prince rides through. Camels, elephants, other fine horses all remain here. The prince is there. Outside the palace, they stand on tiptoe to see. They cannot see. Can see only: the large wooden doors, suspended on their newly greased hinges, pulled shut from the inside.

Madhya in her latticed room looks down at sharp angle into the moonlit courtyard. She sees her prince, no longer on horseback but standing on the courtyard's packed earth. Sees his crown. Knows that were she to see his eyes they would be filled with love. Knows it without the necessity of proof.

The priest extends his arms in front of him, palms up, a cradle. Into that cradle the Prince Dakkar places a small wooden box. Up here: Madhya watches. Down there: the title to her life is being transferred.

She has been told by her older sisters that this is normal. That the less she knows, the more she will understand. It is a paradox, Surya told her, combing out her younger sister's long hair with a brush of thick boar's bristle. *Like the paradox of sex?* Madhya asks. But there are only silences. Silences, or high, silly giggles, as if of pleasure, or of embarrassment vividly recalled.

On this week of weeks Madhya's parents are full of pride, her sisters full of pride and envy. She is about to wed a prince. Her life is about to change forever. What does this mean? Will she still be, a week from now, herself? If—as the elephants, the camels, the horses, all seem to indicate—if she will be, a week from now, a different person in a different place— Who will she be?

This is the culmination of all her father had worked for, and his father before him, and his father before him, as was, as was. This is the moment when the beauty and grace of Madhya's great-grandmother, that legendary beauty and grace, appeared once more, this time with the moon and stars even more propitiously aligned. *Every third generation,* her mother told her, *there is one who justly can aspire.* It was Madhya's mother's mother's mother whose marriage to a successful gold merchant lifted the family from its terrible home. Now it is Madhya. And Madhya's daughter's daughter's daughter. It is hard to imagine. What could be better than to marry a prince? Than to become princess? To stand, with grace and charm, beside him, to bear his children?

There is no better fate. This is what she has been told. This is what she knows. This is what she almost knows.

MADHYA HEARS THE opening of Orchha's inner door. The steps, soft leather on stone. Her father is climbing the stairs. Soon he will knock on the door. He has something to show her. Down in the courtyard: her prince remounts the stallion. Outside the elephants move slowly back, the camels clear a path for the departing prince that he may ride off into the night, to the sound of firecrackers and applause, and, as he gains the wider road, the son et lumière of cannon and sky rockets, trumpets and shouts, echoing far into the silvered night.

Tomorrow night the prince will once more gain the courtyard. Tomorrow night the prince will dismount, and the stallion will remain without rider. She will hear his footsteps on the stairs, his and his alone. The crowd, sated by the day's ceremonies, will have begun its dispersal. That night will be for husband and bride.

Now it is day and now it is hot and the moon is nowhere to be seen in the rippled sky. Only blue sky white smoke and heat.

She remembers the night before her wedding and she remembers her imagining of the night after the wedding, but she cannot, now, recall the day itself. It is too much day, and she needs memories of the night; the sun and flames are far too intense, and she can recall only the lattice, the courtyard, the moon, the full and silvered moon.

The memory no match now for sunlight, heat, flames.

The preparation administered by her amah, a tincture of opiates, has made her slow, lazy. Her head lolls back against the woven restraint. She looks out at odd angle across the field. The town, a good kilometer away, is vague, wispish, distorted by the heat in the air, by the tincture. Nearer, in the foreground, the flames are slow, liquid. There is no middle ground.

Against the terrible heat, against the inevitability of the flames, Madhya's vision again turns inward. A shard of an image, then another, then several. The memories coming more quickly now. They cling and tumble, a kaleidoscope turned by rapid hand. Horses, elephants, robes of flame and saffron. A train quitting the dusty station, gathering force, the engine straining against the weight and inertia, clouds of dense white steam, dense black smoke. And on the train, growing smaller and more distant with each tick of the station clock: a prince, the prince, her prince.

She recalls now her first communication with the man who would become her husband. It was a page torn neatly from a Hoe & Co.'s Premier Diary, printed in Stringers Street in Madras, a compendium of useful facts: calendars fixed, calendars moveable, postal information, registration fees. This particular page, entitled "Postal and Telegraphic Information," contained a Numerical Table: so that correspondents conveying common phrases, common greetings, might send number rather than phrase. (At 2.80 rupees per telegraphed word, economy of language was of the essence.) *Heartiest Diwali Greetings* could be conveyed by sending the numeral "1." *Ib Mubarik* would be "2." *Heartiest Bijoya Greetings* would be "3," *Heartiest Congratulations on your Success in the Examination* would be "10." There were 27 in all. The one against which she placed a near-imperceptible dot of red ink was numeral 16— *May Heaven's Choicest Blessings be Showered on the Young Couple.* She had that neatly torn page conveyed to him by trusted intermediaries. She knew he would understand; and then he did.

The diary page rises, flutters, floats away on memory's wind. Here now is the ivory ball, the white ball in the dark box, the gift tendered to the prince by her father as dowry. It was carved by hands smaller and more precise than Madhya could imagine, an impossibly delicate intaglio. Within the ball was another ball, and within that another. She had assumed that it had been crafted from elephant tusk, but once, speaking of something else, her father had said that this was water ivory, not land ivory. She imagined the whale. The large whale, now spouting on the surface of the waters, now beneath them, larger than any elephant, larger than all the wedding elephants together, they would nest within the whale like the smallest seed of ivory at the center of a carved-out ball. Like the sun, within the wide and final orbit of the outermost planet, the blue planet Neptune.

That ivory ball, that gift, presented to the prince, tied the fate of Madhya to the fate of Prince Dakkar. It was done that night, the night of moon- and torch-light, in a small secluded courtyard while thousands outside held their breath. And because of that night, this day. The children she had borne Prince Dakkar, a boy and a girl— *Hanuman!* and *Rani!*—put to sleep gently one new-moon night and by sun's rise both dead, throats slit wide, tales of British skirmishers clad in black rappelling up the palace wall, committing unspeakable crimes, departing as silently as they'd arrived. (Someone in the palace must have given them a map. Someone in the palace must have been rewarded handsomely. May their souls be forever condemned throughout all time.)

Then, even as she was still in darkest grief—that of mother for dead child, the darkest grief that can be known or imagined—came to Bundelkhand three horsemen from Oudh. They were taken in, their horses fed. They were given tea. And when all were gathered and seated, they gave out their news, the news that Dakkar, Prince Dakkar, Madhya's husband Prince Dakkar, had been killed in battle. Was hit by a curved-trajectory shell, a Mallet's Mortar, designed in

Woolwich to aid in the siege of Sebastopol. The Crimean War ended before the Mallet's Mortar could be deployed but now one of them had found its way to India; and one of the shells hurled by the Mallet's Mortar has found its way to the band of Prince Dakkar. Death to all within range was instantaneous and there were no remains.

Madhya cannot hear their words. Cannot hear anything. See anything. The veil of grief is full, black, and blots out the sun. A day passes. A night, another day. She touches neither food nor water. There is only one certitude now, repeating without cease, until all else has been dispelled.

To live is to die. To die is to live.

The veil of black grief slowly parts, admitting this one ray of sunlight. Illuming the path. The path to Dakkar, to Rani, to Hanuman. It is, to Madhya, the only path. *Sati*. She summons to her chamber only those who cannot defy her will. Tells them in plain words what must be done.

The next morning the widow of the late Prince Dakkar is sedated, is bound, is carried to this field. Her body will be sublimated. Her soul will be freed. He is in another place and so a pyre has been crafted that his wife may join him there.

The pain has increased beyond the recoil of nerve endings. No longer pain but transport.

The first time they were parted the young prince was borne away by steam-engine train. He left land for water, town for globe. Now she is traveling to him, by steam, by fire, by smoke. She loves him, this she knows. The Hindoo holy men who prepared the *sati* had poured substantial quantities of clove and cardamom onto the faggots, aromatic offerings, that her final sensations not be the acrid scorch of her own burnt flesh.

She recalls the cloves from when she was a wife, the rose water from when she was a mother, the cardamom from when she was a princess. But she is no longer mother, princess, wife; and soon there will no longer be a Bundelkhand, for when a prince dies and leaves no heirs the Honourable Company will annex it. 'Tis what they did in Satara, in Jaitpore and Sambalpore, in Nagpore and Jhansi, in Tanjore and Arcot, then in Oudh. 'Tis the Doctrine. And now even Bundelkhand will belong to the Company.

What Madhya recalls now: the high salty pain of children taken from her, the horse-and-saddle musk of the men from Oudh—the Sikh, the bellied merchant—who came to tell her of Dakkar's death. The char and smoke of the burning wood, burning flesh. Compared to all that has come before this seems simple, cleansing, just. The flames are her palanquin, transporting her down a long path, away from the house of suffering which even now recedes in the distance.

Her last thought is not a thought at all, but an image: of a blue and pacific planet, the planet Neptune, discovered just eleven years previous, marking the farthest known reach of bodies trapped by the sun.

FIFTY-SIX

——————❦——————

WHEN THAT FURNACE in La Villette was shut down and the ashes of our sailor were cool enough to touch they were placed in a leather satchel and taken by the lascars from Villette down the rue du Faubourg du Temple, to the rue du Temple, to the rue Ste.-Avoye, to the rue Barre du Bec, down to the quai Pelletier. They proceeded on foot. It was, in effect, a funeral procession, but no one looking at them would know that. They walked slowly as if out for a promenade, not wanting to arouse the attentions of an occupying army.

Then they walked across the pont Notre Dame, past the flower merchants of the quai Desaix where they paused to purchase some white roses. From there they made their way west on the quai de l'Horloge, home to the clockmaker Abraham-Louis Breguet, into whose care Isambard Kingdom Brunel had been entrusted while matriculating at the Lycée Henri-IV. The same Breguet who some twenty-seven years later had been visited by a young Indian prince, and who for that prince had fashioned an exquisite four-footed clock.

When they had gone as far as they could go—the western point of l'île du Palais, under the large and spreading tree—they bent low over the stones and handful by handful scattered the ashes and remains which settled into the river. The river carried them downstream past Le Havre and Honfleur until they were dispersed and mingled with the oceans of the world.

That evening, Monday 30th May, Céline—having at length made her way past and around occupying troops back down to her own quartier—spent the night with her family. When she had shown up at her own door, disheveled and filthy and wounded, she had expected her father to be furious with her. Instead he took her in his arms. Her mother bathed her while her father went out and found a doctor, a medical man who could be trusted. He extracted from her arm a lead bullet, cleaned the wound, debrided the damaged tissue, sewed it up, and wrapped it in a dressing that he'd soaked with carbolic acid. He prescribed that she ingest distilled alcohol and to that end produced from the folds of his jacket a bottle of Vieux Marc. This he shared with the family, even the youngest ones. Monsieur Carbonnel asked for an accounting but the medical man just shook his head, smiled briefly and found his way to the door.

An hour later as she was preparing for bed Céline felt a lump in her skirt and dug into her pocket, finding within its folds a small cloth-wrapped packet. At first it seemed mysterious—*how did it get there?*—but then she recalled she had been given it by the man in the catacombs. In her own room (the room she shared with her four siblings) and in her own bed (the one she shared with her sister Julie) the events of the day seemed both large and distant. *How could so much have happened in so short a period of time?* As she lay in her bed the memories had already started to recede. Trauma and Vieux Marc. All across the city, even as wounds were being wrapped, events were becoming images, images were becoming recollections, until the imagination of a free city was like a dream, the smell and feel and fine detail of which would dissolve quickly in the morning light.

Céline unwrapped the packet. Inside was a small ivory ball, in diameter no larger than the first joint of her thumb. It was carved until it was near-hollow, with a tracery of extraordinarily thin lines holding all together. Who had the skill, or patience, to craft such a thing? There were worlds within worlds. It looked so fragile, as if the slightest pressure would reduce it to dust.

FIFTY-SEVEN

———— ⚓ ————

LATEST BY TELEGRAPH.

—

OVATION TO CYRUS W. FIELD

—

Grand Reception at Great Barrington, Mass.

—

INTERESTING PROCEEDINGS, SPEECHES, &C.

—

Great Barrington, Thursday, Sept. 20.

THIS HAS BEEN a great day here. The occasion was the reception of welcome of CYRUS W. FIELD, Esq., the world-renowned parent of the Atlantic Telegraph Cable scheme, which has been so successfully completed. Little time had been given for preparation, and there was more heart in the demonstration then sought to show itself in display.

A dispatch had been received from Mr. FIELD on Tuesday, stating that he would arrive with Captain HUDSON, of the *Great Eastern*, Mr. ARCHIBALD, British Consul at New York, and Mr. EVERETT, the engineer of the Atlantic Cable Company. Captain HUDSON, however, did not come.

At 2 o'clock a gun from Mount Peter announced that the train bearing Mr. FIELD and his friends was in sight. At that moment the platform at the station and the entire neighborhood was crowded with people to witness the reception. Mr. FIELD's father, the Rev. Dr. FIELD, of Stockbridge, and his wife and four of his children, among them Hon. STEPHEN JOHNSON FIELD, Associate Justice of the Supreme Court of the United States, President HOPKINS of Williams' College, GEO. R. IVES, Esq., DAVID LEAVITT, SHELDEN LEAVITT, and all the principle citizens of Barrington and the surrounding towns were present.

As Mr. FIELD stepped off the train, three rousing cheers were given for him, and the Lee Cornet Band played "Hail to the Chief." A long line of carriages made up a procession, which escorted Mr. FIELD to the Parsonage, the beautiful country seat of GEO. R. IVES, Esq. Here a halt was made, and the party enjoyed the liberal hospitality of Mr. IVES and spent a pleasant half hour, during which Mr. FIELD received many of his old and a host of new friends.

The Company then took their way to Brookside, the princely country seat of DAVID LEAVITT, Esq., where they had dinner. Just before sitting down to the table Mr. FIELD received and announced the contents of a dispatch from London of today's date, announcing the first message that has come over the Atlantic Cable to Old Berkshire, announcing the end of the cholera outbreak in the East End. This happy exemplification of the great undertaking which Mr. FIELD had so gloriously consummated, yielded general gratification to himself as well as to everybody else present.

Shortly after dinner the party took carriages and proceeded to Agricultural Hall, a large building in the close vicinity belonging to the Housatonic Agricultural Society, to which they had a large escort, where a formal meeting was to take place at 6½ o'clock, and where the people of the neighborhood had already proceeded in procession.

The Hall was filled to overflowing. The chair was taken by DAVID LEAVITT, Esq. Messrs. GEORGE R. IVES and A. G. WHITON, the Committee of Arrangements, read sundry letters and dispatches.

The first dispatch was from Captain HUDSON, of the *Great Eastern*, saying that "It is impossible for me to visit Great Barrington on Thursday next. The officers are to go on leaves of absence, the crew are to be paid off, and the ship is to be put out of commission, which I very much regret but cannot alter."

Gov. BANKS telegraphed as follows: "Official duties at Salem alone prevent my joining you in the reception of Mr. Field on Thursday.

No son of Massachusetts has conferred more signal honor or service upon his native State."

The Chairman, in a brief but well-conceived speech, then introduced the business of the occasion and called upon the Hon. INCREASE SUMNER to express the sentiments of the old, warm-hearted, and exultant friends and neighbors of Mr. FIELD towards him in his time of triumph and honor.

Hon. INCREASE SUMNER, in his welcoming speech, said in substance, that the heart of this great Republic—he might add of the whole world—was thrilled with rapture because of the achievement mainly attributable to Mr. FIELD. By his forecast and heroic energy and perseverance space had almost been annihilated between the Old and New Worlds.

The hearts of the people of the Eastern and the Western Continents beat as under one pulsation and with kindred and parental feelings for this sublime and moral triumph, which the world, under Providence, was mainly indebted to Mr. FIELD; its results no man could estimate, but they would be mighty for peace and for good, and as they displayed themselves, the names of their originators would become brighter and brighter on the record of the future, and continue to shine, while the glories of the heroes whose laurels are sprinkled with blood, would face and be forgotten; comparing Mr. FIELD with such benefactors of the human race as CADMUS, EPERMICUS, GALLILEO, COLUMBUS, BACON, NEWTON, FRANKLIN, and WASHINGTON.

Mr. SUMNER said that the tongue of praise never became weary, nor did honest adulation become excessive; for whatever amount of praise was given, a vast space was still left for an additional measure; oratory, poetry, minstrelsy, painting and scripture. Introducing Mr. FIELD to the meeting Mr. SUMNER said: The native boy of our sister town of Stockbridge stands before you, the foremost man of the world, for he has combined all existing discoveries relating to the working of electricity, and through the hidden recesses of the wide ocean made them subservient to human benefit.

Mr. FIELD was received with loud and protracted cheers. Mr. FIELD spoke in reply as follows: Ladies and gentlemen, you can better imagine my feelings than I can describe them. I certainly did not for a moment imagine that I should have such a reception from you, the warm-hearted people of good old Berkshire, the friends of my youth. I had thought that some 50 or 100 of my neighbors would have been present to greet me, but I had no idea of the extent of this demonstration. I am indeed grateful but let me say, without any disparagement of your kindly feelings, that it is not alone on account of any merit of mine you have come here, but because under Providence I have contributed merely my share in the great accomplishment, the benefits of which have been so eloquently alluded to by my friend, Mr. SUMNER.

I beg my friends that you will not forget the deserts of Captain HUDSON of the *Great Eastern*, who has done so much for the successful completion of our great international endeavor. We also acknowledge Prof. WILLIAM THOMPSON, who by virtue of his work on the telegraph is now Sir WILLIAM THOMPSON, FRS. (Cheers.) I pray you not to forget your assignment of credit to my friend near me, who has done everything so well in the perfection of the machinery by which the Atlantic Cable was laid—I allude to my friend Mr. EVERETT of the Atlantic Telegraph Company. (Loud and enthusiastic cheers.)

Nor on this day do we the larger sacrifice still of the late Captain ANDERSON, who gave his life diving from the fore-deck into uncertain and perilous waters to rescue a fellow sailor who had fallen over-board. It is with sadness I acknowledge that neither returned to ship. Captain ANDERSON perished while placing the life of another before his own. In doing so he did show this American the true courage of the Englishman. I shall now observe and encourage you to follow a moment of silence for this sailor and hero.

Though there was no allotment for questions, correspondents from the Massachusetts press, as well as from other journals more distant did, following the observation of silence, speak.

Mr. BRANEGAN, of Boston, did enquire as to the reports that the *Great Eastern* was rent asunder by sea-turbulence. This Mr. FIELD dismissed as rumor and speculation, saying that the ship was the strongest ever built; that the seas, during the voyage, did not challenge her; and that her current drydock was routine.

Mr. HARRISON, of Narragansett, citing first-hand accounts, brought up the reports of piracy, and of mutiny on the high seas, disputing Mr. FIELD's account of Captain ANDERSON's death. Immediately Mr. FIELD did sit down, and the hall rung again with the warm and earnest applause of his friends. After speeches from many other distinguished gentlemen, the assemblage, at a late hour, dispersed.

—*The New York Times.*

21st September.

FIFTY-EIGHT

————⚓————

THE COURSE OF the *Great Eastern* herself—in the years following the grand triumph of thought-by-wire you have just seen so robustly celebrated—will likely offer, for those who have read thus far, little surprise. It was as you can imagine less a course than a descent, into pathos and decay, though perhaps not in that order.

She was, following the cable, put up for sale. There was a mild competition between Charles Louis Napoléon Bonaparte, who wanted the *Great Eastern* to ferry Americans to his Universal Exposition in Paris, and His Transcendent Highness, Sultan Abdul-Aziz of Turkey, who would outfit the *Great Eastern* as a floating palace.

Bonaparte prevailed. Her cable tanks were knocked out, two boilers and a fourth funnel restored, and a steer-by-steam system installed—something that had been in Brunel's original plans, but that Sir Daniel Gooch's penuriousness had prevented.

There was much use of silk and brass to restore former staterooms to their former splendor. Her first outing, from Le Havre to New York, was a red-beef-and-Champagne affair. One of those on board, M. Jules Verne, catalogued the manifest of London bankers, Chicago merchants, Peruvian aristocracy. His impression of the salon was that of "corpulent Americans who swung themselves backward and forward in rocking chairs."

Upon arrival in New York M. Verne cleared customs—it is possible, if nowhere documented, that his examiner at the Custom House Service on Nassau Street was Inspector No. 75, Mr. Herman Melville—and then checked into the Fifth Avenue Hotel.

The return trip, from New York to Le Havre, was far less populated: 191 souls aboard (including our M. Verne), where perhaps ten times that number would be necessary for Bonaparte to turn a profit. He put her up for sale.

Her next owner was the French Cable Company, which again outfitted her to lay wire on the seabed. Under the helm of Robert Halpin, a genial and portly captain out of Wicklow, the *Great Eastern* sailed from Brest. There were storms and squalls, calamities small and large. Deep in the North Atlantic the cable was snagged in, severed by the *Great Eastern*'s propeller. Break; repair; sail on.

Then for two days under lowering glass Captain Halpin was lost: he could see neither sun nor stars, the ship's compass attracted more to Cable than to Pole. When the fog did lift he found himself within sight of Saint-Pierre-et-Miquelon, France's islands in the New World. At 2,584 nautical miles, far and away the longest yet, the French cable was a triumph, even as the *Great Eastern* was showing her miles.

Mr. Field's *grande idée*—a thread of thought between continents— had become less dream than budget item. For the commanders of empire in London, telegraphy had long been the bugbear. Telegraphic cable ran from Old Broad Street under the Channel to Paris, where messages often languished for days if not weeks while French domestic traffic received priority.

From there the missives went across Europe to the Ottoman Empire, where bandit tribes murdered telegraphers for profit, and infidel messages were by officials impounded. The alternative route—Holland, Germany, the Russian State System to Tiflis, Teheran, thence the Persian Gulf—was worse. Russian relay operators spoke no English, and the garbled, unintentionally encrypted results were often published in the *Bombay Gazette* to give the pukka sahibs a decent guffaw over their afternoon gin.

And so the *Great Eastern* set out again: down the Salvage Coast, the Ivory Coast, the Gold Coast, the Slave Coast. Taking up coal at Capetown, then up, through tropical lightning, past the Seychelles to the Indian Sea. The captain had her painted white, stem-to-stern, to reduce the awful heat. When finally she was spotted, coming in on last steam to Bombay, she appeared to be a large and anomalous iceberg, or some variety of ghost.

The workmen of Bombay, like marine workers everywhere,

chanted as they hauled cable up and over and down into the *Great Eastern's* hold.

Good are the cable-wallahs, great are their names!
Good are the cable-wallahs, wah, wah!
Great are the cable-wallahs, wah, wah!

The ship set sail from Bombay on 14th February 1870, on a humid afternoon, just as the banana boats were coming in to harbor. Headed—first leg—for Aden, laying cable on the bed of the Sindhu Sagar. When London and India were by the *Great Eastern* connected by wire, they carried messages of grand congratulations, from the Prince of Wales to the Khedive of Egypt, from Ulysses S. Grant to the Prince. The wife of the Indian Viceroy, in London, cabled her husband, in Bombay:

IN AVAILING MYSELF OF THE SUBMARINE CABLE I FEEL
THE OBLIGATION WHICH SCIENCE IMPOSES UPON THE
WORLD NOT ONLY DOES IT SERVE POLITICAL INTER-
ESTS BUT ASSISTS DOMESTIC RELATIONS IN THUS
ENABLING ME TO SEND YOU ALMOST INSTANTA-
NEOUSLY AN AFFECTIONATE GREETING FROM YOUR
WIFE AND FAMILY

If telegraphy continued to thrive, the ship that laid the cable did not. After many false starts, failed re-imaginings, Sir Daniel Gooch gave her up in 1880. In 1884 in New Orleans a consortium of businessmen, or so they called themselves, raised capital to bring the *Great Eastern* to their city, where she would serve as the world's largest floating faro parlor. They collected $15,000 from Mumm's Champagne and $7,500 from Schweppe's Tonic, but seemed, with hindsight, to have been less interested in the ship than in the funds that might be raised in the contemplation of it. The *Great Eastern* herself remained in Cardiff.

The year subsequent she was once again put up at auction, fetching £26,200 from one Edward de Mattos, who promised, as several had before him, to return *Great Eastern* to her former glory, replacing her rusted plates and scraping what was now a six-inch-thick layer of barnacles from her sub-sea hull. The task of restoring her to seaworthiness proved too daunting, too expensive, or both, and she was taken to Liverpool, though not under her own steam. She was outfitted for advertising. In letters full thirty-feet high on her port hull was written

LADIES SHOULD VISIT LEWIS'S BON MARCHÉ CHURCH STREET
and on the starboard
LEWIS'S ARE THE FRIENDS OF THE PEOPLE

De Mattos then brought onboard, for the delectation of the public, a freak show predicated on the exoticism of the African continent, featuring Bob the Missing Link. In adjoining staterooms he did install yodelers, bell-ringers, conjurors, skipping-rope dancers, each of which could be visited for a separate fee. Each evening, on deck, the citizens of Liverpool could purchase a ticket to see Knockabout Negro Comedians by electrical light.

On 27th October 1887 the *Great Eastern* was sold at auction to scrap metal dealers, an act that might be seen—to any who held the longer view—as a mercy. The scrap dealers, Henry Bath & Sons, commenced by selling her anchors; brass fittings; copper fittings; and her three million rivets. Sold in separate lots and dispersed to the corners of empire. By May of the year 1889 the ship was fully deconstructed. It was only in that month that they found, between Brunel's carefully constructed double hulls, a body, a human body, part skeleton, part long-decayed flesh.

Popular lore has it that the body was that of a riveter who disappeared during the *Great Eastern*'s construction. It is equally possible that the body belonged to our composer, the young Shropham, who at Mile End did see what should not have been seen, and then, soon thereafter, saw no more.

FIFTY-NINE

———— ⚓ ————

THE CAMERA OBSCURA of Bristol is housed in an old structure built
of stone that more resembles a castle than anything else. There is a
one-story building—flat, rectangular—and at the far end a tall and
circular tower. The tower adds perhaps another three stories and is
topped with a crenellated wall. Though it looks—with its commanding view of the river below—as if it might have been a fortification,
it was in fact built as a wind-driven cornmill in 1766, then later
adapted to the grinding of snuff. This it did do until late 1777 when
the mill's canvas sails were left out in a lightning storm and caught
fire.

It lay idle until the late 1820s when it was rented by one William
West, an artist. West installed, atop the tower, telescopes, that were
used by artists of the Bristol School to observe and then draw the
Avon gorge and, on the river's other bank, the Leigh Woods.

In addition to the telescopes, West built a camera obscura—
a dark room in which, once one's eyes become adjusted, one can
see the projected images of the world outside. The earliest *camerae
obscurae* allowed light to pass through a pinhole, casting—inverted
and upside-down—the image of the world outside upon the opposite wall. West's camera obscura made use of a more sophisticated
mechanism, but one still that used the most basic of optics: a convex
lens and a mirror.

The lens that West placed on top of the tower was a small one,
five inches in diameter, pointed outward. Behind it he put a canted
mirror to direct the light downward into the darkened room below.
The entire lens-and-mirror structure was mounted on a gimbal, con-

nected via gears to the room below, so that with the turn of a crank the observer in the darkened room might choose the direction he or she wished to view. (It is, in this, not unlike the omni-scope of a submarine vessel.) The light is thrown downward onto a five-foot table, circular and concave. The image there is neither inverted nor distorted, so that in gazing upon it one feels one is gazing upon a world.

Because one is in this darkened room, removed from all, the silent and liquid image seems like a dream, albeit a dream dense with movement and detail. There is none of the remove one now feels when watching a film or a video—no grain, no artificial "clarity." Just the world as it is—smaller and more quiet—in lovely focus on the table in front of you.

On a fine June day in 1871—scarcely a fortnight after the dismal and murderous events of *la semaine sanglante* in Paris—a visitor makes his way up the winding tower stairs to the darkened room. He moves slowly and with deliberation. He stands with his arms at his side for perhaps ten minutes, his one good eye adjusting to the absence of light (save what comes in via lens and mirror). Then he walks to the table, walks round it. Stares into it. For the longest time. Now—with the apprehension of someone touching a lover's body for the first time—he puts his hand to the crank, turning the view until it displays in full the bridge, the Clifton Suspension Bridge, spanning the Avon Gorge.

The bridge is suspended from wrought-iron chains, chains draped over two tall towers on either side of the gorge. The towers are symmetrical, or nearly so: the Clifton-side tower has cutouts, the Leigh-side tower has more acutely pointed arches. When the bridge was designed in 1831, by the noted British civil engineer Isambard Kingdom Brunel, he'd planned a sphinx atop each tower in keeping with the towers' Egyptian style (though perhaps more influenced by the popular imagination of "Egypt" than by the Khedivate's architecture itself). The towers when they were built were flat at the top, the sphinxes neither carved nor put in place. What we know of those sphinxes we know only from sketches, ink on foolscap, in Brunel's meticulous hand.

Due to the Bristol riots, and various financial difficulties that need not be discussed here, the construction, begun in June of 1831, was halted time and again. The postponements spanned decades. Brunel himself died in 1859—broken, it is said, by the terrible stress of building and attempting to launch the *Great Eastern*—before the bridge had been completed.

The picture our visitor stares at—though picture is hardly the right word, for he is seeing in real time a panorama of life itself— is by any standards magnificent. One can see the trees on the near bank, dense with foliage and in full bloom; the near tower, jutting tall and majestic from the cliffside; the bridge with its long lengths of massive chain suspended in an elegant arc above the river; the bridge's taut deck suspended from some eighty-one tapered vertical rods; the denser foliage on the Leigh side, climbing the far tower; and down to the river itself.

He takes in the full panorama, then works the crank counter-clock until the center of the bridge is in the center of the circular table before him. He takes a bit of time to consider the bridge's wrought-iron chains from which all else depends.

He knows those chains. They were taken from the Hungerford Bridge, another Brunel construction. The Hungerford was a pedestrian bridge that crossed the Thames—midway, more or less, between Waterloo and Westminster. It derived its name from the Hungerford Market on the north side of the Thames, connected by that bridge to South Bank, allowing those who lived below the Thames easily to buy the goods for sale above it. They'd walk across each morning, down to up, enter Charles Fowler's large Italianate building through one of its seven grand arches, leave their coins, return with produce. The very model of what a bridge is for.

In 1859, shortly after Brunel's death-by-stroke, the Hungerford Bridge was bought by a railway company that wished to extend the South Eastern Railway into the newly opened Charing Cross. Though Brunel's brick-pile buttresses were maintained the chains were taken down, replaced by wrought-iron latticework. The chains were not melted down but rather put into storage for reasons lost to history. We do now know who decided—either in homage to Brunel, or out of frugality—to repurpose the Hungerford chains for the Bristol bridge. It says much, though, for the persistence of Brunel: that his design was built, essentially unaltered, even after his death;

and that the metalwork from one Brunel project, lost to the advance of commerce and capital, found its home in another of Brunel's creations.

There are other things to see here: West dug a tunnel from the floor of the Observatory down to Ghyston's Cave, opening onto St. Vincent's Rocks on the cliff face. The tunnel is 2,000 feet long, and is something of an attraction for the tourists.

But in this tunnel our visitor takes no interest. When he has had his fill of the haunting panorama inside this darkened room he walks down the tower steps. He walks with great deliberation, as if he had all the time in the world.

Outside it is very bright and it takes a few moments to accommodate to the sunlight: everything seems glaringly white, near-painful. He blinks—he has one good eye, the other is covered by black patch, pirate-style—and walks away from the river, behind the Observatory, on the path that doubles around to the Clifton-side tower, to the tunnels where the massive chains are anchored.

The tunnels are tapered, some eighty feet long, and plugged with Staffordshire blue brick to prevent the chains from being pulled out of the narrower tunnel mouth. The tunnels were engineered by Brunel to anchor the cables even in the fiercest wind, to withstand centuries of stress.

The visitor spends fully as much time gazing at the tunnel mouth as he did in the panorama. In every aspect they seem to have been built to Brunel's specifications. This seems to please him. He stands beside the epic strands of chain-linked iron, as if recalling another day, another time. Each link is taller than his head, thicker than his thigh.

Our visitor he now walks slowly onto the bridge itself. He passes a cast-metal plaque dedicating the bridge to Brunel's memory but pays it little mind. He wants to tread on the bridge's wooden planks. He wants to cross to the other side and look back at it. He wants to inspect the Leigh Woods end of the Hungerford chains, where they're anchored into the far-side tunnel. But more than that: he wants to know what it feels like, to walk across. To stroll from here to there and perhaps back again, something that was ne'er possible until imagined in the mind of Brunel, and then—this is, of course,

the hard part—designed, engineered, the thousands of small problems and hundreds of large ones solved, and in the most elegant
manner possible.

He walks now. The view from the center of the bridge is fully
magnificent. Above, the cables at their lowest approach, arcing upward in catenary curves toward each tall tower. (He wonders what
they'd have looked like, had the twin sphinxes been commissioned,
carved, lifted into place.) To either side: the city of Bristol, the woods
of Leigh, each of them showing as nicely as they ever had, ever
would.

Can our visitor be Brunel? To even the most percipient among us,
these matters are beyond the ken. Brunel is dead. And yet our visitor
cannot be other than Brunel: by whatever white-shrouded miracle,
expelled by the sea— As a half-sovereign might be coughed up from
a windpipe.

Each death is evasive. A surmise. Provisional 'til proven. And every once in the rarest of whiles: to die is to live.

The visitor continues his slow walk. Takes a cheroot from a battered leather case strapped cross his chest, strikes a match, maintains
the flame in his cupped hands long enough to set the cheroot alight.
His hands are shaking. His right palm bears a faint white scar, a
wound imparted in battle, healed yet leaving its trace. Below him the
River Avon, spring's high currents having abated, flowing quietly,
out past Shirehampton and Pill, out Avonmouth, around Portishead,
past Clevdon and Weston-super-Mare, past Watchet and Minehead
and Linton on the south, Llantwit Major then Swansea on the north,
out the Bristol Channel, into the Celtic Sea.

IT IS NOT possible for us to know anything of his life since last we
left sight of him. But there are things we might infer. That wherever
he has been for the past five years he has chosen now to visit Bristol
to inspect the work that he had imagined, but had not, at the time of
his departure, seen realized. From the lack of ceremony surrounding his visit, and the fact that the historical record does not reflect a
resurrection, we can assume that he is living under a different name
than that which he'd at birth been given. From his demeanor, his

dress, his cheroot case, we may infer a man not fully, or even at all, in the grips of amnesia.

Why did he choose not to reunite with his family? Why did he choose not to resume his former career, reclaim his former standing?

This we know not. It is safe to say that what he had seen, since his body was laid down in Kensal Green, encouraged in him a tendency toward walking solitary on this earth, rather than engaging with the varieties of bond and commerce this world offers up. And it might be supposed, though with no real certainty, that his solitude was a chosen one, his wanderings those of a penitent.

In smashing the electrical ampoule our visitor he did put full-stop to the sub-marine vessel—and in doing so, sealed the fates of all aboard. Two dozen good men on the bottom of the ocean fore'er entombed. Did their deaths yet weigh upon him? With what force, what pressure? How does one measure the column of mercury in any heart's manometer?

We would have one last question. Did he ever reencounter, in the course of his time at sea, or in the years following, the woman he'd as a young man seen on the quai de l'Horloge? Was it possible that in his terrestrial afterlife he found her? That they had joined hands and hearts?

Profoundly unlikely. But so many elements of the life that he had lived, the places in which he'd found himself, were equally improbable. Given the context, the possibility—however small, however dubious—cannot be ruled out. Call it a *château d'Espagne*. (For what of value in this world, large or small, has ever been deemed "likely"?) There was a Hawkins book in his pocket with many white pages remaining.

Twelve years previous—twelve years with the length of twelve long decades—a man in a bottle-green smoking jacket had promised him a lifetime of adventure. From what we know, we can say that the man in the bottle-green jacket did on that promise deliver.

But what of our visitor? Did he, on a beautiful day standing on a bridge of his own devise, look back upon those years as ones of upheaval, ruin, unspeakable disaster? Or with time's retrospect, did he see those years as ones of exploit, escapade, venture, deed, experience?

Our visitor is now closer to Leigh than to Clifton. He is the only person on the bridge this afternoon, a short, contemplative man in his mid-sixties, what was once black hair now gone all white, stark white, with a hat seemingly half his height, a hat that any solitary gust of onshore wind could take, just like that, from atop his head—seize it, lift it, blow it out, between any two of the eighty-one uprights, down to the Avon, or even better, up into the sky.

ACKNOWLEDGEMENTS

―――――⚓―――――

My debts to M. Verne and Mr. Melville are too extensive to repay, or even adequately to acknowledge. Reading their works has made me the writer—and the person—I am today. My theft of their creations is not something I will here try to justify. To put it simply: the worlds that they created have become our worlds. I owe an equal debt of gratitude to so many of the authors whose books formed my library and my universe as I was writing this one. A fuller elaboration of this gratitude can be found at http://howardrodman.com/book/the-great-eastern/.

The staffs of the Brunel Museum in Rotherhithe and the Musée Jules Verne in Nantes were generous and patient when I paid visits to their respective institutions, opening their doors to an American stranger; and on Cape Cod, the staffs of the French Cable Station Museum in Orleans and the Chatham Marconi Maritime Center in North Chatham were no less welcoming. I am greatly indebted to the late Michel Roethel, in whose Paris bookshop dedicated to the work of Jules Verne I spent many fine lost hours, and whose hospitality and conversation were far more inspirational than he would have any way of knowing.

Many provided practical advice; research assistance; editorial suggestions. Others provided small words of encouragement when I needed them the most. I am particularly grateful to Peter Agree, Betsy Amster, Mary Bailey, Antonin Baudry, Rick Berg, Sonja Bolle, Lou Boxer, Leo Braudy, Theodore Braun, Ken Brecher, Jay Cantor, Jenne Casarotto, Michael Chabon, Julie Cline, Anthony Tirado Chase, Micheal Donaldson, Allison Engels, Janet Fitch, Terry Curtis Fox, Peter Gethers, Michael Goldenberg, Brent Green, Maggie Hanbury, Dante Harper, Peter Herman, Doug Headline, Melanie Jackson, Ricky Jay,

Erik Jendresen, Henry Jenkins, Tom Kalin, Steve Katz, Nick Kazan, David King, Dione King, David Kipen, Tim Kittleson, Ken Kwapis, Dan Lansner, Jonathan Lethem, Gloria Loomis, Tom Lutz, Scott McGehee, Maureen McHugh, Walter Mosley, Mimi Munson, Geoff Nicholson, Nicholas Meyer, Dennis Palumbo, Robert Polito, Jon Raymond, Eddie Redmayne, Rebecca Rickman, Adam Rodman, James Schamus, Joan Schenkar, David Siegel, Marisa Silver, John Galbraith Simmons, Dan Simon, Zach Sklar, Tiahna Skye, Steven Soderbergh, Louise Steinman, Robin Swicord, Frank Wuliger, Barry Yourgrau, Wendy Zomparelli.

The support of Steve Erickson has meant everything: Steve was the first person to read any of this manuscript, and he excerpted a chapter for publication in *Black Clock*, in issue no. 10, and again in issue no. 13. He gave me faith to continue this project when I thought that I just can't go on.

The kind guidance of Sandy Dijkstra and Elise Capron of the Sandra Dijkstra Literary Agency was as generous as it was invaluable.

A critical set of revisions was made possible only via the extraordinary hospitality of the Swicord/Kazans, who let me escape to their house on Vashon for two weeks when I needed to be away from the world's other concerns.

The app "Freedom," which suspends one's access to the internet for a specified period of time, was a godsend. The website http://750words .com was deeply useful as goad and incentive. I also, when in need of inspiration, would often consult "Oblique Strategies, or Over One Hundred Worthwhile Dilemmas," the deck created by Brian Eno and Peter Schmidt, 1975 edition. It is one of my most treasured objects.

Without Anne Friedberg, Tristan Rodman, Mary Beth Heffernan: quite simply, no book. Their love, generosity of spirit, and faith as I wrote this manuscript knew no bounds. Their support throughout was in wild excess of what can be acknowledged or repaid. And anyone who knows me knows that the work of the last several years would simply not have been possible without Mary Beth's dogged and literate optimism, which every day continues to inspire.